MW01147208

Ishmael

Emma Dorothy Eliza Nevitte Southworth

Copyright © 2018 Okitoks Press

All rights reserved.

ISBN: 1717272312

ISBN-13: 978-1717272317

Table of Contents

CHAPTER I. 4

CHAPTER II. 6

CHAPTER III. 12

CHAPTER IV. 18

CHAPTER V. 24

CHAPTER VI. 27

CHAPTER VII. 31

CHAPTER VIII. 37

CHAPTER IX. 41

CHAPTER X. 45

CHAPTER XI. 50

CHAPTER XII. 54

CHAPTER XIII. 57

CHAPTER XIV. 60

CHAPTER XV. 63

CHAPTER XVI. 69

CHAPTER XVII. 73

CHAPTER XVIII. 77

CHAPTER XIX. 81

CHAPTER XX. 86

CHAPTER XXI. 91

CHAPTER XXII. 95

CHAPTER XXIII. 101

CHAPTER XXIV. 106

CHAPTER XXV. 110

CHAPTER XXVI. 113

CHAPTER XXVII. 117

CHAPTER XXVIII. 125

CHAPTER XXIX. 129

CHAPTER XXX. 132

CHAPTER XXXI. 138

CHAPTER XXXII. 141

CHAPTER XXXIII. 146

CHAPTER XXXIV. 149

CHAPTER XXXV. 151

CHAPTER XXXVI. 153

CHAPTER XXXVII. 159

CHAPTER XXXVIII. 163

CHAPTER XXXIX. 167

CHAPTER XL. 168

CHAPTER XLI. 171

CHAPTER XLII. 175

CHAPTER XLIII. 180

CHAPTER XLIV. 182

CHAPTER XLV. 187

CHAPTER XLVI. 192

CHAPTER XLVII..196
CHAPTER XLVIII...199
CHAPTER XLIX..202
CHAPTER L...206
CHAPTER LI...210
CHAPTER LII..212
CHAPTER LIII...216
CHAPTER LIV...220
CHAPTER LV..223
CHAPTER LVI...234
CHAPTER LVII..239
CHAPTER LVIII...242
CHAPTER LIX...244
CHAPTER LX..246
CHAPTER LXI...248
CHAPTER LXII..253
CHAPTER LXIII...259
CHAPTER LXIV. 261
CHAPTER LXV. 266
CHAPTER LXVI. 268
CHAPTER LXVII..274

CHAPTER I.

THE SISTERS.

But if thou wilt be constant then,
And faithful of thy word,
I'll make thee glorious by my pen
And famous by my sword.
I'll serve thee in such noble ways
Was never heard before;
I'll crown and deck thee all with bays,
And love thee evermore.
—*James Graham.*

"Well, if there be any truth in the old adage, young Herman Brudenell will have a prosperous life; for really this is a lovely day for the middle of April—the sky is just as sunny and the air as warm as if it were June," said Hannah Worth, looking out from the door of her hut upon a scene as beautiful as ever shone beneath the splendid radiance of an early spring morning.

"And what is that old adage you talk of, Hannah?" inquired her younger sister, who stood braiding the locks of her long black hair before the cracked looking-glass that hung above the rickety chest of drawers.

"Why, la, Nora, don't you know? The adage is as old as the hills and as true as the heavens, and it is this, that a man's twenty-first birthday is an index to his after life:—if it be clear, he will be fortunate; if cloudy, unfortunate."

"Then I should say that young Mr. Brudenell's fortune will be a splendid one; for the sun is dazzling!" said Nora, as she wound the long sable plait of hair around her head in the form of a natural coronet, and secured the end behind with—a thorn! "And, now, how do I look? Aint you proud of me?" she archly inquired, turning with "a smile of conscious beauty born" to the inspection of her elder sister.

That sister might well have answered in the affirmative had she considered personal beauty a merit of high order; for few palaces in this world could boast a princess so superbly beautiful as this peasant girl that this poor hut contained. Beneath those rich sable tresses was a high broad forehead as white as snow; slender black eyebrows so well defined and so perfectly arched that they gave a singularly open and elevated character to the whole countenance; large dark gray eyes, full of light, softened by long, sweeping black lashes; a small, straight nose; oval, blooming cheeks; plump, ruddy lips that, slightly parted, revealed glimpses of the little pearly teeth within; a well-turned chin; a face with this peculiarity, that when she was pleased it was her eyes that smiled and not her lips; a face, in short, full of intelligence and feeling that might become thought and passion. Her form was noble—being tall, finely proportioned, and richly developed.

Her beauty owed nothing to her toilet—her only decoration was the coronet of her own rich black hair; her only hair pin was a thorn; her dress indeed was a masterpiece of domestic manufacture,—the cotton from which it was made having been carded, spun, woven, and dyed by Miss Hannah's own busy hands; but as it was only a coarse blue fabric, after all, it would not be considered highly ornamental; it was new and clean, however, and Nora was well pleased with it, as with playful impatience she repeated her question:

"Say! aint you proud of me now?"

"No," replied the elder sister, with assumed gravity; "I am proud of your dress because it is my own handiwork, and it does me credit; but as for you—"

"I am Nature's handiwork, and I do her credit!" interrupted Nora, with gay self-assertion.

"I am quite ashamed of you, you are so vain!" continued Hannah, completing her sentence.

"Oh, vain, am I? Very well, then, another time I will keep my vanity to myself. It is quite as easy to conceal as to confess, you know; though it may not be quite as good for the soul," exclaimed Nora, with merry perversity, as she danced off in search of her bonnet.

She had not far to look; for the one poor room contained all of the sisters' earthly goods. And they were easily summed up—a bed in one corner, a loom in another, a spinning-wheel in the third, and a corner-cupboard in the fourth; a chest of drawers sat against the wall between the bed and the loom, and a pine table against the opposite wall between the spinning-wheel and the cupboard; four wooden chairs sat just wherever they could be crowded. There was no carpet on the floor, no paper on the walls. There was but one door and one window to the hut, and they were in front. Opposite them at the back of the room was a wide fire-place, with a rude mantle

4

shelf above it, adorned with old brass candlesticks as bright as gold. Poor as this hut was, the most fastidious fine lady need not have feared to sit down within it, it was so purely clean.

The sisters were soon ready, and after closing up their wee hut as cautiously as if it contained the wealth of India, they set forth, in their blue cotton gowns and white cotton bonnets, to attend the grand birthday festival of the young heir of Brudenell Hall.

Around them spread out a fine, rolling, well-wooded country; behind them stood their own little hut upon the top of its bare hill; below them lay a deep, thickly-wooded valley, beyond which rose another hill, crowned with an elegant mansion of white free-stone. That was Brudenell Hall.

Thus the hut and the hall perched upon opposite hills, looked each other in the face across the wooded valley. And both belonged to the same vast plantation—the largest in the county. The morning was indeed delicious, the earth everywhere springing with young grass and early flowers; the forest budding with tender leaves; the freed brooks singing as they ran; the birds darting about here and there seeking materials to build their nests; the heavens benignly smiling over all; the sun glorious; the air intoxicating; mere breath joy; mere life rapture! All nature singing a Gloria in Excelsis! And now while the sisters saunter leisurely on, pausing now and then to admire some exquisite bit of scenery, or to watch some bird, or to look at some flower, taking their own time for passing through the valley that lay between the hut and the hall, I must tell you who and what they were.

Hannah and Leonora Worth were orphans, living alone together in the hut on the hill and supporting themselves by spinning and weaving.

Hannah, the eldest, was but twenty-eight years old, yet looked forty; for, having been the eldest sister, the mother-sister, of a large family of orphan children, all of whom had died except the youngest, Leonora,—her face wore that anxious, haggard, care-worn and prematurely aged look peculiar to women who have the burdens of life too soon and too heavily laid upon them. Her black hair was even streaked here and there with gray. But with all this there was not the least trace of impatience or despondency in that all-enduring face. When grave, its expression was that of resignation; when gay—and even she could be gay at times—its smile was as sunny as Leonora's own. Hannah had a lover as patient as Job, or as herself, a poor fellow who had been constant to her for twelve years, and whose fate resembled her own; for he was the father of all his orphan brothers and sisters as she had been the mother of hers. Of course, these poor lovers could not dream of marriage; but they loved each other all the better upon that very account, perhaps.

Lenora was ten years younger than her sister, eighteen, well grown, well developed, blooming, beautiful, gay and happy as we have described her. She had not a care, or regret, or sorrow in the world. She was a bird, the hut was her nest and Hannah her mother, whose wings covered her. These sisters were very poor; not, however, as the phrase is understood in the large cities, where, notwithstanding the many charitable institutions for the mitigation of poverty, scores of people perish annually from cold and hunger; but as it is understood in the rich lower counties of Maryland, where forests filled with game and rivers swarming with fish afford abundance of food and fuel to even the poorest hutters, however destitute they might be of proper shelter, clothing, or education.

And though these orphan sisters could not hunt or fish, they could buy cheaply a plenty of game from the negroes who did. And besides this, they had a pig, a cow, and a couple of sheep that grazed freely in the neighboring fields, for no one thought of turning out an animal that belonged to these poor girls. In addition, they kept a few fowls and cultivated a small vegetable garden in the rear of their hut. And to keep the chickens out of the garden was one of the principal occupations of Nora. Their spinning-wheel and loom supplied them with the few articles of clothing they required, and with a little money for the purchase of tea, sugar, and salt. Thus you see their living was good, though their dress, their house, and their schooling were so very bad. They were totally ignorant of the world beyond their own neighborhood; they could read and write, but very imperfectly; and their only book was the old family Bible, that might always be seen proudly displayed upon the rickety chest of drawers.

Notwithstanding their lowly condition, the sisters were much esteemed for their integrity of character by their richer neighbors, who would have gladly made them more comfortable had not the proud spirit of Hannah shrunk from dependence.

They had been invited to the festival to be held at Brudenell Hall in honor of the young heir's coming of age and entering upon his estates.

This gentlemen, Herman Brudenell, was their landlord; and it was as his tenants, and not by any means as his equals, that they had been bidden to the feast. And now we will accompany them to the house of rejoicing. They were now emerging from the valley and climbing the opposite hill. Hannah walking steadily on in the calm enjoyment of nature, and Nora darting about like a young bird and caroling as she went in the effervescence of her delight.

CHAPTER II.

Her sweet song died, and a vague unrest
And a nameless longing filled her breast.
—*Whittier.*

The sisters had not seen their young landlord since he was a lad of ten years of age, at which epoch he had been sent to Europe to receive his education. He had but recently been recalled home by his widowed mother, for the purpose of entering upon his estate and celebrating his majority in his patrimonial mansion by giving a dinner and ball in the house to all his kindred and friends, and a feast and dance in the barn to all his tenants and laborers.

It was said that his lady mother and his two young lady sisters, haughty and repellent women that they were, had objected to entertaining his dependents, but the young gentleman was resolved that they should enjoy themselves. And he had his way.

Nora had no recollection whatever of Herman Brudenell, who had been taken to Europe while she was still a baby; so now, her curiosity being stimulated, she plied Hannah with a score of tiresome questions about him.

"Is he tall, Hannah, dear? Is he very handsome?"

"How can I tell? I have not seen him since he was ten years old."

"But what is his complexion—is he fair or dark? and what is the color of his hair and eyes? Surely, you can tell that at least."

"Yes; his complexion, as well as I can recollect it, was freckled, and his hair sandy, and his eyes green."

"Oh-h! the horrid fright! a man to scare bad children into good behavior! But then that was when he was but ten years old; he is twenty-one to-day; perhaps he is much improved."

"Nora, our sheep have passed through here, and left some of their wool on the bushes. Look at that little bird, it has found a flake and is bearing it off in triumph to line its little nest," said Hannah, to change the subject.

"Oh, I don't care about the bird; I wish you to tell me about the young gentleman!" said Nora petulantly, adding the question: "I wonder who he'll marry?"

"Not you, my dear; so you had better not occupy your mind with him," Hannah replied very gravely.

Nora laughed outright. "Oh, I'm quite aware of that; and as for me, I would not marry a prince, if he had red hair and a freckled face; but still one cannot help thinking of one's landlord, when one is going to attend the celebration of his birthday."

They had now reached the top of the hill and come upon a full view of the house and grounds.

The house, as I said, was a very elegant edifice of white free-stone; it was two stories in height, and had airy piazzas running the whole length of the front, both above and below; a stately portico occupied the center of the lower piazza, having on each side of it the tall windows of the drawing-rooms. This portico and all these windows were now wide open, mutely proclaiming welcome to all comers. The beautifully laid out grounds were studded here and there with tents pitched under the shade trees, for the accommodation of the out-door guest, who were now assembling rapidly.

But the more honored guests of the house had not yet begun to arrive.

And none of the family were as yet visible.

On reaching the premises the sisters were really embarrassed, not knowing where to go, and finding no one to direct them.

At length a strange figure appeared upon the scene—a dwarfish mulatto, with a large head, bushy hair, and having the broad forehead and high nose of the European, with the thick lips and heavy jaws of the African; with an ashen gray complexion, and a penetrating, keen and sly expression of the eyes. With this strange combination of features he had also the European intellect with the African utterance. He was a very gifted original, whose singularities of genius and character will reveal themselves in the course of this history, and he was also one of those favored old family domestics whose power in the house was second only to that of the master, and whose will was law to all his fellow servants; he had just completed his fiftieth year, and his name was Jovial.

And he now approached the sisters, saying:

6

"Mornin', Miss Hannah—mornin', Miss Nora. Come to see de show? De young heir hab a fool for his master for de fust time to-day."

"We have come to the birthday celebration; but we do not know where we ought to go—whether to the house or the tents," said Hannah.

The man tucked his tongue into his cheek and squinted at the sisters, muttering to himself:

"I should like to see de mist'ess' face, ef you two was to present yourselves at de house!"

Then, speaking aloud, he said:

"De house be for de quality, an' de tents for de colored gemmen and ladies; an' de barn for de laborin' classes ob de whites. Shall I hab de honor to denounce you to de barn?"

"I thank you, yes, since it is there we are expected to go," said Hannah.

Jovial led the way to an immense barn that had been cleaned out and decorated for the occasion. The vast room was adorned with festoons of evergreens and paper flowers. At the upper end was hung the arms of the Brudenells. Benches were placed along the walls for the accommodation of those who might wish to sit. The floor was chalked for the dancers.

"Dere, young women, dere you is," said Jovial loftily, as he introduced the sisters into this room, and retired.

There were some thirty-five or forty persons present, including men, women, and children, but no one that was known to the sisters. They therefore took seats in a retired corner, from which they watched the company.

"How many people there are! Where could they all have come from?" inquired Nora.

"I do not know. From a distance, I suppose. People will come a long way to a feast like this. And you know that not only were the tenants and laborers invited, but they were asked to bring all their friends and relations as well!" said Hannah.

"And they seemed to have improved the opportunity," added Nora.

"Hush, my dear; I do believe here come Mr. Brudenell and the ladies," said Hannah.

And even as she spoke the great doors of the barn were thrown open, and the young landlord and his family entered.

First came Mr. Brudenell, a young gentleman of medium height, and elegantly rather than strongly built; his features were regular and delicate; his complexion fair and clear; his hair of a pale, soft, golden tint; and in contrast to all this, his eyes were of a deep, dark, burning brown, full of fire, passion, and fascination. There was no doubt about it—he was beautiful! I know that is a strange term to apply to a man, but it is the only true and comprehensive one to characterize the personal appearance of Herman Brudenell. He was attired in a neat black dress suit, without ornaments of any kind; without even a breastpin or a watch chain.

Upon his arm leaned his mother, a tall, fair woman with light hair, light blue eyes, high aquiline features, and a haughty air. She wore a rich gray moire antique, and a fine lace cap.

Behind them came the two young lady sisters, so like their mother that no one could have mistaken them. They wore white muslin dresses, sashes of blue ribbon, and wreaths of blue harebells. They advanced with smiles intended to be gracious, but which were only condescending.

The eyes of all the people in the barn were fixed upon this party, except those of Nora Worth, which were riveted upon the young heir.

And this was destiny!

There was nothing unmaidenly in her regard. She looked upon him as a peasant girl might look upon a passing prince—as something grand, glorious, sunlike, and immeasurably above her sphere; but not as a human being, not as a young man precisely like other young men.

While thus, with fresh lips glowingly apart, and blushing cheeks, and eyes full of innocent admiration, she gazed upon him, he suddenly turned around, and their eyes met full. He smiled sweetly, bowed lowly, and turned slowly away. And she, with childlike delight, seized her sister's arm and exclaimed:

"Oh, Hannah, the young heir bowed to me, he did indeed!"

"He could do no less, since you looked at him so hard," replied the sister gravely.

"But to me, Hannah, to me—just think of it! No one ever bowed to me before, not even the negroes! and to think of him—Mr. Brudenell—bowing to me—me!"

"I tell you he could do no less; he caught you looking at him; to have continued staring you in the face would have been rude; to have turned abruptly away would have been equally so; gentlemen are never guilty of rudeness, and Mr. Brudenell is a gentleman; therefore he bowed to you, as I believe he would have bowed to a colored girl even."

"Oh, but he smiled! he smiled so warmly and brightly, just for all the world like the sun shining out, and as if, as if—"

"As if what, you little goose?"

"Well, then, as if he was pleased."

"It was because he was amused; he was laughing at you, you silly child!"

"Do you think so?" asked Nora, with a sudden change of tone from gay to grave.

"I am quite sure of it, dear," replied the elder sister, speaking her real opinion.

"Laughing at me," repeated Nora to herself, and she fell into thought.

Meanwhile, with a nod to one a smile to another and a word to a third, the young heir and his party passed down the whole length of the room, and retired through an upper door. As soon as they were gone the negro fiddlers, six in number, led by Jovial, entered, took their seats, tuned their instruments, and struck up a lively reel.

There was an, immediate stir; the rustic beaus sought their belles, and sets were quickly formed.

A long, lanky, stooping young man, with a pale, care-worn face and grayish hair, and dressed in a homespun jacket and trousers, came up to the sisters.

"Dance, Hannah?" he inquired.

"No, thank you, Reuben; take Nora out—she would like to."

"Dance, Nora?" said Reuben Gray, turning obediently to the younger sister.

"Set you up with it, after asking Hannah first, right before my very eyes. I'm not a-going to take anybody's cast-offs, Mr. Reuben!"

"I hope you are not angry with, me for that, Nora? It was natural I should prefer to dance with your sister. I belong to her like, you know. Don't be mad with me," said Reuben meekly.

"Nonsense, Rue! you know I was joking. Make Hannah dance; it will do her good; she mopes too much," laughed Nora.

"Do, Hannah, do, dear; you know I can't enjoy myself otherways," said the docile fellow.

"And it is little enjoyment you have in this world, poor soul!" said Hannah Worth, as she rose and placed her hand in his.

"Ah, but I have a great deal, Hannah, dear, when I'm along o' you," he whispered gallantly, as he led her off to join the dancers.

And they were soon seen tritting, whirling, heying, and selling with the best of them—forgetting in the contagious merriment of the music and motion all their cares.

Nora was besieged with admirers, who solicited her hand for the dance. But to one and all she returned a negative. She was tired with her long walk, and would not dance, at least not this set; she preferred to sit still and watch the others. So at last she was left to her chosen occupation. She had sat thus but a few moments, her eyes lovingly following the flying forms of Reuben and Hannah through the mazes of the dance, her heart rejoicing in their joy, when a soft voice murmured at her ear.

"Sitting quite alone, Nora? How is that? The young men have not lost their wits, I hope?"

She started, looked up, and with a vivid blush recognized her young landlord. He was bending over her with the same sweet ingenuous smile that had greeted her when their eyes first met that morning. She drooped the long, dark lashes over her eyes until they swept her carmine cheeks, but she did not answer.

"I have just deposited my mother and sisters in their drawing-room, and I have returned to look at the dancers. May I take this seat left vacant by your sister?" he asked.

"Certainly you may, sir," she faltered forth, trembling with, a vague delight.

"How much they enjoy themselves—do they not?" he asked, as he took the seat and looked upon the dancers with a benevolent delight that irradiated his fair, youthful countenance.

"Oh, indeed they do, sir," said Nora, unconsciously speaking more from her own personal experience of present happiness than from her observation of others.

I wish I could arrive at my majority every few weeks, or else have some other good excuse for giving a great feast. I do so love to see people happy, Nora. It is the greatest pleasure I have in the world."

"Yet you must have a great many other pleasures, sir; all wealthy people must," said Nora, gaining courage to converse with one so amiable as she found her young landlord.

"Yes, I have many others; but the greatest of all is the happiness of making others happy. But why are you not among these dancers, Nora?"

"I was tired with my long walk up and down hill and dale. So I would not join them this set."

"Are you engaged for the next?"

"No, sir."

"Then be my partner for it, will you?"

"Oh, sir!" And the girl's truthful face flashed with surprise and delight.

"Will you dance with me, then, for the next set?"

"Yes, sir, please."

"Thank you, Nora. But now tell me, did you recollect me as well as I remembered you?"

"No, sir."

"But that is strange; for I knew you again the instant I saw you."

"But, sir, you know I was but a baby when you went away?"

"That is true."

"But how, then, did you know me again?" she wonderingly inquired.

"Easily enough. Though you have grown up into such a fine young woman, your face has not changed its character, Nora. You have the same broad, fair forehead and arched brows; the same dark gray eyes and long lashes; the same delicate nose and budding mouth; and the same peculiar way of smiling only with your eyes; in a word—but pardon me, Nora, I forgot myself in speaking to you so plainly. Here is a new set forming already. Your sister and her partner are going to dance together again; shall we join them?" he suddenly inquired, upon seeing that his direct praise, in which he had spoken in ingenuous frankness, had brought the blushes again to Nora's cheeks.

She arose and gave him her hand, and he led her forth to the head of the set that was now forming, where she stood with downcast and blushing face, admired by all the men, and envied by all the women that were present.

This was not the only time he danced with her. He was cordial to all his guests, but he devoted himself to Nora. This exclusive attention of the young heir to the poor maiden gave anxiety to her sister and offense to all the other women.

"No good will come of it," said one.

"No good ever does come of a rich young man paying attention to a poor girl," added another.

"He is making a perfect fool of himself," said a third indignantly.

"He is making a perfect fool of her, you had better say," amended a fourth, more malignant than the rest.

"Hannah, I don't like it! I'm a sort of elder brother-in-law to her, you know, and I don't like it. Just see how he looks at her, Hannah! Why, if I was to melt down my heart and pour it all into my face, I couldn't look at you that-a-way, Hannah, true as I love you. Why, he's just eating of her up with his eyes, and as for her, she looks as if it was pleasant to be swallowed by him!" said honest Reuben Gray, as he watched the ill-matched young pair as they sat absorbed in each other's society in a remote corner of the barn.

"Nor do I like it, Reuben," sighed Hannah.

"I've a great mind to interfere! I've a right to! I'm her brother-in-law to be."

"No, do not, Reuben; it would do more harm than good; it would make her and everybody else think more seriously of these attentions than they deserve. It is only for to-night, you know. After this, they will scarcely ever meet to speak to each other again."

"As you please, Hannah, you are wiser than I am; but still, dear, I must say that a great deal of harm may be done in a day. Remember, dear, that (though I don't call it harm, but the greatest blessing of my life) it was at a corn-shucking, where we met for the first time, that you and I fell in love long of each other, and have we ever fell out of it yet? No, Hannah, nor never will. But as you and I are both poor, and faithful, and patient, and broken in like to bear things cheerful, no harm has come of our falling in love at that corn-shucking. But now, s'pose them there children fall in love long of each other by looking into each other's pretty eyes—who's to hinder it? And that will be the end of it? He can't marry her; that's impossible; a man of his rank and a girl of hers! his mother and sisters would never let him! and if they would, his own pride wouldn't! And so he'd go away and try to forget her, and she'd stop home and break her heart. Hannah, love is like a fire, easy to put out in the beginning, unpossible at the end. You just better let me go and heave a bucket of water on to that there love while it is a-kindling and before the blaze breaks out."

"Go then, good Reuben, and tell Nora that I am going home and wish her to come to me at once."

Reuben arose to obey, but was interrupted by the appearance of a negro footman from the house, who came up to him and said:

"Mr. Reuben, de mistess say will you say to de young marster how de gemmen an' ladies is all arrive, an' de dinner will be sarve in ten minutes, an' how she 'sires his presence at de house immediate."

"Certainly, John! This is better, Hannah, than my interference would have been," said Reuben Gray, as he hurried off to execute his mission.

So completely absorbed in each other's conversation were the young pair that they did not observe Reuben's approach until he stood before them, and, touching his forehead, said respectfully:

"Sir, Madam Brudenell has sent word as the vis'ters be all arrived at the house, and the dinner will be ready in ten minutes, so she wishes you, if you please, to come directly."

"So late!" exclaimed the young man, looking at his watch, and starting up, "how time flies in some society! Nora, I will conduct you to your sister, and then go and welcome our guests at the house; although I had a great deal rather stay where I am," he added, in a whisper.

"If you please, sir, I can take her to Hannah," suggested Reuben.

But without paying any attention to this friendly offer, the young man gave his hand to the maiden and led her down the whole length of the barn, followed by Reuben, and also by the envious eyes of all the assembly.

"Here she is, Hannah. I have brought her back to you quite safe, not even weary with dancing. I hope I have helped her to enjoy herself," said the young heir gayly, as he deposited the rustic beauty by the side of her sister.

"You are very kind, sir," said Hannah coldly.

"Ah, you there, Reuben! Be sure you take good care of this little girl, and see that she has plenty of pleasant partners," said the young gentleman, on seeing Gray behind.

"Be sure I shall take care of her, sir, as if she was my sister, as I hope some day she may be," replied the man.

"And be careful that she gets a good place at the supper-table—there will be a rush, you know."

"I shall see to that, sir."

"Good evening, Hannah; good evening, Nora," said the young heir, smiling and bowing as he withdrew from the sisters.

Nora sighed; it might have been from fatigue. Several country beaus approached, eagerly contending, now that the coast was clear, for the honor of the beauty's hand in the dance. But Nora refused one and all. She should dance no more this evening, she said. Supper came on, and Reuben, with one sister on each arm, led them out to the great tent where it was spread. There was a rush. The room was full and the table was crowded; but Reuben made good places for the sisters, and stood behind their chairs to wait on them. Hannah, like a happy, working, practical young woman in good health, who had earned an appetite, did ample justice to the luxuries placed before them. Nora ate next to nothing. In vain Hannah and Reuben offered everything to her in turn; she would take nothing. She was not hungry, she said; she was tired and wanted to go home.

"But wouldn't you rather stay and see the fireworks, Nora?" inquired Reuben Gray, as they arose from the table to give place to someone else.

"I don't know. Will—will Mr.—I mean Mrs. Brudenell and the young ladies come out to see them, do you think?"

"No, certainly, they will not; these delicate creatures would never stand outside in the night air for that purpose."

"I—I don't think I care about stopping to see the fireworks, Reuben," said Nora.

"But I tell you what, John said how the young heir, the old madam, the young ladies, and the quality folks was all a-going to see the fireworks from the upper piazza. They have got all the red-cushioned settees and arm-chairs put out there for them to sit on."

"Reuben, I—I think I will stop and see the fireworks; that is, if Hannah is willing," said Nora musingly.

And so it was settled.

The rustics, after having demolished the whole of the plentiful supper, leaving scarcely a bone or a crust behind them, rushed out in a body, all the worse for a cask of old rye whisky that had been broached, and began to search for eligible stands from which to witness the exhibition of the evening.

Reuben conducted the sisters to a high knoll at some distance from the disorderly crowd, but from which they could command a fine view of the fireworks, which were to be let off in the lawn that lay below their standpoint and between them and the front of the dwelling-house. Here they sat as the evening closed in. As soon as it was quite dark the whole front of the mansion-house suddenly blazed forth in a blinding illumination. There were stars, wheels, festoons, and leaves, all in fire. In the center burned a rich transparency, exhibiting the arms of the Brudenells.

10

During this illumination none of the family appeared in front, as their forms must have obscured a portion of the lights. It lasted some ten or fifteen minutes, and then suddenly went out, and everything was again dark as midnight. Suddenly from the center of the lawn streamed up a rocket, lighting up with a lurid fire all the scene—the mansion-house with the family and their more honored guests now seated upon the upper piazza, the crowds of men, women, and children, white, black, and mixed, that stood with upturned faces in the lawn, the distant knoll on which were grouped the sisters and their protector, the more distant forests and the tops of remote hills, which all glowed by night in this red glare. This seeming conflagration lasted a minute, and then all was darkness again. This rocket was but the signal for the commencement of the fireworks on the lawn. Another and another, each more brilliant than the last, succeeded. There were stars, wheels, serpents, griffins, dragons, all flashing forth from the darkness in living fire, filling the rustic spectators with admiration, wonder, and terror, and then as suddenly disappearing as if swallowed up in the night from which they had sprung. One instant the whole scene was lighted up as by a general conflagration, the next it was hidden in darkness deep as midnight. The sisters, no more than their fellow-rustics, had never witnessed the marvel of fireworks, so now they gazed from their distant standpoint on the knoll with interest bordering upon consternation.

"Don't you think they're dangerous, Reuben?" inquired Hannah.

"No, dear; else such a larned gentleman as Mr. Brudenell, and such a prudent lady as the old madam, would never allow them," answered Gray.

Nora did not speak; she was absorbed not only by the fireworks themselves, but by the group on the balcony that each illumination revealed; or, to be exact, by one face in that group—the face of Herman Brudenell.

At length the exhibition closed with one grand tableau in many colored fire, displaying the family group of Brudenell, surmounted by their crest, arms, and supporters, all encircled by wreaths of flowers. This splendid transparency illumined the whole scene with dazzling light. It was welcomed by deafening huzzas from the crowd. When the noise had somewhat subsided, Reuben Gray, gazing with the sisters from their knoll upon all this glory, touched Nora upon the shoulder and said:

"Look!"

"I am looking," she said.

"What do you see?"

"The fireworks, of course."

"And what beyond them?"

"The great house—Brudenell Hall."

"And there?"

"The party on the upper piazza."

"With Mr. Brudenell in the midst?"

"Yes."

"Now, then, observe! You see him, but it is across the glare of the fireworks! There is fire between you and him, girl—a gulf of fire! See that you do not dream either he or you can pass it! For either to do so would be to sink one, and that is yourself, in burning fire—in consuming shame! Oh, Nora, beware!"

He had spoken thus! he, the poor unlettered man who had scarcely ever opened his mouth before without a grievous assault upon good English! he had breathed these words of eloquent warning, as if by direct inspiration, as though his lips, like those of the prophet of old, had been touched by the living coal from Heaven. His solemn words awed Hannah, who understood them by sympathy, and frightened Nora, who did not understand them at all. The last rays of the finale were dying out, and with their expiring light the party on the upper piazza were seen to bow to the rustic assembly on the lawn, and then to withdraw into the house.

And thus ended the fête day of the young heir of Brudenell Hall.

The guests began rapidly to disperse.

Reuben Gray escorted the sisters home, talking with Hannah all the way, not upon the splendors of the festival—a topic he seemed willing to have forgotten, but upon crops, stock, wages, and the price of tea and sugar. This did not prevent Nora from dreaming on the interdicted subject; on the contrary, it left her all the more opportunity to do so, until they all three reached the door of the hill hut, where Reuben Gray bade them good-night.

CHAPTER III.

PASSION.

If we are nature's, this is ours—this thorn
Doth to our rose of youth rightly belong;
It is the show and seal of nature's truth
When love's strong passion is impressed in youth.
—*Shakspere*.

What a contrast! the interior of that poor hut to all the splendors they had left! The sisters both were tired, and quickly undressed and went to bed, but not at once to sleep.

Hannah had the bad habit of laying awake at night, studying how to make the two ends of her income and her outlay meet at the close of the year, just as if loss of rest ever helped on the solution to that problem!

Nora, for her part, lay awake in a disturbance of her whole nature, which she could neither understand nor subdue! Nora had never read a poem, a novel, or a play in her life; she had no knowledge of the world; and no instructress but her old maiden sister. Therefore Nora knew no more of love than does the novice who has never left her convent! She could not comprehend the reason why after meeting with Herman Brudenell she had taken such a disgust at the rustic beaus who had hitherto pleased her; nor yet why her whole soul was so very strangely troubled; why at once she was so happy and so miserable; and, above all, why she could not speak of these things to her sister Hannah. She tossed about in feverish excitement.

"What in the world is the matter with you, Nora? You are as restless as a kitten; what ails you?" asked Hannah.

"Nothing," was the answer.

Now everyone who has looked long upon life knows that of all the maladies, mental or physical, that afflict human nature, "nothing" is the most common, the most dangerous, and the most incurable! When you see a person preoccupied, downcast, despondent, and ask him, "What is the matter?" and he answers, "Nothing," be sure that it is something great, unutterable, or fatal! Hannah Worth knew this by instinct, and so she answered:

"Nonsense, Nora! I know there is something that keeps you awake; what is it now?"

"Really—and indeed it is nothing serious; only I am thinking over what we have seen to-day!"

"Oh! but try to go to sleep now, my dear," said Hannah, as if satisfied.

"I can't; but, Hannah, I say, are you and Reuben Gray engaged?"

"Yes, dear."

"How long have you been engaged?"

"For more than twelve years, dear."

"My—good—gracious—me—alive! Twelve years! Why on earth don't you get married, Hannah?"

"He cannot afford it, dear; it takes everything he can rake and scrape to keep his mother and his little brothers and sisters, and even with all that they often want."

"Well, then, why don't he let you off of your promise?"

"Nora!—what! why we would no sooner think of breaking with each other than if we had been married, instead of being engaged all these twelve years!"

"Well, then, when do you expect to be married?"

"I do not know, dear; when his sisters and brothers are all grown up and off his hands, I suppose."

"And that won't be for the next ten years—even if then! Hannah, you will be an elderly woman, and he an old man, before that!"

"Yes, dear, I know that; but we must be patient; for everyone in this world has something to bear, and we must accept our share. And even if it should be in our old age that Reuben and myself come together, what of that? We shall have all eternity before us to live together; for, Nora, dear, I look upon myself as his promised wife for time and eternity. Therefore, you see there is no such thing possible as for me to break with Reuben. We belong to each other forever, and the Lord himself knows it. And now, dear, be quiet and try to sleep; for we must rise early to-morrow to make up by industry for the time lost to-day; so, once more, good-night, dear."

Nora responded to this good-night, and turned her head to the wall—not to sleep, but to muse on those fiery, dark-brown eyes that had looked such mysterious meanings into hers, and that thrilling deep-toned voice that had breathed such sweet praise in her ears. And so musing, Nora fell asleep, and her reverie passed into dreams.

Early the next morning the sisters were up. The weather had changed with the usual abruptness of our capricious climate. The day before had been like June. This day was like January. A dark-gray sky overhead, with black clouds driven by an easterly wind scudding across it, and threatening a rain storm.

The sisters hurried through their morning work, got their frugal breakfast over, put their room in order, and sat down to their daily occupation—Hannah before her loom, Nora beside her spinning-wheel. The clatter of the loom, the whir of the wheel, admitted of no conversation between the workers; so Hannah worked, as usual, in perfect silence, and Nora, who ever before sung to the sound of her humming wheel, now mused instead. The wind rose in occasional gusts, shaking the little hut in its exposed position on the hill.

"How different from yesterday," sighed Nora, at length.

"Yes, dear; but such is life," said Hannah. And there the conversation ended, and only the clatter of the loom and the whir of the wheel was heard again, the sisters working on in silence. But hark! Why has the wheel suddenly stopped and the heart of Nora started to rapid beating?

A step came crashing through the crisp frost, and a hand was on the door-latch.

"It is Mr. Brudenell! What can he want here?" exclaimed Hannah, in a tone of impatience, as she arose and opened the door.

The fresh, smiling, genial face of the young man met her there. His kind, cordial, cheery voice addressed her: "Good morning, Hannah! I have been down to the bay this morning, you see, bleak as it is, and the fish bite well! See this fine rock fish! will you accept it from me? And oh, will you let me come in and thaw out my half-frozen fingers by your fire? or will you keep me standing out here in the cold?" he added, smiling.

"Walk in, sir," said Hannah, inhospitably enough, as she made way for him to enter.

He came in, wearing his picturesque fisherman's dress, carrying his fishing-rod over his right shoulder, and holding in his left hand the fine rock fish of which he had spoken. His eyes searched for and found Nora, whose face was covered with the deepest blushes.

"Good morning, Nora! I hope you enjoyed yourself yesterday. Did they take care of you after I left?" he inquired, going up to her.

"Yes, thank you, sir."

"Mr. Brudenell, will you take this chair?" said Hannah, placing one directly before the fire, and pointing to it without giving him time to speak another word to Nora.

"Thank you, yes, Hannah; and will you relieve me of this fish?"

"No, thank you, sir; I think you had better take it up to the madam," said Hannah bluntly.

"What! carry this all the way from here to Brudenell, after bringing it from the bay? Whatever are you thinking of, Hannah?" laughed the young man, as he stepped outside for a moment and hung the fish on a nail in the wall. "There it is, Hannah," he said, returning and taking his seat at the fire; "you can use it or throw it away, as you like."

Hannah made no reply to this; she did not wish to encourage him either to talk or to prolong his stay. Her very expression of countenance was cold and repellent almost to rudeness. Nora saw this and sympathized with him, and blamed her sister.

"To think," she said to herself, "that he was so good to us when we went to see him; and Hannah is so rude to him, now he has come to see us! It is a shame! And see how well he bears it all, too, sitting there warming his poor white hands."

In fact, the good humor of the young man was imperturbable. He sat there, as Nora observed, smiling and spreading his hands out over the genial blaze and seeking to talk amicably with Hannah, and feeling compensated for all the rebuffs he received from the elder sister whenever he encountered a compassionate glance from the younger, although at the meeting of their eyes her glance was instantly withdrawn and succeeded by fiery blushes. He stayed as long as he had the least excuse for doing so, and then arose to take his leave, half smiling at Hannah's inhospitable surliness and his own perseverance under difficulties. He went up to Nora to bid her good-by. He took her hand, and as he gently pressed it he looked into her eyes; but hers fell beneath his gaze; and with a simple "Good-day, Nora," he turned away.

Hannah stood holding the cottage door wide open for his exit.

"Good morning, Hannah," he said smilingly, as he passed out.

She stepped after him, saying:

"Mr. Brudenell, sir, I must beg you not to come so far out of your way again to bring us a fish. We thank you; but we could not accept it. This also I must request you to take away." And detaching the rock fish from the nail where it hung, she put it in his hands.

He laughed good-humoredly as he took it, and without further answer than a low bow walked swiftly down the hill.

Hannah re-entered the hut and found herself in the midst of a tempest in a tea-pot.

Nora had a fiery temper of her own, and now it blazed out upon her sister—her beautiful face was stormy with grief and indignation as she exclaimed:

"Oh, Hannah! how could you act so shamefully? To think that yesterday you and I ate and drank and feasted and danced all day at his place, and received so much kindness and attention from him besides, and to-day you would scarcely let him sit down and warm his feet in ours! You treated him worse than a dog, you did, Hannah. And he felt it, too. I saw he did, though he was too much of a gentleman to show it! And as for me, I could have died from mortification!"

"My child," answered Hannah gravely, "however badly you or he might have felt, believe me, I felt the worse of the three, to be obliged to take the course I did."

"He will never come here again, never!" sobbed Nora, scarcely heeding the reply of her sister.

"I hope to Heaven he never may!" said Hannah, as she resumed her seat at her loom and drove the shuttle "fast and furious" from side to side of her cloth.

But he did come again. Despite the predictions of Nora and the prayers of Hannah and the inclemency of the weather.

The next day was a tempestuous one, with rain, snow, hail, and sleet all driven before a keen northeast wind, and the sisters, with a great roaring fire in the fireplace between them, were seated the one at her loom and the other at her spinning-wheel, when there came a rap at the door, and before anyone could possibly have had time to go to it, it was pushed open, and Herman Brudenell, covered with snow and sleet, rushed quickly in.

"For Heaven's sake, my dear Hannah, give me shelter from the storm! I couldn't wait for ceremony, you see! I had to rush right in after knocking! pardon me! Was ever such a climate as this of ours! What a day for the seventeenth of April! It ought to be bottled up and sent abroad as a curiosity!" he exclaimed, all in a breath, as he unceremoniously took off his cloak and shook it and threw it over a chair.

"Mr. Brudenell! You here again! What could have brought you out on such a day?" cried Hannah, starting up from her loom in extreme surprise.

"The spirit of restlessness, Hannah! It is so dull up there, and particularly on a dull day! How do you do, Nora? Blooming as a rose, eh?" he said, suddenly breaking off and going to shake hands with the blushing girl.

"Never mind Nora's roses, Mr. Brudenell; attend to me; I ask did you expect to find it any livelier here in this poor hut than in your own princely halls?" said Hannah, as she placed a chair before the fire for his accommodation.

"A great deal livelier, Hannah," he replied, with boyish frankness, as he took his seat and spread out his hands before the cheerful blaze. "No end to the livelier. Why, Hannah, it is always lively where there's nature, and always dull where there's not! Up yonder now there's too much art; high art indeed—but still art! From my mother and sisters all nature seems to have been educated, refined, and polished away. There we all sat this morning in the parlor, the young ladies punching holes in pieces of muslin, to sew them up again, and calling the work embroidery; and there was my mother, actually working a blue lamb on red grass, and calling her employment worsted work. There was no talk but of patterns, no fire but what was shut up close in a horrid radiator. Really, out of doors was more inviting than in. I thought I would just throw on my cloak and walk over here to see how you were getting along this cold weather, and what do I find here? A great open blazing woodfire—warm, fragrant, and cheerful as only such a fire can be! and a humming wheel and a dancing loom, two cheerful girls looking bright as two chirping birds in their nest! This *is* like a nest! and it is worth the walk to find it. You'll not turn me out for an hour or so, Hannah?"

There was scarcely any such thing as resisting his gay, frank, boyish appeal; yet Hannah answered coldly:

"Certainly not, Mr. Brudenell, though I fancy you might have found more attractive company elsewhere. There can be little amusement for you in sitting there and listening to the flying shuttle or the whirling wheel, for hours together, pleasant as you might have first thought them."

"Yes, but it will! I shall hear music in the loom and wheel, and see pictures in the fire," said the young man, settling himself, comfortable.

Hannah drove her shuttle back and forth with a vigor that seemed to owe something to temper.

Herman heard no music and saw no pictures; his whole nature was absorbed in the one delightful feeling of being near Nora, only being near her, that was sufficient for the present to make him happy. To talk to her was impossible, even if he had greatly desired to do so; for the music of which he had spoken made too much noise.

He stayed as long as he possibly could, and then reluctantly arose to leave. He shook hands with Hannah first, reserving the dear delight of pressing Nora's hand for the last.

The next day the weather changed again; it was fine; and Herman Brudenell, as usual, presented himself at the hut; his excuse this time being that he wished to inquire whether the sisters would not like to have some repairs put upon the house—a new roof, another door and window, or even a new room added; if so, his carpenter was even now at Brudenell Hall, attending to some improvements there, and as soon as he was done he should be sent to the hut.

But no; Hannah wanted no repairs whatever. The hut was large enough for her and her sister, only too small to entertain visitors. So with this pointed home-thrust from Hannah, and a glance that at once healed the wound from Nora, he was forced to take his departure.

The next day he called again; he had, unluckily, left his gloves behind him during his preceding visit.

They were very nearly flung at his head by the thoroughly exasperated Hannah. But again he was made happy by a glance from Nora.

And, in short, almost every day he found some excuse for coming to the cottage, overlooking all Hannah's rude rebuffs with the most imperturbable good humor. At all these visits Hannah was present. She never left the house for an instant, even when upon one occasion she saw the cows in her garden, eating up all the young peas and beans. She let the garden be utterly destroyed rather than leave Nora to hear words of love that for her could mean nothing but misery. This went on for some weeks, when Hannah was driven to decisive measures by an unexpected event. Early one morning Hannah went to a village called "Baymouth," to procure coffee, tea, and sugar. She went there, did her errand, and returned to the hut as quickly as she could possibly could. As she suddenly opened the door she was struck with consternation by seeing the wheel idle and Nora and Herman seated close together, conversing in a low, confidential tone. They started up on seeing her, confusion on their faces.

Hannah was thoroughly self-possessed. Putting her parcels in Nora's hands, she said:

"Empty these in their boxes, dear, while I speak to Mr. Brudenell." Then turning to the young man, she said: "Sir, your mother, I believe, has asked to see me about some cloth she wishes to have woven. I am going over to her now; will you go with me?"

"Certainly, Hannah," replied Mr. Brudenell, seizing his hat in nervous trepidation, and forgetting or not venturing to bid good-by to Nora.

When they had got a little way from the hut, Hannah said:

"Mr. Brudenell, why do you come to our poor little house so often?"

The question, though it was expected, was perplexing.

"Why do I come, Hannah? Why, because I like to."

"Because you like to! Quite a sufficient reason for a gentleman to render for his actions, I suppose you think. But, now, another question: 'What are your intentions towards my sister?'"

"My intentions!" repeated the young man, in a thunderstruck manner. "What in the world do you mean, Hannah?"

"I mean to remind you that you have been visiting Nora for the last two months, and that to-day, when I entered the house, I found you sitting together as lovers sit; looking at each other as lovers look; and speaking in the low tones that lovers use; and when I reached you, you started in confusion—as lovers do when discovered at their love-making. Now I repeat my question, 'What are your intentions towards Nora Worth?'"

Herman Brudenell was blushing now, if he had never blushed before; his very brow was crimson. Hannah had to reiterate her question before his hesitating tongue could answer it.

"My intentions, Hannah? Nothing wrong, I do swear to you! Heaven knows, I mean no harm."

"I believe that, Mr. Brudenell! I have always believed it, else be sure that I should have found means to compel your absence. But though you might have meant no harm, did you mean any good, Mr. Brudenell?"

"Hannah, I fear that I meant nothing but to enjoy the great pleasure I derived from—from—Nora's society, and—"

"Stop there, Mr. Brudenell; do not add—mine; for that would be an insincerity unworthy of you! Of me you did not think, except as a marplot! You say you came for the great pleasure you enjoyed in Nora's society! Did it ever occur to you that she might learn to take too much pleasure in yours? Answer me truly."

"Hannah, yes, I believed that she was very happy in my company."

"In a word, you liked her, and you knew you were winning her liking! And yet you had no intentions of any sort, you say; you meant nothing, you admit, but to enjoy yourself! How, Mr. Brudenell, do you think it a manly part for a gentleman to seek to win a poor girl's love merely for his pastime?"

"Hannah, you are severe on me! Heaven knows I have never spoken one word of love to Nora."

"'Never spoken one word!' What of that? What need of words? Are not glances, are not tones, far more eloquent than words? With these glances and tones you have a thousand times assured my young sister that you love her, that you adore her, that you worship her!"

"Hannah, if my eyes spoke this language to Nora, they spoke Heaven's own truth! There! I have told you more than I ever told her, for to her my eyes only have spoken!" said the young man fervently.

"Of what were you talking with your heads so close together this morning?" asked Hannah abruptly.

"How do I know? Of birds, of flowers, moonshine, or some such rubbish. I was not heeding my words."

"No, your eyes were too busy! And now, Mr. Brudenell, I repeat my question: Was yours a manly part—discoursing all this love to Nora, and having no ultimate intentions?"

"Hannah, I never questioned my conscience upon that point; I was too happy for such cross-examination."

"But now the question is forced upon you, Mr. Brudenell, and we must have an answer now and here."

"Then, Hannah, I will answer truly! I love Nora; and if I were free to marry, I would make her my wife to-morrow; but I am not; therefore I have been wrong, and very wrong, to seek her society. I acted, however, from want of thought, not from want of principle; I hope you will believe that, Hannah."

"I do believe it, Mr. Brudenell."

"And now I put myself in your hands, Hannah! Direct me as you think best; I will obey you. What shall I do?"

"See Nora no more; from this day absent yourself from our house."

He turned pale as death, reeled, and supported himself against the trunk of a friendly tree.

Hannah looked at him, and from the bottom of her heart she pitied him; for she knew what love was—loving Reuben.

"Mr. Brudenell," she said, "do not take this to heart so much: why should you, indeed, when you know that your fate is in your own hands? You are master of your own destiny, and no man who is so should give way to despondency. The alternative before you is simply this: to cease to visit Nora, or to marry her. To do the first you must sacrifice your love, to do the last you must sacrifice your pride. Now choose between the courses of action! Gratify your love or your pride, as you see fit, and cheerfully pay down the price! This seems to me to be the only manly, the only rational, course."

"Oh, Hannah, Hannah, you do not understand! you do not!" he cried in a voice full of anguish.

"Yes, I do; I know how hard it would be to you in either case. On the one hand, what a cruel wrench it will give your heart to tear yourself from Nora—"

"Yes, yes; oh, Heaven, yes!"

"And, on the other hand, I know what an awful sacrifice you would make in marrying her—"

"It is not that! Oh, do me justice! I should not think it a sacrifice! She is too good for me! Oh, Hannah, it is not that which hinders!"

"It is the thought of your mother and sisters, perhaps; but surely if they love you, as I am certain they do, and if they see your happiness depends upon this marriage—in time they will yield!"

"It is not my family either, Hannah! Do you think that I would sacrifice my peace—or hers—to the unreasonable pride of my family? No, Hannah, no!"

"Then what is it? What stands in the way of your offering your hand to her to whom you have given your heart?"

"Hannah, I cannot tell you! Oh, Hannah, I feel that I have been very wrong, criminal even! But I acted blindly; you have opened my eyes, and now I see I must visit your house no more; how much it costs me to say this—to do this—you can never know!"

He wiped the perspiration from his pale brow, and, after a few moments given to the effort of composing himself, he asked:

"Shall we go on now?"

She nodded assent and they walked onward.

"Hannah," he said, as they went along, "I have one deplorable weakness."

She looked up suddenly, fearing to hear the confession of some fatal vice.

He continued:

16

"It is the propensity to please others, whether by doing so I act well or ill!"

"Mr. Brudenell!" exclaimed Hannah, in a shocked voice.

"Yes, the pain I feel in seeing others suffer, the delight I have in seeing them enjoy, often leads—leads me to sacrifice not only my own personal interests, but the principles of truth and justice!"

"Oh, Mr. Brudenell!"

"It is so, Hannah! And one signal instance of such a sacrifice at once of myself and of the right has loaded my life with endless regret! However, I am ungenerous to say this; for a gift once given, even if it is of that which one holds most precious in the world, should be forgotten or at least not be grudged by the giver! Ah, Hannah—" He stopped abruptly.

"Mr. Brudenell, you will excuse me for saying that I agree with you in your reproach of yourself. That trait of which you speak is a weakness which should be cured. I am but a poor country girl. But I have seen enough to know that sensitive and sympathizing natures like your own are always at the mercy of all around them. The honest and the generous take no advantage of such; but the selfish and the calculating make a prey of them! You call this weakness a propensity to please others! Mr. Brudenell, seek to please the Lord and He will give you strength to resist the spoilers," said Hannah gravely.

"Too late, too late, at least as far as this life is concerned, for I am ruined, Hannah!"

"Ruined! Mr. Brudenell!"

"Ruined, Hannah!"

"Good Heaven! I hope you have not endorsed for anyone to the whole extent of your fortune?"

"Ha, ha, ha! You make me laugh, Hannah! laugh in the very face of ruin, to think that you should consider loss of fortune a subject of such eternal regret as I told you my life was loaded with!"

"Oh, Mr. Brudenell, I have known you from childhood! I hope, I hope you haven't gambled or—"

"Thank Heaven, no, Hannah! I have never gambled, nor drank, nor—in fact, done anything of the sort!"

"You have not endorsed for anyone, nor gambled, nor drank, nor anything of that sort, and yet you are ruined!"

"Ruined and wretched, Hannah! I do not exaggerate in saying so!"

"And yet you looked so happy!"

"Grasses grow and flowers bloom above burning volcanoes, Hannah."

"Ah, Mr. Brudenell, what is the nature of this ruin then? Tell me! I am your sincere friend, and I am older than you; perhaps I could counsel you."

"It is past counsel, Hannah."

"What is it then?"

"I cannot tell you except this! that the fatality of which I speak is the only reason why I do not overstep the boundary of conventional rank and marry Nora! Why I do not marry anybody! Hush! here we are at the house."

Very stately and beautiful looked the mansion with its walls of white free-stone and its porticos of white marble, gleaming through its groves upon the top of the hill.

When they reached it Hannah turned to go around to the servants' door, but Mr. Brudenell called to her, saying:

"This way! this way, Hannah!" and conducted her up the marble steps to the visitors' entrance.

He preceded her into the drawing-room, a spacious apartment now in its simple summer dress of straw matting, linen covers, and lace curtains.

Mrs. Brudenell and the two young ladies, all in white muslin morning dresses, were gathered around a marble table in the recess of the back bay window, looking over newspapers.

On seeing the visitor who accompanied her son, Mrs. Brudenell arose with a look of haughty surprise.

"You wished to see Hannah Worth, I believe, mother, and here she is," said Herman.

"My housekeeper did. Touch the bell, if you please, Herman."

Mr. Brudenell did as requested, and the summons was answered by Jovial.

"Take this woman to Mrs. Spicer, and say that she has come about the weaving. When she leaves show her where the servants' door is, so that she may know where to find it when she comes again," said Mrs. Brudenell haughtily. As soon as Hannah had left the room Herman said:

"Mother, you need not have hurt that poor girl's feelings by speaking so before her."

"She need not have exposed herself to rebuke by entering where she did."

"Mother, she entered with me. I brought her in."

"Then you were very wrong. These people, like all of their class, require to be kept down—repressed."

"Mother, this is a republic!"

"Yes; and it is ten times more necessary to keep the lower orders down, in a republic like this, where they are always trying to rise, than it is in a monarchy, where they always keep their place," said the lady arrogantly.

"What have you there?" inquired Herman, with a view of changing the disagreeable subject.

"The English papers. The foreign mail is in. And, by the way, here is a letter for you."

Herman received the letter from her hand, changed color as he looked at the writing on the envelope, and walked away to the front window to read it alone.

His mother's watchful eyes followed him.

As he read, his face flushed and paled; his eyes flashed and smoldered; sighs and moans escaped his lips. At length, softly crumpling up the letter, he thrust it into his pocket, and was stealing from the room to conceal his agitation, when his mother, who had seen it all, spoke:

"Any bad news, Herman?"

"No, madam," he promptly answered.

"What is the matter, then?"

He hesitated, and answered:

"Nothing."

"Who is that letter from?"

"A correspondent," he replied, escaping from the room.

"Humph! I might have surmised that much," laughed the lady, with angry scorn.

But he was out of hearing.

"Did you notice the handwriting on the envelope of that letter, Elizabeth?" she inquired of her elder daughter.

"Which letter, mamma?"

"That one for your brother, of course."

"No, mamma, I did not look at it."

"You never look at anything but your stupid worsted work. You will be an old maid, Elizabeth. Did you notice it, Elinor?"

"Yes, mamma. The superscription was in a very delicate feminine handwriting; and the seal was a wounded falcon, drawing the arrow from its own breast—surmounted by an earl's coronet."

"'Tis the seal of the Countess of Hurstmonceux."

CHAPTER IV.

THE FATAL DEED.

I am undone; there is no living, none,
If Bertram be away. It were all one,
That I should love a bright particular star,
And think to wed it, he is so above me.
The hind that would be mated by the lion,
Must die for love. 'Twas pretty though a plague
To see him every hour; to sit and draw
His arched brow, his hawking eyes, his curls
In our heart's table; heart too capable
Of every line and trick of his sweet favor.
—*Shakspere*.

Hannah Worth walked home, laden like a beast of burden, with an enormous bag of hanked yarn on her back. She entered her hut, dropped the burden on the floor, and stopped to take breath.

18

"I think they might have sent a negro man to bring that for you, Hannah," said Nora, pausing in her spinning.

"As if they would do that!" panted Hannah.

Not a word was said upon the subject of Herman Brudenell's morning visit. Hannah forebore to allude to it from pity; Nora from modesty.

Hannah sat down to rest, and Nora got up to prepare their simple afternoon meal. For these sisters, like many poor women, took but two meals a day.

The evening passed much as usual; but the next morning, as the sisters were at work, Hannah putting the warp for Mrs. Brudenell's new web of cloth in the loom, and Nora spinning, the elder noticed that the younger often paused in her work and glanced uneasily from the window. Ah, too well Hannah understood the meaning of those involuntary glances. Nora was "watching for the steps that came not back again!"

Hannah felt sorry for her sister; but she said to herself:

"Never mind, she will be all right in a few days. She will forget him."

This did not happen so, however. As day followed day, and Herman Brudenell failed to appear, Nora Worth grew more uneasy, expectant, and anxious. Ah! who can estimate the real heart-sickness of "hope deferred!" Every morning she said to herself: "He will surely come to-day !" Every day each sense of hearing and of seeing was on the qui vive to catch the first sound or the first sight of his approach. Every night she went to bed to weep in silent sorrow.

All other sorrows may be shared and lightened by sympathy except that of a young girl's disappointment in love. With that no one intermeddles with impunity. To notice it is to distress her; to speak of it is to insult her; even her sister must in silence respect it; as the expiring dove folds her wing over her mortal wound, so does the maiden jealously conceal her grief and die. Days grew into weeks, and Herman did not come. And still Nora watched and listened as she spun—every nerve strained to its utmost tension in vigilance and expectancy. Human nature—especially a girl's nature—cannot bear such a trial for any long time together. Nora's health began to fail; first she lost her spirits, and then her appetite, and finally her sleep. She grew pale, thin, and nervous.

Hannah's heart ached for her sister.

"This will never do," she said; "suspense is killing her. I must end it."

So one morning while they were at work as usual, and Nora's hand was pausing on her spindle, and her eyes were fixed upon the narrow path leading through the Forest Valley, Hannah spoke:

"It will not do, dear; he is not coming! he will never come again; and since he cannot be anything to you, he ought not to come!"

"Oh, Hannah, I know it; but it is killing me!"

These words were surprised from the poor girl; for the very next instant her waxen cheeks, brow, neck, and very ears kindled up into fiery blushes, and hiding her face in her hands she sank down in her chair overwhelmed.

Hannah watched, and then went to her, and began to caress her, saying:

"Nora, Nora, dear; Nora, love; Nora, my own darling, look up!"

"Don't speak to me; I am glad he does not come; never mention his name to me again, Hannah," said the stricken girl, in a low, peremptory whisper.

Hannah felt that this order must be obeyed, and so she went back to her loom and worked on in silence.

After a few minutes Nora arose and resumed her spinning, and for some time the wheel whirled briskly and merrily around. But towards the middle of the day it began to turn slowly and still more slowly.

At length it stopped entirely, and the spinner said:

"Hannah, I feel very tired; would you mind if I should lay down a little while?"

"No, certainly not, my darling. Are you poorly, Nora?"

"No, I am quite well, only tired," replied the girl, as she threw herself upon the bed.

Perhaps Hannah had made a fatal mistake in saying to her sister, "He will never come again," and so depriving her of the last frail plank of hope, and letting her sink in the waves of despair. Perhaps, after all, suspense is not the worst of all things to bear; for in suspense there is hope, and in hope, life! Certain it is that a prop seemed withdrawn from Nora, and from this day she rapidly sunk. She would not take to her bed. Every morning she would insist upon rising and dressing, though daily the effort was more difficult. Every day she would go to her wheel and spin slowly and feebly, until by fatigue she was obliged to stop and throw herself upon the bed. To all Hannah's anxious questions she answered:

"I am very well! indeed there is nothing ails me; only I am so tired!"

One day about this time Reuben Gray called to see Hannah. Reuben was one of the most discreet of lovers, never venturing to visit his beloved more than once in each month.

"Look at Nora!" said Hannah, in a heart-broken tone, as she pointed to her sister, who was sitting at her wheel, not spinning, but gazing from the window down the narrow footpath, and apparently lost in mournful reverie.

"I'll go and fetch a medical man," said Reuben, and he left the hut for that purpose.

But distances from house to house in that sparsely settled neighborhood were great, and doctors were few and could not be had the moment they were called for. So it was not until the next day that Doctor Potts, the round-bodied little medical attendant of the neighborhood, made his appearance at the hut.

He was welcomed by Hannah, who introduced him to her sister.

Nora received his visit with a great deal of nervous irritability, declaring that nothing at all ailed her, only that she was tired.

"Tired," repeated the doctor, as he felt her pulse and watched her countenance. "Yes, tired of living! a serious fatigue this, Hannah. Her malady is more on the mind than the body! You must try to rouse her, take her into company, keep her amused. If you were able to travel, I should recommend change of scene; but of course that is out of the question. However, give her this, according to the directions. I will call in again to see her in a few days." And so saying, the doctor left a bottle of medicine and took his departure.

That day the doctor had to make a professional visit of inspection to the negro quarters at Brudenell Hall; so he mounted his fat little white cob and trotted down the hill in the direction of the valley.

When he arrived at Brudenell Hall he was met by Mrs. Brudenell, who said to him:

"Dr. Potts, I wish before you leave, you would see my son. I am seriously anxious about his health. He objected to my sending for you; but now that you are here on a visit to the quarters, perhaps his objections may give way."

"Very well, madam; but since he does not wish to be attended, perhaps he had better not know that my visit is to him; I will just make you a call as usual."

"Join us at lunch, doctor, and you can observe him at your leisure."

"Thank you, madam. What seems the matter with Mr. Brudenell?"

"A general failure without any particular disease. If it were not that I know better, I would say that something lay heavily upon his mind."

"Humph! a second case of that kind to-day! Well, madam, I will join you at two o'clock," said the doctor, as he trotted off towards the negro quarters.

Punctually at the hour the doctor presented himself at the luncheon table of Mrs. Brudenell. There were present Mrs. Brudenell, her two daughters, her son, and a tall, dark, distinguished looking man, whom the lady named as Colonel Mervin.

The conversation, enlivened by a bottle of fine champagne, flowed briskly and cheerfully around the table. But through all the doctor watched Herman Brudenell. He was indeed changed. He looked ill, yet he ate, drank, laughed, and talked with the best there. But when his eye met that of the doctor fixed upon him, it flashed with a threatening glance that seemed to repel scrutiny.

The doctor, to turn the attention of the lady from her son, said:

"I was at the hut on the hill to-day. One of those poor girls, the youngest, Nora, I think they call her, is in a bad way. She seems to me to be sinking into a decline." As he said this he happened to glance at Herman Brudenell. That gentleman's eyes were fixed upon his with a gaze of wild alarm, but they sank as soon as noticed.

"Poor creatures! that class of people scarcely ever get enough to eat or drink, and thus so many of them die of decline brought on from insufficiency of nourishment. I will send a bag of flour up to the hut to-morrow," said Mrs. Brudenell complacently.

Soon after they all arose from the table.

The little doctor offered his arm to Mrs. Brudenell, and as they walked to the drawing-room he found an opportunity of saying to her:

"It is, I think, as you surmised. There is something on his mind. Try to find out what it is. That is my advice. It is of no use to tease him with medical attendance."

When they reached the drawing room they found the boy with the mail bag waiting for his mistress. She quickly unlocked and distributed its contents.

20

"Letters for everybody except myself! But here is a late copy of the 'London Times' with which I can amuse myself while you look over your epistles, ladies and gentlemen," said Mrs. Brudenell, as she settled herself to the perusal of her paper. She skipped the leader, read the court circular, and was deep in the column of casualties, when she suddenly cried out:

"Good Heaven, Herman! what a catastrophe!"

"What is it, mother?"

"A collision on the London and Brighton Railway, and ever so many killed or wounded, and—Gracious goodness!"

"What, mother?"

"Among those instantly killed are the Marquis and Marchioness of Brambleton and the Countess of Hurstmonceux!"

"No!" cried the young man, rushing across the room, snatching the paper from his mother's hand, and with starting eyes fixed upon the paragraph that she hastily pointed out, seeming to devour the words.

A few days after this Nora Worth sat propped up in an easy-chair by the open window that commanded the view of the Forest Valley and of the opposite hill crowned with the splendid mansion of Brudenell Hall.

But Nora was not looking upon this view; at least except upon a very small part of it—namely, the little narrow footpath that led down her own hill and was lost in the shade of the valley. The doctor's prescriptions had done Nora no good; how should they? Could he, more than others, "minister to a mind diseased"? In a word, she had now grown so weak that the spinning was entirely set aside, and she passed her days propped up in the easy-chair beside the window, through which she could watch that little path, which was now indeed so disused, so neglected and grass grown, as to be almost obliterated.

Suddenly, while Nora's eyes were fixed abstractedly upon this path, she uttered a great cry and started to her feet.

Hannah stopped the clatter of her shuttle to see what was the matter.

Nora was leaning from the window, gazing breathlessly down the path.

"What is it, Nora, my dear? Don't lean so far out; you will fall! What is it?"

"Oh, Hannah, he is coming! he is coming!"

"Who is coming, my darling? I see no one!" said the elder sister, straining her eyes down the path.

"But I feel him coming! He is coming fast! He will be in sight presently! There! what did I tell you? There he is!"

And truly at that moment Herman Brudenell advanced from the thicket and walked rapidly up the path towards the hut.

Nora sank back in her seat, overcome, almost fainting.

Another moment and Herman Brudenell was in the room, clasping her form, and sobbing:

"Nora! Nora, my beloved! my beautiful! you have been ill and I knew it not! dying, and I knew it not! Oh! oh! oh!"

"Yes, but I am well, now that you are here!" gasped the girl, as she thrilled and trembled with returning life. But the moment this confession had been surprised from her she blushed fiery red to the very tips of her ears and hid her face in the pillows of her chair.

"My darling girl! My own blessed girl! do not turn your face away! look at me with your sweet eyes! See, I am here at your side, telling you how deep my own sorrow had been at the separation from you, and how much deeper at the thought that you also have suffered! Look at me! Smile on me! Speak to me, beloved! I am your own!"

These and many other wild, tender, pleading words of love he breathed in the ear of the listening, blushing, happy girl; both quite heedless of the presence of Hannah, who stood petrified with consternation.

At length, however, by the time Herman had seated himself beside Nora, Hannah recovered her presence of mind and power of motion; and she went to him and said:

"Mr. Brudenell! Is this well? Could you not leave her in peace?"

"No, I could not leave her! Yes, it is well, Hannah! The burden I spoke of is unexpectedly lifted from my life! I am a restored man. And I have come here to-day to ask Nora, in your presence, and with your consent, to be my wife!"

"And with your mother's consent, Mr. Brudenell?"

"Hannah, that was unkind of you to throw a damper upon my joy. And look at me, I have not been in such robust health myself since you drove me away!"

As he said this, Nora's hand, which he held, closed convulsively on his, and she murmured under her breath:

"Have you been ill? You are not pale!"

"No, love, I was only sad at our long separation; now you see I am flushed with joy; for now I shall see you every day!" he replied, lifting her hand to his lips.

Hannah was dreadfully disturbed. She was delighted to see life, and light, and color flowing back to her sister's face; but she was dismayed at the very cause of this—the presence of Herman Brudenell. The instincts of her affections and the sense of her duties were at war in her bosom. The latter as yet was in the ascendency. It was under its influence she spoke again.

"But, Mr. Brudenell, your mother?"

"Hannah! Hannah! don't be disagreeable! You are too young to play duenna yet!" he said gayly.

"I do not know what you mean by duenna, Mr. Brudenell, but I know what is due to your mother," replied the elder sister gravely.

"Mother, mother, mother; how tiresome you are, Hannah, everlastingly repeating the same word over and over again! You shall not make us miserable. We intend to be happy, now, Nora and myself. Do we not, dearest?" he added, changing the testy tone in which he had spoken to the elder sister for one of the deepest tenderness as he turned and addressed the younger.

"Yes, but, your mother," murmured Nora very softly and timidly.

"You too! Decidedly that word is infectious, like yawning! Well, my dears, since you will bring it on the tapis, let us discuss and dismiss it. My mother is a very fine woman, Hannah; but she is unreasonable, Nora. She is attached to what she calls her 'order,' my dears, and never would consent to my marriage with any other than a lady of rank and wealth."

"Then you must give up Nora, Mr. Brudenell," said Hannah gravely.

"Yes, indeed," assented poor Nora, under her breath, and turning pale.

"May the Lord give me up if I do!" cried the young man impetuously.

"You will never defy your mother," said Hannah.

"Oh, no! oh, no! I should be frightened to death," gasped Nora, trembling between weakness and fear.

"No, I will never defy my mother; there are other ways of doing things; I must marry Nora, and we must keep the affair quiet for a time."

"I do not understand you," said Hannah coldly.

"Nora does, though! Do you not, my darling?" exclaimed Herman triumphantly.

And the blushing but joyous face of Nora answered him.

"You say you will not defy your mother. Do you mean then to deceive her, Mr. Brudenell?" inquired the elder sister severely.

"Hannah, don't be abusive! This is just the whole matter, in brief. I am twenty-one, master of myself and my estate. I could marry Nora at any time, openly, without my mother's consent. But that would give her great pain. It would not kill her, nor make her ill, but it would wound her in her tenderest points—her love of her son, and her love of rank; it would produce an open rupture between us. She would never forgive me, nor acknowledge my wife."

"Then why do you speak at all of marrying Nora?" interrupted Hannah angrily.

Herman turned and looked at Nora. That mute look was his only answer, and it was eloquent; it said plainly what his lips forbore to speak: "I have won her love, and I ought to marry her; for if I do not, she will die."

Then he continued as if Hannah had not interrupted him:

"I wish to get on as easily as I can between these conflicting difficulties. I will not wrong Nora, and I will not grieve my mother. The only way to avoid doing either will be for me to marry my darling privately, and keep the affair a secret until a fitting opportunity offers to publish it."

"A secret marriage! Mr. Brudenell! is that what you propose to my sister?"

"Why not, Hannah?"

"Secret marriages are terrible things!"

"Disappointed affections, broken hearts, early graves, are more terrible."

"Fudge!" was the word that rose to Hannah's lips, as she looked at the young man; but when she turned to her sister she felt that his words might be true.

"Besides, Hannah," he continued, "this will not be a secret marriage. You cannot call that a secret which will be known to four persons—the parson, you, Nora, and myself. I shall not even bind you or Nora to keep the secret longer than you think it her interest to declare it. She shall have the marriage certificate in her own keeping, and every legal protection and defense; so that even if I should die suddenly—"

Nora gasped for breath.

—"she would be able to claim and establish her rights and position in the world. Hannah, you must see that I mean to act honestly and honorably," said the young man, in an earnest tone.

"I see that you do; but, Mr. Brudenell, it appears to me that the fatal weakness of which you have already spoken to me—the 'propensity to please'—is again leading you into error. You wish to save Nora, and you wish to spare your mother; and to do both these things, you are sacrificing—"

"What, Hannah?"

"Well—fair, plain, open, straight-forward, upright dealing, such as should always exist between man and woman."

"Hannah, you are unjust to me! Am I not fair, plain, open, straight-forward, upright, and all the rest of it in my dealing with you?"

"With us, yes; but—"

"With my mother it is necessary to be cautious. It is true that she has no right to oppose my marriage with Nora; but yet she would oppose it, even to death! Therefore, to save trouble and secure peace, I would marry my dear Nora quietly. Mystery, Hannah, is not necessarily guilt; it is often wisdom and mercy. Do not object to a little harmless mystery, that is besides to secure peace! Come, Hannah, what say you?"

"How long must this marriage, should it take place, be kept a secret?" inquired Hannah uneasily.

"Not one hour longer than you and Nora think it necessary that it should be declared! Still, I should beg your forbearance as long as possible. Come, Hannah, your answer!"

"I must have time to reflect. I fear I should be doing very wrong to consent to this marriage, and yet—and yet—. But I must take a night to think of it! To-morrow, Mr. Brudenell, I will give you an answer!"

With this reply the young man was obliged to be contented. Soon after he arose and took his leave.

When he was quite out of hearing Nora arose and threw herself into her sister's arms, crying:

"Oh, Hannah, consent! consent! I cannot live without him!"

The elder sister caressed the younger tenderly; told her of all the dangers of a secret marriage; of all the miseries of an ill-sorted one; and implored her to dismiss her wealthy lover, and struggle with her misplaced love.

Nora replied only with tears and sobs, and vain repetitions of the words:

"I cannot live without him, Hannah! I cannot live without him!"

Alas, for weakness, willfulness, and passion! They, and not wise counsels, gained the day. Nora would not give up her lover; would not struggle with her love; but would have her own way.

At length, in yielding a reluctant acquiesence, Hannah said:

"I would never countenance this—never, Nora! but for one reason; it is that I know, whether I consent or not, you two, weak and willful and passionate as you are, will rush into this imprudent marriage all the same! And I think for your sake it had better take place with my sanction, and in my presence, than otherwise."

Nora clasped her sister's neck and covered her face with kisses.

"He means well by us, dear Hannah—indeed he does, bless him! So do not look so grave because we are going to be happy."

Had Herman felt sure of his answer the next day? It really seemed so; for when he made his appearance at the cottage in the morning he brought the marriage license in his pocket and a peripatetic minister in his company.

And before the astonished sisters had time to recover their self-possession Herman Brudenell's will had carried his purpose, and the marriage ceremony was performed. The minister then wrote out the certificate, which was signed by himself, and witnessed by Hannah, and handed it to the bride.

"Now, dearest Nora," whispered the triumphant bridegroom, "I am happy, and you are safe!"

But—were either of them really safe or happy?

CHAPTER V.

LOVE AND FATE.

Amid the sylvan solitude
Of unshorn grass and waving wood
And waters glancing bright and fast,
A softened voice was in her ear,
Sweet as those lulling sounds and fine
The hunter lifts his head to hear,
Now far and faint, now full and near—
The murmur of the wood swept pine.
A manly form was ever nigh,
A bold, free hunter, with an eye
Whose dark, keen glance had power to wake
Both fear and love—to awe and charm.
Faded the world that they had known,
A poor vain shadow, cold and waste,
In the warm present bliss alone
Seemed they of actual life to taste.
—*Whittier.*

It was in the month of June they were married; when the sun shone with his brightest splendor; when the sky was of the clearest blue, when the grass was of the freshest green, the woods in their rudest foliage, the flowers in their richest bloom, and all nature in her most luxuriant life! Yes, June was their honeymoon; the forest shades their bridal halls, and birds and flowers and leaves and rills their train of attendants. For weeks they lived a kind of fairy life, wandering together through the depths of the valley forest, discovering through the illumination of their love new beauties and glories in the earth and sky; new sympathies with every form of life. Were ever suns so bright, skies so clear, and woods so green as theirs in this month of beauty, love, and joy!

"It seems to me that I must have been deaf and blind and stupid in the days before I knew you, Herman! for then the sun seemed only to shine, and now I feel that he smiles as well as shines; then the trees only seemed to bend under a passing breeze, now I know they stoop to caress us; then the flowers seemed only to be crowded, now I know they draw together to kiss; then indeed I loved nature, but now I know that she also is alive and loves me!" said Nora, one day, as they sat upon a bank of wild thyme under the spreading branches of an old oak tree that stood alone in a little opening of the forest.

"You darling of nature! you might have known that all along!" exclaimed Herman, enthusiastically pressing her to his heart.

"Oh, how good you are to love me so much! you—so high, so learned, so wealthy; you who have seen so many fine ladies—to come down to me, a poor, ignorant, weaver-girl!" said Nora humbly—for true love in many a woman is ever most humble and most idolatrous, abasing itself and idolizing its object.

"Come down to you, my angel and my queen! to you, whose beauty is so heavenly and so royal that it seems to me everyone should worship and adore you! how could I come down to you! Ah, Nora, it seems to me that it is you who have stooped to me! There are kings on this earth, my beloved, who might be proud to place such regal beauty on their thrones beside them! For, oh! you are as beautiful, my Nora, as any woman of old, for whom heroes lost worlds!"

"Do you think so? do you really think so? I am so glad for your sake! I wish I were ten times as beautiful! and high-born, and learned, and accomplished, and wealthy, and everything else that is good, for your sake! Herman, I would be willing to pass through a fiery furnace if by doing so I could come out like refined gold, for your sake!"

"Hush, hush, sweet love! that fiery furnace of which you speak is the Scriptural symbol for fearful trial and intense suffering! far be it from you! for I would rather my whole body were consumed to ashes than one shining tress of your raven hair should be singed!"

"But, Herman! one of the books you read to me said: 'All that is good must be toiled for; all that is best must be suffered for'; and I am willing to do or bear anything in the world that would make me more worthy of you!"

"My darling, you are worthy of a monarch, and much too good for me!"

24

"How kind you are to say so! but for all that I know I am only a poor, humble, ignorant girl, quite unfit to be your wife! And, oh! sometimes it makes me very sad to think so!" said Nora, with a deep sigh.

"Then do not think so, my own! why should you? You are beautiful; you are good; you are lovely and beloved, and you ought to be happy!" exclaimed Herman.

"Oh, I am happy! very happy now! For whatever I do or say, right or wrong, is good in your eyes, and pleases you because you love me so much. God bless you! God love you! God save you, whatever becomes of your poor Nora!" she said, with a still heavier sigh.

At this moment a soft summer cloud floated between them and the blazing meridian sun, veiling its glory.

"Why, what is the matter, love? What has come over you?" inquired Herman, gently caressing her.

"I do not know; nothing more than that perhaps," answered Nora, pointing to the cloud that was now passing over the sun.

"'Nothing more than that.' Well, that has now passed, so smile forth again, my sun!" said Herman gayly.

"Ah, dear Herman, if this happy life could only last! this life in which we wander or repose in these beautiful summer woods, among rills and flowers and birds! Oh, it is like the Arcadia of which you read to me in your books, Herman! Ah, if it would only last!"

"Why should it not, love?"

"Because it cannot. Winter will come with its wind and snow and ice. The woods will be bare, the grass dry, the flowers all withered, the streams frozen, and the birds gone away, and we—" Here her voice sank into silence, but Herman took up the word:

"Well, and we, beloved! we shall pass to something much better! We are not partridges or squirrels to live in the woods and fields all winter! We shall go to our own luxurious home! You will be my loved and honored and happy wife; the mistress of an elegant house, a fine estate, and many negroes. You will have superb furniture, beautiful dresses, splendid jewels, servants to attend you, carriages, horses, pleasure boats, and everything else that heart could wish, or money buy, or love find to make you happy! Think! Oh, think of all the joys that are in store for you!"

"Not for me! Oh, not for me those splendors and luxuries and joys that you speak of! They are too good for me; I shall never possess them; I know it, Herman; and I knew it even in that hour of heavenly bliss when you first told me you loved me! I knew it even when we stood before the minister to be married, and I know it still! This short summer of love will be all the joy I shall ever have."

"In the name of Heaven, Nora, what do you mean? Is it possible that you can imagine I shall ever be false to you?" passionately demanded the young man, who was deeply impressed at last by the sad earnestness of her manner.

"No! no! no! I never imagine anything unworthy of your gentle and noble nature," said Nora, with fervent emphasis as she pressed closer to his side.

"Then why, why, do you torture yourself and me with these dark previsions?"

"I do not know. Forgive me, Herman," softly sighed Nora, laying her cheek against his own.

He stole his arm around her waist, and as he drew her to his heart, murmured:

"Why should you not enjoy all the wealth, rank, and love to which you are entitled as my wife?"

"Ah! dear Herman, I cannot tell why. I only know that I never shall! Bear with me, dear Herman, while I say this; After I had learned to love you; after I had grieved myself almost to death for your absence; when you returned and asked me to be your wife, I seemed suddenly to have passed from darkness into radiant light! But in the midst of it all I seemed to hear a voice in my heart, saying: 'Poor Moth! you are basking in a consuming fire; you will presently fall to the ground a burnt, blackened, tortured, and writhing thing.' And, Herman, when I thought of the great difference between us; of your old family, high rank, and vast wealth; and of your magnificent house, and your stately lady mother and fine lady sisters, I knew that though you had married me, I never could be owned as your wife—"

"Nora, if it were possible for me to be angry with you, I should be so!" interrupted Herman vehemently; "'you never could be owned as my wife!' I tell you that you can be—and that you shall be, and very soon! It was only to avoid a rupture with my mother that I married you privately at all. Have I not surrounded you with every legal security? Have I not armed you even against myself? Do you not know that even if it were possible for me to turn rascal, and become so mean, and miserable, and dishonored as to desert you, you could still demand your rights as a wife, and compel me to yield them!"

"As if I would! Oh, Herman, as if I would depend upon anything but your dear love to give me all I need! Armed against you, am I? I do not choose to be so! It is enough for me to know that I am your wife. I do not care to be able to prove it; for, Herman, were it possible for you to forsake me, I should not insist upon my 'rights'—I should die. Therefore, why should I be armed with legal proofs against you, my Herman, my life, my soul, my self? I will not continue so!" And with a generous abandonment she drew from her bosom the marriage certificate, tore it to pieces, and scattered it abroad, saying: "There now! I had kept it as a love token, close to my heart, little knowing it was a cold-blooded, cautious, legal proof, else it should have gone before, where it has gone now, to the winds! There now, Herman, I am my own wife, your own Nora, quite unarmed and defenseless before you; trusting only to your faith for my happiness; knowing that you will never willingly forsake me; but feeling that if you do, I should not pursue you, but die!"

"Dear trusting girl! would you indeed deprive yourself of all defenses thus? But, my Nora, did you suppose when I took you to my bosom that I had intrusted your peace and safety and honor only to a scrap of perishable paper? No, Nora, no! Infidelity to you is forever impossible to me; but death is always possible to all persons; and so, though I could never forsake you, I might die and leave you; and to guard against the consequences of such a contingency I surrounded you with every legal security. The minister that married us resides in this county; the witness that attended us lives with you. So that if to-morrow I should die, you could claim, as my widow, your half of my personal property and your life-interest in my estate. And if to-morrow you should become impatient of your condition as a secreted wife, and wish to enter upon all the honors of Bradenell Hall, you have the power to do so!"

"As if I would! As if it was for that I loved you! oh, Herman!"

"I know you would not, love! And I know it was not for that you loved me! I have perfect confidence in your disinterestedness. And I hope you have as much in mine."

"I have, Herman. I have!"

"Then, to go back to the first question, why did you wound me by saying, that though I had married you, you knew you never could be owned as my wife?"

"I spoke from a deep conviction! Oh, Herman, I know you will never willingly forsake me; but I feel you will never acknowledge me!"

"Then you must think me a villain!" said Herman bitterly.

"No, no, no; I think, if you must have my thoughts, you are the gentlest, truest, and noblest among men."

"You cannot get away from the point; if you think I could desert you, you must think I am a villain!"

"Oh, no, no! besides, I did not say you would desert me! I said you would never own me!"

"It is in effect the same thing."

"Herman, understand me: when I say, from the deep conviction I feel, that you will never own me, I also say that you will be blameless."

"Those two things are incompatible, Nora! But why do you persist in asserting that you will never be owned?"

"Ah, dear me, because it is true!"

"But why do you think it is true?"

"Because when I try to imagine our future, I see only my own humble hut, with its spinning-wheel and loom. And I feel I shall never live in Brudenell Hall!"

"Nora, hear me: this is near the first of July; in six months, that is before the first of January, whether I live or die, as my wife or as my widow, you shall rule at Brudenell Hall!"

Nora smiled, a strange, sad smile.

"Listen, dearest," he continued; "my mother leaves Brudenell in December. She thinks the two young ladies, my sisters, should have more society; so she has purchased a fine house in a fashionable quarter of Washington City. The workmen are now busy decorating and furnishing it. She takes possession of it early in December. Then, my Nora, when my mother and sisters are clear of Brudenell Hall, and settled in their town-house, I will bring you home and write and announce our marriage. Thus there can be no noise. People cannot quarrel very long or fiercely through the post. And finally time and reflection will reconcile my mother to the inevitable, and we shall be all once more united and happy."

"Herman dear," said Nora softly, "indeed my heart is toward your mother; I could love and revere and serve her as dutifully as if I were her daughter, if she would only deign to let me. And, at any rate, whether she will or not, I cannot help loving and honoring her, because she is your mother and loves you. And, oh, Herman, if she could look into my heart and see how truly I love you, her son, how gladly I would suffer to make you happy, and how willing I should be to live in utter poverty and obscurity, if it would be for your good, I do think she would love me a little for your sake!"

"Heaven grant it, my darling!"

"But be sure of this, dear Herman. No matter how she may think it good to treat me, I can never be angry with her. I must always love her and seek her favor, for she is your mother."

CHAPTER VI.

A SECRET REVEALED.

Full soon upon that dream of sin
An awful light came bursting in;
The shrine was cold at which she knelt;
The idol of that shrine was gone;
An humbled thing of shame and guilt;
Outcast and spurned and lone,
Wrapt in the shadows of that crime,
With withered heart and burning brain,
And tears that fell like fiery rain,
She passed a fearful time.
—*Whittier.*

Thus in pleasant wandering through the wood and sweet repose beneath the trees the happy lovers passed the blooming months of summer and the glowing months of autumn.

But when the seasons changed again, and with the last days of November came the bleak northwestern winds that stripped the last leaves from the bare trees, and covered the ground with snow and bound up the streams with ice, and drove the birds to the South, the lovers withdrew within doors, and spent many hours beside the humble cottage fireside.

Here for the first time Herman had ample opportunity of finding out how very poor the sisters really were, and how very hard one of them at least worked.

And from the abundance of his own resources he would have supplied their wants and relieved them from this excess of toil, but that there was a reserve of honest pride in these poor girls that forbade them to accept his pressing offers.

"But this is my own family now," said Herman. "Nora is my wife and Hannah is my sister-in-law, and it is equally my duty and pleasure to provide for them."

"No, Herman! No, dear Herman! we cannot be considered as your family until you publicly acknowledge us as such. Dear Herman, do not think me cold or ungrateful, when I say to you that it would give me pain and mortification to receive anything from you, until I do so as your acknowledged wife," said Nora.

"You give everything—you give your hand, your heart, yourself! and you will take nothing," said the young man sadly.

"Yes, I take as much as I give! I take your hand, your heart, and yourself in return for mine. That is fair; but I will take no more until as your wife I take the head of your establishment," said Nora proudly.

"Hannah, is this right? She is my wife; she promised to obey me, and she defies me—I ask you is this right?"

"Yes, Mr. Brudenell. When she is your acknowledged wife, in your house, then she will obey and never 'defy' you, as you call it; but now it is quite different; she has not the shield of your name, and she must take care of her own self-respect until you relieve her of the charge," said the elder sister gravely.

"Hannah, you are a terrible duenna! You would be an acquisition to some crabbed old Spaniard who had a beautiful young wife to look after! Now I want you to tell me how on earth my burning up that old loom and wheel, and putting a little comfortable furniture in this room, and paying you sufficient to support you both, can possibly hurt her self-respect?" demanded Herman.

"It will do more than that! it will hurt her character, Mr. Brudenell; and that should be as dear to you as to herself."

"It is! it is the dearest thing in life to me! But how should what I propose to do hurt either her self-respect or her character? You have not told me that yet!"

"This way, Mr. Brudenell! If we were to accept your offers, our neighbors would talk of us."

"Neighbors! why, Hannah, what neighbors have you? In all the months that I have been coming here, I have not chanced to meet a single soul!"

"No, you have not. And if you had, once in a way, met anyone here, they would have taken you to be a mere passer-by resting yourself in our hut; but if you were to make us as comfortable as you wish, why the very first chance visitor to the hut who would see that the loom and the spinning-wheel and old furniture were gone, and were replaced by the fine carpet, curtains, chairs, and sofa that you wish to give us, would go away and tell the wonder. And people would say: 'Where did Hannah Worth get these things?' or, 'How do they live?' or, 'Who supports those girls?' and so on. Now, Mr. Brudenell, those are questions I will not have asked about myself and my sister, and that you ought not to wish to have asked about your wife!"

"Hannah, you are quite right! You always are! And yet it distresses me to see you living and working as you do."

"We are inured to it, Mr. Brudenell."

"But it will not be for long, Hannah. Very soon my mother and sisters go to take possession of their new house in Washington. When they have left Brudenell I will announce our marriage and bring you and your sister home."

"Not me, Mr. Brudenell! I have said before that in marrying Nora you did not marry all her poor relatives. I have told you that I will not share the splendors of Nora's destiny. No one shall have reason to say of me, as they would say if I went home with you, that I had connived at the young heir's secret marriage with my sister for the sake of securing a luxurious home for myself. No, Mr. Brudenell, Nora is beautiful, and it is not unnatural that she should have made a high match; and the world will soon forgive her for it and forget her humble origin. But I am a plain, rude, hard-working woman; am engaged to a man as poor, as rugged, and toil-worn as myself. We would be strangely out of place in your mansion, subjected to the comments of your friends. We will never intrude there. I shall remain here at my weaving until the time comes, if it ever should come, when Reuben and myself may marry, and then, if possible, we will go to the West, to better ourselves in a better country."

"Well, Hannah, well, if such be your final determination, you will allow me at least to do something towards expediting your marriage. I can advance such a sum to Reuben Gray as will enable him to marry, and take you and all his own brothers and sisters to the rich lands of the West, where, instead of being encumbrances, they will be great helps to him; for there is to be found much work for every pair of hands, young or old, male or female," said the young man, not displeased, perhaps, to provide for his wife's poor relations at a distance from which they would not be likely ever to enter his sphere.

Hannah reflected for a moment and then said:

"I thank you very much for that offer, Mr. Brudenell. It was the wisest and kindest, both for yourself and us, that you could have made. And I think that if we could see our way through repaying the advance, we would gratefully accept it."

"Never trouble yourself about the repayment! Talk to Gray, and then, when my mother has gone, send him up to talk to me," said Herman.

To all this Nora said nothing. She sat silently, with her head resting upon her hand, and a heavy weight at her heart, such as she always felt when their future was spoken of. To her inner vision a heavy cloud that would not disperse always rested on that future.

Thus the matter rested for the present.

Herman continued his daily visits to the sisters, and longed impatiently for the time when he should feel free to acknowledge his beautiful young peasant-wife and place her at the head of his princely establishment.

These daily visits of the young heir to the poor sisters attracted no general attention. The hut on the hill was so remote from any road or any dwelling-house that few persons passed near it, and fewer still entered its door.

It was near the middle of December, when Mrs. Brudenell was busy with her last preparations for her removal, that the first rumor of Herman's visits to the hut reached her.

She was in the housekeeper's room, superintending in person the selection of certain choice pots of domestic sweetmeats from the family stores to be taken to the town-house, when Mrs. Spicer, who was attending her, said:

"If you please, ma'am, there's Jem Morris been waiting in the kitchen all the morning to see you."

"Ah! What does he want? A job, I suppose. Well, tell him to come in here," said the lady carelessly, as she scrutinized the label upon a jar of red currant jelly.

The housekeeper left the room to obey, and returned ushering in an individual who, as he performs an important part in this history, deserves some special notice.

He was a mulatto, between forty-five and fifty years of age, of medium size, and regular features, with a quantity of woolly hair and beard that hung down upon his breast. He was neatly dressed in the gray homespun cloth of the country, and entered with a smiling countenance and respectful manner. Upon the whole he was rather a good-looking and pleasing darky. He was a character, too, in his way. He possessed a fair amount of intellect, and a considerable fund of general information. He had contrived, somehow or other, to read and write; and he would read everything he could lay his hands on, from the Bible to the almanac. He had formed his own opinions upon most of the subjects that interest society, and he expressed them freely. He kept himself well posted up in the politics of the day, and was ready to discuss them with anyone who would enter into the debate.

He had a high appreciation of himself, and also a deep veneration for his superiors. And thus it happened that, when in the presence of his betters, he maintained a certain sort of droll dignity in himself while treating them with the utmost deference. He was faithful in his dealings with his numerous employers, all of whom he looked upon as so many helpless dependents under his protection, for whose well-being in certain respects he was strictly responsible. So much for his character. In circumstances he was a free man, living with his wife and children, who were also free, in a small house on Mr. Brudenell's estate, and supporting his family by such a very great variety of labor as had earned for him the title of "Professor of Odd Jobs." It was young Herman Brudenell, when a boy, who gave him this title, which, from its singular appropriateness, stuck to him; for he could, as he expressed it himself, "do anything as any other man could do." He could shoe a horse, doctor a cow, mend a fence, make a boot, set a bone, fix a lock, draw a tooth, roof a cabin, drive a carriage, put up a chimney, glaze a window, lay a hearth, play a fiddle, or preach a sermon. He could do all these things, and many others besides too numerous to mention, and he did do them for the population of the whole neighborhood, who, having no regular mechanics, gave this "Jack of all Trades" a plenty of work. This universal usefulness won for him, as I said, the title of "Professor of Odd Jobs." This was soon abbreviated to the simple "Professor," which had a singular significance also when applied to one who, in addition to all his other excellencies, believed himself to be pretty well posted up in law, physic, and theology, upon either of which he would stop in his work to hold forth to anyone who would listen.

Finally, there was another little peculiarity about the manner of the professor. In his excessive agreeability he would always preface his answer to any observation whatever with some sort of assent, such as "yes, sir," or "yes, madam," right or wrong.

This morning the professor entered the presence of Mrs. Brudenell, hat in hand, smiling and respectful.

"Well, Morris, who has brought you here this morning?" inquired the lady.

"Yes, madam. I been thinkin' about you, and should a-been here 'fore this to see after your affairs, on'y I had to go over to Colonel Mervin's to give one of his horses a draught, and then to stop at the colored, people's meetin' house to lead the exercises, and afterwards to call at the Miss Worthses to mend Miss Hannah's loom and put a few new spokes in Miss Nora's wheel. And so many people's been after me to do jobs that I'm fairly torn to pieces among um. And it's 'Professor' here, and 'Professor' there, and 'Professor' everywhere, till I think my senses will leave me, ma'am."

"Then, if you are so busy why do you come here, Morris?" said Mrs. Brudenell, who was far too dignified to give him his title.

"Yes, madam. Why, you see, ma'am, I came, as in duty bound, to look after your affairs and see as they were all right, which they are not, ma'am. There's the rain pipes along the roof of the house leaking so the cistern never gets full of water, and I must come and solder them right away, and the lightning reds wants fastenin' more securely, and—"

"Well, but see Grainger, my overseer, about these things; do not trouble me with them."

"Yes, madam. I think overseers ought to be called overlookers, because they oversee so little and overlook so much. Now, there's the hinges nearly rusted off the big barn door, and I dessay he never saw it."

"Well, Morris, call his attention to that also; do whatever you find necessary to be done, and call upon Grainger to settle with you."

"Yes, madam. It wasn't on'y the rain pipes and hinges as wanted attention that brought me here, however, ma'am,"

"What was it, then? Be quick, if you please. I am very much occupied this morning."

"Yes, madam. It was something I heard and felt it my duty to tell you; because, you see, ma'am, I think it is the duty of every honest—"

"Come, come, Morris, I have no time to listen to an oration from you now. In two words, what had you to tell me?" interrupted the lady impatiently.

"Yes, madam. It were about young Mr. Herman, ma'am."

"Mr. Brudenell, if you please, Morris. My son is the head of his family."

"Certainly, madam. Mr. Brudenell."

"Well, what about Mr. Brudenell?"

"Yes, madam. You know he was away from home every day last spring and summer."

"I remember; he went to fish; he is very fond of fishing."

"Certainly, madam; but he was out every day this autumn."

"I am aware of that; he was shooting; he is an enthusiastic sportsman."

"To be sure, madam, so he is; but he is gone every day this winter."

"Of course; hunting; there is no better huntsman in the country than Mr. Brudenell."

"That is very true, madam; do you know what sort of game he is a-huntin' of?" inquired the professor meaningly, but most deferentially.

"Foxes, I presume," said the lady, with a look of inquiry.

"Yes, madam, sure enough; I suppose they is foxes, though in female form," said the professor dryly, but still respectfully.

"Whatever do you mean, Morris?" demanded the lady sternly.

"Well, madam, if it was not from a sense of duty, I would not dare to speak to you on this subject; for I think when a man presumes to meddle with things above his speer, he—"

"I remarked to you before, Morris, that I had no time to listen to your moral disquisitions. Tell me at once, then, what you meant to insinuate by that strange speech," interrupted the lady.

"Yes, madam, certainly. When you said Mr. Brudenell was a hunting of foxes, I saw at once the correctness of your suspicions, madam; for they is foxes."

"Who are foxes?"

"Why, the Miss Worthses, madam."

"The Miss Worths! the weavers! why, what on earth have they to do with what we nave been speaking of?"

"Yes, madam; the Miss Worthses is the foxes that Mr. Brudenell is a-huntin' of."

"The Miss Worths? My son hunting the Miss Worths! What do you mean, sir? Take care what you say of Mr. Brudenell, Morris."

"Yes, madam, certainly; I won't speak another word on the subject; and I beg your pardon for having mentioned it at all; which I did from a sense of duty to your family, madam, thinking you ought to know it; but I am very sorry I made such a mistake, and again I beg your pardon, madam, and I humbly take my leave." And with a low bow the professor turned to depart.

"Stop, fool!" said Mrs. Brudenell. And the "fool" stopped and turned, hat in hand, waiting further orders.

"Do you mean to say that Mr. Brudenell goes after those girls?" asked the lady, raising her voice ominously.

"Yes, madam; leastways, after Miss Nora. You see, madam, young gentlemen will be young gentlemen, for all their mas can say or do; and when the blood is warm and the spirits is high, and the wine is in and the wit is out—"

"No preaching, I say! Pray, are you a clergyman or a barrister? Tell me at once what reason you have for saying that my son goes to Worths' cottage?"

"Yes, madam; I have seen him often and often along of Miss Nora a-walking in the valley forest, when I have been there myself looking for herbs and roots to make up my vegetable medicines with. And I have seen him go home with her. And at last I said, 'It is my bounden duty to go and tell the madam.'"

"You are very sure of what you say?"

"Yes, madam, sure as I am of my life and my death."

"This is very annoying! very! I had supposed Mr. Brudenell to have had better principles. Of course, when a young gentleman of his position goes to see a girl of hers, it can be but with one object. I had thought Herman had better morals, and Hannah at least more sense! This is very annoying! very!" said the lady to herself, as her brows contracted with anger. After a few moments spent in silent thought, she said:

"It is the girl Nora, you say, he is with so much?"

"Yes, madam."

"Then go to the hut this very evening and tell that girl she must come up here to-morrow morning to see me. I thank you for your zeal in my service, Morris, and will find a way to reward you. And now you may do my errand."

30

"Certainly, madam! My duty to you, madam," said the professor, with a low bow, as he left the room and hurried away to deliver his message to Nora Worth.

"This is very unpleasant," said the lady. "But since Hannah has no more prudence than to let a young gentleman visit her sister, I must talk to the poor, ignorant child myself, and warn her that she risks her good name, as well as her peace of mind."

CHAPTER VII.

MOTHER- AND DAUGHTER-IN-LAW.

Your pardon, noble lady!
My friends were poor but honest—so is my love;
Be not offended, for it hurts him not
That he is loved of me. My dearest madam,
Let not your hate encounter with my love
For loving where *you* do.
—*Shakspere.*

The poor sisters had just finished their afternoon meal, cleaned their room, and settled themselves to their evening's work. Nora was spinning gayly, Hannah weaving diligently—the whir of Nora's wheel keeping time to the clatter of Hannah's loom, when the latch was lifted and Herman Brudenell, bringing a brace of hares in his hand, entered the hut.

"There, Hannah, those are prime! I just dropped in to leave them, and to say that it is certain my mother leaves for Washington on Saturday. On Sunday morning I shall bring my wife home; and you, too, Hannah; for if you will not consent to live with us, you must still stop with us until you and Gray are married and ready to go to the West," he said, throwing the game upon the table, and shaking hands with the sisters. His face was glowing from exercise, and his eyes sparkling with joy.

"Sit down, Mr. Brudenell," said Hannah hospitably.

The young man hesitated, and a look of droll perplexity passed over his face as he said:

"Now don't tempt me, Hannah, my dear; don't ask me to stop this evening; and don't even let me do so if I wish to. You see I promised my mother to be home in time to meet some friends at dinner, and I am late now! Good-by, sister; good-by, sweet wife! Sunday morning, Mrs. Herman Brudenell, you will take the head of your own table at Brudenell Hall!"

And giving Hannah a cordial shake of the hand, and Nora a warm kiss, he hurried from the hut.

When he had closed the door behind him, the sisters looked at each other.

"Think of it, Hannah! This is Thursday, and he says that he will take us home on Sunday—in three days! Hannah, do you know I never before believed that this would be! I always thought that to be acknowledged as the wife of Herman Brudenell—placed at the head of his establishment, settled in that magnificent house, with superb furniture and splendid dresses, and costly jewels, and carriages, and horses, and servants to attend me, and to be called Mrs. Brudenell of Brudenell Hall, and visited by the old country families—was a great deal too much happiness, and prosperity, and glory for poor me!"

"Do you believe it now?" inquired Hannah thoughtfully.

"Why, yes! now that it draws so near. There is not much that can happen between this and Sunday to prevent it. I said it was only three days—but in fact it is only two, for this is Thursday evening, and he will take us home on Sunday morning; so you see there is only two whole days—Friday and Saturday—between this and that!"

"And how do you feel about this great change of fortune? Are you still frightened, though no longer unbelieving?"

"No, indeed!" replied Nora, glancing up at the little looking-glass that hung immediately opposite to her wheel; "if I have pleased Herman, who is so fastidious, it is not likely that. I should disgust others. And mind this, too: I pleased Herman in my homespun gown, and when I meet his friends at Brudenell Hall, I shall have all the advantages of splendid dress. No, Hannah, I am no longer incredulous or frightened. And if ever, when sitting at the head of his table when there is a dinner party, my heart should begin to fail me, I will say to

31

myself: 'I pleased Herman—the noblest of you all,' and then I know my courage will return. But, Hannah, won't people be astonished when they find out that I, poor Nora Worth, am really and truly Mrs. Herman Brudenell! What will they say? What will old Mrs. Jones say? And oh! what will the Miss Mervins say? I should like to see their faces when they hear it! for you know it is reported that Colonel Mervin is to marry Miss Brudenell, and that the two Miss Mervins are secretly pulling caps who shall take Herman! Poor young ladies! won't they be dumfounded when they find out that poor Nora Worth has had him all this time! I wonder how long it will take them to get over the mortification, and also whether they will call to see me. Do you think they will, Hannah?"

"I do not know, my dear. The Mervins hold their heads very high," replied the sober elder sister.

"Do they! Well, I fancy they have not much right to hold their heads much higher than the Brudenells of Brudenell Hall hold theirs. Hannah, do you happen to know who our first ancestor was?"

"Adam, my dear, I believe."

"Nonsense, Hannah; I do not mean the first father of all mankind—I mean the head of our house."

"Our house? Indeed, my dear, I don't even know who our grandfather was."

"Fudge, Hannah, I am not talking of the Worths, who of course have no history. I am talking of our family— the Brudenells!"

"Oh!" said Hannah dryly.

"And now do you know who our first ancestor was?"

"Yes; some Norman filibuster who came over to England with William the Conqueror, I suppose. I believe from all that I have heard, that to have been the origin of most of the noble English families and old Maryland ones."

"No, you don't, neither. Herman says our family is much older than the Conquest. They were a noble race of Saxon chiefs that held large sway in England from the time of the first invasion of the Saxons to that of the Norman Conquest; at which period a certain Wolfbold waged such successful war against the invader and held out so long and fought so furiously as to have received the surname of 'Bred-in-hell!'"

"Humph! do you call that an honor, or him a respectable ancestor?"

"Yes, indeed! because it was for no vice or crime that they give him that surname, but because it was said no man born of woman could have exhibited such frantic courage or performed such prodigies of valor as he did. Well, anyway, that was the origin of our family name. From Bred-in-hell it became Bredi-nell, then Bredenell, and finally, as it still sounded rough for the name of a respectable family, they have in these latter generations softened it down into Brudenell. So you see! I should like to detect the Mervins looking down upon us!" concluded Nora, with a pretty assumption of dignity.

"But, my dear, you are not a Brudenell."

"I don't care! My husband is, and Herman says a wife takes rank from her husband! As Nora Worth, or as Mrs. Herman Brudenell, of course I am the very same person; but then, ignorant as I may be, I know enough of the world to feel sure that those who despised Nora Worth will not dare to slight Mrs. Herman Brudenell!"

"Take care! Take care, Nora, dear! 'Pride goeth before a fall, and a haughty temper before destruction!'" said Hannah, in solemn warning.

"Well, I will not be proud if I can help it; yet—how hard to help it! But I will not let it grow on me. I will remember my humble origin and that I am undeserving of anything better."

At this moment the latch of the door was raised and Jem Morris presented himself, taking off his hat and bowing low, as he said:

"Evening, Miss Hannah; evening, Miss Nora. Hopes you finds yourselves well?"

"Why, law, professor, is that you? You have just come in time. Hannah wants you to put a new bottom in her tin saucepan and a new cover on her umbrella, and to mend her coffee-mill; it won't grind at all!" said Nora.

"Yes, miss; soon's ever I gets the time. See, I've got a well to dig at Colonel Mervin's, and a chimney to build at Major Blackistone's, and a hearth to lay at Commodore Burgh's, and a roof to put over old Mrs. Jones'; and see, that will take me all the rest of the week," objected Jem.

"But can't you take the things home with you and do them at night?" inquired Hannah.

"Yes, miss; but you see there's only three nights more this week, and I am engaged for all! To-night I've got to go and sit up long of old Jem Brown's corpse, and to-morrow night to play the fiddle at Miss Polly Hodges' wedding, and the next night I promised to be a waiter at the college ball, and even Sunday night aint free, 'cause our preacher is sick and I've been invited to take his place and read a sermon and lead the prayer! So you see I couldn't possibly mend the coffee-mill and the rest till some time next week, nohow!"

"I tell you what, Morris, you have the monopoly of your line of business in this neighborhood, and so you put on airs and make people wait. I wish to goodness we could induce some other professor of odd jobs to come and settle among us," said Nora archly.

"Yes, miss; I wish I could, for I am pretty nearly run offen my feet," Jem agreed. "But what I was wishing to say to you, miss," he added, "was that the madam sent me here with a message to you."

"Who sent a message, Jem?"

"The madam up yonder, miss."

"Oh! you mean Mrs. Brudenell! It was to Hannah, I suppose, in relation to work," said Nora.

"Yes, miss; but this time it was not to Miss Hannah; it was to you, Miss Nora. 'Go up to the hut on the hill, and request Nora Worth to come up to see me this evening. I wish to have a talk with her?' Such were the madam's words, Miss Nora."

"Oh, Hannah!" breathed Nora, in terror.

"What can she want with my sister?" inquired Hannah.

"Well, yes, miss. She didn't say any further. And now, ladies, as I have declared my message, I must bid you good evening; as they expects me round to old uncle Jem Brown's to watch to-night." And with a deep bow the professor retired.

"Oh, Hannah!" wailed Nora, hiding her head in her sister's bosom.

"Well, my dear, what is the matter?"

"I am so frightened."

"What at?"

"The thoughts of Mrs. Brudenell!"

"Then don't go. You are not a slave to be at that lady's beck and call, I reckon!"

"Yes, but I am Herman's wife and her daughter, and I will not slight her request! I will go, Hannah, though I had rather plunge into ice water this freezing weather than meet that proud lady!" said Nora, shivering.

"Child, you need not do so! You are not bound! You owe no duty to Mrs. Brudenell, until Mr. Brudenell has acknowledged you as his wife and Mrs. Brudenell as her daughter."

"Hannah, it may be so; yet she is my mother-in-law, being dear Herman's mother; and though I am frightened at the thought of meeting her, still I love her; I do, indeed, Hannah! and my heart longs for her love! Therefore I must not begin by disregarding her requests. I will go! But oh, Hannah! what can she want with me? Do you think it possible that she has heard anything? Oh, suppose she were to say anything to me about Herman? What should I do!" cried Nora, her teeth fairly chattering with nervousness.

"Don't go, I say; you are cold and trembling with fear; it is also after sunset, too late for you to go out alone."

"Yes; but, Hannah, I must go! I am not afraid of the night! I am afraid of her! But if you do not think it well for me to go alone, you can go with me, you know. There will be no harm in that, I suppose?"

"It is a pity Herman had not stayed a little longer, we might have asked him; I do not think he would have been in favor of your going."

"I do not know; but, as there is no chance of consulting him, I must do what I think right in the case and obey his mother," said Nora, rising from her position in Hannah's lap and going to make some change in her simple dress. When she was ready she asked:

"Are you going with me, Hannah?"

"Surely, my child," said the elder sister, reaching her bonnet and shawl.

The weather was intensely cold, and in going to Brudenell the sisters had to face a fierce northwest wind. In walking through the valley they were sheltered by the wood; but in climbing the hill upon the opposite side they could scarcely keep their feet against the furious blast.

They reached the house at last. Hannah remembered to go to the servants' door.

"Ah, Hannah! they little think that when next I come to Brudenell it will be in my own carriage, which will draw up at the main entrance," said Nora, with exultant pride, as she blew her cold fingers while they waited to be admitted.

The door was opened by Jovial, who started back at the sight of the sisters and exclaimed:

"Hi, Miss Hannah, and Miss Nora, you here? Loramity sake come in and lemme shet the door. Dere, go to de fire, chillen! Name o' de law what fetch you out dis bitter night? Wind sharp nuff to peel de skin right offen your faces!"

"Your mistress sent word that she wished to see Nora this evening, Jovial. Will you please to let her know that we are here?" asked Hannah, as she and her sister seated themselves beside the roaring hickory fire in the ample kitchen fireplace.

"Sartain, Miss Hannah! Anything to oblige the ladies," said Jovial, as he left the kitchen to do his errand.

Before the sisters had time to thaw, their messenger re-entered, saying:

"Mistess will 'ceive Miss Nora into de drawing-room."

Nora arose in trepidation to obey the summons.

Jovial led her along a spacious, well-lighted passage, through an open door, on the left side of which she saw the dining-room and the dinner-table, at which Mr. Brudenell and his gentlemen guests still sat lingering over their wine. His back was towards the door, so that he could not see her, or know who was at that time passing. But as her eyes fell upon him, a glow of love and pride warmed and strengthened her heart, and she said:

"After all, he is my husband and this is my house! Why should I be afraid to meet the lady mother?"

And with a firm, elastic step Nora entered the drawing-room. At first she was dazzled and bewildered by its splendor and luxury. It was fitted up with almost Oriental magnificence. Her feet seemed to sink among blooming flowers in the soft rich texture of the carpet. Her eyes fell upon crimson velvet curtains that swept in massive folds from ceiling to floor; upon rare full-length pictures that filled up the recesses between the gorgeously draped windows; broad crystal mirrors above the marble mantel-shelves; marble statuettes wherever there was a corner to hold one; soft crimson velvet sofas, chairs, ottomans and stools; inlaid tables; papier-mache stands; and all the thousand miscellaneous vanities of a modern drawing-room.

"And to think that all this is mine! and how little she dreams of it!" said Nora, in an awe-struck whisper to her own heart, as she gazed around upon all this wealth until at last her eye fell upon the stately form of the lady as she sat alone upon a sofa at the back of the room.

"Come here, my girl, if you please," said Mrs. Brudenell.

Nora advanced timidly until she had reached to within a yard of the lady, when she stopped, courtesied, and stood with folded hands waiting, pretty much as a child would stand when called up before its betters for examination.

"Your name is Nora Worth, I believe," said the lady.

"My name is Nora, madam," answered the girl.

"You are Hannah Worth's younger sister?"

"Yes, madam."

"Now, then, my girl, do you know why I have sent for you here to-night?"

"No, madam."

"Are you quite sure that your conscience does not warn you?"

Nora was silent.

"Ah, I have my answer!" remarked the lady in a low voice; then raising her tone she said:

"I believe that my son, Mr. Herman Brudenell, is in the habit of daily visiting your house; is it not so?"

Nora looked up at the lady for an instant and then dropped her eyes.

"Quite sufficient! Now, my girl, as by your silence you have admitted all my suppositions, I must speak to you very seriously. And in the first place I would ask you, if you do not know, that when a gentleman of Mr. Brudenell's high position takes notice of a girl of your low rank, he does so with but one purpose? Answer me!"

"I do not understand you, madam."

"Very well, then, I will speak more plainly! Are you not aware, I would say, that when Herman Brudenell visits Nora Worth daily for months he means her no good?"

Nora paused for a moment to turn this question over in her mind before replying.

"I cannot think, madam, that Mr. Herman Brudenell could mean anything but good to any creature, however humble, whom he deigned to notice!"

"You are a natural fool or a very artful girl, one or the other!" said the lady, who was not very choice in her language when speaking in anger to her inferiors.

"You admit by your silence that Mr. Brudenell has been visiting you daily for months; and yet you imply that in doing so he means you no harm! I should think he meant your utter ruin!"

"Mrs. Brudenell!" exclaimed Nora, in a surprise so sorrowful and indignant that it made her forget herself and her fears, "you are speaking of your own son, your only son; you are his mother, how can you accuse him of a base crime?"

"Recollect yourself, my girl! You surely forget the presence in which you stand! Baseness, crime, can never be connected with the name of Brudenell. But young gentlemen will be young gentlemen, and amuse themselves with just such credulous fools as you!" said the lady haughtily.

"Although their amusement ends in the utter ruin of its subject? Do you not call that a crime?"

"Girl, keep your place, if you please! Twice you have ventured to call me Mrs. Brudenell. To you I am madam. Twice you have asked me questions. You are here to answer, not to ask!"

"Pardon me, madam, if I have offended you through my ignorance of forms," said Nora, bowing with gentle dignity; for somehow or other she was gaining self-possession every moment.

"Will you answer my questions then; or continue to evade them?"

"I can answer you so far, madam—Mr. Brudenell has never attempted to amuse himself at the expense of Nora Worth; nor is she one to permit herself to become the subject of any man's amusement, whether he be gentle or simple!"

"And yet he visits you daily, and you permit his visits! And this has gone on for months! You cannot deny it—you do not attempt to deny it!" She paused, as if waiting some reply; but Nora kept silence.

"And yet you say he is not amusing himself at your expense!"

"He is not, madam; nor would I permit anyone to do so!"

"I do not understand this! Girl! answer me! What are you to my son?"

. Nora was silent.

"Answer me!" said the lady severely.

"I cannot, madam! Oh, forgive me, but I cannot answer you!" said Nora.

The lady looked fixedly at her for a few seconds; something in the girl's appearance startled her; rising, she advanced and pulled the heavy shawl from Nora's shoulders, and regarded her with an expression of mingled hauteur, anger, and scorn.

Nora dropped her head upon her breast and covered her blushing face with both hands.

"I am answered!" said the lady, throwing her shawl upon the floor and touching the bell rope.

Jovial answered the summons.

"Put this vile creature out of the house, and if she ever dares to show her face upon these premises again send for a constable and have her taken up," said Mrs. Brudenell hoarsely and white with suppressed rage, as she pointed to the shrinking girl before her.

"Come, Miss Nora, honey," whispered the old man kindly, as he picked up the shawl and put it over her shoulders and took her hand to lead her from the room; for, ah! old Jovial as well as his fellow-servants had good cause to know and understand the "white heat" of their mistress' anger.

As with downcast eyes and shrinking form Nora followed her conductor through the central passage and past the dining-room door, she once more saw Herman Brudenell still sitting with his friends at the table.

"Ah, if he did but know what I have had to bear within the last few minutes!" she said to herself as she hurried by.

When she re-entered the kitchen she drew the shawl closer around her shivering figure, pulled the bonnet farther over her blushing face, and silently took the arm of Hannah to return home.

The elder sister asked no question. And when they had left the house their walk was as silent as their departure had been. It required all their attention to hold their course through the darkness of the night, the intensity of the cold and the fury of the wind. It was not until they had reached the shelter of their poor hut, drawn the fire-brands together and sat down before the cheerful blaze, that Nora threw herself sobbing into the arms of her sister.

Hannah gathered her child closer to her heart and caressed her in silence until her fit of sobbing had exhausted itself, and then she inquired:

"What did Mrs. Brudenell want with you, dear?"

"Oh, Hannah, she had heard of Herman's visits here! She questioned and cross-questioned me. I would not admit anything, but then I could not deny anything either. I could give her no satisfaction, because you know my tongue was tied by my promise. Then, she suspected me of being a bad girl. And she cross-questioned me more severely than ever. Still I could give her no satisfaction. And her suspicions seemed to be confirmed. And she looked at me—oh! with such terrible eyes, that they seemed to burn me up. I know, not only my poor face, but the very tips of my ears seemed on fire. And suddenly she snatched my shawl off me, and oh! if her look was terrible before, it was consuming now! Hannah, I seemed to shrivel all up in the glare of that look, like some poor worm in the flame!" gasped Nora, with a spasmodic catch of her breath, as she once more clung to the neck of her sister.

"What next?" curtly inquired Hannah.

"She rang the bell and ordered Jovial to 'put this vile creature (meaning me) out'; and if ever I dared to show my face on the premises again, to send for a constable to take me up."

"The insolent woman!" exclaimed the elder sister, with a burst of very natural indignation. "She will have you taken up by a constable if ever you show your face there again, will he? We'll see that! I shall tell Herman Brudenell all about it to-morrow as soon as he comes! He must not wait until his another goes to Washington! He must acknowledge you as his wife immediately. To-morrow morning he must take you up and introduce you as such to his mother. If there is to be an explosion, let it come! The lady must be taught to know who it is that she has branded with ill names, driven from the house and threatened with a constable! She must learn that it is an honorable wife whom she has called a vile creature; the mistress of the house whom she turned out of doors, and finally that it is Mrs. Herman Brudenell whom she has threatened with a constable!" Hannah had spoken with such vehemence and rapidity that Nora had found no opportunity to stop her. She could not, to use a common phrase, "get in a word edgeways." It was only now when Hannah paused for breath that Nora took up the discourse with:

"Hannah! Hannah! Hannah! how you do go on! Tell Herman Brudenell about his own mother's treatment of me, indeed! I will never forgive you if you do, Hannah! Do you think it will be such a pleasant thing for him to hear? Consider how much it would hurt him, and perhaps estrange him from his mother too! And what! shall I do anything, or consent to anything, to set my husband against his own mother? Never, Hannah! I would rather remain forever in my present obscurity. Besides, consider, she was not so much to blame for her treatment of me! You know she never imagined such a thing as that her son had actually married me, and—"

"I should have told her!" interrupted Hannah vehemently. "I should not have borne her evil charges for one moment in silence! I should have soon let her know who and what I was! I should have taken possession of my rightful place then and there! I should have rung a bell and sent for Mr. Herman Brudenell and had it out with the old lady once for all!"

"Hannah, I could not! my tongue was tied by my promise, and besides—"

"It was not tied!" again dashed in the elder sister, whose unusual vehemence of mood seemed to require her to do all the talking herself. "Herman Brudenell—he is a generous fellow with all his faults!—released both you and myself from our promise, and told us at any time when we should feel that the marriage ought not any longer to be kept secret it might be divulged. You should have told her!"

"What! and raised a storm there between mother and son when both those high spirits would have become so inflamed that they would have said things to each other that neither could ever forgive? What! cause a rupture between them that never could be closed? No, indeed, Hannah! Burned and shriveled up as I was with shame in the glare of that lady's scornful look, I would not save myself at such a cost to him and—to her. For though you mayn't believe me, Hannah, I love that lady! I do in spite of her scorn! She is my husband's mother; I love her as I should have loved my own. And, oh, while she was scorching me up with her scornful looks and words, how I did long to show her that I was not the unworthy creature she deemed me, but a poor, honest, loving girl, who adored both her and her son, and who would, for the love I bore them—"

"Die, if necessary, I suppose! That is just about what foolish lovers promise to do for each other," said the elder sister, impatiently.

"Well, I would, Hannah; though that is not what I meant to say; I meant that for the love I bore them I would so strive to improve in every respect that I should at last lift myself to their level and be worthy of them!"

"Humph! and you can rest under this ban of reproach!"

"No, not rest, Hannah! no one can rest in fire! and reproach is fire to me! but I can bear it, knowing it to be undeserved! For, Hannah, even when I stood shriveling in the blaze of that lady's presence, the feeling of innocence, deep in my heart, kept me from death! for I think, Hannah, if I had deserved her reproaches I should have dropped, blackened, at her feet! Dear sister, I am very sorry I told you anything about it. Only I have never kept anything from you, and so the force of habit and my own swelling heart that overflowed with trouble made me do it. Be patient now, Hannah! Say nothing to my dear husband of this. In two days the lady and her daughters will be in Washington. Herman will take us home, acknowledge me and write to his mother. There will then be no outbreak; both will command their tempers better when they are apart! And there will be nothing said or done that need make an irreparable breach between the mother and son, or between her and myself. Promise me, Hannah, that you will say nothing to Herman about it to-morrow!"

"I promise you, Nora; but only because the time draws so very near when you will be acknowledged without any interference on my part."

"And now, dear sister, about you and Reuben. Have you told him of Mr. Brudenell's offer?"

"Yes, dear."

"And he will accept it?"

"Yes."

"And when shall you be married?"

"The very day that you shall be settled in your new home, dear. We both thought that best. I do not wish to go to Brudenell, Nora. Nothing can ever polish me into a fine lady; so I should be out of place there even for a day. Besides it would be awkward on account of the house-servants, who have always looked upon me as a sort of companion, because I have been their fellow-laborer in busy times. And they would not know how to treat me if they found me in the drawing-room or at the dinner-table! With you it is different; you are naturally refined! You have never worked out of our own house; you are their master's wife, and they will respect you as such. But as for me, I am sure I should embarrass everybody if I should go to Brudenell. And, on the other hand, I cannot remain here by myself. So I have taken Reuben's advice and agreed to walk with him to the church the same hour that Mr. Brudenell takes you home."

"That will be early Sunday morning."

"Yes, dear!"

"Well, God bless you, best of mother-sisters! May you have much happiness," said Nora, as she raised herself from Hannah's knees to prepare for rest.

CHAPTER VIII.

END OF THE SECRET MARRIAGE.

Upon her stubborn brow alone
Nor ruth nor mercy's trace is shown,
Her look is hard and stern.
—*Scott.*

After the departure of Nora Worth Mrs. Brudenell seated herself upon the sofa, leaned her elbow upon the little stand at her side, bowed her head upon her hand and fell into deep thought. Should she speak to Herman Brudenell of this matter? No! it was too late; affairs had gone too far; they must now take their course; the foolish girl's fate must be on her own head, and on that of her careless elder sister; they would both be ruined, that was certain; no respectable family would ever employ either of them again; they would starve. Well, so much the better; they would be a warning to other girls of their class, not to throw out their nets to catch gentlemen! Herman had been foolish, wicked even, but then young men will be young men; and then, again, of course it was that artful creature's fault! What could she, his mother, do in the premises? Not speak to her son upon the subject, certainly; not even let him know that she was cognizant of the affair! What then? She was going away with her daughters in a day or two! And good gracious, he would be left alone in the house! to do as he pleased! to keep bachelor's hall! to bring that girl there as his housekeeper, perhaps, and so desecrate his sacred, patrimonial home! No, that must never be! She must invite and urge her son to accompany herself and his sisters to Washington. But if he should decline the invitation and persist in his declination, what then? Why, as a last resort, she would give up the Washington campaign and remain at home to guard the sanctity of her son's house.

Having come to this conclusion, Mrs. Brudenell once more touched the bell, and when Jovial made his appearance she said:

"Let the young ladies know that I am alone, and they may join me now."

In a few minutes Miss Brudenell and Miss Eleanora entered the room, followed by the gentlemen, who had just left the dinner-table.

Coffee was immediately served, and soon after the guests took leave.

The young ladies also left the drawing-room, and retired to their chambers to superintend the careful packing of some fine lace and jewelry. The mother and son remained alone together—Mrs. Brudenell seated upon her favorite back sofa and Herman walking slowly and thoughtfully up and down the whole length of the room.

"Herman," said the lady.

"Well, mother?"

"I have been thinking about our winter in Washington. I have been reflecting that myself and your sisters will have no natural protector there."

"You never had any in Paris or in London, mother, and yet you got on very well."

"That was a matter of necessity, then; you were a youth at college; we could not have your company; but now you are a young man, and your place, until you marry, is with me and my daughters. We shall need your escort, dear Herman, and be happier for your company. I should be very glad if I could induce to accompany us to the city."

"And I should be very glad to do so, dear mother, but for the engagements that bind me here."

She did not ask the very natural question of what those engagements might be. She did not wish to let him see that she knew or suspected his attachment to Nora Worth, so she answered:

"You refer to the improvements and additions you mean, to add to Brudenell Hall. Surely these repairs had better be deferred until the spring, when the weather will be more favorable for such work?"

"My dear mother, all the alterations I mean to have made inside the house can very well be done this winter. By the next summer I hope to have the whole place in complete order for you and my sisters to return and spend the warm weather with me."

The lady lifted her head. She had never known her son to be guilty of the least insincerity. If he had looked forward to the coming of herself and her daughters to Brudenell, to spend the next summer, he could not, of course, be contemplating the removal of Nora Worth to the house.

"Then you really expect us to make this our home, as heretofore, every summer?" she said.

"I have no right to expect such a favor, my dear mother; but I sincerely hope for it," said the son courteously.

"But it is not every young bachelor living on his own estate who cares to be restrained by the presence of his mother and sisters; such generally desire a life of more freedom and gayety than would be proper with ladies in the house," said Mrs. Brudenell.

"But I am not one of those, mother; you know that my habits are very domestic."

"Yes. Well, Herman, it may just as well be understood that myself and the girls will return here to spend the summer. But now—the previous question! Can you not be prevailed on to accompany us to Washington?"

"My dear mother! anything on earth to oblige you I would do, if possible! But see! you go on Saturday, and this is Thursday night. There is but one intervening day. I could not make the necessary arrangements. I have much business to transact with my overseer; the whole year's accounts still to examine, and other duties to do before I could possibly leave home. But I tell you what I can do; I can hurry up these matters and join you in Washington at the end of the week, in full time to escort you and my sisters to that grand national ball of which I hear them incessantly talking."

"And remain with us for the winter?"

"If you shall continue to wish it, and if I can find a builder, decorator, and upholsterer whom I can send down to Brudenell Hall, to make the improvements, and whom I can trust to carry out my ideas."

The lady's heart leaped for joy! It was all right then! he was willing to leave the neighborhood! he had no particular attractions here! his affections were not involved! his acquaintance with that girl had been only a piece of transient folly, of which he was probably sick and tired! These were her thoughts as she thanked her son for his ready acquiescence in her wishes.

Meanwhile what were his purposes? To conciliate his mother by every concession except one! To let her depart from his house with the best feelings towards himself! then to write to her and announce his marriage; plead his great love as its excuse, and implore her forgiveness; then to keep his word and go to Washington, taking Nora with him, and remain in the capital for the winter if his mother should still desire him to do so.

A few moments longer the mother and son remained in the drawing room before separating for the night— Mrs. Brudenell seated on her sofa and Herman walking slowly up and down the floor. Then the lady arose to retire, and Herman lighted a bedroom candle and put it in her hand.

When she had bidden him good night and left the room, he resumed his slow and thoughtful walk. It was very late, and Jovial opened the door for the purpose of entering and putting out the lights; but seeing his master still walking up and down the floor, he retired, and sat yawning while he waited in the hall without.

The clock upon the mantel-piece struck one, and Herman Brudenell lighted his own candle to retire, when his steps were arrested by a sound—a common one enough at other hours and places, only unprecedented at that hour and in that place. It was the roll of carriage wheels upon the drive approaching the house.

Who could possibly be coming to this remote country mansion at one o'clock at night? While Herman Brudenell paused in expectancy, taper in hand, Jovial once more opened the door and looked in.

"Jovial, is that the sound of carriage wheels, or do I only fancy so?" asked the young man.

"Carriage wheels, marser, coming right to de house, too!" answered the negro.

"Who on earth can be coming here at this hour of the night? We have not an acquaintance intimate enough with us to take such a liberty. And it cannot be a belated traveler, for we are miles from any public road."

"Dat's jes' what I been a-sayin' to myself, sir. But we shall find out now directly."

While this short conversation went on, the carriage drew nearer and nearer, and finally rolled up to the door and stopped. Steps were rattled down, someone alighted, and the bell was rung.

Jovial flew to open the door—curiosity giving wings to his feet.

Mr. Brudenell remained standing in the middle of the drawing-room, attentive to what was going on without. He heard Jovial open the door; then a woman's voice inquired:

"Is this Brudenell Hall?"

"In course it is, miss."

"And are the family at home?"

"Yes, miss, dey most, in gen'al, is at dis hour ob de night, dough dey don't expect wisiters."

"Are all the family here?"

"Dey is, miss."

"All right, coachman, you can take off the luggage," said the woman, and then her voice, sounding softer and farther off, spoke to someone still within the carriage: "We are quite right, my lady, this is Brudenell Hall; the family are all at home, and have not yet retired. Shall I assist your ladyship to alight?"

Then a soft, low voice replied:

"Yes, thank you, Phœbe. But first give the dressing-bag to the man to take in, and you carry Fidelle."

"Bub—bub—bub—bub—but," stammered the appalled Jovial, with his arms full of lap-dogs and dressing-bags that the woman had forced upon him, "you better some of you send in your names, and see if it won't be ill-convenient to the fam'ly, afore you 'spects me to denounce a whole coach full of travelers to my masser! Who is you all, anyhow, young woman?"

"My lady will soon let you know who she is! Be careful of that dog! you are squeezing her! and here take this shawl, and this bird-cage, and this carpetbag, and these umbrellas," replied the woman, overwhelming him with luggage. "Here, coachman! bring that large trunk into the hall! And come now, my lady; the luggage is all right."

As for Jovial, he dropped lap-dogs, bird-cages, carpetbags and umbrellas plump upon the hall floor, and rushed into the drawing-room, exclaiming:

"Masser, it's an invasion of de Goffs and Wandalls, or some other sich furriners! And I think the milishy ought to be called out."

"Don't be a fool, if you please. These are travelers who have missed their way, and are in need of shelter this bitter night. Go at once, and show them in here, and then wake up the housekeeper to prepare refreshments," said Mr. Brudenell.

"It is not my wishes to act foolish, marser; but it's enough to constunnate the sensoriest person to be tumbled in upon dis way at dis hour ob de night by a whole raft of strangers—men, and women, and dogs, and cats, and birds included!" mumbled Jovial, as he went to do his errand.

But his services as gentleman usher seemed not to be needed by the stranger, for as he left the drawing-room a lady entered, followed by a waiting maid.

The lady was clothed in deep mourning, with a thick crape veil concealing her face.

As Herman advanced to welcome her she threw aside her veil, revealing a pale, sad, young face, shaded by thick curls of glossy black hair.

At the sight of that face the young man started back, the pallor of death overspreading his countenance as he sunk upon the nearest sofa, breathing in a dying voice:

"Berenice! You here! Is it you? Oh, Heaven have pity on us!"

"Phœbe, go and find out the housekeeper, explain who I am, and have my luggage taken up to my apartment. Then order tea in this room," said the lady, perhaps with the sole view of getting rid of her attendant; for as soon as the latter had withdrawn she threw off her bonnet, went to the overwhelmed young man, sat down beside him, put her arms around him, and drew his head down to meet her own, as she said, caressingly:

"You did not expect me, love? And my arrival here overcomes you."

"I thought you had been killed in that railway collision," came in hoarse and guttural tones from a throat that seemed suddenly parched to ashes.

"Poor Herman! and you had rallied from that shock of grief; but was not strong enough to sustain a shock of joy! I ought not to have given you this surprise! But try now to compose yourself, and give me welcome. I am here; alive, warm, loving, hungry even! a woman, and no specter risen from the grave, although you look at me just as if I were one! Dear Herman, kiss me! I have come a long way to join you!" she said, in a voice softer than the softest notes of the cushat dove.

"How was it that you were not killed?" demanded the young man, with the manner of one who exacted an apology for a grievous wrong.

"My dearest Herman, I came very near being crushed to death; all that were in the same carriage with me perished. I was so seriously injured that I was reported among the killed; but the report was contradicted in the next day's paper."

"How was it that you were not killed, I asked you?"

"My dearest one, I suppose it was the will of Heaven that I should not be. I do not know any other reason."

"Why did you not write and tell me you had escaped?"

"Dear Herman, how hoarsely you speak! And how ill you look! I fear you have a very bad cold!" said the stranger tenderly.

"Why did you not write and tell me of your escape, I ask you? Why did you permit me to believe for months that you were no longer in life?"

"Herman, I thought surely if you should have seen the announcement of my death in one paper, you would see it contradicted, as it was, in half a dozen others. And as for writing, I was incapable of that for months! Among other injuries, my right hand was crushed, Herman. And that it has been saved at all, is owing to a miracle of medical skill!"

"Why did you not get someone else to write, then?"

"Dear Herman, you forget! There was no one in our secret! I had no confidante at all! Besides, as soon as I could be moved, my father took me to Paris, to place me under the care of a celebrated surgeon there. Poor father! he is dead now, Herman! He left me all his money. I am one among the richest heiresses in England. But it is all yours now, dear Herman. When I closed my poor father's eyes my hand was still too stiff to wield a pen! And still, though there was no longer any reason for mystery, I felt that I would rather come to you at once than employ the pen of another to write. That is the reason, dear Herman, why I have been so long silent, and why at last I arrive so unexpectedly. I hope it is satisfactory. But what is the matter, Herman? You do not seem to be yourself! You have not welcomed me! you have not kissed me! you have not even called me by my name, since I first came in! Oh! can it be possible that after all you are not glad to see me?" she exclaimed, rising from her caressing posture and standing sorrowfully before him. Her face that had looked pale and sad from the first was now convulsed by some passing anguish.

He looked at that suffering face, then covered his eyes with his hands and groaned.

"What is this, Herman? Are you sorry that I have come? Do you no longer love me? What is the matter? Oh, speak to me!"

"The matter is—ruin! I am a felon, my lady! And it were better that you had been crushed to death in that railway collision than lived to rejoin me here! I am a wretch, too base to live! And I wish the earth would open beneath our feet and swallow us!"

The lady stepped back, appalled, and before she could think of a reply, the door opened and Mrs. Brudenell, who had been, awakened by the disturbance, sailed into the room.

"It is my mother!" said the young man, struggling for composure. And rising, he took the hand of the stranger and led her to the elder lady, saying:

"This is the Countess of Hurstmonceux, madam; I commend her to your care."

And having done this, he turned and abruptly left the room and the house.

40

CHAPTER IX.

THE VICTIM.

Good hath been born of Evil, many times,
As pearls and precious ambergris are grown,
Fruits of disease in pain and sickness sown,
So think not to unravel, in thy thought,
This mingled tissue, this mysterious plan,
The Alchemy of Good through Evil wrought.
—*Tupper*.

"But one more day, Hannah! but one more day!" gayly exclaimed Nora Worth, as she busied herself in setting the room in order on Friday morning.

"Yes, but one more day in any event! For even if the weather should change in this uncertain season of the year, and a heavy fall of snow should stop Mrs. Brudenell's journey, that shall not prevent Mr. Brudenell from acknowledging you as his wife on Sunday! for it is quite time this were done, in order to save your good name, which I will not have longer endangered!" said the elder sister, with grim determination.

And she spoke with good reason; it was time the secret marriage was made public, for the young wife was destined soon to become a mother.

"Now, do not use any of these threats to Herman, when he comes this morning, Hannah! Leave him alone; it will all be right," said Nora, as she seated herself at her spinning-wheel.

Hannah was already seated at her loom; and there was but little more conversation between the sisters, for the whir of the wheel and the clatter of the loom would have drowned their voices, so that to begin talking, they must have stopped working.

Nora's caution to Hannah was needless; for the hours of the forenoon passed away, and Herman did not appear.

"I wonder why he does not come?" inquired Nora, straining her eyes down the path for the thousandth time that day.

"Perhaps, Nora, the old lady has been blowing him up, also," suggested the elder sister.

"No, no, no—that is not it! Because if she said a word to him about his acquaintance with me, and particularly if she were to speak to him of me as she spoke to me of myself, he would acknowledge me that moment, and come and fetch me home, sooner than have me wrongly accused for an instant. No, Hannah, I will tell you what it is: it is his mother's last day at home, and he is assisting her with her last preparations," said Nora.

"It may be so," replied her sister; and once more whir and clatter put a stop to conversation.

The afternoon drew on.

"It is strange he does not come!" sighed Nora, as she put aside her wheel, and went to mend the fire and hang on the kettle for their evening meal.

Hannah made no comment, but worked on; for she was in a hurry to finish the piece of cloth then in the loom; and so she diligently drove her shuttle until Nora had baked the biscuits, fried the fish, made the tea, set the table, and called her to supper.

"I suppose he has had a great deal to do, Hannah; but perhaps he may get over here later in the evening," sighed Nora, as they took their seats at the table.

"I don't know, dear; but it is my opinion that the old lady, even if she is too artful to blow him up about you, will contrive to keep him busy as long as possible to prevent his coming."

"Now, Hannah, I wish you wouldn't speak so disrespectfully of Herman's mother. If she tries to prevent him from coming to see me, it is because she thinks it her duty to do so, believing of me as badly as she does."

"Yes! I do not know how you can breathe under such a suspicion! It would smother me!"

"I can bear it because I know it to be false, Hannah; and soon to be proved so! Only one day more, Hannah! only one day!" exclaimed Nora, gleefully clapping her hands.

They finished their supper, set the room in order, lighted the candle, and sat down to the knitting that was their usual evening occupation.

Their needles were clicking merrily, when suddenly, in the midst of their work, footsteps were heard outside.

"There he is now!" exclaimed Nora gayly, starting up to open the door.

41

But she was mistaken; there he was not, but an old woman, covered with snow. .

"Law, Mrs. Jones, is this you?" exclaimed Nora, in a tone of disappointment and vexation.

"Yes, child—don't ye see it's me? Le'me come in out'n the snow," replied the dame, shaking herself and bustling in.

"Why, law, Mrs. Jones, you don't mean it's snowing!" said Hannah, mending the fire, and setting a chair for her visitor.

"Why, child, can't you see it's a-snowing—fast as ever it can? been snowing ever since dark—soft and fine and thick too, which is a sure sign it is agoing to be a deep fall; I shouldn't wonder if the snow was three or four feet deep to-morrow morning!" said Mrs. Jones, as she seated herself in the warmest corner of the chimney and drew up the front of her skirt to toast her shins.

"Nora, dear, pour out a glass of wine for Mrs. Jones; it may warm her up, and keep her from taking cold," said Hannah hospitably.

Wine glass there was none in the hut, but Nora generously poured out a large tea-cup full of fine old port that had been given her by Herman, and handed it to the visitor.

Mrs. Jones' palate was accustomed to no better stimulant than weak toddy made of cheap whisky and water, and sweetened with brown sugar. Therefore to her this strong, sweet, rich wine was nectar.

"Now, this ere is prime! Now, where upon the face of the yeth did you get this?" she inquired, as she sniffed and sipped the beverage, that was equally grateful to smell and taste.

"A friend gave it to Nora, who has been poorly, you know; but Nora does not like wine herself, and I would advise you not to drink all that, for it would certainly get in your head," said Hannah.

"Law, child, I wish it would; if it would do my head half as much good as it is a-doing of my insides this blessed minute! after being out in the snow, too! Why, it makes me feel as good as preaching all over!" smiled the old woman, slowly sniffing and sipping the elixir of life, while her bleared eyes shone over the rim of the cup like phosphorus.

"But how came you out in the snow, Mrs. Jones?" inquired Hannah.

"Why, my dear, good child, when did ever I stop for weather? I've been a-monthly nussing up to Colonel Mervin's for the last four weeks, and my time was up to-day, and so I sat out to come home; and first I stopped on my way and got my tea along of Mrs. Spicer, at Brudenell, and now I s'pose I shall have to stop all night along of you. Can you 'commodate me?"

"Of course we can," said Hannah. "You can sleep with me and Nora; you will be rather crowded, but that won't matter on a cold night; anyway, it will be better than for you to try to get home in this snow-storm."

"Thank y', children; and now, to pay you for that, I have got sich a story to tell you! I've been a-saving of it up till I got dry and warm, 'cause I knew if I did but give you a hint of it, you'd be for wanting to know all the particulars afore I was ready to tell 'em! But now I can sit myself down for a good comfortable chat! And it is one, too, I tell you! good as a novel!" said the old woman, nodded her head knowingly.

"Oh, what is it about, Mrs. Jones?" inquired Hannah and Nora in a breath, as they stopped knitting and drew their chairs nearer together.

"Well, then," said the dame, hitching her chair between the sisters, placing a hand upon each of their laps, and looking from one to the other—"what would ye give to know, now?"

"Nonsense! a night's lodging and your breakfast!" laughed Nora.

"And ye'll get your story cheap enough at that! And now listen and open your eyes as wide as ever you can!" said the dame, repeating her emphatic gestures of laying her hands heavily upon the knees of the visitors and looking intently from one eager face to the other. "Mr.—Herman—Brudenell —have—got—a—wife! There, now! What d'ye think o' that! aint you struck all of a heap?"

No, they were not; Hannah's face was perfectly calm; Nora's indeed was radiant, not with wonder, but with joy!

"There, Hannah! What did I tell you!" she exclaimed. "Mrs. Brudenell has spoken to him and he has owned his marriage! But dear Mrs. Jones, tell me—was his mother very, very angry with him about it?" she inquired, turning to the visitor.

"Angry? Dear heart, no! pleased as Punch! 'peared's if a great weight was lifted offen her mind," replied the latter.

"There again, Hannah! What else did I tell you! Herman's mother is a Christian lady! She ill-used me only when she thought I was bad; now Herman has owned his marriage, and she is pleased to find that it is all right! Now isn't that good? Oh, I know I shall love her, and make her love me, too, more than any high-bred, wealthy daughter-in-law ever could! And I shall serve her more than any of her own children ever would! And she will find out the true worth of a faithful, affectionate, devoted heart, that would die to save her or her son, or live to serve both! And she will love me dearly yet!" exclaimed Nora, with a glow of enthusiasm suffusing her beautiful face.

"Now, what upon the face of the yeth be that gal a-talking about? I want to tell my story!" exclaimed Mrs. Jones, who had been listening indignantly, without comprehending entirely Nora's interruption.

"Oh, I beg your pardon, Mrs. Jones," laughed the latter, "I should not have jumped to the conclusion of your story. I should have let you tell it in your own manner; though I doubt if you know all about it either, from the way you talk."

"Don't I, though! I should like to know who knows more."

"Well, now, tell us all about it!"

"You've gone and put me out now, and I don't know where to begin."

"Well, then, I'll help you out—what time was it that Mr. Brudenell acknowledged his private marriage?"

"There now; how did you know it was a private marriage? I never said nothing about it being private yet! Hows'ever, I s'pose you so clever you guessed it, and anyway you guessed right; it were a private marriage. And when did he own up to it, you ask? Why, not as long as he could help it, you may depend! Not until his lawful wife actilly arove up at Brudenell Hall, and that was last night about one o'clock!"

"Oh, there you are very much mistaken; it was but seven in the evening," said Nora.

"There now, again! how do you know anything about it? Somebody's been here afore me and been a-telling of you, I suppose; and a-telling of you wrong, too!" petulantly exclaimed the old woman.

"No, indeed, there has not been a soul here to-day; neither have we heard a word from Brudenell Hall! Still, I think you must be mistaken as to the hour of the wife's arrival, and perhaps as to other particulars, too; but excuse me, dear Mrs. Jones, and go on and tell the story."

"Well, but what made you say it was seven o'clock when his wife arrove?" inquired the gossip.

"Because that was really the hour that I went up to Brudenell. Hannah was with me and knows it."

"Law, honey, were you up to Brudenell yesterday evening?"

"To be sure I was! I thought you knew it! Haven't you just said that the marriage was not acknowledged until his wife arrived?"

"Why, yes, honey; but what's that to do with it? with you being there, I mean? Seems to me there's a puzzlement here between us? Did you stay there till one o'clock, honey?"

"Why, no, of course not! We came away at eight."

"Then I'm blessed if I know what you're a-driving at! For, in course, if you come away at eight o'clock you couldn't a-seen her."

"Seen whom?" questioned Nora.

"Why, laws, his wife, child, as never arrove till one o'clock."

Nora burst out laughing; and in the midst of her mirthfulness exclaimed:

"There, now, Mrs. Jones, I thought you didn't know half the rights of the story you promised to tell us, and now I'm sure of it! Seems like you've heard Mr. Brudenell has acknowledged his marriage; but you haven't even found out who the lady is! Well, I could tell you; but I won't yet, without his leave."

"So you know all about it, after all? How did you find out?"

"Never mind how; you'll find out how I knew it when you hear the bride's name," laughed Nora.

"But I have hearn the bride's name; and a rum un it is, too! Lady, Lady Hoist? no! Hurl? no! Hurt? yes, that is it! Lady Hurt-me-so, that's the name of the lady he's done married!" said the old woman confidently.

"Ha, ha, ha! I tell you what, Hannah, she has had too much wine, and it has got into her poor old head!" laughed Nora, laying her hand caressingly upon the red-cotton handkerchief that covered the gray hair of the gossip.

"No, it aint, nuther! I never drunk the half of what you gin me! I put it up there on the mantel, and kivered it over with the brass candlestick, to keep till I go to bed. No, indeed! my head-piece is as clear as a bell!" said the old woman, nodding.

"But what put it in there, then, that Mr. Herman Brudenell has married a lady with a ridiculous name?" laughed Nora.

"Acause he have, honey! which I would a-told you all about it ef you hadn't a-kept on, and kept on, and kept on interrupting of me!"

43

"Nora," said Hannah, speaking for the first time in many minutes, and looking very grave, "she has something to tell, and we had better let her tell it."

"Very well, then! I'm agreed! Go on, Mrs. Jones!"

"Hem-m-m!" began Mrs. Jones, loudly clearing her throat. "Now I'll tell you, jest as I got it, this arternoon, first from Uncle Jovial, and then from Mrs. Spicer, and then from Madam Brudenell herself, and last of all from my own precious eyesight! 'Pears like Mr. Herman Brudenell fell in long o' this Lady Hurl-my-soul—Hurt-me-so, I mean,—while he was out yonder in forring parts. And 'pears she was a very great lady indeed, and a beautiful young widder besides. So she and Mr. Brudenell, they fell in love long of each other. But law, you see her kinfolks was bitter agin her a-marrying of him—which they called him a commoner, as isn't true, you know, 'cause he is not one of the common sort at all—though I s'pose they being so high, looked down upon him as sich. Well, anyways, they was as bitter against her marrying of him, as his kinfolks would be agin him a-marrying of you. And, to be sure, being of a widder, she a-done as she pleased, only she didn't want to give no offense to her old father, who was very rich and very proud of her, who was his onliest child he ever had in the world; so to make a long rigamarole short, they runned away, so they did, Mr. Brudenell and her, and they got married private, and never let the old man know it long as ever he lived—"

"Hannah! what is she talking about?" gasped Nora, who heard the words, but could not take in the sense of this story.

"Hush! I do not know yet, myself; there is some mistake! listen," whispered Hannah, putting her arms over her young sister's shoulders, for Nora was then seated on the floor beside Hannah's chair, with her head upon Hannah's lap. Mrs. Jones went straight on.

"And so that was easy enough, too; as soon arter they was married, Mr. Herman Brudenell, you know, he was a-coming of age, and so he had to be home to do business long of his guardeens, and take possession of his 'states and so on; and so he come, and kept his birthday last April! And—"

"Hannah! Hannah! what does this all mean? It cannot be true! I know it is not true! And yet, oh, Heaven! every word she speaks goes through my heart like a red hot spear! Woman! do you mean to say that Mr.—Mr. Herman Brudenell left a wife in Europe when he came back here?" cried Nora, clasping her hands in vague, incredulous anguish.

"Hush, hush, Nora, be quiet, my dear. The very question you ask does wrong to your—to Herman Brudenell, who with all his faults is still the soul of honor," murmured Hannah soothingly.

"Yes, I know he is; and yet—but there is some stupid mistake," sighed Nora, dropping her head upon her sister's lap.

Straight through this low, loving talk went the words of Mrs. Jones:

"Well, now, I can't take upon myself to say whether it was Europe or London, or which of them outlandish places; but, anyways, in some on 'em he did leave his wife a-living along of her 'pa. But you see 'bout a month ago, her 'pa he died, a-leaving of all his property to his onliest darter, Lady Hoist, Hurl, Hurt, Hurt-my-toe. No! Hurt-me-so, Lady Hurt-me-so! I never can get the hang of her outlandish name. Well, then you know there wa'n't no call to keep the marriage secret no more. So what does my lady do but want to put a joyful surprise on the top of her husband; so without writing of him a word of what she was a-gwine to do, soon as ever the old man was buried and the will read, off she sets and comes over the sea to New York, and took a boat there for Baymouth, and hired of a carriage and rid over to Brudenell Hall, and arrove there at one o'clock last night, as I telled you afore!"

"Are you certain that all this is true?" murmured Hannah, in a husky undertone.

"Hi, Miss Hannah, didn't Jovial, and Mrs. Spicer, and Madam Brudenell herself tell me? And besides I seen the young cre'tur' myself, with my own eyes, dressed in deep mourning, which it was a fine black crape dress out and out, and a sweet pretty cre'tur' she was too, only so pale!"

"Hannah!" screamed Nora, starting up, "it is false! I know it is false! but I shall go raving mad if I do not prove it so!" And she rushed to the door, tore it open, and ran out into the night and storm.

"What in the name of the law ails her?" inquired Mrs. Jones.

"Nora! Nora! Nora!" cried Hannah, running after her. "Come back! come in! you will get your death! Are you crazy? Where are you going in the snowstorm this time of night, without your bonnet and shawl, too?"

"To Brudenell Hall, to find out the rights of this story" were the words that came from a great distance wafted by the wind.

"Come back! come back!" shrieked Hannah. But there was no answer.

Hannah rushed into the hut, seized her own bonnet and shawl and Nora's, and ran out again.

"Where are you going? What's the matter? What ails that girl?" cried old Mrs. Jones.

Hannah never even thought of answering her, but sped down the narrow path leading into the valley, and through it up towards Brudenell as fast as the dark night, the falling snow, and the slippery ground would permit; but it was too late; the fleet-footed Nora was far in advance.

CHAPTER X.

THE RIVALS.

One word-yes or no! and it means
Death or life! Speak, are you his wife?
—*Anon.*

Heedless as the mad, of night, of storm, and danger, Nora hurried desperately on. She was blinded by the darkness and smothered by the thickly-falling snow, and torn by the thorns and briars of the brushwood; but not for these impediments would the frantic girl abate her speed. She slipped often, hurt herself sometimes, and once she fell and rolled down the steep hill-side until stopped by a clump of cedars. But she scrambled up, wet, wounded, and bleeding, and tore on, through the depths of the valley and up the opposite heights. Panting, breathless, dying almost, she reached Brudenell Hall.

The house was closely shut up to exclude the storm, and outside the strongly barred window-shutters there was a barricade of drifted snow. The roofs were all deeply covered with snow, and it was only by its faint white glare in the darkness that Nora found her way to the house. Her feet sank half a leg deep in the drifts as she toiled on towards the servants' door. All was darkness there! if there was any light, it was too closely shut in to gleam abroad.

For a moment Nora leaned against the wall to recover a little strength, and then she knocked. But she had to repeat the summons again and again before the door was opened. Then old Jovial appeared—his mouth and eyes wide open with astonishment at seeing the visitor.

"Name o' de law, Miss Nora, dis you? What de matter? Is you clean tuk leave of your senses to be a-comin' up here, dis hour of de night in snowstorm?" he cried.

"Let me in, Jovial! Is Mr. Herman Brudenell at home?" gasped Nora, as without waiting for an answer she pushed past him and sunk into the nearest chair.

"Marser Bredinell home? No, miss! Nor likewise been home since late last night. He went away' mediately arter interdoocing de young madam to de ole one; which she tumbled in upon us with a whole raft of waiting maids, and men, and dogs, and birds, and gold fishes, and debil knows what all besides, long arter midnight last night—and so he hasn't been hearn on since, and de fambly is in de greatest 'stress and anxiety. Particular she, poor thing, as comed so far to see him! And we no more s'picioning as he had a wife, nor anything at all, 'til she tumbled right in on top of us! Law, Miss Nora, somefin werry particular must have fetch you out in de snow to-night, and 'deed you do look like you had heard bad news! Has you hearn anything 'bout him, honey?"

"Is it true, then?" moaned Nora, in a dying tone, without heeding his last question.

"Which true, honey?"

"About the foreign lady coming here last night and claiming to be his wife?"

"As true as gospel, honey—which you may judge the astonishment is put on to us all."

"Jovial, where is the lady?"

"Up in de drawing-room, honey, if she has not 'tired to her chamber."

"Show me up there, Jovial, I must see her for myself," Nora wailed, with her head fallen upon her chest.

"Now, sure as the world, honey, you done heard somefin 'bout de poor young marser? Is he come to an accident, honey?" inquired the man very uneasily.

"Who?" questioned Nora vaguely.

"The young marser, honey; Mr. Herman Brudenell, chile!"

"What of him?" cried Nora—a sharp new anxiety added to her woe.

"Why, law, honey, aint I just been a-telling of you? In one half an hour arter de forein lady tumbled in, young marse lef' de house an' haint been seen nor heard on since. I t'ought maybe you'd might a hearn what's become of him. It is mighty hard on her, poor young creatur, to be fairly forsok de very night she come."

45

"Ah!" cried Nora, in the sharp tones of pain—"take me to that lady at once! I must, must see her! I must hear from her own lips—the truth!"

"Come along then, chile! Sure as the worl' you has hearn somefin, dough you won't tell me; for I sees it in your face; you's as white as a sheet, an' all shakin' like a leaf an' ready to drop down dead! You won't let on to me; but mayhaps you may to her," said Jovial, as he led the way along the lighted halls to the drawing-room door, which, he opened, announcing:

"Here's Miss Nora Worth, mistress, come to see Lady Hurt-my-soul."

And as soon as Nora, more like a ghost than a living creature, had glided in, he shut the door, went down on his knees outside and applied his ear to the key-hole.

Meanwhile Nora found herself once more in the gorgeously furnished, splendidly decorated, and brilliantly lighted drawing room that had been the scene of her last night's humiliation. But she did not think of that now, in this supreme crisis of her fate.

Straight before her, opposite the door by which she entered, was an interesting tableau, in a dazzling light—it was a sumptuous fireside picture—the coal-fire glowing between the polished steel bars of the wide grate, the white marble mantel-piece, and above that, reaching to the lofty ceiling, a full-length portrait of Herman Brudenell; before the fire an inlaid mosaic table, covered with costly books, work-boxes, hand-screens, a vase of hot-house flowers, and other elegant trifles of luxury; on the right of this, in a tall easy-chair, sat Mrs. Brudenell; on this side sat the Misses Brudenell; these three ladies were all dressed in slight mourning, if black silk dresses and white lace collars can be termed such; and they were all engaged in the busy idleness of crochet work; but on a luxurious crimson velvet sofa, drawn up to the left side of the fire, reclined a lady dressed in the deepest mourning, and having her delicate pale, sad face half veiled by her long, soft black ringlets.

While Nora gazed breathlessly upon this pretty creature, whom she recognized at once as the stranger, Mrs. Brudenell slowly raised her head and stared at Nora.

"You here, Nora Worth! How dare you? Who had the insolence to let you in?" she said, rising and advancing to the bell-cord. But before she could pull it Nora Worth lifted her hand with that commanding power despair often lends to the humblest, and said:

"Stop, madam, this is no time to heap unmerited scorn upon one crushed to the dust already, and whose life cannot possibly offend you or cumber the earth much longer. I wish to speak to that lady."

"With me!" exclaimed Lady Hurstmonceux, rising upon her elbow and gazing with curiosity upon the beautiful statue that was gliding toward her as if it were moved by invisible means.

Mrs. Brudenell paused with her hand upon the bell-tassel and looked at Nora, whose lovely face seemed to have been thus turned to stone in some moment of mortal suffering, so agonized and yet so still it looked! Her hair had fallen loose and hung in long, wet, black strings about her white bare neck, for she had neither shawl nor bonnet; her clothes were soaked with the melted snow, and she had lost one shoe in her wild night walk.

Mrs. Brudenell shuddered with aversion as she looked at Nora; when she found her voice she said:

"Do not let her approach you, Berenice. She is but a low creature; not fit to speak to one of the decent negroes even; and besides she is wringing wet and will give you a cold."

"Poor thing! she will certainly take one herself, mamma; she looks too miserable to live! If you please, I would rather talk with her! Come here, my poor, poor girl! what is it that troubles you so? Tell me! Can I help you? I will, cheerfully, if I can." And the equally "poor" lady, poor in happiness as Nora herself, put her hand in her pocket and drew forth an elegant portmonnaie of jet.

"Put up your purse, lady! It is not help that I want—save from God! I want but a true answer to one single question, if you will give it to me."

"Certainly, I will, my poor creature; but stand nearer the fire; it will dry your clothes while we talk."

"Thank you, madam, I do not need to."

"Well, then, ask me the question that you wish to have answered. Don't be afraid, I give you leave, you know," said the lady kindly.

Nora hesitated, shivered, and gasped; but could not then ask the question that was to confirm her fate; it was worse than throwing the dice upon which a whole fortune was staked; it was like giving the signal for the ax to fall upon her own neck. At last, however, it came, in low, fearful, but distinct words:

"Madam, are you the wife of Mr. Herman Brudenell?"

"Nora Worth, how dare you? Leave the room and the house this instant, before I send for a constable and have you taken away?" exclaimed Mrs. Brudenell, violently pulling at the bell-cord.

"Mamma, she is insane, poor thing! do not be hard on her," said Lady Hurstmonceux gently; and then turning to poor Nora she answered, in the manner of one humoring a maniac:

46

"Yes, my poor girl, I am the wife of Mr. Herman Brudenell. Can I do anything for you?"

"Nothing, madam," was the answer that came sad, sweet, and low as the wail of an Aeolian harp swept by the south wind.

The stranger lady's eyes were bent with deep pity upon her; but before she could speak again Mrs. Brudenell broke into the discourse by exclaiming:

"Do not speak to her, Berenice! I warned you not to let her speak to you, but you would not take my advice, and now you have been insulted."

"But, mamma, she is insane, poor thing; some great misery has turned her brain; I am very sorry for her," said the kind-hearted stranger.

"I tell you she is not! She is as sane as you are! Look at her! Not in that amazed, pitying manner, but closely and critically, and you will see what she is; one of those low creatures who are the shame of women and the scorn of men. And if she has misery for her portion, she has brought it upon herself, and it is a just punishment."

The eyes of Lady Hurstmonceux turned again upon the unfortunate young creature before her, and this time she did examine her attentively, letting her gaze rove over her form.

This time Nora did not lift up her hands to cover her burning face; that marble face could never burn or blush again; since speaking her last words Nora had remained standing like one in a trance, stone still, with her head fallen upon her breast, and her arms hanging listlessly by her side. She seemed dead to all around her.

Not so Lady Hurstmonceux; as her eyes roved over this form of stone her pale face suddenly flushed, her dark eyes flashed, and she sprang up from the sofa, asking the same question that Mrs. Brudenell had put the evening before.

"Girl! what is it to you whether Mr. Brudenell has a wife or not? What are you to Mr. Herman Brudenell?"

"Nothing, madam; nothing for evermore," wailed Nora, without looking up or changing her posture.

"Humph! I am glad to hear it, I am sure!" grunted Mrs. Brudenell.

"Nothing? you say; nothing?" questioned Lady Hurstmonceux.

"Nothing in this world, madam; nothing whatever! so be at ease." It was another wail of the storm-swept heart-strings.

"I truly believe you; I ought to have believed without asking you; but who, then, has been your betrayer, my poor girl?" inquired the young matron in tones of deepest pity.

This question at length shook the statue; a storm passed through her; she essayed to speak, but her voice failed.

"Tell me, poor one; and I will do what I can to right your wrongs. Who is it?"

"Myself!" moaned Nora, closing her eyes as if to shut out all light and life, while a spasm drew back the corners of her mouth and convulsed her face.

"Enough of this, Berenice! You forget the girls!" said Mrs. Brudenell, putting her hand to the bell and ringing again.

"I beg your pardon, madam; I did indeed forget the presence of the innocent and happy in looking upon the erring and wretched," said Lady Hurstmonceux.

"That will do," said the elder lady. "Here is Jovial at last! Why did you not come when I first rang?" she demanded of the negro, who now stood in the door.

"I 'clare, mist'ess, I never heerd it de fust time, madam."

"Keep your ears open in future, or it will be the worse for you! And now what excuse can you offer for disobeying my express orders, and not only admitting this creature to the house, but even bringing her to our presence?" demanded the lady severely.

"I clare 'fore my 'vine Marster, madam, when Miss Nora come in de storm to de kitchen-door, looking so wild and scared like, and asked to see de young madam dere, I t'ought in my soul how she had some news of de young marster to tell! an' dat was de why I denounced her into dis drawin'-room."

"Do not make such a mistake again! if you do I will make you suffer severely for it! And you, shameless girl! if you presume to set foot on these premises but once again, I will have you sent to the work-house as a troublesome vagrant."

Nora did not seem to hear her; she had relapsed into her stony, trance-like stupor.

"And now, sir, since you took the liberty of bringing her in, put her out—out of the room, and out of the house!" said Mis. Brudenell.

"Mamma! what! at midnight! in the snow-storm?" exclaimed Lady Hurstmonceux, in horror.

"Yes! she shall not desecrate the bleakest garret, or the lowest cellar, or barest barn on the premises!"

"Mamma! It would be murder! She would perish!" pleaded the young lady.

"Not she! Such animals are used to exposure! And if she and all like her were to 'perish,' as you call it, the world would be so much the better for it! They are the pests of society!"

"Mamma, in pity, look at her! consider her situation! She would surely die! and not alone, mamma! think of that!" pleaded Berenice.

"Jovial! am I to be obeyed or not?" sternly demanded the elder lady.

"Come, Miss Nora; come, my poor, poor child," said Jovial, in a low tone, taking the arm of the miserable girl, who turned, mechanically, to be led away.

"Jovial, stop a moment! Mrs. Brudenell, I have surely some little authority in my husband's house; authority that I should be ashamed to claim in the presence of his mother, were it not to be exercised in the cause of humanity. This girl must not leave the house to-night," said Berenice respectfully, but firmly.

"Lady Hurstmonceux, if you did but know what excellent cause you have to loathe that creature, you would not oppose my orders respecting her; if you keep her under your roof this night you degrade yourself; and, finally, if she does not leave the house at once I and my daughters must—midnight and snow-storm, notwithstanding. We are not accustomed to domicile with such wretches," said the old lady grimly.

Berenice was not prepared for this extreme issue; Mrs. Brudenell's threat of departing with her daughters at midnight, and in the storm, shocked and alarmed her; and the other words reawakened her jealous misgivings. Dropping the hand that she had laid protectingly upon Nora's shoulder, she said:

"It shall be as you please, madam. I shall not interfere again."

This altercation had now aroused poor Nora to the consciousness that she herself was a cause of dispute between the two ladies; so putting her hand to her forehead and looking around in a bewildered way, she said:

"No; it is true; I have no right to stop here now; I will go!"

"Jovial," said Berenice, addressing the negro, "have you a wife and a cabin of your own?"

"Yes, madam; at your sarvice."

"Then let it be at my service in good earnest to-night, Jovial; take this poor girl home, and ask your wife to take care of her to-night; and receive this as your compensation," she said, putting a piece of gold in the hand of the man.

"There can be no objection to that, I suppose, madam?" she inquired of Mrs. Brudenell.

"None in the world, unless Dinah objects; it is not every honest negro woman that will consent to have a creature like that thrust upon her. Take her away, Jovial!"

"Come, Miss Nora, honey; my ole 'oman aint agwine to turn you away for your misfortins: we leabes dat to white folk; she'll be a mother to you, honey; and I'll be a father; an' I wish in my soul as I knowed de man as wronged you; if I did, if I didn't give him a skin-full ob broken bones if he was as white as cotton wool, if I didn't, my name aint Mr. Jovial Brudenell, esquire, and I aint no gentleman. And if Mr. Reuben Gray don't hunt him up and punish him, he aint no gentleman, neither!" said Jovial, as he carefully led his half fainting charge along the passages back to the kitchen.

The servants had all gone to bed, except Jovial, whose duty it was, as major-domo, to go all around the house the last thing at night to fasten the doors and windows and put out the fires and lights. So when they reached the kitchen it was empty, though a fine fire was burning in the ample chimney.

"There, my poor hunted hare, you sit down there an' warm yourself good, while I go an' wake up my ole 'oman, an' fetch her here to get something hot for you, afore takin' of you to de cabin, an' likewise to make a fire dere for you; for I 'spects Dinah hab let it go out," said the kind-hearted old man, gently depositing his charge upon a seat in the chimney corner and leaving her there while he went to prepare for her comfort.

When she was alone Nora, who had scarcely heeded a word of his exhortation, sat for a few minutes gazing woefully into vacancy; then she put her hand to her forehead, passing it to and fro, as if to clear away a mist—a gesture common to human creatures bewildered with sorrow; then suddenly crying out:

"My Lord! It is true! and I have no business here! It is a sin and a shame to be here! or anywhere! anywhere in the world!" And throwing up her arms with a gesture of wild despair, she sprang up, tore open the door, and the second time that night rushed out into the storm and darkness.

The warm, light kitchen remained untenanted for perhaps twenty minutes, when Jovial, with his Dinah on his arm and a lantern in his hand, entered, Jovial grumbling:

"Law-a-mity knows, I don't see what she should be a-wantin' to come here for! partic'lar arter de treatment she 'ceived from ole mis'tess las' night! tain't sich a par'dise nohow for nobody—much less for she! Hi, 'oman!"

he suddenly cried, turning the rays of the lantern in all directions, though the kitchen was quite light enough without them.

"What de matter now, ole man?" asked Dinah.

"Where Nora? I lef' her here an' she aint here now! where she gone?"

"Hi, ole man, what you ax me for? how you 'spect I know?"

"Well, I 'clare ef dat don't beat eberyting!"

"Maybe she done gone back in de house ag'in!" suggested Dinah.

"Maybe she hab; I go look; but stop, first let me look out'n de door to see if she went away," said Jovial, going to the door and holding the lantern down near the ground.

"Yes, Dinah, 'oman, here day is; little foot-prints in de snow a-goin' away from de house an' almost covered up now! She done gone! Now don't dat beat eberything? Now she'll be froze to death, 'less I goes out in de storm to look for her; an' maybe she'll be froze anyway; for dere's no sartainty 'bout my findin' of her. Now aint dat a trial for any colored gentleman's narves! Well den, here goes! Wait for me here, ole 'omen, till I come back, and if I nebber comes, all I leabes is yourn, you know," sighed the old man, setting down the lantern and beginning to button up his great coat preparatory to braving the storm.

But at this moment a figure came rushing through the snow towards the kitchen door.

"Here she is now; now, ole 'oman! get de gruel ready!" exclaimed Jovial, as the snow-covered form rushed in. "No, it aint, nyther! Miss Hannah! My goodness, gracious me alibe, is all de worl' gone ravin', starin', 'stracted mad to-night? What de debil fotch you out in de storm at midnight?" he asked, as Hannah Worth threw off her shawl and stood in their midst.

"Oh, Jovial! I am looking for poor Nora! Have you seen anything of her?" asked Hannah anxiously.

"She was here a-sittin' by dat fire, not half an hour ago. And I lef' her to go and fetch my ole 'oman to get somefin hot, and when I come back, jes' dis wery minute, she's gone!"

"Where, where did she go?" asked Hannah, clasping hear hands in the agony of her anxiety.

"Out o' doors, I see by her little foot-prints a-leading away from de door; dough I 'spects dey's filled up by dis time. I was jes' agwine out to look for her."

"Oh, bless you, Jovial!"

"Which way do you think she went, Miss Hannah?"

"Home again, I suppose, poor child."

"It's a wonder you hadn't met her."

"The night is so dark, and then you know there is more than one path leading from Brudenell down into the valley. And if she went that way she took a different path from the one I came by."

"I go look for her now! I won't lose no more time talkin'," and the old man clapped his hat upon his head and picked up his lantern.

"I will go with you, Jovial," said Nora's sister.

"No, Miss Hannah, don't you 'tempt it; tain't no night for no 'oman to be out."

"And dat a fact, Miss Hannah! don't you go! I can't 'mit of it! You stay here long o' me till my ole man fines her and brings her back here; an' I'll have a bit of supper ready, an' you'll both stop wid us all night," suggested Dinah.

"I thank you both, but I cannot keep still while Nora is in danger! I must help in the search for her," insisted Hannah, with the obstinacy of a loving heart, as she wrapped her shawl more closely around her shoulders and followed the old man out in the midnight storm. It was still snowing very fast. Her guide went a step in front with the lantern, throwing a feeble light upon the soft white path that seemed to sink under their feet as they walked. The old man peered about on the right and left and straight before him, so as to miss no object in his way that might be Nora.

"Jovial," said Hannah, as they crept along, "is it true about the young foreign lady that arrived here last night and turned out to be the wife of Mr. Herman?"

"All as true as gospel, honey," replied the old man, who, in his love of gossip, immediately related to Hannah all the particulars of the arrival of Lady Hurstmonceux and the flight of Herman Brudenell. "Seems like he run away at the sight of his wife, honey; and 'pears like she thinks so too, 'cause she's taken of it sorely to heart, scarce' holdin' up her head since. And it is a pity for her, too, poor young thing; for she's a sweet perty young cre'tur', and took Miss Nora's part like an angel when de old madam was a-callin' of her names, and orderin' of her out'n de house."

49

"Calling her names! ordering her out of the house! Did Mrs. Brudenell dare to treat Nora Worth so?" cried Hannah indignantly.

"Well, honey, she did rayther, that's a fact. Law, honey, you know yourself how ha'sh ladies is to poor young gals as has done wrong. A hawk down on a chicken aint nuffin to 'em!"

"But my sister has done no wrong; Nora Worth is as innocent as an angel, as honorable as an empress. I can prove it, and I will prove it, let the consequences to the Brudenells be what they may! Called her ill names, did she? Very well! whether my poor wronged child lives or dies this bitter night, I will clear her character to-morrow, let who will be blackened instead of her! Ordered her out of the house, did she? All right! we will soon see how long the heir himself will be permitted to stop there! There's law in the land, for rich as well as poor, I reckon! Threatened her with a constable, did she? Just so! I wonder how she will feel when her own son is dragged off to prison! That will take her down—"

Hannah's words were suddenly cut short, for Jovial, who was going on before her, fell sprawling over some object that lay directly across the path, and the lantern rolled down the hill.

"What is the matter, Jovial?" she inquired.

"Honey, I done fell—fell over somefin' or oder; it is—law, yes—"

"What, Jovial?"

"It's a 'oman, honey; feels like Miss Nora."

In an instant Hannah was down on her knees beside the fallen figure, clearing away the snow that covered it.

"It is Nora," she said, trying to lift the insensible body; but it was a cold, damp, heavy weight, deeply bedded in the snow, and resisted all her efforts.

"Oh, Jovial, I am afraid she is dead! and I cannot get her up! You come and try!" wept Hannah.

"Well, there now, I knowed it—I jest did; I knowed if she was turned out in de snow-storm this night she'd freeze to death! Ole mist'ess aint no better dan a she-bearess!" grumbled the old man, as he rooted his arms under the cold dead weight of the unfortunate girl, and with much tugging succeeded in raising her.

"Now, den, Miss Hannah, hadn't I better tote her back to my ole 'oman?"

"No; we are much nearer the hut than the hall, and even if it were not so, I would not have her taken back there."

They were in fact going up the path leading to the hut on the top of the hill. So, by dint of much lugging and tugging, and many breathless pauses to rest, the old man succeeded in bearing his lifeless burden to the hut.

CHAPTER XI.

THE MARTYRS OF LOVE.

She woke at length, but not as sleepers wake,
Rather the dead, for life seemed something new,
A strange sensation which she must partake
Perforce, since whatsoever met her view
Struck not her memory; though a heavy ache
Lay at her heart, whose earliest beat, still true,
Brought back the sense of pain, without the cause,
For, for a time the furies made a pause.
—*Byron.*

So Nora's lifeless form was laid upon the bed. Old Mrs. Jones, who had fallen asleep in her chair, was aroused by the disturbance, and stumbled up only half awake to see what was the matter, and to offer her assistance.

Old Jovial had modestly retired to the chimney corner, leaving the poor girl to the personal attention of her sister.

Hannah had thrown off her shawl and bonnet, and was hastily divesting Nora of her wet garments, when the old nurse appeared at her side.

"Oh, Mrs. Jones, is she dead?" cried the elder sister.

"No," replied the oracle, putting her warm hand upon the heart of the patient, "only in a dead faint and chilled to the marrow of her bones, poor heart! Whatever made her run out so in this storm? Where did you find her? had she fallen down in a fit? What was the cause on it?" she went on to hurry question upon question, with the vehemence of an old gossip starving for sensation news.

"Oh, Mrs. Jones, this is no time to talk! we must do something to bring her to life!" wept Hannah.

"That's a fact! Jovial, you good-for-nothing, lazy, lumbering nigger, what are ye idling there for, a-toasting of your crooked black shins? Put up the chunks and hang on the kettle directly," said the nurse with authority.

Poor old Jovial, who was anxious to be of service, waiting only to be called upon, and glad to be set to work, sprung up eagerly to obey this mandate.

Thanks to the huge logs of wood used in Hannah's wide chimney, the neglected fire still burned hotly, and Jovial soon had it in a roaring blaze around the suspended kettle.

"And now, Hannah, you had better get out her dry clothes and a thick blanket, and hang 'em before the fire to warm. And give me some of that wine and some allspice to heat," continued Mrs. Jones.

The sister obeyed, with as much docility as the slave had done, and by their united efforts the patient was soon dressed in warm dry clothes, wrapped in a hot, thick blanket, and tucked up comfortably in bed. But though her form was now limber, and her pulse perceptible, she had not yet spoken or opened her eyes. It was a half an hour later, while Hannah stood bathing her temples with camphor, and Mrs. Jones sat rubbing her hands, that Nora showed the first signs of returning consciousness, and these seemed attended with great mental or bodily pain, it was difficult to tell which, for the stately head was jerked back, the fair forehead corrugated, and the beautiful lips writhen out of shape.

"Fetch me the spiced wine now, Hannah," said the nurse; and when it was brought she administered it by teaspoonfuls. It seemed to do the patient good, for when she had mechanically swallowed it, she sighed as with a sense of relief, sank back upon her pillow and closed her eyes. Her face had lost its look of agony; she seemed perfectly at ease. In a little while she opened her eyes calmly and looked around. Hannah bent over her, murmuring:

"Nora, darling, how do you feel? Speak to me, my pet!"

"Stoop down to me, Hannah! low, lower still, I want to whisper to you."

Hannah put her ear to Nora's lips.

"Oh, Hannah, it was all true! he was married to another woman." And as she gasped out these words with a great sob, her face became convulsed again with agony, and she covered it with her hands.

"Do not take this so much to heart, sweet sister. Heaven knows that you were innocent, and the earth shall know it, too; as for him, he was a villain and a hypocrite not worth a tear," whispered Hannah.

"Oh, no, no, no! I am sure he was not to blame. I cannot tell you why, because I know so little; but I feel that he was faultless," murmured Nora, as the spasm passed off, leaving her in that elysium of physical ease which succeeds great pain.

Hannah was intensely disgusted by Nora's misplaced confidence; but she did not contradict her, for she wished to soothe, not to excite the sufferer.

For a few minutes Nora lay with her eyes closed and her hands crossed upon her bosom, while her watchers stood in silence beside her bed. Then springing up with wildly flaring eyes she seized her sister, crying out:

"Hannah! Oh, Hannah!"

"What is it, child?" exclaimed Hannah, in affright.

"I do believe I'm dying—and, oh! I hope I am."

"Oh, no, ye aint a-dying, nyther; there's more life than death in this 'ere; Lord forgive ye, girl, fer bringing such a grief upon your good sister," said Mrs. Jones grimly.

"Oh, Mrs. Jones, what is the matter with her? Has she taken poison, do you think? She has been in a great deal of trouble to-night!" cried Hannah, in dismay.

"No, it's worse than pi'sen. Hannah, you send that ere gaping and staring nigger right away directly; this aint no place, no longer, for no men-folks to be in, even s'posin they is nothin' but nigger cre-turs.".

Hannah raised her eyes to the speaker. A look of intelligence passed between the two women. The old dame nodded her head knowingly, and then Hannah gently laid Nora back upon her pillow, for she seemed at ease again now, and went to the old man and said:

"Uncle Jovial, you had better go home now. Aunt Dinah will be anxious about you, you know."

"Yes, honey, I knows it, and I was only awaitin' to see if I could be of any more use," replied the old man, meekly rising to obey.

"I thank you very much, dear old Uncle Jovial, for all your goodness to us to-night, and I will knit you a pair of nice warm socks to prove it."

"Laws, child, I don't want nothing of no thanks, nor no socks for a-doin' of a Christian man's duty. And now, Miss Hannah, don't you be cast down about this here misfortin'; it's nothin' of no fault of yours; everybody 'spects you for a well-conducted young 'oman; an' you is no ways 'countable for your sister's mishaps. Why, there was my own Aunt Dolly's step-daughter's husband's sister-in-law's son as was took up for stealin' of sheep. But does anybody 'spect me the less for that? No! and no more won't nobody 'spect you no less for poor misfortinit Miss Nora. Only I do wish I had that ere scamp, whoever he is, by the ha'r of his head! I'd give his blamed neck one twist he wouldn't 'cover of in a hurry," said the old man, drawing himself up stiffly as he buttoned his overcoat.

"And now good-night, chile! I'll send my ole 'oman over early in de mornin', to fetch Miss Nora somefin' nourishin, an' likewise to see if she can be of any use," said Jovial, as he took up his hat to depart.

The snow had ceased to fall, the sky was perfectly clear, and the stars were shining brightly. Hannah felt glad of this for the old man's sake, as she closed the door behind him.

But Nora demanded her instant attention. That sufferer was in a paroxysm of agony stronger than any that had yet preceded it.

There was a night of extreme illness, deadly peril, and fearful anxiety in the hut.

But the next morning, just as the sun arose above the opposite heights of Brudenell, flooding all the cloudless heavens and the snow-clad earth with light and glory, a new life also arose in that humble hut upon the hill.

Hannah Worth held a new-born infant boy in her arms, and her tears fell fast upon his face like a baptism of sorrow.

The miserable young mother lay back upon her pillow—death impressed upon the sunken features, the ashen complexion, and the fixed eyes.

"Oh, what a blessing if this child could die!" cried Hannah, in a piercing voice that reached even the failing senses of the dying girl.

There was an instant change. It was like the sudden flaring up of an expiring light. Down came the stony eyes, melting with tenderness and kindling with light. All the features were softened and illumined.

Those who have watched the dying are familiar with these sudden re-kindlings of life. She spoke in tones of infinite sweetness:

"Oh, do not say so, Hannah! Do not grudge the poor little thing his life! Everything else has been taken from him, Hannah!—father, mother, name, inheritance, and all! Leave him his little life: it has been dearly purchased! Hold him down to me, Hannah; I will give him one kiss, if no one ever kisses him again."

"Nora, my poor darling, you know that I will love your boy, and work for him, and take care of him, if he lives; only I thought it was better if it pleased God that he should go home to the Saviour," said Hannah, as she held the infant down to receive his mother's kiss.

"God love you, poor, poor baby!" said Nora, putting up her feeble hands, and bringing the little face close to her lips. "He will live, Hannah! Oh, I prayed all through the dreadful night that he might live, and the Lord has answered my prayer," she added, as she resigned the child once more to her sister's care.

Then folding her hands over her heart, and lifting her eyes towards heaven with a look of sweet solemnity, and, in a voice so deep, bell-like, and beautiful that it scarcely seemed a human one, she said:

"Out of the Depths have I called to Thee, and Thou hast heard my voice."

And with these sublime words upon her lips she once more dropped away into sleep, stupor, or exhaustion—for it is difficult to define the conditions produced in the dying by the rising and falling of the waves of life when the tide is ebbing away. The beautiful eyes did not close, but rolled themselves up under their lids; the sweet lips fell apart, and the pearly teeth grew dry.

Old Mrs. Jones, who had been busy with a saucepan over the fire, now approached the bedside, saying:

"Is she 'sleep?"

"I do not know. Look at her, and see if she is," replied the weeping sister.

"Well, I can't tell," said the nurse, after a close examination.

And neither could Hippocrates, if he had been there.

"Do you think she can possibly live?" sobbed Hannah.

"Well—I hope so, honey. Law, I've seen 'em as low as that come round again. Now lay the baby down, Hannah Worth, and come away to the window; I want to talk to you without the risk of disturbing her."

Hannah deposited the baby by its mother's side and followed the nurse.

"Now you know, Hannah, you must not think as I'm a hard-hearted ole 'oman; but you see I must go."

"Go! oh, no! don't leave Nora in her low state! I have so little experience in these cases, you know. Stay with her! I will pay you well, if I am poor."

"Child, it aint the fear of losin' of the pay; I'm sure you're welcome to all I've done for you."

"Then do stay! It seems indeed that Providence himself sent you to us last night! What on earth should we have done without you! It was really the Lord that sent you to us."

"'Pears to me it was Old Nick! I know one thing: I shouldn't a-come if I had known what an adventur' I was a-goin' to have," mumbled the old woman to herself.

Hannah, who had not heard her words, spoke again:

"You'll stay?"

"Now, look here, Hannah Worth, I'm a poor old lady, with nothing but my character and my profession; and if I was to stay here and nuss Nora Worth, I should jes' lose both on 'em, and sarve me right, too! What call have I to fly in the face of society?"

Hannah made no answer, but went and reached a cracked tea-pot from the top shelf of the dresser, took from it six dollars and a half, which was all her fortune, and came and put it in the hand of the nurse, saying:

"Here! take this as your fee for your last night's work and go, and never let me see your face again if you can help it."

"Now, Hannah Worth, don't you be unreasonable—now, don't ye; drat the money, child; I can live without it, I reckon; though I can't live without my character and my perfession; here, take it, child—you may want it bad afore all's done; and I'm sure I would stay and take care of the poor gal if I dared; but now you know yourself, Hannah, that if I was to do so, I should be a ruinated old 'oman; for there ain't a respectable lady in the world as would ever employ me again."

"But I tell you that Nora is as innocent as her own babe; and her character shall be cleared before the day is out!" exclaimed Hannah, tears of rage and shame welling to her eyes.

"Yes, honey, I dessay; and when it's done I'll come back and nuss her—for nothing, too," replied the old woman dryly, as she put on her bonnet and shawl.

This done she returned to the side of Hannah.

"Now, you know I have told you everything what to do for Nora; and by-and-by, I suppose, old Dinah will come, as old Jovial promised; and maybe she'll stay and 'tend to the gal and the child; 'twon't hurt her, you know, 'cause niggers aint mostly got much character to lose. There, child, take up your money; I wouldn't take it from you, no more'n I'd pick a pocket. Good-by."

Hannah would have thrown the money after the dame as she left the hut, but that Nora's dulcet tones recalled her:

"Hannah, don't!"

She hurried to the patient's bedside; there was another rising of the waves of life; Nora's face, so dark and rigid a moment before, was now again soft and luminous.

"What is it, sister?" inquired Hannah, bending over her.

"Don't be angry with her, dear; she did all she could for us, you know, without injuring herself—and we had no right to expect that."

"But—her cruel words!"

"Dear Hannah, never mind; when you are hurt by such, remember our Saviour; think of the indignities that were heaped upon the Son of God; and how meekly he bore them, and how freely he forgave them."

"Nora, dear, you do not talk like yourself."

"Because I am dying, Hannah. My boy came in with the rising sun, and I shall go out with its setting."

"No, no, my darling—you are much better than you were. I do not see why you should die!" wept Hannah.

"But I do; I am not better, Hannah—I have only floated back. I am always floating backward and forward, towards life and towards death; only every time I float towards death I go farther away, and I shall float out with the day."

Hannah was too much moved to trust herself to speak.

"Sister," said Nora, in a fainter voice, "I have one last wish."

53

"What is it, my own darling?"

"To see poor, poor Herman once more before I die."

"To forgive him! Yes, I suppose that will be right, though very hard," sighed the elder girl.

"No, not to forgive him, Hannah—for he has never willingly injured me, poor boy; but to lay my hand upon his head, and look into his eyes, and assure him with my dying breath that I know he was not to blame; for I do know it, Hannah."

"Oh, Nora, what faith!" cried the sister.

The dying girl, who, to use her own words, was floating away again, scarcely heard this exclamation, for she murmured on in a lower tone, like the receding voice of the wind:

"For if I do not have a chance of saying this to him, Hannah—if he is left to suppose I went down to the grave believing him to be treacherous—it will utterly break his heart, Hannah; for I know him, poor fellow——-he is as sensitive as—as—any——." She was gone again out of reach.

Hannah watched the change that slowly grew over her beautiful face: saw the grayness of death creep over it—saw its muscles stiffen into stone—saw the lovely eyeballs roll upward out of sight—and the sweet lips drawn away from the glistening teeth.

While she thus watched she heard a sound behind her. She turned in time to see the door pushed open, and Herman Brudenell—pale, wild, haggard, with matted hair, and blood-shot eyes, and shuddering frame—totter into the room.

CHAPTER XII.

HERMAN'S STORY.

Thus lived—thus died she; never more on her
Shall sorrow light or shame. She was not made,
Through years of moons, the inner weight to bear,
Which colder hearts endure 'til they are laid
By age in earth: her days and pleasures were
Brief but delightful—such as had not stayed
Long with her destiny; but she sleeps well
By the sea-shore, whereon she loved to dwell.
—Byron.

Hannah arose, met the intruder, took his hand, led him to the bed of death and silently pointed to the ghastly form of Nora.

He gazed with horror on the sunken features, gray complexion, upturned eyes, and parted lips of the once beautiful girl.

"Hannah, how is this—dying?" he whispered huskily.

"Dying," replied the woman solemnly.

"So best," he whispered, in a choking voice.

"So best," she echoed, as she drew away to the distant window. "So best, as death is better than dishonor. But you! Oh, you villain! oh, you heartless, shameless villain! to pass yourself off for a single man and win her love and deceive her with a false marriage!"

"Hannah! hear me!" cried the young man, in a voice of anguish.

"Dog! ask the judge and jury to hear you when you are brought to trial for your crime! For do you think that I am a-going to let that girl go down to her grave in undeserved reproach? No, you wretch! not to save from ruin you and your fine sisters and high mother, and all your proud, shameful race! No, you devil! if there is law in the land, you shall be dragged to jail like a thief and exposed in court to answer for your bigamy; and all the world shall hear that you are a felon and she an honest girl who thought herself your wife when she gave you her love!"

"Hannah, Hannah, prosecute, expose me if you like! I am so miserable that I care not what becomes of me or mine. The earth is crumbling under my feet! do you think I care for trifles? Denounce, but hear me! Heaven knows I did not willingly deceive poor Nora! I was myself deceived! If she believed herself to be my wife, I as fully believed myself to be her husband."

"You lie!" exclaimed this rude child of nature, who knew no fine word for falsehood.

"Oh, it is natural you should rail at me! But, Hannah, my sharp, sharp grief makes me insensible to mere stinging words. Yet if you would let me, I could tell you the combination of circumstances that deceived us both!" replied Herman, with the patience of one who, having suffered the extreme power of torture, could feel no new wound.

"Tell me, then!" snapped Hannah harshly and incredulously.

He leaned against the window-frame and whispered:

"I shall not survive Nora long; I feel that I shall not; I have not taken food or drink, or rested under a roof, since I heard that news, Hannah. Well, to explain—I was very young when I first met her—-"

"Met who?" savagely demanded Hannah.

"My first wife. She was the only child and heiress of a retired Jew-tradesman. Her beauty fascinated an imbecile old nobleman, who, having insulted the daughter with 'liberal' proposals, that were scornfully rejected, tempted the father with 'honorable' ones, which were eagerly accepted. The old Jew, in his ambition to become father-in-law to the old earl, forgot his religious prejudices and coaxed his daughter to sacrifice herself. And thus Berenice D'Israeli became Countess of Hurstmonceux. The old peer survived his foolish marriage but six months, and died leaving his widow penniless, his debts having swamped even her marriage portion. His entailed estates went to the heir-at-law, a distant relation——"

"What in the name of Heaven do you think I care for your countesses! I want to know what excuse you can give for your base deception of my sister," fiercely interrupted Hannah.

"I am coming to that. It was in the second year of the Countess Hurstmonceux's widowhood that I met her at Brighton. Oh, Hannah, it is not in vanity; but in palliation of my offense that I tell you she loved me first. And when a widow loves a single man, in nine cases out of ten she will make him marry her. She hunted me down, ran me to earth—"

"Oh, you wretch! to say such things of a lady!" exclaimed the woman, with indignation.

"It is true, Hannah, and in this awful hour, with that ghastly form before me, truth and not false delicacy must prevail. I say then that the Countess of Hurstmonceux hunted me down and run me to earth, but all in such feminine fashion that I scarcely knew I was hunted. I was flattered by her preference, grateful for her kindness and proud of the prospect of carrying off from all competitors the most beautiful among the Brighton belles; but all this would not have tempted me to offer her my hand, for I did not love her, Hannah."

"What did tempt you then?" inquired the woman.

"Pity; I saw that she loved me passionately, and—I proposed to her."

"Coxcomb! do you think she would have broken her heart if you hadn't?"

"Yes, Hannah, to tell the truth, I did think so then; I was but a boy, you know; and I had that fatal weakness of which I told you—that which dreaded to inflict pain and delighted to impart joy. So I asked her to marry me. But the penniless Countess of Hurstmonceux was the sole heiress of the wealthy old Jew, Jacob D'Israeli. And he had set his mind upon her marrying a gouty marquis, and thus taking one step higher in the peerage; so of course he would not listen to my proposal, and he threatened to disinherit his daughter if she married me. Then we did what so many others in similar circumstances do—we married privately. Soon after this I was summoned home to take possession of my estates. So I left England; but not until I had discovered the utter unworthiness of the siren whom I was so weak as to make my wife. I did not reproach the woman, but when I sailed from Liverpool it was with the resolution never to return."

"Well, sir! even supposing you were drawn into a foolish marriage with an artful woman, and had a good excuse for deserting her, was that any reason why you should have committed the crime of marrying Nora?" cried the woman fiercely.

"Hannah, it was not until after I had read an account of a railway collision, in which it was stated that the Countess of Hurstmonceux was among the killed that I proposed for Nora. Oh, Hannah, as the Lord in heaven hears me, I believed myself to be a free, single man, a widower, when I married Nora! My only fault was too great haste. I believed Nora to be my lawful wife until the unexpected arrival of the Countess of Hurstmonceux, who had been falsely reported among the killed."

"If this is so," said Hannah, beginning to relent, "perhaps after all you are more to be pitied than blamed."

"Thank you, thank you, Hannah, for saying that! But tell me, does she believe that I willfully deceived her? Yet why should I ask? She must think so! appearances are so strong against me," he sadly reflected.

"But she does not believe it; her last prayer was that she might see you once more before she died, to tell you that she knew you were not to blame," wept Hannah.

"Bless her! bless her!" exclaimed the young man.

Hannah, whose eyes had never, during this interview, left the face of Nora, now murmured:

"She is reviving again; will you see her now?"

Herman humbly bowed his head and both approached the bed.

That power—what is it?—awe?—that power which subdues the wildest passions in the presence of death, calmed the grief of Herman as he stood over Nora.

She was too far gone for any strong human emotion; but her pale, rigid face softened and brightened as she recognized him, and she tried to extend her hand towards him.

He saw and gently took it, and stooped low to hear the sacred words her dying lips were trying to pronounce.

"Poor, poor boy; don't grieve so bitterly; it wasn't your fault," she murmured.

"Oh, Nora, your gentle spirit may forgive me, but I never can forgive myself for the reckless haste that has wrought all this ruin!" groaned Herman, sinking on his knees and burying his face on the counterpane, overwhelmed by grief and remorse for the great, unintentional wrong he had done; and by the impossibility of explaining the cause of his fatal mistake to this poor girl whose minutes were now numbered.

Softly and tremblingly the dying hand arose, fluttered a moment like a white dove, and then dropped in blessing on his head.

"May the Lord give the peace that he only can bestow; may the Lord pity you, comfort you, bless you and save you forever, Herman, poor Herman!"

A few minutes longer her hand rested on his head, and then she removed it and murmured:

"Now leave me for a little while; I wish to speak to my sister."

Herman arose and went out of the hut, where he gave way to the pent-up storm of grief that could not be vented by the awful bed of death.

Nora then beckoned Hannah, who approached and stooped low to catch her words.

"Sister, you would not refuse to grant my dying prayers, would you?"

"Oh, no, no, Nora!" wept the woman.

"Then promise me to forgive poor Herman the wrong that he has done us; he did not mean to do it, Hannah."

"I know he did not, love; he explained it all to me. The first wife was a bad woman who took him in. He thought she had been killed in a railway collision, when he married you, and he never found out his mistake until she followed him home."

"I knew there was something of that sort; but I did not know what. Now, Hannah, promise me not to breathe a word to any human being of his second marriage with me; it would ruin him, you know, Hannah; for no one would believe but that he knew his first wife was living all the time. Will you promise me this, Hannah?"

Even though she spoke with great difficulty, Hannah did not answer until she repeated the question.

Then with a sob and a gulp the elder sister said:

"Keep silence, and let people reproach your memory, Nora? How can I do that?"

"Can reproach reach me—there?" she asked, raising her hand towards heaven.

"But your child, Nora; for his sake his mother's memory should be vindicated!"

"At the expense of making his father out a felon? No, Hannah, no; people will soon forget he ever had a mother. He will only be known as Hannah Worth's nephew, and she is everywhere respected. Promise me, Hannah."

"Nora, I dare not."

"Sister, I am dying; you cannot refuse the prayer of the dying."

Hannah was silent.

"Promise me! promise me! promise me! while my ears can yet take in your voice!" Nora's words fell fainter and fainter; she was failing fast.

"Oh, Heaven, I promise you, Nora—the Lord forgive me for it!" wept Hannah.

"The Lord bless you for it, Hannah." Her voice sunk into murmurs and the cold shades of death crept over her face again; but rallying her fast failing strength she gasped:

"My boy, quick! Oh, quick, Hannah!"

Hannah lifted the babe from his nest and held him low to meet his mother's last kiss.

"There, now, lay him on my arm, Hannah, close to my left side, and draw my hand over him; I would feel him near me to the very last."

With trembling fingers the poor woman obeyed.

And the dying mother held her child to her heart, and raised her glazing eyes full of the agony of human love to Heaven, and prayed:

"O pitiful Lord, look down in mercy on this poor, poor babe! Take him under thy care!" And with this prayer she sank into insensibility.

Hannah flew to the door and beckoned Herman. He came in, the living image of despair. And both went and stood by the bed. They dared not break the sacred spell by speech. They gazed upon her in silent awe.

Her face was gray and rigid; her eyes were still and stony; her breath and pulse were stopped. Was she gone? No, for suddenly upon that face of death a great light dawned, irradiating it with angelic beauty and glory; and once more with awful solemnity deep bell-like tones tolled forth the notes.

"Out of the depths have I called to Thee And Thou hast heard my voice."

And with these holy words upon her lips the gentle spirit of Nora Worth, ruined maiden but innocent mother, winged its way to heaven.

CHAPTER XIII.

THE FLIGHT OF HERMAN.

Tread softly—bow the head—
In reverent silence bow;
There's one in that poor shed,
One by that humble bed,
Greater than thou!

Oh, change! Stupendous change!
Fled the immortal one!
A moment here, so low,
So agonized, and now—
Beyond the sun!
—*Caroline Bowles.*

For some time Hannah Worth and Herman Brudenell remained standing by the bedside, and gazing in awful silence upon the beautiful clay extended before them, upon which the spirit in parting had left the impress of its last earthly smile!

Then the bitter grief of the bereaved woman burst through all outward restraints, and she threw herself upon the bed and clasped the dead body of her sister to her breast, and broke into a tempest of tears and sobs and lamentations.

"Oh, Nora! my darling! are you really dead and gone from me forever? Shall I never hear the sound of your light step coming in, nor meet the beamings of your soft eyes, nor feel your warm arms around my neck, nor listen to your coaxing voice, pleading for some little indulgence which half the time I refused you?

"How could I have refused you, my darling, anything, hard-hearted that I was! Ah! how little did I think how soon you would be taken from me, and I should never be able to give you anything more! Oh, Nora, come back to me, and I will give you everything I have—yes, my eyes, and my life, and my soul, if they could bring you back and make you happy!

"My beautiful darling, you were the light of my eyes and the pulse of my heart and the joy of my life! You were all that I had in the world! my little sister and my daughter and my baby, all in one! How could you die and leave me all alone in the world, for the love of a man? me who loves you more than all the men on the earth could love!

"Nora, I shall look up from my loom and see your little wheel standing still—and where the spinner? I shall sit down to my solitary meals and see your vacant chair—and where my companion? I shall wake in the dark night and stretch out my arms to your empty place beside me—and where my warm loving sister? In the grave! in the cold, dark, still grave!

"Oh, Heaven! Heaven! how can I bear it?—I, all day in the lonely house! all night in the lonely bed! all my life in the lonely world! the black, freezing, desolate world! and she in her grave! I cannot bear it! Oh, no, I cannot bear it! Angels in heaven, you know that I cannot! Speak to the Lord, and ask him to take me!

"Lord, Lord, please to take me along with my child. We were but two! two orphan sisters! I have grown gray in taking care of her! She cannot do without me, nor I without her! We were but two! Why should one be taken and the other left? It is not fair, Lord! I say it is not fair!" raved the mourner, in that blind and passionate abandonment of grief which is sure at its climax to reach frenzy, and break into open rebellion against Omnipotent Power.

And it is well for us that the Father is more merciful than our tenderest thoughts, for he pardons the rebel and heals his wounds.

The sorrow of the young man, deepened by remorse, was too profound for such outward vent. He leaned against the bedpost, seemingly colder, paler, and more lifeless than the dead body before him.

At length the tempest of Hannah's grief raged itself into temporary rest. She arose, composed the form of her sister, and turned and laid her hand upon the shoulder of Herman, saying calmly:

"It is all over. Go, young gentleman, and wrestle with your sorrow and your remorse, as you may. Such wrestlings will be the only punishment your rashness will receive in this world! Be free of dread from me. She left you her forgiveness as a legacy, and you are sacred from my pursuit. Go, and leave me with my dead."

Herman dropped upon his knees beside the bed of death, took the cold hand of Nora between his own, and bowed his head upon it for a little while in penitential homage, and then arose and silently left the hut.

After he had gone, Hannah remained for a few minutes standing where he had left her, gazing in silent anguish upon the dark eyes of Nora, now glazed in death, and then, with reverential tenderness, she pressed down the white lids, closing them until the light of the resurrection morning should open them again.

While engaged in this holy duty, Hannah was interrupted by the re-entrance of Herman.

He came in tottering, as if under the influence of intoxication; but we all know that excessive sorrow takes away the strength and senses as surely as intoxication does. There is such a state as being drunken with grief when we have drained the bitter cup dry!

"Hannah," he faltered, "there are some things which should be remembered even in this awful hour."

The sorrowing woman, her fingers still softly pressing down her sister's eyelids, looked up in mute inquiry.

"Your necessities and—Nora's child must be provided for. Will you give me some writing materials?" And the speaker dropped, as if totally prostrated, into a chair by the table.

With some difficulty Hannah sought and found an old inkstand, a stumpy pen, and a scrap of paper. It was the best she could do. Stationery was scarce in the poor hut. She laid them on the table before Herman. And with a trembling hand he wrote out a check upon the local bank and put it in her hand, saying:

"This sum will provide for the boy, and set you and Gray up in some little business. You had better marry and go to the West, taking the child with you. Be a mother to the orphan, Hannah, for he will never know another parent. And now shake hands and say good-by, for we shall never meet again in this world."

Too thoroughly bewildered with grief to comprehend the purport of his words and acts, Hannah mechanically received the check and returned the pressure of the hand with which it was given.

And the next instant the miserable young man was gone indeed.

Hannah dropped the paper upon the table; she did not in the least suspect that that little strip of soiled foolscap represented the sum of five thousand dollars, nor is it likely that she would have taken it had she known what it really was. Hannah's intellects were chaotic with her troubles. She returned to the bedside and was once more absorbed in her sorrowful task, when she was again interrupted.

This time it was by old Dinah, who, having no hand at liberty, shoved the door open with her foot, and entered the hut.

If "there is but one step between the sublime and the ridiculous," there is no step at all between the awful and the absurd, which are constantly seen side by side. Though such a figure as old Dinah presented, standing in the middle of the death-chamber, is not often to be found in tragic scenes. Her shoulders were bent beneath the burden of an enormous bundle of bed clothing, and her arms were dragged down by the weight of two large baskets of provisions. She was much too absorbed in her own ostentatious benevolence to look at once towards the bed and see what had happened there. Probably, if she glanced at the group at all, she supposed that Hannah was only bathing Nora's head; for instead of going forward or tendering any sympathy or assistance, she just let her huge bundle drop from her shoulders and sat her two baskets carefully upon the table, exclaiming triumphantly:

"Dar! dar's somefin to make de poor gal comfo'ble for a mont' or more! Dar, in dat bundle is two thick blankets and four pa'r o' sheets an' pilly cases, all out'n my own precious chist; an' not beholden to ole mis' for any on 'em," she added, as she carefully untied the bundle and laid its contents, nicely folded, upon a chair.

"An' dar!" she continued, beginning to unload the large basket—"dar's a tukky an' two chickuns offen my own precious roost; nor likewise beholden to ole mis for dem nyder. An' dar! dar's sassidges and blood puddin's out'n our own dear pig as me an' ole man Jov'al ris an' kilt ourselves; an' in course no ways beholden to ole mis'," she concluded, arranging these edibles upon the table.

"An' dar!" she recommenced as she set the smaller basket beside the other things, "dar's a whole raft o"serves an' jellies and pickles as may be useful. An' dat's all for dis time! An' now, how is de poor gal, honey? Is she 'sleep?" she asked, approaching the bed.

"Yes; sleeping her last sleep, Dinah," solemnly replied Hannah.

"De Lor' save us! what does you mean by dat, honey? Is she faint?"

"Look at her, Dinah, and see for yourself!"

"Dead! oh, Lor'-a-mercy!" cried the old woman, drawing back appalled at the sight that met her eyes; for to the animal nature of the pure African negro death is very terrible.

For a moment there was silence in the room, and then the voice of Hannah was heard:

"So you see the comforts you robbed yourself of to bring to Nora will not be wanted, Dinah. You must take them back again."

"Debil burn my poor, ole, black fingers if I teches of 'em to bring 'em home again! S'posin' de poor dear gal is gone home? aint you lef wid a mouf of your own to feed, I wonder? Tell me dat?" sobbed the old woman.

"But, Dinah, I feel as if I should never eat again, and certainly I shall not care what I eat. And that is your Christmas turkey, too, your only one, for I know that you poor colored folks never have more."

"Who you call poor? We's rich in grace, I'd have you to know! 'Sides havin' of a heap o' treasure laid up in heaven, I reckons! Keep de truck, chile; for 'deed you aint got no oder 'ternative! 'Taint Dinah as is a-gwine to tote 'em home ag'n. Lor' knows how dey a'mos' broke my back a-fetchin' of 'em over here. 'Taint likely as I'll be such a consarned fool as to tote 'em all de way back ag'in. So say no more 'bout it, Miss Hannah! 'Sides which how can we talk o' sich wid de sight o' she before our eyes! Ah, Miss Nora! Oh, my beauty! Oh, my pet! Is you really gone an' died an' lef' your poor ole Aunt Dinah behind as lubbed you like de apple of her eye! What did you do it for, honey? You know your ole Aunt Dinah wasn't a-goin' to look down on you for nothin' as is happened of," whined the old woman, stooping and weeping over the corpse. Then she accidentally touched the sleeping babe, and started up in dismay, crying:

"What dis? Oh, my good Lor' in heaben, what dis?"

"It is Nora's child, Dinah. Didn't you know she had one?" said Hannah; with a choking voice and a crimson face.

"Neber even s'picioned! I knowed as she'd been led astray, poor thin', an' as how it was a-breakin' of her heart and a-killin' of her! Leastways I heard it up yonder at de house; but I didn't know nuffin' 'bout dis yere!"

"But Uncle Jovial did."

"Dat ole sinner has got eyes like gimlets, dey bores into eberyting!"

"But didn't he tell you?"

"Not a singly breaf! he know bery well it's much as his ole wool's worf to say a word agin dat gal to me. No, he on'y say how Miss Nora wer' bery ill, an' in want ob eberyting in de worl' an' eberyting else besides. An' how here wer' a chance to 'vest our property to 'vantage, by lendin' of it te de Lor', accordin' te de Scriptur's as 'whoever giveth to the poor lendeth to the Lord.' So I hunted up all I could spare and fotch it ober here, little thinkin' what a sight would meet my old eyes! Well, Lord!"

"But, Dinah," said the weeping Hannah, "you must not think ill of Nora! She does not deserve it. And you must not, indeed."

"Chile, it aint for me to judge no poor motherless gal as is already 'peared afore her own Righteous Judge."

"Yes, but you shall judge her! and judge her with righteous judgment, too! You have known her all your life—all hers, I mean. You put the first baby clothes on her that she ever wore! And you will put the last dress that she ever will! And now judge her, Dinah, looking on her pure brow, and remembering her past life, is she a girl likely to have been 'led astray,' as you call it?"

59

"No, 'fore my 'Vine Marster in heaben, aint she? As I 'members ob de time anybody had a-breaved a s'picion ob Miss Nora, I'd jest up'd an' boxed deir years for 'em good—'deed me! But what staggers of me, honey, is *dat!* How de debil we gwine to 'count for *dat?*" questioned old Dinah, pointing in sorrowful suspicion at the child.

For all answer Hannah beckoned to the old woman to watch her, while she untied from Nora's neck a narrow black ribbon, and removed from it a plain gold ring.

"A wedding-ring!" exclaimed Dinah, in perplexity.

"Yes, it was put upon her finger by the man that married her. Then it was taken off and hung around her neck, because for certain reasons she could not wear it openly. But now it shall go with her to the grave in its right place," said Hannah, as she slipped the ring upon the poor dead finger.

"Lor', child, who was it as married of her?"

"I cannot tell you. I am bound to secrecy."

The old negress shook her head slowly and doubtfully.

"I's no misdoubts as she was innocenter dan a lamb, herself, for she do look it as she lay dar wid de heabenly smile frozen on her face; but I do misdoubts dese secrety marriages; I 'siders ob 'em no 'count. Ten to one, honey, de poor forso'k sinner as married her has anoder wife some'ers."

Without knowing it the old woman had hit the exact truth.

Hannah sighed deeply, and wondered silently how it was that neither Dinah nor Jovial had ever once suspected their young master to be the man.

Old Dinah perceived that her conversation distressed Hannah, and so she threw off her bonnet and cloak and set herself to work to help the poor bereaved sister.

There was enough to occupy both women. There was the dead mother to be prepared for burial, and there was the living child to be cared far.

By the time that they had laid Nora out in her only white dress, and had fed the babe and put it to sleep, and cleaned up the cottage, the winter day had drawn to its close and the room was growing dark.

Old Dinah, thinking it was time to light up, took a home-dipped candle from the cupboard, and seeing a piece of soiled paper on the table, actually lighted her candle with a check for five thousand dollars!

And thus it happened that the poor boy who, without any fault of his mother, had come into the world with a stigma on his birth, now, without any neglect of his father, was left in a state of complete destitution as well as of entire orphanage.

On the Tuesday following her death poor Nora Worth was laid in her humble grave under a spreading oak behind the hut.

This spot was selected by Hannah, who wished to keep her sister's last resting-place always in her sight, and who insisted that every foot of God's earth, enclosed or unenclosed—consecrated or unconsecrated—was holy ground.

Jim Morris, Professor of Odd Jobs for the country side, made the coffin, dug the grave, and managed the funeral.

The Rev. William Wynne, the minister who had performed the fatal nuptial ceremony of the fair bride, read the funeral services over her dead body.

No one was present at the burial but Hannah Worth, Reuben Gray, the two old negroes, Dinah and Jovial, the Professor of Odd Jobs, and the officiating clergyman.

<hr />

CHAPTER XIV.

OVER NORA'S GRAVE.

Oh, Mother Earth! upon thy lap,
Thy weary ones receiving,
And o'er them, silent as a dream,
Thy grassy mantle weaving,
Fold softly, in thy long embrace,
That heart so worn and broken,

And cool its pulse of fire beneath
Thy shadows old and oaken.
Shut out from her the bitter word,
And serpent hiss of scorning:
Nor let the storms of yesterday
Disturb her quiet morning.
—*Whittier.*

When the funeral ceremonies were over and the mourners were coming away from the grave, Mr. Wynne turned to them and said:

"Friends, I wish to have some conversation with Hannah Worth, if you will excuse me."

And the humble group, with the exception of Reuben Gray, took leave of Hannah and dispersed to their several homes. Reuben waited outside for the end of the parson's interview with his betrothed.

"This is a great trial to you, my poor girl; may the Lord support you under it!" said Mr. Wynne, as they entered the hut and sat down.

Hannah sobbed.

"I suppose it was the discovery of Mr. Brudenell's first marriage that killed her?"

"Yes, sir," sobbed Hannah.

"Ah! I often read and speak of the depravity of human nature; but I could not have believed Herman Brudenell capable of so black a crime," said Mr. Wynne, with a shudder.

"Sir," replied Hannah, resolved to do justice in spite of her bleeding heart, "he isn't so guilty as you judge him to be. When he married Norah he believed that his wife had been killed in a great railway crash, for so it was reported in all the newspaper accounts of the accident; and he never saw it contradicted."

"His worst fault then appears to have been that of reckless haste in consummating his second marriage," said Mr. Wynne.

"Yes; and even for that he had some excuse. His first wife was an artful widow, who entrapped him into a union and afterwards betrayed his confidence and her own honor. When he heard she was dead, you see, no doubt he was shocked; but he could not mourn for her as he could for a true, good woman."

"Humph! I hope, then, for the sake of human nature that he is not so bad as I thought him. But now, Hannah, what do you intend to do?"

"About what?" inquired the poor woman sadly.

"About clearing the memory of your sister and the birth of her son from unmerited shame," replied Mr. Wynne gravely.

"Nothing," she answered sadly.

"Nothing?" repeated the minister, in surprise.

"Nothing," she reiterated.

"What! will you leave the stigma of undeserved reproach upon your sister in her grave and upon her child all his life, when a single revelation from you, supported by my testimony, will clear them both?" asked the minister, in almost indignant astonishment.

"Not willingly, the Lord above knows. Oh, I would die to clear Nora from blame!" cried Hannah, bursting into a flood of tears.

"Well, then, do it, my poor woman! do it! You can do it," said the clergyman, drawing his chair to her side and laying his hand kindly on her shoulder. "Hannah, my girl, you have a duty to the dead and to the living to perform. Do not be afraid to attempt it! Do not be afraid to offend that wealthy and powerful family! I will sustain you, for it is my duty as a Christian minister to do so, even though they—the Brudenells—should afterwards turn all their great influence in the parish against me. Yes, I will sustain you, Hannah! What do I say? I? A mightier arm than that of any mortal shall hold you up!"

"Oh, it is of no use! the case is quite past remedying," wept Hannah.

"But it is not, I assure you! When I first heard the astounding news of Brudenell's first marriage with the Countess of Hurstmonceaux, and his wife's sudden arrival at the Hall, and recollected at the same time his second marriage with Nora Worth, which I myself had solemnized, my thoughts flew to his poor young victim, and I pondered what could be done for her, and I searched the laws of the land bearing upon the subject of marriage. And I found that by these same laws—when a man in the lifetime of his wife marries another woman, the said woman being in ignorance of the existence of the said wife, shall be held guiltless by the law, and her

61

child or children, if she have any by the said marriage, shall be the legitimate offspring of the mother, legally entitled to bear her name and inherit her estates. That fits precisely Nora's case. Her son is legitimate. If she had in her own right an estate worth a billion, that child would be her heir-at-law. She had nothing but her good name! Her son has a right to inherit that—unspotted, Hannah! mind, unspotted! Your proper way will be to proceed against Herman Brudenell for bigamy, call me for a witness, establish the fact of Nora's marriage, rescue her memory and her child's birth from the slightest shadow of reproach, and let the consequences fall where they should fall, upon the head of the man! They will not be more serious than he deserves. If he can prove what he asserts—that he himself was in equal ignorance with Nora of the existence of his first wife, he will be honorably acquitted in the court, though of course severely blamed by the community. Come, Hannah, shall we go to Baymouth to-morrow about this business?"

Hannah was sobbing as if her heart would break.

"How glad I would be to clear Nora and her child from shame, no one but the Searcher of Hearts can know! But I dare not! I am bound by a vow! a solemn vow made to the dying! Poor girl! with her last breath she besought me not to expose Mr. Brudenell, and not to breathe one word of his marriage with her to any living soul!" she cried.

"And you were mad enough to promise!"

"I would rather have bitten my tongue off than have used it in such a fatal way! But she was dying fast, and praying to me with her uplifted eyes and clasped hands and failing breath to spare Herman Brudenell. I had no power to refuse her—my heart was broken. So I bound my soul by a vow to be silent. And I must keep my sacred promise made to the dying; I must keep it though, till the Judgment Day that shall set all things right, Nora Worth, if thought of it all, must be considered a fallen girl and her son the child of sin!" cried Hannah, breaking into a passion of tears and sobs.

"The devotion of woman passes the comprehension of man," said the minister reflectively. "But in sacrificing herself thus, had she no thought of the effect upon the future of her child?"

"She said he was a boy; his mother would soon be forgotten; he would be my nephew, and I was respected," sobbed Hannah.

"In a word, she was a special pleader in the interest of the man whose reckless haste had destroyed her!"

"Yes; that was it! that was it! Oh, my Nora! oh, my young sister! it was hard to see you die! hard to see you covered up in the coffin! but it is harder still to know that people will speak ill of you in your grave, and I cannot convince them that they are wrong!" said Hannah, wringing her hands in a frenzy of despair.

For trouble like this the minister seemed to have no word of comfort. He waited in silence until she had grown a little calmer, and then he said:

"They say that the fellow has fled. At least he has not been seen at the Hall since the arrival of his wife. Have you seen anything of him?"

"He rushed in here like a madman the day she died, received her last prayer for his welfare, and threw himself out of the house again, Heaven only knows where!"

"Did he make no provision for this child?"

"I do not know; he said something about it, and he wrote something on a paper; but indeed I do not think he knew what he was about. He was as nearly stark mad as ever you saw a man; and, anyway, he went, off without leaving anything but that bit of paper; and it is but right for me to say, sir, that I would not have taken anything from him on behalf of the child. If the poor boy cannot have his father's family name he shall not have anything else from him with my consent! Those are my principles, Mr. Wynne! I can work for Nora's orphan boy just as I worked for my mother's orphan girl, which was Nora, herself, sir."

"Perhaps you are right, Hannah. But where is that paper. I should much like to see it," said the minister.

"The paper he wrote and left, sir?"

"Yes; show it to me."

"Lord bless your soul, sir, it wasn't of no account; it was the least little scrap, with about three lines wrote on it; I didn't take any care of it. Heavens knows that I had other things to think of than that. But I will try to find it if you wish to look at it," said Hannah, rising.

Her search of course was vain, and after turning up everything in the house to no purpose she came back to the parson, and said:

"I dare say it is swept away or burnt up; but, anyway, it isn't worth troubling one's self about it."

"I think differently, Hannah; and I would advise you to search, and make inquiry, and try your best to find it. And if you do so, just put it away in a very safe place until you can show it to me. And now good-by, my girl; trust in the Lord, and keep up your heart," said the minister, taking his hat and stick to depart.

When Mr. Wynne had gone Reuben Gray, who had been walking about behind the cottage, came in and said:

"Hannah, my dear, I have got something very particular to say to you; but I feel as this is no time to say it exactly, so I only want to ask you when I may come and have a talk with you, Hannah."

"Any time, Reuben; next Sunday, if you like."

"Very well, my dear; next Sunday it shall be! God bless you, Hannah; and God bless the poor boy, too. I mean to adopt that child, Hannah, and cowhide his father within an inch of his life, if ever I find him out!"

"Talk of all this on Sunday when you come, Reuben; not now, oh, not now!"

"Sartinly not now, my dear; I see the impropriety of it. Good-by, my dear. Now, shan't I send Nancy or Peggy over to stay with you?"

"Upon no account, Reuben."

"Just as you say, then. Good-by, my poor dear."

And after another dozen affectionate adieus Reuben reluctantly dragged himself from the hut.

CHAPTER XV.

NORA'S SON.

Look on this babe; and let thy pride take heed,
Thy pride of manhood, intellect or fame,
That thou despise him not; for he indeed,
And such as he in spirit and heart the same,
Are God's own children in that kingdom bright,
Where purity is praise, and where before
The Father's throne, triumphant evermore,
The ministering angels, sons of light,
Stand unreproved because they offer there,
Mixed with the Mediator's hallowing prayer,
The innocence of babes in Christ like this.
—*M.F. Tupper*.

Hannah was left alone with her sorrows and her mortifications.

Never until now had she so intensely realized her bereavement and her solitude. Nora was buried; and the few humble friends who had sympathized with her were gone; and so she was alone with her great troubles. She threw herself into a chair, and for the third or fourth time that day broke into a storm of grief. And the afternoon had faded nearly into night before she regained composure. Even then she sat like one palsied by despair, until a cry of distress aroused her. It was the wail of Nora's infant. She arose and took the child and laid it on her lap to feed it. Even Hannah looked at it with a pity that was almost allied to contempt.

It was in fact the thinnest, palest, puniest little object that had ever come into this world prematurely, uncalled for, and unwelcome. It did not look at all likely to live. And as Hannah fed the ravenous little skeleton she could not help mentally calculating the number of its hours on earth, and wishing that she had thought to request Mr. Wynne, while he was in the house, to baptize the wretched baby, so little likely to live for another opportunity. Nor could Hannah desire that it should live. It had brought sorrow, death, and disgrace into the hut, and it had nothing but poverty, want, and shame for its portion in this world; and so the sooner it followed its mother the better, thought Hannah—short-sighted mortal.

Had Hannah been a discerner of spirits to recognize the soul in that miserable little baby-body!

Or had she been a seeress to foresee the future of that child of sorrow!

Reader, this boy is our hero; a real hero, too, who actually lived and suffered and toiled and triumphed in this land!

"Out of the depths" he came indeed! Out of the depths of poverty, sorrow, and degradation he rose, by God's blessing on his aspirations, to the very zenith of fame, honor, and glory!

He made his name, the only name he was legally entitled to bear—his poor wronged mother's maiden-name—illustrious in the annals of our nation!

But this is to anticipate.

No vision of future glory, however, arose before the poor weaver's imagination as she sat in that old hut holding the wee boy on her lap, and for his sake as well as for her own begrudging him every hour of the few days she supposed he had to live upon this earth. Yes! Hannah would have felt relieved and satisfied if that child had been by his mother's side in the coffin rather than been left on her lap.

Only think of that, my readers; think of the utter, utter destitution of a poor little sickly, helpless infant whose only relative would have been glad to see him dead! Our Ishmael had neither father, mother, name, nor place in the world. He had no legal right to be in it at all; no legal right to the air he breathed, or to the sunshine that warmed him into life; no right to love, or pity, or care; he had nothing—nothing but the eye of the Almighty Father regarding him. But Hannah Worth was a conscientious woman, and even while wishing the poor boy's death she did everything in her power to keep him alive, hoping all would be in vain.

Hannah, as you know, was very, very poor. And with this child upon her hands she expected to be much poorer. She was a weaver of domestic carpets and counterpanes and of those coarse cotton and woolen cloths of which the common clothing of the plantation negroes are made, and the most of her work came from Brudenell Hall. She used to have to go and fetch the yarn, and then carry home the web. She had a piece of cloth now ready to take home to Mrs. Brudenell's housekeeper; but she abhorred the very idea of carrying it there, or of asking for more work.

Nora had been ignominiously turned from the house, cruelly driven out into the midnight storm; that had partly caused her death. And should she, her sister, degrade her womanhood by going again to that house to solicit work, or even to carry back what she had finished, to meet, perhaps, the same insults that had maddened Nora?

No, never; she would starve and see the child starve first. The web of cloth should stay there until Jim Morris should come along, when she would get him to take it to Brudenell Hall. And she would seek work from other planters' wives.

She had four dollars and a half in the house—the money, you know, that old Mrs. Jones, with all her hardness, had yet refused to take from the poor woman. And then Mrs. Brudenell owed her five and a half for the weaving of this web of cloth. In all she had ten dollars, eight of which she owed to the Professor of Odd Jobs for his services at Nora's funeral. The remaining two she hoped would supply her simple wants until she found work. And in the meantime she need not be idle; she would employ her time in cutting up some of poor Nora's clothes to make an outfit for the baby—for if the little object lived but a week it must be clothed—now it was only wrapped up in a piece of flannel.

While Hannah meditated upon these things the baby went to sleep on her lap, and she took it up and laid it in Nora's vacated place in her bed.

And soon after Hannah took her solitary cup of tea, and shut up the hut and retired to bed. She had not had a good night's rest since that fatal night of Nora's flight through the snow storm to Brudenell Hall, and her subsequent illness and death. Now, therefore, Hannah slept the sleep of utter mental and physical prostration.

The babe did not disturb her repose. Indeed, it was a very patient little sufferer, if such a term may be applied to so young a child. But it was strange that an infant so pale, thin, and sickly, deprived of its mother's nursing care besides, should have made so little plaint and given so little trouble. Perhaps in the lack of human pity he had the love of heavenly spirits, who watched over him, soothed his pains, and stilled his cries. We cannot tell how that may have been, but it is certain that Ishmael was an angel from his very birth.

The next day, as Hannah was standing at the table, busy in cutting out small garments, and the baby-boy was lying upon the bed equally busy in sucking his thumb, the door was pushed open and the Professor of Odd Jobs stood in the doorway, with a hand upon either post, and sadness on his usually good-humored and festive countenance.

"Ah, Jim, is that you? Come in, your money is all ready for you," said Hannah on perceiving him.

It is not the poor who "grind the faces of the poor." Jim Morris would have scorned to have taken a dollar from Hannah Worth at this trying crisis of her life.

"Now, Miss Hannah," he answered, as he came in at her bidding, "please don't you say one word to me 'bout de filthy lucre, 'less you means to 'sult me an' hurt my feelin's. I don't 'quire of no money for doin' of a man's duty by a lone 'oman! Think Jim Morris is a man to 'pose upon a lone 'oman? Hopes not, indeed! No, Miss Hannah! I aint a wolf, nor likewise a bear! Our Heabenly Maker, he gib us our lives an' de earth an' all as is on it, for ourselves free! And what have we to render him in turn? Nothing! And what does he 'quire ob us? On'y lub him and lub each oder, like human beings and 'mortal souls made in his own image to live forever! and not to screw and 'press each oder, and devour an' prey on each oder like de wild beastesses dat perish! And I considers, Miss Hannah—"

64

And here, in fact, the professor, having secured a patient hearer, launched into an oration that, were I to report it word for word, would take up more room than we can spare him. He brought his discourse round in a circle, and ended where he had begun.

"And so, Miss Hannah, say no more to me 'bout de money, 'less you want to woun' my feelin's."

"Well, I will not, Morris; but I feel so grateful to you that I would like to repay you in something better than mere words," said Hannah.

"And so you shall, honey, so you shall, soon as eber I has de need and you has de power! But now don't you go and fall into de pop'lar error of misparagin' o' words. Words! why words is de most powerfullist engine of good or evil in dis worl'! Words is to idees what bodies is to souls! Wid words you may save a human from dispair, or you may drive him to perdition! Wid words you may confer happiness or misery! Wid words a great captain may rally his discomforted troops, an' lead 'em on to wictory! wid words a great congressman may change the laws of de land! Wid words a great lawyer may 'suade a jury to hang an innocent man, or to let a murderer go free. It's bery fashionable to misparage words, callin' of 'em 'mere words.' Mere words! mere fire! mere life! mere death! mere heaben! mere hell! as soon as mere words! What are all the grand books in de worl' filled with? words! What is the one great Book called? What is the Bible called? De Word!" said the professor, spreading out his arms in triumph at this peroration.

Hannah gazed in very sincere admiration upon this orator, and when he had finished, said:

"Oh, Morris, what a pity you had not been a white man, and been brought up at a learned profession!"

"Now aint it, though, Miss Hannah?" said Morris.

"You would have made such a splendid lawyer or parson!" continued the simple woman, in all sincerity.

"Now wouldn't I, though?" complained the professor. "Now aint it a shame I'm nyther one nor t'other? I have so many bright idees all of my own! I might have lighted de 'ciety an' made my fortin at de same time! Well!" he continued, with a sigh of resignation, "if I can't make my own fortin I can still lighten de 'ciety if only dey'd let me; an' I'm willin' to du it for nothin'! But people won't 'sent to be lighted by me; soon as ever I begins to preach or to lecture in season, an' out'n season, de white folks, dey shut up my mouf, short! It's trufe I'm a-tellin' of you, Miss Hannah! Dey aint no ways, like you. Dey can't 'preciate ge'nus. Now I mus' say as you can, in black or white! An' when I's so happy as to meet long of a lady like you who can 'preciate me, I'm willin' to do anything in the wide worl' for her! I'd make coffins an' dig graves for her an' her friends from one year's end to de t'other free, an' glad of de chance to do it!" concluded the professor, with enthusiastic good-will.

"I thank you very kindly, Jim Morris; but of course I would not like to give you so much trouble," replied Hannah, in perfect innocence of sarcasm.

"La. It wouldn't be no trouble, Miss Hannah! But then, ma'am, I didn't come over here to pass compliments, nor no sich! I come with a message from old madam up yonder at Brudenell Hall."

"Ah," said Hannah, in much surprise and more disgust, "what may have been her message to me?"

"Well, Miss Hannah, it may have been the words of comfort, such as would become a Christian lady to send to a sorrowing fellow-creatur'; only it wasn't," sighed Jim Morris.

"I want no such hypocritical words from her!" said Hannah indignantly.

"Well, honey, she didn't send none!"

"What did she send?"

"Well, chile, de madam, she 'quested of me to come over here an' hand you dis five dollar an' a half, which she says she owes it to you. An' also to ax you to send by the bearer, which is me, a certain piece of cloth, which she says how you've done wove for her. An' likewise to tell you as you needn't come to Brudenell Hall for more work, which there is no more to give you. Dere, Miss Hannah, dere's de message jes' as de madam give it to me, which I hopes you'll 'sider as I fotch it in de way of my perfession, an' not take no 'fense at me who never meant any towards you," said the professor deprecatingly.

"Of course not, Morris. So far from being angry with you, I am very thankful to you for coming. You have relieved me from a quandary. I didn't know how to return the work or to get the pay. For after what has happened, Morris, the cloth might have stayed here and the money there, forever, before I would have gone near Brudenell Hall!"

Morris slapped his knee with satisfaction, saying:

"Just what I thought, Miss Hannah! which made me the more willing to bring de message. So now if you'll jest take de money an' give me de cloth, I'll be off. I has got some clocks and umberell's to mend to-night. And dat minds me! if you'll give me dat broken coffee-mill o' yourn I'll fix it at de same time," said the professor.

Hannah complied with all his requests, and he took his departure.

He had scarcely got out of sight when Hannah had another visitor, Reuben Gray, who entered the hut with looks of deprecation and words of apology.

"Hannah, woman, I couldn't wait till Sunday! I couldn't rest! Knowing of your situation, I felt as if I must come to you and say what I had on my mind! Do you forgive me?"

"For what?" asked Hannah in surprise.

"For coming afore Sunday."

"Sit down, Reuben, and don't be silly. As well have it over now as any other time."

"Very well, then, Hannah," said the man, drawing a chair to the table at which she sat working, and seating himself.

"Now, then, what have you to say, Reuben?"

"Well, Hannah, my dear, you see I didn't want to make a disturbance while the body of that poor girl lay unburied in the house; but now I ask you right up and down who is the wretch as wronged Nora?" demanded the man with a look of sternness Hannah had never seen on his patient face before.

"Why do you wish to know, Reuben?" she inquired in a low voice.

"To kill him."

"Reuben Gray!"

"Well, what's the matter, girl?"

"Would you do murder?"

"Sartainly not, Hannah; but I will kill the villain as wronged Nora wherever I find him, as I would a mad dog."

"It would be the same thing! It would be murder!"

"No, it wouldn't, Hannah. It would be honest killing. For when a cussed villain hunts down and destroys an innocent girl, he ought to be counted an outlaw that any man may slay who finds him. And if so be he don't get his death from the first comer, he ought to be sure of getting it from the girl's nearest male relation or next friend. And if every such scoundrel knew he was sure to die for his crime, and the law would hold his slayer guiltless, there would be a deal less sin and misery in this world. As for me, Hannah, I feel it to be my solemn duty to Nora, to womankind, and to the world, to seek out the wretch as wronged her and kill him where I find him, just as I would a rattlesnake as had bit my child."

"They would hang you for it, Reuben!" shuddered Hannah.

"Then they'd do very wrong! But they'd not hang me, Hannah! Thank Heaven, in these here parts we all vally our women's innocence a deal higher than we do our lives, or even our honor. And if a man is right to kill another in defense of his own life, he is doubly right to do so in defense of woman's honor. And judges and juries know it, too, and feel it, as has been often proved. But anyways, whether or no," said Reuben Gray, with the dogged persistence for which men of his class are often noted, "I want to find that man to give him his dues."

"And be hung for it," said Hannah curtly.

"No, my dear, I don't want to be hung for the fellow. Indeed, to tell the truth, I shouldn't like it at all; I know I shouldn't beforehand; but at the same time I mustn't shrink from doing of my duty first, and suffering for it afterwards, if necessary! So now for the rascal's name, Hannah!"

"Reuben Gray, I couldn't tell you if I would, and I wouldn't tell you if I could! What! do you think that I, a Christian woman, am going to send you in your blind, brutal vengeance to commit the greatest crime you possibly could commit?"

"Crime, Hannah! why, it is a holy duty!"

"Duty, Reuben! Do you live in the middle of the nineteenth century, in a Christian land, and have you been going to church all your life, and hearing the gospel of peace preached to this end?"

"Yes! For the Lord himself is a God of vengeance. He destroyed Sodom and Gomorrah by fire, and once He destroyed the whole world by water!"

"'The devil can quote Scripture for his purpose,' Reuben! and I think he is prompting you now! What! do you, a mortal, take upon yourself the divine right of punishing sin by death? Reuben, when from the dust of the earth you can make a man, and breathe into his nostrils the breath of life, then perhaps you may talk of punishing sin with death. You cannot even make the smallest gnat or worm live! How then could you dare to stop the sacred breath of life in a man!" said Hannah.

"I don't consider the life of a wretch who has destroyed an innocent girl sacred by any means," persisted Reuben.

"The more sinful the man, the more sacred his life!"

"Well, I'm blowed to thunder, Hannah, if that aint the rummest thing as ever I heard said! the more sinful a man, the more sacred his life! What will you tell me next!"

"Why, this: that if it is a great crime to kill a good man, it is the greatest of all crimes to kill a bad one!"

To this startling theory Reuben could not even attempt a reply. He could only stare at her in blank astonishment. His mental caliber could not be compared with Hannah's in capacity.

"Have patience, dear Reuben, and I will make it all clear to you! The more sinful the man, the more sacred his life should be considered, because in that lies the only chance of his repentance, redemption, and salvation. And is a greater crime to kill a bad man than to kill a good one, because if you kill a good man, you kill his body only; but if you kill a bad man, you kill both his body and his soul! Can't you understand that now, dear Reuben?"

Reuben rubbed his forehead, and answered sullenly, like one about to be convinced against his will:

"Oh, I know what you mean, well enough, for that matter."

"Then you must know, Reuben, why it is that the wicked are suffered to live so long on this earth! People often wonder at the mysterious ways of Providence, when they see a good man prematurely cut off and a wicked man left alive! Why, it isn't mysterious at all to me! The good man was ready to go, and the Lord took him; the bad man was left to his chance of repentance. Reuben, the Lord, who is the most of all offended by sin, spares the sinner a long time to afford him opportunity for repentance! If he wanted to punish the sinner with death in this world, he could strike the sinner dead! But he doesn't do it, and shall we dare to? No! we must bow in humble submission to his awful words—' Vengeance is mine!'"

"Hannah, you may be right; I dare say you are; yes, I'll speak plain—I know you are! but it's hard to put up with such! I feel baffled and disappointed, and ready to cry! A man feels ashamed to set down quiet under such mortification!"

"Then I'll give you a cure for that! It is the remembrance of the Divine Man and the dignified patience with which he bore the insults of the rabble crowd upon his day of trial! You know what those insults were, and how he bore them! Bow down before his majestic meekness, and pay him the homage of obedience to his command of returning good for evil!"

"You're right, Hannah!" said Gray, with a great struggle, in which he conquered his own spirit. "You're altogether right, my girl! So you needn't tell me the name of the wrong-doer! And, indeed, you'd better not; for the temptation to punish him might be too great for my strength, as soon as I am out of your sight and in his!"

"Why, Reuben, my lad, I could not tell you if I were inclined to do so. I am sworn to secrecy!"

"Sworn to secrecy! that's queer too! Who swore you?"

"Poor Nora, who died forgiving all her enemies and at peace with all the world!"

"With him too?"

"With him most of all! And now, Reuben, I want you to listen to me. I met your ideas of vengeance and argued them upon your own ground, for the sake of convincing you that vengeance is wrong even under the greatest possible provocation, such as you believed that we had all had. But, Reuben, you are much mistaken! We have had no provocation!" said Hannah gravely.

"What, no provocation! not in the wrong done to Nora!"

"There has been no intentional wrong done to Nora!"

"What! no wrong in all that villainy?"

"There has been no villainy, Reuben!"

"Then if that wasn't villainy, there's none in the world; and never was any in the world, that's all I have got to say!"

"Reuben, Nora was married to the father of her child. He loved her dearly, and meant her well. You must believe this, for it is as true as Heaven!" said Hannah solemnly.

Reuben pricked up his ears; perhaps he was not sorry to be entirely relieved from the temptation of killing and the danger of hanging.

And Hannah gave him as satisfactory an explanation of Nora's case as she could give, without breaking her promise and betraying Herman Brudenell as the partner of Nora's misfortunes.

At the close of her narrative Reuben Gray took her hand, and holding it, said gravely:

"Well, my dear girl, I suppose the affair must rest where it is for the present. But this makes one thing incumbent upon us." And having said this, Reuben hesitated so long that Hannah took up the word and asked:

"This makes what incumbent upon us, lad?"

"To get married right away!" blurted out the man.

"Pray, have you come into a fortune, Reuben?" inquired Hannah coolly.

"No, child, but——"

"Neither have I," interrupted Hannah.

"I was going to say," continued the man, "that I have my hands to work with——"

"For your large family of sisters and brothers——"

"And for you and that poor orphan boy as well! And I'm willing to do it for you all! And we really must be married right away, Hannah! I must have a lawful right to protect you against the slights as you'll be sure to receive after what's happened, if you don't have a husband to take care of you."

He paused and waited for her reply; but as she did not speak, he began again:

"Come, Hannah, my dear, what do you say to our being married o' Sunday?"

She did not answer, and he continued:

"I think as we better had get tied together arter morning service! And then, you know, I'll take you and the bit of a baby home long o' me, Hannah. And I'll be a loving husband to you, my girl; and I'll be a father to the little lad with as good a will as ever I was to my own orphan brothers and sisters. And I'll break every bone in the skin of any man that looks askance at him, too! Don't you fear for yourself or the child. The country side knows me for a peaceable-disposed man; but it had rather not provoke me for all that, because it knows when I have a just cause of quarrel, I don't leave my work half done! Come, Hannah, what do you say, my dear? Shall it be o' Sunday? You won't answer me? What, crying, my girl, crying! what's that for?"

The tears were streaming from Hannah's eyes. She took up her apron and buried her face in its folds.

"Now what's all that about?" continued Reuben, in distress; then suddenly brightening up, he said: "Oh, I know now! You're thinking of Nancy and Peggy! Don't be afeard, Hannah! They won't do, nor say, nor even so much as look anything to hurt your feelings! and they had better not, if they know which side their bread is buttered! I am the master of my own house, I reckon, poor as it is! And my wife will be the mistress; and my sisters must keep their proper places! Come, Hannah! come, my darling, what do you say to me?"' he whispered, putting his arm over her shoulders, while he tried to draw the apron from her face.

She dropped her apron, lifted her face, looked at him through her falling tears, and answered:

"This is what I have to say to you, dear, dearest, best loved Reuben! I feel your goodness in the very depths of my heart; I thank you with all my soul; I will love you—you only—in silence and in solitude all my life; I will pray for you daily and nightly; but——" She stopped and sobbed.

"But——" said Reuben breathlessly.

"I will never carry myself and my dishonor under your honest roof."

Reuben caught his suspended breath with a sharp gasp and gazed in blank dismay upon the sobbing woman for a few minutes, and then he said:

"Hannah—oh, my Lord! Hannah, you never mean to say that you won't marry me?"

"I mean just that, Reuben."

"Oh, Hannah, what have I done to offend you? I never meant to do it! I don't even know how I've done it! I'm such a blundering animal! But tell me what it is, and I will beg your pardon!"

"It is nothing, you good, true heart! nothing! But you have two sisters——"

"There, I knew it! It's Nancy and Peggy! They've been doing something to hurt your feelings! Well, Hannah, they shall come here and ask your forgiveness, or else they shall leave my home and go to earn their living in somebody's kitchen! I've been a father to them gals; but I won't suffer them to insult my own dear Hannah!" burst forth Reuben.

"Dear Reuben, you are totally mistaken! Your sisters no more than yourself have ever given me the least cause of offense. They could not, dear Reuben! They must be good girls, being your sisters."

"Well, if neither I nor my sisters have hurt your feelings, Hannah, what in the name of sense did you mean by saying—I hate even to repeat the words—that you won't marry me?"

"Reuben, reproach has fallen upon my name—undeserved, indeed, but not the less severe. You have young, unmarried sisters, with nothing but their good names to take them through the world. For their sakes, dear, you must not marry me and my reproach!"

"Is that all you mean, Hannah?"

"All."

"Then I will marry you!"

"Reuben, you must give me up."

"I won't, I say! So there, now."

"Dear Reuben, I value your affection more than I do anything in this world except duty; but I cannot permit you to sacrifice yourself to me," said Hannah, struggling hard to repress the sobs that were again rising in her bosom.

"Hannah, I begin to think you want to drive me crazy or break my heart! What sacrifice would it be for me to marry you and adopt that poor child? The only sacrifice I can think of would be to give you up! But I won't do it! no! I won't for nyther man nor mortal! You promised to marry me, Hannah, and I won't free your promise! but I will keep you to it, and marry you, if I die for it!" grimly persisted Reuben Gray.

And before she could reply they were interrupted by a knock at the door.

"Come in!" said Hannah, expecting to see Mrs. Jones or some other humble neighbor.

The door was pushed gently open, and a woman of exceeding beauty stood upon the threshold.

Her slender but elegant form was clothed in the deepest mourning; her pale, delicate face was shaded by the blackest ringlets; her large, dark eyes were fixed with the saddest interest upon the face of Hannah Worth.

Hannah arose in great surprise to meet her.

"You are Miss Worth, I suppose?" said the young stranger.

"Yes, miss; what is your will with me?"

"I am the Countess of Hurstmonceux. Will you let me rest here a little while?" she asked, with a sweet smile.

Hannah gazed at the speaker in the utmost astonishment, forgetting to answer her question, or offer a seat, or even to shut the door, through which the wind was blowing fiercely.

What! was this beautiful pale young creature the Countess of Hurstmonceux, the rival of Nora, the wife of Herman Brudenell, the "bad, artful woman" who had entrapped the young Oxonian into a discreditable marriage? Impossible!

While Hannah stood thus dumbfounded before the visitor, Reuben came forward with rude courtesy, closed the door, placed a chair before the fire, and invited the lady to be seated.

The countess, with a gentle bow of thanks, passed on, sank into a chair, and let her sable furs slip from her shoulders in a drift around her feet.

CHAPTER XVI.

THE FORSAKEN WIFE.

He prayeth best who loveth most
All things both great and small,
For the good God who loveth us,
He made and loveth all.
—*Coleridge*.

To account for the strange visit of the countess to Hannah Worth we must change the scene to Brudenell Hall.

From the time of her sudden arrival at her husband's house, every hour had been fraught with suffering to Berenice.

In the first instance, where she had expected to give a joyful surprise, she had only given a painful shock; where she had looked for a cordial welcome, she had received a cold repulse; finally, where she had hoped her presence would confer happiness, it had brought misery!

On the very evening of her arrival her husband, after meeting her with reproaches, had fled from the house, leaving no clew to his destination, and giving no reason for his strange proceeding.

Berenice did not understand this. She cast her memory back through all the days of her short married life spent with Herman Brudenell, and she sought diligently for anything in her conduct that might have given him offense. She could find nothing. Neither in all their intercourse had he ever accused her of any wrong-doing. On the contrary, he had been profuse in words of admiration, protestations of love and fidelity. Now what had caused this fatal change in his feelings and conduct towards her? Berenice could not tell. Her mind was as thoroughly perplexed as her heart was deeply wounded. At first she did not know that he was gone forever. She thought that he would return in an hour or two and openly accuse her of some fault, or that he would in some manner betray the cause of offense which he must suppose she had given him. And then, feeling sure of her innocence, she knew she could exonerate herself from every shadow of blame—except from that of loving him too well, if he should consider that a fault.

Therefore she waited patiently for his return; but when the night passed and he had not come, she grew more and more uneasy, and when the next day had passed without his making his appearance her uneasiness rose to intolerable anxiety.

The visit of poor Nora at night had aroused at once her suspicions, her jealousy, and her compassion. She half believed that in this girl she saw her rival in her husband's affections, the cause of her own repudiation and—what was more bitter still to the childless Hebrew wife—the mother of his children! This had been very terrible! But to the Jewish woman the child of her husband, even if it is at the same time the child of her rival, is as sacred as her own. Berenice was loyal, conscientious, and compassionate. In the anguish of her own deeply wounded and bleeding heart she had pitied and pleaded for poor Nora—had even asserted her own authority as mistress of the house, for the sake of protecting Nora: her husband's other wife, as in the merciful construction of her gentle spirit she had termed the unhappy girl! But then, my readers, you must remember that Berenice was a Jewess. This poor unloved Leah would have sheltered the beloved Rachel. We all know how her generous intentions were carried out. A second and a third day passed, and still there came no news of Herman.

Berenice, prostrated with the heart-wasting sickness of hope deferred, kept her own room. Mrs. Brudenell was indignant at her son, not for his neglect of his lovely young wife, but for his indifference to a wealthy countess! She deferred her journey to Washington in consideration of her noble daughter-in-law, and in the hope of her son's speedy reappearance and reconciliation with his wife, when, she anticipated, they would all go to Washington together, where the Countess of Hurstmonceux would certainly be the lioness and the Misses Brudenell the belles of the season.

On the evening of the fourth day, while Berenice lay exhausted upon the sofa of her bedroom, her maid entered the chamber saying:

"Please, my lady, you remember the young woman that was here on Friday evening?"

"Yes!" Berenice was up on her elbow in an instant, looking eagerly into the girl's face.

"Your ladyship ordered me to make inquiries about her, but I could get no news except from the old man who took her home out of the snowstorm and who came back and said she was ill."

"I know! I know! You told me that before. But you have heard something else. What is it?"

"My lady, the old woman Dinah, who went to nurse her, never came back till to-day; that is the reason I couldn't hear any more news until to-night."

"Well, well, well? Your news! Out with it, girl!"

"My lady, she is dead and buried!"

"Who?"

"The young woman, my lady. She died on Saturday. She was buried to-day."

Berenice sank back on the sofa and covered her face with her hands. So! her dangerous rival was gone; the poor unhappy girl was dead! Berenice was jealous, but pitiful. And she experienced in the same moment a sense of infinite relief and a feeling of the deepest compassion.

Neither mistress nor maid spoke for several minutes. The latter was the first to break silence.

"My lady!"

"Well, Phœbe!"

"There was something else I had to tell you."

"What was it?"

"The young woman left a child, my lady."

"A child!" Again Berenice was up on her elbow, her eyes fixed upon the speaker and blazing with eager interest.

"It is a boy, my lady; but they don't think it will live!"

"A boy! He shall live! He is mine—my son! I will have him. Since his mother is dead, it is I who have the best right to him!" exclaimed the countess vehemently, rising to her feet.

The maid recoiled—she thought her mistress had suddenly gone mad.

"Phœbe," said the countess eagerly, "what is the hour?"

"Nearly eleven, my lady."

"Has it cleared off?"

"No, my lady; it has come on to rain hard; it is pouring."

The countess went to the windows of her room, but they were too closely shut and warmly curtained to give her any information as to the state of the weather without. Then she hurried impatiently into the passage where the one end window remained with its shutters still unclosed, and she looked out. The rain was lashing the glass with fury. She turned away and sought her own room again—complaining:

"Oh, I can never go to-night! It is too late and too stormy! Mrs. Brudenell would think me crazy, and the woman at the hut would never let me have my son. Yet, oh! what would I not give to have him on my bosom to-night," said Berenice, pacing feverishly about the room.

"My lady," said the maid uneasily, "I don't think you are well at all this evening. Won't you let me give you some salvolatile?"

"No, I don't want any!" replied the countess, without stopping in her restless walk.

"But, my lady, indeed you are not well!" persisted the affectionate creature.

"No, I am not well, Phœbe! My heart is sore, sore, Phœig;be! But that child would be a balm to it! If I could press my son to my bosom, Phœbe, he would draw out all the fire and pain!"

"But, my lady, he is not your son!" said the maid, with tears of alarm starting in her eyes.

"He is, girl! Now that his mother is dead he is mine! Who has a better right to him than I, I wonder? His mother is gone! his father—" Here the countess suddenly recollected herself, and as she looked into her maid's astonished face she felt how far apart were the ideas of the Jewish matron and the Christian maiden. She controlled her emotion, took her seat, and said:

"Don't be alarmed, Phœbe. I am only a little nervous to-night, my girl. And I want something more satisfactory than a little dog to pet."

"I don't think, my lady, you could get anything in the world more grateful, or more faithful, or more easy to manage, than a little dog. Certainly not a baby. Babies is awful, my lady. They aint got a bit of gratitude or faithfulness in them; and after you have toted them about all day, you may tote them about all night. And then they are bawling from the first day of January until the thirty-first day of December. Take my advice, my lady, and stick to the little dogs, and let babies alone, if you love your peace."

The countess smiled faintly and kept silence. But—she kept her resolution also.

The last words that night spoken after she was in bed, and when she was about to dismiss her maid, were these:

"Phœbe, mind that you are not to say one word to any human being of the subject of our conversation to-night. But you are to call me at eight o'clock, have my breakfast brought to me here at half-past eight, and the carriage at the door at nine. Do you hear?"

"Yes, my lady," answered the girl, who immediately went to the small room adjoining her mistress' chamber, where she usually sat by day and slept by night.

The countess could only sleep in perfect darkness; so when Phœbe had put out all the lights she took advantage of that darkness to leave her door open, so that she could listen if her mistress was restless or wakeful. The maid soon discovered that her mistress was wakeful and restless.

The countess could not sleep for contemplating her project of the morning. According to her Jewish ideas, the motherless son of her husband was as much hers as though she had brought him into the world. And thus she, poor, unloved and childless wife, was delighted with the son that she thought had dropped from heaven into her arms.

That anyone should venture to raise the slightest objection to her taking possession of her own son never entered the mind of Berenice. She imagined that even Mrs. Brudenell, who had treated the mother with the utmost scorn and contumely, must turn to the son with satisfaction and desire.

In cautioning Phœbe to secrecy she had not done so in dread of opposition from any quarter, but with the design of giving Mrs. Brudenell a pleasant surprise.

She intended to go out in the morning as if for a drive, to go to the hut, take possession of the boy, bring him home and lay him in his grandmother's lap. And she anticipated for her reward her child's affection, her husband's love, and her mother's cordial approval.

Full of excitement from these thoughts, Berenice could not sleep; but tossed from side to side in her bed like one suffering from pain or fever.

Her faithful attendant, who had loved her mistress well enough to leave home and country and follow her across the seas to the Western World, lay awake anxiously listening to her restless motions until near morning, when, overcome by watching, she fell asleep.

The maid, who had been the first to close her eyes, was the first to open them. Remembering her mistress' order to be called at eight o'clock, she sprang out of bed and looked at her watch. To her consternation she found that it was half-past nine.

She flew to her mistress' room and threw open the blinds, letting in a flood of morning light.

And then she went to the bedside and drew back the curtains and looked upon the face of the sleeper. Such a pale, sad, worn-looking face! with the full lips closed, the long black lashes lying on the waxen cheeks, the slender black brows slightly contracted, and the long purplish black hair flowing down each side and resting upon the swelling bosom; her arms were thrown up over the pillow, and her hands clasped over her head. This attitude added to the utter sadness and weariness of her aspect.

Phœbe slowly shook her head, murmuring:

"I can't think why a lady having beauty and wealth and rank should break her heart about any scamp of a man! Why couldn't she have purchased an estate with her money and settled down in Old England? And if she must have married, why didn't she marry the marquis? Lack-a-daisy-me! I wish she had never seen this young scamp! She didn't sleep the whole night! I know it was after four o'clock in the morning that I dropped off, and the last thing I knew was trying to keep awake and listen to her tossing! Well, whatever her appointment was this morning, she has missed it by a good hour and a half; that she has, and I'm glad of it. Sleep is the best part of life, and there isn't anything in this world worth waking up for, as I've found out yet! Let her sleep on; she's dead for it, anyway. So let her sleep on, and I'll take the blame."

And with this the judicious Phœbe carefully drew the bed curtains again, closed the window shutters, and withdrew to her own room to complete her toilet.

After a little while Phœbe went below to get her breakfast, which she always took in the housekeeper's room.

Mrs. Spicer had breakfasted long before, and so she met the girl with a sharp rebuke for keeping late hours.

"Pray," she inquired mockingly, "is it the fashion in the country you came from for servants to be abed until ten o'clock in the morning?"

"That depends on circumstances," answered Phœbe, with assumed gravity; "the servants of noble families like the Countess of Hurstmonceux's lie late; but the servants of common folks like yours have to get up early."

"Like ours, you impudent minx! I'll have you to know that our family—the Brudenells—are as good as any other family in the world! But it is not the custom here for the maids to lie in bed until all hours of the morning, and that you'll find!" cried Mrs. Spicer in a passion.

"You'll find yourself discharged if you go on in this way! You seem to forget that my lady is the mistress of this house," said Phœbe, seating herself at the table, which was covered with the litter of the housekeeper's breakfast.

Before the housekeeper had time to reply, or the lady's maid had time to pour out her cold coffee, the drawing-room bell rang. And soon after Jovial entered to say that Mrs. Brudenell required the attendance of Phœbe. The girl rose at once and went up to the drawing room.

"How is the countess this morning?" was the first question of Mrs. Brudenell.

"My lady is sleeping; she has had a bad night; I thought it best not to awake her," answered Phœbe.

"You did right. Let me know when she is awake and ready to receive me. You may go now."

Phœbe returned to her cold and comfortless breakfast, and had but just finished it when a second bell rang. This time it was her mistress, and she hurried to answer it.

The countess was already in her dressing-gown and slippers, seated before her toilet-table, and holding a watch in her hand.

"Oh, Phœbe," she exclaimed, "how could you have disobeyed me so! It is after ten o'clock!"

"My lady, I will tell you the truth. You were so restless last night that you could not sleep, and I was so anxious for fear you were going to be ill, that indeed I could not. And so I lay awake listening at you till after four o'clock this morning, when I dropped off out of sheer exhaustion, and so I overslept myself until half-past nine; and then my lady, I thought, as you had had such a bad night, and as it was too late for you to keep your appointment with yourself, and as you were sleeping so finely, I had better not wake you. I beg your pardon, my lady, if I did wrong, and I hope no harm has been done."

"Not much harm, Phœbe; but something that should have been finished by this time is yet to begin—that is all. In future, Phœbe, try to obey me."

"Indeed I will, my lady."

"And now do my hair as quickly as possible."

Phœbe's nimble fingers soon accomplished their task.

"And now go order the carriage to come round directly; and then bring me a cup of coffee," said the lady, rising to adjust her own dress.

Phœbe hurried off to obey, and soon returned, bringing a delicate little breakfast served on a tray.

By the time the countess had drunk the coffee and tasted the rice waffles and broiled partridge, the carriage was announced.

Mrs. Brudenell met her in the lower hall.

"Ah, Berenice, my dear, I am glad to see that you are going for an airing at last. The morning is beautiful after the storm," she said.

"Yes, mamma," replied the countess, rather avoiding the interview.

"Which way will you drive, my dear?"

"I think through the valley; it is sheltered from the wind there. Good-morning!"

And the lady entered the carriage and gave her order.

The carriage road through the valley was necessarily much longer and more circuitous than the footpath with which we are so familiar. The footpath, we know, went straight down the steep precipice of Brudenell hill, across the bottom, and then straight up the equally steep ascent of Hut hill. Of course this route was impracticable for any wheeled vehicle. The carriage therefore turned off to the left into a road that wound gradually down the hillside and as gradually ascended the opposite heights. The carriage drew up at a short distance from the hut, and the countess alighted and walked to the door. We have seen what a surprise her arrival caused, and now we must return to the interview between the wife of Herman and the sister of Nora.

<hr>

CHAPTER XVII.

THE COUNTESS AND THE CHILD.

With no misgiving thought or doubt
Her fond arms clasped his child about
In the full mantle of her love;
For who so loves the darling flowers
Must love the bloom of human bowers,
The types of brightest things above.
One day—one sunny winter day—
She pressed it to her tender breast;
The sunshine of its head there lay
As pillowed on its native rest.
—*Thomas Buchanan Reed.*

Lady Hurstmonceux and Hannah Worth sat opposite each other in silence. The lady with her eyes fixed thoughtfully on the floor—Hannah waiting for the visitor to disclose the object of her visit.

Reuben Gray had retired to the farthest end of the room, in delicate respect to the lady; but finding that she continued silent, it at last dawned upon his mind that his absence was desirable. So he came forward with awkward courtesy, saying:

"Hannah, I think the lady would like to be alone with you; so I will bid you good-day, and come again to-morrow."

"Very well, Reuben," was all that the woman could answer in the presence of a third person.

And after shaking Hannah's hand, and pulling his forelock to the visitor, the man went away.

As soon as he was clearly gone the countess turned to the weaver and said:

"Hannah—your name is Hannah, I think?"

"Yes, madam."

"Well, Hannah, I have come to thank you for your tender care of my son, and to relieve you of him!" said the countess.

"Madam!" exclaimed the amazed woman, staring point-blank at the visitor.

"Why, what is the matter, girl? What have I said that you should glare at me in that way?" petulantly demanded the lady.

"Madam, you astonish me! Your son is not here. I know nothing about your son; not even that you had a son," replied Hannah.

"Oh, I see," said the lady, with a faint smile; "you are angry because I have left him on your hands so many days. That is pardonable in you. But, you see, my girl, it was not my fault. I never even heard of the little fellow's existence until late last night. I could not sleep for thinking of him. And I came here as soon as I had had my breakfast."

"Madam, can a lady have a son and not know it?" exclaimed Hannah, her amazement fast rising to alarm, for she was beginning to suppose her visitor a maniac escaped from Bedlam.

"Nonsense, Hannah; do not be so hard to propitiate, my good woman! I have explained to you how it happened! I came as soon as I could! I am willing to reward you liberally for all the trouble you have had with him. So now show me my son, there's a good soul."

"Poor thing! poor, poor thing! so young and so perfectly crazy!" muttered Hannah, looking at the countess with blended pity and fear.

"Come, Hannah, show me my son, and have done with this!" said the visitor, rising.

"Don't, my lady; don't go on in this way; you know you have no son; be good, now, and tell me if you really are the Countess of Hurstmonceux; or if not, tell me who you are, and where you live, and let me take you back to your friends," pleaded Hannah, taking her visitor by the hands.

"Oh, there he is now!" exclaimed the countess, shaking Hannah off, and going towards the bed where she saw the babe lying.

Hannah sprang after her, clasped her around the waist, and holding her tightly, cried out in terror:

"Don't, my lady! for Heaven's sake, don't hurt the child! He is such a poor little mite; he cannot live many days; he must die, and it will be a great blessing that he does; but still, for all that, I mustn't see him killed before my very face. No, you shan't, my lady! you shan't go anigh him! You shan't, indeed!" exclaimed Hannah, as the countess struggled once to free herself.

"How dare you hold me?" exclaimed Berenice.

"Because I am strong enough to do so, my lady, without your leave! And because you are not yourself, my lady, and you might kill the child," said Hannah resolutely enough, though, to tell the truth, she was frightened almost out of her senses.

"Not myself? Are you crazy, woman?" indignantly demanded Berenice.

"No, my lady, but you are! Oh, do try to compose your mind, or you may do yourself a mischief!" pleaded Hannah.

Berenice suddenly ceased to struggle, and became perfectly quiet. Hannah was resolved not to be deceived, and held her firmly as ever.

"Hannah," said the countess, "I begin to see how it is that you think me mad. You, a Christian maid, and I, a Jewish matron, do not understand each other. We think, and look, and speak from different points of view. You think I mean to say that the child upon the bed is the son of my own bosom!"

"You said so, my lady."

"No, I said he was my son—I meant my son by marriage and by adoption."

"I do not understand you, madam."

"Well, I fear you don't. I will try to explain. He is"—the lady's voice faltered and broke down—"he is my husband's son, and so, his mother being dead, he becomes mine," breathed Berenice, in a faint voice.

"Madam!" exclaimed Hannah, drawing back and reddening to the very edge of her hair.

"He is the son of Herman Brudenell, and so—"

"My lady! how dare you say such a thing as that?" fiercely interrupted Hannah.

"Because, oh, Heaven! it is true," moaned Berenice; "it is true, Hannah! Would to the Lord it were not!"

"Lady Hurstmonceux—"

"Stop! listen to me first, Hannah! I do not blame your poor sister. Heaven knows I pitied her very much, and did all I could to protect her the night she came to Brudenell Hall."

"I know you did, madam," said Hannah, her heart softening at the recollection of what she had heard of the countess' share in the scene between Nora and Mrs. Brudenell.

"She knew nothing of me when she met my husband, and she could not help loving him any more than I could—any more than I could," she repeated lowly to herself; "and so, though it wrings my heart to think of it, I cannot blame her, Hannah—"

"My lady, you have no right to blame her," interrupted Nora's sister.

"I know it," meekly replied the wronged wife.

"You have no right to blame her, because she was perfectly blameless in the sight of Heaven."

Berenice looked up in surprise, sighed and continued:

"However that may be, Hannah, I am not her judge, and do not presume to arraign her. May she rest in peace! But her child! Herman's child! my child! It is of him I wish to speak! Oh, Hannah, give him to me! I want him so much! I long for him so intensely! My heart warms to him so ardently! He will be such a comfort, such a blessing, such a salvation to me, Hannah! I will love him so well, and rear him so carefully, and make him so happy! I will educate him, provide for all his wants, and give him a profession. And if I am never reconciled to my husband—" Here again her voice faltered and broke down; but after a dry sob, she resumed: "If I am never reconciled to my husband, I will make his son my heir; for I hold all my large property in my own right, Hannah! Say, will you give me my husband's son?"

"But, my lady—"

"Ah, do not refuse me!" interrupted the countess. "I am so unhappy! I am alone in the world, with no one for me to love, and no one to love me!"

"You have many blessings, madam."

"I have rank and wealth and good looks, if you mean them. But, ah! do you think they make a woman happy?"

"No, madam."

"Listen, Hannah! My poor father was an apostate to his faith. My nation cast me off for being his daughter and for marrying a Christian. My parents are dead. My people are estranged. My husband alienated. But still I have one comfort and one hope! My comfort is—the—the simple existence of my husband! Yes, Hannah! alienated as he is, it is a comfort to me to know that he lives. If it were not for that, I myself should die! Oh, Hannah! it is common enough to talk of being willing to die for one we love! It is easy to die—much easier sometimes than to live: the last is often very hard! I will do more than die for my love: I will live for him! live through long years of dreary loneliness, taking my consolation in rearing his son, if you will give me the boy, and hoping in some distant future for his return, when I can present his boy to him, and say to him: 'If you cannot love me for my own sake, try to love me a little for his!' Oh, Hannah! do not dash this last hope from me! give me the boy!"

Hannah bent her head in painful thought. To grant Lady Hurstmonceux's prayer would be to break her vow, by virtually acknowledging the parentage of Ishmael and betraying Herman Brudenell—and without effecting any real good to the lady or the child, since in all human probability the child's hours were already numbered.

"Hannah! will you speak to me?" pleaded Berenice.

"Yes, my lady. I was wishing to speak to you all along; but you would not give me a chance. If you had, my lady, you would not have been compelled to talk so much. I wished to ask you then what I wish to ask you now: What reason have you for thinking and speaking so ill of my sister as you do?"

"I do not blame her; I told you so."

"You cover her errors with a veil of charity; that is what you mean, my lady! She needs no such veil! My sister is as innocent as an angel. And you, my lady, are mistaken."

"Mistaken? as to—to—Oh, Hannah! how am I mistaken?" asked the countess, with sudden eagerness, perhaps with sudden hope.

"If you will compose yourself, my lady, and come and sit down, I will tell you the truth, as I have told it to everybody."

Lady Hurstmonceux went and dropped into her chair, and gazed at Hannah with breathless interest.

Hannah drew another forward and sat down opposite to the countess.

"Now then," said Berenice eagerly.

"My lady, what I have to tell is soon said. My sister was buried in her wedding-ring. Her son was born in wedlock."

The Countess of Hurstmonceux started to her feet, clasped her hands and gazed into Hannah's very soul! The light of an infinite joy irradiated her face.

"Is this true?" she exclaimed.

"It is true."

"Then I have been mistaken! Oh, how widely mistaken! Thank Heaven! Oh, thank Heaven!"

And the Countess of Hurstmonceux sank back in her chair, covered her face with her hands, and burst into tears.

Hannah felt very uncomfortable; her conscience reproached her; she was self-implicated in a deception; and this to one of her integrity of character was very painful. Literally, she had spoken the truth; but the countess had drawn false inferences and deceived herself; and she could not undeceive her without breaking her oath to Nora and betraying Herman Brudenell.

Then she pitied that beautiful, pale woman who was weeping so violently. And she arose and poured out the last of poor Nora's bottle of wine and brought it to her, saying:

"Drink this, my lady, and try and compose yourself."

Berenice drank the wine and thanked the woman, and then said:

"I was very wrong to take up such fancies as I did; but then, you do not know how strong the circumstances were that led me to such fancies. I am glad and sorry and ashamed, all at once, Hannah! Glad to find my own and my mother-in-law's suspicions all unfounded; sorry that I ever entertained them against my dear husband; and ashamed—oh, how much ashamed—that I ever betrayed them to anyone."

"You were seeking to do him a service, my lady, when you did so," said Hannah remorsefully and compassionately.

"Yes, indeed I was! And then I was not quite myself! Oh, I have suffered so much in my short life, Hannah! And I met such a cruel disappointment on my arrival here! But there! I am talking too much again! Hannah, I entreat you to forget all that I have said to you. And if you cannot forget it, I implore you most earnestly never to repeat it to anyone."

"I will not indeed, madam."

The Countess of Hurstmonceux arose and walked to the bed, turned down the shawl that covered the sleeping child, and gazed pitifully upon him. Hannah did not now seek to prevent her.

"Oh, poor little fellow, how feeble he looks! Hannah, it seems such a pity that all the plans I formed for his future welfare should be lost because he is not what I supposed him to be; it seems hard that the revelation which has made me happy should make him unfortunate; or, rather, that it should prevent his good fortune! And it shall not do so entirely. It is true, I cannot now adopt him,—the child of a stranger,—and take him home and rear him as my own, as I should have done had he been what I fancied him to be. Because it might not be right, you know, and my husband might not approve it. And, oh, Hannah, I have grown so timid lately that I dread, I dread more than you can imagine, to do anything that he might not like. Not that he is a domestic tyrant either. You have lived on his estate long enough to know that Herman Brudenell is all that is good and kind. But then you see I am all wrong—and always was so. Everything I do is ill done—and always so. It is all my own fault, and I must try to amend it, if ever I am to hope for happiness. So I must not do anything unless I am sure that it will not displease him, therefore I must not take this child of a stranger home, and rear him as my own. But I will do all that I can for him here. At present his little wants are all physical. Take this purse, dear woman, and make him as comfortable as you can. I think he ought to have medical attendance; procure it for him; get everything he needs; and when the purse is empty bring it to me to be replenished. So much for the present. If he lives I will pay for his schooling, and see that he is apprenticed to some good master to learn a trade."

And with these words the countess held out a well-filled purse to Hannah.

With a deep blush Hannah shook her head and put the offered bounty back, saying:

"No, my lady, no. Nora's child must not become the object of your charity. It will not do. My nephew's wants are few, and will not be felt long; I can supply them all while he lives, I thank you all the same, madam."

Berenice looked seriously disappointed. Again she pressed her bounty upon Hannah, saying:

"I do not really think you are right to refuse assistance that is proffered to this poor child."

But Hannah was firm as she replied:

"I know that I am right, madam. And so long as I am able and willing to supply all his wants myself, and so long as I do supply them, I do him no injury in refusing for him the help of others."

"But do you have to supply all his wants? I suppose that his father must be a poor man, but is he so poor as not to be able to render you some assistance?"

Hannah paused a moment in thought before answering this question, then she said:

"His father is dead, my lady." (Dead to him was her mental reservation.)

"Poor orphan," sighed the countess, with the tears springing to her eyes; "and you will not let me do anything for him?"

"I prefer to take care of him myself, madam, for the short time that he will need care," replied Hannah.

"Well, then," sighed the lady, as she restored her purse to her pocket, "remember this—if from any circumstances whatever you should change your mind, and be willing to accept my protection for this child, come to me frankly, and you will find that I have not changed my mind. I shall always be glad to do anything in my power for this poor babe."

"I thank you, my lady; I thank you very much," said Hannah, without committing herself to any promise.

What instinct was it that impelled the countess to stoop and kiss the brow of the sleeping babe, and then to catch him up and press him fondly to her heart? Who can tell?

The action awoke the infant, who opened his large blue eyes to the gaze of the lady.

"Hannah, you need not think this boy is going to die. He is only a skeleton; but in his strong, bright eyes there is no sign of death—but certainty of life! Take the word of one who has the blood of a Hebrew prophetess in her veins for that!" said Berenice, with solemnity.

"It will be as the Lord wills, my lady," Hannah reverently replied.

The countess laid the infant back upon the bed and then drew her sable cloak around her shoulders, shook hands with Hannah, and departed.

Hannah Worth stood looking after the lady for some little space of time. Hannah was an accurate reader of character, and she had seen at the first glance that this pale, sad, but most beautiful woman could not be the bad, artful, deceitful creature that her husband had been led to believe and to represent her. And she wondered what mistake it could possibly have been that had estranged Herman Brudenell from his lovely wife and left his heart vacant for the reception of another and a most fatal passion.

"Whatever it may have been, I have nothing to do with it. I pity the gentle lady, but I cannot accept her bounty for Nora's child," said Hannah, dismissing the subject from her thoughts and returning to her work.

In this manner, from one plausible motive or another, was all help rejected for the orphan boy.

It seemed as if Providence were resolved to cast the infant helpless upon life, to show the world what a poor boy might make of himself, by God's blessing on his own unaided efforts!

CHAPTER XVIII.

BERENICE.

Her cheeks grew pale and dim her eye,
Her voice was low, her mirth was stay'd;
Upon her heart there seemed to lie
The darkness of a nameless shade;
She paced the house from room to room,
Her form became a walking gloom.
—*Read.*

It was yet early in the afternoon when Berenice reached Brudenell Hall.

Before going to her own apartments she looked into the drawing room, and seeing Mrs. Brudenell, inquired:

"Any news of Herman yet, mamma, dear?"

"No, love, not yet. You've had a pleasant drive, Berenice?"

"Very pleasant."

"I thought so; you have more color than when you went. You should go out every morning, my dear."

"Yes, mamma," said the young lady, hurrying away.

Mrs. Brudenell recalled her.

"Come in here, if you please, my love; I want to have a little conversation with you."

Berenice threw her bonnet, cloak, and muff upon the hall table and entered the drawing room.

Mrs. Brudenell was alone; her daughters had not yet come down; she beckoned her son's wife to take the seat on the sofa by her side.

And when Berenice had complied she said:

"It is of yourself and Herman that I wish to speak to you, my dear."

"Yes, mamma."

The lady hesitated, and then suddenly said:

"It is now nearly a week since my son disappeared; he left his home abruptly, without explanation, in the dead of night, at the very hour of your arrival! That was very strange."

"Very strange," echoed the unloved wife.

"What was the meaning of it, Berenice?"

"Indeed, mamma, I do not know."

"What, then, is the cause of his absence?"

"Indeed, indeed, I do not know."

"Berenice! he fled from your presence. There is evidently some misunderstanding or estrangement between yourself and your husband. I cannot ask him for an explanation. Hitherto I have forborne to ask you. But now that a week has passed without any tidings of my son, I have a right to demand the explanation. Give it to me."

"Mamma, I cannot; for I know no more than yourself," answered Berenice, in a tone of distress.

"You do not know; but you must suspect. Now what do you suspect to be the cause of his going?"

"I do not even suspect, mamma."

"What do you conjecture, then?" persisted the lady.

"I cannot conjecture; I am all lost in amazement, mamma; but I feel—I feel—that it must be some fault in myself," faltered Berenice.

"What fault?"

"Ah, there again I am lost in perplexity; faults I have enough, Heaven knows; but what particular one is strong enough to estrange my husband I do not know, I cannot guess."

"Has he never accused you?"

"Never, mamma."

"Nor quarreled with you?"

"Never!"

"Nor complained of you at all?"

"No, mamma! The first intimation that I had of his displeasure was given me the night of my arrival, when he betrayed some annoyance at my coming upon him suddenly without having previously written. I gave him what I supposed to be sufficient reasons for my act—the same reasons that I afterwards gave you."

"They were perfectly satisfactory. And even if they had not been so, it was no just cause for his behavior. Did he find fault with any part of your conduct previous to your arrival?"

"No, mamma; certainly not. I have told you so before."

"And this is true?"

"As true as Heaven, mamma."

"Then it is easy to fix upon the cause of his bad conduct. That girl. It is a good thing she is dead," hissed the elder lady between her teeth.

She spoke in a tone too low to reach the ears of Berenice, who sat with her weeping face buried in her handkerchief.

There was silence for a little while between the ladies. Berenice was the first to break it, by asking:

"Mamma, can you imagine where he is?"

"No, my love! And if I do not feel so anxious about him as you feel, it is because I know him better than you do. And I know that it is some unjustifiable caprice that is keeping him from his home. When he comes to his senses he will return. In the meanwhile, we must not, by any show of anxiety, give the servants or the neighbors any cause to gossip of his disappearance. And I must not have my plans upset by his whims. I have already delayed my departure for Washington longer than I like; and my daughters have missed the great ball of the season. I am not willing to remain here any longer at all. And I think, also, that we shall be more likely to meet Herman by going to town than by staying here. Washington is the great center of attraction at this season of the year. Everyone goes there. I have a pleasant furnished house on Lafayette Square. It has been quite ready for our reception for the last fortnight. Some of our servants have already gone up. So, my love, I have fixed our departure for Saturday morning, if you think you can be ready by that time. If not, I can wait a day or two."

"I thank you, mamma; I thank you very much; but pray do not inconvenience yourself on my account. I cannot go to town. I must stay here and wait my husband's return—if he ever returns," murmured Berenice to herself.

"But suppose he is in Washington?"

"Still, mamma, as he has not invited me to follow him, I prefer to stay here."

"But surely, child, you need no invitation to follow your husband, wherever he may be."

"Indeed I do, mamma. I came to him from Europe here, and my doing so displeased him and drove him away from his home. And I myself would return to my native country, only, now that I am in my husband's house, I feel that to leave it would be to abandon my post of duty and expose myself to just censure. But I cannot follow him farther, mamma. I cannot! I must not obtrude myself upon his presence. I must remain here and pray and hope for his return," sighed the poor young wife.

"Berenice, this is all wrong; you are morbid; not fit, in your present state of mind, to guide yourself. Be guided by me. Come with me to Washington. You will really enjoy yourself there—you cannot help it. Your beauty will make you the reigning belle; your taste will make you the leader of fashion; and your title will constitute you the lioness of the season; for, mark you, Berenice, there is nothing, not even the 'almighty dollar,' that our consistent republicans fall down and worship with a sincerer homage than a title! All your combined attractions will make you whatever you please to be."

"Except the beloved of my husband," murmured Berenice, in a low voice.

"That also! for, believe me, my dear, many men admire and love through other men's eyes. My son is one of the many. Nothing in this world would bring him to your side so quickly as to see you the center of attraction in the first circles of the capital."

"Ah, madam, the situation would lack the charm of novelty to him; he has been accustomed to seeing me fill similar ones in London and in Paris," said the countess, with a proud though mournful smile.

Mrs. Brudenell's face flushed as she became conscious of having made a blunder—a thing she abhorred, so she hastened to say:

"Oh, of course, my dear, I know, after the European courts, our republican capital must seem an anti-climax! Still, it is the best thing I can offer you, and I counsel you to accept it."

"I feel deeply grateful for your kindness, mamma; but you know I could not enter society, except under the auspices of my husband," replied Berenice.

"You can enter society under the auspices of your husband's mother, the very best chaperone you could possibly have," said the lady coldly.

"I know that, mamma."

"Then you will come with us?"

"Excuse me, madam; indeed I am not thankless of your thought of me. But I cannot go; for even if I had the spirits to sustain the role of a woman of fashion in the gay capital this winter, I feel that in doing so I should still further displease and alienate my husband. No, I must remain here in retirement, doing what good I can, and hoping and praying for his return," sighed Berenice.

Mrs. Brudenell hastily rose from her seat. She was not accustomed to opposition; she was too proud to plead further; and she was very much displeased with Berenice for disappointing her cherished plan of introducing her daughter, the Countess of Hurstmonceux, to the circles of Washington.

"The first dinner bell has rung some time ago, my dear. I will not detain you longer. Myself and daughters leave for town on Saturday."

Berenice bowed gently, and went upstairs to change her dress for dinner.

On Saturday, according to programme, Mrs. Brudenell and her daughters went to town, traveling in their capacious family carriage, and Berenice was left alone. Yes, she was left alone to a solitude of heart and home difficult to be understood by beloved and happy wives and mothers. The strange, wild country, the large, empty house, the grotesque black servants, were enough in themselves to depress the spirits and sadden the heart of the young English lady. Added to these were the deep wounds her affections had received by the contemptuous desertion of her husband; there was uncertainty of his fate, and keen anxiety for his safety; and the slow, wasting soul-sickness of that fruitless hope which is worse than despair.

Every morning, on rising from her restless bed, she would say to herself:

"Herman will return or I shall get a letter from him to-day."

Every night, on sinking upon her sleepless pillow, she would sigh:

"Another dreary day has gone and no news of Herman!"

Thus in feverish expectation the days crept into weeks. And with the extension of time hope grew more strained, tense, and painful.

On Monday morning she would murmur:

"This week I shall surely hear from Herman, if I do not see him."

And every Saturday night she would groan:

"Another miserable week, and no tidings of my husband."

And thus the weeks slowly crept into months.

Mrs. Brudenell wrote occasionally to say that Herman was not in Washington, and to ask if he was at Brudenell. That was all. The answer was always, "Not yet."

Berenice could not go out among the poor, as she had designed; for in that wilderness of hill and valley, wood and water, the roads even in the best weather were bad enough—but in mid-winter they were nearly impassable except by the hardiest pedestrians, the roughest horses, and the strongest wagons. Very early in January there came a deep snow, followed by a sharp frost, and then by a warm rain and thaw, that converted the hills into seamed and guttered precipices; the valleys into pools and quagmires; and the roads into ravines and rivers—quite impracticable for ordinary passengers.

Berenice could not get out to do her deeds of charity among the suffering poor; nor could the landed gentry of the neighborhood make calls upon the young stranger. And thus the unloved wife had nothing to divert her thoughts from the one all-absorbing subject of her husband's unexplained abandonment. The fire, that was consuming her life—the fire of "restless, unsatisfied longing"—burned fiercely in her cavernous dark eyes and the hollow crimson cheeks, lending wildness to the beauty of that face which it was slowly burning away.

As spring advanced the ground improved. The hills dried first. And every day the poor young stranger would wander up the narrow footpath that led over the summit of the hill at the back of the house and down to a stile at a point on the turnpike that commanded a wide sweep of the road. And there, leaning on the rotary cross, she would watch morbidly for the form of him who never came back.

Gossip was busy with her name, asking, Who this strange wife of Mr. Brudenell really was? Why he had abandoned her? And why Mrs. Brudenell had left the house for good, taking her daughters with her? There were some uneducated women among the wives and daughters of the wealthy planters, and these wished to know, if the strange young woman was really the wife of Herman Brudenell, why she was called Lady Hurstmonceux? and they thought that looked very black indeed; until they were laughed at and enlightened by their better informed friends, who instructed them that a woman once a peeress is always by courtesy a peeress, and retains her own title even though married to a commoner.

Upon the whole the planters' wives decided to call upon the countess, once at least, to satisfy their curiosity. Afterwards they could visit or drop her as might seem expedient.

Thus, as soon as the roads became passable, scarcely a day went by in which a large, lumbering family coach, driven by a negro coachman and attended by a negro groom on horseback, did not arrive at Brudenell.

To one and all of these callers the same answer was returned:

"The Countess of Hurstmonceux is engaged, and cannot receive visitors."

The tables were turned. The country ladies, who had been debating with themselves whether to "take up" or "drop" this very questionable stranger, received their congée from the countess herself from the threshold of her own door. The planters' wives were stunned! Each was a native queen, in her own little domain, over her own black subjects, and to meet with a repulse from a foreign countess was an incomprehensible thing!

The reverence for titled foreigners, for which we republicans have been justly laughed at, is confined exclusively to those large cities corrupted by European intercourse. It does not exist in the interior of the country. For instance, in Maryland and Virginia the owner of a large plantation had a domain greater in territorial extent, and a power over his subjects more absolute, than that of any reigning grand-duke or sovereign prince in Germany or Italy. The planter was an absolute monarch, his wife was his queen-consort; they saw no equals and knew no contradiction in their own realm. Their neighbors were as powerful as themselves. When they met, they met as peers on equal terms, the only precedence being that given by courtesy. How, then, could the planter's wife appreciate the dignity of a countess, who, on state occasions, must walk behind a marchioness, who must walk behind a duchess, who must walk behind a queen? Thus you see how it was that the sovereign ladies of Maryland thought they were doing a very condescending thing in calling upon the young stranger whose husband had deserted her, and whose mother and sisters-in-law had left her alone; and that her ladyship had committed a great act of ill-breeding and impertinence in declining their visits.

At the close of the Washington season Mrs. Brudenell and her daughters returned to the Hall. She told her friends that her son was traveling in Europe; but she told her daughter-in-law that she only hoped he was doing so; that she really had not heard a word from him, and did not know anything whatever of his whereabouts.

Mrs. Brudenell and her daughters received and paid visits; gave and attended parties, and made the house and the neighborhood very gay in the pleasant summer time.

Berenice did not enter into any of these amusements. She never accepted an invitation to go out. And even when company was entertained at the house she kept her own suite of rooms and had her meals brought to her there. Mrs. Brudenell was excessively displeased at a course of conduct in her daughter-in-law that would naturally give rise to a great deal of conjecture. She expostulated with Lady Hurstmonceux; but to no good purpose: for Berenice shrunk from company, replying to all arguments that could be urged upon her:

"I cannot—I cannot see visitors, mamma! It is quite—quite impossible."

And then Mrs. Brudenell made a resolution, which she also kept—never to come to Brudenell Hall for another summer until Herman should return to his home and Berenice to her senses. And having so decided, she abridged her stay and went away with her daughters to spend the remainder of the summer at some pleasant watering-place in the North.

And Berenice was once more left to solitude.

Now, Lady Hurstmonceux was not naturally cold, or proud, or unsocial; but as surely as brains can turn, and hearts break, and women die of grief, she was crazy, heart-broken, and dying.

She turned sick at the sight of every human face, because the one dear face she loved and longed for was not near. The pastor of the parish, with the benevolent perseverance of a true Christian, continued to call at the Hall long after every other human creature had ceased to visit the place. But Lady Hurstmonceux steadily refused to receive him.

She never went to church. Her cherished sorrow grew morbid; her hopeless hope became a monomania; her life narrowed down to one mournful routine. She went nowhere but to the turnstile on the turnpike, where she leaned upon the rotary cross, and watched the road.

Even to this day the pale, despairing, but most beautiful face of that young watcher is remembered in that neighborhood.

Only very recently a lady who had lived in that vicinity said to me, in speaking of this young forsaken wife—this stranger in our land:

"Yes, every day she walked slowly up that narrow path to the turnstile, and stood leaning on the cross and gazing up the road, to watch for him—every day, rain or shine; in all weathers and seasons; for months and years."

CHAPTER XIX.

NOBODY'S SON.

Not blest? not saved? Who dares to doubt all well
With holy innocence? We scorn the creed
And tell thee truer than the bigots tell,—
That infants all are Jesu's lambs indeed.
—*Martin F. Tupper*.

But thou wilt burst this transient sleep,
And thou wilt wake my babe to weep;
The tenant of a frail abode,
Thy tears must flow as mine have flowed:
And thou may'st live perchance to prove
The pang of unrequited love.
—*Byron*.

Ishmael lived. Poor, thin, pale, sick; sent too soon into the world; deprived of all that could nurture healthy infant life; fed on uncongenial food; exposed in that bleak hut to the piercing cold of that severe winter; tended only by a poor old maid who honestly wished his death as the best good that could happen to him—Ishmael lived.

One day it occurred to Hannah that he was created to live. This being so, and Hannah being a good churchwoman, she thought she would have him baptized. He had no legal name; but that was no reason why he should not receive a Christian one. The cruel human law discarded him as nobody's child; the merciful Christian law claimed him as one "of the kingdom of Heaven." The human law denied him a name; the Christian law offered him one.

The next time the pastor in going his charitable rounds among his poor parishioners, called at the hut, the weaver mentioned the subject and begged him to baptize the boy then and there.

But the reverend gentleman, who was a high churchman, replied:

"I will cheerfully administer the rites of baptism to the child; but you must bring him to the altar to receive them. Nothing but imminent danger of death can justify the performance of those sacred rites at any other place. Bring the boy to church next Sabbath afternoon."

"What! bring this child to church!—before all the congregation! I should die of mortification!" said Hannah.

"Why? Are you to blame for what has happened? Or is he? Even if the boy were what he is supposed to be,—the child of sin,—it would not be his fault. Do you think in all the congregation there is a soul whiter than that of this child? Has not the Saviour said, 'Suffer little children to come unto me and forbid them not, for of such is the kingdom of Heaven?' Bring the boy to church, Hannah! bring the boy to church," said the pastor, as he took up his hat and departed.

Accordingly the next Sabbath afternoon Hannah Worth took Ishmael to the church, which was, as usual, well filled.

Poor Hannah! Poor, gentle-hearted, pure-spirited old maid! She sat there in a remote corner pew, hiding her child under her shawl and hushing him with gentle caresses during the whole of the afternoon service. And when after the last lesson had been read the minister came down to the font and said: "Any persons present having children to offer for baptism will now bring them forward," Hannah felt as if she would faint. But summoning all her resolution, she arose and came out of her pew, carrying the child. Every eye in the church turned full upon her. There was no harm meant in this; people will gaze at every such a little spectacle; a baby going to be baptized, if nothing else is to be had. But to Hannah's humbled spirit and sinking heart, to carry that child up that aisle under the fire of those eyes seemed like running a blockade of righteous indignation that appeared to surround the altar. But she did it. With downcast looks and hesitating steps she approached and stood at the font—alone—the target of every pair of eyes in the congregation. Only a moment she stood thus, when a countryman, with a start, left one of the side benches and came and stood by her side.

It was Reuben Gray, who, standing by her, whispered:

"Hannah, woman, why didn't you let me know? I would have come and sat in the pew with you and carried the child."

"Oh, Reuben, why will you mix yourself up with me and my miseries?" sighed Hannah.

"'Cause we are one, my dear woman, and so I can't help it," murmured the man.

There was no time for more words. The minister began the services. Reuben Gray offered himself as sponsor with Hannah, who had no right to refuse this sort of copartnership.

The child was christened Ishmael Worth, thus receiving both given and surname at the altar.

When the afternoon worship was concluded and they left the church, Reuben Gray walked beside Hannah, begging for the privilege of carrying the child—a privilege Hannah grimly refused.

Reuben, undismayed, walked by her side all the way from Baymouth church to the hut on the hill, a distance of three miles. And taking advantage of that long walk, he pleaded with Hannah to reconsider her refusal and to become his wife.

"After a bit, we can go away and take the boy with us and bring him up as our'n. And nobody need to know any better," he pleaded.

But this also Hannah grimly refused.

When they reached the hut she turned upon him and said:

"Reuben Gray, I will bear my miseries and reproaches myself! I will bear them alone! Your duty is to your sisters. Go to them and forget me." And so saying she actually shut the door in his face!

Reuben went away crestfallen.

But Hannah! poor Hannah! she never anticipated the full amount of misery and reproach she would have to bear alone!

A few weeks passed and the money she had saved was all spent. No more work was brought to her to do. A miserable consciousness of lost caste prevented her from going to seek it. She did not dream of the extent of her misfortune; she did not know that even if she had sought work from her old employers, it would have been refused her.

One day when the Professor of Odd Jobs happened to be making a professional tour in her way, and called at the hut to see if his services might be required there, she gave him a commission to seek work for her among the neighboring farmers and planters—a duty that the professor cheerfully undertook.

But when she saw him again, about ten days after, and inquired about his success in procuring employment for her, he shook his head, saying:

"There's a plenty of weaving waiting to be done everywhere, Miss Hannah—which it stands to reason there would be at this season of the year. There's all the cotton cloth for the negroes' summer clothes to be wove; but, Miss Hannah, to tell you the truth, the ladies as I've mentioned it to refuses to give the work to you."

"But why?" inquired the poor woman, in alarm.

"Well, Miss Hannah, because of what has happened, you know. The world is very unjust, Miss Hannah! And women are more unjust than men. If 'man's inhumanity to man makes countless thousands mourn,' I'm sure women's cruelty to women makes angels weep!" And here the professor, having lighted upon a high-toned subject and a helpless hearer, launched into a long oration I have not space to report. He ended by saying:

"And now, Miss Hannah, if I were you I would not expose myself to affronts by going to seek work."

"But what can I do, Morris? Must I starve, and let the child starve?" asked the weaver, in despair.

"Well, no, Miss Hannah; me and my ole 'oman must see what we can do for you. She aint as young as she used to be, and she mustn't work so hard. She must part with some of her own spinning and weaving to you. And I must work a little harder to pay for it. Which I am very willing to do; for I say, Hannah, when an able-bodied man is not willing to shift the burden off his wife's shoulders on to his own, he is unworthy to be——"

Here the professor launched into a second oration, longer than the first. In conclusion, he said:

"And so, Miss Hannah, we will give you what work we have to put out. And you must try and knock along and do as well as you can this season. And before the next the poor child will die, and the people will forget all about it, and employ you again."

"But the child is not a-going to die!" burst forth Hannah, in exasperation. "If he was the son of rich parents, whose hearts lay in him, and who piled comforts and luxuries and elegances upon him, and fell down and worshiped him, and had a big fortune and a great name to leave him, and so did everything they possibly could to keep him alive, he'd die! But being what he is, a misery and shame to himself and all connected with him, he'll live! Yes, half-perished as he is with cold and famine, he'll live! Look at him now!"

The professor did turn and look at the little, thin, wizen-faced boy who lay upon the bed, contentedly sucking his skinny thumb, and regarding the speaker with big, bright, knowing eyes, that seemed to say:

"Yes, I mean to suck my thumb and live!"

"To tell you the truth, I think so, too," said the professor, scarcely certain whether he was replying to the words of Hannah or to the looks of the child.

It is certain that the dread of death and the desire of life is the very earliest instinct of every animate creature. Perhaps this child was endowed with excessive vitality. Certainly, the babe's persistence in living on "under difficulties" might have been the germ of that enormous strength and power of will for which the man was afterwards so noted.

The professor kept his word with Hannah, and brought her some work. But the little that he could afford to pay for it was not sufficient to supply one-fourth of Hannah's necessities.

At last came a day when her provisions were all gone. And Hannah locked the child up alone in the hut and set off to walk to Baymouth, to try to get some meal and bacon on credit from the country shop where she had dealt all her life.

Baymouth was a small port, at the mouth of a small bay making up from the Chesapeake. It had one church, in charge of the Episcopal minister who had baptized Nora's child. And it had one large, country store, kept by a general dealer named Nutt, who had for sale everything to eat, drink, wear, or wield, from sugar and tea to meat and fish; from linen cambric to linsey-woolsey; from bonnets and hats to boots and shoes; from new milk to old whisky; from fresh eggs to stale cheese; and from needles and thimbles to plows and harrows.

Hannah, as I said, had been in the habit of dealing at this shop all her life, and paying cash for everything she got. So now, indeed, she might reasonably ask for a little credit, a little indulgence until she could procure work.

Yet, for all that, she blushed and hesitated at having to ask the unusual favor. She entered the store and found the dealer alone. She was glad of that, as she rather shrank from preferring her humble request before witnesses. Mr. Nutt hurried forward to wait on her. Hannah explained her wants, and then added:

"If you will please credit me for the things, Mr. Nutt, I will be sure to pay you the first of the month."

The dealer looked at the customer and then looked down at the counter, but made no reply.

Hannah, seeing his hesitation, hastened to say that she had been out of work all the winter and spring, but that she hoped soon to get some more, when she would be sure to pay her creditor.

"Yes, I know you have lost your employment, poor girl, and I fear that you will not get it again," said the dealer, with a look of compassion.

"But why, oh! why should I not be allowed to work, when I do my work so willingly and so well?" exclaimed Hannah, in, despair.

"Well, my dear girl, if you do not know the reason, I cannot be the man to tell you."

"But if I cannot get work, what shall I do? Oh! what shall I do? I cannot starve! And I cannot see the child starve!" exclaimed Hannah, clasping her hands and raising her eyes in earnest appeal to the judgment of the man who had known her from infancy: who was old enough to be her father, and who had a wife and grown daughter of his own:

"What shall I do? Oh! what shall I do?" she repeated.

Mr. Nutt still seemed to hesitate and reflect, stealing furtive glances at the anxious face of the woman. At last he bent across the counter, took her hand, and, bending his head close to her face, whispered:

"I'll tell you what, Hannah. I will let you have the articles you have asked for, and anything else in my store that you want, and I will never charge you anything for them—"

"Oh, sir, I couldn't think of imposing on your goodness so: The Lord reward you, sir! but I only want a little credit for a short time," broke out Hannah, in the warmth of her gratitude.

"But stop, hear me out, my dear girl! I was about to say you might come to my store and get whatever you want, at any time, without payment, if you will let me drop in and see you sometimes of evenings," whispered the dealer.

"Sir!" said Hannah, looking up in innocent perplexity.

The man repeated his proposal with a look that taught even Hannah's simplicity that she had received the deepest insult a woman could suffer. Hannah was a rude, honest, high-spirited old maid. And she immediately obeyed her natural impulses, which were to raise her strong hands and soundly box the villain's ears right and left, until he saw more stars in the firmament than had ever been created. And before he could recover from the shock of the assault she picked up her basket and strode from the shop. Indignation lent her strength and speed, and she walked home in double-quick time. But once in the shelter of her own hut she sat down, threw her apron over her head, and burst into passionate tears and sobs, crying:

"It's all along of poor Nora and that child, as I'm thought ill on by the women and insulted by the men! Yes, it is, you miserable little wretch!" she added, speaking to the baby, who had opened his big eyes to see the cause of the uproar. "It's all on her account and yourn, as I'm treated so! Why do you keep on living, you poor little shrimp? Why don't you die? Why can't both of us die? Many people die who want to live! Why should we live who want to die? Tell me that, little miserable!" But the baby defiantly sucked his thumb, as if it held the elixir of life, and looked indestructible vitality from his great, bright eyes.

Hannah never ventured to ask another favor from mortal man, except the very few in whom she could place entire confidence, such as the pastor of the parish, the Professor of Odd Jobs, and old Jovial. Especially she shunned Nutt's shop as she would have shunned a pesthouse; although this course obliged her to go two miles farther to another village to procure necessaries whenever she had money to pay for them.

Nutt, on his part, did not think it prudent to prosecute Hannah for assault. But he did a base thing more fatal to her reputation. He told his wife how that worthless creature, whose sister turned out so badly, had come running after him, wanting to get goods from his shop, and teasing him to come to see her; but that he had promptly ordered her out of the shop and threatened her with a constable if ever she dared to show her face there again.

False, absurd, and cruel as this story was, Mrs. Nutt believed it, and told all her acquaintants what an abandoned wretch that woman was. And thus poor Hannah Worth lost all that she possessed in the world—her good name. She had been very poor. But it would be too dreadful now to tell in detail of the depths of destitution and misery into which she and the child fell, and in which they suffered and struggled to keep soul and body together for years and years.

It is wonderful how long life may be sustained under the severest privations. Ishmael suffered the extremes of hunger and cold; yet he did not starve or freeze to death; he lived and grew in that mountain hut as pertinaciously as if he had been the pampered pet of some royal nursery.

At first Hannah did not love him. Ah, you know, such unwelcome children are seldom loved, even by their parents. But this child was so patient and affectionate, that it must have been an unnatural heart that would not have been won by his artless efforts to please. He bore hunger and cold and weariness with baby heroism. And if you doubt whether there is any such a thing in the world as "baby heroism", just visit the nursery hospitals of New York, and look at the cheerfulness of infant sufferers from disease.

Ishmael was content to sit upon the floor all day long, with his big eyes watching Hannah knit, sew, spin, or weave, as the case might be. And if she happened to drop her thimble, scissors, spool of cotton, or ball of yarn, Ishmael would crawl after it as fast as his feeble little limbs would take him, and bring it back and hold it up to her with a smile of pleasure, or, if the feat had been a fine one, a little laugh of triumph. Thus, even before he could walk, he tried to make himself useful. It was his occupation to love Hannah, and watch her, and crawl after anything she dropped and restore it to her. Was this such a small service? No; for it saved the poor woman the trouble of getting up and deranging her work to chase rolling balls of yarn around the room. Or was it a small pleasure to the lonely old maid to see the child smile lovingly up in her face as he tendered her these baby services? I think not. Hannah grew to love little Ishmael. Who, indeed, could have received all his innocent overtures of affection and not loved him a little in return? Not honest Hannah Worth. It was thus, you see, by his own artless efforts that he won his grim aunt's heart. This was our boy's first success. And the truth may as well be told of him now, that in the whole course of his eventful life he gained no earthly good which he did not earn by his own merits. But I must hurry over this part of my story.

When Ishmael was about four years old he began to take pleasure in the quaint pictures of the old family Bible, that I have mentioned as the only book and sole literary possession of Hannah Worth. A rare old copy it was, bearing the date of London, 1720, and containing the strangest of all old old-fashioned engravings. But to the keenly appreciating mind of the child these pictures were a gallery of art. And on Sunday afternoons, when Hannah had leisure to exhibit them, Ishmael never wearied of standing by her side, and gazing at the illustrations of "Cain and Abel," "Joseph Sold by his Brethren," "Moses in the Bulrushes," "Samuel Called by the Lord," "John the Baptist and the Infant Jesus," "Christ and the Doctors in the Temple," and so forth.

"Read me about it," he would say of each picture.

And Hannah would have to read these beautiful Bible stories. One day, when he was about five years old, he astonished his aunt by saying:

"And now I want to read about them for myself!"

But Hannah found no leisure to teach him. And besides she thought it would be time enough some years to come for Ishmael to learn to read. So thought not our boy, however, as a few days proved.

One night Hannah had taken home a dress to one of the plantation negroes, who were now her only customers, and it was late when she returned to the hut. When she opened the door a strange sight met her eyes. The Professor of Odd Jobs occupied the seat of honor in the arm chair in the chimney corner. On his knees lay the open Bible; while by his side stood little Ishmael, holding an end of candle in his hand, and diligently conning the large letters on the title page. The little fellow looked up with his face full of triumph, exclaiming:

"Oh, aunty, I know all the letters on this page now! And the professor is going to teach me to read! And I am going to help him gather his herbs and roots every day to pay him for his trouble!"

The professor looked up and smiled apologetically, saying:

"I just happened in, Miss Hannah, to see if there was anything wanting to be done, and I found this boy lying on the floor with the Bible open before him trying to puzzle out the letters for himself. And as soon as he saw me he up and struck a bargain with me to teach him to read. And I'll tell you what, Miss Hannah, he's going to make a man one of these days! You know I've been a colored schoolmaster, among my other professions, and I tell you I never came across such a quick little fellow as he is, bless his big head! There now, my little man, that's learning enough for one sitting. And besides the candle is going out," concluded the professor, as he arose and closed the book and departed.

But again Ishmael held a different opinion from his elders; and lying down before the fire-lit hearth, with the book open before him, he went over and over his lesson, grafting it firmly in his memory lest it should escape him. In this way our boy took his first step in knowledge. Two or three times in the course of the week the professor would come to give him another lesson. And Ishmael paid for his tuition by doing the least of the little odd jobs for the professor of that useful art.

"You see I can feel for the boy like a father, Miss Hannah," said the professor, after giving his lesson one evening; "because, you know, I am in a manner self-educated myself. I had to pick up reading, writing, and 'rithmetick any way I could from the white children. So I can feel for this boy as I once felt for myself. All my children are girls; but if I had a son I couldn't feel more pride in him than I do in this boy. And I tell you again, he is going to make a man one of these days."

Ishmael thought so too. He had previsions of future success, as every very intelligent lad must have; but at present his ambition took no very lofty flights. The greatest man of his acquaintance was the Professor of Odd Jobs. And to attain the glorious eminence occupied by the learned and eloquent dignitary was the highest aspiration of our boy's early genius.

"Aunty," he said one day, after remaining in deep thought for a long time, "do you think if I was to study very hard indeed, night and day, for years and years, I should ever be able to get as much knowledge and make as fine speeches as the professor?"

"How do I know, Ishmael? You ask such stupid questions. All I can say is, if it aint in you it will never come out of you," answered the unappreciating aunt.

"Oh, if that's all, it is in me; there's a deal more in me than I can talk about; and so I believe I shall be able to make fine speeches like the professor some day."

Morris certainly took great pains with his pupil; and Ishmael repaid his teacher's zeal by the utmost devotion to his service.

By the time our boy had attained his seventh year he could read fluently, write legibly, and work the first four rules in arithmetic. Besides this, he had glided into a sort of apprenticeship to the odd-job line of business, and was very useful to his principal. The manner in which he helped his master was something like this: If the odd job on hand happened to be in the tinkering line, Ishmael could heat the irons and prepare the solder; if it were in the carpentering and joining branch, he could melt the glue; if in the brick-laying, he could mix the mortar; if in the painting and glazing, he could roll the putty.

When he was eight years old he commenced the study of grammar, geography, and history, from old books lent him by his patron; and he also took a higher degree in his art, and began to assist his master by doing the duties of clerk and making the responses, whenever the professor assumed the office of parson and conducted the church services to a barn full of colored brethren; by performing the part of mourner whenever the professor undertook to superintend a funeral; and by playing the tambourine in accompaniment to the professor's violin whenever the latter became master of ceremonies for a colored ball!

In this manner he not only paid for his own tuition, but earned a very small stipend, which it was his pride to carry to Hannah, promising her that some day soon he should be able to earn enough to support her in comfort.

Thus our boy was rapidly progressing in the art of odd jobs and bidding fair to emulate the fame and usefulness of the eminent professor himself, when an event occurred in the neighborhood that was destined to change the direction of his genius.

CHAPTER XX.

NEWS FROM HERMAN.

But that which keepeth us apart is not
Distance, nor depth of wave, nor space of earth,
But the distractions of a various lot,
As various as the climates of our birth.

My blood is all meridian—were it not
I had not left my clime, nor should I be,
In spite of tortures, ne'er to be forgot,
A slave again of love, at least of thee!
—*Byron*.

The life of Berenice was lonely enough. She had perseveringly rejected the visits of her neighbors, until at length they had taken her at her word and kept away from her house.

She had persistently declined the invitations of Mrs. Brudenell to join the family circle at Washington every winter, until at last that lady had ceased to repeat them and had also discontinued her visits to Brudenell Hall.

Berenice passed her time in hoping and praying for her husband's return, and in preparing and adorning her home for his reception; in training and improving the negroes; in visiting and relieving the poor; and in walking to the turnstile and watching the high-road.

Surely a more harmless and beneficent life could not be led by woman; yet the poisonous alchemy of detraction turned all her good deeds into evil ones.

Poor Berenice—poor in love, was rich in gold, and she lavished it with an unsparing hand on the improvement of Brudenell. She did not feel at liberty to pull down and build up, else had the time-worn old mansion house disappeared from sight and a new and elegant villa had reared its walls upon Brudenell Heights. But she did everything else she could to enhance the beauty and value of the estate.

The house was thoroughly repaired, refurnished, and decorated with great luxury, richness, and splendor. The grounds were laid out, planted, and adorned with all the beauty that taste, wealth, and skill could produce. Orchards and vineyards were set out. Conservatories and pineries were erected. The negroes' squalid log-huts were replaced with neat stone cottages, and the shabby wooden fences by substantial stone walls.

And all this was done, not for herself, but for her husband, and her constant mental inquiry was:

"After all, will Herman be pleased?"

Yet when the neighbors saw this general renovation, of the estate, which could not have been accomplished without considerable expenditure of time, money, and labor, they shook their heads in strong disapprobation, and predicted that that woman's extravagance would bring Herman Brudenell to beggary yet.

She sought to raise the condition of the negroes, not only by giving them neat cottages, but by comfortably furnishing their rooms, and encouraging them to keep their little houses and gardens in order, rewarding them for neatness and industry, and established a school for their children to learn to read and write. But the negroes—hereditary servants of the Brudenells—looked upon this stranger with jealous distrust, as an interloping foreigner who had, by some means or other, managed to dispossess and drive away the rightful family from the old place. And so they regarded all her favors as a species of bribery, and thanked her for none of them. And this was really not ingratitude, but fidelity. The neighbors denounced these well-meant efforts of the mistress as dangerous innovations, incendiarisms, and so forth, and thanked Heaven that the Brudenell negroes were too faithful to be led away by her!

She went out among the poor of her neighborhood and relieved their wants with such indiscriminate and munificent generosity as to draw down upon herself the rebuke of the clergy for encouraging habits of improvidence and dependence in the laboring classes. As for the subjects of her benevolence, they received her bounty with the most extravagant expressions of gratitude and the most fulsome flattery. This was so distasteful to Berenice that she oftened turned her face away, blushing with embarrassment at having listened to it. Yet such was the gentleness of her spirit, that she never wounded their feelings by letting them see that she distrusted the sincerity of these hyperbolical phrases.

"Poor souls," she said to herself, "it is the best they have to offer me, and I will take it as if it were genuine."

Berenice was right in her estimate of their flattery. Astonished at her lavish generosity, and ignorant of her great wealth, which made alms-giving easy, her poor neighbors put their old heads together to find out the solution of the problem. And they came to the conclusion that this lady must have been a great sinner, whose husband had abandoned her for some very good reason, and who was now endeavoring to atone for her sins by a life of self-denial and benevolence. This conclusion seemed too probable to be questioned. This verdict was brought to the knowledge of Berenice in a curious way. Among the recipients of her bounty was Mrs. Jones, the ladies' nurse. The old woman had fallen into a long illness, and consequently into extreme want. Her case came to the knowledge of Berenice, who hastened to relieve her. When the lady had made the invalid comfortable and was about to take leave, the latter said:

"Ah, 'charity covers a multitude of sins,' ma'am! Let us hope that all yours may be so covered."

Berenice stared in surprise. It was not the words so much as the manner that shocked her. And Phœbe, who had attended her mistress, scarcely got well out of the house before her indignation burst forth in the expletives:

"Old brute! Whatever did she mean by her insolence? My lady, I hope you will do nothing more for the old wretch."

Berenice walked on in silence until they reached the spot where they had left their carriage, and when they had re-entered it, she said:

"Something like this has vaguely met me before; but never so plainly and bluntly as to-day; it is unpleasant; but I must not punish one poor old woman for a misapprehension shared by the whole community."

So calmly and dispassionately had the countess answered her attendant's indignant exclamation. But as soon as Berenice reached her own chamber she dismissed her maid, locked her door, and gave herself up to a passion of grief.

It was but a trifle—that coarse speech of a thoughtless old woman—a mere trifle; but it overwhelmed her, coming, as it did, after all that had gone before. It was but the last feather, you know, only a single feather laid on the pack that broke the camel's back. It was but a drop of water, a single drop, that made the full cup overflow!

Added to bereavement, desertion, loneliness, slander, ingratitude, had come this little bit of insolence to overthrow the firmness that had stood all the rest. And Berenice wept.

She had left home, friends, and country for one who repaid the sacrifice by leaving her. She had lavished her wealth upon those who received her bounty with suspicion and repaid her kindness with ingratitude. She had lived a life as blameless and as beneficent as that of any old time saint or martyr, and had won by it nothing but detraction and calumny. Her parents were dead, her husband gone, her native land far away, her hopes were crushed. No wonder she wept. And then the countess was out of her sphere; as much out of her sphere in the woods of Maryland as Hans Christian Andersen's cygnet was in the barnyard full of fowls. She was a swan, and they took her for a deformed duck. And at last she herself began to be vaguely conscious of this.

"Why do I remain here?" she moaned; "what strange magnetic power is it that holds my very will, fettered here, against my reason and judgment? That has so held me for long years? Yes, for long, weary years have I been bound to this cross, and I am not dead yet! Heavenly Powers! what are my nerves and brain and heart made of that I am not dead, or mad, or criminal before this? Steel, and rock, and gutta percha, I think! Not mere flesh and blood and bone like other women's? Oh, why do I stay here? Why do I not go home? I have lost everything else; but I have still a home and country left! Oh, that I could break loose! Oh, that I could free myself! Oh, that I had the wings of a dove, for then I would fly away and be at rest!'" she exclaimed, breaking into the pathetic language of the Psalmist.

A voice softly stole upon her ear, a low, plaintive voice singing a homely Scotch song:

"'Oh, it's hame, hame, hame,
Hame fain would I be;
But the wearie never win back
To their ain countrie.'"

Tears sprang again to the eyes of the countess as she caught up and murmured the last two lines:

"'But the wearie never win back
To their ain countrie.'"

Phœbe, for it was she who was singing, hushed her song as she reached her lady's door, and knocked softly. The countess unlocked the door to admit her.

"It is only the mail bag, my lady, that old Jovial has just brought from the post office," said the girl.

Lady Hurstmonceux listlessly looked over its contents. Several years of disappointment had worn out all expectation of hearing from the only one of whom she cared to receive news. There were home and foreign newspapers that she threw carelessly out. And there was one letter at the bottom of all the rest that she lifted up and looked at with languid curiosity. But as soon as her eyes fell upon the handwriting of the superscription the letter dropped from her hand and she sank back in her chair and quietly fainted away.

Phœbe hastened to apply restoratives, and after a few minutes the lady recovered consciousness and rallied her faculties.

"The letter! the letter, girl! give me the letter!" she gasped in eager tones.

Phœbe picked it up from the carpet, upon which it had fallen, and handed it to her mistress.

Berenice, with trembling fingers, broke the seal and read the letter. It was from Herman Brudenell, and ran as follows:

"London, December 1, 18—

"Lady Hurstmonceux: If there is one element of saving comfort in my lost, unhappy life, it is the reflection that, though in an evil hour I made you my wife, you are not called by my name; but that the courtesy of custom continues to you the title won by your first marriage with the late Earl of Hurstmonceux; and that you cannot therefore so deeply dishonor my family.

"Madam, it would give me great pain to write to any other woman, however guilty, as I am forced to write to you; because on any woman I should feel that I was inflicting suffering, which you know too well I have not-- never had the nerve to do; but you, I know, cannot be hurt; you are callous. If your early youth had not shown you to be so, the last few years of your life would have proved it. If you had not been so insensible to shame as you are to remorse, how could you, after your great crime, take possession of my house and, by so doing, turn my mother and sisters from their home and banish me from my country? For well you know that, while you live at Brudenell Hall, my family cannot re-enter its walls! Nay, more—while you choose to reside in America, I must remain an exile in Europe. The same hemisphere is not broad enough to contain the Countess of Hurstmonceux and Herman Brudenell.

"I have given you a long time to come to your senses and leave my house. Now my patience is exhausted, and I require you to depart. You are not embarrassed for a home or a support: if you were I should afford you both, on condition of your departure from America. But my whole patrimony would be but a mite added to your treasures.

"You have country-seats in England, Scotland, and Ireland, as well as a town house in London, a marine villa at Boulougne, and a Swiss cottage on Lake Leman. All these are your own; and you shall never be molested by me in your exclusive possession of them. Choose your residence from among them, and leave me in peaceable possession of the one modest countryhouse I have inherited in my native land. I wish to sell it.

"But you doubtless have informed yourself before this time, that by the laws of the State in which my property is situated, a man cannot sell his homestead without the consent of his wife. Your co-operation is therefore necessary in the sale of Brudenell Hall. I wish you to put yourself in immediate communication with my solicitors, Messrs. Kage & Kage, Monument Street, Baltimore, who are in possession of my instructions. Do this promptly, and win from me the only return you have left it in my power to make you—oblivion of your crimes and of yourself.

"Herman Brudenell."

With the calmness of despair Berenice read this cruel letter through to the end, and dropped it on her lap, and sat staring at it in silence. Then, as if incredulous of its contents, or doubtful of its meaning, she took it up and read it again, and again let it fall. And yet a third time—after rapidly passing her hand to and fro across her forehead, as if that action would clear her vision—she raised, re-perused, and laid aside the letter. Then she firmly set her teeth, and slowly nodded her head, while for an instant a startling light gleamed from her deep black eyes.

Her faithful attendant, while seeming to be busy arranging the flasks on the dressing-table, furtively and anxiously watched her mistress, who at last spoke:

"Phœbe!"

"Yes, my lady."

"Bring me a glass of wine."

The girl brought the required stimulant, and in handing it to her mistress noticed how deadly white her face had become. And as the countess took the glass from the little silver waiter her hand came in contact with that of Phœbe, and the girl felt as if an icicle had touched her, so cold it was.

"Now wheel my writing-desk forward," said the countess, as she sipped her wine.

The order was obeyed.

"And now," continued the lady, as she replaced the glass and opened her desk, "pack up my wardrobe and jewels, and your own clothes. Order the carriage to be at the door at eight o'clock, to take us to Baymouth. We leave Baymouth for New York to-morrow morning, and New York for Liverpool next Saturday."

"Now, glory be to Heaven for that, my lady; and I wish it had been years ago instead of to-day!" joyfully exclaimed the girl, as she went about her business.

"And so do I! And so do I, with all my heart and soul!" thought Berenice, as she arranged her papers and took up a pen to write. In an instant she laid it down again, and arose and walked restlessly up and down the floor, wringing her hands, and muttering to herself:

"And this is the man for whose sake I sacrificed home, friends, country, and the most splendid prospects that ever dazzled the imagination of woman! This is the man whom I have loved and watched and prayed for, all these long years, hoping against hope, and believing against knowledge. If he had ceased to love me, grown tired of me, and wished to be rid of me, could he not have told me so, frankly, from the first? It would have been less cruel than to have inflicted on me this long anguish of suspense! less cowardly than to have attempted to justify his desertion of me by a charge of crime! What crime—he knows no more than I do! Oh, Herman! Herman! how could you fall so low? But I will not reproach you even in my thoughts. But I must, I must forget you!"

She returned to her desk, sat down and took up her pen; but again she dropped it, bowed her head upon her desk, and wept:

"Oh, Herman! Herman! must I never hope to meet you again? never look into your dark eyes, never clasp your hand, or hear your voice again? never more? never more! Must mine be the hand that writes our sentence of separation? I cannot! oh! I cannot do it, Herman! And yet!—it is you who require it!"

After a few minutes she took up his letter and read it over for the fourth time. Its ruthless implacability seemed to give her the strength necessary to obey its behests. As if fearing another failure of her resolution, she wrote at once:

"Brudenell Hall, December 30, 18—

"Mr. Brudenell: Your letter has relieved me from an embarrassing position. I beg your pardon for having been for so long a period an unconscious usurper of your premises. I had mistaken this place for my husband's house and my proper home. My mistake, however, has not extended to the appropriation of the revenues of the estate. You will find every dollar of those placed to your credit in the Planters' Bank of Baymouth. My mistake has been limited to the occupancy of the house. For that wrong I shall make what reparation remains in my power. I shall leave this place this Friday evening; see your solicitors on Monday; place in their hands a sum equivalent to the full value of Brudenell Hall, as a compensation to you for my long use of the house; and then sign whatever documents may be necessary to renounce all claim upon yourself and your estate, and to free you forever from

"Berenice, Countess of Hurstmonceux."

She finished the letter and threw down the pen. What it had cost her to write thus, only her own loving and outraged woman's heart knew.

By the time she had sealed her letter Phœbe entered to say that the dinner was served—that solitary meal at which she had sat down, heart-broken, for so many weary years.

She answered, "Very well," but never stirred from her seat.

Phœbe fidgeted about the room for a while, and then, with the freedom of a favorite attendant, she came to the side of the countess and, smiling archly, said:

"My lady."

"Well, Phœbe?"

"People needn't starve, need they, because they are going back to their 'ain countrie'?"

Lady Hurstmonceux smiled faintly, roused herself, and went down to dinner.

On her return to her room she found her maid locking the last trunks.

"Is everything packed, Phœbe?"

"Except the dress you have on, my lady; and I can lay that on the top of this trunk after you put on your traveling dress."

"And you are glad we are going home, my girl?"

"Oh, my lady, I feel as if I could just spread out my arms and fly for joy."

"Then I am, also, for your sake. What time is it now?"

"Five o'clock, my lady."

"Three hours yet. Tell Mrs. Spicer to come here."

Phœbe locked the trunk she had under her hand and went out to obey. When Mrs. Spicer came in she was startled by the intelligence that her lady was going away immediately, and that the house was to be shut up until the arrival of Mr. Brudenell or his agents, who would arrange for its future disposition.

When Lady Hurstmonceux had finished these instructions she placed a liberal sum of money in the housekeeper's hands, with orders to divide it among the house-servants.

Next she sent for Grainger, the overseer, and having given him the same information, and put a similar sum of money in his hands for distribution among the negroes, she dismissed both the housekeeper and the overseer. Then she enclosed a note for a large amount in a letter addressed to the pastor of the parish, with a request that he would appropriate it for the relief of the suffering poor in that neighborhood. Finally, having completed all her preparations, she took a cup of tea, bade farewell to her dependents, and, attended by Phœbe, entered the carriage and was driven to Baymouth, where she posted her two letters in time for the evening mail, and where the next morning she took the boat for Baltimore, en route for the North. She stopped in Baltimore only long enough to arrange business with Mr. Brudenell's solicitors, and then proceeded to New York, whence, at the end of the same week, she sailed for Liverpool. Thus the beautiful young English Jewess, who had dropped for a while like some rich exotic flower transplanted to our wild Maryland woods, returned to her native land, where, let us hope, she found in an appreciating circle of friends some consolation for the loss of that domestic happiness that had been so cruelly torn from her.

We shall meet with Berenice, Countess of Hurstmonceux, again; but it will be in another sphere, and under other circumstances.

90

It was in the spring succeeding her departure that the house-agents and attorneys came down to appraise and sell Brudenell Hall. Since the improvements bestowed upon the estate by Lady Hurstmonceux, the property had increased its value, so that a purchaser could not at once be found. When this fact was communicated to Mr. Brudenell, in London, he wrote and authorized his agent to let the property to a responsible tenant, and if possible to hire the plantation negroes to the same party who should take the house.

All this after a while was successfully accomplished. A gentleman from a neighboring State took the house, all furnished as it was, and hired all the servants of the premises.

He came early in June, but who or what he was, or whence he came, none of the neighbors knew. The arrival of any stranger in a remote country district is always the occasion of much curiosity, speculation, and gossip. But when such a one brings the purse of Fortunatus in his pocket, and takes possession of the finest establishment in the country—house, furniture, servants, carriages, horses, stock and all, he becomes the subject of the wildest conjecture.

It does not require long to get comfortably to housekeeping in a ready-made home; so it was soon understood in the neighborhood that the strangers were settled in their new residence, and might be supposed to be ready to receive calls.

But the neighbors, though tormented with curiosity, cautiously held aloof, and waited until the Sabbath, when they might expect to see the newcomers, and judge of their appearance and hear their pastor's opinion of them.

So, on the first Sunday after the stranger's settlement at Brudenell Hall the Baymouth Church was crowded to excess. But those of the congregation who went there with other motives than to worship their Creator were sadly disappointed. The crimson-lined Brudenell pew remained vacant, as it had remained for several years.

"Humph! not church-going people, perhaps! We had an English Jewess before, perhaps we shall have a Turkish Mohammedan next!" was the speculation of one of the disappointed.

The conjecture proved false.

The next Sunday the Brudenell pew was filled. There was a gentleman and lady, and half-a-dozen girls and boys, all dressed in half-mourning, except one little lady of about ten years old, whose form was enveloped in black bombazine and crape, and whose face, what could be seen of it, was drowned in tears. It needed no seer to tell that she was just left motherless, and placed in charge of her relations.

After undergoing the scrutiny of the congregation, this family was unanimously, though silently, voted to be perfectly respectable.

CHAPTER XXI.

ISHMAEL'S ADVENTURE.

I almost fancy that the more
He was cast out from men,
Nature had made him of her store
A worthier denizen;
As if it pleased her to caress
A plant grown up so wild,
As if his being parentless
Had made him more *her* child.
—*Monckton Milnes.*

At twelve years of age Ishmael was a tall, thin, delicate-looking lad, with regular features, pale complexion, fair hair, and blue eyes. His great, broad forehead and wasted cheeks gave his face almost a triangular shape. The truth is, that up to this age the boy had never had enough food to nourish the healthy growth of the body. And that he lived at all was probably due to some great original vital force in his organization, and also to the purity of his native air, of which at least he got a plenty.

He had learned all the professor could teach him; had read all the books that Morris could lend him; and was now hungering and thirsting for more knowledge. At this time a book had such a fascination for Ishmael that when he happened to be at Baymouth he would stand gazing, spellbound, at the volumes exposed for sale in the shop windows, just as other boys gaze at toys and sweetmeats.

But little time had the poor lad for such peeps into Paradise, for he was now earning about a dollar a week, as Assistant-Professor of Odd Jobs to Jem Morris, and his professional duties kept him very busy.

Baymouth had progressed in all these years, and now actually boasted a fine new shop, with this sign over the door:

BOOK, STATIONERY, AND FANCY BAZAAR.

And this to Ishmael seemed a very fairy palace. It attracted him with an irresistible glamour.

It happened one burning Saturday afternoon in August that the boy, having a half-holiday, resolved to make the most of it and enjoy himself by walking to Baymouth and standing before that shop to gaze at his leisure upon the marvels of literature displayed in its windows.

The unshaded village street was hot and dusty, and the unclouded August sun was blazing down upon it; but Ishmael did not mind that, as he stood devouring with his eyes the unattainable books.

While he was thus occupied, a small, open, one-horse carriage drove up and stopped before the shop door. The gentleman who had driven it alighted and handed out a lady and a little girl in deep mourning. The lady and the little girl passed immediately into the shop. And oh! how Ishmael envied them! They were perhaps going to buy some of those beautiful books!

The gentleman paused with the reins in his hands, and looked up and down the bare street, as if in search of some person. At last, in withdrawing his eyes, they fell upon Ishmael, and he called him.

The boy hastened to his side.

"My lad, do you think you can hold my horse?"

"Oh, yes, sir."

"Well, and can you lead him out of the road to that stream there under the trees, and let him drink and rest?"

"Yes, sir."

"Very well, go on, then, and mind and watch the carriage well, while we are in the shop; because, you see, there are tempting parcels in it."

"Yes, sir," again said the boy.

The gentleman gave him the reins and followed the ladies into the shop. And Ishmael led the horse off to the grove stream, a place much frequented by visitors at Baymouth to rest and water their horses.

The thirsty horse had drank his fill, and the kind boy was engaged in rubbing him down with cool, fresh dock leaves, when a voice near the carriage attracted Ishmael's attention.

"Oh, cricky, Ben! if here isn't old Middy's pony-chaise standing all alone, and full of good nuggs he's been a buying for that tea-party! Come, let's have our share beforehand."

Ishmael who was partly concealed by his stooping position behind the horse, now raised his head, and saw two young gentlemen of about twelve and fourteen years of age, whom he recognized as the sons of Commodore Burghe, by having seen them often at church in the commodore's pew.

"Oh, I say, Ben, here's a hamper chock full of oranges and figs and nuts and raisins and things! let's get at them," said the elder boy, who had climbed upon one wheel and was looking into the carriage.

"Oh, no, Alf! don't meddle with them! Mr. Middleton would be mad," replied the younger.

"Who cares if he is? Who's afraid? Not I!" exclaimed Alf, tearing off the top of the hamper and helping himself.

All this passed in the instant that Ishmael was rising up.

"You must not touch those things, young gentlemen! You must not, indeed! Put those figs back again, Master Alfred," he said.

"Who the blazes are you, pray?" inquired Master Alfred contemptuously, as he coolly proceeded to fill his pockets.

"I am Ishmael Worth, and I am set here to watch this horse and carriage, and I mean to do it! Put those figs back again, Master Alfred."

"Oh! you are Ishmael Worth, are you? The wearer woman's boy and Jem Morris's 'prentice! Happy to know you, sir!" said the lad sarcastically, as he deliberately spread his handkerchief on the ground and began to fill it with English walnuts.

"Return those things to the hamper, Master Alfred, while times are good," said Ishmael slowly and distinctly.

"Oh, I say, Ben, isn't he a nice one to make acquaintance with? Let's ask him to dinner!" jeered the boy, helping himself to more walnuts.

"You had better return those things before worse comes of it," said Ishmael, slowly pulling off his little jacket and carefully folding it up and laying it on the ground.

"I say, Ben! Jem Morris's apprentice is going to fight! Ar'n't you scared?" sneered Master Alfred, tying up his handkerchief full of nuts.

"Will you return those things or not?" exclaimed Ishmael, unbuttoning his little shirt collar and rolling up his sleeves.

"Will you tell me who was your father?" mocked Master Alfred.

That question was answered by a blow dashed full in the mouth of the questioner, followed instantly by another blow into his right eye and a third into his left. Then Ishmael seized him by the collar and, twisting it, choked and shook him until he dropped his plunder. But it was only the suddenness of the assault that had given Ishmael a moment's advantage. The contest was too unequal. As soon as Master Alfred had dropped his plunder he seized his assailant. Ben also rushed to the rescue. It was unfair, two boys upon one. They soon threw Ishmael down upon the ground and beat his breath nearly out of his body. They were so absorbed in their cowardly work that they were unconscious of the approach of the party from the shop, until the gentleman left the ladies and hurried to the scene of action, exclaiming:

"What's this? What's this? What's all this, young gentlemen? Let that poor lad alone! Shame on you both!"

The two culprits ceased their blows and started up panic-stricken. But only for a moment. The ready and reckless falsehood sprang to Alfred's lips.

"Why, sir, you see, we were walking along and saw your carriage standing here and saw that boy stealing the fruit and nuts from it. And we ordered him to stop and he wouldn't, and we pitched into him and beat him. Didn't we, Ben"

"Yes, we beat him," said Ben evasively.

"Humph! And he stole the very articles that he was put here to guard! Sad! sad! but the fault was mine! He is but a child! a poor child, and was most likely hungry. I should not have left the fruit right under his keen young nose to tempt him! Boys, you did very wrong to beat him so! You, who are pampered so much, know little of the severe privations and great temptations of the poor. And we cannot expect children to resist their natural appetites," said the gentleman gently, as he stooped to examine the condition of the fallen boy.

Ishmael was half stunned, exhausted, and bleeding; but his confused senses had gathered the meaning of the false accusation made against him. And, through the blood bursting from his mouth, he gurgled forth the words:

"I didn't, sir! The Lord above, he knows I didn't!"

"He did! he did! Didn't he, Ben?" cried Master Alfred.

Ben was silent.

"And we beat him! Didn't we, Ben?" questioned the young villain, who well understood his weak younger brother.

"Yes," replied Ben, who was always willing to oblige his elder brother if he could do so without telling an out and out falsehood; "we did beat him."

The gentleman raised the battered boy to his feet, took a look at him and murmured to himself:

"Well! if this lad is a thief and a liar, there is no truth in phrenology or physiognomy either."

Then, speaking aloud, he said:

"My boy! I am very sorry for what has just happened! You were placed here to guard my property. You betrayed your trust! You, yourself, stole it! And you have told a falsehood to conceal your theft. No! do not attempt to deny it! Here are two young gentlemen of position who are witnesses against you!"

Ishmael attempted to gurgle some denial, but his voice was drowned in the blood that still filled his mouth.

"My poor boy," continued the gentleman—"for I see you are poor, if you had simply eaten the fruit and nuts, that would have been wrong certainly, being a breach of trust; but it would have been almost excusable, for you might have been hungry and been tempted by the smell of the fruit and by the opportunity of tasting it. And if you had confessed it frankly, I should as frankly have forgiven you. But I am sorry to say that you have attempted to conceal your fault by falsehood. And do you know what that falsehood has done? It has converted the act, that I should have construed as mere trespass, into a theft!"

Ishmael stooped down and bathed his bloody face in the stream and then wiped it clean with his coarse pocket handkerchief. And then he raised his head with a childish dignity most wonderful to see, and said:

"Listen to me, sir, if you please. I did not take the fruit or the nuts, or anything that was yours. It is true, sir, as you said, that I am poor. And I was hungry, very hungry indeed, because I have had nothing to eat since six o'clock this morning. And the oranges and figs did smell nice, and I did want them very much. But I did not touch them, sir! I could better bear hunger than I could bear shame! And I should have suffered shame if I had taken your things! Yes, even though you might have never found out the loss of them. Because—I should have known myself to be a thief, and I could not have borne that, sir! I did not take your property, sir, I hope you will believe me."

"He did! he did! he did! didn't he now, Ben?" cried Alfred.

Ben was silent.

"And we beat him for it, didn't we, Ben?"

"Yes," said Ben.

"There now you see, my boy! I would be glad to believe you; but here are two witnesses against you! two young gentlemen of rank, who would not stoop to falsehood!" said the gentleman sadly.

"Sir," replied Ishmael calmly, "be pleased to listen to me, while I tell you what really happened. When you left me in charge of this horse I led him to this stream and gave him water, and I was rubbing him down with a handful of fresh dock-leaves when these two young gentlemen came up. And the elder one proposed to help himself to the contents of the hamper. But the younger one would not agree to the plan. And I, for my part, told him to let the things alone. But he wouldn't mind me. I insisted, but he laughed at me and helped himself to the oranges, figs, walnuts, and raisins. I told him to put them back directly; but he wouldn't. And then I struck him and collared him, sir; for I thought it was my duty to fight for the property that had been left in my care. But he was bigger than I was, and his brother came to help him, and they were too many for me, and between them they threw me down. And then you came up. And that is the whole truth, sir."

"It isn't! it isn't! He stole the things, and now he wants to lay it on us! that is the worst of all! But we can prove that he did it, because we are two witnesses against one!" said Master Alfred excitedly.

"Yes; that is the worst of all, my boy; it was bad to take the things, but you were tempted by hunger; it was worse to deny the act, but you were tempted by fear; it is the worst of all to try to lay your fault upon the shoulders of others. I fear I shall be obliged to punish you," said the gentleman.

"Sir, punish me for the loss of the fruit if you please; but believe me; for I speak the truth," said Ishmael firmly.

At that moment he felt a little soft hand steal into his own, and heard a gentle voice whisper in his ear:

"I believe you, poor boy, if they don't."

He turned, and saw at his side the little orphan girl in deep mourning. She was a stately little lady, with black eyes and black ringlets, and with the air of a little princess.

"Come, Claudia! Come away, my love," said the lady, who had just arrived at the spot.

"No, aunt, if you please; I am going to stand by this poor boy here! He has got no friend! He is telling the truth, and nobody will believe him!" said the little girl, tossing her head, and shaking back her black ringlets haughtily.

It was easy to see that this little lady had had her own royal will, ever since she was one day old, and cried for a light until it was brought.

"Claudia, Claudia, you are very naughty to disobey your aunt," said the gentleman gravely.

The little lady lifted her jetty eyebrows in simple surprise.

"'Naughty,' uncle! How can you say such things to me? Mamma never did; and papa never does! Pray do not say such things again to me, uncle! I have not been used to hear them."

The gentleman shrugged his shoulders, and turned to Ishmael, saying:

"I am more grieved than angry, my boy, to see you stand convicted of theft and falsehood."

"I was never guilty of either in my life, sir," said Ishmael.

"He was! he was! He stole the things, and then told stories about it, and tried to lay it on us! But we can prove it was himself! We are two witnesses against one! two genteel witnesses against one low one! We are gentleman's sons; and who is he? He's a thief! He stole the things, didn't he, Ben?" questioned Master Alfred.

Ben turned away.

"And we thrashed him well for it, didn't we, Ben?"

"Yes," said Ben.

"So you see, sir, it is true! there are two witnesses against you; do not therefore make your case quite hopeless by a persistence in falsehood," said the gentleman, speaking sternly for the first time.

Ishmael dropped his head, and the Burghe boys laughed.

Little Claudia's eyes blazed.

"Shame on you, Alfred Burghe! and you too, Ben! I know that you have told stories yourselves, for I see it in both your faces, just as I see that this poor boy has told the truth by his face!" she exclaimed. Then putting her arm around Ishmael's neck in the tender, motherly way that such little women will use to boys in distress, she said:

"There! hold up your head, and look them in the face. It is true, they are all against you; but, then, what of that, when I am on your side. It is a great thing, let me tell you, to have me on your side. I am Miss Merlin, my father's heiress; and he is the Chief Justice of the Supreme Court. And I am not sure but that I might make my papa have these two bad boys hanged if I insisted upon it! And I stand by you because I know you are telling the truth, and because my mamma always told me it would be my duty, as the first lady in the country, to protect the poor and the persecuted! So hold up your head, and look them in the face, and answer them!" said the young lady, throwing up her own head and shaking back her rich ringlets.

CHAPTER XXII.

ISHMAEL GAINS HIS FIRST VERDICT.

Honor and shame from no condition rise;
Act well your part, there all the honor lies.
Worth makes the man, and want of it the fellow,
The rest is all but leather and prunella.
—*Pope*.

So conjured, Ishmael lifted his face and confronted his accusers. It was truth and intellect encountering falsehood and stupidity. Who could doubt the issue?

"Sir," said the boy, "if you will look into the pockets of that young gentleman, Master Alfred, you will find the stolen fruit upon him."

Alfred Burghe started and turned to run. But the gentleman was too quick to let him escape, and caught him by the arm.

"What, sir! Mr. Middleton, would you search me at his bidding? Search the son of Commodore Burghe at the bidding of—nobody's son?" exclaimed the youth, struggling to free himself, while the blood seemed ready to burst from his red and swollen face.

"For your vindication, young sir! For your vindication," replied Mr. Middleton, proceeding to turn out the young gentleman's pockets, when lo! oranges, figs, and nuts rolled upon the ground.

"It is infamous—so it is!" exclaimed Master Alfred, mad with shame and rage.

"Yes, it is infamous," sternly replied Mr. Middleton.

"I mean it is infamous to treat a commodore's son in this way!"

"And I mean it is infamous in anybody's son to behave as you have, sir!"

"I bought the things at Nutt's shop! I bought them with my own money! They are mine! I never touched your things. That fellow did! He took them, and then told falsehoods about it."

"Sir," said Ishmael, "if you will examine that bundle, lying under that bush, you will find something there to prove which of us two speaks the truth."

Master Alfred made a dash for the bundle; but again Mr. Middleton was too quick for him, and caught it up. It was a red bandanna silk handkerchief stuffed full of parcels and tied at the corners. The handkerchief had the name of Alfred Burghe on one corner; the small parcel of nuts and raisins it contained were at once recognized by Mr. Middleton as his own.

"Oh, sir, sir!" began that gentleman severely, turning upon the detected culprit; but the young villain was at bay!

"Well?" he growled in defiance; "what now? what's all the muss about? Those parcels were what I took off his person when he was running away with them. Didn't I, Ben?"

Ben grumbled some inaudible answer, which Alfred assumed to be assent, for he immediately added:

"And I tied them up in my handkerchief to give them back to you. Didn't I, Ben?"

Ben mumbled something or other.

"And then I beat him for stealing. Didn't I, Ben?"

"Yes, you beat him," sulkily answered the younger brother.

Mr. Middleton gazed at the two boys in amazement; not that he entertained the slightest doubt of the innocence of Ishmael and the guilt of Alfred, but that he was simply struck with consternation at this instance of hardened juvenile depravity.

"Sir," continued the relentless young prosecutor, "if you will please to question Master Ben, I think he will tell you the truth. He has not told a downright story yet."

"What! why he has been corroborating his brother's testimony all along!" said Mr. Middleton.

"Only as to the assault, sir; not as to the theft. Please question him, sir, to finish this business."

"I will! Ben, who stole the fruit and nuts from my carriage?"

Ben dug his hands into his pockets and turned sullenly away.

"Did this poor boy steal them? For if I find he did, I will send him to prison. And I know you wouldn't like to see an innocent boy sent to prison. So tell me the truth. Did he, or did he not, steal the articles in question?"

"He did not; not so much as one of them," replied the younger Burghe.

"Did Alfred take them?"

Ben was sullenly silent.

"Did Alfred take them?" repeated Mr. Middleton.

"I won't tell you! So there now! I told you that fellow didn't! but I won't tell you who did! It is real hard of you to want me to tell on my own brother!" exclaimed Master Ben, walking off indignantly.

"That is enough; indeed the finding of the articles upon Alfred's person was enough," said Mr. Middleton.

"I think this poor boy's word ought to have been enough!" said Claudia.

"And now, sir!" continued Mr. Middleton, turning to Master Burghe; "you have been convicted of theft, falsehood, and cowardice—yes, and of the meanest falsehood and the basest cowardice I ever heard of. Under these circumstances, I cannot permit your future attendance upon my school. You are no longer a proper companion for my pupils. To-morrow I shall call upon your father, to tell him what has happened and advise him to send you to sea, under some strict captain, for a three or five years' cruise!"

"If you blow me to the governor, I'll be shot to death if I don't knife you, old fellow!" roared the young reprobate.

"Begone, sir!" was the answer of Mr. Middleton.

"Oh, I can go! But you look out! You're all a set of radicals, anyhow! making equals of all the rag, tag, and bobtail about. Look at Claudia there! What would Judge Merlin say if he was to see his daughter with her arm around that boy's neck!"

Claudia's eyes kindled dangerously, and she made one step towards the offender, saying:

"Hark you, Master Alfred Burghe. Don't you dare to take my name between your lips again! and don't you dare to come near me as long as you live, or even to say to anybody that you were ever acquainted with me! If you do I will make my papa have you hanged! For I do not choose to know a thief, liar, and coward!"

"Claudia! Claudia! Claudia! You shock me beyond all measure, my dear!" exclaimed the lady in a tone of real pain; and then lowering her voice she whispered—"'Thief, liar, coward!' what shocking words to issue from a young lady's lips."

"I know they are not nice words, Aunt Middleton, and if you will only teach me nicer ones I will use them instead. But are there any pretty words for ugly tricks?"

As this question was a "poser" that Mrs. Middleton did not attempt to answer, the little lady continued very demurely:

"I will look in 'Webster' when I get home and see if there are."

"My boy," said Mr. Middleton, approaching our lad, "I have accused you wrongfully. I am sorry for it and beg your pardon."

Ishmael looked up in surprise and with an "Oh, sir, please don't," blushed and hung his head. It seemed really dreadful to this poor boy that this grave and dignified gentleman should ask his pardon! And yet Mr. Middleton lost no dignity in this simple act, because it was right; he had wronged the poor lad, and owed an apology just as much as if he had wronged the greatest man in the country.

"And now, my boy," continued the gentleman, "be always as honest, as truthful, and as fearless as you have shown yourself to-day, and though your lot in life may be very humble—aye, of the very humblest—yet you will be respected in your lowly sphere." Here the speaker opened his portmonnaie and took from it a silver dollar, saying, "Take this, my boy, not as a reward for your integrity,—that, understand, is a matter of more worth than to be rewarded with money,—but simply as payment for your time and trouble in defending my property."

"Oh, sir, please don't. I really don't want the money," said Ishmael, shrinking from the offered coin.

"Oh, nonsense, my boy! You must be paid, you know," said Mr. Middleton, urging the dollar upon him.

"But I do not want pay for a mere act of civility," persisted Ishmael, drawing back.

"But your time and trouble, child; they are money to lads in your line of life."

"If you please, sir, it was a holiday, and I had nothing else to do."

"But take this to oblige me."

"Indeed, sir, I don't want it. The professor is very freehearted and pays me well for my work."

"The professor? What professor, my boy? I thought I had the honor to be the only professor in the neighborhood," said the gentleman, smiling.

"I mean Professor Jim Morris, sir," replied Ishmael, in perfect good faith.

"Oh! yes, exactly; I have heard of that ingenious and useful individual, who seems to have served his time at all trades, and taken degrees in all arts and sciences; but I did not know he was called a professor. So you are a student in his college!" smiled Mr. Middleton.

"I help him, sir, and he pays me," answered the boy.

"And what is your name, my good little fellow?"

"Ishmael Worth, sir."

"Oh, yes, exactly; you are the son of the little weaver up on Hut Hill, just across the valley from Brudenell Heights?"

"I am her nephew, sir."

"Are your parents living?"

"No, sir; I have been an orphan from my birth."

"Poor boy! And you are depending on your aunt for a home, and on your own labor for a support?"

"Yes, sir."

"Well, Ishmael, as you very rightly take pay from my brother professor, I do not know why you should refuse it from me."

Ishmael perhaps could not answer that question to his own satisfaction. At all events, he hesitated a moment before he replied:

"Why, you see, sir, what I do for the other professor is all in the line of my business; but the small service I have done for you is only a little bit of civility that I am always so glad to show to any gentleman—I mean to anybody at all, sir; even a poor wagoner, I often hold horses for them, sir! And, bless you, they couldn't pay me a penny."

"But I can, my boy! and besides you not only held my horse, and watered him, and rubbed him down, and watched my carriage, but you fought a stout battle in defense of my goods, and got yourself badly bruised by the thieves, and unjustly accused by me. Certainly, it is a poor offering I make in return for your services and sufferings in my interests. Here, my lad, I have thought better of it; here is a half eagle. Take it and buy something for yourself."

"Indeed, indeed, sir, I cannot. Please don't keep on asking me," persisted Ishmael, drawing back with a look of distress and almost of reproach on his fine face.

Now, why could not the little fellow take the money that was pressed upon him? He wanted it badly enough, Heaven knows! His best clothes were all patches, and this five dollar gold piece would have bought him a new suit. And besides there was an "Illustrated History of the United States" in that book-shop, that really and truly Ishmael would have been willing to give a finger off either of his hands to possess; and its price was just three dollars. Now, why didn't the little wretch take the money and buy the beautiful book with which his whole soul was enamored? The poor child did not know himself. But you and I know, reader, don't we? We know that he could not take the money, with the arm of that black-eyed little lady around his neck!

Yes, the arm of Claudia was still most tenderly and protectingly encircling his neck, and every few minutes she would draw down his rough head caressingly to her own damask cheek.

Shocking, wasn't it? And you wonder how her aunt and uncle could have stood by and permitted it. Because they couldn't help it. Miss Claudia was a little lady, angel born, who had never been contradicted in her life. Her father was a crochety old fellow, with a "theory," one result of which was that he let his trees and his daughter grow up unpruned as they liked.

But do not mistake Miss Claudia, or think her any better or any worse than she really was. Her caresses of the peasant boy looked as if she was republican in her principles and "fast" in her manners. She was neither the one nor the other. So far from being republican, she was just the most ingrained little aristocrat that ever lived! She was an aristocrat from the crown of her little, black, ringletted head to the sole of her tiny, gaitered foot; from her heart's core to her scarf-skin; so perfect an aristocrat that she was quite unconscious of being so. For instance, she looked upon herself as very little lower than the angels; and upon the working classes as very little higher than the brutes; if in her heart she acknowledged that all in the human shape were human, that was about the utmost extent of her liberalism. She and they were both clay, to be sure, but she was of the finest porcelain clay and they of the coarsest potter's earth. This theory had not been taught her, it was born in her, and so entirely natural and sincere that she was almost unconscious of its existence; certainly unsuspicious of its fallacy.

Thus, you see, she caressed Ishmael just exactly as she would have caressed her own Newfoundland dog; she defended his truth and honesty from false accusation just as she would have defended Fido's from a similar charge; she praised his fidelity and courage just as she would have praised Fido's; for, in very truth, she rated the peasant boy not one whit higher than the dog! Had she been a degree less proud, had she looked upon Ishmael as a human being with like passions and emotions as her own, she might have been more reserved in her manner. But being as proud as she was, she caressed and protected the noble peasant boy as a kind-hearted little lady would have caressed and protected a noble specimen of the canine race! Therefore, what might have been considered very forward and lowering in another little lady, was perfectly graceful and dignified in Miss Merlin.

But, meanwhile, the poor, earnest, enthusiastic boy! He didn't know that she rated him as low as any four-footed pet! He thought she appreciated him, very highly, too highly, as a human being! And his great little heart burned and glowed with joy and gratitude! And he would no more have taken pay for doing her uncle a service than he would have picked a pocket or robbed a henroost! He just adored her lovely clemency, and he was even turning over in his mind the problem how he, a poor, poor boy, hardly able to afford himself a halfpenny candle to read by, after dark, could repay her kindness—what could he find, invent, or achieve to please her!

Of all this Miss Claudia only understood his gratitude; and it pleased her as the gratitude of Fido might have done.

And she left his side for a moment, and raised herself on tiptoe and whispered to her uncle:

"Uncle, he is a noble fellow—isn't he, now? But he loves me better than he does you. So let me give him something."

Mr. Middleton placed the five dollar piece in her hand.

"No, no, no—not that! Don't you see it hurts his feelings to offer him that?"

"Well—but what then?"

"I'll tell you: When we drove up to Hamlin's I saw him standing before the shop, with his hands in his pockets, staring at the books in the windows, just as I have seen hungry children stare at the tarts and cakes in a pastry cook's. And I know he is hungry for a book! Now uncle, let me give him a book."

"Yes; but had not I better give it to him, Claudia?"

"Oh, if you like, and he'll take it from you! But, you know, there's Fido now, who sometimes gets contrary, and won't take anything from your hand, but no matter how contrary he is, will always take anything from mine. But you may try, uncle—you may try!"

This conversation was carried on in a whisper. When it was ended Mr. Middleton turned to Ishmael and said:

"Very well, my boy; I can but respect your scruples. Follow us back to Hamlin's."

And so saying, he helped his wife and his niece into the pony chaise, got in himself, and took the reins to drive on.

Miss Claudia looked back and watched Ishmael as he limped slowly and painfully after them. The distance was very short, and they soon reached the shop.

"Which is the window he was looking in, Claudia?" inquired Mr. Middleton.

"This one on the left hand, uncle."

"Ah! Come here, my boy; look into this window now, and tell me which of these books you would advise me to buy for a present to a young friend of mine?"

The poor fellow looked up with so much perplexity in his face at the idea of this grave, middle-aged gentleman asking advice of him, that Mr. Middleton hastened to say:

"The reason I ask you, Ishmael, is because, you being a boy would be a better judge of another boy's tastes than an old man like me could be. So now judge by yourself, and tell me which book you think would please my young friend best. Look at them all, and take time."

"Oh, yes, sir. But I don't want time! Anybody could tell in a minute which book a boy would like!"

"Which, then?"

"Oh, this, this, this! 'History of the United States,' all full of pictures!"

"But here is 'Robinson Crusoe,' and here is the 'Arabian Nights'; why not choose one of them?"

"Oh, no, sir—don't! They are about people that never lived, and things that aren't true; and though they are very interesting, I know, there is no solid satisfaction in them like there is in this——"

"Well, now 'this.' What is the great attraction of this to a boy? Why, it's nothing but dry history," said Mr. Middleton, with an amused smile, while he tried to "pump" the poor lad.

"Oh, sir, but there's so much in it! There's Captain John Smith, and Sir Walter Raleigh, and Jamestown, and Plymouth, and the Pilgrim Fathers, and John Hancock, and Patrick Henry, and George Washington, and the Declaration of Independence, and Bunker's Hill, and Yorktown! Oh!" cried Ishmael with an ardent burst of enthusiasm.

"You seem to know already a deal more of the history of our country than some of my first-class young gentlemen have taken the trouble to learn," said Mr. Middleton, in surprise.

"Oh, no, I don't, sir. I know no more than what I have read in a little thin book, no bigger than your hand, sir, that was lent to me by the professor; but I know by that how much good there must be in this, sir."

"Ah! a taste of the dish has made you long for a feast."

"Sir?"

"Nothing, my boy, but that I shall follow your advice in the selection of a book," said the gentleman, as he entered the shop. The lady and the little girl remained in the carriage, and Ishmael stood feasting his hungry eyes upon the books in the window.

Presently the volume he admired so much disappeared.

"There! I shall never see it any more!" said Ishmael, with a sigh; "but I'm glad some boy is going to get it! Oh, won't he be happy to-night, though! Wish it was I! No, I don't neither; it's a sin to covet!"

And a few minutes after the gentleman emerged from the shop with an oblong packet in his hand.

"It was the last copy he had left, my boy, and I have secured it! Now do you really think my young friend will like it?" asked Mr. Middleton.

"Oh, sir, won't he though, neither!" exclaimed Ishmael, in sincere hearty sympathy with the prospective happiness of another.

"Well, then, my little friend must take it," said Mr. Middleton, offering the packet to Ishmael.

"Sir!" exclaimed the latter.

"It is for you, my boy."

"Oh, sir, I couldn't take it, indeed! It is only another way of paying me for a common civility," said Ishmael, shrinking from the gift, yet longing for the book.

"It is not; it is a testimonial of my regard for you, my boy! Receive it as such."

"I do not deserve such a testimonial, and cannot receive it, sir," persisted Ishmael.

"There, uncle, I told you so!" exclaimed Claudia, springing from the carriage and taking the book from the hand of Mr. Middleton.

She went to the side of Ishmael, put her arm around his neck, drew his head down against hers, leaned her bright cheek against his, and said:

"Come, now, take the book; I know you want it; take it like a good boy; take it for my sake,"

Still Ishmael hesitated a little.

Then she raised the parcel and pressed it to her lips and handed it to him again, saying:

"There, now, you see I've kissed it. Fido would take anything I kissed; won't you?"

Ishmael now held out his hands eagerly for the prize, took it and pressed it to his jacket, exclaiming awkwardly but earnestly:

"Thank you, miss! Oh, thank you a thousand, thousand times, miss! You don't know how much I wanted this book, and how glad I am!"

"Oh, yes, I do. I'm a witch, and know people's secret thoughts. But why didn't you take the book when uncle offered it?"

"If you are a witch, miss, you can tell."

"So I can; it was because you don't love uncle as well as you love me! Well, Fido doesn't either. But uncle is a nice man for all that."

"I wonder who 'Fido' is," thought the poor boy. "I do wonder who he is; her brother, I suppose."

"Come, Claudia, my love, get into the carriage; we must go home," said Mr. Middleton, as he assisted his niece to her seat.

"I thank you very much, sir, for this very beautiful book," said Ishmael, going up to Mr. Middleton and taking off his hat.

"You are very welcome, my boy; so run home now and enjoy it," replied the gentleman, as he sprang into the carriage and took the reins.

"'Run home?' how can he run home, uncle? If he lives at the weaver's, it is four miles off! How can he run it, or even walk it? Don't you see how badly hurt he is? Why, he could scarcely limp from the pond to the shop! I think it would be only kind, uncle, to take him up beside you. We pass close to the hut, you know, in going home, and we could set him down."

"Come along, then, my little fellow! The young princess says you are to ride home with us, and her highness' wishes are not to be disobeyed!" laughed Mr. Middleton, holding out his hand to help the boy into the carriage.

Ishmael made no objection to this proposal: but eagerly clambered up to the offered seat beside the gentleman.

The reins were moved, and they set off at a spanking pace, and were soon bowling along the turnpike road that made a circuit through the forest toward Brudenell Heights.

The sun had set, a fresh breeze had sprung up, and, as they were driving rapidly in the eye of the wind, there was scarcely opportunity for conversation. In little more than an hour they reached a point in the road within a few hundred yards of the weaver's hut.

"Here we are, my boy! Now, do you think you can get home without help?" inquired Mr. Middleton, as he stopped the carriage.

"Oh, yes, sir, thank you!" replied Ishmael, as he clambered down to the ground. He took off his hat beside the carriage, and making his best Sabbath-school bow, said:

"Good-evening, sir; good-evening, madam and miss, and thank you very much."

"Good-evening, my little man; there get along home with you out of the night air," said Mr. Middleton.

Mrs. Middleton and the little lady nodded and smiled their adieus.

And Ishmael struck into the narrow and half hidden footpath that led from the highway to the hut.

The carriage started on its way.

"A rather remarkable boy, that," said Mr. Middleton, as they drove along the forest road encircling the crest of the hills towards Brudenell Heights, that moonlit, dewy evening; "a rather remarkable boy! He has an uncommonly fine head! I should really like to examine it! The intellect and moral organs seem wonderfully developed! I really should like to examine it carefully at my leisure."

"He has a fine face, if it were not so pale and thin," said Mrs. Middleton.

"Poor, poor fellow," said Claudia, in a tone of deep pity, "he is thin and pale, isn't he? And Fido is so fat and sleek! I'm afraid he doesn't get enough to eat, uncle!"

"Who, Fido?"

"No, the other one, the boy! I say I'm afraid he don't get enough to eat. Do you think he does?"

"I—I'm afraid not, my dear!"

"Then I think it is a shame, uncle! Rich people ought not to let the poor, who depend upon them, starve! Papa says that I am to come into my mamma's fortune as soon as I am eighteen. When I do, nobody in this world shall want. Everybody shall have as much as ever they can eat three times a day. Won't that be nice?"

"Magnificent, my little princess, if you can only carry out your ideas," replied her uncle.

"Oh! but I will! I will, if it takes every dollar of my income! My mamma told me that when I grew up I must be the mother of the poor! And doesn't a mother feed her children?"

Middleton laughed.

"And as for that poor boy on the hill, he shall have tarts and cheese cakes, and plum pudding, and roast turkey, and new books every day; because I like him; I like him so much; I like him better than I do anything in the world except Fido!"

"Well, my dear," said Mr. Middleton, seizing this opportunity of administering an admonition, "like him as well as Fido, if you please; but do not pet him quite as freely as you pet Fido."

"But I will, if I choose to! Why shouldn't I?" inquired the young lady, erecting her haughty little head.

"Because he is not a dog!" dryly answered her uncle.

"Oh! but he likes petting just as much as Fido! He does indeed, uncle; I assure you! Oh, I noticed that."

"Nevertheless, Miss Claudia, I must object in future to your making a pet of the poor boy, whether you or he like it or not."

"But I will, if I choose!" persisted the little princess, throwing back her head and shaking all her ringlets.

Mr. Middleton sighed, shook his head, and turned to his wife, whispering, in a low tone:

"What are we to do with this self-willed elf? To carry out her father's ideas, and let her nature have unrestrained freedom to develop itself, will be the ruin of her! Unless she is controlled and guided she is just the girl to grow up wild and eccentric, and end in running away with her own footman."

These words were not intended for Miss Claudia's ears; but notwithstanding, or rather because of, that, she heard every syllable, and immediately fired up, exclaiming:

"Who are you talking of marrying a footman? Me! me! me! Do you think that I would ever marry anyone beneath me?' No, indeed! I will live to be an old maid, before I will marry anybody but a lord! that I am determined upon!"

"You will never reach that consummation of your hopes, my dear, by petting a peasant boy, even though you do look upon him as little better than a dog," said Mr. Middleton, as he drew up before the gates of Brudenell.

A servant was in attendance to open them. And as the party were now at home, the conversation ceased for the present.

Claudia ran in to exhibit her purchases.

Her favorite, Fido, ran to meet her, barking with delight.

CHAPTER XXIII.

ISHMAEL'S PROGRESS.

Athwart his face when blushes pass
To be so poor and weak,
He falls into the dewy grass,
To cool his fevered cheek;
And hears a music strangely made,
That you have never heard,
A sprite in every rustling blade,
That sings like any bird!
—*Monckton Milnes.*

Meanwhile on that fresh, dewy, moonlight summer evening, along the narrow path leading through the wood behind the hut, Ishmael limped—the happiest little fellow, despite his wounds and bruises, that ever lived. He was so happy that he half suspected his delight to be all unreal, and feared to wake up presently and find it was but a dream, and see the little black-eyed girl, the ride in the carriage, and, above all, the new "Illustrated History of the United States" vanish into the land of shades.

In this dazed frame of mind he reached the hut and opened the door.

The room was lighted only by the blazing logs of a wood fire, which the freshness of the late August evening on the hills made not quite unwelcome.

The room was in no respect changed in the last twelve years. The well-cared-for though humble furniture was still in its old position.

Hannah, as of old, was seated at her loom, driving the shuttle back and forth with a deafening clatter. Hannah's face was a little more sallow and wrinkled, and her hair a little more freely streaked with gray than of yore: that was all the change visible in her personal appearance. But long continued solitude had rendered her as taciturn and unobservant as if she had been born deaf and blind.

She had not seen Reuben Gray since that Sunday when Ishmael was christened and Reuben insisted on bringing the child home, and when, in the bitterness of her woe and her shame, she had slammed the door in his face. Gray had left the neighborhood, and it was reported that he had been promoted to the management of a rich farm in the forest of Prince George's.

"There is your supper on the hearth, child," she said, without ceasing her work or turning her head as Ishmael entered.

Hannah was a good aunt; but she was not his mother; if she had been, she would at least have turned around to look at the boy, and then she would have seen he was hurt, and would have asked an explanation. As it was she saw nothing.

And Ishmael was very glad of it. He did not wish to be pitied or praised; he wished to be left to himself and his own devices, for this evening at least, when he had such a distinguished guest as his grand new book to entertain!

Ishmael took up his bowl of mush and milk, sat down, and with a large spoon shoveled his food down his throat with more dispatch than delicacy—just as he would have shoveled coal into a cellar. The sharp cries of a hungry stomach must be appeased, he knew; but with as little loss of time as possible, particularly when there was a hungry brain waiting to set to work upon a rich feast already prepared for it!

So in three minutes he put away his bowl and spoon, drew his three-legged stool to the corner of the fireplace, where he could see to read, seated himself, opened his packet, and displayed his treasure. It was a large, thick, octavo volume, bound in stout leather, and filled with portraits and pictured battle scenes. And on the fly-leaf was written:

"Presented to Ishmael Worth, as a reward of merit, by his friend James Middleton."

Ishmael read that with a new accession of pleasure. Then he turned the leaves to peep at the hidden jewels in this intellectual casket. Then he closed the book and laid it on his knees and shut his eyes and held his breath for joy.

He had been enamored of this beauty for months and months. He had fallen in love with it at first sight, when he had seen its pages open, with a portrait of George Washington on the right and a picture of the Battle of Yorktown on the left, all displayed in the show window of Hainlin's book shop. He had loved it and longed for it with a passionate ardor ever since. He had spent all his half holidays in going to Baymouth and standing before Hamlin's window and staring at the book, and asking the price of it, and wondering if he should ever be able to save money enough to buy it. Now, to be in love with an unattainable woman is bad enough, the dear knows! But to be in love with an unattainable book—Oh, my gracious! Lover-like, he had thought of this book all day, and dreamt of it all night; but never hoped to possess it!

And now he really owned it! He had won it as a reward for courage, truth, and honesty! It was lying there on his knees. It was all his own! His intense satisfaction can only be compared to that of a youthful bridegroom who has got his beloved all to himself at last! It might have been said of the one, as it is often said of the other, "It was the happiest day of his life!"

Oh, doubtless in after years the future statesman enjoyed many a hard-won victory. Sweet is the breath of fame! Sweet the praise of nations! But I question whether, in all the vicissitudes, successes, failures, trials, and triumphs of his future life, Ishmael Worth ever tasted such keen joy as he did this night in the possession of this book.

He enjoyed it more than wealthy men enjoy their great libraries. To him, this was the book of books, because it was the history of his own country.

There were thousands and thousands of young men, sons of gentlemen, in schools and colleges, reading this glorious history of the young republic as a task, with indifference or disgust, while this poor boy, in the hill-top hut, pored over its pages with all the enthusiasm of reverence and love! And why—what caused this difference? Because they were of the commonplace, while he was one in a million. This was the history of the rise and progress of the United States; Ishmael Worth was an ardent lover and worshiper of his country, as well as of all that was great and good! He had the brain to comprehend and the heart to reverence the divine idea embodied in the Federal Union. He possessed these, not by inheritance, not by education, but by the direct inspiration of Heaven, who, passing over the wealthy and the prosperous, ordained this poor outcast boy, this despised, illegitimate son of a country weaver, to become a great power among the people! a great pillar of the State.

No one could guess this now. Not even the boy himself. He did not know that he was any richer in heart or brain than other boys of his age. No, most probably, by analogy, he thought himself in this respect as well as in all others, poorer than his neighbors. He covered his book carefully, and studied it perseveringly; studied it not only while it was a novelty, but after he had grown familiar with its incidents.

I have dwelt so long upon this subject because the possession of this book at this time had a signal effect in forming Ishmael Worth's character and directing the current of the boy's whole future life. It was one of the first media of his inspiration. Its heroes, its warriors, and its statesmen were his idols, his models, and his exemplars. By studying them he became himself high-toned, chivalrous, and devoted. Through the whole autumn he worked hard all day, upheld with the prospect of returning home at night to—his poor hut and his silent aunt?—oh, no, but to the grand stage upon which the Revolutionary struggle was exhibited and to the company of its heroes—Washington, Putnam, Marion, Jefferson, Hancock, and Henry! He saw no more for some time of his friends at Brudenell Hall. He knew that Mr. Middleton had a first-class school at his house, and he envied the privileged young gentlemen who had the happiness to attend it: little knowing how unenviable a privilege the said young gentlemen considered that attendance and how a small portion of happiness they derived from it.

The winter set in early and severely. Hannah took a violent cold and was confined to her bed with inflammatory rheumatism. For many weeks she was unable to do a stroke of work. During this time of trial Ishmael worked for both—rising very early in the morning to get the frugal breakfast and set the house in order before going out to his daily occupation of "jobbing" with the professor—and coming home late at night to get the supper and to split the wood and to bring the water for the next day's supply. Thus, as long as his work lasted, he was the provider as well as the nurse of his poor aunt.

But at last there came one of the heaviest falls of snow ever known in that region. It lay upon the ground for many weeks, quite blocking up the roads, interrupting travel, and of course putting a stop to the professor's jobbing and to Ishmael's income. Provisions were soon exhausted, and there was no way of getting more. Hannah and Ishmael suffered hunger. Ishmael bore this with great fortitude. Hannah also bore it patiently as long as the tea lasted. But when that woman's consolation failed she broke down and complained bitterly.

The Baymouth turnpike was about the only passable road in the neighborhood. By it Ishmael walked on to the village, one bitter cold morning, to try to get credit for a quarter of a pound of tea.

But Nutt would see him hanged first.

Disappointed and sorrowful, Ishmael turned his steps from the town. He had come about a mile on his homeward road, when something glowing like a coal of fire on the glistening whiteness of the snow caught his eye.

It was a red morocco pocketbook lying in the middle of the road. There was not a human creature except Ishmael himself on the road or anywhere in sight. Neither had he passed anyone on his way from the village. Therefore it was quite in vain that he looked up and down and all around for the owner of the pocketbook as he raised it from the ground. No possible claimant was to be seen. He opened it and examined its contents. It contained a little gold and silver, not quite ten dollars in all; but a fortune for Ishmael, in his present needy condition. There was no name on the pocketbook and not a scrap of paper in it by which the owner might be discovered. There was nothing in it but the untraceable silver and gold. It seemed to have dropped from heaven for Ishmael's own benefit! This was his thought as he turned with the impulse to fly directly back to the village and invest a portion of the money in necessaries for Hannah.

What was it that suddenly arrested his steps? The recollection that the money was not his own! that to use it even for the best purpose in the world would be an act of dishonesty.

He paused and reflected. The devil took that opportunity to tempt him—whispering:

"You found the pocketbook and you cannot find the owner; therefore it is your own, you know."

"You know it isn't," murmured Ishmael's conscience.

"Well, even so, it is no harm to borrow a dollar or two to get your poor sick aunt a little tea and sugar. You could pay it back again before the pocketbook is claimed, even if it is ever claimed," mildly insinuated the devil.

"It would be borrowing without leave," replied conscience.

"But for your poor, sick, suffering aunt! think of her, and make her happy this evening with a consoling cup of tea! Take only half a dollar for that good purpose. Nobody could blame you for that," whimpered the devil, who was losing ground.

"I would like to make dear Aunt Hannah happy to-night. But I am sure George Washington would not approve of my taking what don't belong to me for that or any other purpose. And neither would Patrick Henry, nor John Hancock. And so I won't do it," said Ishmael, resolutely putting the pocketbook in his vest pocket and buttoning his coat tight over it, and starting at brisk pace homeward.

You see his heroes had come to his aid and saved him in the first temptation of his life.

"Ah, you may be sure that in after days the rising politician met and resisted many a temptation to sell his vote, his party, or his soul for a "consideration"; but none more serious to the man than this one was to the boy.

When Ishmael had trudged another mile of his homeward road, it suddenly occurred to him that he might possibly meet or overtake the owner of the pocketbook, who would know his property in a moment if he should see it. And with this thought he took it from his pocket and carried it conspicuously in his hand until he reached home, without having met a human being.

It was about twelve meridian when he lifted the latch and entered. Hannah was in bed; but she turned her hungry eyes anxiously on him—as she eagerly inquired:

"Did you bring the tea, Ishmael?"

"No, Aunt Hannah; Mr. Nutt wouldn't trust me," replied the boy sadly, sinking down in a chair; for he was very weak from insufficient food, and the long walk had exhausted him.

Hannah began to complain piteously. Do not blame her, reader. You would fret, too, if you were sick in bed, and longing for a cup of tea, without having the means of procuring it.

To divert her thoughts Ishmael went and showed the pocketbook, and told her the history of his finding it.

Hannah seized it with the greedy grasp with which the starving catch at money. She opened it, and counted the gold and silver.

"Where did you say you found it, Ishmael?"

"I told you a mile out of the village."

"Only that little way! Why didn't you go back and buy my tea?" she inquired, with an injured look.

"Oh, aunt! the money wasn't mine, you know!" said Iahmael.

"Well, I don't say it was. But you might have borrowed a dollar from it, and the owner would have never minded, for I dare say he'd be willing to give two dollars as a reward for finding the pocketbook. You might have bought my tea if you had eared for me! But nobody cares for me now! No one ever did but Reuben—poor fellow!"

"Indeed, Aunt Hannah, I do care for you a great deal! I love you dearly; and I did want to take some of the money and buy your tea."

"Why didn't you do it, then?"

"Oh, Aunt Hannah, the Lord has commanded, 'Thou shalt not steal.'"

"It wouldn't have been stealing; it would have been borrowing."

"But I know Patrick Henry and John Hancock wouldn't have borrowed what didn't belong to them!"

"Plague take Patrick Hancock and John Henry, I say! I believe they are turning your head! What have them dead and buried old people to do with folks that are alive and starving?"

"Oh, Aunt Hannah! scold me as much as you please, but don't speak so of the great men!" said Ishmael, to whom all this was sheer blasphemy and nothing less.

"Great fiddlesticks' ends! No tea yesterday, and no tea for breakfast this morning, and no tea for supper to-night! And I laying helpless with the rheumatism, and feeling as faint as if I should sink and die; and my head aching ready to burst! And I would give anything in the world for a cup of tea, because I know it would do me so much good, and I can't get it! And you have money in your pocket and won't buy it for me! No, not if I die for the want of it! You, that I have been a mother to! That's the way you pay me, is it, for all my care?"

"Oh, Aunt Hannah, dear, I do love you, and I would do anything in the world for you; but, indeed, I am sure Patrick Henry—"

"Hang Patrick Henry! If you mention his name to me again I'll box your ears!"

Ishmael dropped his eyes to the ground and sighed deeply.

"After all I have done for you, ever since you were left a helpless infant on my hands, for you to let me lie here and die, yes, actually die, for the want of a cup of tea, before you will spend one quarter of a dollar to get it for me! Oh! Oh! Oh! Oo-oo-oo!"

And Hannah put her hands to her face, and cried like a baby.

You see Hannah was honest; but she was not heroic; her nerves were very weak, and her spirits very low. Inflammatory rheumatism is often more or less complicated with heart disease. And the latter is a great demoralizer of mind as well as body. And that was Hannah's case. We must make every excuse for the weakness of the poor, over-tasked, all enduring, long-suffering woman, broken down at last.

But not a thought of blaming her entered Ishmael's mind. Full of love, he bent over her, saying:

"Oh, Aunt Hannah, don't, don't cry! You shall have your tea this very evening; indeed you shall!" And he stooped and kissed her tenderly.

Then he put on his cap and went and took his only treasure, his beloved "History," from its place of honor on the top of the bureau; and cold, hungry, and tired as he was, he set off again to walk the four long miles to the village, to try to sell his book for half price to the trader.

Reader! I am not fooling you with a fictitious character here. Do you not love this boy? And will you not forgive me if I have already lingered too long over the trials and triumphs of his friendless but heroic boyhood! He who in his feeble childhood resists small temptations, and makes small sacrifices, is very apt in his strong manhood to conquer great difficulties and achieve great successes.

Ishmael, with his book under his arm, went as fast as his exhausted frame would permit him on the road towards Baymouth. But as he was obliged to walk slowly and pause to rest frequently, he made but little progress, so that it was three o'clock in the afternoon before he reached Hamlin's book shop.

There was a customer present, and Ishmael had to wait until the man was served and had departed, before he could mention his own humble errand. This short interview Ishmael spent in taking the brown paper cover off his book, and looking fondly at the cherished volume. It was like taking a last leave of it. Do not blame this as a weakness. He was so poor, so very poor; this book was his only treasure and his only joy in life. The tears arose to his eyes, but he kept them from falling.

When the customer was gone, and the bookseller was at leisure, Ishmael approached and laid the volume on the counter, saying:

"Have you another copy of this work in the shop, Mr. Hamlin?"

"No; I wish I had half-a-dozen; for I could sell them all; but I intend to order some from Baltimore to-day."

"Then maybe you would buy this one back from me at half price? I have taken such care of it, that it is as good as new, you see. Look at it for yourself."

"Yes, I see it looks perfectly fresh; but here is some writing on the fly leaf; that would have to be torn out, you know; so that the book could never be sold as a new one again; I should have to sell it as a second hand one, at half price; that would be a dollar and a half, so that you see I would only give you a dollar for it."

"Sir?" questioned Ishmael, in sad amazement.

"Yes; because you know, I must have my own little profit on it."

"Oh, I see; yes, to be sure," assented Ishmael, with a sigh.

But to part with his treasure and get no more than that! It was like Esau selling his birthright for a mess of pottage.

However, the poor cannot argue with the prosperous. The bargain was soon struck. The book was sold and the boy received his dollar. And then the dealer, feeling a twinge of conscience, gave him a dime in addition.

"Thank you, sir; I will take this out in paper and wafers, if you please. I want some particularly," said Ishmael.

Having received a half dozen sheets of paper and a small box of wafers, the lad asked the loan of pen and ink; and then, standing at the counter, he wrote a dozen circulars as follows:

FOUND, A POCKET-BOOK.

On the Baymouth Turnpike Road, on Friday morning, I picked up a pocketbook, which the owner can have by coming to me at the Hill Hut and proving his property.

Ishmael Worth.

Having finished these, he thanked the bookseller and left the shop, saying to himself:

"I won't keep that about me much longer to be a constant temptation and cross."

He first went and bought a quarter of a pound of tea, a pound of sugar, and a bag of meal from Nutt's general shop for Hannah; and leaving them there until he should have got through his work, he went around the village and wafered up his twelve posters at various conspicuous points on fences, walls, pumps, trees, etc.

Then he called for his provisions, and set out on his long walk home.

CLAUDIA TO THE RESCUE.

Let me not now ungenerously condemn
My few good deeds on impulse—half unwise
And scarce approved by reason's colder eyes;
I will not blame, nor weakly blush for them;
The feelings and the actions then stood right;
And if regret, for half a moment sighs
That worldly wisdom in its keener sight
Had ordered matters so and so, my heart,
Still, in its fervor loves a warmer part
Than Prudence wots of; while my faithful mind,
Heart's consort, also praises her for this;
And on our conscience little load I find
If sometimes we have helped another's bliss,
At some small cost of selfish loss behind.
—*M.F. Tupper.*

As Ishmael left the village by the eastern arm of the road a gay sleighing party dashed into it from the western one. Horses prancing, bells ringing, veils flying, and voices chattering, they drew up before Hamlin's shop. The party consisted of Mr. Middleton, his wife, and his niece.

Mr. Middleton gave the reins to his wife and got out and went into the shop to make a few purchases.

When his parcels had been made up and paid for, he turned to leave the shop; but then, as if suddenly recollecting something, he looked back and inquired:

"By the way, Hamlin, have those Histories come yet?"

"No, sir; but I shall write for them again by this evening's mail; I cannot think what has delayed them. However, sir, there is one copy that I can let you have, if that will be of any service."

"Certainly, certainly; it is better than nothing; let me look at it," said Mr. Middleton, coming back from the counter and taking the book from Hamlin's hands.

In turning over the leaves he came to the presentation page, on which he recognized his own handwriting in the lines:

"Presented to Ishmael Worth, as a reward of merit, by his friend James Middleton."

"Why, this is the very copy I gave to that poor little fellow on the hill, last August! How did you come by it again?" asked Mr. Middleton, in astonishment.

"He brought it here to sell about an hour ago, sir, and as it was a perfectly fresh copy, and I knew you were in a hurry for some of them, I bought it of him," replied the dealer.

"But why should the lad have sold his book?"

"Why, law, sir, you cannot expect boys of his class to appreciate books. I dare say he wanted his money to spend in tops or marbles, or some such traps!" replied the dealer.

"Very like, very like! though I am sorry to think so of that little fellow. I had hoped better things of him," assented Mr. Middleton.

"Law, sir, boys will be boys."

"Certainly; well, put the book in paper for me, and say what you are going to ask for it."

"Well, sir, it is as good as new, and the work is much called for just about now in this neighborhood. So I s'pose I shall have to ask you about three dollars."

"That is the full price. Did you give the boy that?" inquired the gentleman.

"Well, no, sir; but you know I must have my own little profit," replied the dealer, reddening.

"Certainly," assented Mr. Middleton, taking out his purse—a delicate, effeminate-looking article, that seemed to have been borrowed from his wife, paying Hamlin and carrying off the book.

As he got into the sleigh and took the reins with one hand, hugging up his parcels and his purse loosely to his breast with the other, Mrs. Middleton said:

"Now, James, don't go and plant my purse on the road, as you did your pocketbook this morning!"

"My dear, pray don't harp on that loss forever! It was not ruinous! There was only nine dollars in it."

"And if there had been nine hundred, it would have been the same thing!" said the lady.

Her husband laughed, put away his purse, stowed away his parcels, and then, having both hands at liberty, took the reins and set off for home.

As he dashed along the street a poster caught his attention. He drew up, threw the reins to Mrs. Middleton, jumped out, pulled down the poster, and returned to his seat in the sleigh.

"Here we are, my dear, all right; the pocketbook is found," he smiled, as he again took possession of the reins.

"Found?" she echoed.

"Yes, by that boy, Worth, you know, who behaved so well in that affair with the Burghes."

"Oh, yes! and he found the pocketbook?"

"Yes, and advertised it in this way, poor little fellow!"

And Mr. Middleton drove slowly while he read the circular to his wife.

"Well, we can call by the hut as we go home, and you can get out and get it, and you will not forget to reward the poor boy for his honesty. He might have kept it, you know; for there was nothing in it that could be traced."

"Very well; I will do as you recommend; but I have a quarrel with the young fellow, for all that," said Mr. Middleton.

"Upon what ground?" inquired his wife.

"Why, upon the ground of his just having sold the book I gave him last August as a reward of merit."

"What did he do that for?"

"To get money to buy tops and marbles."

"It is false!" burst out Claudia, speaking for the first time.

"Claudia! Claudia! Claudia! How dare you charge your uncle with falsehood?" exclaimed Mrs. Middleton, horrified.

"I don't accuse him, aunt. He don't know anything about it! Somebody has told him falsehoods about poor Ishmael, and he believes it just as he did before," exclaimed the little lady with flashing eyes.

"Well, then, what did he sell it for, Claudia?" inquired her uncle, smiling.

"I don't believe he sold it at all!" said Miss Claudia.

Her uncle quietly untied the packet, and placed the book before her, open at the fly-leaf, upon which the names of the donor and the receiver were written.

"Well, then, I believe he must have sold it to get something to eat," said Ishmael's obstinate little advocate; "for I heard Mr. Rutherford say that there was a great deal of suffering among the frozen-out working classes this winter."

"It may be as you say, my dear. I do not know."

"Well, uncle, you ought to know, then! It is the duty of the prosperous to find out the condition of the poor! When I come into my fortune—"

"Yes, I know; we have heard all that before; the millennium will be brought about, of course. But, if I am not mistaken, there is your little protégé on the road before us!" said Mr. Middleton, slacking his horse's speed, as he caught sight of Ishmael.

"Yes, it is he! And look at him! does he look like a boy who is thinking of playing marbles and spinning tops?" inquired Miss Claudia.

Indeed, no! no one who saw the child could have connected childish sports with him. He was creeping wearily along, bent under the burden of the bag of meal he carried on his back, and looking from behind more like a little old man than a boy.

Mr. Middleton drove slowly as he approached him.

Ishmael drew aside to let the sleigh pass.

But Mr. Middleton drew up to examine the boy more at his leisure.

The stooping gait, the pale, broad forehead, the hollow eyes, the wasted cheeks and haggard countenance, so sad to see in so young a lad, spoke more eloquently than words could express the famine, the cold, the weariness, and illness he suffered.

"Oh, uncle, if you haven't got a stone in your bosom instead of a heart, you will call the poor fellow here and give him a seat with us! He is hardly able to stand! And it is so bitter cold!" said Miss Claudia, drawing her own warm, sable cloak around her.

"But—he is such an object! His clothes are all over patches," said Mr. Middleton, who liked sometimes to try the spirit of his niece.

"But, uncle, he is so clean! just as clean as you are, or even as I am," said Miss Claudia.

"And he has got a great bag on his back!"

"Well, uncle, that makes it so much harder for him to walk this long, long road, and is so much the more reason for you to take him in. You can put the bag down under your feet. And now if you don't call him here in one minute, I will—so there now! Ishmael! Ishmael, I say! Here, sir! here!" cried the little lady, standing up in the sleigh.

"Ishmael! come here, my boy," called Mr. Middleton.

Our boy came as fast as his weakness and his burden would permit him,

"Get in here, my boy, and take this seat beside me. We are going the same way that you are walking, and we can give you a ride without inconveniencing ourselves. And besides I want to talk with you," said Mr. Middleton, as Ishmael came up to the side of the sleigh and took off his hat to the party. He bowed and took the seat indicated, and Mr. Middleton started his horses, driving slowly as he talked.

"Ishmael, did you ever have a sleigh-ride before?" inquired Claudia, bending forward and laying her little gloved hand upon his shoulder, as he sat immediately before her.

"No, miss."

"Oh, then, how you'll enjoy it! It is so grand! But only wait until uncle is done talking and we are going fast! It is like flying! You'll see! But what do you think, Ishmael! Do you think somebody—I know it was that old Hamlin—didn't go and tell uncle that you went and——"

"Claudia, Claudia, hold your little tongue, my dear, for just five minutes, if you possibly can, while I speak to this boy myself!" said Mr. Middleton.

"Ah, you see uncle don't want to hear of his mistakes. He is not vain of them."

"Will you hold your tongue just for three minutes, Claudia?"

"Yes, sir, to oblige you; but I know I shall get a sore throat by keeping my mouth open so long."

And with that, I regret to say, Miss Merlin put out her little tongue and literally "held" it between her thumb and finger as she sank back in her seat.

"Ishmael," said Mr. Middleton, "I have seen your poster about the pocketbook. It is mine; I dropped it this forenoon, when we first came out."

"Oh, sir, I'm so glad I have found the owner, and that it is you!" exclaimed Ishmael, putting his hand in his pocket to deliver the lost article.

"Stop, stop, stop, my impetuous little friend! Don't you know I must prove my property before I take possession of it? That is to say, I must describe it before I see it, so as to convince you that it is really mine?"

"Oh, sir, but that was only put in my poster to prevent imposters from claiming it," said Ishmael, blushing.

"Nevertheless, it is better to do business in a business-like way," persisted Mr. Middleton, putting his hand upon that of the boy to prevent him from drawing forth the pocketbook. "Imprimis—a crimson pocketbook, with yellow silk lining; items—in one compartment three quarter eagles in gold; in another two dollars in silver. Now is that right?"

"Oh, yes, sir; but it wasn't necessary; you know that!" said Ishmael, putting the pocketbook in the hand of its owner.

Mr. Middleton opened it, took out a piece of gold and would have silently forced it in the hand of the poor boy, but Ishmael respectfully but firmly put back the offering.

"Take it, my boy; it is usual to do so, you know," said Mr. Middleton, in a low voice.

"Not for me, sir; please do not offer me money again unless I have earned it," replied the boy, in an equally low tone.

"But as a reward for finding the pocketbook," persisted Mr. Middleton.

"That was a piece of good fortune, sir, and deserved no reward," replied Ishmael.

"Then for restoring it to me."

"That was simple honesty, sir, and merited nothing either."

"Still, there would be no harm in your taking this from me," insisted Mr. Middleton, pressing the gold upon the boy.

"No, sir; perhaps there would not be; but I am sure—I am very sure—that Thomas Jefferson when he was a boy would never have let anybody pay him for being honest!"

"Who?" demanded Mr. Middleton, with a look of perplexity.

"Thomas Jefferson, sir, who wrote the Declaration of Independence, that I read of in that beautiful history you gave me."

"Oh!" said Mr. Middleton, ceasing to press the money upon the boy, but putting it in his pocketbook and returning the pocketbook to his pocket. "Oh! and by the way, I am told that you have sold that history to-day."

"Yes! for money to buy spinning-tops and marbles with!" put in Miss Claudia.

Ishmael looked around in dismay for a moment, and then burst out with:

"Oh, sir! indeed, indeed I did not!"

"What! you didn't sell it?" exclaimed Mr. Middleton.

"Oh, yes, sir, I sold it!" said Ishmael, as the irrepressible tears rushed to his eyes. "I sold it! I was obliged to do so! Patrick Henry would have done it, sir!"

"But you did not sell it to get money to buy toys with?"

"Oh, no, no, no, sir! It was a matter of life and death, else I never would have parted with my book!"

"Tell me all about it, my boy."

"My Aunt Hannah has been ill in bed all the winter. I haven't been able to earn anything for the last month. We got out of money and provisions. And Mr. Nutt wouldn't trust us for anything—"

"Uncle, mind you, don't deal with that horrid man any more!" interrupted Claudia.

"Did you owe him much, my boy?" inquired Mr. Middleton.

"Not a penny, sir! We never went in debt and never even asked for credit before."

"Go on."

"Well, sir, to-day Aunt Hannah wanted a cup of tea so badly that she cried for it, sir—cried like any little baby, and said she would die if she didn't get it; and so I brought my book to town this afternoon and sold it to get the money to buy what she wanted."

"But you had the pocketbook full of money; why didn't you take some of that?"

"The Lord says 'Thou shalt not steal!'"

"But that would have been only taking in advance what would certainly have been offered to you as a reward."

"I did think of that when aunt was crying for tea; but then I knew John Hancock never would have done so, and I wouldn't, so I sold my book."

"There, uncle! I said so! Now! now! what do you think now?" exclaimed Claudia.

"It must have cost you much to part with your treasure, my boy!" said Mr. Middleton, without heeding the interruption of Claudia.

Ishmael's features quivered, his eyes filled with tears and his voice failed in the attempt to answer.

"There is your book, my lad! It would be a sin to keep it from you," said Mr. Middleton, taking a packet from the bottom of the sleigh and laying it upon Ishmael's knees.

"My book! my book again! Oh, oh, sir! I—" His voice sank; but his pale face beamed with surprise, delight, and gratitude.

"Yes, it is yours, my boy, my noble boy! I give it to you once more; not as any sort of a reward; but simply because I think it would be a sin to deprive you of that which is yours by a sacred right. Keep it, and make its history still your study, and its heroes still your models," said Mr. Middleton, with emotion.

Ishmael was trembling with joy! His delight at recovering his lost treasure was even greater than his joy at first possessing it had been. He tried to thank the donor; but his gratitude was too intense to find utterance in words.

"There, there, I know it all as well as if you had expressed it with the eloquence of Cicero, my boy," said Mr. Middleton.

"Uncle, you are such a good old gander that I would hug and kiss you if I could do so without climbing over aunt," said Claudia.

"Mr. Middleton, do let us get along a little faster! or we shall not reach home until dark," said the lady.

"My good, little old wife, it will not be dark this night. The moon is rising, and between the moon above and the snow beneath, we shall have it as light as day all night. However, here goes!" And Mr. Middleton touched up his horse and they flew as before the wind.

It was a glorious ride through a glorious scene! The setting sun was kindling all the western sky into a dazzling effulgence, and sending long golden lines of light through the interstices of the forest on one hand, and the rising moon was flooding the eastern heavens with a silvery radiance on the other. The sleigh flew as if drawn by winged horses.

"Isn't it grand, Ishmael?" inquired Claudia.

"Oh, yes, indeed, miss!" responded the boy, with fervor.

In twenty minutes they had reached the turnpike road from which started the little narrow foot-path leading through the forest to the hut.

"Well, my boy, here we are! jump out! Good-night! I shall not lose sight of you!" said Mr. Middleton, as he drew up to let Ishmael alight.

"Good-night, sir; good-night, madam; good-night, Miss Claudia. I thank you more than I can express, sir; but, indeed, indeed, I will try to deserve your kindness," said Ishmael, as he bowed, and took his pack once more upon his back and sped on through the narrow forest-path that led to his humble home. His very soul within him was singing for joy.

CHAPTER XXV.

A TURNING POINT IN ISHMAEL'S LIFE.

There is a thought, so purely blest,
That to its use I oft repair,
When evil breaks my spirit's rest,
And pleasure is but varied care;
A thought to light the darkest skies,
To deck with flowers the bleakest moor,
A thought whose home is paradise,
The charities of Poor to Poor.
—*Richard Monckton Milnes.*

Ishmael lifted the latch and entered the hut, softly lest Hannah should have fallen asleep and he should awaken her.

He was right. The invalid had dropped into one of those soft, refreshing slumbers that often visit and relieve the bed-ridden and exhausted sufferer.

Ishmael closed the door, and moving about noiselessly, placed his treasured book on the bureau; put away his provisions in the cupboard; rekindled the smoldering fire; hung on the teakettle; set a little stand by Hannah's bedside, covered it with a white napkin and arranged a little tea service upon it; and then drew his little three-legged stool to the fire and sat down to warm and rest his cold and tired limbs, and to watch the teakettle boil.

Poor child! His feeble frame had been fearfully over-tasked, and so the heat of the fire and the stillness of the room, both acting upon his exhausted nature, sent him also to sleep, and he was soon nodding.

He was aroused by the voice of Hannah, who had quietly awakened.

"Is that you, Ishmael?" she said.

"Yes, aunt," he exclaimed, starting up with a jerk and rubbing his eyes; "and I have got the tea and things; and the kettle is boiling; but I thought I wouldn't set the tea to draw until you woke up, for fear it should be flat."

"Come here, my child," said Hannah, in a kindly voice, for you see the woman had had a good sleep and had awakened much refreshed, with calmer nerves and consequently better temper.

"Come to me, Ishmael," repeated Hannah; for the boy had delayed obeying long enough to set the tea to draw, and cut a slice of bread and set it down to toast.

When Ishmael went to her she raised herself up, took his thin face between her hands and gazed tenderly into it, saying:

"I was cross to you, my poor lad, this morning; but, oh, Ishmael, I felt so badly I was not myself."

"I know that, Aunt Hannah; because when you are well you are always good to me; but let me run and turn your toast now, or it will burn; I will come back to you directly." And the practical little fellow flew off to the fireplace, turned the bread and flew back to Hannah.

"But where did you get the tea, my child?" she inquired.

Ishmael told her all about it in a few words.

"And so you walked all the way back again to Baymouth, tired and hungry as you were; and you sold your precious book, much as you loved it, all to get tea for me! Oh, my boy, my boy, how unjust I have been to you! But I am so glad Mr. Middleton bought it back and gave it to you again! And the pocketbook was his! and you gave it to him and would not take any reward for finding it! That was right, Ishmael; that was right! And it seems to me that every good thing you have ever got in this world has come through your own right doing," was the comment of Hannah upon all this.

"Well, aunt, now the tea is drawn and the toast is ready, let me fix it on the stand for you," said Ishmael, hurrying off to perform this duty.

That evening Hannah enjoyed her tea and dry toast only as a woman long debarred from these feminine necessaries could enjoy them.

When Ishmael also had had his supper and had cleared away the tea service, he took down his book, lighted his little bit of candle, and—as his aunt was in a benignant humor, he went to her for sympathy in his studies—saying:

"Now, aunt, don't mope and pine any more! George Washington didn't, even when the army was at Valley Forge and the snow was so deep and the soldiers were barefooted! Let me read you something out of my book to amuse you! Come, now, I'll read to you what General Marion did when—"

"No, don't, that's a good boy," exclaimed Hannah, interrupting him in alarm, for she had a perfect horror of books. "You know it would tire me to death, dear! But just you sit down by me and tell me about Mrs. Middleton and Miss Merlin and how they were dressed. For you know, dear, as I haven't been able to go to church these three months, I don't even know what sort of bonnets ladies wear."

This requirement was for a moment a perfect "poser" to Ishmael. He wasn't interested in bonnets! But, however, as he had the faculty of seeing, understanding, and remembering everything that fell under his observation in his own limited sphere, he blew out his candle, sat down and complied with his aunt's request, narrating and describing until she went to sleep. Then he relighted his little bit of candle and sat down to enjoy his book in comfort.

That night the wind shifted to the south and brought in a mild spell of weather.

The next day the snow began to melt. In a week it was entirely gone. In a fortnight the ground had dried. All the roads became passable. With the improved weather, Hannah grew better. She was able to leave her bed in the morning and sit in her old arm-chair in the chimney-corner all day.

The professor came to look after his pupil.

Poor old odd-jobber! In his palmiest days he had never made more than sufficient for the support of his large family; he had never been able to lay up any money; and so, during this long and severe winter, when he was frozen out of work, he and his humble household suffered many privations; not so many as Hannah and Ishmael had; for you see, there are degrees of poverty even among the very poor.

And the good professor knew this; and so on that fine March morning, when he made his appearance at the hut, it was with a bag of flour on his back and a side of bacon in his hand.

After the primitive manners of the neighborhood, he dispensed with rapping, and just lifted the latch and walked in.

He found Hannah sitting propped up in her arm-chair in the chimney-corner engaged in knitting and glancing ruefully at the unfinished web of cloth in the motionless loom, at which she was not yet strong enough to work.

Ishmael was washing his own clothes in a little tub in the other corner.

"Morning, Miss Hannah! Morning, young Ishmael!" said the professor, depositing both his bag and bacon on the floor. "I thought I had better just drop in and see after my 'prentice. Work has been frozen up all winter, and now, like the rivers and the snow-drifts, it is thawed and coming with a rush! I'm nigh torn to pieces by the people as has been sending after me; and I thought I would just take young Ishmael on again to help me. And—as I heard how you'd been disabled along of the rheumatism, Miss Hannah, and wasn't able to do no weaving, and as I knowed young Ishmael would be out of work as long as I was, I just made so free, Miss Hannah, as to bring you this bag of flour and middling of bacon, which I hope you'll do me the honor of accepting from a well-wisher."

"I thank you, Morris; I thank you, very much; but I cannot think of accepting such assistance from you; I know that even you and your family must have suffered something from this long frost; and I cannot take the gift."

"Law, Miss Hannah," interrupted the honest fellow, "I never presumed to think of such a piece of impertinence as to offer it to you as a gift! I only make free to beg you will take it as an advance on account of young Ishmael's wages, as he'll be sure to earn; for, bless you, miss, work is a-pouring in on top of me like the cataract of Niagara itself! And I shall want all his help. And as I mayn't have the money to pay him all at once, I would consider of it as a favor to a poor man if you would take this much of me in advance," said the professor.

Now whether Hannah was really deceived by the benevolent diplomacy of the good professor or not, I do not know; but at any rate her sensitive pride was hushed by the prospect held out of Ishmael's labor paying for the provisions, and—as she had not tasted meat for three weeks and her very soul longed for a savory "rasher," she replied:

"Oh, very well, Morris, if you will take the price out of Ishmael's wages, I will accept the things and thank you kindly too; for to be candid with so good a friend as yourself, I was wanting a bit of broiled bacon."

"Law, Miss Hannah! It will be the greatest accommodation of me as ever was," replied the unscrupulous professor.

Ishmael understood it all.

"Indeed, professor," he said, "I think Israel Putnam would have approved of you."

"Well, young Ishmael, I don't know; when I mean well, my acts often work evil; and sometimes I don't even mean well! But it wasn't to talk of myself as I came here this morning; but to talk to you. You see I promised to go over to Squire Hall's and do several jobs for him to-morrow forenoon; and to-morrow afternoon I have got to go to old Mr. Truman's; and to-morrow night I have to lead the exercises at the colored people's missionary meeting at Colonel Mervin's. And as all that will be a long day's work I shall have to make a pretty early start in the morning; and of course as I shall want you to go with me, I shall expect you to be at my house as early as six o'clock in the morning! Can you do it?"

"Oh, yes, professor," answered Ishmael, so promptly and cheerfully that Morris laid his hand upon the boy's head and smiled upon him as he said, addressing Hannah:

"I take great comfort in this boy, Miss Hannah! I look upon him a'most as my own son and the prop of my declining years; and I hope to prepare him to succeed me in my business, when I know he will do honor to the profession. Ah, Miss Hannah, I feel that I am not as young as I used to be; in fact that I am rather past my first youth; being about fifty-two years of age; professional duties wear a man, Miss Hannah! But when I look at this boy I am consoled! I say to myself, though I have no son, I shall have a successor who will do credit to my memory, my teachings, and my profession! I say, that, fall when it may, my mantle will fall upon his shoulders!" concluded Jim with emotion. And like all other great orators, after having produced his finest effect, he made his exit.

The next morning, according to promise, Ishmael rendered himself at the appointed hour at the professor's cottage. They set out together upon their day's round of professional visits. The forenoon was spent at Squire Hall's in mending a pump, fitting up some rain pipes, and putting locks on some of the cabin doors. Then they got their dinner. The afternoon was spent at old Mr. Truman's in altering the position of the lightning rod, laying a hearth, and glazing some windows. And there they got their tea. The evening was spent in leading the exercises of the colored people's missionary meeting at Colonel Mervin's. As the session was rather long, it was after ten o'clock before they left the meetinghouse on their return home. The night was pitch dark; the rain, that had been threatening all day long, now fell in torrents.

They had a full four miles walk before them; but the professor had an ample old cotton umbrella that sheltered both himself and his pupil; so they trudged manfully onward, cheering the way with lively talk instead of overshadowing it with complaints.

"Black as pitch! not a star to be seen! but courage, my boy! we shall enjoy the light of the fireside all the more when we get home," said the professor.

"Yes! there's one star, professor, just rising,—rising away there on the horizon beyond Brudenell Hall," said Ishmael.

"So there is a star, or—something! it looks more like the moon rising; only there's no moon," said Morris, scrutinizing the small dull red glare that hung upon the skirts of the horizon.

"It looks more like a bonfire than either, just now," added the boy, as the lurid red light suddenly burst into flame.

"It is! it is a large fire!" cried the professor, as the whole sky became suddenly illuminated with a red glare.

"It is Brudenell Hall in flames!" exclaimed Ishmael Worth, in horror. "Let us hurry on and see if we can do any good."

CHAPTER XXVI.

THE FIRE AT BRUDENELL HALL.

Seize then the occasion; by the forelock take
That subtle power the never halting time,
Lest a mere moment's putting off should make
Mischance almost as heavy as a crime.
—*Wordsworth.*

Through the threefold darkness of night, clouds, and rain they hurried on towards that fearful beacon light which flamed on the edge of the horizon.

The rain, which continued to pour down in torrents, appeared to dampen without extinguishing the fire, which blazed and smoldered at intervals.

"Professor?" said the boy, as they toiled onward through the storm.

"Well, young Ishmael?"

"It seems to me the fire is inside the house."

"Why so, young Ishmael?"

"Because if it wasn't, this storm would put it out at once! Why, if it had been the roof that caught from a burning chimney this driving rain would have quenched it in no time."

"The roof couldn't catch, young Ishmael; it is all slate."

"Oh!" ejaculated Ishmael, as they increased their speed. They proceeded in silence for a few minutes, keeping their eyes fixed on the burning building, when Ishmael suddenly exclaimed:

"The house is burning inside, professor! You can see now the windows distinctly shaped out in fire against the blackness of the building!"

"Just so, young Ishmael!"

"Now, then, professor, we must run on as fast as ever we can if we expect to be of any use. George Washington was always prompt in times of danger. Remember the night he crossed the Delaware. Come, professor, let us run on!"

"Oh yes, young Ishmael, it is all very well for you to say—run on! but how the deuce am I to do it, with the rain and wind beating this old umbrella this way and that way, until, instead of being a protection to our persons, it is a hindrance to our progress!" said the professor, as he tried in vain to shelter himself and his companion from the fury of the floods of rain.

"I think you had better let it down, professor," suggested the boy.

"If I did we should get wet to the skin, young Ishmael," objected Morris.

"All right, professor. The wetter we get the better we shall be prepared to fight the fire."

"That is true enough, young Ishmael," admitted Morris.

"And besides, if you let the umbrella down you can furl it and use it for a walking-stick, and instead of being a hindrance it will be a help to you."

"That is a good idea, young Ishmael. Upon my word, I think if you had been born in a higher speer of society, young Ishmael, your talents would have caused you to be sent to the State's legislature, I do indeed. And you might even have come to be put on the Committee of Ways and Means."

"I hope that is not a committee of mean ways, professor."

"Ha, ha, ha! There you are again! I say it and I stand to it, if you had been born in a more elevated speer you would have ris' to be something!"

"Law, professor!"

"Well, I do! and it is a pity you hadn't been! As it is, my poor boy, you will have to be contented to do your duty 'in that station to which the Lord has been pleased to call you,' as the Scriptur' says."

"As the catechism says, professor! The Scripture says nothing about stations. The Lord in no respecter of persons."

"Catechism, was it? Well, it's all the same."

"Professor! look how the flames are pouring from that window! Run! run!" And with these words Ishmael took to his heels and ran as fast as darkness, rain, and wind would permit him.

The professor took after him; but having shorter wind, though longer legs, than his young companion, he barely managed to keep up with the flying boy.

When they arrived upon the premises a wild scene of confusion lighted up by a lurid glare of fire met their view. The right wing of the mansion was on fire; the flames were pouring from the front windows at that end. A crowd of frightened negroes were hurrying towards the building with water buckets; others were standing on ladders placed against the wall; others again were clinging about the eaves, or standing on the roof; and all these were engaged in passing buckets from hand to hand, or dashing water on the burning timbers; all poor ineffectual efforts to extinguish the fire, carried on amid shouts, cries, and halloos that only added to the horrible confusion.

A little further removed, the women and children of the family, heedless of the pouring rain, were clinging together under the old elm tree. The master of the house was nowhere to be seen; nor did there appear to be any controlling head to direct the confused mob; or any system in their work.

"Professor, they have got no hose! they are trying to put the fire out with buckets of water! that only keeps it under a little; it will not put it out. Let me run to your house and get the hose you wash windows and water trees with, and we can play it right through that window into the burning room," said Ishmael breathlessly. And without waiting for permission, he dashed away in the direction of Morris' house.

"Where the deuce is the master?" inquired the professor, as he seized a full bucket of water from a man on the ground, and passed it up to the overseer, Grainger, who was stationed on the ladder.

"He went out to an oyster supper at Commodore Burghe's, and he hasn't got back yet," answered the man, as he took the bucket and passed it to a negro on the roof.

"How the mischief did the fire break out?" inquired the professor, handing up another bucket.

"Nobody knows. The mistress first found it out. She was woke up a-smelling of smoke, and screeched out, and alarmed the house, and all run out here. Be careful there, Jovial! Don't be afraid of singing your old wool nor breaking your old neck either! because if you did you'd only be saving the hangman and the devil trouble. Go nearer to that window! dash the water full upon the flames!"

"Are all safe out of the house?" anxiously inquired the professor.

"Every soul!" was the satisfactory answer.

At this moment Ishmael came running up with the hose, exclaiming:

"Here, professor! if you will take this end, I will run and put the sucker to the spout of the pump."

"Good fellow, be off then!" answered Morris.

The hose was soon adjusted and played into the burning room.

At this moment there was a sudden outcry from the group of women and children, and the form of Mrs. Middleton was seen flying through the darkness towards the firemen.

"Oh, Grainger!" she cried, as soon as she had reached the spot, "oh, Grainger! the Burghe boys are still in the house. I thought they had been out! I thought I had seen them out but it was two negro boys I mistook in the dark for them! I have just found out my mistake! Oh, Grainger, they will perish! What is to be done?"

"'Pends on what room they're in, ma'am," hastily replied the overseer, while all the others stood speechless with intense anxiety.

"Oh, they are in the front chamber there, immediately above the burning room!" cried Mrs. Middleton, wringing her hands in anguish, while those around suspended their breath in horror.

"More than a man's life would be worth to venture, ma'am. The ceiling of that burning room is on fire; it may fall in any minute, carrying the floor of the upper room with it!"

"Oh, Grainger! but the poor, poor lads! to perish so horribly in their early youth!"

"It's dreadful, ma'am; but it can't be helped! It's as much as certain death to any man as goes into that part of the building!"

"Grainger! Grainger! I cannot abandon these poor boys to their fate! Think of their mother! Grainger, I will give any man his freedom who will rescue those two boys! It is said men will risk their lives for that. Get up on the ladder where you can be seen and heard and proclaim this—shout it forth: 'Freedom to any slave who will save the Burghe boys!'"

114

The overseer climbed up the ladder, and after calling the attention of the whole mob by three loud whoops and waiting a moment until quiet was restored, he shouted:

"Freedom to any slave who will save the Burghe boys from the burning building!"

He paused and waited a response; but the silenqe was unbroken.

"They won't risk it, ma'am; life is sweet," said the overseer, coming down from his post.

"I cannot give them up, Grainger! I cannot for their poor mother's sake! Go up once more! Shout forth that I offer liberty to any slave with his wife and children—if he will save those boys!" said Mrs. Middleton.

Once more the overseer mounted his post and thundered forth the proclamation:

"Freedom to any slave with his wife and children, who will rescue the Burghe boys!"

Again he paused for a response; and nothing but dead silence followed.

"I tell you they won't run the risk, ma'am! Life is sweeter than anything else in this world!" said the overseer, coming down.

"And the children will perish horribly in the fire and their mother will go raving mad; for I know I should in her place!" cried Mrs. Middleton, wildly wringing her hands, and gazing in helpless anguish upon the burning house.

"And oh! poor fellows! they are such naughty boys that they will go right from this fire to the other one!" cried Claudia Merlin, running up, burying her face in her aunt's gown, and beginning to sob.

"Oh! oh! oh! that I should live to see such a horrible sight! to stand here and gaze at that burning building and know those boys are perishing inside and not be able to help them. Oh! oh! oh!" And here Mrs. Middleton broke into shrieks and cries in which she was joined by all the women and children present.

"Professor! I can't stand this any longer! I'll do it!" exclaimed Ishmael.

"Do what?" asked the astonished artist.

"Get those boys out."

"You will kill yourself for nothing."

"No, there's a chance of saving them, professor, and I'll risk it!" said Ishmael, preparing for a start.

"You are mad; you shall not do it!" exclaimed the professor, seizing the boy and holding him fast.

"Let me go, professor! Let me go, I tell you! Let me go, then! Israel Putman would have done it, and so will I!" cried Ishmael, struggling, breaking away, and dashing into the burning building.

"But George Washington wouldn't, you run mad maniac, he would have had more prudence!" yelled the professor, beside himself with grief and terror.

But Ishmael was out of hearing. He dashed into the front hall, and up the main staircase, through volumes of smoke that rolled down and nearly suffocated him. Ishmael's excellent memory stood him in good stead now. He recollected to have read that people passing through burning houses filled with smoke must keep their heads as near the floor as possible, in order to breathe. So when he reached the first landing, where the fire in the wing was at its worst, and the smoke was too dense to be inhaled at all, he ducked his head quite low, and ran through the hall and up the second flight of stairs to the floor upon which the boys slept.

He dashed on to the front room and tried the door. It was fastened within. He rapped and called and shouted aloud. In vain! The dwellers within were dead, or dead asleep, it was impossible to tell which. He threw himself down upon the floor to get a breath of air, and then arose and renewed his clamor at the door. He thumped, kicked, shrieked, hoping either to force the door or awake the sleepers. Still in vain! The silence of death reigned within the chamber; while volumes of lurid red smoke began to fill the passage. This change in the color of the smoke warned the brave young boy that the flames were approaching. At this moment, too, he heard a crash, a fall, and a sudden roaring up of the fire, somewhere near at hand. Again in frantic agony he renewed his assault upon the door. This time it was suddenly torn open by the boys within.

And horrors of horrors! what a scene met his appalled gaze! One portion of the floor of the room had fallen in, and the flames were rushing up through the aperture from the gulf of fire beneath. The two boys, standing at the open door, were spell-bound in a sort of panic.

"What is it?" asked one of them, as if uncertain whether this were reality or nightmare.

"It is fire! Don't you see! Quick! Seize each of you a blanket! Wrap yourselves up and follow me! Stoop near the floor when you want to breathe! Shut your eyes and mouths when the flame blows too near. Now then!"

It is marvelous how quickly we can understand and execute when we are in mortal peril. Ishmael was instantly understood and obeyed. The lads quick as lightning caught up blankets, enveloped themselves, and rushed from the sinking room.

It was well! In another moment the whole floor, with a great, sobbing creak, swayed, gave way, and fell into the burning gulf of fire below. The flames with a horrible roar rushed up, filling the upper space where the chamber floor had been; seizing on the window-shutters, mantel-piece, door-frames, and all the timbers attached to the walls; and finally streaming out into the passage as if in pursuit of the flying boys.

They hurried down the hot and suffocating staircase to the first floor, where the fire raged with the utmost fury. Here the flames were bursting from the burning wing through every crevice into the passage. Ishmael, in his wet woollen clothes, and the boys in their blankets, dashed for the last flight of stairs—keeping their eyes shut to save their sight, and their lips closed to save their lungs—and so reached the ground floor.

Here a wall of flame barred their exit through the front door; but they turned and made their escape through the back one.

They were in the open air! Scorched, singed, blackened, choked, breathless, but safe!

Here they paused a moment to recover breath, and then Ishmael said:

"We must run around to the front and let them know that we are out!" The two boys that he had saved obeyed him as though he had been their master.

Extreme peril throws down all false conventional barriers and reduces and elevates all to their proper level. In this supreme moment Ishmael instinctively commanded, and they mechanically obeyed.

They hurried around to the front. Here, as soon as they were seen and recognized, a general shout of joy and thanksgiving greeted them.

Ishmael found himself clasped in the arms of his friend, the professor, whose tears rained down upon him as he cried:

"Oh, my boy! my boy! my brave, noble boy! there is not your like upon this earth! no, there is not! I would kneel down and kiss your feet! I would! There isn't a prince in this world like you! there isn't, Ishmael! there isn't! Any king on this earth might be proud of you for his son and heir, my great-hearted boy!" And the professor bowed his head over Ishmael and sobbed for joy and gratitude and admiration.

"Was it really so well done, professor?" asked Ishmael simply.

"Well done, my boy? Oh, but my heart is full! Was it well done? Ah! my boy, you will never know how well done, until the day when the Lord shall judge the quick and the dead!"

"Ah, if your poor young mother were living to see her boy now!" cried the professor, with emotion.

"Don't you suppose mother does live, and does see me, professor? I do," answered Ishmael, in a sweet, grave tone that sounded like Nora's own voice.

"Yes, I do! I believe she does live and watch over you, my boy."

Meanwhile Mrs. Middleton, who had been engaged in receiving and rejoicing over the two rescued youths, and soothing and composing their agitated spirits, now came forward to speak to Ishmael.

"My boy," she said, in a voice shaking with emotion, "my brave, good boy! I cannot thank you in set words; they would be too poor and weak to tell you what I feel, what we must all ever feel towards you, for what you have done to-night. But we will find some better means to prove how much we thank, how highly we esteem you."

Ishmael held down his head, and blushed as deeply as if he had been detected in some mean act and reproached for it.

"You should look up and reply to the madam!" whispered the professor.

Ishmael raised his head and answered:

"My lady, I'm glad the young gentlemen are saved and you are pleased. But I do not wish to have more credit than I have a right to; for I feel very sure George Washington wouldn't."

"What do you say, Ishmael? I do not quite understand you," said the lady.

"I mean, ma'am, as it wasn't altogether myself as the credit is due to."

"To whom else, then, I should like to know?" inquired the lady in perplexity.

"Why, ma'am, it was all along of Israel Putnam. I knew he would have done it, and so I felt as if I was obliged to!"

"What a very strange lad! I really do not quite know what to make of him!" exclaimed the lady, appealing to the professor for want of a better oracle.

"Why, you see, ma'am, Ishmael is a noble boy and a real hero; but he is a bit of a heathen for all that, with a lot of false gods, as he is everlasting a-falling down and a-worshiping of! And the names of his gods are Washington, Jefferson, Putnam, Marion, Hancock, Henry, and the lot! The History of the United States is his Bible, ma'am, and its warriors and statesmen are his saints and prophets. But by-and-by, when Ishmael grows older, ma'am, he will learn, when he does any great or good action, to give the glory to God, and not to those dead and gone old heroes who were only flesh and blood like himself," said the professor.

Mrs. Middleton looked perplexed, as if the professor's explanation itself required to be explained. And Ishmael, who seemed to think that a confession of faith was imperatively demanded of him, looked anxious—as if eager, yet ashamed, to speak. Presently he conquered his shyness, and said:

"But you are mistaken, professor. I am not a heathen. I wish to be a Christian. And I do give the glory of all that is good and great to the Lord, first of all. I do honor the good and great men; but I do glorify and worship the Lord who made them." And having said this, Ishmael collapsed, hung his head, and blushed.

"And I know he is not a heathen, you horrid old humbug of a professor! He is a brave, good boy, and I love him!" said Miss Claudia, joining the circle and caressing Ishmael.

But, ah! again it was as if she had caressed Fido, and said that he was a brave, good dog, and she loved him.

"It was glorious in you to risk your life to save those good-for-nothing boys, who were your enemies besides! It was so! And it makes my heart burn to think of it! Stoop down and kiss me, Ishmael!"

Our little hero had the instincts of a gallant little gentleman. And this challenge was to be in no wise rejected. And though he blushed until his very ears seemed like two little flames, he stooped and touched with his lips the beautiful white forehead that gleamed like marble beneath its curls of jet. The storm, which had abated for a time, now arose with redoubled violence. The party of women and children, though gathered under a group of cedars, were still somewhat exposed to its fury.

Grainger, the overseer, who with his men had been unremitting in his endeavors to arrest the progress of the flames, now came up, and taking off his hat to Mrs. Middleton, said:

"Madam, I think, please the Lord, we shall bring the fire under presently and save all of the building except that wing, which must go. But, if you please, ma'am, I don't see as you can do any good standing here looking on. So, now that the young gentlemen are safe, hadn't you all better take shelter in my house? It is poor and plain; but it is roomy and weather-tight, and altogether you and the young gentlemen and ladies would be better off there than here."

"I thank you, Grainger. I thank you for your offer as well as for your efforts here to-night, and I will gladly accept the shelter of your roof for myself and young friends. Show us the way. Come, my children. Come, you also, Ishmael."

"Thank you very much, ma'am; but, if I can't be of any more use here, I must go home. Aunt Hannah will be looking for me." And with a low bow the boy left the scene.

CHAPTER XXVII.

ISHMAEL'S FIRST STEP ON THE LADDER.

There is a proud modesty in merit
Averse to asking, and resolved to pay
Ten times the gift it asks.
—Dryden.

Early the next morning the professor made his appearance at the Hill Hut. Ishmael and Hannah had eaten breakfast, and the boy was helping his aunt to put the warp in the loom for a new piece of cloth.

"Morning, Miss Hannah; morning, young Ishmael! You are wanted, sir, up to the Hall this morning, and I am come to fetch you," said the professor, as he stood within the door, hat in hand.

"Yes, I thought I would be; there must be no end of the rubbish to clear away, and the work to do up there now, and I knew you would be expecting me to help you, and so I meant to go up to your house just as soon as ever I had done helping aunt to put the warp in her loom," answered Ishmael simply.

"Oh, you think you are wanted only to be set to work, do you? All right! But now as we are in a hurry, I'll just lend a hand to this little job, and help it on a bit." And with that the artist, who was as expert at one thing as at another, began to aid Hannah with such good will that the job was soon done.

"And now, young Ishmael, get your hat and come along. We must be going."

But now, Hannah, who had been far too much interested in her loom to stop to talk until its arrangements were complete, found time to ask:

"What about that fire at Brudenell Hall?"

"Didn't young Ishmael tell you, ma'am?" inquired the professor.

"Very little! I was asleep when he came in last night, and this morning, when I saw that his clothes were all scorched, and his hair singed, and his hands and face red and blistered, and I asked him what in the world he had been doing to himself, he told me there had been a fire at the Hall; but that it was put out before any great damage had been done; nothing but that old wing, that they talked about pulling down, burnt, as if to save them the trouble," answered Hannah.

"Well, ma'am, that was a cheerful way of putting it, certainly; and it was also a true one; there wasn't much damage done, as the wing that was burnt was doomed to be pulled down this very spring. But did young Ishmael tell you how he received his injuries?"

"No; but I suppose of course he got them, boy-like, bobbing about among the firemen, where he had no business to be!"

"Ma'am, he got burned in saving Commodore Burghe's sons, who were fast asleep in that burning wing! Mrs. Middleton offered freedom to any slave who would venture through the house to wake them up, and get them out. Not a man would run the risk! Then she offered freedom, not only to any slave, but also to the wife and children of any slave who would go in and save the boys. Not a man would venture! And when all the women were a-howling like a pack of she-wolves, what does your nephew do but rush into the burning wing, rouse up the boys and convoy them out! Just in time, too! for they were sleeping in the chamber over the burning room, and in two minutes after they got out the floor of that room fell in!" said Morris.

"You did that! You!" exclaimed Hannah vehemently. "Oh! you horrid, wicked, ungrateful, heartless boy! to do such a thing as that, when you knew if you had been burnt to death, it would have broken my heart! And you, professor! you are just as bad as he is! yes, and worse too, because you are older and ought to have more sense! The boy was in your care! pretty care you took of him to let him rush right into the fire."

"Ma'am, if you'll only let me get in a word edgeways like, I'll tell you all about it! I did try to hinder him! I reasoned with him, and I held him tight, until the young hero—rascal, I mean—turned upon me and hit me in the face; yes, ma'am, administered a 'scientific' right into my left eye, and then broke from me and rushed into the burning house——"

"Well, but I thought it better the professor should have a black eye than the boys should be burned to death," put in the lad, edgeways.

"Oh, Ishmael, Ishmael, this is dreadful! You will live to be hung, I know you will!" sobbed Hannah.

"Well, aunty, maybe so; Sir William Wallace did," coolly replied the boy.

"What in the name of goodness set you on to do such a wild thing? And all for old Burghe's sons! Pray, what were they to you that you should rush through burning flames for them?"

"Nothing, Aunt Hannah; only I felt quite sure that Israel Putnam or Francis Marion would have done just as I did, and so——"

"Plague take Francis Putnam and Israel Marion, and also Patrick Handcock, and the whole lot of 'em, I say! Who are they that you should run your head into the fire for them? They wouldn't do it for you, that I know," exclaimed Hannah.

"Aunt Hannah," said Ishmael pathetically, "you have got their names all wrong, and you always do! Now, if you would only take my book and read it while you are resting in your chair, you would soon learn all their names, and——"

"I'll take the book and throw it into the fire the very first time I lay my hands on it! The fetched book will be your ruin yet!" exclaimed Hannah, in a rage.

"Now, Miss Worth," interposed the professor, "if you destroy that boy's book, I'll never do another odd job for you as long as ever I live."

"Whist! professor," whispered Ishmael. "You don't know my Aunt Hannah as well as I do. Her bark is a deal worse than her bite! If you only knew how many times she has threatened to 'shake the life out of' me, and to 'be the death of me', and to 'flay' me 'alive,' you would know the value of her words."

"Well, young Ishmael, you are the best judge of that matter, at least. And now are you ready? For, indeed, we haven't any more time to spare. We ought to have been at the Hall before this."

"Why, professor, I have been ready and waiting for the last ten minutes."

"Come along, then. And now, Miss Hannah, you take a well-wisher's advice and don't scold young Ishmael any more about last night's adventur'. He has done a brave act, and he has saved the commodore's sons without coming to any harm by it. And, if he hasn't made his everlasting fortun', he has done himself a great deal of credit and made some very powerful friends. And that I tell you! You wait and see!" said the professor, as he left the hut, followed by Ishmael.

The morning was clear and bright after the rain. As they emerged into the open air Ishmael naturally raised his eyes and threw a glance across the valley to Brudenell Heights. The main building was standing intact, though darkened; and a smoke, small in volume but dense black in hue, was rising from the ruins of the burnt wing.

Ishmael had only time to observe this before they descended the narrow path that led through the wooded valley. They walked on in perfect silence until the professor, noticing the unusual taciturnity of his companion, said:

"What is the matter with you, young Ishmael? You haven't opened your mouth since we left the hut."

"Oh, professor, I am thinking of Aunt Hannah. It is awful to hear her rail about the great heroes as she does. It is flat blasphemy," replied the boy solemnly.

"Hum, ha, well, but you see, young Ishmael, though I wouldn't like to say one word to dampen your enthusiasm for great heroism, yet the truth is the truth; and that compels me to say that you do fall down and worship these same said heroes a little too superstitiously. Why, law, my boy, there wasn't one of them, at twelve years of age, had any more courage or wisdom than you have—even if as much."

"Oh, professor, don't say that—don't! it is almost as bad as anything Aunt Hannah says of them. Don't go to compare their great boyhood with mine. History tells what they were, and I know myself what I am."

"I doubt if you do, young Ishmael."

"Yes! for I know that I haven't even so much as the courage that you think I have; for, do you know, professor, when I was in that burning house I was frightened when I saw the red smoke rolling into the passage and heard the fire roaring so near me? And once—I am ashamed to own it, but I will, because I know George Washington always owned his faults when he was a boy—once, I say, I was tempted to run away and leave the boys to their fate."

"But you didn't do it, my lad. And you were not the less courageous because you knew the danger that you freely met. You are brave, Ishmael, and as good and wise as you are brave."

"Oh, professor, I know you believe so, else you wouldn't say it; but I cannot help thinking that if I really were good I shouldn't vex Aunt Hannah as often as I do."

"Humph!" said the professor.

"And then if I were wise, I would always know right from wrong."

"And don't you?"

"No, professor; because last night when I ran into the burning house to save the boys I thought I was doing right; and when the ladies so kindly thanked me, I felt sure I had done right; but this morning, when Aunt Hannah scolded me, I doubted."

"My boy, listen to the oracles of experience. Do what your own conscience assures you to be right, and never mind what others think or say. I, who have been your guide up to this time, can be so no longer. I can scarcely follow you at a distance, much less lead you. A higher hand than Old Morris' shall take you on. But here we are now at the Hall," said the professor, as he opened the gates to admit himself and his companion.

They passed up the circular drive leading to the front of the house, paused a few minutes to gaze upon the ruins of the burnt wing, of which nothing was now left but a shell of brick walls and a cellar of smoking cinders, and then they entered the house by the servant's door.

"Mr. Middleton and the Commodore are in the library, and you are to take the boy in there," said Grainger, who was superintending the clearing away of the ruins.

"Come along, young Ishmael!" said the professor, and as he knew the way of the house quite as well as the oldest servant in it, he passed straight on to the door of the library and knocked.

"Come in," said the voice of Mr. Middleton.

And the professor, followed by Ishmael, entered the library.

It was a handsome room, with the walls lined with book-cases; the windows draped with crimson curtains; the floor covered with a rich carpet; a cheerful fire burning in the grate; and a marble-top table in the center of the room, at which was placed two crimson velvet arm-chairs occupied by two gentlemen—namely, Mr. Middleton and Commodore Burghe. The latter was a fine, tall, stout jolly old sailor, with a very round waist, a very red face, and a very white head, who, as soon as ever he saw Ishmael enter, got up and held out his broad hand, saying:

"This is the boy, is it? Come here, my brave little lad, and let us take a look at you!"

119

Ishmael took off his hat, advanced and stood before the commodore.

"A delicate little slip of a fellow to show such spirit!" said the old sailor, laying his hand on the flaxen hair of the boy and passing his eyes down from Ishmael's broad forehead and thin cheeks to his slender figure. "Never do for the army or navy, sir! be rejected by both upon account of physical incapacity, sir. Eh?" he continued, appealing to Mr. Middleton.

"The boy is certainly very delicate at present; but that may be the fault of his manner of living; under better regimen he may outgrow his fragility," said Mr. Middleton.

"Yes, yes, so he may; but now as I look at him, I wonder where the deuce the little fellow got his pluck from! Where did you, my little man, eh?" inquired the old sailor, turning bluffly to Ishmael.

"Indeed I don't know, sir; unless it was from George Washington and——" Ishmael was going on to enumerate his model heroes, but the commodore, who had not stopped to hear the reply, turned to Mr. Middleton again and said:

"One is accustomed to associate great courage with great size, weight, strength, and so forth!" And he drew up his own magnificent form with conscious pride.

"Indeed, I do not know why we should, then, when all nature and all history contradicts the notion! Nature shows us that the lion is braver than the elephant, and history informs us that all the great generals of the world have been little men——"

"And experience teaches us that schoolmasters are pedants!" said the old man, half vexed, half laughing; "but that is not the question. The question is how are we to reward this brave little fellow?"

"If you please, sir, I do not want any reward," said Ishmael modestly.

"Oh, yes, yes, yes; I know all about that! Your friend, Mr. Middleton, has just been telling me some of your antecedents —how you fought my two young scapegraces in defense of his fruit baskets. Wish you had been strong enough to have given hem a good thrashing. And about your finding the pocketbook, forbearing to borrow a dollar from it, though sorely tempted by want. And then about your refusing any reward for being simply honest. You see I know all about you. So I am not going to offer you money for risking your life to save my boys. But I am going to give you a start in the world, if I can. Come, now, how shall I do it?"

Ishmael hesitated, looked down and blushed.

"Would you like to go to sea and be a sailor, eh?"

"No, sir, thank you."

"Like to go for a soldier, eh? You might be a drummerboy, you know."

"No, thank you, sir."

"Neither sailor nor soldier; that's queer, too! I thought all lads longed to be one or the other! Why don't you, eh?"

"I would not like to leave my Aunt Hannah, sir; she has no one but me."

"What the deuce would you like, then?" testily demanded the old sailor.

"If you please, sir, nothing; do not trouble yourself."

"But you saved the life of my boys, you proud little rascal and do you suppose I am going to let that pass unrepaid?"

"Sir, I am glad the young gentlemen are safe; that is enough for me."

"But I'll be shot if it is enough for me!"

"Commodore Burghe, sir, will you allow me to suggest something?" said the professor, coming forward, hat in hand.

"And who the deuce are you? Oh, I see! the artist-in-general to the country side! Well, what do you suggest?" laughed the old man.

"If I might be so bold, sir, it would be to send young Ishmael to school."

"Send him to school! Ha, ha, ha! ho, ho, ho! why, he'd like that least of anything else! why, he'd consider that the most ungrateful of all returns to make for his services! Boys are sent to school for punishment, not for reward!" laughed the commodore.

"Young Ishmael wouldn't think it a punishment, sir," mildly suggested the professor.

"I tell you he wouldn't go, my friend! punishment or no punishment! Why, I can scarcely make my own fellows go! Bosh! I know boys; school is their bugbear."

"But, under correction, sir, permit me to say I don't think you know young Ishmael."

"I know he is a boy; that is enough!"

"But, sir, he is rather an uncommon boy."

"In that case he has an uncommon aversion to school."

"Sir, put it to him, whether he would like to go to school."

"What's the use, when I know he'd rather be hung?"

"But, pray, give him the choice, sir," respectfully persisted the professor.

"What a solemn, impertinent jackanapes you are, to be sure, Morris! But I will 'put it to him,' as you call it! Here, you young fire-eater, come here to me."

The boy, who had modestly withdrawn into the background, now came forward.

"Stand up before me; hold up your Head; look me in the face! Now, then, answer me truly, and don't be afraid. Would you like to go to school, eh?"

Ishmael did not speak, but the moonlight radiance of his pale beaming face answered for him.

"Have you no tongue, eh?" bluffly demanded the old sailor.

"If you please, sir, I should like to go to school more than anything in the world, if I was rich enough to pay for it."

"Humph! what do you think of that, Middleton, eh? what do you think of that? A boy saying that he would like to go to school! Did you ever hear of such a thing in your life? Is the young rascal humbugging us, do you think?" said the commodore, turning to his friend.

"Not in the least, sir; he is perfectly sincere. I am sure of it, from what I have seen of him myself. And look at him, sir! he is a boy of talent; and if you wish to reward him, you could not do so in a more effectual way than by giving him some education," said Mr. Middleton.

"But what could a boy of his humble lot do with an education if he had it?" inquired the commodore.

"Ah! that I cannot tell, as it would depend greatly upon future circumstances; but this we know, that the education he desires cannot do him any harm, and may do him good."

"Yes! well, then, to school he shall go. Where shall I send him" inquired the old sailor.

"Here; I would willingly take him."

"You! you're joking! Why, you have one of the most select schools in the State."

"And this boy would soon be an honor to it! In a word, commodore, I would offer to take him freely myself, but that I know the independent spirit of the young fellow could not rest under such an obligation. You, however, are his debtor to a larger amount than you can ever repay. From you, therefore, even he cannot refuse to accept an education."

"But your patrons, my dear sir, may object to the association for their sons," said the commodore, in a low voice.

"Do you object?"

"Not I indeed! I like the little fellow too well."

"Very well, then, if anyone else objects to their sons keeping company with Ishmael Worth, they shall be at liberty to do so."

"Humph! but suppose they remove their sons from the school? what then, eh?" demanded the commodore.

"They shall be free from any reproach from me. The liberty I claim for myself I also allow others. I interfere with no man's freedom of action, and suffer no man to interfere with mine," returned Middleton.

"Quite right! Then it is settled the boy attends the school. Where are you, you young fire-bravo! you young thunderbolt of war! Come forward, and let us have a word with you!" shouted the commodore.

Ishmael, who had again retreated behind the shelter of the professor's stout form, now came forward, cap in hand, and stood blushing before the old sailor.

"Well, you are to be 'cursed with a granted prayer,' you young Don Quixote. You are to come here to school, and I am to foot the bills. You are to come next Monday, which being the first of April and all-fool's-day, I consider an appropriate time for beginning. You are to tilt with certain giants, called Grammar, Geography, and History. And if you succeed with them, you are to combat certain dragons and griffins, named Virgil, Euclid, and so forth. And if you conquer them, you may eventually rise above your present humble sphere, and perhaps become a parish clerk or a constable—who knows? Make good use of your opportunities, my lad! Pursue the path of learning, and there is no knowing where it may carry you. 'Big streams from little fountains flow. Great oaks from little acorns grow;' and so forth. Good-by! and God bless you, my lad," said the commodore, rising to take his leave.

Ishmael bowed very low, and attempted to thank his friend, but tears arose to his eyes, and swelling emotion choked his voice; and before he could speak, the commodore walked up to Mr. Middleton, and said:

"I hope your favor to this lad will not seriously affect your school; but we will talk further of the matter on some future occasion. I have an engagement this morning. Good-by! Oh, by the way—I had nearly forgotten: Mervin, and Turner, and the other old boys are coming down to my place for an oyster roast on Thursday night. I won't ask you if you will come. I say to you that you must do so; and I will not stop to hear any denial. Good-by!" and the commodore shook Mr. Middleton's hand and departed.

Ishmael stood the very picture of perplexity, until Mr. Middleton addressed him.

"Come here, my brave little lad. You are to do as the commodore has directed you, and present yourself here on Monday next. Do you understand?"

"Yes, sir, I understand very well; but——"

"But—what, my lad? Wouldn't you like to come?"

"Oh, yes, sir! more than anything in the world. I would like it, but——"

"What, my boy?"

"It would be taking something for nothing; and I do not like to do that, sir."

"You are mistaken, Ishmael. It would be taking what you have a right to take. It would be taking what you have earned a hundred-fold. You risked your life to save Commodore Burghe's two sons, and you did save them."

"Sir, that was only my duty."

"Then it is equally the commodore's duty to do all that he can for you. And it is also your duty to accept his offers."

"Do you look at it in that light, sir?"

"Certainly I do."

"And—do you think John Hancock and Patrick Henry would have looked at it in that light?"

Mr. Middleton laughed. No one could have helped laughing at the solemn, little, pale visage of Ishmael, as he gravely put this question.

"Why, assuredly, my boy. Every hero and martyr in sacred or profane history would view the matter as the commodore and myself do."

"Oh, then, sir, I am so glad! and indeed, indeed, I will do my very best to profit by my opportunities, and to show my thankfulness to the commodore and you," said Ishmael fervently.

"Quite right. I am sure you will. And now, my boy, you may retire," said Mr. Middleton, kindly giving Ishmael his hand.

Our lad bowed deeply and turned towards the professor, who, with a sweeping obeisance to all the literary shelves, left the room.

"Your everlastin' fortin's made, young Ishmael! You will learn the classmatics, and all the fine arts; and it depends on yourself alone, whether you do not rise to be a sexton or a clerk!" said the professor, as they went out into the lawn.

They went around to the smoking ruins of the burnt wing, where all the field negroes were collected under the superintendence of the overseer, Grainger, and engaged in clearing away the rubbish.

"I have a hundred and fifty things to do," said the professor; "but, still, if my assistance is required here it must be given. Do you want my help, Mr. Grainger?"

"No, Morris, not until the rubbish is cleared away. Then, I think, we shall want you to put down a temporary covering to keep the cellar from filling with rain until the builder comes," was the reply.

"Come along, then, young Ishmael; I guess I will not linger here any longer; and as for going over to Mr. Martindale's, to begin to dig his well to-day, it is too late to think of such a thing. So I will just walk over home with you, to see how Hannah receives your good news," said the professor, leading the way rapidly down the narrow path through the wooded valley.

When they reached the hut they found Hannah sitting in her chair before the fire, crying.

In a moment Ishmael's thin arm was around her neck and his gentle voice in her ear, inquiring:

"What is the matter?"

"Starvation is the matter, my child! I cannot weave. It hurts my arms too much. What we are to do for bread I cannot tell! for of course the poor little dollar a week that you earn is not going to support us," said Hannah, sobbing.

Ishmael looked distressed; the professor dismayed. The same thought occurred to both—Hannah unable to work, Ishmael's "poor little dollar a week" would not support them; but yet neither could it be dispensed with, since it would be the only thing to keep them both from famine, and since this was the case, Ishmael would be obliged to continue to earn that small stipend, and to do so he must give up all hopes of going to school—at least for the present, perhaps forever. It was a bitter disappointment, but when was the boy ever known to hesitate between right and wrong? He swallowed his rising tears and kissed his weeping relative saying:

"Never mind, Aunt Hannah! Don't cry; maybe if I work hard I may be able to earn more."

"Yes; times is brisk; I dare say, young Ishmael will be able to bring you as much as two dollars a week for a while," chimed in the professor.

Hannah dropped her coarse handkerchief and lifted her weeping face to ask:

"What did they want with you up at the Hall, my dear?"

"The commodore wanted to send me to school, Aunt Hannah; but it don't matter," said Ishmael firmly.

Hannah sighed.

And the professor, knowing now that he should have no pleasure in seeing Hannah's delight in her nephew's advancement, since the school plan was nipped in the bud, took up his hat to depart.

"Well, young Ishmael, I shall start for Mr. Martindale's to-morrow, to dig that well. I shall have a plenty for you to do, so you must be at my house as usual at six o'clock in the morning," he said.

"Professor, I think I will walk with you. I ought to tell Mr. Middleton at once. And I shall have no more time after to-day," replied the boy rising.

They went out together and in silence retraced their steps to Brudenell Heights. Both were brooding over Ishmael's defeated hopes and over that strange fatality in the lot of the poor that makes them miss great fortunes for the lack of small means.

The professor parted with his companion at his own cottage door. But Ishmael, with his hands in his pockets, walked slowly and thoughtfully on towards Brudenell Heights.

To have the cup of happiness dashed to the ground the very moment it was raised to his lips! It was a cruel disappointment. He could not resign himself to it. All his nature was in arms to resist it. His mind was laboring with the means to reconcile his duty and his desire. His intense longing to go to school, his burning thirst for knowledge, the eagerness of his hungry and restless intellect for food and action, can scarcely be appreciated by less gifted beings. While earnestly searching for the way by which he might supply Hannah with the means of living, without sacrificing his hopes of school, he suddenly hit upon a plan. He quickened his footsteps to put it into instant execution. He arrived at Brudenell Hall and asked to see Mrs. Middleton. A servant took up his petition and soon returned to conduct him to that lady's presence. They went up two flights of stairs, when the man, turning to the left, opened a door, and admitted the boy to the bed-chamber of Mrs. Middleton.

The lady, wrapped in a dressing gown and shawl, reclined in an arm-chair in the chimney corner.

"Come here, my dear," she said, in a sweet voice. And when Ishmael had advanced and made his bow, she took his hand kindly and said: "You are the only visitor whom I would have received to-day, for I have taken a very bad cold from last night's exposure, my dear; but you I could not refuse. Now sit down in that chair opposite me, and tell me what I can do for you. I hear you are coming to school here; I am glad of it."

"I was, ma'am; but I do not know that I am", replied the boy.

"Why, how is that?"

"I hope you won't be displeased with me, ma'am—"

"Certainly not, my boy. What is it that you wish to say?"

"Well, ma'am, my Aunt Hannah cannot weave now, because her wrists are crippled with rheumatism; and, as she cannot earn any money in that way, I shall be obliged to give up school—unless—" Ishmael hesitated.

"Unless what, my boy?"

"Unless she can get some work that she can do. She can knit and sew very nicely, and I thought maybe, ma'am—I hope you won't be offended—"

"Certainly not."

"I thought, then, maybe you might have some sewing or some knitting to put out."

"Why, Ishmael, I have been looking in vain for a seamstress for the last three or four weeks. And I thought I really should have to go to the trouble and expense of sending to Baltimore or Washington for one; for all our spring and summer sewing is yet to do. I am sure I could keep one woman in fine needlework all the year round."

"Oh, ma'am, how glad I would be if Aunt Hannah would suit you."

"I can easily tell that. Does she make your clothes?"

"All of them, ma'am, and her own too."

"Come here, then, and let me look at her sewing."

Ishmael went to the lady, who took his arm and carefully examined the stitching of his jacket and shirt sleeve.

"She sews beautifully. That will do, my boy. Ring that bell for me."

Ishmael obeyed and a servant answered the summons.

"Jane," she said, "hand me that roll of linen from the wardrobe."

The woman complied, and the mistress put the bundle in the hands of Ishmael, saying:

"Here, my boy: here are a dozen shirts already cut out, with the sewing cotton, buttons, and so forth rolled up in them. Take them to your aunt. Ask her if she can do them, and tell her that I pay a dollar apiece."

"Oh! thank you, thank you, ma'am! I know Aunt Hannah will do them very nicely!" exclaimed the boy in delight, as he made his bow and his exit.

He ran home, leaping and jumping as he went.

He rushed into the hut and threw the bundle on the table, exclaiming gleefully:

"There, Aunt Hannah! I have done it!"

"Done what, you crazy fellow?" cried Hannah, looking up from the frying pan in which she was turning savory rashers of bacon for their second meal.

"I have got you—'an engagement,' as the professor calls a big lot of work to do. I've got it for you, aunt; and I begin to think a body may get any reasonable thing in this world if they will only try hard enough for it!" exclaimed Ishmael.

Hannah sat down her frying pan and approached the table, saying:

"Will you try to be sensible now, Ishmael; and tell me where this bundle of linen came from?"

Ishmael grew sober in an instant, and made a very clear statement of his afternoon's errand, and its success, ending as he had begun, by saying: "I do believe in my soul, Aunt Hannah, that anybody can get any reasonable thing in the world they want, if they only try hard enough for it! And now, dear Aunt Hannah, I would not be so selfish as to go to school and leave all the burden of getting a living upon your shoulders, if I did not know that it would be better even for you by-and-by! For if I go to school and get some little education, I shall be able to work at something better than odd jobbing. The professor and Mr. Middleton, and even the commodore himself, thinks that if I persevere, I may come to be county constable, or parish clerk, or schoolmaster, or something of that sort; and if I do, you know, Aunt Hannah, we can live in a house with three or four rooms, and I can keep you in splendor! So you won't think your boy selfish in wanting to go to school, will you, Aunt Hannah?"

"No, my darling, no. I love you dearly, my Ishmael. Only my temper is tried when you run your precious head into the fire, as you did last night."

"But, Aunt Hannah, Israel Putnam, or Francis——"

"Now, now, Ishmael—don't, dear, don't! If you did but know how I hate the sound of those old dead and gone men's names, you wouldn't be foreverlasting dinging of them into my ears!" said Hannah nervously.

"Well, Aunt Hannah—I'll try to remember not to name them to you again. But for all that I must follow where they lead me!" said this young aspirant and unconscious prophet. For I have elsewhere said, what I now with emphasis repeat, that "aspirations are prophecies," which it requires only faith to fulfill.

Hannah made no reply. She was busy setting the table for the supper, which the aunt and nephew presently enjoyed with the appreciation only to be felt by those who seldom sit down to a satisfactory meal.

When it was over, and the table was cleared, Hannah, who never lost time, took the bundle of linen, unrolled it, sat down, and commenced sewing.

Ishmael with his book of heroes sat opposite to her.

The plain deal table, scrubbed white as cream, stood between them, lighted by one tallow candle.

"Aunt Hannah," said the boy, as he watched her arranging her work, "is that easier than weaving?"

"Very much easier, Ishmael."

"And is it as profitable to you?"

"About twice as profitable, my dear; so, if the lady really can keep me in work all the year round, there will be no need of your poor little wages, earned by your hard labor," answered Hannah.

"Oh, I didn't think it hard at all, you see, because Israel Put——I beg your pardon, Aunt Hannah—I won't forget again," said the boy, correcting himself in time, and returning to the silent reading of his book.

Some time after he closed his book, and looked up.

"Aunt Hannah!"

"Well, Ishmael?"

"You often talk to me of my dear mother in heaven, but never of my father. Who was my father, Aunt Hannah?"

For all answer Hannah arose and boxed his ears.

CHAPTER XXVIII.

ISHMAEL AND CLAUDIA.

I saw two children intertwine
Their arms about each other,
Like the lithe tendrils of the vine
Around its nearest brother;
And ever and anon,
As gayly they ran on,
Each looked into the other's face,
Anticipating an embrace.
—*Richard Monckton Milnes.*

Punctually at nine o'clock on Monday morning Ishmael Worth rendered himself at Brudenell Hall. Mr. Middleton's school was just such a one as can seldom, if ever, be met with out of the Southern States. Mr. Middleton had been a professor of languages in one of the Southern universities; and by his salary had supported and educated a large family of sons and daughters until the death of a distant relative enriched him with the inheritance of a large funded property.

He immediately resigned his position in the university, and—as he did not wish to commit himself hastily to a fixed abode in any particular neighborhood by the purchase of an estate—he leased the whole ready-made establishment at Brudenell Hall, all furnished and officered as it was. There he conveyed his wife and ten children—that is, five girls and five boys, ranging from the age of one year up to fifteen years of age. Added to these was the motherless daughter of his deceased sister, Beatrice Merlin, who had been the wife of the chief-justice of the Supreme Court of the State.

Claudia Merlin had been confided to the care of her uncle and aunt in preference to being sent to a boarding school during her father's absence on official duty at the capital.

Mr. and Mrs. Middleton had found, on coming to Brudenell Hall, that there was no proper school in the neighborhood to which they could send their sons and daughters. They had besides a strong prejudice in favor of educating their children under their own eyes. Mr. Middleton, in his capacity of professor, had seen too much of the temptations of college life to be willing to trust his boys too early to its dangers. And as for sending the girls away from home, Mrs. Middleton would not hear of it for an instant.

After grappling with the difficulty for a while, they conquered it by concluding to engage a graduate of the university as tutor, to ground young people in what are called the fundamental parts of an English education, together with the classics and mathematics; and also to employ an accomplished lady to instruct them in music and drawing. This school was always under the immediate supervision of the master and mistress of the house. One or the other was almost always present in the schoolroom. And even if this had not been so, the strictest propriety must have been preserved; for the governess was a discreet woman, nearly fifty years of age; and the tutor, though but twenty-five, was the gravest of all grave young men.

The classroom was arranged in a spare back parlor on the first floor—a spacious apartment whose windows looked out upon the near shrubberies and the distant woods. Here on the right hand were seated the five boys under their tutor; and on the left were gathered the girls under their governess. But when a class was called up for recitation, before the tutor, boys and girls engaged in the same studies, and in the same stage of progress stood up together, that their minds might be stimulated by mutual emulation.

Often Mrs. Middleton occupied a seat in an arm-chair near one of the pleasant windows overlooking the shrubberies, and employed herself with some fine needlework while superintending the school. Sometimes, also, Mr. Middleton came in with his book or paper, and occasionally, from force of habit, he would take a classbook and hear a recitation. It was to keep his hand in, he said, lest some unexpected turn of the wheel of fortune should send him back to his old profession again.

Thus, this was in all respects a family school.

But when the neighbors became acquainted with its admirable working, they begged as a favor the privilege of sending their children as day pupils; and Mr. Middleton, in his cordial kindness, agreed to receive the new pupils; but only on condition that their tuition fees should be paid to augment the salaries of the tutor and the governess, as he—Mr. Middleton—did not wish, and would not receive, a profit from the school.

Among the newcomers were the sons of Commodore Burghe. Like the other new pupils, they were only day scholars. For bad conduct they had once been warned away from the school; but had been pardoned and received back at the earnest entreaty of their father.

Their presence at Brudenell Hall on the nearly fatal night of the fire had been accidental. The night had been stormy, and Mrs. Middleton had insisted upon their remaining.

These boys were now regular attendants at the school, and their manners and morals were perceptibly improving. They now sat with the Middleton boys and shared their studies.

Into this pleasant family schoolroom, on the first Monday in April, young Ishmael Worth was introduced. His own heroic conduct had won him a place in the most select and exclusive little school in the State.

Ishmael was now thirteen years of age, a tall, slender boy, with a broad full forehead, large prominent blue eyes, a straight well-shaped nose, full, sweet, smiling lips, thin, wasted-looking cheeks, a round chin and fair complexion. His hands and feet were small and symmetrical, but roughened with hard usage. He was perfectly clean and neat in his appearance. His thin, pale face was as delicately fair as any lady's; his flaxen hair was parted at the left side and brushed away from his big forehead; his coarse linen was as white as snow, and his coarser homespun blue cloth jacket and trousers were spotless; his shoes were also clean.

Altogether, Nora's son was a pleasing lad to look upon as he stood smilingly but modestly, hat in hand, at the schoolroom door, to which he had been brought by Jovial.

The pupils were all assembled—the boys gathered around their tutor, on the right; the girls hovering about their governess on the left.

Mr. and Mrs. Middleton were both present, sitting near a pleasant window that the mild spring morning had invited them to open. They were both expecting Ishmael, and both arose to meet him.

Mrs. Middleton silently shook his hand.

Mr. Middleton presented him to the school, saying:

"Young gentlemen, this is your new companion, Master Ishmael Worth, as worthy a youth as it has ever been my pleasure to know. I hope you will all make him welcome among you."

There was an instant and mysterious putting together of heads and buzzing of voices among the pupils.

"Walter, come here," said Mr. Middleton.

A youth of about fifteen years of age arose and approached.

"Ishmael, this is my eldest son, Walter. I hope you two may be good friends. Walter, take Ishmael to a seat beside you; and when the recreation hour comes, make him well acquainted with your companions. Mind, Walter, I commit him to your charge."

Walter Middleton smiled, shook hands with Ishmael, and led him away to share his own double desk.

Mr. Middleton then called the school to order and opened the exercises with the reading of the Scripture and prayer.

This over, he came to Ishmael and laid an elementary geography before him, with the first lesson marked out on it, saying:

"There, my lad; commit this to memory as soon as you can, and then take your book up for recitation to Mr. Green. He will hear you singly for some time until you overtake the first class, which I am sure you will do very soon; it will depend upon yourself how soon."

And with these kind words Mr. Middleton left the room.

How happy was Ishmael! The schoolroom seemed an elysium! It is true that this was no ordinary schoolroom; but one of the pleasantest places of the kind to be imagined; and very different from the small, dark, poor hut. Ishmael was delighted with its snow-white walls, its polished oak floor, its clear open windows with their outlook upon the blue sky and the green trees and variegated shrubs. He was pleased with his shining mahogany desk, with neat little compartments for slate, books, pen, pencils, ink, etc. He was in love with his new book with its gayly colored maps and pictures and the wonders revealed to him in its lessons. He soon left off reveling in the sights and sounds of the cheerful schoolroom to devote himself to his book. To him study was not a task, it was an all-absorbing rapture. His thirsty intellect drank up the knowledge in that book as eagerly as ever parched lips quaffed cold water. He soon mastered the first easy lesson, and would have gone up immediately for recitation, only that Mr. Green was engaged with a class. But Ishmael could not stop; he went on to the second lesson and then to the third, and had committed the three to memory before Mr. Green was disengaged. Then he went up to recite. At the end of the first lesson Mr. Green praised his accuracy and began to mark the second.

"If you please, sir, I have got that into my head, and also the third one," said Ishmael, interrupting him.

"What! do you mean to say that you have committed three of these lessons to memory?" inquired the surprised tutor.

"Yes, sir, while I was waiting for you to be at leisure."

"Extraordinary! Well, I will see if you can recite them," said Mr. Green, opening the book.

Ishmael was perfect in his recitation.

All schoolmasters delight in quick and intelligent pupils; but Mr. Green especially did so; for he had a true vocation for his profession. He smiled radiantly upon Ishmael as he asked:

"Do you think, now, you can take three of these ordinary lessons for one every day?"

"Oh, yes, sir; if it would not be too much trouble for you to hear me," answered our boy.

"It will be a real pleasure; I shall feel an interest in seeing how fast a bright and willing lad like yourself can get on. Now, then, put away your geography, and bring me the Universal History that you will find in your desk."

In joy, Ishmael went back to his seat, lifted the lid of his desk, and found in the inside a row of books, a large slate, a copy-book, pens, ink, and pencils, all neatly arranged.

"Am I to use these?" he inquired of Walter Middleton.

"Oh, yes; they are all yours; my mother put them all in there for you this morning. You will find your name written on every one of them," replied the youth.

What treasures Ishmael had! He could scarcely believe in his wealth and happiness! He selected the Universal History and took it up to the tutor, who, in consideration of his pupil's capacity and desire, set him a very long lesson.

In an hour Ishmael had mastered this task also, and taken it up to his teacher.

His third book that morning was Murray's English Grammar.

"I do not think I shall set you a lesson of more than the ordinary length this time, Ishmael. I cannot allow you to devour grammar in such large quantities as you have taken of geography and history at a meal. For, grammar requires to be digested as well as swallowed; in other words, it needs to be understood as well as remembered," said Mr. Green, as he marked the lesson for his pupil.

Ishmael smiled as he went back to his seat.

To ordinary boys the study of grammar is very dry work. Not so to Ishmael. For his rare, fine, intellectual mind the analysis of language had a strange fascination. He soon conquered the difficulties of his initiatory lesson in this science, and recited it to the perfect satisfaction of his teacher.

And then the morning's lessons were all over.

This had been a forenoon of varied pleasures to Ishmael. The gates of the Temple of Knowledge had been thrown open to him. All three of his studies had charmed him: the marvelous description of the earth's surface, the wonderful history of the human race, the curious analysis of language—each had in its turn delighted him. And now came the recreation hour to refresh him.

The girls all went to walk on the lawn in front of the house.

The boys all went into the shrubberies in the rear; and the day pupils began to open their dinner baskets.

Ishmael took a piece of bread from his pocket. That was to be his dinner.

But presently a servant came out of the house and spoke to Walter Middleton; and Walter called our boy, saying:

"Come, Ishmael; my father has sent for you."

Ishmael put his piece of bread in his pocket and accompanied the youth into the house and to the dining-room, where a plain, substantial dinner of roast mutton, vegetables, and pudding was provided for the children of the family.

"You are to dine with my children every day, Ishmael," said Mr. Middleton, in those tones of calm authority that admitted of no appeal from their decision.

Ishmael took the chair that was pointed out to him, and you may be sure he did full justice to the nourishing food placed before him.

When dinner was over the boys had another hour's recreation in the grounds, and then they returned to the schoolroom for afternoon exercises. These were very properly of a lighter nature than those of the morning—being only penmanship, elocution, and drawing.

At six o'clock the school was dismissed. And Ishmael went home, enchanted with his new life, but wondering where little Claudia could be; he had not seen her that day. And thus ended his first day at school.

When he reached the hut Hannah had supper on the table.

"Well, Ishmael, how did you get on?" she asked.

"Oh, Aunt Hannah, I have had such a happy day!" exclaimed the boy. And thereupon he commenced and poured upon her in a torrent of words a description of the schoolroom, the teachers, the studies, the dinner, the recreations, and, in short, the history of his whole day's experiences.

"And so you are charmed?" said Hannah.

"Oh, aunt, so much!" smiled the boy.

"Hope it may last, that's all! for I never yet saw the lad that liked school after the first novelty wore off," observed the woman.

The next morning Ishmael awoke with the dawn, and sprang from his pallet in the loft as a lark from its nest in the tree.

He hurried downstairs to help Hannah with the morning work before he should prepare for school.

He cut wood, and brought water enough to last through the day, and then ate his frugal breakfast, and set off for school.

He arrived there early—almost too early, for none of the day pupils had come, and there was no one in the schoolroom but the young Middletons and Claudia Merlin.

She was sitting in her seat, with her desk open before her, and her black ringletted head half buried in it. But as soon she heard the door open she glanced up, and seeing Ishmael, shut down the desk and flew to meet him.

"I am so glad you come to school, Ishmael! I wasn't here yesterday, because I had a cold; but I knew you were! And oh! how nice you do look. Indeed, if I did not know better, I should take you to be the young gentleman, and those Burghes to be workman's sons!" she said, as she held his hand, and looked approvingly upon his smooth, light hair, his fair, broad forehead, clear, blue eyes, and delicate features; and upon his erect figure and neat dress.

"Thank you, miss," answered Ishmael, with boyish embarrassment.

"Come here, Bee, and look at him," said Miss Merlin, addressing some unknown little party, who did not at once obey the behest.

With a reddening cheek, Ishmael gently essayed to pass to his seat; but the imperious little lady held fast his hand, as, with a more peremptory tone, she said:

"Stop! I want Bee to see you! Come here, Bee, this instant, and look at Ishmael!"

This time a little golden-haired, fair-faced girl came from the group of children collected at the window, and stood before Claudia.

"There, now, Bee, look at the new pupil! Does he look like a common boy—a poor laborer's son?"

The little girl addressed as Bee was evidently afraid to disobey Claudia and ashamed to obey her. She therefore stood in embarrassment.

"Look at him, can't you? he won't bite you!" said Miss Claudia.

Ishmael felt reassured by the very shyness of the little new acquaintance that was being forced upon him, and he said, very gently:

"I will not frighten you, little girl; I am not a rude boy."

"I know you will not; it is not that," murmured the little maiden, encouraged by the sweet voice, and stealing a glance at the gentle, intellectual countenance of our lad.

"There, now, does he look like a laborer's son?" inquired Claudia.

"No," murmured Bee.

"But he is, for all that! He is the son of—of—I forget; but some relation of Hannah Worth, the weaver. Who was your father, Ishmael? I never heard—or if I did I have forgotten. Who was he?"

Ishmael's face grew crimson. Yet he could not have told, because he did not know, why this question caused his brow to burn as though it had been smitten by a red-hot iron.

"Who was your father, I ask you, Ishmael?" persisted the imperious little girl.

"I do not remember my father, Miss Claudia," answered the boy, in a low, half-stifled voice.

"And now you have hurt his feelings, Claudia; let him alone," whispered the fair child, in a low voice, as the tears of a vague but deep sympathy, felt but not understood, arose to her eyes.

Before another word could be said Mrs. Middleton entered the room.

"Ah, Bee, so your are making acquaintance with your new schoolmate! This is my oldest daughter, Miss Beatrice, Ishmael. We call her Bee, because it is the abbreviation of Beatrice, and because she is such a busy, helpful little lady," she said, as she shook hands with the boy and patted the little girl on the head.

The entrance of the teachers and the day pupils broke up this little group; the children took their seats and the school was opened, as before, with prayer. This morning the tutor led the exercises. Mr. Middleton was absent on business. This day passed much as the previous one, except that at its close there was Claudia to shake hands with Ishmael; to tell him that he was a bright, intelligent boy, and that she was proud of him; and all with the air of a princess rewarding some deserving peasant.

CHAPTER XXIX.

YOUNG LOVE.

Have you been out some starry night,
And found it joy to bend
Your eyes to one particular light
Till it became a friend?
And then so loved that glistening spot,
That whether it were far,
Or more, or less, it mattered not—
It still was your own star?
Thus, and thus only, can you know
How I, even lowly I,
Can live in love, though set so low,
And my lady-love no high!
—*Richard Monckton Milnes.*

Ishmael's improvement was marked and rapid; both as to his bodily and mental growth and progress. His happiness in his studies; his regular morning and evening walks to and from school; his abundant and nutritious noontide meals with the young Middletons; even his wood-cutting at the hut; his whole manner of life, in fact, had tended to promote the best development of his physical organization. He grew taller, stronger, and broader-shouldered; he held himself erect, and his pale complexion cleared and became fair. He no longer ate with a canine rapacity; his appetite was moderate, and his habits temperate, because his body was well nourished and his health was sound.

His mental progress was quite equal to his bodily growth. He quickly mastered the elementary branches of education, and was initiated into the rudiments of Latin, Greek, and mathematics. He soon overtook the two Burghes and was placed in the same class with them and with John and James Middleton—Mr. Middleton's second and third sons. When he entered the class, of course he was placed at the foot; but he first got above Ben Burghe, and then above Alfred Burghe, and he was evidently resolved to remain above them, and to watch for an opportunity for getting above James and John Middleton, who were equally resolved that no such opportunity should be afforded him. This was a generous emulation encouraged by Mr. Middleton, who was accustomed to say, laughingly, to his boys:

"Take care, my sons! You know Ishmael is a dead shot! Let him once bring you down, and you will never get up again!"

And to Ishmael:

"Persevere, my lad! Some fine day you will catch them tripping, and take a step higher in the class." And he declared to Mrs. Middleton that his own sons had never progressed so rapidly in their studies as now that they had found in Ishmael Worth a worthy competitor to spur them on. Upon that very account, he said, the boy was invaluable in the school.

Well, John and James had all Ishmael's industry and ambition, but they had not his genius! consequently they were soon distanced in the race by our boy. Ishmael got above James, and kept his place; then he got above John, at the head of the class, and kept that place also; and finally he got so far ahead of all his classmates that, not to retard his progress, Mr. Middleton felt obliged to advance him a step higher and place him beside Walter who, up to this time, had stood alone, unapproached and unapproachable, at the head of the school.

John and James, being generous rivals, saw this well-merited advancement without "envy, hatred or malice"; but to Alfred ind Benjamin Burghe it was as gall and wormwood.

Walter was, of course, as yet much in advance of Ishmael; but, in placing the boys together, Mr. Middleton had said:

"Now, Walter, you are about to be put upon your very best mettle. Ishmael will certainly overtake you, and if you are not very careful he will soon surpass you."

The noble boy laughed as he replied:

"After what I have seen of Ishmael for the last two or three years, father, I dare not make any promises! I think I am a fair match for most youths of my age; and I should not mind competing with industry alone, or talent alone, or with a moderate amount of both united in one boy; but, really, when it comes to competing with invincible genius combined with indomitable perseverence, I do not enter into the contest with any very sanguine hopes of success."

The youth's previsions proved true. Before the year was out Ishmael stood by his side, his equal, and bidding fair to become his superior.

Mr. Middleton had too much magnanimity to feel any little paternal jealousy on this account. He knew that his own son was highly gifted in moral and intellectual endowments, and he was satisfied; and if Ishmael Worth was even his son's superior in these respects, the generous man only rejoiced the more in contemplating the higher excellence.

Commodore Burghe was also proud of his protégé. He was not very well pleased that his own sons were eclipsed by the brighter talents of the peasant boy; but he only shrugged his shoulders as he said:

"You know the Bible says that 'gifts are divers,' my friend. Well, my two boys will never be brilliant scholars, that is certain; but I hope, for that very reason, Alf may make the braver soldier and Ben the bolder sailor." And having laid this flattering unction to his soul, the old man felt no malice against our boy for outshining his own sons.

Not so the Burghe boys themselves. Their natures were essentially low; and this low nature betrayed itself in their very faces, forms, and manners. They were short and thickset, with bull necks, bullet heads, shocks of thick black hair, low foreheads, large mouths, dark complexions, and sullen expressions. They were very much alike in person and in character. The only difference being that Alf was the bigger and the wickeder and Ben the smaller and the weaker.

Against Ishmael they had many grudges, the least of which was cause enough with them for lifelong malice. First, on that memorable occasion of the robbed carriage, he had exposed their theft and their falsehood. Secondly, he had had the good luck to save their lives and win everlasting renown for the brave act; and this, to churlish, thankless, and insolent natures like theirs, was the greater offense of the two; and now he had had the unpardonable impudence to eclipse them in the school. He! the object of their father's bounty, as they called him. They lost no opportunity of sneering at him whenever they dared to do so.

Ishmael Worth could very well afford to practice forbearance towards these ill-conditioned lads. He was no longer the poor, sickly, and self-doubting child he had been but a year previous. Though still delicate as to his physique, it was with an elegant, refined rather than a feeble and sickly delicacy. He grew very much like his father, who was one of the handsomest men of his day; but it was from his mother that he derived his sweet voice and his beautiful peculiarity of smiling only with his eyes. His school-life had, besides, taught him more than book learning; it had taught him self-knowledge. He had been forced to measure himself with others, and find out his relative moral and intellectual standing. His success at school, and the appreciation he received from others, had endowed him with a self-respect and confidence easily noticeable in the modest dignity and grace of his air and manner. In these respects also his deportment formed a favorable contrast to the shame-faced, half-sullen, and half-defiant behavior of the Burghes. These boys were the only enemies Ishmael possessed in the school; his sweetness of spirit had, on the contrary, made him many friends. He was ever ready to do any kindness to anyone; to give up his own pleasure for the convenience of others; to help forward a backward pupil, or to enlighten a dull one. This goodness gained him grateful partisans among the boys; but he had, also, disinterested ones among the girls.

Claudia and Beatrice were his self-constituted little lady-patronesses.

The Burghes did not dare to sneer at Ishmael's humble position in their presence. For, upon the very first occasion that Alfred had ventured a sarcasm at the expense of Ishmael in her hearing, Claudia had so shamed him for insulting a youth to whose bravery he was indebted for his life, that even Master Alfred had had the grace to blush, and ever afterward had avoided exposing himself to a similar scorching.

In this little world of the schoolroom there was a little unconscious drama beginning to be performed.

I said that Claudia and Beatrice had constituted themselves the little lady-patronesses of the poor boy. But there was a difference in their manner towards their protégé.

The dark-eyed, dark-haired, imperious young heiress patronized him in a right royal manner, trotting him out, as it were, for the inspection of her friends, and calling their attention to his merits—so surprising in a boy of his station; very much, I say, as she would have exhibited the accomplishments of her dog, Fido, so wonderful in a brute! very much, ah! as duchesses patronize promising young poets.

This was at times so humiliating to Ishmael that his self-respect must have suffered terribly, fatally, but for Beatrice.

The fair-haired, blue-eyed, and gentle Bee had a much finer, more delicate, sensitive, and susceptible nature than her cousin; she understood Ishmael better, and sympathized with him more than Claudia could. She loved and respected him as an elder brother, and indeed more than she did her elder brothers; for he was much superior to both in physical, moral, and intellectual beauty. Bee felt all this so deeply that she honored in Ishmael her ideal of what a boy ought to be, and what she wished her brothers to become.

In a word, the child-woman had already set up an idol in her heart, an idol never, never, in all the changes and chances of this world, to be thrown from its altar. Already she unconsciously identified herself with his successes. He was now the classmate, equal, and competitor of her eldest brother; yet in the literary and scholastic rivalship and struggle between the two, it was not for Walter, but for Ishmael that she secretly trembled; and in their alternate triumphs and defeats, it was not with Walter, but Ishmael, that she sorrowed or rejoiced.

Bee was her mother's right hand woman in all household affairs; she would have been the favorite, if Mrs. Middleton's strict sense of justice had permitted her to have one among the children. It was Bee who was always by her mother's side in the early morning, helping her to prepare the light, nutritious puddings for dinner.

On these occasions Bee would often beg for some special kind of tart or pie, not for the gratification of her own appetite, but because she had noticed that Ishmael liked that dish. So early she became his little household guardian.

And Ishmael? He was now nearly sixteen years old, and thoughtful beyond his years. Was he grateful for this little creature's earnest affection? Very grateful he was indeed! He had no sister; but as the dearest of all dear sisters he loved this little woman of twelve summers.

But she was not his idol! Oh, no! The star of his boyish worship was Claudia! Whether it was from youthful perversity, or from prior association, or, as is most likely, by the attraction of antagonism, the fair, gentle, intellectual peasant boy adored the dark, fiery, imperious young patrician who loved, petted, and patronized him only as if he had been a wonderfully learned pig or very accomplished parrot! Bee knew this; but the pure love of her sweet spirit was incapable of jealousy, and when she saw that Ishmael loved Claudia best, she herself saw reason in that for esteeming her cousin higher than she had ever done before! If Ishmael loved Claudia so much, then Claudia must be more worthy than ever she had supposed her to be! Such was the reasoning of Beatrice.

Did Mr. and Mrs. Middleton observe this little domestic drama?

Yes; but they attached no importance to it. They considered it all the harmless, shallow, transient friendships of childhood. They had left their own youth so far behind that they forgot what serious matters—sometimes affecting the happiness of many years, sometimes deciding the destiny of a life—are commenced in the schoolroom.

Ishmael was felt to be perfectly trustworthy; therefore he was allowed the privilege of free association with these little girls—an honor not accorded to other day pupils.

This "unjust partiality," as they called the well-merited confidence bestowed upon our boy, greatly incensed the Burghes, and increased their enmity against Ishmael.

Master Alfred, who was now a very forward youth of eighteen, fancied himself to be smitten with the charms of the little beauty of fifteen. Whether he really was so or not it is impossible to say; but it is extremely probable that he was more alive to the fortune of the heiress than to the beauty of the girl. Avarice is not exclusively the passion of the aged, nor is it a whit less powerful than the passion of love. Thus young Alfred Burghe was as jealous of Ishmael's approach to Claudia, as if he—Alfred—had loved the girl instead of coveting her wealth.

Early, very early, marriages were customary in that neighborhood; so that there was nothing very extravagant in the dream of that fast young gentleman, that in another year—namely, when he should be nineteen and she sixteen—he might marry the heiress, and revel in her riches. But how was he to marry her if he could not court her? And how was he to court her if he was never permitted to associate with her? He was forbidden to approach her, while "that cur of a weaver boy" was freely admitted to her society! He did not reflect that the "weaver boy" had earned his own position; had established a character for truth, honesty, fidelity; was pure in spirit, word, and deed, and so was fit company for the young. But Alfred was quite incapable of appreciating all this; he thought the preference shown to Ishmael unjust, indecent, outrageous, and he resolved to be revenged upon his rival, by exposing, taunting, and humiliating him in the presence of Claudia, the very first time chance should throw them all three together.

Satan, who always assists his own, soon sent the opportunity.

It was near the first of August; there was to be an examination, exhibition, and distribution of prizes at the school. And the parents and friends of the pupils were invited to attend.

Walter Middleton and Ishmael Worth were at the head of the school and would compete for the first prizes with equal chance of success. The highest prize—a gold watch—was to be awarded to the best written Greek thesis. Walter and Ishmael were both ordered to write for this prize, and for weeks previous to the examination all their leisure time was bestowed upon this work. The day before the examination each completed his own composition. And then, like good, confidential, unenvying friends as they were, they exchanged papers and gave each other a sight of their work. When each had read and returned his rival's thesis, Walter said with a sigh:

"It will be just as I foreboded, Ishmael. I said you would take the prize, and now I know it."

Ishmael paused some time before he answered calmly:

"No, Walter, I will not take it."

"Not take it! nonsense! if you do not take it, it will be because the examiners do not know their business! Why, Ishmael, there can be no question as to the relative merits of your composition and mine! Mine will not bear an instant's comparison with yours."

"Your thesis is perfectly correct; there is not a mistake in it," said Ishmael encouragingly.

"Oh, yes, it is correct enough; but yours, Ishmael, is not only that, but more! for it is strong, logical, eloquent! Now I can be accurate enough, for that matter; but I cannot be anything more! I cannot be strong, logical, or eloquent in my own native and living language, much less in a foreign and a dead one! So, Ishmael, you will gain the prize."

"I am quite sure that I shall not," replied our boy.

"Then it will be because our examiners will know no more of Greek than I do, and not so much as yourself! And as that cannot possibly be the case, they must award you the prize, my boy. And you shall be welcome to it for me! I have done my duty in doing the very best I could; and if you excel me by doing better still, Heaven forbid that I should be so base as to grudge you the reward you have so well earned. So God bless you, old boy," said Walter, as he parted from his friend.

CHAPTER XXX.

ISHMAEL AND CLAUDIA.

And both were young—yet not alike in youth;
As the sweet moon upon the horizon's verge,
The maid was on the eve of womanhood;
The boy had no more summers; but his heart
Had far out-grown his years, and to his eye
There was but one beloved face on earth,
And that was shining on him.
—*Byron.*

The first of August, the decisive day, arrived. It was to be a fête day for the whole neighborhood—that quiet neighbourhood, where fêtes, indeed, were so unusual as to make a great sensation when they did occur. There was to be the examination in the forenoon, followed by the distribution of prizes in the afternoon, and a dance in the evening. "The public" were invited to attend in the morning and afternoon, and the parents, friends, and guardians of the pupils were invited to remain for the dinner and ball in the evening. All the young people were on the qui vive for this festival; and their elders were not much less excited.

Everywhere they were preparing dresses as well as lessons.

Poor Hannah Worth, whose circumstances were much improved since she had been seamstress in general to Mrs. Middleton's large family, had strained every nerve to procure for Ishmael a genteel suit of clothes for this occasion. And she had succeeded. And this summer morning saw Ishmael arrayed, for the first time in his life, in a neat, well-fitting dress suit of light gray cassimere, made by the Baymouth tailor. Hannah was proud of her nephew, and Ishmael was pleased with himself. He was indeed a handsome youth, as he stood smiling there for the inspection of his aunt. Every vestige of ill health had left him, but left him with a delicacy, refinement, and elegance in his person, manners, and speech very rare in any youth, rarer still in youth of his humble grade. But all this was of the soul.

"You will do, Ishmael—you will do very well indeed!" said Hannah, as she drew the boy to her bosom and kissed him with blended feelings of affection, admiration, and remorse. Yes, remorse; for Hannah remembered how often, in his feeble infancy, she had wished him dead, and had been impatient for his death.

"I hope you will do yourself credit to-day, Ishmael," she said, as she released him from her embrace.

"I shall try to do you credit, Aunt Hannah," replied the smiling youth, as he set off gayly for the fête at the school.

It was a splendid morning, but promised to be a sultry day.

When he reached Brudenell Hall he found the young ladies and gentlemen of the school, about twenty in all, assembled on the front lawn before the house. The young gentlemen in their holiday suits were sauntering lazily about among the parterres and shrubberies. The young ladies in their white muslin dresses and pink sashes were grouped under the shade of that grove of flowering locusts that stood near the house—the same grove that had sheltered some of them on the night of the fire.

As Ishmael came up the flagged walk leading to the house Claudia saw him and called out:

"Come here, Ishmael, and let us look at you!"

The youth, blushing with the consciousness of his new clothes, and the criticisms they would be sure to provoke from his honored but exasperating little patroness, advanced to the group of white-robed girls.

Claudia, with her glittering black ringlets, her rich crimson bloom, and glorious dark eyes, was brilliantly beautiful, and at fifteen looked quite a young woman, while Ishmael at sixteen seemed still a boy.

Her manner, too, was that of a young lady towards a mere lad.

She took him by the hand, and looked at him from head to foot, and turned him around; and then, with a triumphant smile, appealed to her companions, exclaiming:

"Look at him now! Isn't he really elegant in his new clothes? Light gray becomes him—his complexion is so fair and clear! There isn't another boy in the neighborhood that wouldn't look as yellow as a dandelion in gray! Isn't he handsome, now?"

This was a very severe ordeal for Ishmael. The young ladies had all gathered around Claudia, and were examining her favourite. Ishmael felt his face burn until it seemed as if the very tips of his ears would take fire.

"Isn't he handsome, now, Bee?" pursued the relentless Claudia, appealing to her cousin.

Beatrice was blushing in intense sympathy with the blushing youth.

"I say, isn't he handsome, Bee?" persevered the implacable critic, turning him around for her cousin's closer inspection.

"Yes! he is a very handsome dog! I wonder you do not get a collar and chain for him, for fear he should run away, or someone should steal him from you, Claudia!" suddenly exclaimed the distressed girl, bursting into indignant tears.

"Consternation! what is the matter now?" inquired the heiress, dropping her victim, from whom general attention was now diverted.

"What is the matter, Bee? what is the matter?" inquired all the young ladies, gathering around the excited girl.

Beatrice could only sob forth the words:

"Nothing, only Claudia vexes me."

"Jealous little imp!" laughed Miss Merlin.

"I am not jealous, I am only vexed," sobbed Beatrice.

"What at? what at?" was the general question.

But Beatrice only answered by tears and sobs. This gentlest of all gentle creatures was in a passion! It was unprecedented; it was wonderful and alarming!

"I should really like to know what is the matter with you, you foolish child! Why are you so angry with me? It is very unkind!" said Miss Merlin, feeling, she knew not why, a little ashamed.

"I would not be angry with you if you would treat him properly, like a young gentleman, and not like a dog! You treat him for all the world as you treat Fido," said this little lady of so few years, speaking with an effort of moral courage that distressed her more than her companions could have guessed, as she turned and walked away.

Ishmael stepped after her. There were moments when the boy's soul arose above all the embarrassments incident to his age and condition.

He stepped after her, and taking her hand, and pressing it affectionately, said:

"Thank you, Bee! Thank you, dear, dearest, Bee! It was bravely done!"

She turned her tearful, smiling face towards the youth, and replied:

"But do not blame Claudia. She means well always; but, she is——"

"What is she?" inquired the youth anxiously; for there was no book in his collection that he studied with so much interest as Claudia. There was no branch of knowledge that he wished so earnestly to be thoroughly acquainted with as with the nature of Claudia.

"What is she?" he again eagerly inquired.

"She is blind, where you are concerned."

"I think so too," murmured Ishmael, as he pressed the hand of his little friend and left her.

Was Ishmael's allegiance to his "elect lady" turned aside? Ah, no! Claudia might misunderstand, humiliate, and wound him; but she was still "his own star," the star of destiny. He went straight back to her side. But before a word could be exchanged between them the bell rang that summoned the young ladies to their places in the classroom.

The long drawing room, which was opened only once or twice in the year, for large evening parties, had been fitted up and decorated for this fête.

The room being in its summer suit of straw matting, lace curtains, and brown holland chair and sofa covering, needed but little change in its arrangements.

At the upper end of the room was erected a stage; upon that was placed a long table; behind the table were arranged the seats of the examining committee; and before it, and below the stage, were ranged, row behind row, the benches for the classes, a separate bench being appropriated to each class. The middle of the room was filled up with additional chairs, arranged in rows, for the accommodation of the audience. The walls were profusely decorated with green boughs and blooming flowers, arranged in festoons and wreaths.

At twelve o'clock precisely, the examining committee being in their places, the classbooks on the table before them, the classes ranged in order in front of them, and the greater part of the company assembled, the business of the examination commenced in earnest.

The examining committee was composed of the masters of a neighboring collegiate school, who were three in number—namely, Professor Adams, Doctor Martin, and Mr. Watkins. The school was divided into three classes. They began with the lowest class and ascended by regular rotation to the highest. The examination of these classes passed off fairly enough to satisfy a reasonable audience. Among the pupils there was the usual proportion of "sharps, flats, and naturals"—otherwise of bright, dull, and mediocre individuals. After the examination of the three classes was complete, there remained the two youths, Walter Middleton and Ishmael Worth, who, far in advance of the other pupils, were not classed with them, and, being but two, could not be called a class of themselves. Yet they stood up and were examined together, and acquitted themselves with alternating success and equal honor. For instance, in mathematics Walter Middleton had the advantage; in belles-lettres Ishmael excelled; in modern languages both were equal; and nothing now remained but the reading of the two Greek theses to establish the relative merits of these generous competitors. These compositions had been placed in the hands of the committee, without the names of their authors; so that the most captious might not be able to complain that the decision of the examiners had been swayed by fear or favor. The theses were to be read and deliberated upon by the examiners alone, and while this deliberation was going on there was a recess, during which the pupils were dismissed to amuse themselves on the lawn, and the audience fell into easy disorder, moving about and chatting among themselves.

In an hour a bell was rung, the pupils were called in and arranged in their classes, the audience fell into order again, and the distribution of prizes commenced. This was arranged on so liberal a scale that each and all received a prize for something thing or other—if it were not for scholastic proficiency, or exemplary deportment, then it was for personal neatness or something else. The two Burghes, who were grossly ignorant, slothful, perverse, and slovenly, got prizes for the regular attendance, into which they were daily dragooned by their father.

Walter Middleton received the highest prize in mathematics; Ishmael Worth took the highest in belles-lettres; both took prizes in modern languages; so far they were head and head in the race; and nothing remained but to award the gold watch which was to confer the highest honors of the school upon its fortunate recipient. But before awarding the watch the two theses were to be read aloud to the audience for the benefit of the few who were learned enough to understand them. Professor Adams was the reader. He arose in his place and opened the first paper; it proved to be the composition of Ishmael Worth. As he read the eyes and ears of the two young competitors, who were sitting together, were strained upon him.

"Oh, I know beforehand you will get the prize! And I wish you joy of it, my dear fellow!" whispered Walter.

"Oh, no, I am sure I shall not! You will get it! You will see!" replied Ishmael.

Walter shook his head incredulously. But as the reading proceeded Walter looked surprised, then perplexed, and then utterly confounded. Finally he turned and inquired:

"Ish., what the mischief is the old fellow doing with your composition? He is reading it all wrong."

"He is reading just what is written, I suppose," replied Ishmael.

"But he isn't, I tell you! I ought to know, for I have read it myself, you remember! and I assure you he makes one or two mistakes in every paragraph! The fact is, I do not believe he knows much of Greek, and he will just ruin us both by reading our compositions in that style!" exclaimed Walter.

"He is reading mine aright," persisted Ishmael.

And before Walter could reply again, the perusal of Ishmael's thesis was finished, the paper was laid upon the table, and Walter's thesis was taken up.

"Now then; I wonder if he is going to murder mine in the same manner," said Walter.

The reader commenced and went on smoothly to the end without having miscalled a word or a syllable.

"That is a wonder; I do not understand it at all!" said young Middleton.

Ishmael smiled; but did not reply.

Professor Adams rapped upon the table and called the school to order; and then, still retaining Walter's thesis in his hand, he said:

"The highest prize in the gift of the examiners—the gold watch—is awarded to the author of the thesis I hold in my hand. The young gentleman will please to declare himself, walk forward, and receive the reward."

"There, Walter! what did I tell you? I wish you joy now, old fellow! There! 'go where glory awaits you,'" smilingly whispered Ishmael.

"I understand it all now, Ish.! I fully understand it! But I will not accept the sacrifice, old boy," replied Walter.

"Will the young gentleman who is the author of the prize thesis step up and be invested with this watch?" rather impatiently demanded the wearied Professor Adams.

Walter Middleton arose in his place.

"I am the author of the thesis last read; but I am not entitled to the prize; there has been a mistake."

"Walter!" exclaimed his father, in a tone of rebuke.

The examiners looked at the young speaker in surprise, and at each other in perplexity.

"Excuse me, father; excuse me, gentlemen; but there has been a serious mistake, which I hope to prove to you, and which I know you would not wish me to profit by," persisted the youth modestly, but firmly.

"Don't, now, Walter! hush, sit down," whispered Ishmael in distress.

"I will," replied young Middleton firmly.

"Walter, come forward and explain yourself; you certainly owe these gentlemen both an explanation and an apology for your unseemly interruption of their proceedings and your presumptuous questioning of their judgment," said Mr. Middleton.

"Father, I am willing and anxious to explain, and my explanation in itself will be my very best apology; but, before I can go on, I wish to beg the favor of a sight of the thesis that was first read," said Walter, coming up to the table of the examiners.

The paper was put in his hands. He cast his eyes over it and smiled.

"Well, my young friend, what do you mean by that?" inquired Professor Adams.

"Why, sir, I mean that it is just as I surmised; that this paper which I hold in my hand is not the paper that was prepared for the examining committee; this, sir, must be the original draft of the thesis, and not the fair copy which was intended to compete for the gold watch," said Walter firmly.

"But why do you say this, sir? What grounds have you for entertaining such an opinion?" inquired Professor Adams. Young Middleton smiled confidently as he replied:

"I have seen and read the fair copy; there was not a mistake in it; and it was in every other respect greatly superior to my own."

"If this is true, and of course I know it must be so, since you say it, my son, why was not the fair copy put in our hands? By what strange inadvertence has this rough draft found its way to us?" inquired Mr. Middleton.

"Father," replied Walter, in a low voice, "by no inadvertence at all! Ishmael has done this on purpose that your son might receive the gold watch. I am sure of it; but I cannot accept his noble sacrifice! Father, you would not have me do it."

"No, Walter; no, my boy; not if a kingdom instead of a gold watch were at stake. You must not profit by his renunciation, if there has been any renunciation. But are you sure that there has been?"

"I will prove it to your satisfaction, sir. Yesterday, in my great anxiety to know how my chances stood for the first prize, I asked Ishmael for a sight of his thesis, and I tendered him a sight of mine. Ishmael did not refuse me. We exchanged papers and read each other's compositions. Ishmael's was fairly written, accurate, logical, and very eloquent. Mine was very inferior in every respect except literal accuracy. Ishmael must have seen, after comparing the two, that he must gain the prize. I certainly knew he would; I expressed my conviction strongly to that effect; and I congratulated him in anticipation of a certain triumph. But, though I wished him joy, I must have betrayed the mortification that was in my own heart; for Ishmael insisted that I should be sure to get the medal myself. And this is the way in which he has secured the fulfillment of his own prediction: by suppressing his fair copy that must have taken the prize, and sending up that rough draft on purpose to lose it in my favor."

"Can this be true?" mused Mr. Middleton.

"You can test its truth for yourself, sir. Call up Ishmael Worth. You know that he will not speak falsely. Ask him if he has not suppressed the fair copy and exhibited the rough draft. You have authority over him, sir. Order him to produce the suppressed copy, that his abilities may be justly tested," said Walter.

Mr. Middleton dropped his head upon his chest and mused. Meanwhile the audience were curious and impatient to know what on earth could be going on around the examiner's table. Those only who were nearest had heard the words of Walter Middleton when he first got up to disclaim all right to the gold watch. But after he had gone forward to the table no more was heard, the conversation being carried on in a confidential tone much too low to be heard beyond the little circle around the board.

After musing for a few minutes, Mr. Middleton lifted his head and said:

"I will follow your advice, my son." Then, raising his voice, he called out:

"Ishmael Worth come forward."

Ishmael, who had half suspected what was going on around that table, now arose, approached and stood respectfully waiting orders.

Mr. Middleton took the thesis from the hands of Walter and placed it in those of Ishmael, saying:

"Look over that paper and tell me if it is not the first rough draft of your thesis."

"Yes, sir, it is," admitted the youth, as with embarrassment he received the paper.

"Have you a fair copy?" inquired Mr. Middleton.

"Yes, sir."

"Where is it? anywhere in reach?"

"It is in the bottom of my desk in the schoolroom, sir."

"Go and fetch it, that we may examine it and fairly test your abilities," commanded the master.

Ishmael left the drawing-room, and after an absence of a few minutes returned with a neatly folded paper, which he handed to Mr. Middleton.

That gentleman unfolded and looked at it. A very cursory examination served to prove the great superiority of this copy over the original one. Mr. Middleton refolded it, and, looking steadily and almost sternly into Ishmael's face, inquired:

"Was the rough draft sent to the examiners, instead of this fair copy, through any inadvertence of yours? Answer me truly."

"No, sir," replied Ishmael, looking down.

"It was done knowingly, then?"

"Yes, sir."

"For what purpose, may I ask you, did you suppress the fair copy, which most assuredly must have won you the watch, and substitute this rough draft, that as certainly must have lost it?"

Still looking down, Ishmael remained silent and embarrassed.

"Young man, I command you to reply to me," said the master.

"Sir, I thought I had a right to do as I pleased with my own composition," replied Ishmael, lifting his head and looking straight into the face of the questioner, with that modest confidence which sometimes gained the victory over his shyness.

"Unquestionably; but that is not an answer to my question, as to why the substitution was made."

"I wish you would not press the question, sir."

"But I do, Ishmael, and I enjoin you to answer it."

"Then, sir, I suppressed the fair copy, and sent up the rough draft, because I thought there was one who, for his great diligence, had an equal or better right to the watch than I had, and who would be more pained by losing it than I should, and I did not wish to enter into competition with him; for indeed, sir, if I had won the watch from my friend I should have been more pained by his defeat than pleased at my own victory," said Ishmael, his fine face clearing up under the consciousness of probity. (But, reader, mark you this—it was the amiable trait inherited from his father—the pain in giving pain; the pleasure in giving pleasure. But we know that this propensity which had proved so fatal to the father was guided by conscience to all good ends in the son.)

While Ishmael gave this little explanation, the examiners listened, whispered, and nodded to each other with looks of approval.

And Walter came to his friend's side, and affectionately took and pressed his hand, saying:

"I knew it, as soon as I had heard both theses read, and saw that they seemed to make mistakes only in yours. It was very generous in you, Ishmael; but you seemed to leave out of the account the fact that I ought not to have profited by such generosity; and also that if I had lost the prize, and you had won it, my mortification would have been alleviated by the thought that you, the best pupil in the school, and my own chosen friend, had won it."

"Order!" said Mr. Middleton, interrupting this whispered conversation. "Ishmael," he continued, addressing the youth, "your act was a generous one, certainly; whether it was a righteous one is doubtful. There is an old proverb which places 'justice before generosity.' I do not know that it does not go so far as even to inculcate justice to ourselves before generosity to our fellows. You should have been just to yourself before being generous to your friend. It only remains for us now to rectify this wrong." Then turning to Professor Adams, he said:

"Sir, may I trouble you to take this fair copy and read it aloud?"

Professor Adams bowed in assent as he received the paper. Ishmael and Walter returned to their seats to await the proceedings.

Professor Adams arose in his place, and in a few words explained how it happened that in the case of the first thesis read to them, he had given the rough draft instead of the fair copy, which in justice to the young writer he should now proceed to read.

Now, although not half a dozen persons in that room could have perceived any difference in the two readings of a thesis written in a language of which even the alphabet was unknown known to them, yet every individual among them could keenly appreciate the magnanimity of Ishmael, who would have sacrificed his scholastic fame for his friend's benefit, and the quickness and integrity of Walter in discovering the generous ruse and refusing the sacrifice. They put their heads together whispering, nodding, and smiling approval. "Damon and Pythias," "Orestes and Pylades," were the names bestowed upon the two friends. But at length courtesy demanded that the audience should give some little attention to the reading of the Greek thesis, whether they understood a word of it or not. Their patience was not put to a long test. The reading was a matter of about fifteen minutes, and at its close the three examiners conversed together for a few moments.

And then Professor Adams arose and announced the young author of the thesis which he had just read as the successful competitor for the highest honors of the school, and requested him to come forward and be invested with the prize.

"Now it is my time to wish you joy, and to say, 'Go where glory waits you,' Ishmael!" whispered Walter, pressing his friend's hand and gently urging him from his seat.

137

Ishmael yielded to the impulse and the invitation, and went up to the table. Professor Adams leaned forward, threw the slender gold chain, to which the watch was attached, around the neck of Ishmael, saying:

"May this well-earned prize be the earnest of future successes even more brilliant than this."

Ishmael bowed low in acknowledgment of the gold watch and the kind words, and amid the hearty applause of the company returned to his seat.

The business of the day was now finished, and as it was now growing late in the afternoon, the assembly broke up. The "public" who had come only for the examination returned home. The "friends" who had been invited to the ball repaired first to the dining room to partake of a collation, and then to chambers which had been assigned them, to change their dresses for the evening.

CHAPTER XXXI.

ISHMAEL HEARS A SECRET FROM AN ENEMY.

Shame come to Romeo? Blistered be thy tongue
For such a wish! He was not born to shame;
Upon his brow shame is ashamed to sit;
For 'tis a throne where honor may be crowned,
Sole monarch of the universal earth!
—*Shakspere*.

In the interval the drawing room was rapidly cleared out and prepared for dancing. The staging at the upper end, which had been appropriated to the use of the examining committee, was now occupied by a band of six negro musicians, headed by the Professor of Odd Jobs. They were seated all in a row, engaged in tuning their instruments under the instructions of Morris. The room wore a gay, festive, and inviting aspect. It was brightly lighted up; its white walls were festooned with wreaths of flowers; its oak floor was polished and chalked for the dancers; and its windows were all open to admit the pleasant summer air and the perfume of flowers, so much more refreshing in the evening than at any other time of the day.

At a very early hour the young ladies and gentlemen of the school, whose gala dresses needed but the addition of wreaths and bouquets for the evening, began to gather in the drawing room; the girls looking very pretty in their white muslin dresses, pink sashes, and coronets of red roses; and the boys very smart in their holiday clothes, with rosebuds stuck into their buttonholes. Ishmael was made splendid by the addition of his gold watch and chain, and famous by his success of the morning. All the girls, and many of the boys, gathered around him, sympathizing with his triumph and complimenting him upon his abilities. Ishmael was clearly the hero of the evening; but he bore himself with an aspect half of pleasure, half of pain, until Walter Middleton approached him, and taking his arm walked him down the room, until they were out of earshot from the others, when he said:

"Now do, Ishmael, put off that distressed look and enjoy your success as you ought! Make much of your watch, my boy! I know if it were not for thoughts of me, you would enjoy the possession of it vastly—would you not, now?"

"Yes," said Ishmael, "I would."

"You would not be a 'human boy,' if you didn't. I know well enough I was near losing my wits with delight in the first watch I possessed, although it was but a trumpery little silver affair! Well, now, Ishmael, enjoy your possession without a drawback. I assure you, upon record, I am very glad you got the prize. You deserved the honor more than I did, and you needed the watch more. For see here, you know I have a gold one of my own already—my mother's gift to me on my last birthday," continued Walter, taking out and displaying his school watch. "Now what could I do with two? So, Ishmael, let me see you enjoy yours, or else I shall feel unhappy," he concluded, earnestly pressing his friend's hand.

"Walter Middleton, what do you mean, sir, by stealing my thunder in that way? It is my property that you are carrying off! Ishmael is my protégé, my liege subject. Bring him back, sir! I want to show his watch to my companions," spoke the imperious voice of Miss Merlin.

"Come, Ishmael; you must make a spectacle of yourself again, I suppose, to please that little tyrant," laughed Walter, as he turned back with his friend towards the group of young girls.

Now in this company was one who looked with the envious malignity of Satan upon the well-merited honors of the poor peasant boy. This enemy was Alfred Burghe, and he was now savagely waiting his opportunity to inflict upon Ishmael a severe mortification.

As Walter and Ishmael, therefore, approached the group of young ladies, Alfred, who was loitering near them, lying in wait for his victim, drew away with an expression of disgust upon his face, saying:

"Oh, if that fellow is to join our circle, I shall feel obliged to leave it. It is degrading enough to be forced to mix with such rubbish in the schoolroom, without having to associate with him in the drawing room."

"What do you mean by that, sir?" demanded Miss Merlin, flashing upon him the lightning of her eyes, before Ishmael had drawn near enough to overhear the words of Alfred.

"I mean that fellow is not fit company for me."

"No; Heavens knows that he is not!" exclaimed Claudia pointedly.

"Never mind, Miss Merlin; do not be angry with him; the beaten have a right to cry out," said Ishmael, who had now come up, and stood smiling among them, totally unconscious of the humiliation that was in store for him.

"I am not angry; I am never angry with such dull pups; though I find it necessary to punish them sometimes," replied Claudia haughtily.

"I say he is no fit company for me; and when I say that, I mean to say that he is no fit company for any young gentleman, much less for any young lady!" exclaimed Alfred.

Ishmael looked on with perfect good humor, thinking only that his poverty was sneered at, and feeling immeasurably above the possibility of humiliation or displeasure upon that account.

Claudia thought as he did, that only his lowly fortunes had exposed him to contempt; so putting her delicate white gloved hand in that of Ishmael, she said:

"Ishmael Worth is my partner in the first dance; do you dare to hint that the youth I dance with is not proper company for any gentleman, or any lady, either?"

"No, I don't hint it; I speak it out in plain words; he is not only not fit company for any gentleman or lady, but he is not even fit company for any decent negro!"

Ishmael, strong in conscious worth, and believing the words of Alfred to be only reckless assertion, senseless abuse, laughed aloud with sincere, boyish mirthfulness at its absurdity.

But Claudia's cheeks grew crimson, and her eyes flashed—bad signs these for the keeping of her temper towards "dull pups."

"He is honest, truthful, intelligent, industrious, and polite. These are qualities which, of course, unfit him for such society as yours, Mr. Burghe; but I do not see why they should unfit him for that of ladies and gentlemen," said Claudia severely.

"He is a ——," brutally exclaimed Alfred, using a coarse word, at which all the young girls started and recoiled, as if each had received a wound, while all the boys exclaimed simultaneously:

"Oh, fie!" or "Oh, Alf, how could you say such a thing!"

"For shame!"

As for Walter Middleton, he had collared the young miscreant before the word was fairly out of his mouth. But an instant's reflection caused the young gentleman to release the culprit, with the words:

"My father's house and the presence of these young ladies protect you for the present, sir."

Ishmael stood alone, in the center of a shocked and recoiling circle of young girls; so stunned by the epithet that had been hurled at him that he scarcely yet understood its meaning or felt that he was wounded.

"What did he say, Walter?" he inquired, appealing to his friend.

Walter Middleton put his strong arm around the slender and elegant form of Ishmael, and held him firmly; but whether in a close embrace or light restraint, or both, it was hard to decide, as he answered:

"He says what will be very difficult for him to explain, when he shall be called to account to-morrow morning; but what, it is quite needless to repeat."

"I say he is a ——! His mother was never married! and no one on earth knows who his father was—or if he ever had a father!" roared Alfred brutally.

Walter's arm closed convulsively upon Ishmael. There was good reason. The boy had given one spasmodic bound forward, as if he would have throttled his adversary on the spot; but the restraining arm of Walter Middleton held him back; his face was pale as marble; a cold sweat had burst upon his brow; he was trembling in every limb as he gasped:

139

"Walter, this cannot be true! Oh, say it is not true!"

"True! no! I believe it is as false—as false as that young villain's heart! and nothing can be falser than that!" indignantly exclaimed young Middleton.

"It is! it is true! The whole county knows it is true!" vociferated Alfred. "And if anybody here doubts it, let them ask old Hannah Worth if her nephew isn't a ——"

"Leave the room, sir!" exclaimed Walter, interrupting him before he could add another word. "Your language and manners are so offensive as to render your presence entirely inadmissible here! Leave the room, instantly!"

"I won't!" said Alfred stoutly.

Walter was unwilling to release Ishmael from the tight, half-friendly, half-masterly embrace in which he held him; else, perhaps, he might himself have ejected the offender. As it was, he grimly repeated his demand.

"Will you leave the room?"

"No!" replied Alfred.

"James, do me the favor to ring the bell."

James Middleton rang a peal that brought old Jovial quickly to the room.

"Jovial, will you go and ask your master if he will be kind enough to come here; his presence is very much needed," said Walter.

Jovial bowed and withdrew.

"I shall go and complain to my father of the insults I have received!" said Alfred, turning to leave the room; for he had evidently no wish to meet the impending interview with Mr. Middleton.

"I anticipated that you would reconsider your resolution of remaining here!" laughed Walter, as he let this sarcasm off after his retreating foe.

He had scarcely disappeared through one door before Mr. Middleton entered at another.

"What is all this about, Walter?" he inquired, approaching the group of panic-stricken girls and wondering boys.

"Some new rudeness of Alfred Burghe, father; but he has just taken himself off, for which I thank him; so there is no use in saying more upon the subject for the present," replied Walter.

"There is no use, in any case, to disturb the harmony of a festive evening, my son; all complaints may well be deferred until the morning, when I shall be ready to hear them," replied Mr. Middleton, smiling, and never suspecting how serious the offense of Alfred Burghe had been.

"And now," he continued, turning towards the band, "strike up the music, professor! The summer evenings are short, and the young people must make the most of this one. Walter, my son, you are to open the ball with your cousin."

"Thank you very much, uncle; thank you, Walter, but my hand is engaged for this set to Ishmael Worth; none but the winner of the first prize for me!" said Claudia gayly, veiling the kindness that prompted her to favor the mortified youth under a sportive assumption of vanity.

"Very well, then, where is the hero?" said Mr. Middleton.

But Ishmael had suddenly disappeared, and was nowhere to be found.

"Where is he, Walter? He was standing by you," said Claudia.

"I had my arm around him to prevent mischief, and I released him only an instant since; but he seems to have slipped away," answered Walter, in surprise.

"He has gone after Alfred! and there will be mischief done; and no one could blame Ishmael if there was!" exclaimed Claudia.

"It was young Worth, then, that Burghe assailed?" inquired Mr. Middleton.

"Yes, uncle! and if Mr. Burghe is permitted to come to the house after his conduct this evening, I really shall feel compelled to write to my father, and request him to remove me, for I cannot, indeed, indeed, I cannot expose myself to the shock of hearing such language as he has dared to use in my presence this evening!" said Claudia excitedly.

"Compose yourself, my dear girl; he will not trouble us after this evening; he does not return to school after the vacation; he goes to West Point," said her uncle.

"And where I hope the discipline will be strict enough to keep him in order!" exclaimed Claudia.

"But now someone must go after Ishmael. Ring for Jovial, Walter."

"Father, old Jovial will be too slow. Had I not better go myself?" asked Walter, seizing his hat.

Mr. Middleton assented, and the young man went out on his quest.

He hunted high and low, but found no trace of Ishmael. He found, however, what set his mind at ease upon the subject of a collision between the youths; it was the form of Alfred Burghe, stretched at length upon the thick and dewy grass.

"Why do you lie there? You will take cold. Get up and go home," said Walter, pitying his discomfiture and loneliness; for the generous are compassionate even to the evil doer.

Alfred did not condescend to reply.

"Get up, I say; you will take cold," persisted Walter.

"I don't care if I do! I had as lief die as not! I have no friends! nobody cares for me," exclaimed the unhappy youth, in the bitterness of spirit common to those who have brought their troubles upon themselves.

"If you would only reform your manners, Alfred, you would find friends enough, from the Creator, who only requires of you that 'you cease to do evil and learn to do well,' down to the humblest of his creatures—down to that poor boy whom you so heartlessly insulted to-night; but whose generous nature would bear no lasting malice against you," said Walter gravely.

"It is deuced hard, though, to see a fellow like that taking the shine out of us all," grumbled Alfred.

"No, it isn't! it is glorious, glorious indeed, to see a poor youth like that struggling up to a higher life—as he is struggling. He won the prize from me, me, his senior in age and in the school, and my heart burns with admiration for the boy when I think of it! How severely he must have striven to have attained such proficiency in these three years. How hard he must have studied; how much of temptation to idleness he must have resisted; how much of youthful recreation, and even of needful rest, he must have constantly denied himself; not once or twice, but for months and years! Think of it! He has richly earned all the success he has had. Do not envy him his honors, at least until you have emulated his heroism," said Walter, with enthusiasm.

"I think I will go home," said Alfred, to whom the praises of his rival was not the most attractive theme in the world.

"You may return with me to the house now, if you please, since my friend Ishmael has gone home. Keep out of the way of Miss Merlin, and no one else will interfere with you," said Walter, who, when not roused to indignation, had all his father's charity for "miserable" sinners.

Alfred hesitated for a minute, looking towards the house, where the light windows and pealing music of the drawing room proved an attraction too strong for his pride to resist. Crestfallen and sheepish, he nevertheless returned to the scene of festivity, where the young people were now all engaged in dancing, and where, after a while, they all with the happy facility of youth forgot his rudeness and drew him into their sports. All except Claudia, who would have nothing on earth to say to him, and Beatrice, who, though ignorant of his assault upon Ishmael, obeyed the delicate instincts of her nature that warned her to avoid him.

On observing the return of Alfred, Mr. Middleton took the first opportunity of saying to his son:

"I see that you have brought Burghe back."

"Yes, father; since Ishmael is not here to be pained by his presence, I thought it better to bring him back; for I remembered your words spoken of him on a former occasion: 'That kindness will do more to reform such a nature as his than reprobation could.'"

"Yes—very true! But poor Ishmael! Where is he?"

Aye! where, indeed?

CHAPTER XXXII.

AT HIS MOTHER'S GRAVE.

He sees her lone headstone,
'Tis white as a shroud;
Like a pall hangs above it
The low, drooping cloud.

'Tis well that the white ones
Who bore her to bliss,
Shut out from her new life

The sorrows of this.

Else sure as he stands here,
And speaks of his love,
She would leave for his darkness
Her glory above.
—*E.H. Whittier.*

Giddy, faint, reeling from the shock he had received, Ishmael tottered from the gay and lighted rooms and sought the darkness and the coolness of the night without.

He leaned against the great elm tree on the lawn, and wiped the beaded sweat from his brow.

"It is not true," he said. "I know it is not true! Walter said it was false; and I would stake my soul that it is. My dear mother is an angel in heaven; I am certain of that; for I have seen her in my dreams ever since I can remember. But yet—but yet—why did they all recoil from me? Even she—even Claudia Merlin shrank from me as from something unclean and contaminating, when Alfred called me that name. If they had not thought there was some truth in the charge, would they all have recoiled from me so? Would she have shrunk from me as if I had had the plague? Oh, no! Oh, no! And then Aunt Hannah! Why does she act so very strangely when I ask her about my parents? If I ask her about my father she answers me with a blow. If I ask her about my mother, she answers that my mother was a saint on earth and is now an angel in heaven. Oh! I do not need to be told that; I know it already. I always knew it of my dear mother. But to only know it no longer satisfies me; I must have the means of proving it. And to-night, yes, to-night, Aunt Hannah, before either of us sleep, you shall tell me all that you know of my angel mother and my unknown father."

And having recovered his severely shaken strength, Ishmael left the grounds of Brudenell Hall and struck into the narrow foot-path leading down the heights and through the valley to the Hut hill.

Hannah was seated alone, enjoying her solitary cup of tea, when Ishmael opened the door and entered.

"What, my lad, have you come back so early? I did not think the ball would have been over before twelve or one o'clock, and it is not ten yet; but I suppose, being a school ball, it broke up early. Did you get any premiums? How many did you get?" inquired Hannah, heaping question upon question without waiting for reply, as was her frequent custom.

Ishmael drew a chair to the other side of the table and sunk heavily into it.

"You are tired, poor fellow, and no wonder! I dare say, for all the good things you got at the ball, that a cup of tea will do you no harm," said Hannah, pouring out and handing him one.

Ishmael took it wearily and sat it by his side.

"And now tell me about the premiums," continued his aunt.

"I got the first premium in belles-lettres, aunt; and it was Hallam's 'History of Literature.' And I got the first in languages, which was Irving's 'Life of Washington'—two very valuable works, Aunt Hannah, that will be treasures to me all my life."

"Why do you sigh so heavily, my boy? are you so tired as all that? But one would think, as well as you love books, those fine ones would 'liven you up. Where are they? Let me see them."

"I left them at the school, Aunt Hannah. I will go and fetch them to-morrow."

"There's that sigh again! What is the matter with you, child? Are you growing lazy? Who got the gold medal?"

"It wasn't a medal, Aunt Hannah. Mr. Middleton wanted to give something useful as well as costly for the first prize; and he said a medal was of no earthly use to anybody, so he made the prize a gold watch and chain."

"But who got it?"

"I did, aunt; there it is," said Ishmael, taking the jewel from his neck and laying it on the table.

"Oh! what a beautiful watch and chain! and all pure gold! real yellow guinea gold! This must be worth almost a hundred dollars! Oh, Ishmael, we never had anything like this in the house before. I am so much afraid somebody might break in and steal it!" exclaimed Hannah, her admiration and delight at sight of the rich prize immediately modified by the cares and fears that attend the possession of riches.

Ishmael did not reply; but Hannah went on reveling in the sight of the costly bauble, until, happening to look up, she saw that Ishmael, instead of drinking his tea, sat with his head drooped upon his hand in sorrowful abstraction.

"There you are again! There is no satisfying some people. One would think you would be as happy as a king with all your prizes. But there you are moping. What is the matter with you, boy? Why don't you drink your tea?"

"Aunt Hannah, you drink your own tea, and when you have done it I will have a talk with you."

"Is it anything particular?"

"Very particular, Aunt Hannah; but I will not enter upon the subject now," said Ishmael, raising his cup to his lips to prevent further questionings.

But when the tea was over and the table cleared away, Ishmael took the hand of his aunt and drew her towards the door, saying:

"Aunt Hannah, I want you to go with me to my mother's grave. It will not hurt you to do so; the night is beautiful, clear and dry, and there is no dew."

Wondering at the deep gravity of his words and manner, Hannah allowed him to draw her out of the house and up the hill behind it to Nora's grave at the foot of the old oak tree. It was a fine, bright, starlight night, and the rough headstone, rudely fashioned and set up by the professor, gleamed whitely out from the long shadowy grass.

Ishmael sank down upon the ground beside the grave, put his arms around the headstone, and for a space bowed his head.

Hannah seated herself upon a fragment of rock near him. But both remained silent for a few minutes.

It was Hannah who broke the spell.

"Ishmael, my dear," she said, "why have you drawn me out here, and what have you to say to me of such a serious nature that it can be uttered only here?"

But Ishmael still was silent—being bowed down with thought or grief.

Reflect a moment, reader: At this very instant of time his enemy—he who had plunged him in this grief—was in the midst of all the light and music of the ball at Brudenell Hall; but could not enjoy himself, because the stings of conscience irritated him, and because the frowns of Claudia Merlin chilled and depressed him.

Ishmael was out in the comparative darkness and silence of night and nature. Yet he, too, had his light and music—light and music more in harmony with his mood than any artificial substitutes could be; he had the holy light of myriads of stars shining down upon him, and the music of myriads of tiny insects sounding around him. Mark you this, dear reader—in light and music is the Creator forever worshiped by nature. When the sun sets, the stars shine; and when the birds sleep, the insects sing!

This subdued light and music of nature's evening worship suited well the saddened yet exalted mood of our poor boy. He knew not what was before him, what sort of revelation he was about to invoke, but he knew that, whatever it might be, it should not shake his resolve, "to deal justly, love mercy, and walk humbly" with his God.

Hannah, spoke again:

"Ishmael, will you answer me—why have you brought me here? What have you to say to me so serious as to demand this grave for the place of its hearing?"

"Aunt Hannah," began the boy, "what I have to say to you is even more solemn than your words import."

"Ishmael, you frighten me."

"No, no; there is no cause of alarm."

"Why don't you tell me what has brought us here, then?"

"I am about to do so," said Ishmael solemnly. "Aunt Hannah, you have often told me that she whose remains lie below us was a saint on earth and is an angel in heaven!"

"Yes, Ishmael. I have told you so, and I have told you truly."

"Aunt Hannah, three years ago I asked you who was my father. You replied by a blow. Well, I was but a boy then, and so of course you must have thought that that was the most judicious answer you could give. But now, Aunt Hannah, I am a young man, and I demand of you, Who was my father?"

"Ishmael, I cannot tell you!"

With a sharp cry of anguish the youth sprang up; but governing his strong excitement he subsided to his seat, only gasping out the question:

"In the name of Heaven, why can you not?"

Hannah's violent sobs were the only answer.

"Aunt Hannah! I know this much—that your name is Hannah Worth; that my dear mother was your sister; that her name was Nora Worth; and that mine is Ishmael Worth! Therefore I know that I bear yours and my mother's maiden name! I always took it for granted that my father belonged to the same family; that he was a relative, perhaps a cousin of my mother, and that he bore the same name, and therefore did not in marrying my mother give her a new one. That was what I always thought, Aunt Hannah; was I right?"

Hannah sobbed on in silence.

"Aunt Hannah! by my mother's grave, I adjure you to answer me! Was I right?"

"No, Ishmael, you were not!" wailed Hannah.

"Then I do not bear my father's name?"

"No."

"But only my poor mother's?"

"Yes."

"Oh, Heaven! how is that?"

"Because you have no legal right to your father's; because the only name to which you have any legal right is your poor, wronged mother's!"

With a groan that seemed to rend body and soul asunder, Ishmael threw himself upon his mother's grave.

"You said she was an angel! And I know that she was!" he cried, as soon as he had recovered the power of speech.·

"I said truly, and you know the truth!" wept Hannah.

"How, then, is it, that I, her son, cannot bear my father's name?"

"Ishmael, your mother was the victim of a false marriage!"

Ishmael sprang up from his recumbent posture, and gazed at his aunt with a fierceness that pierced through the darkness.

"And so pure and proud was she, that the discovery broke her heart!"

Ishmael threw himself once more upon the grave, and clasping the mound in his arms, burst into a passionate flood of tears, and wept long and bitterly. And, after a while, through this shower of tears, came forth in gusty sobs these words:

"Oh, mother! Oh, poor, young, wronged, and broken-hearted mother! sleep in peace; for your son lives to vindicate you. Yes, if he has been spared, it was for this purpose—to honor, to vindicate, to avenge you!" And after these words his voice was again lost and drowned in tears and sobs.

Hannah kneeled down beside him, took his hand, and tried to raise him, saying:

"Ishmael, my love, get up, dear! There was no wrong done, no crime committed, nothing to avenge. Your father was as guiltless as your mother, my boy; there was no sin; nothing from first to last but great misfortune. Come into the house, my Ishmael, and I will tell you all about it."

"Yes; tell me all! tell me every particular; have no more concealments from me!" cried Ishmael, rising to follow his aunt.

"I will not; but oh, my boy! gladly would I have kept the sorrowful story concealed from you forever, but that I know from what I have seen of you to-night, that some rude tongue has told you of your misfortune—and told you wrong besides!" said Hannah, as they re-entered the hut.

They sat down beside the small wood fire that the chill night made not unwelcome, even in August. Hannah sat in her old arm-chair, and Ishmael on the three-legged stool at her feet, with his head in her lap. And there, with her hand caressing his light brown hair, Hannah told him the story of his mother's love and suffering and death.

At some parts of her story his tears gushed forth in floods, and his sobs shook his whole frame. Then Hannah would be forced to pause in her narrative, until he had regained composure enough to listen to the sequel.

Hannah told him all; every particular with which the reader is already acquainted; suppressing nothing but the name of his miserable father.

At the close of the sad story both remained silent for some time; the deathly stillness of the room broken only by Ishmael's deep sighs. At last, however, he spoke:

"Aunt Hannah, still you have not told me the name of him my poor mother loved so fatally."

"Ishmael, I have told you that I cannot; and now I will tell you why I cannot."

And then Hannah related the promise that she had made to her dying sister, never to expose the unhappy but guiltless author of her death.

"Poor mother! poor, young, broken-hearted mother! She was not much older than I am now when she died—was she, Aunt Hannah?"

"Scarcely two years older, my dear."

"So young!" sobbed Ishmael, dropping his head again upon Hannah's knee, and bursting into a tempest of grief.

She allowed the storm to subside a little, and then said:

"Now, my Ishmael, I wish you to tell me what it was that sent you home so early from the party, and in such a sorrowful mood. I knew, of course, that something must have been said to you about your birth. What was said, and who said it?"

"Oh, Aunt Hannah! it was in the very height of my triumph that I was struck down! I was not proud, Heaven knows, that I should have had such a fall! I was not proud—I was feeling rather sad upon account of Walter's having missed the prize; and I was thinking how hard it was in this world that nobody could enjoy a triumph without someone else suffering a mortification. I was thinking and feeling so, as I tell you, until Walter came up and talked me out of my gloom. And then all my young companions were doing me honor in their way, when—"

Ishmael's voice was choked for a moment; but with an effort he regained his composure and continued, though in a broken and faltering voice:

"Alfred Burghe left the group, saying that I was not a proper companion for young ladies and gentlemen. And when—she—Miss Merlin, angrily demanded why I was not, he—Oh! Aunt Hannah!" Ishmael suddenly ceased and dropped his face into his hands.

"Compose yourself, my dear boy, and go on," said the weaver.

"He said that I was a—No! I cannot speak the word! I cannot!"

"A young villain! If ever I get my hands on him, I will give him as good a broomsticking as ever a bad boy had in this world! He lied, Ishmael! You are not what he called you. You are legitimate on your mother's side, because she believed herself to be a lawful wife. You bear her name, and you could lawfully inherit her property, if she had left any. Tell them that when they insult you!" exclaimed Hannah indignantly.

"Ah! Aunt Hannah, they would not believe it without proof!"

"True! too true! and we cannot prove it, merely because your mother bound me by a promise never to expose the bigamy of your father. Oh, Ishmael, to shield him, what a wrong she did to herself and to you!" wept the woman.

"Oh, Aunt Hannah, do not blame her! she was so good!" said this loyal son. "I can bear reproach for myself, but I will not bear it for her! Say anything you like to me, dear Aunt Hannah! but never say a word against her!"

"But, poor boy! how will you bear the sure reproach of birth that you are bound to hear from others? Ah, Ishmael, you must try to fortify your mind, my dear, to bear much unjust shame in this world. Ishmael, the brighter the sun shines the blacker the shadow falls. The greater your success in the world, the bitterer will be this shame! See, my boy, it was in the hour of your youthful triumph that this reproach was first cast in your face! The envious are very mean, my boy. Ah, how will you answer their cruel reproaches!"

"I will tell you, Aunt Hannah! Let them say what they like of me; I will try to bear with them patiently; but if any man or boy utters one word of reproach against my dear mother—" The boy ceased to speak, but his face grew lived.

"Now, now, what would you do?" exclaimed Hannah, in alarm.

"Make him recant his words, or silence him forever!"

"Oh, Ishmael! Ishmael! you frighten me nearly to death! Good Heaven, men are dreadful creatures! They never receive an injury but they must needs think of slaying! Oh, how I wish you had been a girl! Since you were to be, how I do wish you had been a girl! Boys are a dreadful trial and terror to a lone woman! Oh, Ishmael! promise me you won't do anything violent!" exclaimed Hannah, beside herself with terror.

"I cannot, Aunt Hannah! For I should be sure to break such a promise if the occasion offered. Oh, Aunt Hannah! you don't know all my mother is to me! You don't! You think because she died the very day that I was born that I cannot know anything about her and cannot love her; but I tell you, Aunt Hannah, I know her well! and I love her as much as if she was still in the flesh. I have seen her in my dreams ever since I can remember anything. Oh! often, when I was very small and you used to lock me up alone in the hut, while you went away for all day to Baymouth, I have been strangely soothed to sleep and then I have seen her in my dreams!"

"Ishmael, you rave!"

"No, I don't; I will prove it to you, that I see my mother. Listen, now; nobody ever described her to me; not even you; but I will tell you how she looks—she is tall and slender; she has a very fair skin and very long black

145

hair, and nice slender black eyebrows and long eyelashes, and large dark eyes—and she smiles with her eyes only! Now, is not that my mother? For that is the form that I see in my dreams," said Ishmael triumphantly, and for the moment forgetting his grief.

"Yes, that is like what she was; but of course you must have heard her described by someone, although you may have forgotten it. Ishmael, dear, I shall pray for you to-night, that all thoughts of vengeance may be put out of your mind. Now let us go to bed, my child, for we have to be up early in the morning. And, Ishmael?"

"Yes, Aunt Hannah."

"Do you also pray to God for guidance and help."

"Aunt Hannah, I always do," said the boy, as he bade his relative good-night and went up to his loft.

Long Ishmael lay tumbling and tossing upon his restless bed. But when at length he fell asleep a heavenly dream visited him.

He dreamed that his mother, in her celestial robe, stood by his bed and breathed sweetly forth his name:

"Ishmael, my son."

And in his dream he answered:

"I am here, mother."

"Listen, my child: Put thoughts of vengeance from your soul! In this strong temptation think not what Washington, Jackson, or any of your warlike heroes would have done; think what the Prince of Peace, Christ, would have done; and do thou likewise!" And so saying, the heavenly vision vanished.

CHAPTER XXXIII.

LOVE AND GENIUS.

Her face was shining on him; he had looked
Upon it till it could not pass away;
He had no breath, no being but in hers;
She was his voice: he did not speak to her,
But trembled on her words: she was his sight;
For his eye followed hers and saw with hers,
Which colored all his objects.
—*Byron.*

Early the next morning Ishmael walked over to Brudenell Hall with the threefold purpose of making an apology for his sudden departure from the ball; taking leave of the family for the holidays; and bringing home the books he had won as prizes.

As he approached the house he saw Mr. Middleton walking on the lawn.

That gentleman immediately advanced to meet Ishmael, holding out his hand, and saying, with even more than his usual kindness of manner:

"Good-morning, my dear boy; you quite distinguished yourself yesterday; I congratulate you."

"I thank you, sir; I thank you very much; but I fear that I was guilty of great rudeness in leaving the party so abruptly last night; but I hope, when you hear my explanation, you will excuse me, sir," said Ishmael, deeply flushing.

Mr. Middleton kindly drew the boy's arm within his own, and walked him away from the house down a shady avenue of elms, and when they had got quite out of hearing of any chance listener, he said gravely:

"My boy, I have heard the facts from Walter, and I do not require any explanation from you. I hold you entirely blameless in the affair, Ishmael, and I can only express my deep regret that you should have received an insult while under my roof. I trust, Ishmael, that time and reflection will convince young Burghe of his great error, and that the day may come when he himself will seek you to make a voluntary apology for his exceeding rudeness."

Ishmael did not reply; his eyes were fixed upon the ground, and his very forehead was crimson. Mr. Middleton saw all this, divined his thoughts, and so gently continued:

"You will be troubled no more with Alfred Burghe or his weak brother; both boys left this morning; Alfred goes to the Military Academy at West Point; Ben to the Naval School at Annapolis; so you will be quite free from annoyance by them."

Still Ishmael hung his head, and Mr. Middleton added:

"And now, my young friend, do not let the recollection of that scapegrace's words trouble you in the slightest degree. Let me assure you, that no one who knows you, and whose good opinion is worth having, will ever esteem your personal merits less, upon account of—" Mr. Middleton hesitated for a moment, and then said, very softly—"your poor, unhappy mother."

Ishmael sprang aside, and groaned as if he had received a stab; and then with a rush of emotion, and in an impassioned manner, he exclaimed:

"My poor, unhappy mother! Oh, sir, you have used the right words! She was very poor and very unhappy! most unhappy; but not weak! not foolish! not guilty! Oh, believe it, sir! believe it, Mr. Middleton! For if you were to doubt it, I think my spirit would indeed be broken! My poor, young mother, who went down to the grave when she was but little older than her son is now, was a pure, good, honorable woman. She was, sir! she was! and I will prove it to the world some day, if Heaven only lets me live to do it! Say you believe it, Mr. Middleton! Oh, say you believe it!"

"I do believe it, my boy," replied Mr. Middleton, entirely carried away by the powerful magnetism of Ishmael's eager, earnest, impassioned manner.

"Heaven reward you, sir," sighed the youth, subsiding into the modest calmness of his usual deportment.

"How do you intend to employ your holidays, Ishmael?" inquired his friend.

"By continuing my studies at home, sir," replied the youth.

"I thought so! Well, so that you do not overwork yourself, you are right to keep them up. These very long vacations are made for the benefit of the careless and idle, and not for the earnest and industrious. But, Ishmael, that little cot of yours is not the best place for your purpose; studies can scarcely be pursued favorably where household work is going on constantly; so I think you had better come here every day as usual, and read in the schoolroom. Mr. Brown will be gone certainly; but I shall be at home, and ready to render you any assistance."

"Oh, sir, how shall I thank you?" joyfully began Ishmael.

"By just making the best use of your opportunities to improve yourself, my lad," smiled his friend, patting him on the shoulder.

"But, sir—in the vacation—it will give you trouble—"

"It will afford me pleasure, Ishmael! I hope you can take my word for that?"

"Oh, Mr. Middleton! Indeed you—how can I ever prove myself grateful enough?"

"By simply getting on as fast as you can, boy! as I told you before. And let me tell you now, that there is good reason why you should now make the best possible use of your time; it may be short."

"Sir?" questioned Ishmael in perplexity and vague alarm.

"I should rather have said it must be short! I will explain. You know Mr. Herman Brudenell?"

"Mr—Herman—Brudenell," repeated the unconscious son, slowly and thoughtfully; then, as a flash of intelligence lighted up his face, he exclaimed: "Oh, yes, sir, I know who you mean; the young gentleman who owns Brudenell Hall, and who is now traveling in Europe."

"Yes! but he is not such a very young gentleman now; he must be between thirty-five and forty years of age. Well, my boy, you know, of course, that he is my landlord. When I rented this place, I took it by the year, and at a very low price, as the especial condition that I should leave it at six months' warning. Ishmael, I have received that warning this morning. I must vacate the premises on the first of next February."

Ishmael looked confounded. "Must vacate these premises the first of next February," he echoed, in a very dreary voice.

"Yes, my lad; but don't look so utterly sorrowful; we shall not go out of the world, or even out of the State; perhaps not out of the county, Ishmael; and our next residence will be a permanent one; I shall purchase, and not rent, next time; and I shall not lose sight of your interests; besides the parting is six months off yet; so look up, my boy. Bless me, if I had known it was going to depress you in this way, I should have delayed the communication as long as possible; in fact, my only motive for making it now, is to give a good reason why you should make the most of your time while we remain here."

"Oh, sir, I will; believe me, I will; but I am so sorry you are ever going to leave us," said the boy, with emotion.

147

"Thank you, Ishmael; I shall not forget you; and in the meantime, Mr. Brudenell, who is coming back to the Hall, and is a gentleman of great means and beneficence, cannot fail to be interested in you; indeed, I myself will mention you to him. And now come in, my boy, and take luncheon with us. We breakfasted very early this morning in order to get the teachers off in time for the Baltimore boat; and so we require an early luncheon," said Mr. Middleton, as he walked his young friend off to the house.

Mrs. Middleton and all her children and Claudia were already seated around the table in the pleasant morning room, where all the windows were open, admitting the free summer breezes, the perfume of flowers, and the songs of birds.

The young people started up and rushed towards Ishmael; for their sympathies were with him; and all began speaking at once.

"Oh, Ishmael! why did you disappoint me of dancing with the best scholar in the school?" asked Claudia.

"What did you run away for?" demanded James.

"I wouldn't have gone for him," said John.

"Oh, Ishmael, it was such a pleasant party," said little Fanny.

"Alf was a bad boy," said Baby Sue.

"It was very impolite in you to run away and leave me when I was your partner in the first quadrille! I do not see why you should have disappointed me for anything that fellow could have said or done!" exclaimed Claudia.

As all were speaking at once it was quite impossible to answer either, so Ishmael looked in embarrassment from one to the other.

Bee had not spoken; she was spreading butter on thin slices of bread for her baby sisters; but now, seeing Ishmael's perplexity, she whispered to her mother:

"Call them off, mamma dear; they mean well; but it must hurt his feelings to be reminded of last night."

Mrs. Middleton thought so too; so she arose and went forward and offered Ishmael her hand, saying:

"Good-morning, my boy; I am glad to see you; draw up your chair to the table. Children, take your places. Mr. Middleton, we have been waiting for you."

"I know you have, my dear, but cold lunch don't grow colder by standing; if it does, so much the better this warm weather."

"I have been taking a walk with my young friend here," said the gentleman, as he took his seat.

Ishmael followed his example, but not before he had quietly shaken hands with Beatrice.

At luncheon Mr. Middleton spoke of his plan, that Ishmael should come every day during the holidays to pursue his studies as usual in the schoolroom.

"You know he cannot read to any advantage in the little room where Hannah is always at work," explained Mr. Middleton.

"Oh, no! certainly not," agreed his wife.

The family were all pleased that Ishmael was still to come.

"But, my boy, I think you had better not set in again until Monday. A few days of mental rest is absolutely necessary after the hard reading of the last few months. So I enjoin you not to open a classbook before next Monday."

As Mrs. Middleton emphatically seconded this move, our boy gave his promise to refrain, and after luncheon was over he went and got his books, took a respectful leave of his friends and returned home.

"Aunty," he said, as he entered the hut, where he found Hannah down on her knees scrubbing the floor, "what do you think? Mr. Middleton and his family are going away from the Hall. They have had warning to quit at the end of six months."

"Ah," said Hannah indifferently, going on with her work.

"Yes; they leave on the first of February, and the owner of the place, young Mr. Herman Brudenell, you know, is coming on to live there for good!"

"Ah!" cried Hannah, no longer indifferently, but excitedly, as she left off scrubbing, and fixed her keen black eyes upon the boy.

"Yes, indeed! and Mr. Middleton—oh, he is so kind—says he will mention me to Mr Herman Brudenell."

"Oh! will he?" exclaimed Hannah, between her teeth.

"Yes; and—Mr. Herman Brudenell is a very kind gentleman, is he not?"

"Very," muttered Hannah.

"You were very well acquainted with him, were you not?"

"Yes."

"You answer so shortly, Aunt Hannah. Didn't you like young Mr. Herman Brudenell?"

"I—don't know whether I did or not; but, Ishmael, I can't scrub and talk at the same time. Go out and chop me some wood; and then go and dig some potatoes, and beets, and cut a cabbage—a white-head mind! and then go to the spring and bring a bucket of water; and make haste; but don't talk to me any more, if you can help it."

Ishmael went out immediately to obey, and as the sound of his ax was heard Hannah muttered to herself:

"Herman Brudenell coming back to the Hall to live!" And she fell into deep thought.

Ishmael was intelligent enough to divine that his Aunt Hannah did not wish to talk of Mr. Herman Brudenell.

"Some old grudge, connected with their relations as landlord and tenant, I suppose," said Ishmael to himself. And as he chopped away at the wood he resolved to avoid in her presence the objectionable name.

The subject was not mentioned between the aunt and nephew again. Ishmael assisted her in preparing their late afternoon meal of dinner and supper together, and then, when the room was made tidy and Hannah was seated at her evening sewing, Ishmael, for a treat, showed her his prize books; at which Hannah was so pleased, that she went to bed and dreamed that night that Ishmael had risen to the distinction of being a country schoolmaster.

The few days of mental rest that Mr. Middleton had enjoined upon the young student were passed by Ishmael in hard manual labor that did him good. Among his labors, as he had now several valuable books, he fitted up some book shelves over the little low window of his loft, and under the window he fixed a sloping board, that would serve him for a writing-desk.

CHAPTER XXXIV.

UNDER THE OLD ELM TREE.

She was his life,
The ocean to the river of his thoughts,
Which terminated all; upon a tone,
A touch of hers, his blood would ebb and flow,
And his cheek change tempestuously—his heart
Unknowing of its cause of agony.
—*Byron.*

On Monday morning he resumed his attendance at Brudenell Hall. He was received very kindly by the family, and permitted to go up to the empty schoolroom and take his choice among all the vacant seats, and to make the freest use of the school library, maps, globes, and instruments.

Ishmael moved his own desk up under one of the delightful windows, and there he sat day after day at hard study. He did not trouble Mr. Middleton much; whenever it was possible to do so by any amount of labor and thought, he puzzled out all his problems and got over all his difficulties alone.

He kept up the old school hours; punctually, and exactly at noon, he laid aside his books and went out on the lawn for an hour's recreation before lunch.

There he often met his young friends, and always saw Claudia. It was Miss Merlin's good pleasure to approve and encourage this poor but gifted youth; and she took great credit, to herself for her condescension. She seemed to herself like some high and mighty princess graciously patronizing some deserving young peasant. She often called him to her side; interested himself in his studies and in his health, praised his assiduity, but warned him not to confine himself too closely to his books, as ambitious students had been known before now to sacrifice their lives to the pursuit of an unattainable fame. She told him that she meant to interest her father in his fortunes; and that she hoped in another year the judge would be able to procure for him the situation of usher in some school, or tutor in some family. Although she was younger than Ishmael, yet her tone and manner in addressing him was that of an elder as well as of a superior; and blended the high authority of a young queen with the deep tenderness of a little mother. For instance, when he would come out at noon, she would often beckon him to her side, as she sat in her garden chair, under the shadow of the great elm tree, with a book of poetry or a piece of needlework in her hands. And when he came, she would make him sit down on the grass at her feet, and she would put her small, white hand on his burning forehead, and look in his face with her beautiful, dark eyes, and murmur softly:

"Poor boy; your head aches; I know it does. You have been sitting under the blazing sun in that south window of the schoolroom, so absorbed in your studies that you forgot to close your shutters."

And she would take a vial of eau-de-cologne from her pocket, pour a portion of it upon a handkerchief, and with her own fair hand bathe his heated brows; at the same time administering a queenly reprimand, or a motherly caution, as pride or tenderness happened to predominate in her capricious mood.

This royal or maternal manner in this beautiful girl would not have attracted the hearts of most men; but Ishmael, at the age of seventeen, was yet too young to feel that haughty pride of full-grown manhood which recoils from the patronage of women, and most of all from that of the woman they love.

To him, this proud and tender interest for his welfare added a greater and more perilous fascination to the charms of his beautiful love; it drew her nearer to him; it allowed him to worship her, though mutely; it permitted him to sit at her feet, and in that attitude do silent homage to her as his queen; it permitted him to receive the cool touch of her fingers on his heated brow; to hear the soft murmur of her voice close to his ear; to meet the sweet questioning of her eyes.

And, oh, the happiness of sitting at her feet, under the green shadows of that old elm tree! The light touch of her soft fingers on his brow thrilled him to his heart's core; the sweet sound of her voice in his ears filled his soul with music; the earnest gaze of her beautiful dark eyes sent electric shocks of joy through all his sensitive frame.

Ishmael was intensely happy. This earth was no longer a commonplace world, filled with commonplace beings; it was a paradise peopled with angels.

Did Mr. and Mrs. Middleton fear no harm in the close intimacy of this gifted boy of seventeen and this beautiful girl of sixteen?

Indeed, no! They believed the proud heiress looked upon, the peasant boy merely as her protégé, her pet, her fine, intelligent dog! they believed Claudia secure in her pride and Ishmael absorbed in his studies. They were three-quarters right, which is as near the correct thing as you can expect imperfect human nature to approach; that is, they were wholly right as to Claudia and half right as to Ishmael. Claudia was secure in her pride; and half of Ishmael's soul—the mental half—was absorbed in his studies; his mind was given to his books; but his heart was devoted to Claudia. And in this double occupation there was no discord, but the most perfect harmony.

But though Claudia, whom he adored, was his watchful patroness, Bee, whom he only loved, was his truest friend. Claudia would warn him against danger; but Bee would silently save him from it. While Claudia would be administering a queenly rebuke to the ardent young student for exposing himself to a sunstroke by reading under the blazing sun in an open south window, Bee, without saying a word, would go quietly into the schoolroom, close the shutters of the sunny windows, and open those of the shady ones, so that the danger might not recur in the afternoon.

In September the school was regularly reopened for the reception of the day pupils. Their parents were warned, however, that this was to be the last term; that the school must necessarily be broken up at Christmas, as the house must be given up on the first of February. The return of the pupils, although they filled the schoolroom during study hours, and made the lawn a livelier scene during recess, did not in the least degree interrupt the intimacy of Ishmael and Claudia. He still sat at her feet beneath the green shadows of the old elm tree, often reading to her while she worked her crochet; or strumming upon his old guitar an accompaniment to her song. For long ago the professor had taught Ishmael to play, and loaned him the instrument.

It is not to be supposed that Claudia's favor of Ishmael could be witnessed by his companions without exciting their envy and dislike of our youth. But the more strongly they evinced their disapproval of her partiality for Ishmael, the more ostentatiously she displayed it.

Many were the covert sneers leveled at "Nobody's Son." And often Ishmael felt his heart swell, his blood boil, and his cheek burn at these cowardly insults. And it was well for all concerned that the youth was "obedient" to that "heavenly vision" which had warned him, in these sore trials, not to ask himself—as had been his boyish custom—what Marion, Putnam, Jackson, or any of the "great battle-ax heroes" would have done in a similar crisis; but what Christ, the Prince of Peace, would have done; for Ishmael knew that all these great historical warriors held the "bloody code of honor" that would oblige them to answer insult with death; but that the Saviour of the world "when reviled, reviled not again"; and that he commended all his followers to do likewise, returning "good for evil," "blessings for cursings."

All this was very hard to do; and the difficulty of it finally sent Ishmael to study his Bible with a new interest, to seek the mystery of the Saviour's majestic meekness. In the light of a new experience, he read the amazing story of the life, sufferings, and death of Christ. Oh, nothing in the whole history of mankind could approach this, for beauty, for sublimity, and for completeness; nothing had ever so warmed, inspired, and elevated his soul as this; this was perfect; answering all the needs of his spirit. The great heroes and sages of history might be very good and useful as examples and references in the ordinary trials and temptations of life; but only Christ could teach him how to meet the great trial from the world without, where envy and hate assailed him; or how to resist the dark temptations from the world within, in whose deep shadows rage and murder lurked! Henceforth the Saviour became his own exemplar and the gospel his only guidebook. Such was the manner in which Ishmael was called of the Lord. He became proof against the most envenomed shafts of malice. The reflection: What would Christ have done? armed him with a sublime and invincible meekness and courage.

CHAPTER XXXV.

THE DREAM AND THE AWAKENING.

The lover is a god,—the ground
He treads on is not ours;
His soul by other laws is bound,
Sustained by other powers;
His own and that one other heart
Form for himself a world apart.
—*Milnes*.

Time went on. Autumn faded into winter: the flowers wore withered; the grass dried; the woods bare. Miss Merlin no longer sat under the green shadows of the old elm tree; there were no green shadows there; the tree was stripped of its leaves and seemed but the skeleton of itself, and the snow lay around its foot.

The season, far from interrupting the intimacy between the heiress and her favorite, only served to draw them even more closely together. This was the way of it. At the noon recess all the pupils of the school would rush madly out upon the lawn to engage in the rough, healthful, and exciting game of snowballing each other—all except Claudia, who was far too fine a lady to enter into any such rude sport, and Ishmael, whose attendance upon her own presence she would peremptorily demand.

While all the others were running over each other in their haste to get out, Claudia would pass into the empty drawing room, and seating herself in the deep easy chair, would call to her "gentleman in waiting," saying:

"Come, my young troubadour, bring your guitar and sit down upon this cushion at my feet and play an accompaniment to my song, as I sing and work."

And Ishmael, filled with joy, would fly to obey the royal mandate; and soon seated at the beauty's feet, in the glow of the warm wood fire and in the glory of her heavenly presence, he would lose himself in a delicious dream of love and music. No one ever interrupted their tête-à-tête. And Ishmael grew to feel that he belonged to his liege lady; that they were forever inseparate and inseparable. And thus his days passed in one delusive dream of bliss until the time came when he was rudely awakened.

One evening, as usual, he took leave of Claudia. It was a bitter cold evening, and she took off her own crimson Berlin wool scarf and with her own fair hands wound it around Ishmael's neck, and charged him to hasten home, because she knew that influenza would be lying in wait to seize any loitering pedestrian that night.

Ishmael ran home, as happy as it was in the power of man to make him. How blest he felt in the possession of her scarf—her fine, soft, warm scarf, deliciously filled with the aroma of Claudia's own youth, beauty, and sweetness. He felt that he was not quite separated from her while he had her scarf—her dear scarf, with the warmth and perfume of her own neck yet within its meshes! That night he only unwound it from his throat to fold it and lay it on his pillow that his cheek might rest upon it while he slept—slept the sweetest sleep that ever visited his eyes.

Ah, poor, pale sleeper! this was the last happy night he was destined to have for many weeks and months.

In the morning he arose early as usual to hasten to school and—to Claudia. He wound her gift around his neck and set off at a brisk pace. The weather was still intensely cold; but the winter sky was clear and the sunshine glittered "keen and bright" upon the crisp white snow. Ishmael hurried on and reached Brudenell Hall just in time to see a large fur-covered sleigh, drawn by a pair of fine horses, shoot through, the great gates and disappear down the forest road.

A death-like feeling, a strange spasm, as if a hand of ice had clutched his heart, caught away Ishmael's breath at the sight of that vanishing sleigh. He could not rationally account for this feeling; but soon as he recovered his breath he inquired of old Jovial, who stood gazing after the sleigh.

"Who has gone away?"

"Miss Claudia, sir; her pa came after her last night—"

"Claudia—gone!" echoing Ishmael, reeling and supporting himself against the trunk of the bare old elm tree.

"It was most unexpected, sir; mist'ess sat up most all night to see to the packing of her clothes—"

"Gone—gone—Claudia gone!" breathed Ishmael, in a voice despairing, yet so low, that it did not interrupt the easy flow of Jovial's narrative.

"But you see, sir, the judge, he said how he hadn't a day to lose, 'cause he'd have to be at Annapolis to-morrow to open his court—"

"Gone—gone!" wailed Ishmael, dropping his arms.

"And 'pears the judge did write to warn master and mist'ess to get Miss Claudia ready to go this morning; but seems like they never got the letter—"

"Oh, gone!" moaned Ishmael.

—"Anyways, it was all, 'Quick! march!' and away they went. And the word does go around as, after the court term is over, the judge he means to take Miss Claudia over the seas to forrin parts to see the world."

"Which—which road did they take, Jovial?" gasped Ishmael, striving hard to recover breath and strength and the power of motion.

"Law, sir, the Baymouth road, to be sure! where they 'spects to take the 'Napolis boat, which 'ill be a nigh thing if they get there in time to meet it, dough dey has taken the sleigh an' the fast horses."

Ishmael heard no more. Dropping his books, he darted out of the gate, and fled along the road taken by the travelers. Was it in the mad hope of overtaking the sleigh? As well might he expect to overtake an express train! No—he was mad indeed! maddened by the suddenness of his bereavement; but not so mad as that; and he started after his flying love in the fierce, blind, passionate instinct of pursuit. A whirl of wild hopes kept him up and urged him on—hopes that they might stop on the road to water the horses, or to refresh themselves, or that they might be delayed at the toll-gate to make change, or that some other possible or impossible thing might happen to stop their journey long enough for him to overtake them and see Claudia once more; to shake hands with her, bid her good-by, and receive from her at parting some last word of regard—some last token of remembrance! This was now the only object of his life; this was what urged him onward in that fearful chase! To see Claudia once more—to meet her eyes—to clasp her hand—to hear her voice—to bid her farewell!

On and on he ran; toiling up hill, and rushing down dale; overturning all impediments that lay in his way; startling all the foot-passengers with the fear of an escaped maniac! On and on he sped in his mad flight, until he reached the outskirts of the village. There a sharp pang and sudden faintness obliged him to stop and rest, grudging the few moments required for the recovery of his breath. Then he set off again, and ran all the way into the village—ran down the principal street, and turned down the one leading to the wharf.

A quick, breathless glance told him all. The boat had left the shore, and was steaming down the bay.

He ran down to the water's edge, stretching his arms out towards the receding steamer, and with an agonizing cry of "Claudia! Claudia!" fell forward upon his face in a deep swoon.

A crowd of villagers gathered around him.

"Who is he?"

"What is the matter with him!"

"Is he ill?"

"Has he fainted?"

"Has he been hurt?"

"Has an accident happened?"

"Is there a doctor to be had?"

All these questions were asked in the same breath by the various individuals of the crowd that had collected around the insensible boy; but none seemed ready with an answer.

"Is there no one here who can tell who he is?" inquired a tall, gray-haired, mild-looking man, stooping to raise the prostrate form.

"Yes; it is Ishmael Worth!" answered Hamlin, the bookseller, who was a newcomer upon the scene.

"Ishmael Worth? Hannah Worth's nephew?"

"Yes; that is who he is."

"Then stand out of the way, friends; I will take charge of the lad," said the gray-haired stranger, lifting the form of the boy in his arms, and gazing into his face.

"He is not hurt; he is only in a dead faint, and I had better take him home at once," continued the old man, as he carried his burden to a light wagon that stood in the street in charge of a negro, and laid him carefully on the cushions. Then he got in himself, and took the boy's head upon his knees, and directed the negro to drive gently along the road leading to the weaver's. And with what infinite tenderness the stranger supported the light form; with what wistful interest he contemplated the livid young face. And so at an easy pace they reached the hill hut.

CHAPTER XXXVI.

DARKNESS.

With such wrong and woe exhausted, what I suffered and occasioned—
As a wild horse through a city, runs, with lightning in his eyes,
And then dashing at a church's cold and passive wall impassioned,
Strikes the death into his burning brain, and blindly drops and dies—
So I fell struck down before her! Do you blame me, friends, for weakness?
'Twas my strength of passion slew me! fell before her like a stone;
Fast the dreadful world rolled from me, on its roaring wheels of blackness!
When the light came, I was lying in this chamber—and alone.
—E.B. Browning.

Hannah Worth was sitting over her great wood fire and busily engaged in needlework when the door was gently pushed open and the gray-haired man entered, bearing the boy in his arms.

Hannah looked calmly up, then threw down her work and started from her chair, exclaiming:

"Reuben Gray! you back again! you! and—who have you got there—Ishmael? Good Heavens! what has happened to the poor boy?"

"Nothing to frighten you, Hannah, my dear; he has fainted, I think, that is all," answered Reuben gently, as he laid the boy carefully upon the bed.

"But, oh, my goodness, Reuben, how did it happen? where did you find him?" cried Hannah, frantically seizing first one hand and then the other of the fainting boy, and clapping and rubbing them vigorously.

"I picked him up on the Baymouth wharf about half an hour ago, Hannah, my dear, and—"

"The Baymouth wharf! that is out of all reason! Why it is not more than two hours since he started to go to Brudenell Hall," exclaimed Hannah, as she violently rubbed away at the boy's hands.

Reuben was standing patiently at the foot of the bed, with his hat in his hands, and he answered slowly:

"Well, Hannah, I don't know how that might be; but I know I picked him up where I said."

"But what caused all this, Reuben Gray? What caused it? that's what I want to know! can't you speak?" harshly demanded the woman, as she flew to her cupboard, seized a vinegar cruet, and began to bathe Ishmael's head and face with its stimulating contents.

"Well, Hannah, I couldn't tell exactly; but 'pears to me someone went off in the boat as he was a-pining after."

"Who went off in the boat?" asked Hannah impatiently.

"Law, Hannah, my dear, how can I tell? Why, there wasn't less than thirty or forty passengers, more or less, went off in that boat!"

"What do I care how many restless fools went off in the boat? Tell me about the boy!" snapped Hannah, as she once more ran to the cupboard, poured out a little precious brandy (kept for medicinal purposes) and came and tried to force a teaspoonful between Ishmael's lips.

"Hannah, woman, don't be so unpatient. Indeed, it wasn't my fault. I will tell you all I know about it."

"Tell me, then."

"I am going to. Well, you see, I had just taken some of the judge's luggage down to the boat and got it well on, and the boat had just started, and I was just a-getting into my cart again when I see a youth come a-tearin'

153

down the street like mad, and he whips round the corner like a rush of wind, and streaks it down to the wharf and looks after the boat as if it was a-carrying off every friend he had upon the yeth; and then he stretches out both his arms and cries out aloud, and falls on his face like a tree cut down. And a crowd gathered, and someone said how the lad was your nephew, so I picked him up and laid him in my cart to bring him home. And I made Bob drive slow; and I bathed the boy's face and hands with some good whisky, and tried to make him swallow some; but it was no use."

While Reuben spoke, Ishmael gave signs of returning consciousness, and then suddenly opened his eyes and looked around him.

"Drink this, my boy; drink this, my darling Ishmael," said Hannah, raising his head with one hand while she held the brandy to his lips with the other.

Ishmael obediently drank a little and then sank back upon his pillow. He gazed fixedly at Hannah for a few moments, and then suddenly threw his arms around her neck, as she stooped over him, and cried out in a voice piercing shrill with anguish:

"Oh, Aunt Hannah! she is gone; she is gone forever!"

"Who is gone, my boy?" asked Hannah sympathetically.

"Claudia! Claudia!" he wailed, covering his convulsed face with his hands.

"How, my ban upon Brudenell Hall and all connected with it!" exclaimed Hannah bitterly, as the hitherto unsuspected fact of Ishmael's fatal love flashed upon her mind; "my blackest ban upon Brudenell Hall and all its hateful race! It was built for the ruin of me and mine! I was a fool, a weak, wicked fool, ever to have allowed Ishmael to enter its unlucky doors! My curse upon them!"

The boy threw up his thin hand with a gesture of deprecation.

"Don't! don't! don't, Aunt Hannah! Every word you speak is a stab through my heart." And the sentence closed with a gasp and a sob, and he covered his face with his hands.

"What can I do for him?" said Hannah, appealing to Reuben.

"Nothing, my dear, but what you have done. Leave him alone to rest quietly. It is easy to see that he has been very much shaken both in body and hind; and perfect rest is the only thing as will help him," answered Gray.

Ishmael's hands covered his quivering face; but they saw that his bosom was heaving convulsively. He seemed to be struggling valiantly to regain composure. Presently, as if ashamed of having betrayed his weakness, he uncovered his face and said, in a faltering and interrupted voice:

"Dear Aunt Hannah, I am so sorry that I have disturbed you; excuse me; and let me lie here for half an hour to recover myself. I do not wish to be self-indulgent; but I am exhausted. I ran all the way from Brudenell Hall to Baymouth to get—to see—to see———" His voice broke down with a sob, he covered his face with his hands, and shook as with an ague.

"Never mind, my dear, don't try to explain; lie as long as you wish, and sleep if you can," said Hannah.

But Ishmael looked up again, and with recovered calmness, said:

"I will rest for half an hour, Aunt Hannah, no longer; and then I will get up and cut the wood, or do any work you want done."

"Very well, my boy," said Hannah, stooping and kissing him. Then she arranged the pillow, covered him up carefully, drew the curtains and came away and left him.

"He will be all right in a little while, Hannah, my dear," said Reuben, as he walked with her to the fireplace.

"Sit down there, Reuben, and tell me about yourself, and where you have been living all this time," said Hannah, seating herself in her arm-chair and pointing to another.

Reuben slowly took the seat and carefully deposited his hat on the floor by his side.

"I am sorry I spoke so sharply to you about the lad, Reuben; it was a thankless return for all your kindness in taking care of him and bringing him home; but indeed I am not thankless, Reuben; but I have grown to be a cross old woman," she said.

"Have you, indeed, Hannah, my dear?" exclaimed Reuben, raising his eyebrows in sincere astonishment and some consternation.

"It appears to me that you might see that I have," replied Hannah plainly.

"Well, no; seems to me, my dear, you're the same as you allers was, both as to looks and as to temper."

"I feel that I am very much changed. And so are you, Reuben! How gray your hair is!" she said, looking critically at her old admirer.

"Gray! I believe you! Ain't it though?" exclaimed Reuben, smiling, and running his fingers through his blanched locks.

"But you haven't told me all about yourself, yet; where you have been living; how you have been getting along, and what brought you back to this part of the country," said Hannah, with an air of deep interest.

"Why, Hannah, my dear, didn't you know all how and about it?"

"No; I heard long ago, of course, that you had got a place as overseer on the plantation of some rich gentleman up in the forest; but that was all; I never even heard the name of the place or the master."

"Well, now, that beats all! Why, Hannah, woman, as soon as I got settled, I set down and writ you a letter, and all how and about it, and axed you, if ever you changed your mind about what—about the—about our affairs, you know—to drop me a line and I'd come and marry you and the child, right out of hand, and fetch you both to my new home."

"I never got the letter."

"See that, now! Everything, even the post, goes to cross a feller's love! But Hannah, woman, if you had a-got the letter, would you a-called me back?" asked Gray eagerly.

"No, Reuben, certainly not," said Hannah decidedly.

"Then it is just as well you didn't get it," sighed this most faithful, though most unfortunate of suitors.

"Yes; just as well, Reuben," assented Hannah; "but that fact does not lessen my interests in your fortunes, and as I never got the letter I am still ignorant of your circumstances."

"Well, Hannah, my dear, I'm thankful as you feel any interest in me at all; and I'll tell you everything. Let me see, what was it you was wanting to know, now? all about myself; where I was living; how I was getting along; and what fotch me back here; all soon told, Hannah, my dear. First about myself: You see, Hannah, that day as you slammed the door in my face I felt so distressed in my mind as I didn't care what on earth became of me; first I thought I'd just 'list for a soldier; then I thought I'd ship for a sailor; last I thought I'd go and seek my fortun' in Californy; but then the idea of the girls having no protector but myself hindered me; hows'evar, anyways I made up my mind, as come what would I'd leave the neighborhood first opportunity; and so, soon after, as I heard of a situation as overseer at Judge Merlin's plantation up in the forest of Prince George's County, I sets off and walks up there, and offers myself for the place; and was so fort'nate as to be taken; so I comes back and moves my family, bag and baggage, up there. Now as to the place where I live, it is called Tanglewood, and a tangle it is, as gets more and more tangled every year of its life. As to how I'm getting on, Hannah, I can't complain; for if I have to do very hard work, I get very good wages. As to what brought me back to the neighborhood, Hannah, it was to do some business for the judge, and to buy some stock for the farm. But there, my dear! that boy has slipped out, and is cutting the wood; I'll go and do it for him," said Reuben, as the sound of Ishmael's ax fell upon his ears.

Hannah arose and followed Gray to the door, and there before it stood Ishmael, chopping away at random, upon the pile of wood, his cheeks flushed with fever and his eyes wild with excitement.

"Hannah, he is ill; he is very ill; he doesn't well know what he is about," said Reuben, taking the ax from the boy's hand.

"Ishmael, Ishmael, my lad, come in; you are not well enough to work," said Hannah anxiously.

Ishmael yielded up the ax and suffered Reuben to draw him into the house.

"It is only that I am so hot and dizzy and weak, Mr. Middleton; but I am sure I shall be able to do it presently," said Ishmael apologetically, as he put his hand to his head and looked around himself in perplexity.

"I'll tell you what, the boy is out of his head, Hannah, and it's my belief as he's a going to have a bad illness," said Reuben, as he guided Ishmael to the bed and laid him on it.

"Oh, Reuben! what shall we do?" exclaimed Hannah.

"I don't know, child! wait a bit and see."

They had not long to wait; in a few hours Ishmael was burning with fever and raving with delirium.

"This is a-gwine to be a bad job! I'll go and fetch a doctor," said Reuben Gray, hurrying away for the purpose.

Reuben's words proved true. It was a "bad job." Severe study, mental excitement, disappointment and distress had done their work upon his extremely sensitive organization, and Ishmael was prostrated by illness.

We will not linger over the gloomy days that followed. The village doctor brought by Reuben was as skillful as if he had been the fashionable physician of a large city, and as attentive as if his poor young patient had been a millionaire. Hannah devoted herself with almost motherly love to the suffering boy; and Reuben remained in the neighborhood and came every day to fetch and carry, chop wood and bring water, and help Hannah to nurse Ishmael. And Hannah was absolutely reduced to the necessity of accepting his affectionate services. Mr. Middleton, as soon as he heard of his favorite's illness, hurried to the hut to inquire into Ishmael's condition and to offer every assistance in his power to render; and he repeated his visits as often as the great pressure of his affairs permitted him to do. Ishmael's illness was long protracted; Mr. Middleton's orders to vacate Brudenell

155

Hall on or before the first day of February were peremptory; and thus it followed that the whole family removed from the neighborhood before Ishmael was in a condition to bid them farewell.

The day previous to their departure, however, Mr. and Mrs. Middleton, with Walter and Beatrice, came to take leave of him. As Mrs. Middleton stooped over the unconscious youth her tears fell fast and warm upon his face, so that in his fever dream he murmured:

"Claudia, it is beginning to rain, let us go in."

At this Beatrice burst into a flood of tears and was led away to the carriage by her father.

After the departure of the Middletons it was currently reported in the neighborhood that the arrival of Mr. Herman Brudenell was daily expected. Hannah became very much disturbed with an anxiety that was all the more wearing because she could not communicate it to anyone. The idea of remaining in the neighborhood with Mr. Brudenell, and being subjected to the chance of meeting him, was unsupportable to her; she would have been glad of any happy event that might take her off to a distant part of the State, and she resolved, in the event of poor Ishmael's death, to go and seek a home and service somewhere else. Reuben Gray stayed on; and in answer to all Hannah's remonstrances he said:

"It is of no use talking to me now, Hannah! You can't do without me, woman; and I mean to stop until the poor lad gets well or dies."

But our boy was not doomed to die; the indestructible vitality, the irrepressible elasticity of his delicate and sensitive organization, bore him through and above his terrible illness, and he passed the crisis safely and lived. After that turning point his recovery was rapid. It was a mild, dry mid-day in early spring that Ishmael walked out for the first time. He bent his steps to the old oak tree that overshadowed his mother's grave, and seated himself there to enjoy the fresh air while he reflected.

Ishmael took himself severely to task for what he called the blindness, the weakness, and the folly with which he had permitted himself to fall into a hopeless, mad, and nearly fatal passion for one placed so high above him that indeed he might as well have loved some "bright particular star," and hoped to win it. And here on the sacred turf of his mother's grave he resolved once for all to conquer this boyish passion, by devoting himself to the serious business of life.

Hannah and Reuben were left alone in the hut.

"Now, Reuben Gray," began Hannah, "no tongue can tell how much I feel your goodness to me and Ishmael; but, my good man, you mustn't stay in this neighborhood any longer; Ishmael is well and does not need you; and your employer's affairs are neglected and do need you. So, Reuben, my friend, you had better start home as soon as possible."

"Well, Hannah, my dear, I think so too, and I have thought so for the last week, only I did not like to hurry you," said Reuben acquiescently.

"Didn't like to hurry me, Reuben? how hurry me? I don't know what you mean," said Hannah, raising her eyes in astonishment.

"Why, I didn't know as you'd like to get ready so soon; or, indeed, whether the lad was able to bear the journey yet," said Reuben calmly and reflectively.

"Reuben, I haven't the least idea of your meaning."

"Why, law, Hannah, my dear, it seems to me it is plain enough; no woman likes to be hurried at such times, and I thought you wouldn't like to be neither; I thought you would like a little time to get up some little finery; and also the boy would be the better for more rest before taking of a long journey; but hows'ever, Hannah, if you don't think all these delays necessary, why I wouldn't be the man to be a-making of them. Because, to tell you the truth, considering the shortness of life, I think the delays have been long enough; and considering our age, I think we have precious little time to lose. I'm fifty-one years of age, Hannah; and you be getting on smart towards forty-four; and if we ever mean to marry in this world, I think it is about time, my dear."

"Reuben Gray, is that what you mean?"

"Sartin, Hannah! You didn't think I was a-going away again without you, did you now?"

"And so that was what you meant, was it?"

"That was what I meant, and that was what I still mean, Hannah, my dear."

"Then you must be a natural fool!" burst forth Hannah.

"Now stop o' that, my dear! 'taint a bit of use! all them hard words might o' fooled me years and years agone, when you kept me at such a distance that I had no chance of reading your natur'; but they can't fool me now, as I have been six weeks in constant sarvice here, Hannah, and obsarving of you close. Once they might have made me think you hated me; but now nothing you can say will make me believe but what you like old Reuben to-day just as well as you liked young Reuben that day we first fell in love long o' one another at the harvest home.

And as for me, Hannah, the Lord knows I have never changed towards you. We always liked each other, Hannah, and we like each other still. So don't try to deceive yourself about it, for you can't deceive me!"

"Reuben Gray, why do you talk so to me?"

"Because it is right, dear."

"I gave you your answer years ago."

"I know you did, Hannah; because there were sartain circumstances, as you chose to elewate into obstacles against our marriage; but now, Hannah, all these obstacles are removed. Nancy and Peggy married and went to Texas years ago. And Kitty married and left me last summer. She and her husband have gone to Californy; where, they do tell me, that lumps of pure gold lay about the ground as plenty as stones do around here! Anyways, they've all gone! all the little sisters as I have worked for, and cared for, and saved for—all gone, and left me alone in my old age!"

"That was very ungrateful, and selfish, and cruel of them, Reuben! They should have taken you with them! At least little Kitty and her husband should have done so," said Hannah, with more feeling than she had yet betrayed.

"Law, Hannah, why little Kitty and her husband couldn't! Why, child, it takes mints and mints of money to pay for a passage out yonder to Californy! and it takes nine months to go the v'y'ge—they have to go all around Cape—Cape Hoof, no, Horn—Cape Horn! I knowed it wor somethin' relating to cattle. Yes, Hannah—hundreds of dollars and months of time do it take to go to that gold region! and so, 'stead o' them being able to take me out, I had to gather up all my savings to help 'em to pay their own passage."

"Poor Reuben! poor, poor Reuben!" said Hannah, with the tears springing to her eyes.

"Thank you, thank you, dear; but I shall not be poor Reuben, if you will be mine," whispered Gray.

"Reuben, dear, I would—indeed I would—if I were still young and good-looking; but I am not so, dear Reuben; I am middle-aged and plain."

"Well, Hannah, old sweetheart, while you have been growing older, have I been going bac'ards and growing younger? One would think so to hear you talk. No, Hannah! I think there is just about the same difference in our ages now as there was years ago; and besides, if you were young and handsome, Hannah, I would never do such a wrong as to ask you to be the wife of a poor old man like me! It is the fitness of our ages and circumstances, as well as our long attachment, that gives me the courage to ask you even at this late day, old friend, to come and cheer my lonely home. Will you do so, Hannah?"

"Reuben, do you really think that I could make you any happier than you are, or make your home any more comfortable than it is?" asked Hannah, in a low, doubting voice.

"Sartain, my dear."

"But, Reuben, I am not good-tempered like I used to be; I am very often cross; and—"

"That is because you have been all alone, with no one to care for you, Hannah, my dear. You couldn't be cross, with me to love you," said Reuben soothingly.

"But, indeed, I fear I should; it is my infirmity; I am cross even with Ishmael, poor dear lad."

"Well, Hannah, even if you was to be, I shouldn't mind it much. I don't want to boast, but I do hope as I've got too much manhood to be out of patience with women; besides, I aint easy put out, you know."

"No, you good fellow; I never saw you out of temper in my life."

"Thank you, Hannah! Then it's a bargain?"

"But, Reuben! about Ishmael?"

"Lord bless you, Hannah, why, I told you years ago, when the lad was a helpless baby, that he should be as welcome to me as a son of my own; and now, Hannah, at his age, with his larnin', he'll be a perfect treasure to me," said Reuben, brightening up.

"In what manner, Reuben?"

"Why, law, Hannah, you know I never could make any fist of reading, writing, and 'rithmetic; and so the keeping of the farm-books is just the one torment of my life. Little Kitty used to keep them for me before she was married (you know I managed to give the child a bit of schooling); but since she have been gone they haven't been half kept, and if I hadn't a good memory of my own I shouldn't be able to give no account of nothing. Now, Ishmael, you know, could put all the books to rights for me, and keep them to rights."

"If that be so, it will relieve my mind very much, Reuben," replied Hannah.

The appearance of Ishmael's pale face at the door put an end to the conversation for the time being. And Reuben took up his hat and departed.

That evening, after Reuben had bid them good-night, and departed to the neighbor's house where he slept, Hannah told Ishmael all about her engagement to Gray. And it was with the utmost astonishment the youth learned they were all to go to reside on the plantation of Judge Merlin—Claudia's father! Well! to live so near her house would make his duty to conquer his passion only the more difficult, but he was still resolved to effect his purpose.

Having once given her consent, Hannah would not compromise Reuben's interest with his employer by making any more difficulties or delays. She spent the remainder of that week in packing up the few effects belonging to herself and Ishmael. The boy himself employed his time in transplanting rosebushes from the cottage-garden to his mother's grave, and fencing it around with a rude but substantial paling. On Sunday morning Reuben and Hannah were married at the church; and on Monday they were to set out for their new home.

Early on Monday morning Ishmael arose and went out to take leave of his mother's grave; and, kneeling there, he silently renewed his vow to rescue her name from reproach and give it to honor.

Then he returned and joined the traveling party.

Before the cottage door stood Reuben's light wagon, in which were packed the trunks with their wearing apparel, the hamper with their luncheon, and all the little light effects which required care. Into this Gray placed Hannah and Ishmael, taking the driver's seat himself. A heavier wagon behind this one contained all Hannah's household furniture, including her loom and wheel and Ishmael's home-made desk and book-shelf, and in the driver's seat sat the negro man who had come down in attendance upon the overseer.

The Professor of Odd Jobs stood in the door of the hut, with his hat in his hand, waving adieu to the departing travelers. The professor had come by appointment to see them off and take the key of the hut to the overseer at the Hall.

The sun was just rising above the heights of Brudenell Hall and flooding all the vale with light. The season was very forward, and, although the month was March, the weather was like that of April. The sky was of that clear, soft, bright blue of early spring; the sun shone with dazzling splendor; the new grass was springing up everywhere, and was enameled with early violets and snow-drops; the woods were budding with the tender green of young vegetation. Distant, sunny hills, covered with apple or peach orchards all in blossom, looked like vast gardens of mammoth red and white rose trees.

Even to the aged spring brings renewal of life, but to the young—not even poets have words at command to tell what exhilaration, what ecstatic rapture, it brings to the young, who are also sensitive and sympathetic.

Ishmael was all these; his delicate organization was susceptible of intense enjoyment or suffering. He had never in his life been five miles from his native place; he had just risen from a sick-bed as from a grave; he was going to penetrate a little beyond his native round of hills, and see what was on the other side; the morning was young, the season was early, the world was fresh; this day seemed a new birth to Ishmael; this journey a new start in his life; he intensely enjoyed it all; to him all was delightful: the ride through the beautiful, green, blossoming woods; the glimpses of the blue sky through the quivering upper leaves; the shining of the sun; the singing of the birds; the fragrance of the flowers.

To him the waving trees seemed bending in worship, the birds trilling hymns of joy, and the flowers wafting offerings of incense! There are times when earth seems heaven and all nature worshipers. Ishmael was divinely happy; even the lost image of Claudia reappeared now surrounded with a halo of hope, for to-day aspirations seemed prophecies, will seemed power, and all things possible. And not on Ishmael alone beamed the blessed influence of the spring weather. Even Hannah's care-worn face was softened into contentment and enjoyment. As for Reuben's honest phiz, it was a sight to behold in its perfect satisfaction. Even the negro driver of the heavy wagon let his horses take their time as he raised his ear to catch some very delicate trill in a bird's song, or turned his head to inhale the perfume from some bank of flowers.

Onward they journeyed at their leisure through all that glad morning landscape.

At noon they stopped at a clearing around a cool spring in the woods, and while the negro fed and watered the horses, they rested and refreshed themselves with a substantial luncheon, and then strolled about through the shades until "Sam" had eaten his dinner, re-packed the hamper, and put the horses to the wagons again. And then they all returned to their seats and recommenced their journey.

On and on they journeyed through the afternoon; deeper and deeper they descended into the forest as the sun declined in the west. When it was on the edge of the horizon, striking long golden lines through the interstices of the woods, Hannah grew rather anxious, and she spoke up:

"It seems to me, Reuben, that we have come ten miles since we saw a house or a farm."

"Yes, my dear. We are now in the midst of the old forest of Prince George's, and our home is yet about five miles off. But don't be afraid, Hannah, woman; you have got me with you, and we will get home before midnight."

"I am only thinking of the runaway negroes, Reuben; they all take refuge in these thick woods, you know; and they are a very desperate gang; their hands against everybody and everybody's hands against them, you may say."

"True, Hannah; they are desperate enough, for they have everything to fear and nothing to hope, in a meeting with most of the whites; but there is no danger to us, child."

"I don't know; they murdered a harmless peddler last winter, and attacked a peaceable teamster this spring."

"Still, my dear, there is no danger; we have a pair of double-barreled pistols loaded, and also a blunderbuss; and we are three men, and you are as good as a fourth; so don't be afraid."

Hannah was silenced, if not reassured.

They journeyed on at a rate as fast as the rather tired horses could be urged to make. When the sun had set it grew dark, very dark in the forest. There was no moon; and although it was a clear, starlight night, yet that did not help them much. They had to drive very slowly and carefully to avoid accidents, and it was indeed midnight when they drove up to the door of Hannah's new home. It was too dark to see more of it than that it was a two-storied white cottage with a vine-clad porch, and that it stood in a garden on the edge of the wood.

CHAPTER XXXVII.

THE NEW HOME.

It is a quiet picture of delight,
The humble cottage, hiding from the sun
In the thick woods. You see it not till then,
When at its porch. Rudely, but neatly wrought,
Four columns make its entrance; slender shafts,
The rough bark yet upon them, as they came
From the old forest. Prolific vines
Have wreathed them well and half obscured the rinds
Original, that wrap them. Crowding leaves
Or glistening green, and clustering bright flowers
Of purple, in whose cups, throughout the day,
The humming bird wantons boldly, wave around
And woo the gentle eye and delicate touch.
This is the dwelling, and 'twill be to them
Quiet's especial temple.
—*W.G. Simms*.

"Welcome home, Hannah! welcome home, dearest woman! No more hard work now, Hannah! and no more slaving at the everlasting wheel and loom! Nothing to do but your own pretty little house to keep, and your own tidy servant girl to look after! And no more anxiety about the future, Hannah; for you have me to love you and care for you! Ah, dear wife! this is a day I have looked forward to through all the gloom and trouble of many years. Thank God, it has come at last, more blessed than I ever hoped it would be, and I welcome you home, my wife!" said Reuben Gray, as he lifted his companion from the wagon, embraced her, and led her through the gate into the front yard.

"Oh, you dear, good Reuben, what a nice, large house this is! so much better than I had any reason to expect," said Hannah, in surprise and delight.

"You'll like it better still by daylight, my dear," answered Gray.

"How kind you are to me, dear Reuben."

"It shall always be my greatest pleasure to be so, Hannah."

A negro girl at this moment appeared at the door with a light, and the husband and wife entered the house.

159

Ishmael sprang down from his seat, stretched his cramped limbs, and gazed about him with all the curiosity and interest of a stranger in a strange scene.

The features of the landscape, as dimly discerned by starlight, were simple and grand.

Behind him lay the deep forest from which they had just emerged. On its edge stood the white cottage, surrounded by its garden. Before him lay the open country, sloping down to the banks of a broad river, whose dark waves glimmered in the starlight.

So this was Judge Merlin's estate—and Claudia's birthplace!

"Well, Ishmael, are you waiting for an invitation to enter? Why, you are as welcome as Hannah herself, and you couldn't be more so!" exclaimed the hearty voice of Reuben Gray, as he returned almost immediately after taking Hannah in.

"I know it, Uncle Reuben. You are very good to me; and I do hope to make myself very useful to you," replied the boy.

"You'll be a fortun' to me, lad—an ample fortun' to me! But why don't you go in out of the midnight air? You ain't just as strong as Samson, yet, though you're agwine to be," said Gray cheerily.

"I only stopped to stretch my limbs, and—to help in with the luggage," said Ishmael, who was always thoughtful, practical, and useful, and who now stopped to load himself with Hannah's baskets and bundles before going into the house.

"Now, then, Sam," said Gray, turning to the negro, "look sharp there! Bring in the trunks and boxes from the light wagon; take the furniture from the heavy one, and pile it in the shed, where it can stay until morning; put both on 'em under cover, feed and put up the horses; and then you can go to your quarters."

The negro bestirred himself to obey these orders, and Reuben Gray and Ishmael entered the cottage garden.

They passed up a gravel walk bordered each side with lilac bushes, and entered by a vine-shaded porch into a broad passage, that ran through the middle of the house from the front to the back door.

"There are four large rooms on this floor, Ishmael, and this is the family sitting room," said Gray, opening a door on his right.

It was a very pleasant front room, with a bright paper on its walls, a gay homespun carpet on the floor; pretty chintz curtains at the two front windows; chintz covers of the same pattern on the two easy-chairs and the sofa; a bright fire burning in the open fireplace, and a neat tea-table set out in the middle of the floor.

But Hannah was nowhere visible.

"She has gone in her room, Ishmael, to take off her bonnet; it is the other front one across the passage, just opposite to this; and as she seems to be taking of her time, I may as well show you your'n, Ishmael. Just drop them baskets down anywhere, and come with me, my lad," said Gray, leading the way into the passage and up the staircase to the second floor. Arrived there, he opened a door, admitting himself and his companion into a chamber immediately over the sitting-room.

"This is your'n, Ishmael, and I hope as you'll find it comfortable and make yourself at home," said Reuben, hastily, as he introduced Ishmael to this room.

It was more rudely furnished than the one below. There was no carpet except the strip laid down by the bedside; the bed itself was very plain, and covered with a patchwork quilt; the two front windows were shaded with dark green paper blinds; and the black walnut bureau, washstand, and chairs were very old. Yet all was scrupulously clean; and everywhere were evidences that the kindly care of Reuben Gray had taken pains to discover Ishmael's habits and provide for his necessities. For instance, just between the front windows stood an old-fashioned piece of furniture, half book-case and half writing-desk, and wholly convenient, containing three upper shelves well filled with books, a drawer full of stationery, and a closet for waste paper.

Ishmael walked straight up to this.

"Why, where did you get this escritoire, and all these books, Uncle Reuben?" he inquired, in surprise.

"Why, you see, Ishmael, the screwtwar, as you call it, was among the old furnitur' sent down from the mansion-house here, to fit up this place when I first came into it; you see, the housekeeper up there sends the cast-off furniture to the overseer, same as she sends the cast-off finery to the niggers."

"But the books, Uncle Reuben; they are all law books," said the boy, examining them.

"Exactly; and that's why I was so fort'nate as to get 'em. You see, I was at the sale at Colonel Mervin's to see if I could pick up anything nice for Hannah; and I sees a lot of books sold—laws! why, the story books all went off like wildfire; but when it come to these, nobody didn't seem to want 'em. So I says to myself: These will do to fill up the empty shelves in the screwtwar, and I dare say as our Ishmael would vally them. So I up and bought the lot for five dollars; and sent 'em up here by Sam, with orders to put 'em in the screwtwar, and move the screwtwar out'n the sitting room into this room, as I intended for you."

160

"Ah, Uncle Reuben, how good you are to me! Everybody is good to me."

"Quite nat'rel, Ishmael, since you are useful to everybody. And now, my lad, I'll go and send Sam up with your box. And when you have freshed up a bit you can come down to supper," said Gray, leaving Ishmael in possession of his room.

In a few minutes after the negro Sam brought in the box that contained all Ishmael's worldly goods.

"Missus Gray say how the supper is all ready, sir," said the man, setting down the box.

As Ishmael was also quite ready, he followed the negro downstairs into the sitting room.

Hannah was already in her seat at the head of the table; while behind her waited a neat colored girl. Reuben stood at the back of his own chair at the foot of the table, waiting for Ishmael before seating himself. When the boy took his own place, Reuben asked a blessing, and the meal commenced. The tired travelers did ample justice to the hot coffee, broiled ham and eggs and fresh bread and butter before them.

After supper they separated for the night.

Ishmael went up to his room and went to bed, so very tired that his head was no sooner laid upon his pillow than his senses were sunk in sleep.

He was awakened by the caroling of a thousand birds. He started up, a little confused at first by finding himself in a strange room; but as memory quickly returned he sprang from his bed and went and drew up his blind and looked out from his window.

It was early morning; the sun was just rising and flooding the whole landscape with light. A fine, inspiring scene lay before him—orchards of apple, peach, and cherry trees in full blossom; meadows of white and red clover; fields of wheat and rye, in their pale green hue of early growth; all spreading downwards towards the banks of the mighty Potomac that here in its majestic breadth seemed a channel of the sea; while far away across the waters, under the distant horizon, a faint blue line marked the southern shore.

Sailing up and down the mighty river were ships of all nations, craft of every description, from the three-decker East India merchantman, going or returning from her distant voyage, to the little schooner-rigged fishermen trading up and down the coast. These were the sights. The songs of birds, the low of cattle, the hum of bees, and the murmur of the water as it washed the sands—these were the sounds. All the joyous life of land, water, and sky seemed combined at this spot and visible from this window.

"This is a pleasant place to live in; thank the Lord for it!" said Ishmael fervently, as he stood gazing from the window. Not long, however, did the youth indulge his love of nature; he turned away, washed and dressed himself quickly and went downstairs to see if he could be useful.

The windows were open in the sitting room, which was filled with the refreshing fragrance of the lilacs. The breakfast table was set; and Phillis, the colored girl, was bringing in the coffee. Almost at the same moment Hannah entered from the kitchen and Reuben from the garden.

"Good-morning, Ishmael!" said Reuben gayly. "How do you like Woodside? Woodside is the name of our little home, same as Tanglewood is the name of the judge's house, a half a mile back in the forest, you know. How do you like it by daylight?"

"Oh, very much, indeed, uncle. Don't you like it, Aunt Hannah? Isn't it pleasant?" exclaimed the youth, appealing to Mrs. Gray.

"Very pleasant, indeed, Ishmael!" she said. "Ah, Reuben," she continued, turning to her husband, "you never let me guess what a delightful home you were bringing me to! I had no idea but that it was just like the cottages of other overseers that I have known—a little house of two or three small rooms."

"Ha, ha, ha!" laughed Gray, "I knew you too well, Hannah! I knew if I had let you know how well off I was, you would never have taken me; your pride would have been up in arms and you would have thought besides as how I was comfortable enough without you, which would have been an idee as I never could have got out of your head! No, Hannah, I humored your pride, and let you think as how you were marrying of a poor, miserable, desolate old man, as would be apt to die of neglect and privations if you didn't consent to come and take care of him. And then I comforted myself with thinking what a pleasant surprise I had in store for you when I should fetch you here. Enjoy yourself, dear woman! for there isn't a thing as I have done to this house I didn't do for your sake!"

"But, Reuben, how is it that you have so much better a house than other men of your station ever have?"

"Well, Hannah, my dear, it is partly accident and partly design in the judge. You see, this house used to be the mansion of the planters theirselves, until the present master, when he was first married, built the great house back in the woods, and then, 'stead of pulling this one down, he just 'pointed it to be the dwelling of the overseer; for it is the pleasure of the judge to make all his people as comfortable as it is possible for them to be," answered Reuben. As he spoke, Phillis placed the last dish upon the table, and they all took their seats and commenced breakfast.

As soon as the meal was over, Ishmael said:

"Now, Uncle Reuben, if you will give me those farm books you were wanting me to arrange, I will make a commencement."

"No, you won't, Ishmael, my lad. You have worked yourself nearly to death this winter and spring, and now, please the Lord, you shall do no more work for a month. When I picked you up for dead that day, I promised the Almighty Father to be a father to you; so, Ishmael, you must regard me as such, when I tell you that you are to let the books alone for a whole month longer, until your health is restored. So just get your hat and come with us; I am going to show your aunt over the place."

Ishmael smiled and obeyed. And all three went out together. And oh! with how much pride Reuben displayed the treasures of her little place to his long-loved Hannah. He showed her her cows and pigs and sheep; and her turkeys and geese and hens; and her beehives and garden and orchard.

"And this isn't all, either, Hannah, my dear! We can have as much as we want for family use, of all the rare fruits and vegetables from the greenhouses and hotbeds up at Tanglewood; and, besides that, we have the freedom of the fisheries and the oyster beds, too; so you see, my dear, you will live like any queen! Thank the Lord!" said Reuben, reverently raising his hat.

"And oh, Reuben, to think that you should have saved all this happiness for me, poor, faded, unworthy me!" sighed his wife.

"Why, law, Hannah, who else should I have saved it for but my own dear old sweetheart? I never so much as thought of another."

"With all these comforts about you, you might have married some blooming young girl."

"Lord, dear woman, I ha'n't much larnin', nor much religion, more's the pity; but I hope I have conscience enough to keep me from doing any young girl so cruel a wrong as to tempt her to throw away her youth and beauty on an old man like me; and I am sure I have sense enough to prevent me from doing myself so great an injustice as to buy a young wife, who, in the very natur' of things, would be looking for'ard to my death as the beginning of her life; for I've heard as how the very life of a woman is love, and if the girl-wife cannot love her old husband—Oh, Hannah, let us drop the veil—the pictur' is too sickening to look at. Such marriages are crimes. Ah, Hannah, in the way of sweethearting, age may love youth, but youth can't love age. And another thing I am sartin' sure of—as a young girl is a much more delicate cre'tur' than a young man, it must be a great deal harder for her to marry an old man than it would be for him to marry an old woman, though either would be horrible."

"You seem to have found this out somehow, Reuben."

"Well, yes, my dear; it was along of a rich old fellow, hereaway, as fell in love with my little Kitty's rosy cheeks and black eyes, and wanted to make her Mrs. Barnabas Winterberry. And I saw how that girl was at the same time tempted by his money and frightened by his age; and how in her bewitched state, half-drawn and half-scared, she fluttered about him, for all the world like a humming-bird going right into the jaws of a rattlesnake. Well, I questioned little Kitty, and she answered me in this horrid way—'Why, brother, he must know I can't love him; for how can I? But still he teases me to marry him, and I can do that; and why shouldn't I, if he wants me to?' Then in a whisper—'You know, brother, it wouldn't be for long; because he is ever so old, and he would soon die; and then I should be a rich young widow, and have my pick and choose out of the best young men in the country side.' Such, Hannah, was the evil state of feeling to which that old man's courtship had brought my simple little sister! And I believe in my soul it is the natural state of feeling into which every young girl falls who marries an old man."

"That is terrible, Reuben."

"Sartinly it is."

"What did you say to your sister?"

"Why, I didn't spare the feelings of little Kitty, nor her doting suitor's nyther, and that I can tell you! I talked to little Kitty like a father and mother, both; I told her well what a young traitress she was a-planning to be; and how she was fooling herself worse than she was deceiving her old beau, who had got into the whit-leathar age, and would be sartin' sure to live twenty-five or thirty years longer, till she would be an old woman herself, and I so frightened her, by telling her the plain truth in the plainest words, that she shrank from seeing her old lover any more, and begged me to send him about his business. And I did, too, 'with a flea in his ear,' as the saying is; for I repeated to him every word as little Kitty had said to me, as a warning to him for the futur' not to go tempting any more young girls to marry him for his money and then wish him dead for the enjoyment of it."

"I hope it did him good."

"Why, Hannah, he went right straight home, and that same day married his fat, middle-aged housekeeper, who, to tell the solemn truth, he ought to have married twenty years before! And as for little Kitty, thank Heaven! she was soon sought as a wife by a handsome young fellow, who was suited to her in every way, and who really did love her and win her love; and they were married and went to Californy, as I told you. Well, after I was left alone, the neighboring small farmers with unprovided daughters, seeing how comfortable I was fixed, would often say to me—'Gray, you ought to marry.' 'Gray, why don't you marry?' 'Gray, your nice little place only needs one thing to make it perfect, a nice little wife.' 'Why don't you drop in and see the girls some evening, Gray? They would always be glad to see you.' And all that. I understood it all, Hannah, my dear; but I didn't want any young girls who would marry me only for a home. And, besides, the Lord knows I never thought of any woman, young or old, except yourself, who was my first love and my only one, and whose whole life was mixed up with my own, as close as ever warp and woof was woven in your webs, Hannah."

"You have been more faithful to me than I deserved, Reuben; but I will try to make you happy," said Hannah, with much emotion.

"You do make me happy, dear, without trying. And now where is Ishmael?" inquired Reuben, who never in his own content forgot the welfare of others.

Ishmael was walking slowly and thoughtfully at some distance behind them. Reuben called after him:

"Walk up, my lad. We are going in to dinner now; we dine at noon, you know."

Ishmael, who had lingered behind from the motives of delicacy that withheld him from intruding on the confidential conversation of the newly-married pair, now quickened his steps and joined them, saying, with a smile:

"Uncle Reuben, when you advised me not to study for a whole month you did not mean to counsel me to rust in idleness for four long weeks? I must work, and I wish you would put me to that which will be the most useful to you."

"And most beneficial to your own health, my boy! What would you say to fishing? Would that meet your wishes?"

"Oh, I should like that very much, if I could really be of use in that way, Uncle Reuben," said the youth.

"Why, of course you could; now I'll tell you what you can do; you can go this afternoon with Sam in the sailboat as far down the river as Silver Sands, where he hopes to hook some fine rock fish. Would that meet your views?"

"Exactly," laughed Ishmael, as his eyes danced with the eagerness of youth for the sport.

They went into the house, where Phillis had prepared a nice dinner, of bacon and sprouts and apple dumplings, which the whole party relished.

Afterwards Ishmael started on his first fishing voyage with Sam. And though it was a short one, it had for him all the charms of novelty added to the excitement of sport, and he enjoyed the excursion excessively. The fishing was very successful, and they filled their little boat and got back home by sunset. At supper Ishmael gave a full account of the expedition and received the hearty congratulations of Reuben. And thus ended the holiday of their first day at home.

The next morning Reuben Gray went into the fields to resume his oversight of his employer's estate.

Hannah turned in to housework, and had all the furniture she had brought from the hill hut moved into the cottage and arranged in one of the empty rooms upstairs.

Ishmael, forbidden to study, employed himself in useful manual labor in the garden and in the fields.

And thus in cheerful industry passed the early days of spring.

CHAPTER XXXVIII.

ISHMAEL'S STRUGGLES

Yet must my brow be paler! I have vowed
To clip it with the crown that shall not fade
When it is faded. Not in vain ye cry,
Oh, glorious voices, that survive the tongue
From whence was drawn your separate sovereignty,

For I would stand beside you!

—*E.B. Browning.*

Ishmael continued his work, yet resumed his studies. He managed to do both in this way—all the forenoon he delved in the garden; all the afternoon he went over the chaotic account-books of Reuben Gray, to bring them into order; and all the evening he studied in his own room. He kept up his Greek and Latin. And he read law.

No time to dream of Claudia now.

One of the wisest of our modern philosophers says that we are sure to meet with the right book at the right time. Now whether it were chance, fate, or Providence that filled the scanty shelves of the old escritoire with a few law books, is not known; but it is certain that their presence there decided the career of Ishmael Worth.

As a young babe, whose sole object in life is to feed, pops everything it can get hold of into its mouth, so this youthful aspirant, whose master-passion was the love of learning, read everything he could lay his hands on. Prompted by that intellectual curiosity which ever stimulated him to examine every subject that fell under his notice, Ishmael looked into the law books. They were mere text-books, probably the discarded property of some young student of the Mervin family, who had never got beyond the rudiments of the profession; but had abandoned it as a "dry study."

Ishmael did not find it so, however. The same ardent soul, strong mind, and bright spirit that had found "dry history" an inspiring heroic poem, "dry grammar" a beautiful analysis of language, now found "dry law" the intensely interesting science of human justice. Ishmael read diligently, for the love of his subject!—at first it was only for the love of his subject, but after a few weeks of study he began to read with a fixed purpose—to become a lawyer. Of course Ishmael Worth was no longer unconscious of his own great intellectual power; he had measured himself with the best educated youth of the highest rank, and he had found himself in mental strength their master. So when he resolved to become a lawyer, he felt a just confidence that he should make a very able one. Of course, with his clear perceptions and profound reflections he saw all the great difficulties in his way; but they did not dismay him. His will was as strong as his intellect, and he knew that, combined, they would work wonders, almost miracles.

Indeed, without strength of will, intellect is of very little effect; for if intellect is the eye of the soul, will is the hand; intellect is wisdom, but will is power; intellect may be the monarch, but will is the executive minister. How often we see men of the finest intellect fail in life through weakness of will! How often also we see men of very moderate intellect succeed through strength of will!

In Ishmael Worth intellect and will were equally strong. And when in that poor chamber he set himself down to study law, upon his own account, with the resolution to master the profession and to distinguish himself in it, he did so with the full consciousness of the magnitude of the object and of his own power to attain it. Day after day he worked hard, night after night he studied diligently.

Ishmael did not think this a hardship; he did not murmur over his poverty, privations, and toil; no, for his own bright and beautiful spirit turned everything to light and loveliness. He did not, indeed, in the pride of the Pharisee, thank God that he was not as other men; but he did feel too deeply grateful for the intellectual power bestowed upon him, to murmur at the circumstances that made it so difficult to cultivate that glorious gift.

One afternoon, while they were all at tea, Reuben Gray said:

"Now, Ishmael, my lad, Hannah and me are going over to spend the evening at Brown's, who is overseer at Rushy Shore; and you might's well go with us; there's a nice lot o' gals there. What do you say?"

"Thank you, Uncle Reuben, but I wish to read this evening," said the youth.

"Now, Ishmael, what for should you slave yourself to death?"

"I don't, uncle. I work hard, it is true; but then, you know, youth is the time for work, and besides I like it," said the young fellow cheerfully.

"Well, but after hoeing and weeding and raking and planting in the garden all the morning, and bothering your brains over them distracting 'count books all the afternoon, what's the good of your going and poring over them stupid books all the evening?"

"You will see the good of it some of these days, Uncle Reuben," laughed Ishmael.

"You will wear yourself out before that day comes, my boy, if you are not careful," answered Reuben.

"I always said the fetched books would be his ruin, and now I know it," put in Hannah.

Ishmael laughed good-humoredly; but Reuben sighed.

"Ishmael, my lad," he said, "if you must read, do, pray, read in the forenoon, instead of working in the garden."

"But what will become of the garden?" inquired Ishmael, with gravity.

"Oh, I can put one of the nigger boys into it."

"And have to pay for his time and not have the work half done at last."

"Well, I had rather it be so, than you should slave yourself to death."

"Oh, but I do not slave myself to death! I like to work in the garden, and I am never happier than when I am engaged there; the garden is beautiful, and the care of it is a great pleasure as well as a great benefit to me; it gives me all the outdoor exercise and recreation that I require to enable me to sit at my writing or reading all the rest of the day."

"Ah, Ishmael, my lad, who would think work was recreation except you? But it is your goodness of heart that turns every duty into a delight," said Reuben Gray; and he was not very far from the truth.

"It is his obstinacy as keeps him everlasting a-working himself to death! Reuben Gray, Ishmael Worth is one of the obstinatest boys that ever you set your eyes on! He has been obstinate ever since he was a baby," said Hannah angrily. And her mind reverted to that old time when the infant Ishmael would live in defiance of everybody.

"I do believe as Ishmael would be as firm as a rock in a good cause; but I don't believe that he could be obstinate in a bad one," said Reuben decidedly.

"Yes, he could! else why does he persist in staying home this evening when we want him to go with us?" complained Hannah.

Now, strength of will is not necessarily self-will. Firmness of purpose is not always implacability. The strong need not be violent in order to prove their strength. And Ishmael, firmly resolved as he was to devote every hour of his leisure to study, knew very well when to make an exception to his rule, and sacrifice his inclinations to his duty. So he answered:

"Aunt Hannah, if you really desire me to go with you, I will do so of course."

"I want you to go because I think you stick too close to your books, you stubborn fellow; and because I know you haven't been out anywhere for the last two months; and because I believe it would do you good to go," said Mrs. Gray.

"All right, Aunt Hannah. I will run upstairs and dress," laughed Ishmael, leaving the tea-table.

"And be sure you put on your gold watch and chain," called out Hannah.

Hannah also arose and went to her room to change her plain brown calico gown for a fine black silk dress and mantle that had been Reuben Gray's nuptial present to her, and a straw bonnet trimmed with blue.

In a few minutes Ishmael, neatly attired, joined her in the parlor.

"Have you put on your watch, Ishmael?"

"Yes, Aunt Hannah; but I'm wearing it on a guard. I don't like to wear the chain; it is too showy for my circumstances. You wear it, Aunt Hannah; and always wear it when you go out; it looks beautiful over your black silk dress," said Ishmael, as he put the chain around Mrs. Gray's neck and contemplated the effect.

"What a good boy you are!" said Hannah; but she would not have been a woman if she had not been pleased with the decoration.

Reuben Gray came in, arrayed in his Sunday suit, and smiled to see how splendid Hannah was, and then drawing his wife's arm proudly within his own, and calling Ishmael to accompany them, set off to walk a mile farther up the river and spend a festive evening with his brother overseer. They had a pleasant afternoon stroll along the pebbly beach of the broad waters. They sauntered at their leisure, watching the ships sail up or down the river; looking at the sea-fowl dart up from the reeds and float far away; glancing at the little fish leaping up and disappearing in the waves; and pausing once in a while to pick up a pretty shell or stone; and so at last they reached the cottage of the overseer Brown, which stood just upon the point of a little promontory that jutted out into the river.

They spent a social evening with the overseer and his wife and their half a dozen buxom boys and girls. And about ten o'clock they walked home by starlight.

Twice a week Reuben Gray went up the river to a little waterside hamlet called Shelton to meet the mail. Reuben's only correspondent was his master, who wrote occasionally to make inquiries or to give orders. The day after his evening out was the regular day for Reuben to go to the post office.

So immediately after breakfast Reuben mounted the white cob which he usually rode and set out for Shelton.

He was gone about two hours, and returned with a most perplexed countenance. Now "the master's" correspondence had always been a great bother to Reuben. It took him a long time to spell out the letters and a longer time to indite the answers. So the arrival of a letter was always sure to unsettle him for a day or two.

165

Still, that fact did not account for the great disturbance of mind in which he reached home and entered the family sitting-room.

"What's the matter, Reuben? Any bad news?" anxiously inquired Hannah.

"N-n-o, not exactly bad news; but a very bad bother," said Gray, sitting down in the big arm-chair and wiping the perspiration from his heated face.

"What is it, Reuben?" pursued Hannah.

"Where's Ishmael?" inquired Gray, without attempting to answer her question.

"Working in the garden, of course. But why can't you tell me what's the matter?"

"Botheration is the matter, Hannah, my dear. Just go call Ishmael to me."

Hannah left the house to comply with his request, and Reuben sat and wiped his face and pondered over his perplexities. Reuben had lately given to rely very much upon Ishmael's judgment, and to appeal to him in all his difficulties. So he looked up in confidence as the youth entered with Hannah.

"What is it, Uncle Reuben?" inquired the boy cheerfully.

"The biggest botheration as ever was, Ishmael, my lad!" answered Gray.

"Well, take a mug of cool cider to refresh yourself, and then tell me all about it," said Ishmael.

Hannah ran and brought the invigorating drink, and after quaffing it Gray drew a long breath and said:

"Why, I've got the botherationest letter from the judge as ever was. He says how he has sent down a lot of books, as will be landed at our landing by the schooner 'Canvas Back,' Capt'n Miller; and wants me to take the cart and go and receive them, and carry them up to the house, and ask the housekeeper for the keys of the liber-airy and put them in there," said Reuben, pausing for breath.

"Why, that is not much bother, Uncle Reuben. Let me go and get the books for you," smiled Ishmael.

"Law, it aint that; for I don't s'pose it's much more trouble to cart books than it is to cart bricks. You didn't hear me out: After I have got the botheration things into the liber-airy, he wants me to unpack them, and also take down the books as is there already, and put the whole lot on 'em in the middle of the floor, and then pick 'em out and 'range 'em all in separate lots, like one would sort vegetables for market, and put each sort all together on a different shelf, and then write all their names in a book, all regular and in exact order! There, now, that's the work as the judge has cut out for me, as well as I can make out his meaning from his hard words and crabbed hand; and I no more fit to do it nor I am to write a sarmon or to build a ship; and if that aint enough, to bother a man's brains I don't know what is, that's all."

"But it is no part of your duty as overseer to act as his librarian," said Ishmael.

"I know it aint; but, you see, the judge he pays me liberal, and he gives me a fust-rate house and garden, and the liberty of his own orchards and vineyards, and a great many other privileges besides, and he expects me to 'commodate him in turn by doing of little things as isn't exactly in the line of my duty," answered Gray.

"But," demurred Ishmael, "he ought to have known that you were not precisely fitted for this new task he has set you."

"Well, my lad, he didn't; 'cause, you see, the gals as I edicated, you know, they did everything for me as required larning, like writing letters and keeping 'counts; and as for little Kitty, she used to do them beautiful, for Kitty was real clever; and I do s'pose the judge took it for granted as the work was all my own, and so he thinks I can do this job too. Now, if the parish school wa'n't broke up for the holidays, I might get the schoolmaster to do it for me and pay him for it; but, you see, he is gone North to visit his mother and he won't be back until September, so the mischief knows what I shall do. I thought I'd just ask your advice, Ishmael, because you have got such a wonderful head of your own."

"Thank you, Uncle Reuben. Don't you be the least distressed. I can do what is required to be done, and do it in a manner that shall give satisfaction, too," said Ishmael.

"You! you, my boy! could you do that everlasting big botheration of a job?"

"Yes, and do it well, I hope."

"Why, I don't believe the professor himself could!" exclaimed Gray, in incredulous astonishment.

"Nor I, either," laughed Ishmael; "but I know that I can."

"But, my boy, it is such a task!"

"I should like it, of all things, Uncle Reuben! You could not give me a greater treat than the privilege of overhauling all those books and putting them in order and making the catalogue," said the youth eagerly.

And besides he was going to Claudia's house!

Reuben looked more and more astonished as Ishmael went on; but Hannah spoke up:

166

"You may believe him, Reuben! He is book-mad; and it is my opinion, that when he gets into that musty old library, among the dusty books, he will fancy himself in heaven."

Reuben looked from the serious face of Hannah to the smiling eyes of Ishmael, and inquired doubtfully:

"Is that the truth, my boy?"

"Something very near it, Uncle Reuben," answered Ishmael.

"Very well, my lad," exclaimed the greatly relieved overseer, gleefully slapping his knees, "very well! as sure as you are horn, you shall go to your heaven."

CHAPTER XXXIX.

ISHMAEL IN TANGLEWOOD.

Into a forest far, they thence him led
Where stood the mansion in a pleasant glade,
With great hills round about environèd
And mighty woods which did the valley shade,
And like a stately theater it made,
Spreading itself into a spacious plain,
And in the midst a little river played
Amongst the pumy stones which seemed to 'plain
With gentle murmur that his course they did restrain.
—*Spenser*.

The next morning Ishmael Worth went down to the shore, carrying' a spy-glass to look out for the "Canvas Back." There was no certainty about the passing of these sailing packets; a dead calm or a head wind might delay them for days and even weeks; but on this occasion there was no disappointment and no delay, the wind had been fair and the little schooner was seen flying before it up the river. Ishmael seated himself upon the shore and drew a book from his pocket to study while he waited for the arrival of the schooner. In less than an hour she dropped anchor opposite the landing, and sent off a large boat laden with boxes, and rowed by four stout seamen. As they reached the sands Ishmael blew a horn to warn Reuben Gray of their arrival.

Three or four times the boat went back and forth between the schooner and the shore, each time bringing a heavy load. By the time the last load was brought and deposited upon the beach, Reuben Gray arrived at the spot with his team. The sailors received a small gratuity from Gray and returned to the schooner, which immediately raised anchor and continued her way up the river.

Ishmael, Reuben, and Sam, the teamster, loaded the wagon with the boxes and set out for Tanglewood, Sam driving the team, Ishmael and Reuben walking beside it.

Through all the fertile and highly cultivated fields that lay along the banks of the river they went, until they reached the borders of the forest, where Reuben's cottage stood. They did not pause here, but passed it and entered the forest. What a forest it was! They had scarcely entered it when they became so buried in shade that they might have imagined themselves a thousand miles deep in some primeval wilderness, where never the foot of man had trod. The road along which they went was grass-grown. The trees, which grew to an enormous size and gigantic height, interwove their branches thickly overhead. Sometimes these branches intermingled so low that they grazed the top of the wagon as it passed, while men and horses had to bow their heads.

"Why isn't this road cleared, Uncle Reuben?" inquired Ishmael.

"Because it is as much as a man's place is worth to touch a tree in this forest, Ishmael," replied Reuben.

"But why is that? The near branches of these trees need lopping away from the roadside; we can scarcely get along."

"I know it, Ishmael; but the judge won't have a tree in Tanglewood so much as touched; it is his crochet."

"True, for you, Marse Gray," spoke up Sam; "last time I trimmed away the branches from the sides of this here road, ole marse threatened if I cut off so much as a twig from one of the trees again he'd take off a joint of one of my fingers to see how I'd like to be 'trimmed', he said."

Ishmael laughed and remarked:

"But the road will soon be closed unless the trees are cut away."

"Sartin it will; but he don't care for consequences; he will have his way; that's the reason why he never could keep any overseer but me; there was always such a row about the trees and things, as he always swore they should grow as they had a mind to, in spite of all the overseers in the world. I let him have his own will; it's none of my business to contradict him," said Reuben.

"But what will you do when the road closes, how will you manage to get heavy boxes up to the house?" laughed Ishmael.

"Wheel 'em up in a hand-barrow, I s'pose, and if the road gets too narrow for that, unpack 'em and let the niggers tote the parcels up piece-meal."

Thicker and thicker grew the trees as they penetrated deeper into the forest; more obstructed and difficult became the road. Suddenly, without an instant's warning, they came upon the house, a huge, square building of gray stone, so overgrown with moss, ivy, and creeping vines that scarcely a glimpse of the wall could be seen. Its colors, therefore, blended so well with the forest trees that grew thickly and closely around it, that one could scarcely suspect the existence of a building there.

"Here we are," said Reuben, while Sam dismounted and began to take off the boxes.

The front door opened and a fat negro woman, apparently startled by the arrival of the wagon, made her appearance, asking:

"What de debbil all dis, chillun?"

"Here are some books that are to be put into the library, Aunt Katie, and this young man is to unpack and arrange them," answered the overseer.

"More books: my hebbinly Lord, what ole marse want wid more books, when he nebber here to read dem he has got?" exclaimed the fat woman, raising her hands in dismay.

"That is none of our business, Katie! What we are to do is to obey orders; so, if you please, let us have the keys," replied Gray.

The woman disappeared within the house and remained absent for a few minutes, during which the men lifted the boxes from the wagon.

By the time they had set down the last one Katie reappeared with her heavy bunch of keys and beckoned them to follow her.

Ishmael obeyed, by shouldering a small box and entering the house, while Reuben Gray and Sam took up a heavy one between them and came after.

It was a noble old hall, with its walls hung with family pictures and rusty arms and trophies of the chase; with doors opening on each side into spacious apartments; and with a broad staircase ascending from the center.

The fat old negro housekeeper, waddling along before the men, led them to the back of the hall, and opened a door on the right, admitting them into the library of Tanglewood.

Here the men set down the boxes. And when they had brought them all in, and Sam, under the direction of Gray, had forced off all the tops, laying the contents bare to view, the latter said:

"Now then, Ishmael, we will leave you to go to work and unpack; but don't you get so interested in the work as to disremember dinner time at one o'clock precisely; and be sure you are punctual, because we've got veal and spinnidge."

"Thank you, Uncle Reuben, I will not keep you waiting," replied the youth.

Gray and his assistant departed, and Ishmael was left alone with the wealth of books around him.

CHAPTER XL.

THE LIBRARY.

Round the room are shelves of dainty lore,
And rich old pictures hang upon the walls,
Where the slant light falls on them; and wrought gems,
Medallions, rare mosaics and antiques
From Herculaneum, the niches fill;

And on a table of enamel wrought
With a lost art in Italy, do lie
Prints of fair women and engravings rare.
—*N.P. Willis.*

It was a noble room; four lofty windows—two on each side—admitting abundance of light and air; at one end was a marble chimney-piece, over which hung a fine picture of Christ disputing with the doctors in the temple; on each side of this chimney-piece were glass cases filled with rare shells, minerals, and other curiosities; all the remaining spaces along the walls and between the windows were filled up with book-cases; various writing tables, reading stands, and easy-chairs occupied the center of the floor.

After a curious glance at this scene, Ishmael went to work at unpacking the boxes. He found his task much easier than he had expected to find it. Each box contained one particular set of books. On the top of one of the boxes he found a large strong blank folio, entitled—"Library Catalogue."

Ishmael took this book and sat down at one of the tables and divided it into twelve portions, writing over each portion the name of the subject to which he proposed to devote it, as "Theology," "Physics," "Jurisprudence," etc. The last portion he headed "Miscellaneous." Next he divided the empty shelves into similar compartments, and headed each with thy corresponding names. Then he began to make a list of the books, taking one set at a time, writing their names in their proper portion of the catalogue and then arranging them in their proper compartment of the library.

Ishmael had just got through with "Theology," and was about to begin to arrange the next set of books in rotation, when he bethought himself to look at the timepiece, and seeing that it was after twelve, he hurried back to Woodside to keep his appointment with Reuben.

But he returned in the afternoon and recommenced work; and not only on this day, but for several succeeding days, Ishmael toiled cheerfully at this task. To arrange all these books in perfect order and neatness was to Ishmael a labor of real love; and so when one Saturday afternoon he had completed his task, it was with a feeling half of satisfaction at the results of his labor, half of regret at leaving the scene of it, that he locked up the library, returned the key to Aunt Katie, and took leave of Tanglewood.

Walking home through the forest that evening Ishmael thought well over his future prospects. He had read and mastered all those text-books of law that he had found in the old escritoire of his bedroom; and now he wanted more advanced books on the same subject. Such books he had seen in the library at Tanglewood; and he had been sorely tempted to linger as long as possible there for the sake of reading them: but honest and true in thought and act, he resisted the temptation to appropriate the use of the books, or the time that he felt was not his own.

On this evening, therefore, he meditated upon the means of obtaining the books that he wanted. He was now about eighteen years of age, highly gifted in physical beauty and in moral and intellectual excellence; but he was still as poor as poverty could make him. He worked hard, much harder than many who earned liberal salaries; but he earned nothing, absolutely nothing, beyond his board and clothing.

This state of things he felt must not continue longer. It was now nearly nine months since he had left Mr. Middleton's school, and there was no chance of his ever entering another; so now he felt he must turn the education he had received to some better account than merely keeping Reuben Gray's farm books; that he must earn something to support himself and to enable him to go on with his law studies; and he must earn this "something" in this neighborhood, too; for the idea of leaving poor Reuben with no one to keep his accounts never entered the unselfish mind of Ishmael.

Various plans of action as to how he should contrive to support himself and pursue his studies without leaving the neighborhood suggested themselves to Ishmael. Among the rest, he thought of opening a country school. True, he was very young, too young for so responsible a post; but in every other respect, except that of age, he was admirably well qualified for the duty. While he was still meditating upon this subject, he unexpectedly reached the end of his walk and the gate of the cottage.

Reuben and Hannah were standing at the gate. Reuben's left arm was around Hannah, and his right hand held an open letter, over which both their heads were bent. Hannah was helping poor Reuben to spell out its contents.

Ishmael smiled as he greeted them, smiled with his eyes only, as if his sweet bright spirit had looked out in love upon them; and thus it was that Ishmael always met his friends.

"Glad you've come home so soon, Ishmael—glad as ever I can be! Here's another rum go, as ever was!" said Gray, looking up from his letter.

"What is it, Uncle Reuben?"

"Why, it's a sort of notice from the judge. 'Pears like he's gin up his v'y'ge to forrin parts; and 'stead of gwine out yonder for two or three years, he and Miss Merlin be coming down here to spend the summer—leastways, what's left of it," said Gray.

Ishmael's face flushed crimson, and then went deadly white, as he reeled and leaned against the fence for support. Much as he had struggled to conquer his wild passion for the beautiful and high-born heiress, often as he had characterized it as mere boyish folly, or moon-struck madness, closely as he had applied himself to study in the hope of curing his mania, he was overwhelmed by the sudden announcement of her expected return: overwhelmed by a shock of equally blended joy and pain—joy at the prospect of soon meeting her, pain at the thought of the impassable gulf that yawned them—"so near and yet so far!"

His extreme agitation was not observed by either Reuben or Hannah, whose heads were again bent over the puzzling letter. While he was still in that half-stunned, half-excited and wholly-confused state of feeling, Reuben went slowly on with his explanations:

"'Pears like the judge have got another gov'ment 'pointment, or some sich thing, as will keep him here in his natyve land; so he and Miss Claudia, they be a-coming down here to stop till the meeting of Congress in Washington. So he orders me to tell Katie to get the house ready to receive them by the first of next week; and law! this is Saturday! Leastways, that is all me and Hannah can make out'n this here letter, Ishmael; but you take it and read it yourself," said Gray, putting the missive into Ishmael's hands.

With a great effort to recover his self-possession, Ishmael took the letter and read it aloud.

It proved to be just what Reuben and Hannah had made of it, but Ishmael's clear reading rendered the orders much plainer.

"Now, if old Katie won't have to turn her fat body a little faster than she often does, I don't know nothing!" exclaimed Gray, when Ishmael had finished the reading.

"I will go up myself this evening and help her," said Hannah kindly.

"No, you won't, neither, my dear! Old Katie has lots of young maid servants to help her, and she's as jealous as a pet cat of all interference with her affairs. But we will walk over after tea and let her know what's up," said Gray.

After tea, accordingly, Reuben, Hannah, and Ishmael took a pleasant evening stroll through the forest to Tanglewood, and told Katie what was at hand.

"And you'll have to stir round, old woman, and that I tell you, for this is Saturday night, and they may be here on Monday evening," said Gray.

"Law, Marse Reuben, you needn't tell me nuffin 'tall 'bout Marse Judge Merlin! I knows his ways too well; I been too long use to his popping down on us, unexpected, like the Day of Judgment, for me to be unprepared! The house is all in fust-rate order; only wantin' fires to be kindled to correct de damp, and windows to be opened to air de rooms; and time 'nuff for dat o' Monday," grinned old Katie, taking things easy.

"Very well, only see to it! Come, Hannah, let us go home," said Gray.

"But, Uncle Reuben, have you no directions for the coachman to meet the judge at the landing?" inquired Ishmael.

"No, my lad. The judge never comes down by any of these little sailing packets as pass here. He allers comes by the steamboat to Baymouth, and then from there to here by land."

"Then had you not better send the carriage to Baymouth immediately, that it may be there in time to meet him? It will be more comfortable for the judge and—and Miss—and his daughter to travel in their own easy carriage than in those rough village hacks."

"Well, now, Ishmael, that's a rale good idee, and I'll follow it, and the judge will thank you for it. If he'd took a thought, you see, he'd a-gin me the order to do just that thing. But law! he's so took up along of public affairs, as he never thinks of his private comfort, though he is always pleased as possible when anybody thinks of it for him."

"Then, Uncle Reuben, had you not better start Sam with the carriage this evening? It is a very clear night, the roads are excellent, and the horses are fresh; so he could easily reach Baymouth by sunrise, and put up at the 'Planter's Rest,' for Sunday, and wait there for the boat."

"Yes, Ishmael, I think I had better do so; we'll go home now directly and start Sam. He'll be pleased to death! If there's anything that nigger likes, it's a journey, particular through the cool of the night; but he'll sleep all day to-morrow to make up for his lost rest," returned Reuben, as they turned to walk back to the cottage.

Sam was found loitering near the front gate. When told what he was to do, he grinned and started with alacrity to put the horses to the carriage and prepare the horse feed to take along with him.

And meanwhile Hannah packed a hamper full of food and drink to solace the traveler on his night journey.

In half an hour from his first notice to go, Sam drove the carriage up to the cottage gate, received his hamper of provisions and his final orders, and departed.

Hannah and Reuben, leaning over the gate, watched him out of sight, and then sat down in front of their cottage door, to enjoy the coolness of the summer evening, and talk of the judge's expected arrival.

Ishmael went up to his room, lighted a candle, and sat down to try to compose his agitated heart and apply his mind to study. But in vain; his eyes wandered over the pages of his book; his mind could not take in the meaning. The thought of Claudia filled his whole soul, absorbed his every faculty to the exclusion of every other idea.

"Oh, this will never, never do! It is weakness, folly, madness! What have I to do with Miss Merlin that she takes possession of my whole being in this manner! I must, I will conquer this passion!" he exclaimed, at last, starting up, throwing aside his book, and pacing the floor.

"Yes, with the Lord's help, I will overcome this infatuation!" he repeated, as he paused in his hasty walk, bowed his head, and folded his hands in prayer to God for deliverance from the power of inordinate and vain affections.

This done, he returned to his studies with more success. And long after he heard Hannah and Reuben re-enter the cottage and retire to their room, he continued to sit up and read. He read on perseveringly, until he had wearied himself out enough to be able to sleep. And his last resolution on seeking his bed was:

"By the Lord's help I will conquer this passion! I will combat it with prayer, and study, and work!"

CHAPTER XLI.

CLAUDIA.

But she in those fond feelings had no share;
Her sighs were not for him; to her he was
Even as a brother; but no more; 'twas much,
For brotherless she was save in the name
Her girlish friendship had bestowed on him;
Herself the solitary scion left
Of a time-honored race.
—*Byron's Dream*.

Ishmael applied himself diligently to active outdoor work during the morning and to study during the evening hours.

Thus several days passed. Nothing was heard from Sam, the carriage, or the judge.

Reuben Gray expressed great anxiety—not upon account of the judge, or Miss Merlin, who, he averred, were both capable of taking care of themselves and each other, but on account of Sam and his valuable charge that he feared had in some way or other come to harm.

Ishmael tried to reassure him by declaring his own opinion that all was right, and that Sam was only waiting at Baymouth for the arrival of his master.

Reuben Gray only shook his head and predicted all sorts of misfortunes.

But Ishmael's supposition was proved to be correct, when late Wednesday night, or rather—for it was after midnight—early Thursday morning, the unusual sound of carriage wheels passing the road before the cottage waked up all its inmates, and announced to them the arrival of the judge and his daughter.

Reuben Gray started up and hurried on his clothes.

Ishmael sprang out of bed and looked forth from the window. But the carriage without pausing for a moment rolled on its way to Tanglewood House.

The startled sleepers finding their services not required returned to bed again.

Early that morning, while the family were at the breakfast table, Sam made his appearance and formally announced the arrival of the judge and Miss Merlin at Tanglewood.

"How long did you have to wait for them at Baymouth?" inquired Reuben Gray.

"Not a hour, sar. I arrove about sunrise at the 'Planter's,' just the 'Powhatan' was a steaming up to the wharf; and so I druv on to the wharf to see if de judge and his darter was aboard, and sure nuff dere dey was! And mightily 'stonished was dey to see me and de carriage and de horses; and mightily pleased, too. So de judge he put his darter inter de inside, while I piled on de luggage a-hind and a-top; and so we goes back to de 'Planters,'" said Sam.

"But what kept you so long at Baymouth?"

"Why, law bless you, de judge, he had wisits to pay in de neighborhood; and having of me an' de carriage dere made it all de more convenienter. O' Monday we went over to a place called de Burrow, and dined long of one Marse Commodore Burghe; and o' Tuesday we went and dined at Brudenell Hall with young Mr. Herman Brudenell."

At this name Hannah started and turned pale; but almost immediately recovered her composure.

Sam continued:

"And o' Wednesday, that is yesterday morning airly, we started for home. We laid by during the heat of the day at Horse-head, and started again late in de arternoon; dat made it one o'clock when we arrove at home last night, or leastways this morning."

"Well, and what brought you down here? Has the judge sent any messages to me?"

"Yes, he have; he want you to come right up to de house and fetch de farm books, so he can see how the 'counts stands."

"Very well; they're all right!" said Reuben confidently, as he arose from the table, put on his hat, took two account-books from the shelf, and went out followed by Sam.

Ishmael as usual went into the garden to work, and tried to keep his thoughts from dwelling upon Claudia.

At dinner-time Gray returned, and Ishmael met him at the table. And Gray could talk of nothing but the improvement, beauty, and the grace of Miss Merlin.

"She is just too beautiful for this world, Hannah," he concluded, after having exhausted all his powers of description upon his subject.

After dinner Ishmael went upstairs to his books, and Hannah took advantage of his absence to say to Gray:

"Reuben, I wish you would never mention Miss Claudia Merlin's name before Ishmael."

"Law! why?" inquired Gray.

"Because I want him to forget her."

"But why so?"

"Oh, Reuben, how dull you are! Well, if I must tell you, he likes her."

"Well, so do I! and so do everyone!" said honest Reuben.

"But he likes her too well! he loves her, Reuben!"

"What! Ishmael love Judge Merlin's daughter! L-a-w! Why I should as soon think of falling in love with a royal princess!" exclaimed the honest man, in extreme astonishment.

"Reuben, hush! I hate to speak of it; but it is true. Pray, never let him know that we even suspect the truth; and be careful not to mention her name in his presence. I can see that he is struggling to conquer his feelings; but he can never do it while you continue to ding her name into his ears foreverlasting."

"I'll be mum! Ishmael in love with Miss Merlin! I should as soon suspicion him of being in love with the Queen of Spain! Good gracious! how angry she'd be if she knew it."

After this conversation Reuben Gray was very careful to avoid all mention of Claudia Merlin in the hearing of Ishmael.

The month of August was drawing to a close. Ishmael had not once set eyes on Claudia, though he had chanced to see the judge on horseback at a distance several times. Ishmael busied himself in seeking out a room in the neighborhood, in which to open a school on the first of September. He had not as yet succeeded in his object, when one day an accident occurred that, as he used it, had a signal effect on his future life.

It was a rather cool morning in the latter part of August when he, after spending an hour or two of work in the garden, dressed himself in his best clothes and set off to walk to Rushy Shore farm, where he heard there was a small schoolhouse ready furnished with rough benches and desks, to be had at low rent. His road lay along the high banks of the river, above the sands. He had gone about a mile on his way when he heard the sound of carriage wheels behind him, and in a few minutes caught a glimpse of an open barouche, drawn by a pair of fine, spirited gray horses, as it flashed by him. Quickly as the carriage passed, he recognized in the distinguished looking young lady seated within it—Claudia!—recognized her with an electric shock that thrilled his whole being, paralyzed him where he stood and bound him to the spot! He gazed after the flying vehicle until it vanished from his sight. Then he sank down where he stood and covered his face with his hands and strove to calm the rising emotion that swelled his bosom. It was minutes before he recovered self-possession enough to arise and go on his way.

In due time he reached the farm—Rushy Shore—where the schoolhouse was for rent. It was a plain little log house close to the river side and shaded by cedars. It had been built for the use of a poor country master who had worn out his life in teaching for small pay the humbler class of country children. He rested from his earthly labors, and the school was without a teacher. Ishmael saw only the overseer of the farm, who informed him that he had authority to let the schoolroom only until Christmas, as the whole estate had just been sold and the new owner was to take possession at the new year.

"Who is the new owner?" inquired Ishmael.

"Well, sir, his name is Middleton—Mr. James Middleton, from St. Mary's County; though I think I did hear as he was first of all from Virginia."

"Mr. Middleton! Mr. James Middleton!" exclaimed Ishmael, catching his breath for joy.

"Yes, sir; that is the gentleman; did you happen to know him?"

"Yes: intimately; he is one of the best and most honored friends I have in the world!" said Ishmael warmly.

"Then, sir, maybe he wouldn't be for turning you out of the schoolhouse even when the time we can let it for is up?"

"No, I don't think he would," said Ishmael, smiling, as he took his leave and started on his return. He walked rapidly on his way homeward, thinking of the strange destiny that threw him again among the friends of his childhood, when he was startled by a sound as of the sudden rush of wheels. He raised his head and beheld a fearful sight! Plunging madly towards the brink of the high bank were the horses of Claudia's returning carriage. The coachman had dropped the reins, which were trailing on the ground, sprung from his seat and was left some distance behind. Claudia retained hers, holding by the sides of the carriage; but her face was white as marble; her eyes were starting from their sockets; her teeth were firmly set; her lips drawn back; her hat lost and her black hair streaming behind her! On rushed the maddened beasts towards the brink of the precipice! another moment, and they would have dashed down into certain destruction!

Ishmael saw and hurled himself furiously forward between the rushing horses and the edge of the precipice, seizing the reins as the horses dashed up to him, and threw all his strength into the effort to turn them aside from their fate.

He did turn them from the brink of destruction, but alas! alas! as they were suddenly and violently whirled around they threw him down and passed, dragging the carriage with them, over his prostrate body!

At the same moment some fishermen on the sands below, who had seen the impending catastrophe, rushed up the bank, headed the maddened horses and succeeded in stopping them.

Then Miss Merlin jumped from the carriage, and ran to the side of Ishmael.

In that instant of deadly peril she had recognized him; but all had passed so instantaneously that she had not had time to speak, scarcely to breathe.

Now she kneeled by his side and raised his head. He was mangled, bleeding, pallid, and insensible.

"Oh, for the love of God, leave those horses and come here, men! Come instantly!" cried Claudia, who with trembling hands was seeking on the boy's face and bosom for some signs of life.

Two of the men remained with the horses, but three rushed to the side of the young lady.

"Oh, Heaven! he is crushed to death, I fear! He was trampled down by the horses, and the whole carriage seemed to have passed over him! Oh, tell me! tell me! is he killed? is he quite, quite dead?" cried Claudia breathlessly, wringing her hands in anguish, as she arose from her kneeling posture to make room for the man.

The three got down beside him and began to examine his condition.

"Is he dead? Oh! is he dead?" cried Claudia.

"It's impossible to tell, miss," answered one of the men, who had his hand on Ishmael's wrist; "but he haint got no pulse."

"And his leg is broken, to begin with," said another, who was busy feeling the poor fellow's limbs.

"And I think his ribs be broken, too," added the third man, who had his hand in the boy's bosom.

With a piercing scream Claudia threw herself down on the ground, bent over the fallen body, raised the poor, ghastly head in her arms, supported it on her bosom, snatched a vial of aromatic vinegar from her pocket, and began hastily to bathe the blanched face; her tears falling fast as she cried:

"He must not die! Oh, he shall not die! Oh, God have mercy on me, and spare his life! Oh, Saviour of the world, save him! Sweet angels in heaven, come to his aid! Oh, Ishmael, my brother! my treasure! my own, dear boy, do not die! Better I had died than you! Come back! come back to me, my own! my beautiful boy, come back to me! You are mine!"

Her tears fell like rain; and utterly careless of the eyes gazing in wonder upon her, she covered his cold, white face with kisses.

Those warm tears, those thrilling kisses, falling on his lifeless, face, might have called back the boy's spirit, had it been waiting at the gates of heaven!

To Claudia's unutterable joy his sensitive features quivered, his pale cheeks flushed, his large, blue eyes opened, and with a smile of ineffable satisfaction he recognized the face that was bending over him. Then the pallid lips trembled and unclosed with the faintly uttered inquiry:

"You are safe, Miss Merlin?"

"Quite safe, my own dear boy! but oh! at what a cost to you!" she answered impulsively and fervently.

He closed his eyes, and while that look of ineffable bliss deepened on his face, he murmured some faint words that she stooped to catch:

"I am so happy—so happy—I could wish to die now!" he breathed.

"But you shall not die, dear Ishmael! God heard my cry and sent you back to me! You shall live!"

Then turning to the gaping men, she said:

"Raise him gently, and lay him in the barouche. Stop a moment!—I will get in first and arrange the cushions for him."

And with that she tenderly laid the boy's head back upon the ground, and entered the carriage, and with her own hands took all the cushions from the tops of the seats, and arranged them so as to make a level bed for the hurt boy. Then she placed herself in the back seat, and, as they lifted him into the carriage, she took his head and shoulders and supported them upon her lap.

But Ishmael had fainted from the pain of being moved. And oh! what a mangled form he seemed, as she held him in her arms upon her bosom, while his broken limbs lay out upon the pile of cushions.

"One of you two now take the horses by the head, and lead them slowly, by the river road, towards Tanglewood House. It is the longest road, but the smoothest," said Miss Merlin.

Two of the men started to obey this order, saying that it might take more than one to manage the horses if they should grow restive again.

"That is very true; besides, you can relieve each other in leading the horses. And now one of the others must run directly to the house of the Overseer Gray, and tell him what has happened, and direct him to ride off immediately to Shelton and fetch Dr. Jarvis to Tanglewood."

All three of the remaining men started off zealously upon this errand. Meanwhile Sam, the craven coachman, came up with a crestfallen air to the side of the carriage, whimpering:

"Miss Claudia, I hope nobody was dangerous hurt?"

"Nobody dangerously hurt? Ishmael Worth is killed for aught I know! Keep out of my way, you cowardly villain!" exclaimed Claudia angrily, for you know the heiress was no angel.

"'Deed and 'deed, Miss Claudia, I didn't know what I was a-doing of no more than the dead when I jumped out'n the b'rouche! 'Clare to my Marster in heben I didn't!" whined Sam.

"Perhaps not; but keep out of my way!" repeated Claudia, with her eyes kindling. .

"But please, miss, mayn't I drive you home now?"

"What? after nearly breaking my neck, which was saved only at the cost of this poor boy's life, perhaps?"

"Please, Miss Claudia, I'll be careful another time—"

"Careful of your own life!"

"Please, miss, let me drive you home this once."

"Not to save your soul!"

"But what'll ole Marse say?" cried Sam, in utter dismay.

"That is your affair. I advise you to keep out of his way also! Begone from my sight! Go on, men!" finally ordered Miss Merlin.

Sam, more ashamed of himself than ever, slunk away.

And the fishermen started to lead the horses and carriage towards Tanglewood.

Meanwhile the messengers dispatched by Claudia hurried on towards Reuben Gray's cottage. But before they got in sight of the house they came full upon Reuben, who was mounted on his white cob, and riding as if for a wager.

"Hey! hallo! stop!" cried the foremost man, throwing up his arms before the horse, which immediately started and shied.

"Hush, can't ye! Don't stop me now! I'm in a desp'at hurry! I'm off for the doctor! My wife's taken bad, and may die before I get back!" exclaimed Reuben, with a scared visage, as he tried to pass the messengers.

"Going for the doctor! There's just where we were going to send you! Go as fast as you can, and if your wife isn't very bad indeed, send him first of all to Tanglewood, where he is wanted immediately."

"Who is ill there?" inquired Reuben anxiously.

"Nobody! but your nephew has been knocked down and trampled nearly to death while stopping Miss Merlin's horses that were running away with her."

"Ishmael hurt! Good gracious! there's nothing but trouble in this world! Where is the poor lad?"

"Miss Merlin has taken him to Tanglewood. The doctor is wanted there."

"I'll send him as soon as ever I can; but I must get him to Hannah first! I must indeed!" And with that Reuben put whip to his horse and rode away; but in a moment he wheeled again and rode back to the fishermen, saying:

"Hallo, Simpson! are you going past our place?"

"Yes," replied the man.

"Well, then, mind and don't breathe a word about Ishmael's accident to Hannah, or to anybody about the place as might tell her; because she's very ill, and the shock might be her death, you know," said Reuben anxiously.

"All right! we'll be careful," replied the man. And Reuben rode off.

He was so fortunate as to find Dr. Jarvis at his office and get him to come immediately to Woodside. But not until the doctor had seen Hannah and had given her a little medicine, and declared that his farther services would not be required by her for several hours yet, did Reuben mention to him the other case that awaited his attention at Tanglewood. And Dr. Jarvis, with a movement of impatience at the unnecessary delay, hurried thither.

CHAPTER XLII.

ISHMAEL AT TANGLEWOOD.

There was an ancient mansion, and before
Its walls there was a steed caparisoned.
Within an antique oratory lay
The boy of whom I spake; he was alone,
And pale and tossing to and fro . . . .
—*Byron.*

Meanwhile the carriage traveling slowly reached Tanglewood. Slowly pacing up and down the long piazza in front of the house was Judge Merlin. He was a rather singular-looking man of about forty-five years of age. He was very tall, thin, and bony, with high aquiline features, dark complexion, and iron-gray hair, which he wore long and parted in the middle. He was habited in a loose jacket, vest, and trousers of brown linen, and wore a broad-brimmed straw hat on his head, and large slippers, down at the heel, on his feet. He carried in his hand a lighted pipe of common clay, and he walked with a slow, swinging gait, and an air of careless indifference to all around him. Altogether, he presented the idea of a civilized Indian chief, rather than that of a Christian gentleman. Tradition said that the blood of King Powhatan flowed in Randolph Merlin's veins, and certainly his personal appearance, character, tastes, habits, and manners favored the legend.

On seeing the carriage approach he had taken the clay pipe from his mouth and sauntered forward. On seeing the strange burden that his daughter supported in her arms, he came down to the side of the carriage, exclaiming:

"Who have you got there, Claudia?"

"Oh, papa, it is Ishmael Worth! He has killed himself, I fear, in saving me! My horses ran away, ran directly towards the steeps above the river, and would have plunged over if he had not started forward and turned their heads in time; but the horses, as they turned, knocked him down and ran over him!" cried Claudia, in almost breathless vehemence.

"What was Sam doing all this time?" inquired the judge, as he stood contemplating the insensible boy.

"Oh, papa, he sprang from the carriage as soon as the horses became unmanageable and ran away! But don't stop here asking useless questions! Lift him out and take him into the house! Gently, papa! gently," said Claudia, as Judge Merlin slipped his long arms under the youth's body and lifted him from the carriage.

"Now, then, what do you expect me to do with him?" inquired Judge Merlin, looking around as if for a convenient place to lay him on the grass.

"Oh, papa, take him right into the spare bedroom on the lower floor! and lay him on the bed. I have sent for a doctor to attend him here," answered Claudia, as she sprang from the carriage and led the way into the very room she had indicated.

"He is rather badly hurt," said the judge, as he laid Ishmael upon the bed and arranged his broken limbs as easily as he could.

"'Rather badly!' he is crushed nearly to death! I told you the whole carriage passed over him!" cried Claudia, with a hysterical sob, as she bent over the boy.

"Worse than I thought," continued the judge, as he proceeded to unbutton Ishmael's coat and loosen his clothes. "Did you say you sent for a doctor?"

"Yes! as soon as it happened! He ought to be here in an hour from this!" replied Claudia, wringing her hands.

"His clothes must be cut away from him; it might do his fractured limbs irreparable injury to try to draw off his coat and trousers in the usual manner. Leave him to me, Claudia, and go and tell old Katie to come here and bring a pair of sharp shears with her," ordered the judge.

Claudia stooped down quickly, gave one wistful, longing, compassionate gaze at the still, cold white face of the sufferer, and then hurried out to obey her father's directions. She sent old Katie in, and then threw off her hat and mantle and sat down on the step of the door to watch for the doctor's approach, and also to be at hand to hear any tidings that might come from the room of the wounded boy.

More than an hour Claudia remained on the watch without seeing anyone. Then, when suspense grew intolerable, she impulsively sprang up and silently hastened to the door of the sick-room and softly rapped.

The judge came and opened it.

"Oh, papa, how is he?"

"Breathing, Claudia, that is all! I wish to Heaven the doctor would come! Are you sure the messenger went after him!"

"Oh, yes, papa, I am sure! Do let me come in and see him!"

"It is no place for you, Claudia; he is partially undressed; I will take care of him."

And with these words the judge gently closed the door in his daughter's face.

Claudia went back to her post.

"Why don't the doctor come! And oh! why don't Reuben Gray or Hannah come? It is dreadful to sit here and wait!" she exclaimed, as with a sudden resolution she sprang up again, seized her hat and ran out of the house with the intention of proceeding directly to the Gray's cottage.

But a few paces from the house she met the doctor's gig.

"Oh, Doctor Jarvis, I am so glad you have come at last!" she cried.

"Who is it that is hurt?" inquired the doctor.

"Ishmael Worth, our overseer's nephew!"

"How did it happen?"

"Didn't they tell you?"

"No."

"Oh, poor boy! He threw himself before my horses to stop them as they were running down the steeps over the river; and he turned them aside, but they knocked him down and ran over him!"

"Bad! very bad! poor fellow!" said the doctor, jumping from his gig as he drew up before the house.

Claudia ran in before him, leading the way to the sick chamber, at the door of which she rapped to announce the arrival. This time old Katie opened the door, and admitted the doctor.

Claudia, excluded from entrance, walked up and down the hall in a fever of anxiety.

Once old Katie came out and Claudia arrested her.

"What does the doctor say, Katie?"

"He don't say nothing satisfactory, Miss Claudia. Don't stop me, please! I'm sent for bandages and things!"

And Katie hurried on her errand, and presently reappeared with her arms full of linen and other articles, which she carried into the sick-room. Later, the doctor came out attended by the judge.

Claudia waylaid them with the questions:

"What is the nature of his injuries? are they fatal?"

"Not fatal; but very serious. One leg and arm are broken; and he is very badly bruised; but worst of all is the great shock to his very sensitive nervous system," was the reply of Doctor Jarvis.

"When will you see him again, sir?" anxiously inquired Claudia.

"In the course of the evening. I am not going back home for some hours, perhaps not for the night; I have a case at Gray's."

"Indeed! that is the reason, then, I suppose, why no one has answered my message to come up and see Ishmael. But who is sick there?" inquired Claudia.

"Mrs. Gray. Good-afternoon, Miss Merlin," said the doctor shortly, as he walked out of the house attended by the judge.

Claudia went to the door of Ishmael's room and rapped softly.

Old Katie answered the summons.

"Can I come in now, Katie?" asked Miss Merlin, a little impatiently.

"Oh, yes, I s'pose so; I s'pose you'd die if you didn't!" answered this privileged old servant, holding open the door for Claudia's admittance.

She passed softly into the darkened room, and approached the bedside. Ishmael lay there swathed in linen bandages and extended at full length, more like a shrouded corpse than a living boy. His eyes were closed and his face was livid.

"Is he asleep?" inquired Claudia, in a tone scarcely above her breath.

"Sort o' sleep. You see, arter de doctor done set his arm an' leg, an' splintered of 'em up, an' boun' up his wounds an' bruises, he gib him some'at to 'pose his nerves and make him sleep, an' it done hev him into dis state; which you see yourse'f is nyder sleep nor wake nor dead nor libe."

Claudia saw indeed that he was under the effects of morphia. And with a deep sigh of strangely blended relief and apprehension, Claudia sank into a chair beside his bed.

And old Katie took that opportunity to slip out and eat her "bit of dinner," leaving Claudia watching.

At the expiration of an hour Katie returned to her post. But Claudia did not therefore quit hers. She remained seated beside the wounded boy. All that day he lay quietly, under the influence of morphia. Once the judge looked in to inquire the state of the patient, and on being told that the boy still slept, he went off again. Late in the afternoon the doctor came again, saw that his patient was at ease, left directions for his treatment, and then prepared to depart.

"How is the sick woman at Gray's?" inquired Claudia.

"Extremely ill. I am going immediately back there to remain until it is over; if I should be particularly wanted here, send there for me," said the doctor.

"Yes; but I am very sorry Mrs. Gray is so ill! She is Ishmael's aunt. What is the matter with her?"

"Humph!" answered the doctor. "Good-night, Miss Claudia. You will know where to send for me, if I am wanted here."

"Yes; but I am so sorry about Gray's wife! Is she in danger?" persisted Claudia.

"Yes."

"I am very sorry; but what ails her?" persevered Claudia.

"Good-evening, Miss Merlin," replied the doctor, lifting his hat and departing.

"The man is half asleep; he has not answered my question," grumbled Claudia, as she returned to her seat by the sick-bed.

Just then the bell rung for the late dinner, and Claudia went out and crossed the hall to the dining room, where she joined her father. And while at dinner she gave him a more detailed account of her late danger, and the manner in which she was saved.

Once more in the course of that evening Claudia looked in upon the wounded boy, to ascertain his condition before retiring to her room. He was still sleeping.

"If he should wake up, you must call me, no matter what time of night it is, Katie," said Miss Merlin, as she left the sick-chamber.

"Yes, miss," answered Katie, who nevertheless made up her mind to use her own discretion in the matter of obedience to this order.

Claudia Merlin was not, as Ishmael was, of a religious disposition, yet nevertheless before she retired to bed she did kneel and pray for his restoration to life and health; for, somehow, the well-being of the peasant youth was very precious to the heiress. Claudia could not sleep; she lay tumbling and tossing upon a restless and feverish couch. The image of that mangled and bleeding youth as she first saw him on the river bank was ever before her. The gaze of his intensely earnest eyes as he raised them to hers, when he inquired, "Are you safe?"—and the deep smile of joy with which they closed again when she answered, "I am safe"—haunted her memory and troubled her spirit. Those looks, those tones, had made a revelation to Claudia!—That the peasant boy presumed to love her!—her! Claudia Merlin, the heiress, angel-born, who scarcely deemed there was in all democratic America a fitting match for her!

During the excitement and terror of the day, while the extent of Ishmael's injuries was still unknown and his life seemed in extreme danger, Claudia had not had leisure to receive the fact of Ishmael's love, much less to reflect upon its consequences. But now that all was known and suspense was over, now in the silence and solitude of her bed-chamber, the images and impressions of the day returned to her with all their revelations and tendencies, and filled the mind of Claudia with astonishment and consternation! That Ishmael Worth should be capable of loving her, seemed to Miss Merlin as miraculous as it would be for Fido to be capable of talking to her! And in the wonder of the affair she almost lost sight of its presumption!

But how should she deal with this presuming peasant boy, who had dared to love her, to risk his life to save hers, and to let the secret of his love escape him?

For a long time Claudia could not satisfactorily answer this question, and this was what kept her awake all night. To neglect him, or to treat him with marked coldness, would be a cruel return for the sacrifice he had rendered her; it would be besides making the affair of too much importance; and finally, it would be "against the grain" of Claudia's own heart; for in a queenly way she loved this Ishmael very dearly indeed; much more dearly than she loved Fido, or any four-footed pet she possessed; and if he had happened to have been killed in her service, Claudia would have abandoned herself to grief for weeks afterwards, and she would have had a headstone recording his heroism placed over his grave.

After wearying herself out with conjectures as to what would be the becoming line of conduct in a young princess who should discover that a brave peasant had fallen in love with her, Claudia at length determined to ignore the fact that had come to her knowledge and act just as if she had never discovered or even suspected its existence.

"My dignity cannot suffer from his presumptuous folly, so long as I do not permit him to see that I know it; and as for the rest, this love may do his character good; may elevate it!" And having laid this balm to her wounded pride, Claudia closed her eyes.

So near sunrise was it when Miss Merlin dropped off that, once asleep, she continued to sleep on until late in the day.

Meanwhile all the rest of the family were up and astir. The doctor came early and went in to see his patient. The judge breakfasted alone, and then joined the doctor in the sick-room. Ishmael was awake, but pale, languid, and suffering. The doctor was seated beside him. He had just finished dressing his wounds, and had ordered some light nourishment, which old Katie had left the room to bring.

"How is your patient getting along, doctor?" inquired the judge.

"Oh, he is doing very well—very well indeed," replied the doctor, putting the best face on a bad affair, after the manner of his class.

"How do you feel, my lad?" inquired the judge, bending over the patient.

"In some pain; but no more than I can very well bear, thank you, sir," said Ishmael courteously. But his white and quivering lip betrayed the extremity of his suffering, and the difficulty he experienced in speaking at all.

"I must beg, sir, that you will not talk to him; he must be left in perfect quietness," whispered the doctor.

At this moment old Katie returned with a little light jelly on a plate. The doctor slowly administered a few teaspoonfuls to his patient, and then returned the plate to the nurse.

"Miss Claudia ordered me to call her as soon as the young man woke; and now as his wounds is dressed, and he has had somethin' to eat, I might's well go call her," suggested Katie.

At the hearing of Claudia's name Ishmael's eyes flew open, and a hectic spot blazed upon his pale cheek. The doctor, who had his eye upon his patient, noticed this, as he replied:

"Upon no account! Neither Miss Merlin nor anyone else must be permitted to enter his room for days to come—not until I give leave. You will see this obeyed, judge?" he inquired, turning to his host.

178

"Assuredly," replied the latter.

At these words the color faded from Ishmael's face and the light from his eyes.

The doctor arose and took leave.

The judge attended him to the door, saw him depart, and was in the act of turning into his own house when he perceived Reuben Gray approaching.

Judge Merlin paused to wait for his overseer. Reuben Gray came up, took off his hat, and stood before his employer with the most comical blending of emotions on his weather-beaten countenance, where joy, grief, satisfaction, and anxiety seemed to strive for the mastery.

"Well, Gray, what is it?" inquired the judge.

"Please, sir, how is Ishmael?" entreated Reuben, anxiety getting the upper hand for the moment.

"He is badly hurt, Gray; but doing very well, the doctor says."

"Please, sir, can I see him?"

"Not upon any account for the present; he must be left in perfect quiet. But why haven't you been up to inquire after him before this?"

"Ah, sir, the state of my wife."

"Oh, yes, I heard she was ill; but did not know that she was so ill as to prevent your coming to see after your poor boy. I hope she is better now?"

"Yes, sir, thank Heaven, she is well over it!" said Reuben, satisfaction now expressed in every lineament of his honest face.

"What was the matter with her? Was it the cholera morbus, that is so prevalent at this season?"

Reuben grinned from ear to ear; but did not immediately reply.

The judge looked as if he still expected an answer. Reuben scratched his gray head, and looked up from the corner of his eye, as he at length replied:

"It was a boy and a gal, sir!"

"A what?" questioned the judge—perplexity.

"A boy and a gal, sir; twins, sir, they is," replied Reuben Gray, joy getting the mastery over every other expression in his beaming countenance.

"Why—you don't mean to tell me that your wife has presented you with twins?" exclaimed the judge, both surprised and amused at the announcement.

"Well, yes, sir," said Reuben proudly.

"But you are such an elderly couple!" laughed the judge.

"Well, yes, sir, so we is! And that, I take it, is the very reason on't. You see, I think, sir, because we married very late in life—poor Hannah and me—natur' took a consideration on to it, and, as we hadn't much time before us, she sent us two at once! at least, if that aint the reason, I can't account for them both in any other way!" said Reuben, looking up.

"That's it! You've hit it, Reuben!" said the judge, laughing. "And mind, if they live, I'll stand godfather to the babies at the christening. Are they fine healthy children?"

"As bouncing babies, sir, as ever you set eyes on!" answered Reuben triumphantly.

"Count on me, then, Gray."

"Thank you, sir! And, your honor—"

"Well, Gray?"

"Soon as ever Ishmael is able to hear the news, tell him, will you, please? I think it will set him up, and help him on towards his recovery."

"I think so, too," said the judge.

Reuben touched his hat and withdrew. And the judge returned to the house.

Claudia had come down and breakfasted, but was in a state of great annoyance because she was denied admittance to the bedside of her suffering favorite.

The judge, to divert her thoughts, told her of the bountiful present nature had made to Hannah and Reuben Gray. At which Miss Claudia was so pleased that she got up and went to hunt through all her finery for presents for the children.

CHAPTER XLIII.

THE HEIRESS.

Trust me, Clara Vere de Vere,
From yon blue heavens above us bent,
The grand old gardener and his wife
Smile at the claims of long descent,
Howe'er it be, it seems to me,
'Tis only noble to be good;
Kind hearts are more than coronets,
And simple faith than Norman blood.
—*Tennyson.*

Almost any other youth than Ishmael Worth would have died of such injuries as he had sustained. But owing to that indestructible vitality and irrepressible elasticity of organization which had carried him safely through the deadly perils of his miserable infancy, he survived.

About the fourth day of his illness the irritative fever of his wounds having been subdued, Judge Merlin was admitted to see and converse with him.

Up to this morning the judge had thought of the victim only as the overseer's nephew, a poor, laboring youth about the estate, who had got hurt in doing his duty and stopping Miss Merlin's runaway horses; and he supposed that he, Judge Merlin, had done his part in simply taking the suffering youth into his own house and having him properly attended to. And now the judge went to the patient with the intention of praising his courage and offering him some proper reward for his services—as, for instance, a permanent situation to work on the estate for good wages.

And so Judge Merlin entered the sick-chamber, which was no longer darkened, but had all the windows open to admit the light and air.

He took a chair and seated himself by the bedside of the patient, and for the first time took a good look at him.

Ishmael's handsome face, no longer distorted by suffering, was calm and clear; his eyes were closed in repose but not in sleep, for the moment the judge "hemmed" he raised his eyelids and greeted his host with a gentle smile and nod.

Judge Merlin could not but be struck with the delicacy, refinement, and intellectuality of Ishmael's countenance.

"How do you feel yourself this morning, my lad?" he inquired, putting the usual commonplace question.

"Much easier, thank you, sir," replied the youth, in the pure, sweet, modulated tones of a highly-cultivated nature.

The judge was surprised, but did not show that he was so, as he said:

"You have done my daughter a great service; but at the cost of much suffering to yourself, I fear, my lad."

"I consider myself very fortunate and happy, sir, in having had the privilege of rendering Miss Merlin any service, at whatever cost to myself," replied Ishmael, with graceful courtesy.

More and more astonished at the words and manner of the young workman, the judge continued:

"Thank you, young man; very properly spoken—very properly: but for all that, I must find some way of rewarding you."

"Sir," said Ishmael, with gentle dignity, "I must beg you will not speak to me of reward for a simple act of instinctive gallantry that any man, worthy of the name, would have performed."

"But with you, young man, the case was different," said the judge loftily.

"True, sir," replied our youth, with sweet and courteous dignity, "with me the case was very different; because, with me, it was a matter of self-interest; for the service rendered to Miss Merlin was rendered to myself."

"I do not understand you, young man," said the judge haughtily.

"Pardon me, sir. I mean that in saving Miss Merlin from injury I saved myself from despair. If any harm had befallen her I should have been miserable; so you perceive, sir, that the act you are good enough to term a great service was too natural and too selfish to be praised or rewarded; and so I must beseech you to speak of it in that relation no more."

"But what was my daughter to you that you should risk your life for her, more than for another? or that her maimed limbs or broken neck should affect you more than others?"

"Sir, we were old acquaintances; I saw her every day when I went to Mr. Middleton's, and she was ever exceedingly kind to me," replied Ishmael.

"Oh! and you lived in that neighborhood?" inquired Judge Merlin, who immediately jumped to the conclusion that Ishmael had been employed as a laborer on Mr. Middleton's estate; though still he could not possibly account for the refinement in Ishmael's manner nor the excellence of his language.

"I lived in that neighborhood with my Aunt Hannah until Uncle Reuben married her, when I accompanied them to this place," answered Ishmael.

"Ah! and you saw a great deal of Mr. Middleton and—and his family?"

"I saw them every day, sir; they were very, very kind to me."

"Every day! then you must have been employed about the house," said the judge.

An arch smile beamed in the eyes of Ishmael as he answered:

"Yes, sir, I was employed about the house—that is to say, in the schoolroom."

"Ah! to sweep it out and keep it in order, I suppose; and, doubtless, there was where you contracted your superior tone of manners and conversation," thought the judge to himself, but he replied aloud:

"Well, young man, we will say no more of rewards, since the word is distasteful to you; but as soon as you can get strong again, I should be pleased to give you work about the place at fair wages. Our miller wants a white boy to go around with the grist. Would you like the place?"

"I thank you, sir, no; my plans for the future are fixed; that is, as nearly fixed as those of short-sighted mortals can be," smiled Ishmael.

"Ah, indeed!" exclaimed the judge, raising his eyebrows, "and may I, as one interested in your welfare, inquire what those plans may be?"

"Certainly, sir, and I thank you very much for the interest you express, as well as for all your kindness to me." Ishmael paused for a moment and then added:

"On the first of September I shall open the Rushy Shore schoolhouse, for the reception of day pupils."

"Whe-ew!" said the judge, with a low whistle, "and do you really mean to be a schoolmaster?"

"For the present, sir, until a better one can be found to fill the place; then, indeed, I shall feel bound in honor and conscience to resign my post, for I do not believe teaching to be my true vocation."

"No! I should think not, indeed!" replied Judge Merlin, who of course supposed the overseer's nephew, notwithstanding the grace and courtesy of his speech and manner, to be fit for nothing but manual labor. "What ever induces you to try school-keeping?" he inquired.

"I am driven to it by my own necessities, and drawn to it by the necessities of others. In other words, I need employment, and the neighborhood needs a teacher—and I think, sir, that one who conscientiously does his best is better than none at all. Those are the reasons, sir, why I have taken the school, with the intention of keeping it until a person more competent than myself to discharge its duties shall be found, when I shall give it up; for, as I said before, teaching is not my ultimate vocation."

"What is your 'ultimate vocation,' young man? for I should like to help you to it," said the judge, still thinking only of manual labor in all its varieties; "what is it?"

"Jurisprudence," answered Ishmael.

"Juris—what?" demanded the judge, as if he had not heard aright.

"Jurisprudence—the science of human justice; the knowledge of the laws, customs, and rights of man in communities; the study above all others most necessary to the due administration of justice in human affairs, and even in divine, and second only to that of theology," replied Ishmael, with grave enthusiasm.

"But—you don't mean to say that you intend to become a lawyer?" exclaimed the judge, in a state of astonishment that bordered on consternation.

"Yes, sir; I intend to be a lawyer, if it please the Lord to bless my earnest efforts," replied the youth reverently.

"Why—I am a lawyer!" exclaimed the judge.

"I am aware that you are a very distinguished one, sir, having risen to the bench of the Supreme Court of your native State," replied the youth respectfully.

The judge remained in a sort of panic of astonishment. The thought in his mind was this: What—you? you, the nephew of my overseer, have you the astounding impudence, the madness, to think that you can enter a profession of which I am a member?

Ishmael saw that thought reflected in his countenance and smiled to himself.

"But—how do you propose ever to become a lawyer?" inquired the judge, aloud.

"By reading law," answered Ishmael simply.

"What! upon your own responsibility?"

"Upon my own responsibility for a while. I shall try afterwards to enter the office of some lawyer. I shall use every faculty, try every means and improve every opportunity that Heaven grants me for this end. And thus I hope to succeed," said Ishmael gravely.

"Are you aware," inquired the judge, with a little sarcasm in his tone, "that some knowledge of the classics is absolutely necessary to the success of a lawyer?"

"I am aware that a knowledge of the classics is very desirable in each and all of what are termed the 'learned professions'; but I did not know, and I do not think, that it can be absolutely necessary in every grade of each of these; but if so, it is well for me that I have a fair knowledge of Latin and Greek," replied Ishmael.

"What did you say?" inquired the judge, with ever-increasing wonder.

Ishmael blushed at the perception that while he only meant to state a fact, he might be suspected of making a boast.

"Did you say that you knew anything of Latin and Greek?" inquired the judge, in amazement.

"Something of both, sir," replied Ishmael modestly.

"But surely you never picked up a smattering of the classics while sweeping out Middleton's family schoolroom!"

"Oh, no, sir!" laughed Ishmael.

"Where then?"

Ishmael's reply was lost in the bustling entrance of Doctor Jarvis, whom Judge Merlin arose to receive.

The doctor examined the condition of his patient, found him with an accession of fever, prescribed a complete repose for the remainder of the day, left some medicine with directions for its administration, and departed. The judge accompanied the doctor to the door.

"That is a rather remarkable boy," observed Judge Merlin, as they went out together.

"A very remarkable one! Who is he?" asked Doctor Jarvis.

"The nephew of my overseer, Reuben Gray. That is absolutely all I know about it."

"The nephew of Gray? Can it be so? Why, Gray is but an ignorant boor, while this youth has the manners and education of a gentleman—a polished gentleman!" exclaimed the doctor, in astonishment.

"It is true, and I can make nothing of it," said Judge Merlin, shaking his head.

"How very strange," mused the doctor, as he mounted his horse, bowed and rode away.

CHAPTER XLIV.

CLAUDIA'S PERPLEXITIES.

Oh, face most fair, shall thy beauty compare
With affection's glowing light?
Oh, riches and pride, how fade ye beside
Love's wealth, serene and bright.
—*Martin F. Tupper.*

Judge Merlin went into his well-ordered library, rang the bell, and sent a servant to call his daughter.

The messenger found Claudia walking impatiently up and down the drawing-room floor and turning herself at each wall with an angry jerk. Claudia had not yet been admitted to see Ishmael. She had just been refused again by old Katie, who acted upon the doctor's authority, and Claudia was unreasonably furious with everybody.

Claudia instantly obeyed the summons. She entered the library with hasty steps, closed the door with a bang, and stood before her father with flushed cheeks, sparkling eyes, and heaving bosom.

"Hey, dey! what's the matter?" asked the judge, taking his pipe from his mouth and staring at his daughter.

"You sent for me, papa! I hope it is to take me in to see that poor, half-crushed boy! What does old Katie mean by forever denying me entrance? It is not every day that a poor lad risks his life and gets himself crushed nearly to death in my service, that I should be made to appear to neglect him in this way! What must the boy think of me? What does old Katie mean, I ask?"

"If your nature requires a vehement expression, of course I am not the one to repress it! Still, in my opinion, vehemency is unworthy of a rational being, at all times, and especially when, as now, there is not the slightest occasion for it. You have not willfully neglected the young man; it is not of the least consequence whether he thinks you have, or not; and, finally, Katie means to obey the doctor's orders, which are to keep every living soul out of the sick-room to secure the patient needful repose. I believe I have answered you, Miss Merlin," replied the judge, smiling and coolly replacing his pipe in his mouth.

"Papa, what a disagreeable wet blanket you are, to be sure!"

"It is my nature to be so, my dear; and I am just what you need to dampen the fire of your temperament."

"Are those the orders of the doctor?"

"What, wet blankets for you?"

"No; but that everybody must be excluded from Ishmael's room?"

"Yes; his most peremptory orders, including even me for the present."

"Then I suppose they must be submitted to?"

"For the present, certainly."

Claudia shrugged her shoulders with an impatient gesture, and then said:

"You sent for me, papa. Was it for anything particular?"

"Yes; to question you. Have you been long acquainted with this Ishmael Gray?"

"Ishmael Worth, papa! Yes, I have known him well ever since you placed me with my Aunt Middleton," replied Claudia, throwing herself into a chair.

The judge was slowly walking up and down the library, and he continued his walk as he conversed with his daughter.

"Who is this Ishmael Worth, then?"

"You know, papa; the nephew of Reuben Gray, or rather of his wife; but it is the same thing."

"I know he is the nephew of Reuben Gray; but that explains nothing! Gray is a rude, ignorant, though well-meaning boor; but this lad is a refined, graceful, and cultivated young man."

Claudia made no comment upon this.

"Now, if you have known him so many years, you ought to be able to explain this inconsistency. One does not expect to find nightingales in crows' nests," said the judge.

Still Miss Merlin was silent.

"Why don't you speak, my dear?"

Claudia blushed over her face, neck, and bosom as she answered:

"Papa, what shall I say? You force me to remember things I would like to forget. Socially, Ishmael Worth was born the lowest of all the low. Naturally, he was endowed with the highest moral and intellectual gifts. He is in a great measure self-educated. In worldly position he is beneath our feet: in wisdom and goodness he is far, far above our heads. He is one of nature's princes, but one of society's outcasts."

"But how has the youth contrived to procure the means of such education as he has?" inquired the judge, seating himself opposite his daughter.

"Papa, I will tell you all I know about him," replied Claudia. And she commenced and related the history of Ishmael's struggles, trials, and triumphs, from the hour of her first meeting with him in front of Hamlin's book shop to that of his self-immolation to save her from death. Claudia spoke with deep feeling. As she concluded her bosom was heaving, her cheeks were flushed, and her eyes tearful with emotion.

"And now, papa," she said, as she finished her narrative, "you will understand why it is that I cannot, must not, will not, neglect him! As soon as he can bear visitors I must be admitted to his room, to do for him all that a young sister might do for her brother; no one could reasonably cavil at that. Papa, Ishmael believes in me more than anyone else in the world does. He thinks more highly of me than others do. He knows that there is something better in me than this mere outside beauty that others praise so foolishly. And I would not like to lose his good opinion, papa. I could not bear to have him think me cold, selfish, or ungrateful. So I must and I will help to nurse him."

"Miss Merlin, you have grown up very much as my trees have, with every natural eccentricity of growth untrimmed; but I hope you will not let your branches trail upon the earth."

"What do you mean, papa?"

"I hope you do not mean to play Catherine to this boy's Huon in a new version of the drama of 'Love; or, The Countess and the Serf!"

"Papa! how can you say such things to your motherless daughter! You know that I would die first!" exclaimed the imperious girl indignantly, as she bounced up and flung herself into a passion and out of the room. She left the door wide open; but had scarcely disappeared before her place in the doorway was filled up by the tall, gaunt figure, gray head, and smiling face of Reuben.

"Well, Gray?"

"Well, sir, I have brought the farm books all made up to the first of this month, sir," said the overseer, laying the volumes on the table before his master.

"And very neatly and accurately done, too," remarked the judge, as he turned over the pages and examined the items. "It is not your handwriting, Gray?"

"Dear, no, sir! not likely!"

"Nor little Kitty's?"

"Why, law, sir! little Kitty has been in Californy a year or more! How did you like the 'rangement of your liber-airy, sir?" inquired Gray, with apparent irrelevance, as he glanced around upon the book-lined walls.

"Very much, indeed, Gray! I never had my books so well classified. It was the work of young Ramsey, the schoolmaster, I suppose, and furnished him with employment during the midsummer holidays. You must tell him that I am very much pleased with the work and that he must send in his account immediately."

"Law bless you, sir; it was not Master Ramsey as did it," said Gray, with a broad grin.

"Who, then? Whoever it was, it is all the same to me; I am pleased with the work, and willing to testify my approval by a liberal payment."

"It was the same hand, sir, as made out the farm-books."

"And who was that?"

"It was my nephew, Ishmael Worth, sir," replied Reuben, with a little pardonable pride.

"Ishmael Worth again!" exclaimed the judge.

"Yes, sir; he done 'em both."

"That is an intelligent lad of yours, Gray."

"Well, sir, he is just a wonder."

"How do you account for his being so different from—from—"

"From me and Hannah?" inquired the simple Reuben, helping the judge out of his difficulty. "Well, sir, I s'pose as how his natur' were diff'ent, and so he growed up diff'ent accordin' to his natur'. Human creeters differ like wegetables, sir; some one sort and some another. Me and Hannah, sir, we's like plain 'tatoes; but Ishmael, sir, is like a rich, bright blooming peach! That's the onliest way as I can explain it, sir."

"A very satisfactory explanation, Gray! How are Hannah and those wonderful twins?"

"Fine, sir; fine, thank Heaven! Miss Claudia was so good as to send word as how she would come to see Hannah as soon as she was able to see company. Now Hannah is able to-day, sir, and would be proud to see Miss Claudia and to show her the babbies."

"Very well, Gray! I will let my daughter know," said the judge, rising from his chair.

Reuben took this as a hint that his departure was desirable, and so he made his bow and his exit.

In another moment, however, he reappeared, holding his hat in his hand and saying:

"I beg your pardon, sir."

"Well, what now? what is it, Gray? What's forgotten?"

"If you please, sir, to give my duty to Miss Claudia, and beg her not to let poor Hannah know as Ishmael has been so badly hurt. When she missed him we told her how he was staying up here long of your honor, and she naturally thinks how he is a-doing some more liber-airy work for you; and we dar'n't tell her any better or how the truth is, for fear of heaving of her back, sir."

"Very well; I will caution Miss Merlin."

"And I hope, sir, as you and Miss Claudia will pardon the liberty I take in mentioning of the matter; which I wouldn't go for to do it, if poor Hannah's safety were not involved."

"Certainly, certainly, Gray, I can appreciate your feelings as a husband and father."

"Thank your honor," said Reuben, as he departed.

The judge kept his word to the overseer, and the same hour conveyed to his daughter the invitation and the caution.

Claudia was moped half to death, and desired nothing better than a little amusement. So the same afternoon she set out on her walk to Woodside, followed by her own maid Mattie, carrying a large basket filled with fine laces, ribbons, and beads to deck the babies, and wines, cordials, and jellies to nourish the mother.

On arriving at Woodside Cottage Miss Merlin was met by Sally, the colored maid of all work, and shown immediately into a neat bedroom on the ground floor, where she found Hannah sitting in state in her resting-chair beside her bed, and contemplating with maternal satisfaction the infant prodigies that lay in a cradle at her feet.

"Do not attempt to rise! I am so glad to see you looking so well, Mrs. Gray! I am Miss Merlin," was Claudia's frank greeting, as she approached Hannah, and held out her hand.

"Thank you, miss; you are very good to come; and I am glad to see you," said the proud mother, heartily shaking the hand offered by the visitor.

"I wish you much joy of your fine children, Mrs. Gray."

"Thank you very much, miss. Pray sit down. Sally, hand a chair."

The maid of all work brought one, which Claudia took, saying:

"Now let me see the twins."

Hannah stooped and raised the white dimity coverlet, and proudly displayed her treasures—two fat, round, red-faced babies, calmly sleeping side by side.

What woman or girl ever looked upon sleeping infancy without pleasure? Claudia's face brightened into beaming smiles as she contemplated these children, and exclaimed:

"They are beauties! I want you to let me help to dress them up fine, Mrs. Gray! I have no little brothers and sisters, nor nephews and nieces; and I should like so much to have a part property in these!"

"You are too good, Miss Merlin."

"I am not good at all. I like to have my own way. I should like to pet and dress these babies. I declare, for the want of a little brother or sister to pet, I could find it in my heart to dress a doll! See, now, what I have brought for these babies! Let the basket down, Mattie, and take the things out."

Miss Merlin's maid obeyed, and displayed to the astonished eyes of Hannah yards of cambric, muslin, and lawn, rolls of lace, ribbon, and beads, and lots of other finery.

Hannah's eyes sparkled. That good woman had never been covetous for herself, but for those children she could become so. She had too much surly pride to accept favors for herself, but for those children she could do so; not, however, without some becoming hesitation and reluctance.

"It is too much, Miss Merlin. All these articles are much too costly for me to accept, or for the children to wear," she began.

But Claudia silenced her with:

"Nonsense! I know very well that you do not in your heart think that there is anything on earth too fine for those babies to wear. And as for their being costly, that is my business. Mattie, lay these things on Mrs. Gray's bureau."

Again Mattie obeyed her mistress, and then set the empty basket down on the floor.

"Now, Mattie, the other basket."

Mattie brought it.

"Mrs. Gray, these wines, cordials, and jellies are all of domestic manufacture—Katie's own make; and she declares them to be the best possible supports for invalids in your condition," said Miss Merlin, uncovering the second basket.

"But really and indeed, miss, you are too kind. I cannot think of accepting all these good things from you."

"Mattie, arrange all those pots, jars, and bottles on the mantel shelf, until somebody comes to take them away," said Claudia, without paying the least attention to Hannah's remonstrances.

When this order was also obeyed, and Mattie stood with both baskets on her arms, waiting for further instructions, Miss Merlin arose, saying:

"And now, Mrs. Gray, I must bid you good-afternoon. I cannot keep papa waiting dinner for me. But I will come to see you again to-morrow, if you will allow me to do so."

"Miss Merlin, I should be proud and happy to see you as often as you think fit to come."

"And, mind, I am to stand god-mother to the twins."

"Certainly, miss, if you please to do so."

"By the way, what is to be their names?"

"John and Mary, miss—after Reuben's father and my mother."

"Very well; I will be spiritually responsible for John and Mary! Good-by, Mrs. Gray."

"Good-by, and thank you, Miss Merlin."

Claudia shook hands and departed. She had scarcely got beyond the threshold of the chamber door when she heard the voice of Hannah calling her back:

"Miss Merlin!"

Claudia returned.

"I beg your pardon, miss; but I hear my nephew, Ishmael Worth, is up at the house, doing something for the judge."

"He is up there," answered Claudia evasively.

"Well, do pray tell him, my dear Miss Merlin, if you please, that I want to see him as soon as he can possibly get home. Oh! I beg your pardon a thousand times for taking the liberty of asking you, miss."

"I will tell him," said Claudia, smiling and retiring.

When Miss Merlin had gone Hannah stooped and contemplated her own two children with a mother's insatiable pride and love. Suddenly she burst into penitential tears and wept.

Why?

She was gazing upon her own two fine, healthy, handsome babies, that were so much admired, so well beloved, and so tenderly cared for; and she was remembering little Ishmael in his poor orphaned infancy—so pale, thin, and sickly, so disliked, avoided, and neglected! At this remembrance her penitent heart melted in remorseful tenderness. The advent of her own children had shown to Hannah by retrospective action all the cruelty and hardness of heart she had once felt and shown towards Ishmael.

"But I will make it all up to him—poor, dear boy! I will make it all up to him in the future! Oh, how hard my heart was towards him! as if he could have helped being born, poor fellow! How badly I treated him! Suppose now, as a punishment for my sin, I was to die and leave my babes to be despised, neglected, and wished dead by them as had the care of 'em! How would I feel? although my children are so much healthier and stronger, and better able to bear neglect than ever Ishmael was, poor, poor fellow! It is a wonder he ever lived through it all. Surely, only God sustained him, for he was bereft of nearly all human help. Oh, Nora! Nora! I never did my duty to your boy; but I will do it now, if God will only forgive and spare me for the work!" concluded Hannah, as she raised both her own children to her lap.

Meanwhile, attended by her maid, Miss Merlin went on her way homeward. She reached Tanglewood in time for dinner, at six o'clock.

At table the judge said to her:

"Well, Claudia! the doctor has been here on his evening visit, and he says that you may see our young patient in the morning, after he has had his breakfast; but that no visitor must be admitted to his chamber at any later hour of the day."

"Very well, papa. I hope you will give old Katie to understand that, so she may not give me any trouble when I apply at the door," smiled Claudia.

"Katie understands it all, my dear," said the judge.

And so it was arranged that Claudia should visit her young preserver on the following morning.

CHAPTER XLV.

The lady of his love re-entered there;
She was serene and smiling then, and yet
She knew she was by him beloved—she knew,
For quickly comes such knowledge, that his heart
Was darken'd by her shadow; and she saw
That he was wretched; but she saw not all.
He took her hand, a moment o'er his face
A tablet of unutterable thoughts
Was traced, and then it faded as it came.
—*Byron*.

It was as yet early morning; but the day promised to be sultry, and all the windows of Ishmael's chamber were open to facilitate the freest passage of air. Ishmael lay motionless upon his cool, white bed, letting his glances wander abroad, whither his broken limbs could no longer carry him.

His room, being a corner one, rejoiced in four large windows, two looking east and two north. Close up to these windows grew the clustering woods. Amid their branches even the wildest birds built nests, and their strange songs mingled with the rustle of the golden green leaves as they glimmered in the morning sun and breeze.

It was a singular combination, that comfortable room, abounding in all the elegancies of the highest civilization, and that untrodden wilderness in which the whip-poor-will cried and the wild eagle screamed.

And Ishmael, as he looked through the dainty white-draped windows into the tremulous shadows of the wood, understood how the descendant of Powhatan, weary of endless brick walls, dusty streets, and crowded thoroughfares, should, as soon as he was free from official duties, fly to the opposite extreme of all these—to his lodge in this unbroken forest, where scarcely a woodman's ax had sounded, where scarcely a human foot had fallen. He sympathized with the "monomania" of Randolph Merlin in not permitting a thicket to be thinned out, a road to be opened, or a tree to be trimmed on his wild woodland estate; so that here at least, nature should have her own way, with no hint of the world's labor and struggle to disturb her vital repose.

As these reveries floated through the clear, active brain of the invalid youth, the door of his chamber softly opened.

Why did Ishmael's heart bound in his bosom, and every pulse throb?

She stood within the open doorway! How lovely she looked, with her soft, white muslin morning dress floating freely around her graceful form, and her glittering jet black ringlets shading her snowy forehead, shadowy eyes, and damask cheeks!

She closed the door as softly as she had opened it, and advanced into the room.

Old Katie arose from some obscure corner and placed a chair for her near the head of Ishmael's bed on his right side.

Claudia sank gently into this seat and turned her face towards Ishmael, and attempted to speak; but a sudden, hysterical rising in her throat choked her voice.

Her eyes had taken in all at a glance!—the splintered leg, the bandaged arm, the plastered chest, the ashen complexion, the sunken cheeks and the hollow eyes of the poor youth; and utterance failed her!

But Ishmael gently and respectfully pressed the hand she had given him, and smiled as he said:

"It is very kind of you to come and see me, Miss Merlin. I thank you earnestly." For, however strong Ishmael's emotions might have been, he possessed the self-controlling power of an exalted nature.

"Oh, Ishmael!" was all that Claudia found ability to say; her voice was choked, her bosom heaving, her face pallid.

"Pray, pray, do not disturb yourself, Miss Merlin; indeed I am doing very well," said the youth, smiling. The next instant he turned away his face; it was to conceal a spasm of agony that suddenly sharpened all his features, blanched his lips, and forced the cold sweat out on his brow. But Claudia had seen it.

"Oh, I fear you suffer very much," she said.

The spasm had passed as quickly as it came. He turned to her his smiling eyes.

"I fear you suffer very, very much," she repeated, looking at him.

"Oh, no, not much; see how soon the pain passed away."

"Ah! but it was so severe while it lasted! I saw that it caught your breath away! I saw it, though you tried to hide it! Ah! you do suffer, Ishmael! and for me! me," she cried, forgetting her pride in the excess of her sympathy.

The smile in Ishmael's dark blue eyes deepened to ineffable tenderness and beauty as he answered softly:

"It is very, very sweet to suffer for—one we esteem and honor."

"I am not worth an hour of your pain!" exclaimed Claudia, with something very like self-reproach.

"Oh, Miss Merlin, if you knew how little I should value my life in comparison with your safety." Ishmael paused; for he felt that perhaps he was going too far.

"I think that you have well proved how ready you are to sacrifice your life for the preservation, not only of your friends, but of your very foes! I have not forgotten your rescue of Alf and Ben Burghe," said the heiress emphatically, yet a little coldly, as if, while anxious to give him the fullest credit and the greatest honor for courage, generosity, and magnanimity, she was desirous to disclaim any personal interest he might feel for herself.

"There is a difference, Miss Merlin," said Ishmael, with gentle dignity.

"Oh, I suppose there is; one would rather risk one's life for a friend than for an enemy," replied Claudia icily.

"I have displeased you, Miss Merlin; I am very sorry for it. Pray, forgive me," said Ishmael, with a certain suave and stately courtesy, for which the youth was beginning to be noted.

"Oh, you have not displeased me, Ishmael! How could you, you who have just risked and almost sacrificed your life to save mine! No, you have not displeased; but you have surprised me! I would not have had you run any risk for me, Ishmael, that you would not have run for the humblest negro on my father's plantation; that is all."

"Miss Merlin, I would have run any risk to save anyone at need; but I might not have borne the after consequences in all cases with equal patience—equal pleasure. Ah, Miss Merlin, forgive me, if I am now happy in my pain! forgive me this presumption, for it is the only question at issue between us," said the youth, with a pleading glance.

"Oh, Ishmael, let us not talk any more about me! Talk of yourself. Tell me how you are, and where you feel pain."

"Nowhere much, Miss Merlin."

"Papa told me that two of your limbs were broken and your chest injured, and now I see all that for myself."

"My injuries are doing very well. My broken bones are knitting together again as fast as they possibly can, my physician says."

"But that is a very painful process I fear," said Claudia compassionately.

"Indeed, no; I do not find it so."

"Ah! your face shows what you endure. It is your chest, then, that hurts you?"

"My chest is healing very rapidly. Do not distress your kind heart, Miss Merlin; indeed, I am doing very well."

"You are very patient, and therefore you will do well, if you are not doing so now. Ishmael, now that I am permitted to visit you, I shall come every day. But they have limited me to fifteen minutes' stay this morning, and my time is up. Good-morning, Ishmael."

"Good-morning, Miss Merlin. May the Lord bless you," said Ishmael, respectfully pressing the hand she gave him.

"I will come again to-morrow; and then if you continue to grow better, I may be allowed to remain with you for half an hour," she said, rising.

"Thank you, Miss Merlin; I shall try to grow better; you have given me a great incentive to improvement."

Claudia's face grew grave again. She bowed coldly and left the room.

As soon as the door had closed behind her Ishmael's long-strained nerves became relaxed, and his countenance changed again in one of those awful spasms of pain to which he was now so subject. The paroxysm, kept off by force of will, for Claudia's sake, during her stay, now took its revenge by holding the victim longer in its grasp. A minute or two of mortal agony and then is was past, and the patient was relieved.

"I don't know what you call pain; but if dis'ere aint pain, I don't want to set no worser de longest day as ever I live!" exclaimed Katie, who stood by the bedside wiping the deathly dew from the icy brow of the sufferer.

"But you see—it lasts so short a time—it is already gone," gasped Ishmael faintly. "It is no sooner come than gone," he added, with a smile.

"And no sooner gone, nor come again! And a-most taking of your life when it do come!" said Katie, placing a cordial to the ashen lips of the sufferer.

The stimulant revived his strength, brought color to his cheeks and light to his eyes.

Ishmael's next visitor was Reuben Gray, who was admitted to see him for a few minutes only. This was Reuben's first visit to the invalid, and as under the transient influence of the stimulant Ishmael looked brighter than usual, Reuben thought that he must be getting on remarkably well, and congratulated him accordingly.

Ishmael smilingly returned the compliment by wishing Gray joy of his son and daughter.

Reuben grinned with delight and expatiated on their beauty, until it was time for him to take leave.

"Your Aunt Hannah don't know as you've been hurt, my boy; we dar'n't tell her, for fear of the consequences. But now as you really do seem to be getting on so well, and as she is getting strong so fast, and continually asking arter you, I think I will just go and tell her all about it, and as how there is no cause to be alarmed no more," said Reuben, as he stood, hat in hand, by Ishmael's bed.

"Yes, do, Uncle Reuben, else she will think I neglect her," pleaded Ishmael.

Reuben promised, and then took his departure.

That was the last visit Ishmael received that day.

Reuben kept his word, and as soon as he got home he gradually broke to Hannah the news of Ishmael's accident, softening the matter as much as possible, softening it out of all truth, for when the anxious woman insisted on knowing exactly the extent of her nephew's injuries, poor Reuben, alarmed for the effect upon his wife's health, boldly affirmed that there was nothing worse in Ishmael's case than a badly sprained ankle, that confined him to the house! And it was weeks longer before Hannah heard the truth of the affair.

The next day Claudia Merlin repeated her visit to Ishmael, and remained with him for half an hour.

And from that time she visited his room daily, increasing each day the length of her stay.

Ishmael's convalescence was very protracted. The severe injuries that must have caused the death of a less highly vitalized human creature really confined Ishmael for weeks to his bed and for months to the house. It was four weeks before he could leave his bed for a sofa. And it was about that time that Hannah got out again; and incredulous, anxious, and angry all at once, walked up to Tanglewood to find out for herself whether it was a "sprained ankle" only that kept her nephew confined there.

Mrs. Gray was shown at once to the convalescent's room, where Ishmael, whose very breath was pure truth, being asked, told her all about his injuries.

Poor Hannah wept tears of retrospective pity; but did not in her inmost heart blame Gray for the "pious fraud" he had practiced with the view of saving her own feelings at a critical time. She would have had Ishmael conveyed immediately to Woodside, that she might nurse him herself; but neither the doctor, the judge, nor the heiress would consent to his removal; and so Hannah had to submit to their will and leave her nephew where he was. But she consoled herself by walking over every afternoon to see Ishmael.

Claudia usually spent several hours of the forenoon in Ishmael's company. He was still very weak, pale, and thin. His arm was in a sling, and as it was his right arm, as well as his right leg that had been broken, he could not use a crutch; so that he was confined all day to the sofa or the easy-chair, in which his nurse would place him in the morning.

Claudia devoted herself to his amusement with all a sister's care. She read to him; sung to him, accompanying her song with the guitar; and she played chess—Ishmael using his left hand to move the pieces.

Claudia knew that this gifted boy worshiped her with a passionate love that was growing deeper, stronger, and more ardent every day. She knew that probably his peace of mind would be utterly wrecked by his fatal passion. She knew all this, and yet she would not withdraw herself, either suddenly or gradually. The adoration of this young, pure, exalted soul was an intoxicating incense that had become a daily habit and necessity to the heiress. But she tacitly required it to be a silent offering. So long as her lover worshiped her only with his eyes, tones, and manners, she was satisfied, gracious, and cordial; but the instant he was betrayed into any words of admiration or interest in her, she grew cold and haughty, she chilled and repelled him.

And yet she did not mean to trifle with his affections or destroy his peace; but—it was very dull in the country, and Claudia had nothing else to occupy and interest her mind and heart. Besides, she really did appreciate and admire the wonderfully endowed peasant boy as much as she possibly could in the case of one so immeasurably far beneath her in rank. And she really did take more pride and delight in the society of Ishmael than in that of any other human being she had ever met. And yet, had it been possible that Ishmael should have been acknowledged by his father and invested with the name, arms, and estate of Brudenell, Claudia Merlin, in her present mood of mind, would have died and seen him die, before she would have given her hand to one upon whose birth a single shade of reproach was even suspected to rest.

Meanwhile Ishmael reveled in what would have been a fool's paradise to most young men in similar circumstances,—but which really was not such to him, dreaming those dreams of youth, the realization of which would have been impossible to nine hundred and ninety-nine in a thousand situated as he was, but which intellect and will made quite probable for him. With his master mind and heart he read Claudia Merlin thoroughly, and understood her better than she understood herself. In his secret soul he knew that every inch of progress made in her favor was a permanent conquest never to be yielded up. And loving her as loyally as ever knight loved lady, he let her deceive herself by thinking she was amusing herself at his expense, for he was certain of ultimate victory.

Other thoughts also occupied Ishmael. The first of September, the time for opening the Rushy Shore school, had come, and the youth was still unable to walk. Under these circumstances, he wrote a note to the agent, Brown, and told him that it would be wrong to leave the school shut up while the children of the neighborhood remained untaught, and requested him to seek another teacher.

It cost the youth some self-sacrifice to give up this last chance of employment; but we already know that Ishmael never hesitated a moment between duty and self-interest.

September passed. Those who have watched surgical cases in military hospitals know how long it takes a crushed and broken human body to recover the use of its members. It was late in October before Ishmael's right arm was strong enough to support the crutch that was needed to relieve the pressure upon his right leg when he attempted to walk.

It was about this time that Judge Merlin was heard often to complain of the great accumulation of correspondence upon his hands.

Ishmael, ever ready to be useful, modestly tendered his services to assist.

After a little hesitation, the judge thanked the youth and accepted his offer. And the next day Ishmael was installed in a comfortable leather chair in the library, with his crutch beside him and a writing table covered with letters to be read and answered before him. These letters were all open, and each had a word or a line penciled upon it indicating the character of the answer that was to be given. Upon some was simply written the word "No"; upon others, "Yes"; upon others again, "Call on me when I come to town"; and so forth. All this, of course, Ishmael had to put into courteous language, using his own judgment after reading the letters.

Of course it was the least important part of his correspondence that Judge Merlin put into his young assistant's hands; but, notwithstanding that, the trust was a very responsible one. Even Ishmael doubted whether he could discharge such unfamiliar duties with satisfaction to his employer.

He worked diligently all that day, however, and completed the task that had been laid out for him before the bell rung for the late dinner. Then he arose and respectfully called the judge's attention to the finished work, and bowed and left the room.

With something like curiosity and doubt the judge went up to the table and opened and read three or four of the letters written for him by his young amanuensis. And as he read, surprise and pleasure lighted up his countenance.

"The boy is a born diplomatist! I should not wonder if the world should hear of him some day, after all!" he said, as he read letter after letter that had been left unsealed for his optional perusal. In these letters he found his own hard "No's" expressed with a courtesy that softened them even to the most bitterly disappointed; his arrogant "Yes's," with a delicacy that could not wound the self-love of the most sensitive petitioner; and his intermediate, doubtful answers rendered with a clearness of which by their very nature they seemed incapable.

"The boy is a born diplomatist," repeated the judge in an accession of astonishment.

But he was wrong in his judgment of Ishmael. If the youth's style of writing was gracious, courteous, delicate, it was because his inmost nature was pure, refined, and benignant. If his letters denying favors soothed rather than offended the applicant, and of those granting favors flattered rather than humiliated the petitioner, it was because of that angelic attribute of Ishmael's soul that made it so painful to him to give pain, so delightful to impart delight. There was no thought of diplomatic dealing in all Ishmael's truthful soul.

The judge was excessively pleased with his young assistant. Judge Merlin was an excellent lawyer, but no orator, and never had been, nor could be one. He had not himself the gift of eloquence either in speaking or writing; and, therefore, perhaps he was the more astonished and pleased to find it in the possession of his letter-writer. He was pleased to have his correspondence well written, for it reflected credit upon himself.

Under the influence of his surprise and pleasure he took up his hand full of letters and went directly to Ishmael's room. He found the youth seated in his arm-chair engaged in reading.

"What have you there?" inquired Judge Merlin.

Ishmael smiled and turned the title-page to his questioner.

"Humph! 'Coke upon Lyttleton.' Lay it down, Ishmael, and attend to me," said the judge, drawing a chair and seating himself beside the youth.

Ishmael immediately closed the book and gave the most respectful attention.

"I am very much pleased with the manner in which you have accomplished your task, Ishmael. You have done your work remarkably well! So well that I should like to give you longer employment," he said.

Ishmael's heart leaped in his bosom.

"Thank you, sir; I am very glad you are satisfied with me," he replied.

"Let us see now, this is the fifteenth of October; I shall remain here until the first of December, when we go to town; a matter of six weeks; and I shall be glad, Ishmael, during the interval of my stay here, to retain you as my assistant. What say you?"

"Indeed, sir, I shall feel honored and happy in serving you."

"I will give you what I consider a fair compensation for so young a beginner. By the way, how old are you?"

"I shall be nineteen in December."

"Very well; I will give you twenty dollars a month and your board."

"Judge Merlin," said Ishmael, as his pale face flushed crimson, "I shall feel honored and happy in serving you; but from you I cannot consent to receive any compensation."

The judge stared at the speaker with astonishment that took all power of reply away; but Ishmael continued:

"Consider, sir, the heavy obligations under which I already rest towards you, and permit me to do what I can to lighten the load."

"What do you mean? What the deuce are you talking about?" at last asked the judge.

"Sir, I have been an inmate of your house for nearly three months, nursed, tended, and cared for as if I had been a son of the family. What can I render you for all these benefits? Sir, my gratitude and services are due to you, are your own. Pray, therefore, do not mention compensation to me again," replied the youth.

"Young man, you surprise me beyond measure. Your gratitude and services due to me? For what, pray? For taking care of you when you were dangerously injured in my service? Did you not receive all your injuries in saving my daughter from a violent death? After that, who should have taken care of you but me? 'Taken care of you?' I should take care of all your future! I should give you a fortune, or a profession, or some other substantial compensation for your great service, to clear accounts between us!" exclaimed the judge.

Ishmael bowed his head. Oh, bitterest of all bitter mortifications! To hear her father speak to him of reward for saving Claudia's life! To think how everyone was so far from knowing that in saving Claudia he had saved himself! He had a right to risk his life for Claudia, and no one, not even her father, had a right to insult him by speaking of reward! Claudia was his own; Ishmael knew it, though no one on earth, not even the heiress herself, suspected it.

The judge watched the youth as he sat with his fine young forehead bowed thoughtfully upon his hand; and Judge Merlin understood Ishmael's reluctance to receive pay; but did not understand the cause of it.

"Come, my boy," he said; "you are young and inexperienced. You cannot know much of life. I am an old man of the world, capable of advising you. You should follow my advice."

"Indeed, I will gratefully do so, sir," said Ishmael, raising his head, glad, amid all his humiliation, to be advised by Claudia's father.

"Then, my boy, you must reflect that it would be very improper for me to avail myself of your really valuable assistance without giving you a reasonable compensation; and that, in short, I could not do it," said the judge firmly.

"Do you regard the question in that light, sir?" inquired Ishmael doubtingly.

"Most assuredly. It is the only true light in which to regard it."

"Then I have no option but to accept your own terms, sir. I will serve you gladly and gratefully, to the best of my ability," concluded the youth.

And the affair was settled to their mutual satisfaction.

CHAPTER XLVI.

NEW LIFE.

Oh, mighty perseverance!
Oh, courage, stern and stout!
That wills and works a clearance
Of every troubling doubt,
That cannot brook denial
And scarce allows delay,
But wins from every trial
More strength for every day!
—*M.F. Tupper*.

When the judge met his daughter at dinner that evening, he informed her of the new arrangement affected with Ishmael Worth.

Miss Merlin listened in some surprise, and then asked:

"Was it well done, papa?"

"What, Claudia?"

"The making of that engagement with Ishmael."

"I think so, my dear, as far as I am interested, at least, and I shall endeavor to make the arrangement profitable also to the youth."

"And he is to remain with us until we go to town?"

"Yes, my dear; but you seem to demur, Claudia. Now what is the matter? What possible objection can there be to Ishmael Worth remaining here as my assistant until we go to town?"

"Papa, it will be accustoming him to a society and style that will make it very hard for him to return to the company of the ignorant men and women who have hitherto been his associates," said Claudia.

"But why should he return to them? Young Worth is very talented and well educated. He works to enable him to study a profession. There is no reason on earth why he should not succeed. He looks like a gentleman, talks like a gentleman, and behaves like a gentleman! And there is nothing to prevent his becoming a gentleman."

"Oh, yes, there is, papa! Yes, there is!" exclaimed Claudia, with emotion.

"To what do you allude, my dear?"

"To his—low birth, papa!" exclaimed Claudia, with a gasp.

"His low birth? Claudia! do we live in a republic or not? If we do, what is the use of our free institutions, if a deserving young man is to be despised on account of his birth? Claudia, in the circle of my acquaintance there are at least half-a-dozen prosperous men who were the sons of poor but respectable parents."

"Yes! poor, but—respectable!" ejaculated Claudia, with exceeding bitterness.

"My daughter, what do you mean by that? Surely young Worth's family are honest people?" inquired the judge.

"Ishmael's parents were not respectable! his mother was never married! I heard this years ago, but did not believe it. I heard it confirmed to-day!" cried Claudia, with a gasp and a sob, as she sank back in her chair and covered her burning face with her hands.

The judge laid down his knife and fork and gazed at his daughter, muttering:

"That is unfortunate; very unfortunate! No, he will never get over that reproach; so far, you are right, Claudia."

"Oh, no, I am wrong; basely wrong! He saved my life, and I speak these words of him, as if he were answerable for the sins of others—as if his great misfortune was his crime! Poor Ishmael! Poor, noble-hearted boy! He saved my life, papa, at the price of deadly peril and terrible suffering to himself. Oh, reward him well, lavishly, munificently; but send him away! I cannot bear his presence here!" exclaimed the excited girl.

"Claudia, it is natural that you should be shocked at hearing such a piece of news; which, true or false, certainly ought never to have been brought to your ear. But, my dear, there is no need of all this excitement on your part. I do not understand its excess. The youth is a good, intelligent, well-mannered boy, when all is said. Of course he can never attain the position of a gentleman; but that is no reason why he should be utterly cast out. And as to sending him away, now, there are several reasons why I cannot do that: In the first place, he is not able to go; in the second, I need his pen; in the third, I have made an engagement with him which I will not break. As for the rest, Claudia, you need not be troubled with a sight of him; I will take care that he does not intrude upon your presence," said the judge, as he arose from the table.

Claudia threw on her garden hat and hurried out of the house to bury herself in the shadows of the forest. That day she had learned, from the gossip of old Mrs. Jones, who was on a visit to a married daughter in the neighborhood, Ishmael's real history, or what was supposed to be his real history. She had struggled for composure all day long, and only utterly lost her self-possession in the conversation with her father at the dinner-table. Now she sought the depths of the forest, because she could not bear the sight of a human face. Her whole nature was divided and at war with itself. All that was best in Claudia Merlin's heart and mind was powerfully and constantly attracted by the moral and intellectual excellence of Ishmael Worth; but all the prejudices of her rank and education were revolted by the circumstances attending his birth, and were up in arms against the emotions of her better nature.

In what consists the power of the quiet forest shades to calm fierce human passions? I know not; but it is certain that, after walking two or three hours through their depths communing with her own spirit, Claudia Merlin returned home in a better mood to meet her father at the tea-table.

"Papa," she said, as she seated herself at the head of the table and made tea, "you need not trouble yourself to keep Ishmael out of my way. Dreadful as this discovery is, he is not to blame, poor boy. And I think we had better not make any change in our treatment of him; he would be wounded by our coldness; he would not understand it and we could not explain. Besides, the six weeks will soon be over, and then we shall be done with him."

"I am glad to hear you say so, my dear; especially as I had invited Ishmael to join us at tea this evening, and forgotten to tell you of it until this moment. But, Claudia, my little girl," said the judge, scrutinizing her pale cheeks and heavy eyes, "you must not take all the sin and sorrows of the world as much to heart as you have this case; for, if you do, you will be an old woman before you are twenty years of age."

Claudia smiled faintly; but before she could reply the regular monotonous thump of a crutch, was heard approaching the door, and in another moment Ishmael stood within the room.

There was nothing in that fine intellectual countenance, with its fair, broad, calm forehead, thoughtful eyes, and finely curved lips, to suggest the idea of an ignoble birth. With a graceful bow and sweet smile and a perfectly well-bred manner, Ishmael approached and took his seat at the table. The judge took his crutch and set it up in the corner, saying:

"I see you have discarded one crutch, my boy! You will be able to discard the other in a day or so."

"Yes, sir; I only retain this one in compliance with the injunctions of the doctor, who declares that I must not bear full weight upon the injured limb yet," replied Ishmael courteously.

No one could have supposed from the manner of the youth that he had not been accustomed to mingle on equal terms in the best society.

Claudia poured out the tea. She was not deficient in courtesy; but she could not bring herself, as yet, to speak to Ishmael with her usual ease and freedom. When tea was over she excused herself and retired. Claudia was not accustomed to seek Divine help. And so, in one of the greatest straits of her moral experience, without one word of prayer, she threw herself upon her bed, where she lay tossing about, as yet too agitated with mental conflict to sleep.

Ishmael improved in health and grew in favor with his employer. He walked daily from his chamber to the library without the aid of a crutch. He took his meals with the family. And oh! ruinous extravagance, he wore his Sunday suit every day! There was no help for it, since he must sit in the judge's library and eat at the judge's table.

Claudia treated him well; with the inconsistency of girlish nature, since she had felt such a revulsion towards him, and despite of it resolved to be kind to him, she went to the extreme and treated him better than ever.

The judge was unchanged in his manner to the struggling youth.

And so the time went on and the month of November arrived.

Ishmael kept the Rushy Shore schoolhouse in mind. Up to this time no schoolmaster had been found to undertake its care. And Ishmael resolved if it should remain vacant until his engagement with the judge should be finished, he would then take it himself.

All this while Ishmael, true to the smallest duty, had not neglected Reuben Gray's account-books. They had been brought to him by Gray every week to be posted up. But it was the second week in November before Ishmael was able to walk to Woodside to see Hannah's babes, now fine children of nearly three months of age. Of course Ishmael, in the geniality of his nature, was delighted with them; and equally, of course, he delighted their mother with their praises.

The last two weeks in November were devoted by the judge and his family to preparations for their departure.

As the time slipped and the interval of their stay grew shorter and shorter, Ishmael began to count the days, treasuring each precious day that still gave him to the sight of Claudia.

On the last day but one before their departure, all letters having been finished, the judge was in his library, selecting books to be packed and sent off to his city residence. Ishmael was assisting him. When their task was completed, the judge turned to the youth and said:

"Now, Ishmael, I will leave the keys of the library in your possession. You will come occasionally to see that all is right here; and you will air and dust the books, and in wet weather have a fire kindled to keep them from molding, for in the depths of this forest it is very damp in winter. In recompense for your care of the library, Ishmael, I will give you the use of such law books as you may need to continue your studies. Here is a list of works that I recommend you to read in the order in which they are written down," said the judge, handing the youth a folded paper.

"I thank you, sir; I thank you very much," answered Ishmael fervently.

"You can either read them here, or take them home with you, just as you please," continued the judge.

"You are very kind, and I am very grateful, sir."

"It seems to me I am only just, and scarcely that, Ishmael! The county court opens at Shelton on the first of December. I would strongly recommend you to attend its sessions and watch its trials; it will be a very good school for you, and a great help to the progress of your studies."

"Thank you, sir, I will follow your advice."

"And after a while I hope you will be able to go for a term or two to one of the good Northern law schools."

"I hope so, sir; and for that purpose I must work hard."

"And if you should ever succeed in getting admitted to the bar, Ishmael, I should advise you to go to the Far West. It may seem premature to give you this counsel now, but I give it, while I think of it, because after parting with you I may never see you again."

"Again I thank you, Judge Merlin; but if ever that day of success should come for me, it will find me in my native State. I have an especial reason for fixing my home here; and here I must succeed or fail!" said Ishmael earnestly, as he thought of his mother's early death and unhonored grave, and his vow to rescue her memory from reproach.

"It appears to me that your native place would be the last spot on earth where you, with your talents, would consent to remain," said the judge significantly.

"I have a reason—a sacred reason, sir," replied Ishmael earnestly, yet with some reserve in his manner.

"A reason 'with which the stranger intermeddleth not,' I suppose?"

Ishmael bowed gravely, in assent.

"Very well, my young friend; I will not inquire what it may be," said Judge Merlin, who was busying himself at his writing bureau, among some papers, from which he selected one, which he brought forward to the youth, saying:

"Here, Ishmael—here is a memorandum of your services, which I have taken care to keep; for I knew full well that if I waited for you to present me a bill, I might wait forever. You will learn to do such things, however, in time. Now I find by my memorandum that I owe you about sixty dollars. Here is the money. There, now, do not draw back and flush all over your face at the idea of taking money you have well earned. Oh, but you will get over that in time, and when you are a lawyer you will hold out your hand for a thumping fee before you give an opinion on a case!" laughed the judge, as he forced a roll of banknotes into Ishmael's hands, and left the library.

The remainder of the day was spent in sending off wagon loads of boxes to the landing on the river side, where they were taken off by a rowboat, and conveyed on board the "Canvas Back," that lay at anchor opposite Tanglewood, waiting for the freight, to transport it to the city.

On the following Saturday morning the judge and his daughter left Tanglewood for Washington. They traveled in the private carriage, driven by the heroic Sam, and attended by a mounted groom. The parting, which shook Ishmael's whole nature like a storm, nearly rending soul and body asunder, seemed to have but little effect upon Miss Merlin. She went through it with great decorum, shaking hands with Ishmael, wishing him success, and hoping to see him, some fine day, on the bench!

This Claudia said laughing, as with good-humored raillery.

But Ishmael bowed very gravely, and though his heart was breaking, answered calmly:

"I hope so too, Miss Merlin. We shall see."

"Au revoir!" said Claudia, her eyes sparkling with mirth.

"Until we meet!" answered Ishmael solemnly, as he closed the carriage door and gave the coachman the word to drive off.

As the carriage rolled away the beautiful girl, who was its sole passenger, and whose eyes had been sparkling with mirth but an instant before, now threw her hands up to her face, fell back in her seat, and burst into a tempest of sobs and tears.

Ignorant of what was going on within its curtained inclosure, Ishmael remained standing and gazing after the vanishing carriage, which was quickly lost to view in the deep shadows of the forest road, until Judge Merlin, who at the last moment had decided to travel on horseback, rode up to take leave of him and follow the carriage.

"Well, good-by, my young friend! Take care of yourself," were the last adieus of the judge, as he shook hands with Ishmael, and rode away.

"I wish you a pleasant journey, sir," were the final words of Ishmael, sent after the galloping horse.

Then the young man, with desolation in his heart, turned into the house to set the library in order, lock it up, and remove his own few personal effects from the premises.

Reuben Gray, who had come up to assist the judge, receive his final orders, and see him off, waited outside with his light wagon to take Ishmael and his luggage home to Woodside. Reuben helped Ishmael to transfer his books, clothing, etc., to the little wagon. And then Ishmael, after having taken leave of Aunt Katie, and left a small present in her hand, jumped into his seat and was driven off by Reuben.

The arrangement at Tanglewood had occupied nearly the whole of the short winter forenoon, so that it was twelve o'clock meridian when they reached Woodside.

They found a very comfortable sitting room awaiting them. Reuben in the pride of paternity had refurnished it. There was a warm red carpet on the floor; warm red curtains at the windows; a bright fire burning in the fireplace; a neat dinner-table set out, and, best of all, Hannah seated in a low rocking chair, with one rosy babe on her lap and another in the soft, white cradle bed by her side. Hannah laid the baby she held beside its brother in the cradle, and arose and went to Ishmael, warmly welcoming him home again, saying:

"Oh, my dear boy, I am so glad you have come back! I will make you happier with us, lad, than you have ever been before."

"You have always been very good to me, Aunt Hannah," said Ishmael warmly, returning her embrace.

"No, I haven't, Ishmael, no, I haven't, my boy; but I will be. Sally, bring in the fish directly. You know very well that Ishmael don't like rock-fish boiled too much," she said by way of commencement.

The order was immediately obeyed, and the family sat down to the table. The thrifty overseer's wife had provided a sumptuous dinner in honor of her nephew's return. The thriving overseer could afford to be extravagant once in a while. Ah! very different were those days of plenty at Woodside to those days of penury at the Hill hut. And Hannah thought of the difference, as she dispensed the good things from the head of her well-supplied table. The rock-fish with egg sauce was followed by a boiled ham and roast ducks with sage dressing, and the dinner was finished off with apple pudding and mince pies and new cider.

Ishmael tried his best to do justice to the luxuries affection had provided for him; but after all he could not satisfy the expectation of Hannah, who complained bitterly of his want of appetite.

After dinner, when the young man had gone upstairs to arrange his books and clothes in his own room, and had left Hannah and Reuben alone, Hannah again complained of Ishmael's derelictions to the duty of the dinner-table.

"It's no use talking, Hannah; he can't help it. His heart is so full—so full, that he aint got room in his insides for no victuals! And that's just about the truth on't. 'Twas the same with me when I was young and in love long o' you! And wa'n't you contrary nyther? Lord, Hannah, why when you used to get on your high horse with me, I'd be offen my feed for weeks and weeks together. My heart would be swelled up to my very throat, and my stomach wouldn't be nowhar!"

"Reuben, don't be a fool, it's not becoming in the father of a family," said Mrs. Hannah, proudly glancing at the twins.

"Law, so it isn't, so it isn't, Hannah, woman. But surely I was only a-telling of you what ailed Ishmael, as he was off his feed."

"But what foolishness and craziness and sottishness for Ishmael to be in love with Miss Merlin!" exclaimed Hannah impatiently.

"Law, woman, who ever said love was anything else but craziness and the rest of it," laughed Gray.

"But Miss Merlin thinks no more of Ishmael than she does of the dirt under her feet," said Hannah bitterly.

"Begging your pardon, she thinks a deal more of him than she'd like anybody to find out," said honest Reuben, winking.

"How did you find it out then?" inquired his wife.

"Law, Hannah, I haven't been fried and froze, by turn, with all sorts of fever and ague love fits, all the days of my youth, without knowing of the symptoms. And I tell you as how the high and mighty heiress, Miss Claudia Merlin, loves the very buttons on our Ishmael's coat better nor she loves the whole world and all the people in it besides. And no wonder! for of all the young men as ever I seed, gentlemen or workingmen, Ishmael Worth is the handsomest in his looks, and his manners, and his speech, and all. And I believe, though I am not much of a judge, as he is the most intelligentest and book-larnedest. I never seed his equal yet. Why, Hannah, I don't believe as there is e'er a prince a-livin' as has finer manners—I don't!"

"But, Reuben, do you mean what you say? Do you really think Miss Claudia Merlin condescends to like Ishmael? I have heard of ladies doing such strange things sometimes; but Miss Claudia Merlin!"

"I told you, and I tell you again, as she loves the very buttons offen Ishmael's coat better nor she loves all the world besides. But she is as proud as Lucifer, and ready to tear her own heart out of her bosom for passion and spite, because she can't get Ishmael out of it! She'll never marry him, if you mean that; though I know sometimes young ladies will marry beneath them for love; but Miss Merlin will never do that. She would fling herself into burning fire first!"

The conversation could go no farther, for the subject of it was heard coming down the stairs, and the next moment he opened the door and entered the room.

He took a seat near Hannah, smiling and saying:

"For this one afternoon I will take a holiday, Aunt Hannah, and enjoy the society of yourself and the babies."

"So do, Ishmael," replied the pleased and happy mother. And in the very effort to shake off his gloom and please and be pleased, Ishmael found his sadness alleviated.

He was never weary of wondering at Hannah and her children. To behold his maiden aunt in the character of a wife had been a standing marvel to Ishmael. To contemplate her now as a mother was an ever-growing delight to the genial boy. She had lost all her old-maidish appearance. She was fleshier, fairer, and softer to look upon. And she wore a pretty bobbinet cap and a bright-colored calico wrapper, and she busied herself with needlework while turning the cradle with her foot, and humming a little nursery song. As for Reuben, he arose as Ishmael sat down, stood contemplating his domestic bliss for a few minutes, and then took his hat and went out upon his afternoon rounds among the field laborers. A happy man was Reuben Gray!

CHAPTER XLVII.

RUSHY SHORE.

He feels, he feels within him
That courage self-possessed,—
That force that ye shall win him,
The brightest and the best,—
The stalwarth Saxon daring
That steadily steps on,
Unswerving and unsparing
Until the goal be won!
—*M.F. Tupper*.

The first thing Ishmael did when he found himself again settled at Woodside, and had got over the anguish of his parting with Claudia and the excitement of his removal from Tanglewood, was to walk over to Rushy Shore and inquire of Overseer Brown whether a master had yet been heard of for the little school.

"No, nor aint a-gwine to be! There aint much temptation to anybody as knows anything about this 'ere school to take it. The chillun as comes to it,—well there, they are just the dullest, headstrongest, forwardest set o' boys and gals as ever was; and their fathers and mothers, take 'em all together, are the bad-payingest! The fact is, cansarning this school, one may say as the wexation is sartain and the wages un-sartain," answered Brown, whom Ishmael found, as usual, sauntering through the fields with his pipe in his mouth.

"Well, then, as I am on my feet again, and no other master can be found, I will take it myself—that is to say, if I can have it," said Ishmael.

"Well, I reckon you can. Mr. Middleton, he sent his lawyer down here to settle up affairs arter he had bought the property, and the lawyer, he told me, as I had been so long used to the place as I was to keep on a-managing of it for the new master; and as a-letting out of this schoolhouse was a part of my business, I do s'pose as I can let you have it, if you like to take it."

"Yes, I should, and I engage it from the first of January. There are now but two weeks remaining until the Christmas holidays. So it is not worth while to open the school until these shall be over. But meanwhile, Brown, you can let your friends and neighbors know that the schoolhouse will be ready for the reception of pupils on Monday, the third of January."

"Very well, sir; I'll let them all know."

"And now, Brown, tell me, is Mr. Middleton's family coming in at the first of the year?" inquired Ishmael anxiously.

"Oh, no, sir! the house is a deal too damp. In some places it leaks awful in rainy weather. There be a lot of repairs to be made. So it won't be ready for the family much afore the spring, if then."

"I am sorry to hear that. Will you give me Mr. Middleton's address?"

"His—which, sir?"

"Tell me where I can write to him."

"Oh! he is at Washington, present speaking; Franklin Square, Washington City; that will find him."

"Thank you." And shaking hands with the worthy overseer Ishmael departed.

And the same day he wrote and posted a letter to Mr. Middleton.

The intervening two weeks between that day and Christmas were spent by Ishmael, as usual, in work and study. He made up the whole year's accounts for Reuben Gray, and put his farm books in perfect order. While Ishmael was engaged in this latter job, it occurred to him that he could not always be at hand to assist Reuben, and that it would be much better for Gray to learn enough of arithmetic and bookkeeping to make him independent of other people's help in keeping his accounts.

So when Ishmael brought him his books one evening and told him they were all in order up to that present day, and Reuben said:

"Thank you, Ishmael! I don't know what I should do without you, my lad!" Ishmael answered him, saying very earnestly:

"Uncle Reuben, all the events of life are proverbially very uncertain; and it may happen that you may be obliged to do without me; in which case, would it not be well for you to be prepared for such a contingency?"

"What do you mean, Ishmael?" inquired Gray, in alarm.

"I mean—had you not better learn to keep your books yourself, in case you should lose me?"

"Oh, Ishmael, I do hope you are not going to leave us!" exclaimed Reuben, in terror.

"Not until duty obliges me to do so, and that may not be for years. It is true that I have taken the Rushy Shore schoolhouse, which I intend to open on the third of January; but then I shall continue to reside here with you, and walk backward and forward between this and that."

"What! every day there and back, and it such a distance!"

"Yes, Uncle Reuben; I can manage to do so, by rising an hour earlier than usual," said Ishmael cheerfully.

"You rise airly enough now, in all conscience! You're up at daybreak. If you get up airlier nor that, and take that long walk twice every day, it will wear you out and kill you—that is all."

"It will do me good, Uncle Reuben! It will be just the sort of exercise in the open air that I shall require to antidote the effect of my sedentary work in the schoolroom," said Ishmael cheerfully.

"That's you, Ishmael! allers looking on the bright side of everything, and taking hold of all tools by the smooth handle! I hardly think any hardship in this world as could be put upon you, would be took amiss by you, Ishmael."

"I am glad you think so well of me, Uncle Reuben; I must try to retain your good opinion; it was not of myself I wished to speak, however, but of you. I hope you will learn to keep your own accounts, so as to be independent of anybody else's assistance. If you would give me a half an hour's attention every night, I could teach you to do it well in the course of a few weeks or months."

"Law, Ishmael, that would give you more trouble than keeping the books yourself."

"I can teach you, and keep the books besides, until you are able to do it yourself."

"Law, Ishmael, how will you ever find the time to do all that, and keep school, and read law, and take them long walks besides?"

"Why, Uncle Reuben, I can always find time to do every, duty I undertake," replied the persevering boy.

"One would think your days were forty-eight hours long, Ishmael, for you to get through all the work as you undertake."

"But how about the lessons, Uncle Reuben?"

"Oh, Ishmael, I'm too old to larn; it aint worth while now; I'm past fifty, you know."

"Well, but you are a fine, strong, healthy man, and may live to be eighty or ninety. Now, if I can teach you in two or three months an art which will be useful to you every day of your life, for thirty or forty years, don't you think that it is quite worth while to learn it?"

"Well, Ishmael, you have got a way of putting things as makes people think they're reasonable, whether or no, and convinces of folks agin' their will. I think, after all, belike you oughter be a lawyer, if so be you'd turn a judge and jury round your finger as easy as you turn other people. I'll e'en larn of you, Ishmael, though it do look rum like for an old man like me to go to school to a boy like you."

"That is right, Uncle Reuben. You'll be a good accountant yet before the winter is over," laughed Ishmael.

Christmas came; but it would take too long to tell of the rustic merry-makings in a neighborhood noted for the festive style in which it celebrates its Christmas holidays. There were dinner, supper, and dancing parties in all the cottages during the entire week. Reuben Gray gave a rustic ball on New Year's evening. And all the country beaus and belles of his rank in society came and danced at it. And Ishmael, in the geniality of his nature, made himself so agreeable to everybody that he unconsciously turned the heads of half the girls in the room, who unanimously pronounced him "quite the gentleman."

This was the last as well as the gayest party of the holidays. It broke up at twelve midnight, because the next day was Sunday.

On Monday Ishmael arose early and walked over to Rushy Shore, opened his schoolhouse, lighted a fire in it, and sat down at his teacher's desk to await the arrival of his pupils.

About eight or nine o'clock they began to come, by ones, twos, and threes; some attended by their parents and some alone. Rough-looking customers they were, to be sure; shock-headed, sun-burned, and freckle-faced girls and boys of the humblest class of "poor whites," as they were called in the slave States.

Ishmael received them, each and all, with that genial kindness which always won the hearts of all who knew him.

In arranging his school and classifying his pupils, Ishmael found the latter as ignorant, stubborn, and froward as they had been represented to him.

Sam White would not go into the same class with Pete Johnson because Pete's father got drunk and was "had up" for fighting. Susan Jones would not sit beside Ann Bates because Ann's mother "hired out." Jem Ellis, who was a big boy that did not know his ABC's, insisted on being put at the head of the highest class because he was the tallest pupil in the school. And Sarah Brown refused to go into any class at all, because her father was the overseer of the estate, and she felt herself above them all!

These objections and claims were all put forth with loud voices and rude gestures.

But Ishmael, though shocked, was not discouraged. "In patience he possessed his soul" that day. And after a while he succeeded in calming all these turbulent spirits and reducing his little kingdom to order.

It was a very harassing day, however, and after he had dismissed his school and walked home, and given Reuben Gray his lesson, and posted the account-book, and read a portion of his "Coke," he retired to bed, thoroughly wearied in mind and body and keenly appreciative of the privilege of rest. From this day forth Ishmael worked harder and suffered more privations than, perhaps, he had ever done at any former period of his life.

He rose every morning at four o'clock, before any of the family were stirring; dressed himself neatly, read a portion of the Holy Scriptures by candle-light, said his prayers, ate a cold breakfast that had been laid out for him the night before, and set off to walk five miles to his schoolhouse.

He usually reached it at half-past six; opened and aired the room, and made the fire; and then sat down to read law until the arrival of the hour for the commencement of the studies.

He taught diligently until twelve o'clock; then he dismissed the pupils for two hours to go home and get their dinners; he ate the cold luncheon of bread and cheese or meat that he had brought with him; and set off to walk briskly the distance of a mile and a half to Shelton, where the court was in session, and where he spent an hour watching their proceedings and taking notes. He got back to his school at two o'clock; called in his pupils for the afternoon session, and taught diligently until six o'clock in the afternoon, when he dismissed them for the day, shut up the schoolhouse, and set off to walk home.

He usually reached Woodside at about seven o'clock, where he found them waiting tea for him. As this was the only meal Ishmael could take home, Hannah always took care that it should be a comfortable and abundant one. After tea he would give Reuben his lesson in bookkeeping, post up the day's accounts, and then retire to his room to study for an hour or two before going to bed. This was the history of five days out of every week of Ishmael's life.

On Saturdays, according to custom, the school had a holiday; and Ishmael spent the morning in working in the garden. As it was now the depth of winter, there was but little to do, and half a day's work in the week sufficed to keep all in order. Saturday afternoons Ishmael went over to open and air the library at Tanglewood, and to return the books he had read and bring back new ones. Saturday evenings he spent very much as he did the preceding ones of the week—in giving Reuben his lesson, in posting up the week's accounts, and in reading law until bed time.

On Sundays Ishmael rested from worldly labors and went to church to refresh his soul. But for this Sabbath's rest, made obligatory upon him by the Christian law, Ishmael must have broken down under his severe labors. As it was, however, the benign Christian law of the Sabbath's holy rest proved his salvation.

CHAPTER XLVIII.

ONWARD.

The boldness and the quiet,
That calmly go ahead,
In spite of wrath and riot,
In spite of quick and dead—
Warm energy to spur him,
Keen enterprise to guide.
And conscience to upstir him,
And duty by his side,
And hope forever singing
Assurance of success,
And rapid action springing
At once to nothing less!
—*M.F. Tupper.*

In this persevering labor Ishmael cheerfully passed the winter months.

He had not heard one word of Claudia, or of her father, except such scant news as reached him through the judge's occasional letters to the overseer.

He had received an encouraging note from Mr. Middleton in answer to the letter he had written to that gentleman. About the first of April Ishmael's first quarterly school bills began to be due.

Tuition fees were not high in that poor neighborhood, and his pay for each pupil averaged about two dollars a quarter. His school numbered thirty pupils, about one-third of whom never paid, consequently at the end of the first three months his net receipts were just forty-two dollars. Not very encouraging this, yet Ishmael was pleased and happy, especially as he felt that he was really doing the little savages intrusted to his care a great deal of good.

Half of this money Ishmael would have forced upon Hannah and Reuben; but Hannah flew into a passion and demanded if her nephew took her for a money-grub; and Reuben quietly assured the young man that his services overpaid his board, which was quite true.

One evening about the middle of April Ishmael sat at his school desk mending pens, setting copies, and keeping an eye on a refractory boy who had been detained after school hours to learn a lesson he had failed to know in his class.

Ishmael had just finished setting his last copy and was engaged in piling the copy-books neatly, one on top of another, when there came a soft tap at the door.

"Come in," said Ishmael, fully expecting to see some of the refractory boy's friends come to inquire after him.

The door opened and a very young lady, in a gray silk dress, straw hat, and blue ribbons entered the schoolroom.

Ishmael looked up, gave one glance at the fair, sweet face, serious blue eyes, and soft light ringlets, and dropped his copy-books, came down from his seat and hurried to meet the visitor, exclaiming:

"Bee! Oh, dear, dear Bee, I am so glad to see you!"

"So am I you, Ishmael," said Beatrice Middleton, frankly giving her hand to be shaken.

"Bee! oh, I beg pardon! Miss Middleton I mean! it is such a happiness to me to see you again!"

"So it is to me to see you, Ishmael," frankly answered Beatrice.

"You will sit down and rest, Bee?—Miss Middleton!" exclaimed Ishmael, running to bring his own school chair for her accommodation.

"I will sit down, Bee. None of my old schoolmates call me anything else, Ishmael, and I should hardly know my little self by any other name," said Bee, taking the offered seat.

"I thank you very much for letting me call you so! It really went against all old feelings of friendship to call you otherwise."

"Why certainly it did."

"I hope your father and all the family are well?"

"All except mamma, who, you know, is very delicate."

"Yes, I know. They are all down here, of course?"

"No; no one but myself and one man- and maid-servant."

"Indeed!"

"Yes; I came down to see to the last preparations, so as to have everything in order and comfortable for mamma when she comes."

"Still 'mamma's right-hand woman,' Bee!"

"Well, yes; I must be so. You know her health is very uncertain, and there are so many children—two more since you left us, Ishmael! And they are all such a responsibility! And as mamma is so delicate and I am the eldest daughter, I must take much of the care of them all upon myself," replied the girl-woman very gravely.

"Yes, I suppose so; and yet—" Ishmael hesitated and Bee took up the discourse:

—"I know what you are thinking of, Ishmael! That some other than myself ought to have been found to come down to this uninhabited house to make the final preparations for the reception of the family; but really now, Ishmael, when you come to think of it, who could have been found so competent as myself for this duty? To be sure, you know, we sent an upholsterer down with the new furniture, and with particular instructions as to its arrangement: every carpet, set of curtains, and suit of furniture marked with the name of the room for which it was destined. But then, you know, there are a hundred other things to be done, after the upholsterer has quitted the house, that none but a woman and a member of the family would know how to do—cut glass and china and cutlery to be taken out of their cases and arranged in sideboards and cupboards; and bed and table linen to be unpacked and put into drawers and closets; and the children's beds to be aired and made up; and mamma's own chamber and nursery made ready for her; and, last of all, for the evening that they are expected to arrive, a nice delicate supper got. Now, who was there to attend to all this but me?" questioned Beatrice, looking gravely into Ishmael's face. And as she waited for an answer, Ishmael replied:

"Why—failing your mamma, your papa might have done it, without any derogation from his manly dignity. When General Washington was in Philadelphia, during his first Presidential term, with all the cares of the young nation upon his shoulders, he superintended the fitting up of his town house for the reception of Mrs. Washington; descending even to the details of hanging curtains and setting up mangles!"

Beatrice laughed, as she said:

"Law, Ishmael! haven't you got over your habit of quoting your heroes yet? And have you really faith enough to hope that modern men will come up to their standard? Of course, George Washington was equal to every human duty from the conquering of Cornwallis to—the crimping of a cap-border, if necessary! for he was a miracle! But my papa, God bless him, though wise and good, is but a man, and would no more know how to perform a woman's duties than I should how to do a man's! What should he know of china-closets and linen chests? Why, Ishmael, he doesn't know fi'penny bit cotton from five shilling linen, and would have been as apt as not to have ordered the servants' sheets on the children's beds and vice versa; and for mamma's supper he would have been as likely to have fried pork as the broiled spring chickens that I shall provide! No, Ishmael; gentlemen may be great masters in Latin and Greek; but they are dunces in housekeeping matters."

200

"As far as your experience goes, Bee."

"Of course, as far as my experience goes."

"When did you reach Rushy Shore, Bee?"

"Last night about seven o'clock. Matty came with me in the carriage, and Jason drove us. We spent all day in unpacking and arranging the things that had been sent down on the 'Canvas Back' a week or two ago. And this afternoon I thought I would walk over here and see what sort of a school you had. Papa read your letter to us, and we were all interested in your success here."

"Thank you, dear Bee; I know that you are all among my very best friends; and some of these days, Bee, I hope, I trust, to do credit to your friendship."

"That you will, Ishmael! What do you think my papa told my uncle Merlin?—that 'that young man (meaning you) was destined to make his mark on this century.'"

A deep blush of mingled pleasure, bashfulness, and aspiration mantled Ishmael's delicate face. He bowed with sweet, grave courtesy, and changed the subject of conversation by saying:

"I hope Judge Merlin and his daughter are quite well?"

"Quite. They are still at Annapolis. Papa visited them there for a few days last week. The judge is stopping at the Stars and Stripes hotel, and Claudia is a parlor boarder at a celebrated French school in the vicinity. Claudia will not 'come out' until next winter, when her father goes to Washington. For next December Claudia will be eighteen years of age, and will enter upon her mother's large property, according to the terms of the marriage settlement and the mother's will. I suppose she will be the richest heiress in America, for the property is estimated at more than a million! Ah! it is fine to be Claudia Merlin—is it not, Ishmael?"

"Very," answered the young man, scarcely conscious amid the whirl of his emotions what he was saying.

"And what a sensation her entrée into society will make! I should like to be in Washington next winter when she comes out. Ah, but after all—what a target for fortune-hunters she will be, to be sure!" sighed Bee.

"She is beautiful and accomplished, and altogether lovely enough to be sought for herself alone!" exclaimed Ishmael, in the low and faltering tones of deep feeling.

"Ah, yes, if she were poor; but who on earth could see whether the heiress of a million were pretty or plain, good or bad, witty or stupid?"

"So young and so cynical!" said Ishmael sadly.

"Ah, Ishmael, whoever reads and observes must feel and reflect; and whoever feels and reflects must soon lose the simple faith of childhood. We shall see!" said Bee, rising and drawing her gray silk scarf around her shoulders.

"You are not going?"

"Yes; I have much yet to do."

"Can I not help you?"

"Oh, no; there is nothing that I have to do that a classical and mathematical scholar and nursling lawyer could understand."

"Then, at least, allow me to see you safely home. The nursling-lawyer can do that, I suppose? If you will be pleased to sit down until I hear this young hopeful say his lesson, I will close up the schoolroom and be at your service."

"Thank you very much; but I have to call at Brown's, the overseer's, and I would much rather you would not trouble yourself, Ishmael. Good-by. When we all get settled up at the house, which must be by next Saturday night, at farthest, you must come often to see us. It was to say this that I came here."

"Thank you, dearest Bee! I shall esteem it a great privilege to come."

"Prove it," laughed Bee, as she waved adieu, and tripped out of the schoolroom.

Ishmael called up his pupil for recitation.

The little savage could not say his lesson, and began to weep and rub his eyes with the sleeve of his jacket.

"You mought let me off this once, anyways," he sobbed.

"But why should I?" inquired Ishmael.

"A-cause of the pretty lady a-coming."

Ishmael laughed, and for a moment entertained the thought of admitting this plea and letting the pleader go. But Ishmael was really too conscientious to suffer himself to be lured aside from the strict line of duty by any passing fancy or caprice; so he answered:

"Your plea is an ingenious one, Eddy; and since you have wit enough to make it, you must have sense enough to learn your lesson. Come, now, let us sit down and put our heads together, and try again, and see what we can do."

And with the kindness for which he was ever noted, the young master sat down beside his stupid pupil and patiently went over and over the lesson with him, until he had succeeded in getting it into Eddy's thick head.

"There, now! now you know the difference between a common noun and a proper one! are you not glad?" asked Ishmael, smiling.

"Yes; but they'll all be done supper, and the hominy'll be cold!" said the boy sulkily.

"Oh, no, it will not. I know all about the boiling of hominy. They'll keep the pot hanging over the fire until bed-time, so you can have yours hot as soon as you get home. Off with you, now!" laughed Ishmael.

His hopeful pupil lost no time in obeying the order, but set off on a run.

Ishmael arranged his books, closed up his schoolroom, and started to walk home.

There he delighted Hannah with the news that her former friend and patron, Mrs. Middleton, was soon expected at Rushy Shore. And he interested both Reuben and Hannah with the description of beautiful Bee's visit to the school.

"I wonder why he couldn't have fallen in love with her?" thought Hannah.

<hr />

CHAPTER XLIX.

STILL ONWARD.

His, all the mighty movements
That urge the hero's breast,
The longings and the lovings,
The spirit's glad unrest,
That scorns excuse to tender,
Or fortune's favor ask,
That never will surrender
Whatever be the task!
—*M.F. Tupper.*

Beatrice did not come again to the schoolroom to see Ishmael. The memory of old school-day friendship, as well as the prompting of hospitality and benevolence, had brought her there on her first visit. She had not thought of the lapse of time, or the change that two years must have made in him as well as in herself, and so, where she expected to find a mere youth, she found a young man; and maiden delicacy restrained her from repeating her visit.

On Thursday\morning, however, as Ishmael was opening his schoolroom he heard a brisk step approaching, and Mr. Middleton was at his side. Their hands flew into each other and shook mutually before either spoke. Then, with beaming eyes and hearty tones, both exclaimed at once:

"I am so glad to see you!"

"Of course you arrived last night! I hope you had a pleasant journey, and that Mrs. Middleton has recovered her fatigue," said Ishmael, placing a chair for his visitor.

"A very pleasant journey. The day was delightfully cool, and even my wife did not suffer from fatigue. She is quite well this morning, and quite delighted with her new home. But, see here, Ishmael, how you have changed! You are taller than I am! You must be near six feet in height—are you not?"

"I suppose so," smiled Ishmael.

"And your hair is so much darker. Altogether, you are so much improved."

"There was room for it."

"There always is, my boy. Well, I did not come here to pay compliments, my young friend. I came to tell you that, thanks to my little Bee's activity, we are all comfortably settled at home now; and we should be happy if you would come on Friday evening and spend with us Saturday and Sunday, your weekly holidays."

"I thank you, sir; I thank you very much. I should extremely like to come, but—"

"Now, Ishmael, hush! I do not intend to take a denial. When I give an invitation I am very much in earnest about it; and to show you how much I am in earnest about this, I will tell you that I reflected that this was Thursday, and that if I asked you to-day you could tell your friends when you get home this evening, and come to-morrow morning prepared to remain over till Monday. Otherwise if I had not invited you till to-morrow morning, you would have had to walk all the way back home to-morrow evening to tell your friends before coming to see us. So you see how much I wished to have you come, Ishmael, and how I studied ways and means. Mrs. Middleton and all your old schoolmates are equally anxious to see you, so say no more about it, but come!"

"Indeed, I earnestly thank you, Mr. Middleton, and I was not about to decline your kind invitation in toto, but only to say that I am occupied with duties that I cannot neglect on Friday evenings and Saturday mornings; but on Saturday evening I shall be very happy to come over and spend Sunday."

"Very well, then, Ishmael; so be it; I accept so much of your pleasant company, since no more of it is to be had. By the way, Ishmael!"

"Yes, sir."

"That was a gallant feat and a narrow escape of yours as it was described to me by my niece Claudia. Nothing less than the preservation of her life could have justified you in such a desperate act."

"I am grateful to Miss Merlin for remembering it, sir."

"As if she could ever forget it! Good Heaven! Well, Ishmael, I see that your pupils are assembling fast. I will not detain you from your duties longer. Good-morning; and remember that we shall expect you on Saturday evening."

"Good-morning, sir! I will remember; pray give my respects to Mrs. Middleton and all the family."

"Certainly," said Mr. Middleton, as he walked away.

Ishmael re-entered the schoolroom, rang the bell to call the pupils in, and commenced the duties of the day.

On Saturday afternoon, all his weekly labors being scrupulously finished, Ishmael walked over to Rushy Shore Beacon, as Mr. Middleton's house was called.

It was a very large old edifice of white stone, and stood upon the extreme point of a headland running out into the river. There were many trees behind it, landward; but none before it, seaward; so that really the tall white house, with its many windows, might well serve as a beacon to passing vessels.

Around the headland upon which it was situated the waters swept with a mighty impetus and a deafening roar that gave the place its descriptive name of Rushy Shore. As the air and water here were mildly salt, the situation was deemed very healthy and well suited to such delicate lungs as required a stimulating atmosphere, and yet could not bear the full strength of the sea breezes. As such the place had been selected by Mr. Middleton for the residence of his invalid wife.

When Ishmael approached the house he found the family all assembled in the long front porch to enjoy the fine view.

Walter Middleton, who was the first to spy Ishmael's approach, ran down the steps and out to meet him, exclaiming, as he caught and shook his hand:

"How are you, old boy, how are you? Looking in high health and handsomeness, at any rate! I should have come down to school to see you, Ishmael, only, on the very morning after our arrival, I had to mount my horse and ride down to Baymouth to attend to some business for my father, and I did not get back until late last night. Come, hurry on to the house! My mother is anxious to see her old favorite."

And so, overpowering Ishmael with the cordiality of his greeting, Walter drew his friend's arm within his own, and took him upon the porch in the midst of the family group, that immediately surrounded and warmly welcomed him.

"How handsome and manly you have grown, my dear," said Mrs. Middleton, with almost motherly pride in her favorite.

Ishmael blushed and bowed in reply to this direct compliment. And soon he was seated among them, chatting pleasantly.

This was but the first of many delightful visits to Bushy Shore enjoyed by Ishmael. Mr. Middleton liked to have him there, and often pressed him to come. And Ishmael, who very well knew the difference between invitations given from mere politeness and those prompted by a sincere desire for his company, frequently accepted them.

One day Mr. Middleton, who took a deep interest in the struggles of Ishmael, said to him:

"You should enter some law school, my young friend."

"I intend to do so, sir, as soon as I have accomplished two things."

"And what are they?"

"Saved money enough to defray my expenses and found a substitute for myself as master of this little school."

"Oh, bother the school! you must not always be sacrificing yourself to the public welfare, Ishmael," laughed Mr. Middleton, who sometimes permitted himself to use rough words.

"But to duty, sir?"

"Oh, if you make it a question of duty, I have no more to say," was the concluding remark of Ishmael's friend.

Thus, in diligent labor and intellectual intercourse, the young man passed the summer months.

One bright hope burned constantly before Ishmael's mental vision—of seeing Claudia; but, ah! this hope was destined to be deferred from week to week, and finally disappointed.

Judge Merlin did not come to Tanglewood as usual this summer. He took his daughter to the seaside instead, where they lived quietly at a private boarding house, because it was not intended that Miss Merlin should enter society until the coming winter at Washington.

To Ishmael this was a bitter disappointment, but a bitter tonic, too, since it served to give strength to his mind.

Late in September his friend Walter Middleton, who was a medical student, left them to attend the autumn and winter course of lectures in Baltimore. Ishmael felt the loss of his society very much; but as usual consoled himself by hard work through all the autumn months.

He heard from Judge Merlin and his daughter through their letters·to the Middletons. They were again in Annapolis, where Miss Merlin was passing her last term at the finishing school, but they were to go to Washington at the meeting of Congress in December.

As the month of November drew to a close Ishmael began to compute the labors, progress, and profits of the year. He found that he had brought his school into fine working order; he had brought his pupils on well; he had made Reuben Gray a very good reader, penman, arithmetician, and bookkeeper; and lastly, he had advanced himself very far in his chosen professional studies. But he had made but little money, and saved less than a hundred dollars. This was not enough to support him, even by the severest economy, at any law school. Something else, he felt, must be done for the next year, by which more money might be made. So after reflecting upon the subject for some time, he wrote out two advertisements—one for a teacher, competent to take charge of a small country school, and the other for a situation as bookkeeper, clerk, or amanuensis. In the course of a week the first advertisement was answered by a Methodist preacher living in the same neighborhood, who proposed to augment the small salary he received for preaching on Sundays, by teaching a day school all the week. Ishmael had an interview with this gentleman, and finding him all that could be desired in a clergyman and country schoolmaster, willingly engaged to relinquish his own post in favor of the new candidate on the first of the coming year.

His second advertisement was not yet answered; but Ishmael kept it on and anxiously awaited the result.

At length his perseverance was crowned with a success greater than he could have anticipated. It was about the middle of December, a few days before the breaking up of his school for the Christmas holidays, that he called at the Shelton post office to ask if there were any letters for "X.Y.Z.," those being the initials he had signed to his second advertisement. A letter was handed him; at last, then, it had come! Without scrutinizing the handwriting or the superscription, Ishmael tore it open and read:

"Washington, December 14.

"Mr. 'X.Y.Z.'—I have seen your advertisement in the Intelligencer. I am in want of an intelligent and well-educated young man to act as my confidential secretary and occasional amanuensis. If you will write to me, enclosing testimonials and references as to your character and competency, and stating the amount of salary you will expect to receive, I hope we may come to satisfactory arrangement.

"Respectfully yours,

"RANDOLF MERLIN."

It was from Claudia's father, then! It was a stroke of fate, or so it seemed to the surprised and excited mind of Ishmael.

Trembling with joy, he retired to the private parlor of the quiet little village inn to answer the letter, so that it might go off to Washington by the mail that started that afternoon. He smiled to himself as he wrote that Judge Merlin himself had had ample opportunity of personally testing the character and ability of the advertiser, but that if further testimony were needed, he begged to refer to Mr. James Middleton, of Rushy Shore. Finally, he left the question of the amount of salary to be settled by the judge himself. He signed, sealed, and directed this letter, and hurried to the post office to post it before the closing of the mail.

And then he went home in a maze of delight.

Three anxious days passed, and then Ishmael received his answer. It was a favorable and a conclusive one. The judge told him that from the post office address given in the advertisement, as well as from other circumstances, he had supposed the advertiser to be Ishmael himself, but could not be sure until he had received his letter, when he was glad to find his supposition correct, as he should much rather receive into his family, in a confidential capacity, a known young man like Mr. Worth than any stranger, however well recommended the latter might be; he would fix the salary at three hundred dollars, with board and lodging, if that would meet the young gentleman's views; if the terms suited, he hoped Mr. Worth would lose no time in joining him in Washington, as he, the writer, was overwhelmed with correspondence that was still accumulating.

Ishmael answered this second letter immediately, saying that he would be in Washington on the following Tuesday.

After posting his letter he walked rapidly homeward, calling at Rushy Shore on his way to inform his friends, the Middletons, of his change of fortune. As Ishmael was not egotistical enough to speak of himself and his affairs until it became absolutely needful for him to do so, he had never told Mr. Middleton of his plan of giving up the school to the Methodist minister and seeking another situation for himself. And during the three days of his correspondence with Judge Merlin he had not even seen Mr. Middleton, whom he only took time to visit on Saturday evenings.

Upon this afternoon he reached Rushy Shore just as the family were sitting down to dinner. They were as much surprised as pleased to see him at such an unusual time as the middle of the week. Mr. Middleton got up to shake hands with him; Mrs. Middleton ordered another plate brought; Bee saw that room was made for another chair; and so Ishmael was welcomed by acclamation, and seated among them at the table.

"And now, young gentleman, tell us what it all means. For glad as we are to see you, and glad as you are to see us, we know very well that you did not take time to come here in the middle of the week merely to please yourself or us; pleasure not being your first object in life, Ishmael," said Mr. Middleton.

"I regret to say, sir, that I came to tell you, I am going away on Monday morning," replied Ishmael gravely, for at the moment he felt a very real regret at the thought of leaving such good and true friends.

"Going away!" exclaimed all the family in a breath, and in consternation; for this boy, with his excellent character and charming manners had always deeply endeared himself to all his friends. "Going away!" they repeated.

"I am sorry to say it," said Ishmael.

"But this is so unexpected, so sudden!" said Mrs. Middleton.

"What the grand deuce is the matter? Have you enlisted for a soldier, engaged as a sailor, been seized with the gold fever?"

"Neither, sir; I will explain," said Ishmael. And forthwith he told all his plans and prospects, in the fewest possible words.

"And so you are going to Washington, to be Randolph Merlin's clerk! Well, Ishmael, as he is a thorough lawyer, though no very brilliant barrister, I do not know that you could be in a better school. Heaven prosper you, my lad! By the way, Ishmael, just before you came in, we were all talking of going to Washington ourselves."

"Indeed! and is there really a prospect of your going?" inquired Ishmael, in pleased surprise.

"Well, yes. You see the judge wishes a chaperone for his daughter this winter, and has invited Mrs. Middleton, and in fact all the family, to come and spend the season with them in Washington. He says that he has taken the old Washington House, which is large enough to accommodate our united families, and ten times as many."

"And you will go?" inquired Ishmael anxiously.

"Well, yes—I think so. You see, this place, so pre-eminently healthy during eight months of the year, is rather too much exposed and too bleak in the depth of winter to suit my wife. She begins to cough already. And as Claudia really does need a matronly friend near her, and as the judge is very anxious for us to come, I think all interests will be best served by our going."

"I hope you will go very soon," said Ishmael.

"In a week or ten days," replied Mr. Middleton.

Ishmael soon after arose and took his leave, for he had a long walk before him, and a momentous interview with Hannah to brave at the end of it.

After tea that evening Ishmael broke the news to Reuben and Hannah. Both were considerably startled and bewildered, for they, no more than the Middletons, had received any previous hint of the young man's intentions. And now they really did not know whether to congratulate Ishmael on going to seek his fortune or to condole with him for leaving home. Reuben heartily shook hands with Ishmael and said how sorry he should be to part with him, but how glad he was that the young man was going to do something handsome for himself.

Hannah cried heartily, but for the life of her, could not have told whether it was for joy or sorrow. To her apprehension, to go to Washington and be Judge Merlin's clerk seemed to be one of the greatest honors that any young man could attain; so she was perfectly delighted with that part of the affair. But, on the other hand, Ishmael had been to her like the most affectionate and dearest of sons, and to part with him seemed more than she could bear; so she wept vehemently and clung to her boy.

Reuben sought to console her.

"Never mind, Hannah, woman, never mind. It is the law of nature that the young bird must leave his nest and the young man his home. But never you mind! Washing-town-city aint out'n the world, and any time as you want to see your boy very bad, I'll just put Dobbin to the wagon and cart you and the young uns up there for a day or two. Law, Hannah, my dear, you never should shed a tear if I could help it. 'Cause I feel kind o' guilty when you cry, Hannah, as if I ought to help it somehow!" said the good fellow.

"As if you could, Reuben! But it is I myself who do wrong to cry for anything when I am blessed with the love of such a heart as yours, Reuben! There, I will not cry any more. Of course, Ishmael must go to the city and make his fortune, and I ought to be glad, and I am glad, only I am sich a fool. Ishmael, my dear, this is Wednesday night, and you say you are going o' Monday morning; so there aint no time to make you no new shirts and things before you go, but I'll make a lot of 'em, my boy, and send 'em up to you," said Hannah, wiping her eyes.

Ishmael opened his mouth to reply; but Reuben was before him with:

"So do, Hannah, my dear; that will be one of the best ways of comforting yourself, making up things for the lad; and you shan't want for money, for the fine linen nyther, Hannah, my dear! And when you have got them all done, you and I can take them up to him when we go to see him! So think of that, and you won't be fretting after him. And now, childun, it is bedtime!"

On Friday evening Ishmael, in breaking up his school for the Christmas holidays, also took a final leave of his pupils. The young master had so endeared himself to his rough pupils that they grieved sincerely at the separation. The girls wept, and even rude boys sobbed. Our stupid little friend, Eddy, who could not learn grammar, had learned to love his kind young teacher, and at the prospect of parting with him and having the minister for a master roared aloud, saying:

"Master Worth have allers been good to us, so he have; but the minister—he'll lick us, ever so much!"

Ishmael distributed such parting gifts as his slender purse would afford, and so dismissed his pupils.

On Sunday evening he took leave of his friends, the Middletons, who promised to join him in Washington in the course of a week.

And on Monday morning he took leave of Hannah and Reuben, and walked to Baymouth to meet the Washington steamboat.

CHAPTER L.

CLAUDIA'S CITY HOME.

How beautiful the mansion's throned
Behind its elm tree's screen,
With simple attic cornice crowned
All graceful and serene.
—*Anon.*

Just north of the Capitol park, upon a gentle eminence, within its own well-shaded and well-cultivated grounds, stood a fine, old, family mansion that had once been the temporary residence of George Washington.

The house was very large, with many spacious rooms and broad passages within, and many garden walks and trellised arbors around it.

In front were so many evergreen trees and in the rear was so fine a conservatory of blooming flowers, that even in the depth, of winter it seemed like summer there.

The house was so secluded within its many thick trees and high garden walls that the noise of the city never reached its inmates, though they were within five minutes' walk of the Capitol and ten minutes' drive of the President's mansion.

Judge Merlin had been very fortunate in securing for the season this delightful home, where he could be within easy reach of his official business and at the same time enjoy the quiet so necessary to his temperament.

That winter he had been appointed one of the judges of the Supreme Court of the United States, and it was very desirable to have so pleasant a dwelling place within such easy reach of the Capitol, where the court was held. At the head of this house his young daughter had been placed as its mistress. She had not yet appeared anywhere in public. She was reserving herself for two events: the arrival of her chaperone and the first evening reception of the President. Her presence in the city was not even certainly known beyond her own domestic circle; though a vague rumor, started no one knew by whom, was afloat, to the effect that Miss Merlin, the young Maryland heiress and beauty, was expected to come out in Washington during the current season.

Meanwhile she remained in seclusion in her father's house.

It was to this delightful town house, so like the country in its isolation, that Ishmael Worth was invited.

It was just at sunrise on Tuesday morning that the old steamer "Columbia," having Ishmael on board, landed at the Seventh Street wharf, and the young man, destined some future day to fill a high official position in the Federal government, took his humble carpetbag in his hand and entered the Federal city.

Ah! many thousands had entered the National capital before him, and many more thousands would enter it after him, only to complain of it, to carp over it, to laugh at it, for its "magnificent distances," its unfinished buildings, its muddy streets, and its mean dwellings.

But Ishmael entered within its boundaries with feelings of reverence and affection. It was the City of Washington, the sacred heart of the nation.

He had heard it called by shallow-brained and short-sighted people a sublime failure! It was a sublime idea, indeed, he thought, but no failure! Failure? Why, what did those who called it so expect? Did they expect that the great capital of the great Republic should spring into full-grown existence as quickly as a hamlet around a railway station, or village at a steamboat landing? Great ideas require a long time for their complete embodiment. And those who sneered at Washington were as little capable of foreseeing its future as the idlers about the steamboat wharf were of foretelling the fortunes of the modest-looking youth, in country clothes, who stood there gazing thoughtfully upon the city.

"Can you tell me the nearest way to Pennsylvania Avenue?" at length he asked of a bystander.

"Just set your face to the north and follow your nose for about a mile, and you'll fetch up to the broadest street as ever you see; and that will be it," was the answer.

With this simple direction Ishmael went on until he came to the avenue, which he recognized at once from the description.

The Capitol, throned in majestic grandeur upon the top of its wooded hill at the eastern extremity of the Avenue, and gleaming white in the rays of the morning sun, seeming to preside over the whole scene, next attracted Ishmael's admiration. As his way lay towards it, he had ample time to contemplate its imposing magnificence and beauty.

As he drew near it, however, he began to throw his eyes around the surrounding country in search of Judge Merlin's house. He soon identified it—a large old family mansion, standing in a thick grove of trees on a hill just north of the Capitol grounds. He turned to the left, ascended the hill, and soon found himself at the iron gate leading to the grounds.

Here his old acquaintance, Sam, being on duty as porter, admitted him, and, taking him by a winding gravel walk that turned and twisted among groves and parterres, led him up to the house and delivered him into the charge of a black footman, who was at that early hour engaged in opening the doors and windows.

He was the same Jim who used to wait on the table at Tanglewood.

"Good-morning, Mr. Ishmael, sir," he said, advancing in a friendly and respectful manner, to receive the new arrival.

"The judge expected me this morning, Jim?" inquired Ishmael, when he had returned the greeting of the man.

"Oh, yes, sir; and ordered your room got ready for you. The family aint down yet, sir; but I can show you your room," said Jim, taking Ishmael's carpetbag from him, and leading the way upstairs.

They went up three flights of stairs, to a small front room in the third story, with one window, looking west.

Here Jim sat down the carpetbag, saying:

"It's rather high up, sir; but you see we are expecting Mrs. Middleton and all her family, and of course the best spare rooms has to be given up to the ladies. I think you will find everything you could wish for at hand, sir; but if there should be anything else wanted, you can ring, and one of the men servants will come up." And with this, Jim bowed and left the room.

Ishmael looked around upon his new domicile.

It was a very plain room with simple maple furniture, neatly arranged; a brown woolen carpet on the floor; white dimity curtains at the window; and a small coal fire in the grate. Yet it was much better than Ishmael had been accustomed to at home, and besides, the elevated position of the room, and the outlook from the only window, compensated for all deficiencies.

Ishmael walked up to this window, put aside the dainty white curtain, and looked forth: the whole city of Washington, Georgetown, the winding of the Potomac and Anacostia rivers, Anacostia Island, and the undulating hills of the Virginia and Maryland shores lay spread like a vast panorama before him.

As the thicket was a necessity to Judge Merlin's nature, so the widely extended prospect was a need of Ishmael's spirit; his eyes must travel when his feet could not.

Feeling perfectly satisfied with his quarters, Ishmael at last left the window and made his toilet, preparatory to meeting the judge and—Claudia!

"Oh, beating heart, be still! be still!" he said to himself, as the anticipation of that latter meeting, with all its disturbing influences, sent the blood rioting through his veins.

Without being the very least dandyish, Ishmael was still fastidiously nice in his personal appointments; purity and refinement pervaded his presence.

He had completed his toilet, and was engaged in lightly brushing some lint from his black coat, when a knock at his door attracted his attention.

It was Jim, who had come to announce breakfast and show him the way to the morning room.

Down the three flights of stairs they went again, and across the central hall to a front room on the left that looked out upon the winter garden of evergreen trees. Crimson curtained and crimson carpeted, with a bright coal fire in the polished steel grate, and a glittering silver service on the white draped breakfast table, this room had a very inviting aspect on this frosty December morning.

The judge stood with his back to the fire, and a damp newspaper open in his hand. Claudia was nowhere visible—a hasty glance around the room assured Ishmael that she had not yet entered it. Ishmael's movements were so noiseless that his presence was not observed until he actually went up to the judge, and, bowing, accosted him with the words:

"I am here according to appointment, Judge Merlin; and hope I find you well."

"Ah, yes; good-morning! how do you do, Ishmael?" said the judge laying aside his paper and cordially shaking hands with the youth. "Punctual, I see. Had a pleasant journey?"

"Thank you, sir; very pleasant," returned Ishmael.

"Feel like setting to work this morning? There is quite an accumulation of correspondence groaning to be attended to."

"I am ready to enter upon my duties whenever you please, sir."

"All right," said the judge, touching a bell that presently summoned Jim to his presence.

"Let us have breakfast immediately. Where is Miss Merlin? Let her know that we are waiting for her."

"'Miss Merlin' is here, papa," said a rich voice at the door.

Ishmael's heart bounded and throbbed, and Claudia entered the breakfast room.

Such a picture of almost Oriental beauty, luxury, and splendor as she looked! She wore a morning robe of rich crimson foulard silk, fastened up the front with garnet buttons, each a spark of fire. The dress was open at the throat and wrists, revealing glimpses of the delicate cambric collar and cuffs confined by the purest pearl studs. Her luxuriant hair was carried away from her snowy temples and drooped in long, rich, purplish, black ringlets from the back of her stately head. But her full, dark eyes and oval crimson cheeks and lips glowed with a fire too vivid for health as she advanced and gave her father the morning kiss.

"I am glad you have come, my dear! I have been waiting for you!" said the judge.

"You shall not have to do so another morning, papa,'" she answered.

"Here is Ishmael, Claudia," said her father, directing her attention to the youth, who had delicately withdrawn into the background; but who, at the mention of his own name, came forward to pay his respects to the heiress.

"I am glad to see you, Mr. Worth," she said, extending her hand to him as he bowed before her; and then quickly detecting a passing shade of pain in his expressive face, she added, smiling:

"You know we must begin to call you Mr. Worth some time, and there can be no better time than this, when you make your first appearance in the city and commence a new career in life."

"I had always hoped to be 'Ishmael' with my friends," he replied.

"'Times change and we change with them,' said one of the wisest of sages," smiled Claudia.

"And coffee and muffins grow cold by standing; which is more to the present purpose," laughed Judge Merlin, handing his daughter to her seat at the head of the table, taking his own at the foot, and pointing his guest to one at the side.

When all were seated, Claudia poured out the coffee and the breakfast commenced. But to the discredit of the judge's consistency, it might have been noticed that, after he had helped his companion to steak, waffles, and other edibles, he resumed his newspaper; and, regardless that coffee and muffins grew cold by standing, recommended reading the debates in Congress.

At length, when he finished reading and saw that his companions had finished eating, he swallowed his muffin in two bolts, gulped his coffee in two draughts, and started up from the table, exclaiming:

"Now, then, Ishmael, if you are ready?"

Ishmael arose, bowed to Claudia, and turned to follow his employer.

The judge led him upstairs to a sort of office or study, immediately over the breakfast room, having an outlook over the Capitol grounds, and fitted up with a few book-cases, writing desks, and easy-chairs.

The judge drew a chair to the central table, which was covered with papers, and motioned Ishmael to take another seat at the same table. As soon as Ishmael obeyed, Judge Merlin began to initiate him into his new duties, which, in fact, were so much of the same description with those in which he had been engaged at Tanglewood, that he very soon understood and entered upon them.

The first few days of Ishmael's sojourn were very busy ones. There was a great arrearage of correspondence; and he worked diligently, day and night, until he had brought up all arrears to the current time.

When this was done, and he had but two mails to attend to in one day, he found that five hours in the morning and five in the evening sufficed for the work, and left him ample leisure for the pursuit of his legal studies, and he devoted himself to them, both by diligent reading and by regular attendance upon the sessions of the circuit court, where he watched, listened, and took notes, comparing the latter with the readings. Of course he could not do all this without reducing his labors to a perfect system, and he could not constantly adhere to this system without practicing the severest self-denial. I tell you, young reader of this story, that in this republic there is no "royal road" to fame and honor. The way is open to each and all of you; but it is steep and rugged, yes, and slippery; and you must toil and sweat and watch if you would reach the summit.

Would you know exactly how Ishmael managed this stage of his toilsome ascent? I will tell you. He arose at four o'clock those winter mornings, dressed quickly and went into the judge's study, where he made the fire himself, because the servants would not be astir for hours; then he sat down with the pile of letters that had come by the night's mail; he looked over the judge's hints regarding them, and then went to work and answered letters or copied documents for four hours, or until the breakfast bell rung, when he joined Claudia and her father at table. After breakfast he attended the judge in his study; submitted to his inspection the morning's work; then took them to the post office, posted them, brought back the letters that arrived by the morning's mail, and left them with the judge to be read. This would bring him to about eleven o'clock, when he went to the City Hall, to watch the proceedings of the circuit court, making careful notes and comparing them with his own private readings of law. He returned from the circuit court about two o'clock; spent the afternoon in answering the letters left for him by the judge; dined late with the family; took the second lot of letters to the post office, and returned with those that came by the evening mail; gave them to the judge for examination, and then went up to his room to spend the evening in reading law and comparing notes. He allowed himself no recreation and but little rest. His soul was sustained by what Balzac calls "the divine patience of genius." And the more he was enabled to measure himself with other men, the more confidence he acquired in his own powers. This severe mental labor took away much of the pain of his "despised love." Ishmael was one to love strongly, ardently, constantly. But he was not one to drivel over a hopeless passion. He loved Claudia: how deeply, how purely, how faithfully, all his future life was destined to prove. And he knew that Claudia loved him; but that all the prejudices of her rank, her character, and her education were warring in her bosom against this love. He knew that she appreciated his personal worth, but scorned his social position. He felt that she had resolved never, under any circumstances whatever, to marry him; but he trusted in her honor never to permit her, while loving him, to marry another. And in the meantime years of toil would pass; he would achieve greatness; and when the obscurity of his origin should be lost in the light of his fame, then he would woo and win Miss Merlin!

Such were the young man's dreams, whenever in his busy, crowded, useful life he gave himself time to dream.

And meanwhile, what was the conduct of the heiress to her presumptuous lover? Coldly proud, but very respectful. For, mark you this: No one who was capable of appreciating Ishmael Worth could possibly treat him otherwise than with respect.

CHAPTER LI.

HEIRESS AND BEAUTY.

'Tis hard upon the dawn, and yet
She comes not from the ball.
The night is cold and bleak and wet,
And the snow lies over all.

I praised her with her diamonds on!
And as she went she smiled,
And yet I sighed when she was gone,
I sighed like any child.
—*Meredith.*

Meanwhile all Claudia Merlin's time was taken up with milliners, mantua makers, and jewelers. She was to make her first appearance in society at the President's first evening reception, which was to be held on Friday, the sixth of January. It was now very near the New Year, and all her intervening time was occupied in preparations for the festivities that were to attend it.

On the twenty-third of December, two days before Christmas, Mr. and Mrs. Middleton and all their family arrived. They came up by the "Columbia," and reached Judge Merlin's house early in the morning. Consequently they were not fatigued, and the day of their arrival was a day of unalloyed pleasure and of family jubilee.

Ishmael took sympathetic part in all the rejoicings, and was caressed by Mr. and Mrs. Middleton and all their younger children as a sort of supplementary son and brother.

On Christmas Eve, also, Reuben Gray, Hannah, and her children came to town in their wagon. Honest Reuben had brought a load of turkeys for the Christmas market, and had "put up" at a plain, respectable inn, much frequented by the farmers, near the market house; but in the course of the day he and his wife, leaving the children in the care of their faithful Sally, who had accompanied them in the character of nurse, called on Ishmael and brought him his trunk of wearing apparel.

The judge, in his hearty, old-fashioned, thoughtless hospitality, would have had Reuben and his family come and stop at his own house. But Reuben Gray, with all his simplicity, had the good sense firmly to decline this invitation and keep to his tavern.

"For you know, Hannah, my dear," he said to his wife, when they found themselves again, at the Plow, "we would bother the family more'n the judge reckoned on. What could they do with us? Where could they put us? As to axing of us in the drawing room or sitting of us down in the dining room, with all his fine, fashionable friends, that wasn't to be thought on! And as to you being put into the kitchen, along of the servants, that I wouldn't allow! Now the judge, he didn't think of all these things: but I did; and I was right to decline the invitation, don't you think so?"

"Of course you were, Reuben, and if you hadn't declined it, I would, and that I tell you," answered Mrs. Gray.

"And so, Hannah, my dear, we will just keep our Christmas where we are! We won't deprive Ishmael of his grand Christmas dinner with his grand friends; but we will ax him to come over and go to the playhouse with us and see the play, and then we'll all come back and have a nice supper all on us together. We'll have a roast turkey and mince pie and egg-nog and apple toddy, my dear, and make a night of it, once in a way! What do you think?"

"I think that will be all very well, Reuben, so that you don't take too much of that same egg-nog and apple toddy," replied Mrs. Gray.

"Now, Hannah, did you ever know me to do such a thing?" inquired Reuben, with an injured air.

"No, Reuben, I never did. But I think that a man that even so much as touches spiritable likkers is never safe until he is in his grave," said Mrs. Gray solemnly.

"Where he can never get no more," sighed Reuben; and as he had to attend the market to sell his turkeys that night, he left Hannah and went to put his horses to the wagon.

So fine a trade did Reuben drive with his fat turkeys that he came home at ten with an empty wagon and full pocketbook, and told Hannah that she might have a new black silk "gownd," and Sally should have a red calico "un," and as for the children, they should have an outfit from head to foot.

Christmas morning dawned gloriously. All the little Middleton's were made happy by the fruit of the Christmas tree. In the many kind interchanges of gifts Ishmael was not entirely forgotten. Some loving heart had remembered him. Some skillful hand had worked for him. When he went up to his room after breakfast on Christmas morning, he saw upon his dressing table a packet directed to himself. On opening it he found a fine pocket-handkerchief neatly hemmed and marked, a pair of nice gloves, a pair of home-knit socks, and a pair of embroidered slippers. Here was no useless fancy trumpery; all were useful articles; and in the old-fashioned, housewifely present Ishmael recognized the thoughtful heart and careful hand of Bee, and grateful, affectionate tears filled his eyes. He went below stairs to a back parlor, where he felt sure he should find Bee presiding over the indoor amusements of her younger brothers and sisters.

And, sure enough, there the pretty little motherly maiden was among the children.

Ishmael went straight up to her, saying, in fervent tones:

"I thank you, Bee; I thank you for remembering me."

"Why, who should remember you if not I, Ishmael? Are you not like one of ourselves? And should I forget you any sooner than I should forget Walter, or James, or John?" said Bee, with a pleasant smile.

"Ah, Bee! I have neither mother nor sister to think of me at festive times; but you, dear Bee, you make me forget the need of either."

"You have 'neither mother nor sister,' Ishmael? Now, do not think so, while my dear mother and myself live; for I am sure she loves you as a son, Ishmael, and I love you—as a brother," answered Bee, speaking comfort to the lonely youth from the depths of her own pure, kind heart. But ah! the intense blush that followed her words might have revealed to an interested observer how much more than any brother she loved Ishmael Worth.

Judge Merlin, Claudia, Mr. and Mrs. Middleton, and Ishmael went to church.

Bee stayed home to see that the nurses took proper care of the children.

They had a family Christmas dinner.

And after that Ishmael excused himself, and went over to the Plow to spend the evening with Reuben and Hannah. That evening the three friends went to the theater, and saw their first play, "the Comedy of Errors," together. And it did many an old, satiated play-goer good to see the hearty zest with which honest Reuben enjoyed the fun. Nor was Hannah or Ishmael much behind him in their keen appreciation of the piece; only, at those passages at which Hannah and Ishmael only smiled, Reuben rubbed his knees, and laughed aloud, startling all the audience.

"It's a good thing I don't live in the city, Hannah, my dear, for I would go to the play every night!" said Reuben, as they left the theater at the close of the performance.

"And it is a good thing you don't, Reuben, for it would be the ruination of you!" admitted Hannah.

They went back to the Plow, where the Christmas supper was served for them in the plain little private sitting room. After partaking moderately of its delicacies, Ishmael bade them good-night, and returned home.

Reuben and Hannah stayed a week in the city. Reuben took her about to see all the sights and to shop in all the stores. And on New Year's day, when the President received the public, Reuben took Hannah to the White House, to "pay their duty" to the chief magistrate of the nation. And the day after New Year's day they took leave of Ishmael and of all their friends, and returned home, delighted with the memory of their pleasant visit to the city.

Ishmael, after all these interruptions, returned with new zest to his duties, and, as before, worked diligently day and night.

Claudia went deeper into her preparations for her first appearance in society at the President's first drawing room of the season.

The night of nights for the heiress came. After dinner Claudia indulged herself in a long nap, so that she might be quite fresh in the evening. When she woke up she took a cup of tea, and immediately retired to her chamber to dress.

Mrs. Middleton superintended her toilet.

Claudia wore a rich point-lace dress over a white satin skirt. The wreath that crowned her head, the necklace that reposed upon her bosom, the bracelets that clasped her arms, the girdle that enclosed her waist, and the bunches of flowers that festooned her upper lace dress, were all of the same rich pattern—lilies of the valley, whose blossoms were formed of pearl, whose leaves were of emeralds, and whose dew was of diamonds. Snowy gloves and snowy shoes completed this toilet, the effect of which was rich, chaste, and elegant beyond description. Mrs. Middleton wore a superb dress of ruby-colored velvet.

When they were both quite ready, they went down into the drawing room, where Judge Merlin, Mr. Middleton, and Ishmael were awaiting them, and where Claudia's splendid presence suddenly dazzled them. Mr. Middleton and Judge Merlin gazed upon the radiant beauty with undisguised admiration. And Ishmael looked on with a deep, unuttered groan. How dared he love this stately, resplendent queen? How dared he hope she would ever deign to notice him? But the next instant he reproached himself for the groan and the doubt— how could he have been so fooled by a mere shimmer of satin and glitter of jewels?

Judge Merlin and Mr. Middleton were in the conventional evening dress of gentlemen, and were quite ready to attend the ladies. They had nothing to do, therefore, but to hand them to the carriage, which they accordingly did. The party of four, Mr. and Mrs. Middleton, Judge Merlin, and Claudia, drove off.

Ishmael and Beatrice remained at home. Ishmael to study his law books; Beatrice to give the boys their supper and see that the nurses took proper care of the children.

CHAPTER LII.

AN EVENING AT THE PRESIDENT'S.

There was a sound of revelry by night—
"Columbia's" capital had gathered then
Her beauty and her chivalry: and bright
The lamps shone o'er fair women and brave men.
A thousand hearts beat happily; and when
Music arose with its voluptuous swell,
Soft eyes looked love to eyes that spoke again,
And all went merry as a marriage bell.
—*Byron*.

The carriage rolled along Pennsylvania Avenue. The weather had changed since sunset, and the evening was misty with a light, drizzling rain. Yet still the scene was a gay, busy, and enlivening one; the gas lamps that lighted the Avenue gleamed brightly through the rain drops like smiles through tears; the sidewalks were filled with pedestrians, and the middle of the street with vehicles, all going in one direction, to the President's palace.

A decorously slow drive of fifteen minutes brought our party through this gay scene to a gayer one at the north gate of the President's park, where a great crowd of carriages were drawn up, waiting their turn to drive in.

The gates were open and lighted by four tall lamps placed upon the posts, and which illuminated the whole scene.

Judge Merlin's carriage drew up on the outskirts of this crowd of vehicles, to wait his turn to enter; but he soon found himself enclosed in the center of the assemblage by other carriages that had come after his own. He had to wait full fifteen minutes before he could fall into the procession that was slowly making its way through the right-hand gate, and along the lighted circular avenue that led up to the front entrance of the palace. Even on this misty night the grounds were gayly illuminated and well filled. But crowded as the scene was, the utmost order prevailed. The carriages that came up the right-hand avenue, full of visitors, discharged them at the entrance hall and rolled away empty down the left-hand avenue, so that there was a continuous procession of full carriages coming up one way and empty carriages going down the other.

At length Judge Merlin's carriage, coming slowly along in the line, drew up in its turn before the front of the mansion. The whole façade of the White House was splendidly illuminated, as if to express in radiant light a smiling welcome. The halls were occupied by attentive officers, who received the visitors and ushered them into cloakrooms. Within the house also, great as the crowd of visitors was, the most perfect order prevailed.

212

Judge Merlin and his party were received by a civil, respectable official, who directed them to a cloakroom, and they soon found themselves in a close, orderly crowd moving thitherward. When the gentlemen had succeeded in conveying their ladies safely to this bourne and seen them well over its threshold, they retired to the receptacle where they were to leave their hats and overcoats before coming back to take their parties into the saloon.

In the ladies' cloakroom Claudia and her chaperone found themselves in a brilliant, impracticable crowd. There were about half-a-dozen tall dressing glasses in the place, and about half-a-hundred young ladies were trying to smooth braids and ringlets and adjust wreaths and coronets by their aid. And there were about half-a-hundred more in the center of the room; some taking off opera cloaks, shaking out flounces, and waiting their turns to go to the mirrors; and some, quite ready and waiting the appearance of their escort at the door to take them to the saloon; and beside these some were coming in and some were passing out continually; and through the open doors the crowds of those newly arriving and the crowds of those passing on to the reception rooms, were always visible.

Claudia looked upon this seething multitude with a shudder.

"What a scene!" she exclaimed.

"Yes, but with it all, what order! There has never been such order and system in these crowded receptions as now under the management of Mrs. ------," said Mrs. Middleton, naming the accomplished lady who, that season, ruled the domestic affairs of the White House.

As Mrs. Middleton and Claudia had finished their toilets, to the sticking of the very last pin, before leaving their dressing rooms at home, they had now nothing to do but to give their opera cloaks to a woman in attendance, and then stand near the door to watch for the appearance of Judge Merlin and Mr. Middleton. They had but a few minutes to wait. The gentlemen soon came and gave their arms to their ladies and led them to join the throng that were slowly making its way through the crowded halls and anterooms towards the audience chamber, where the President received his visitors. It was a severe ordeal, the passage of those halls. Our party, like all their companions, were pressed forward in the crowd until they were fairly pushed into the presence chamber, known as the small crimson drawing room, in which the President and his family waited to receive their visitors.

Yes, there he stood, the majestic old man, with his kingly gray head bared, and his stately form clothed in the republican citizen's dress of simple black. There he stood, fresh from the victories of a score of well-fought fields, receiving the meed of honor won by his years, his patriotism, and his courage. A crowd of admirers perpetually passed before him; by the orderly arrangement of the ushers they came up on the right-hand side, bowed or courtesied before him, received a cordial shake of the hand, a smile, and a few kind words, and then passed on to the left towards the great saloon commonly known as the East Room. Perhaps never has any President since Washington made himself so much beloved by the people as did General —— during his short administration. Great love-compelling power had that dignified and benignant old man! Fit to be the chief magistrate of a great, free people he was! At least so thought Judge Merlin's daughter, as she courtesied before him, received the cordial shake of his hand, heard the kind tones of his voice say, "I am very glad to see you, my dear," and passed on with the throng who were proceeding toward the East Room.

Once arrived in that magnificent room, they found space enough even for that vast crowd to move about in. This room is too well known to the public to need any labored description. For the information of those who have never seen it, it is sufficient to say that its dimensions are magnificent, its decorations superb, its furniture luxurious, and its illuminations splendid. Three enormous chandeliers, like constellations, flooded the scene with light, and a fine brass band, somewhere out of sight, filled the air with music. A brilliant company enlivened, but did not crowd, the room. There were assembled beautiful girls, handsome women, gorgeous old ladies; there were officers of the army and of the navy in their full-dress uniforms; there were the diplomatic corps of all foreign nations in the costumes of their several ranks and countries; there were grave senators and wise judges and holy divines; there were Indian chiefs in their beads and blankets; there were adventurous Poles from Warsaw; exiled Bourbons from Paris; and Comanché braves from the Cordilleras! There was, in fact, such a curious assemblage as can be met with nowhere on the face of the earth but in the east drawing room of our President's palace on a great reception evening!

Into this motley but splendid assemblage Judge Merlin led his beautiful daughter. At first her entrance attracted no attention; but when one, and then another, noticed the dazzling new star of beauty that had so suddenly risen above their horizon, a whisper arose that soon grew into a general buzz of admiration that attended Claudia in her progress through the room and heralded her approach to those at the upper end. And—
—

"Who is she?" "Who can she be?" were the low-toned questions that reached her ear as her father led her to a sofa and rested her upon it. But these questions came only from those who were strangers in Washington. Of course all others knew the person of Judge Merlin, and surmised the young lady on his arm to be his daughter.

Soon after the judge and his party were seated, his friends began to come forward to pay their respects to him, and to be presented to his beautiful daughter.

Claudia received all these with a self-possession, grace, and fascination peculiarly her own.

There was no doubt about it—Miss Merlin's first entrance into society had been a great success; she had made a sensation.

Among those presented to Miss Merlin on that occasion was the Honorable ---- ———, the British minister. He was young, handsome, accomplished, and a bachelor. Consequently he was a target for all the shafts of Cupid that ladies' eyes could send.

He offered his arm to Miss Merlin for a promenade through the room. She accepted it, and became as much the envy of every unmarried lady present as if the offer made and accepted had been for a promenade through life.

No such thought, however, was in the young English minister's mind; for after making the circuit of the room two or three times, he brought his companion back, and, with a smile and a bow, left her in the care of her father.

But if the people were inclined to feed their envy, they found plenty of food for that appetite. A few minutes after Miss Merlin had resumed her seat a general buzz of voices announced some new event of interest. It turned out to be the entrance of the President and his family into the East Room.

For some good reason or other, known only to his own friendly heart, the President, sauntering leisurely, dispensing bows, smiles, and kind words as he passed, went straight up to the sofa whereon his old friend, Judge Merlin, sat, took a seat beside him, and entered into conversation.

Ah! their talk was not about state affairs, foreign or domestic policy, duties, imports, war, peace—no! their talk was of their boyhood's days, spent together; of the holidays they had had; of the orchards they had robbed; of the well-merited thrashings they had got; and of the good old schoolmaster, long since dust and ashes, who had lectured and flogged them!

Claudia listened, and loved the old man more, that he could turn from the memory of his bloody victories, the presence of his political cares, and the prospects of a divided cabinet, to refresh himself with the green reminiscences of his boyhood's days. It was impossible for the young girl to feel so much sympathy without betraying it and attracting the attention of the old man. He looked at her. He had shaken hands with her, and said that he was glad to see her, when she was presented to him in his presence chamber; but he had not really seen her; she had been only one of the passing crowd of courtesiers for whom he felt a wholesale kindness and expressed a wholesale good-will; now, however, he looked at her—now he saw her.

Sixty-five years had whitened the hair of General ———, but he was not insensible to the charms of beauty; nor unconscious of his own power of conferring honor upon beauty.

Rising, therefore, with all the stately courtesy of the old school gentleman, he offered his arm to Miss Merlin for a promenade through the rooms.

With a sweet smile, Claudia arose, and once more became the cynosure of all eyes and the envy of all hearts. A few turns through the rooms, and the President brought the beauty back, seated her, and took his own seat beside her on the sofa.

But the cup of bitterness for the envious was not yet full. Another hum and buzz went around the room, announcing some new event of great interest; which seemed to be a late arrival of much importance.

Presently the British minister and another gentleman were seen approaching the sofa where sat the President, Judge Merlin, Miss Merlin, and Mr. and Mrs. Middleton. They paused immediately before the President, when the minister said:

"Your Excellency, permit me to present to you the Viscount Vincent, late from London."

The President arose and heartily shook hands with the young foreigner, cordially saying:

"I am happy to see you, my lord; happy to welcome you to Washington."

The viscount bowed low before the gray-haired old hero, saying, in a low tone:

"I am glad to see the President of the United States; but I am proud to shake the hand of the conqueror of—of——"

The viscount paused, his memory suddenly failed him, for the life and soul of him he could not remember the names of those bloody fields where the General had won his laurels.

The President gracefully covered the hesitation of the viscount and evaded the compliment at the same time by turning to the ladies of his party and presenting his guest, saying:

"Mrs. Middleton, Lord Vincent. Miss Merlin, Lord Vincent."

The viscount bowed low to these ladies, who courtesied in turn and resumed their seats.

"My old friend, Judge Merlin, Lord Vincent," then said the plain, matter-of-fact old President.

The judge and the viscount simultaneously bowed, and then, these formalities being over, seats were found for the two strangers, and the whole group fell into an easy chat—subject of discussion the old question that is sure to be argued whenever the old world and the new meet—the rival merits of monarchies and republics. The discussion grew warm, though the disputants remained courteous. The viscount grew bored, and gradually dropped out of the argument, leaving the subject in the hands of the President and the minister, who, of course, had taken opposite sides, the minister representing the advantages of a monarchical form of government, and the President contending for a republican one. The viscount noticed that a large portion of the company were promenading in a procession round and round the room to the music of one of Beethoven's grand marches. It was monotonous enough; but it was better than sitting there and listening to the vexed question whether "the peoples" were capable of governing themselves. So he turned to Miss Merlin with a bow and smile, saying:

"Shall we join the promenade? Will you so far honor me?"

"With pleasure, my lord," replied Miss Merlin.

And he rose and gave her his arm, and they walked away. And for the third time that evening Claudia became the target of all sorts of glances—glances of admiration, glances of hate. She had been led out by the young English minister; then by the old President; and now she was promenading with the lion of the evening, the only titled person at this republican court, the Viscount Vincent. And she a newcomer, a mere girl, not twenty years old! It was intolerable, thought all the ladies, young and old, married or single.

But if the beautiful Claudia was the envy of all the women, the handsome Vincent was not less the envy of all the men present. "Puppy"; "coxcomb"; "Jackanape"; "swell"; "Viscount, indeed! more probably some foreign blackleg or barber"; "It is perfectly ridiculous the manner in which American girls throw themselves under the feet of these titled foreign paupers," were some of the low-breathed blessings bestowed upon young Lord Vincent. And yet these expletives were not intended to be half so malignant as they might have sounded. They were but the impulsive expressions of transient vexation at seeing the very pearl of beauty, on the first evening of her appearance, carried off by an alien.

In truth, the viscount and the heiress were a very handsome couple; and notwithstanding all the envy felt for them, all eyes followed them with secret admiration. The beautiful Claudia was a rare type of the young American girl—tall, slender, graceful, dark-haired, dark-eyed, with a rich, glowing bloom on cheeks and lips. And her snow white dress of misty lace over shining satin, and her gleaming pearls and sparkling diamonds, set off her beauty well. Vincent was a fine specimen of the young English gentleman—tall, broad-chouldered, deep-chested; with a stately head; a fair, roseate complexion; light-brown, curling hair and beard; and clear, blue eyes. And his simple evening dress of speckless black became him well. His manners were graceful, his voice pleasant, and his conversation brilliant; but, alas, for Claudia! the greatest charm he possessed for her was—his title! Claudia knew another, handsomer, more graceful, more brilliant than this viscount; but that other was unknown, untitled, and unnamed in the world. The viscount was so engaged with his beautiful companion that it was some time before he observed that the company was dropping off and the room was half empty. He then led Miss Merlin back to her party, took a slight leave of them all, bowed to the President, and departed.

Judge Merlin, who had only waited for his daughter, now arose to go. His party made their adieus and left the saloon. As so many of the guests had already gone, they found the halls and anterooms comparatively free of crowds, and easily made their way to the gentlemen's cloakroom and the ladies' dressing room, and thence to the entrance hall. Mr. Middleton went out to call the carriage, which was near at hand. And the whole party entered and drove homeward. The sky had not cleared, the drizzle still continued; but the lamps gleamed brightly through the raindrops, and the Avenue was as gay at midnight as it had been at midday. As the carriage rolled along, Judge Merlin and Mr. and Mrs. Middleton discussed the reception, the President, the company, and especially the young English viscount.

"He is the son and heir of the Earl of Hurstmonceux, whose estates lie somewhere in the rich county of Sussex. The title did not come to the present earl in the direct line of descent. The late earl died childless, at a very advanced age; and the title fell to his distant relation, Lord Banff, the father of this young man, whose estates lie away up in the north of Scotland somewhere. Thus the Scottish Lord Banff became Earl of Hurstmonceux, and his eldest son, our new acquaintance, took the second title in the family, and became Lord Vincent," said Judge Merlin.

"The English minister gave you this information?" inquired Mr. Middleton.

"Yes, he did; I suppose he thought it but right to put me in possession of all such facts in relation to a young foreigner whom he had been instrumental in introducing to my family. But, by the way, Middleton—Hurstmonceux? Was not that the title of the young dowager countess whom Brudenell married, and parted with, years ago?"

"Yes; and I suppose that she was the widow of that very old man, the late Earl of Hurstmonceux, who died childless; in fact, she must have been."

"I wonder whatever became of her?"

"I do not know; I know nothing whatever about the last Countess of Hurstmonceux; but I know very well who has a fair prospect of becoming the next Countess of Hurstmonceux, if She pleases!" replied Mr. Middleton, with a merry glance at his niece.

Claudia, who had been a silent, thoughtful, and attentive listener to their conversation, did not reply, but smothered a sigh and turned to look out of the window. The carriage was just drawing up before their own gate.

The whole face of the house was closed and darkened except one little light that burned in a small front window at the very top of the house.

It was Ishmael's lamp; and, as plainly as if she had been in the room, Claudia in imagination saw the pale young face bent studiously over the volume lying open before him.

With another inward sigh Claudia gave her hand to her uncle, who had left the carriage to help her out. And then the whole party entered the house, where they were admitted by sleepy Jim.

And in another half hour they were all in repose.

CHAPTER LIII.

THE VISCOUNT VINCENT.

A king may make a belted knight,
A marquis, duke and a' that,
But an honest man's aboon his might
Gude faith he mauna fa' that!
For a' that and a' that,
Their dignities and a' that,
The pith o' sense and pride o' worth
Are higher ranks than a' that.
—*Robert Burns*.

The next morning Ishmael and Bee, the only hard workers in the family, were the first to make their appearance in the breakfast room. They had both been up for hours—Ishmael in the library, answering letters, and Bee in the nursery, seeing that the young children were properly washed, dressed, and fed. And now, at the usual hour, they came down, a little hungry, and impatient for the morning meal. But for some time no one joined them. All seemed to be sleeping off the night's dissipation. Bee waited nearly an hour, and then said:

"Ishmael, I will not detain you longer. I know that you wish to go to the courthouse, to watch the Emerson trial; so I will ring for breakfast. Industrious people must not be hindered by the tardiness of lazy ones," she added, with a smile, as she put her hand to the bell-cord.

Ishmael was about to protest against the breakfast being hurried on his account, when the matter was settled by the entrance of Judge Merlin, followed by Mr. Middleton and Claudia. After the morning salutations had passed, the judge said:

"You may ring for breakfast, Claudia, my dear. We will not wait for your aunt, since your uncle tells us that she is too tired to rise this morning."

But as Bee had already rung, the coffee and muffins were soon served, and the family gathered around the table.

Beside Claudia's plate lay a weekly paper, which, as soon as she had helped her companions to coffee, she took up and read. It was a lively gossiping little paper of that day, published every Saturday morning, under the somewhat sounding title of "The Republican Court Journal," and it gave, in addition to the news of the world, the doings of the fashionable circles. This number of the paper contained a long description of the President's drawing room of the preceding evening. And as Claudia read it, she smiled and broke in silvery laughter.

Everyone looked up.

"What is it, my dear?" inquired the judge.

"Let us have it, Claudia," said Mr. Middleton.

"Oh, papa! oh, uncle! I really cannot read it out—it is too absurd! Is there no way, I wonder, of stopping these reporters from giving their auction-book schedule of one's height, figure, complexion, and all that? Here, Bee—you read it, my dear," said Claudia, handing it to her cousin.

Bee took the paper and cast her eyes over the article in question; but as she did so her cheek crimsoned with blushes, and she laid the paper down.

"Read it, Bee," said Claudia.

"I cannot," answered Beatrice coldly.

"Why not?"

"It makes my eyes burn even to see it! Oh, Claudia, how dare they take such liberties with your name?"

"Why, every word of it is praise—high praise."

"It is fulsome, offensive flattery."

"Oh, you jealous little imp!" said Miss Merlin, laughing.

"Yes, Claudia, I am jealous! not of you; but for you—for your delicacy and dignity," said Beatrice gravely.

"And you think, then, I have been wronged by this public notice?" inquired the heiress, half wounded and half offended by the words of her cousin.

"I do," answered Beatrice gravely.

"As if I cared! Queens of society, like other sovereigns, must be so taxed for their popularity, Miss Middleton!" said Claudia, half laughingly and half defiantly.

Bee made no reply.

But Mr. Middleton extended his hand, saying:

"Give me the paper. Claudia is a little too independent, and Bee a little too fastidious, for either to be a fair judge of what is right and proper in this matter; so we will see for ourselves."

Judge Merlin nodded assent.

Mr. Middleton read the article aloud. It was really a very lively description of the President's evening reception—interesting to those who had not been present; more interesting to those who had; and most interesting of all to those who found themselves favorably noticed. To the last-mentioned the notice was fame—for a day. The article was two or three columns in length; but we will quote only a few lines. One paragraph said:

"Among the distinguished guests present was the young Viscount Vincent, eldest son and heir of the earl of Hurstmonceux and Banff. He was presented by the British minister."

Another paragraph alluded to Claudia in these terms:

"The belle of the evening, beyond all competition, was the beautiful Miss M——n, only daughter and heiress of Judge M——n, of the Supreme Court. It will be remembered that the blood of Pocahontas runs in this young beauty's veins, giving luster to her raven black hair, light to her dusky eyes, fire to her brown cheeks, and majesty and grace to all her movements. She is truly an Indian princess."

"Well!" said Mr. Middleton, laying down the paper, "I agree with Bee. It is really too bad to be trotted out in this way, and have all your points indicated, and then be dubbed with a fancy name besides. Why, Miss Merlin, they will call you the 'Indian' Princess' to the end of time, or of your Washington campaign."

Claudia tossed her head.

"What odds?" she asked. "I am rather proud to be of the royal lineage of Powhatan. They may call me Indian princess, if they like. I will accept the title."

"Until you get a more legitimate one!" laughed Mr. Middleton.

"Until I get a more legitimate one," assented Claudia.

"But I will see McQuill, the reporter of the 'Journal,' and ask him as a particular favor to leave my daughter's name out of his next balloon full of gas!" laughed the judge, as he arose from the table.

The other members of the family followed. And each went about his or her own particular business. This day being the next following the first appearance of Miss Merlin in society, was passed quietly in the family.

The next day, being Sunday, they all attended church.

But on Monday a continual stream of visitors arrived, and a great number of cards were left at Judge Merlin's door.

In the course of a week Claudia returned all these calls, and thus she was fairly launched into fashionable life.

She received numerous invitations to dinners, evening parties, and balls; but all these she civilly excused herself from attending; for it was her whim to give a large party before going to any. To this end, she forced her Aunt Middleton to issue cards and make preparations on a grand scale for a very magnificent ball.

"It must eclipse everything else that has been done, or can be done, this season!" said Claudia.

"Humph!" answered Mrs. Middleton.

"We must have Dureezie's celebrated band for the music, you know!"

"My dear, he charges a thousand dollars a night to leave New York and play for anyone!"

"Well? what if it were two thousand—ten thousand? I will have him. Tell Ishmael to write to him at once."

"Very well, my dear. You are spending your own money, remember."

"Who cares? I will be the only one who engages Dureezie's famous music. And, Aunt Middleton?"

"Well, my dear?"

"Vourienne must decorate the rooms."

"My dear, his charges are enormous."

"So is my fortune, Aunt Middleton," laughed Claudia.

"Very well," sighed the lady.

"And—aunt?"

"Yes, dear?"

"Devizac must supply the supper."

"Claudia, you are mad! Everything that man touches turns to gold—for his own pocket."

Claudia shrugged her shoulders.

"Aunt, what do I care for all that. I can afford it. As long as he can hold out to charge, I can hold out to pay. I mean to enjoy my fortune, and live while I live."

"Ah, my dear, wealth was given for other purposes than the enjoyment of its possessor!" sighed Mrs. Middleton.

"I know it, aunty. It was given for the advancement of its possessor. I have another object besides enjoyment in view. I say, aunty!"

"Well, my child?"

"We must be very careful whom we have here."

"Of course, my dear."

"We must have the best people."

"Certainly."

"We must invite the diplomatic corps."

"By all means."

"And—all foreigners of distinction, who may be present in the city."

"Yes, my love."

"We must not forget to invite—"

"Who, my dear?"

"Lord Vincent."

"Humph! Has he called here?"

"He left his card a week ago."

The day succeeding this conversation the cards of invitation to the Merlin ball were issued.

And in ten days the ball came off.

It was—as Miss Merlin had resolved it should be—the most splendid affair of the kind that has ever been seen in Washington, before or since. It cost a small fortune, of course, but it was unsurpassed and unsurpassable. Even to this day it is remembered as the great ball. As Claudia had determined, Vourienne superintended the decorations of the reception, dancing, and supper rooms; Devizac furnished the refreshment, and Dureezie the music. The élite of the city were present. The guests began to assemble at ten o'clock, and by eleven the rooms were crowded.

Among the guests was he for whom all this pageantry had been got up—the Viscount Vincent.

With excellent taste, Claudia had on this occasion avoided display in her own personal appointments. She wore a snow-white, mist-like tulle over white glacé silk, that floated cloud-like around her with every movement of her graceful form. She wore no jewelry, but upon her head a simple withe of the cypress vine, whose green leaves and crimson buds contrasted well with her raven black hair. Yet never in all the splendor of her richest dress and rarest jewels had she looked more beautiful. The same good taste that governed her unassuming toilet withheld her from taking any prominent part in the festivities of the evening. She was courteous to all, solicitous for the comfort of her guests, yet not too officious. As if only to do honor to the most distinguished stranger present, she danced with the Viscount Vincent once; and after that declined all invitations to the floor. Nor did Lord Vincent dance again. He seemed to prefer to devote himself to his lovely young hostess for the evening. The viscount was the lion of the party, and his exclusive attention to the young heiress could not escape observation. Everyone noticed and commented upon it. Nor was Claudia insensible to the honor of being the object of this exclusive devotion from his lordship. She was flattered, and when Claudia was in this state her beauty became radiant.

Among those who watched the incipient flirtation commencing between the viscount and the heiress was Beatrice Middleton. She had come late. She had had all the children to see properly fed and put to bed before she could begin to dress herself. And one restless little brother had kept her by his crib singing songs and telling stories until ten o'clock before he finally dropped off to sleep, and left her at liberty to go to her room and dress herself for the ball. Her dress was simplicity itself—a plain white tarletan with white ribbons; but it well became the angelic purity of her type of beauty. Her golden ringlets and sapphire eyes were the only jewels she wore, the roses on her cheeks the only flowers. When she entered the dancing room she saw four quadrilles in active progress on the floor; and about four hundred spectators crowded along the walls, some sitting, some standing, some reclining, and some grouped. She passed on, greeting courteously those with whom she had a speaking acquaintance, smiling kindly upon others, and observing all. In this way she reached the group of which Claudia Merlin and Lord Vincent formed the center. A cursory glance showed her that one for whom she looked was not among them. With a bow and a smile to the group she turned away and went up to where Judge Merlin stood for the moment alone.

"Uncle," she said, in a tone slightly reproachful, "is not Ishmael to be with us this evening?"

"My dear, I invited him to join us, but he excused himself."

"Of course, naturally he would do so at first, thinking doubtless that you asked him as a mere matter of form. Uncle, considering his position, you ought to have pressed him to come. You ought not to have permitted him to excuse himself, if you really were in earnest with your invitation. Were you in earnest, sir?"

"Why, of course I was, my dear! Why shouldn't I have been? I should have been really glad to see the young man here enjoying himself this evening."

"Have I your authority for saying so much to Ishmael, even now, uncle?" inquired Bee eagerly.

"Certainly, my love. Go and oust him from his den. Bring him down here, if you like—and if you can," said the judge cheerily.

Bee left him, glided like a spirit through the crowd, passed from the room and went upstairs, flight after flight, until she reached the third floor, and rapped at Ishmael's door.

"Come in," said the rich, deep, sweet voice—always sweet in its tones, whether addressing man, woman, or child—human being or bumb brute; "come in."

Bee entered the little chamber, so dark after the lighted rooms below.

In the recess of the dormer window, at a small table lighted by one candle, sat Ishmael, bending over an open volume. His cheek was pale, his expression weary. He looked up, and recognizing Bee, arose with a smile to meet her.

"How dark you are up here, all alone, Ishmael," she said, coming forward.

Ishmael snuffed his candle, picked the wick, and sat it up on his pile of books that it might give a better light, and then turned again smilingly towards Bee, offered her a chair and stood as if waiting her command.

"What are you doing up here alone, Ishmael?" she inquired, with her hand upon the back of the chair that she omitted to take.

"I am studying 'Kent's Commentaries,'" answered the young man.

"I wish you would study your own health a little more, Ishmael! Why are you not down with us?"

"My dear Bee, I am better here."

"Nonsense, Ishmael! You are here too much. You confine yourself too closely to study. You should remember the plain old proverb—proverbs are the wisdom of nations, you know—the old proverb which says: 'All work and no play makes Jack a dull boy.' Come!"

"My dear friend, Bee, you must excuse me."

"But I will not."

"Bee—"

"I insist upon your coming, Ishmael."

"Bee, do not. I should be the wrong man in the wrong place."

"Now, why do you say that?"

"Because I have no business in a ballroom, Bee."

"You have as much business there as anyone else."

"What should I do there, Bee?"

"Dance! waltz! polka! At our school balls you were one of the best dancers we had, I recollect. Now, with your memory and your ear for music, you would do as well as then."

"But who would dance with me in Washington, dear Bee? I am a total stranger to everyone out of this family. And I have no right to ask an introduction to any of the belles," said Ishmael.

"I will dance with you, Ishmael, to begin with, if you will accept me as a partner. And I do not think you will venture to refuse your little adopted sister and old playmate. Come, Ishmael."

"Dearest little sister, do you know that I declined Judge Merlin's invitation?"

"Yes; he told me so, and sent me here to say to you, that he will not excuse you, that he insists upon your coming. Come, Ishmael!"

"Dear Bee, you constrain me. I will come. Yes, I confess I am glad to be 'constrained.' Sometimes, dear, we require to be compelled to do as we like; or, in other words, our consciences require just excuses for yielding certain points to our inclinations. I have been secretly wishing to be with you all the evening. The distant sound of the music has been alluring me very persuasively. (That is a magnificent band of Dureezie's, by the way.) I have been longing to join the festivities. And I am glad, my little liege lady, that you lay your royal commands on me to do so."

"That is right, Ishmael. I must say that you yield gracefully. Well, I will leave you now to prepare your toilet. And—Ishmael?"

"Yes, Bee?"

"Ring for more light! You will never be able to render yourself irresistible with the aid of a single candle on one side of your glass," said Bee, as she made her laughing exit.

Ishmael followed her advice in every particular, and soon made himself ready to appear in the ball. When just about to leave the room he thought of his gloves, and doubted whether he had a pair for drawing-room use. Then suddenly he recollected Bee's Christmas present that he had laid away as something too sacred for use. He went and took from the parcel the straw-colored kid gloves she had given him, and drew them on as he descended the stairs, whispering to himself:

"Even for these I am indebted to her—may Heaven bless her!"

CHAPTER LIV.

ISHMAEL AT THE BALL.

Yes! welcome, right welcome—and give us your hand,
You shall not stand "out in the cold"!
If new friends are true friends, I can't understand
Why hearts should hold out till they're old;
Then come with all welcome and fear not to fling
Reserve to the winds and the waves,
For thou never canst live, the cold-blooded thing

Society makes of its slaves.
—*M.F. Tupper.*

A very handsome young fellow was Ishmael Worth as he entered the drawing room that evening. He had attained his full height, over six feet, and he had grown broad-shouldered and full-chested, with the prospect of becoming the athletic man of majestic presence that he appeared in riper years. His hair and eyes were growing much darker; you might now call the first dark brown and the last dark gray. His face was somewhat fuller; but his forehead was still high, broad, and massive, and the line of his profile was clear-cut, distinct, and classic; his lips were full and beautifully curved; and, to sum up, he still retained the peculiar charm of his countenance—the habit of smiling only with his eyes. How intense is the light of a smile that is confined to the eyes only. His dress is not worth notice. All gentlemen dress alike for evening parties; all wear the stereotyped black dress coat, light kid gloves, etc., etc., etc., and he wore the uniform for such cases made and provided. Only everything that Ishmael put on looked like the costume of a prince.

He entered the lighted and crowded drawing room very hesitatingly, looking over that splendid but confused assemblage until he caught the eye of Judge Merlin, who immediately came forward to meet him, saying in a low tone:

"I am glad you changed your mind and decided to come down. You must become acquainted with some of my acquaintances. You must make friends, Ishmael, as well as gain knowledge, if you would advance yourself. Come along!"

And the judge led him into the thick of the crowd.

Little more than a year before the judge had said, in speaking of Ishmael: "Of course, owing to the circumstances of his birth, he never can hope to attain the position of a gentleman, never." But the judge had forgotten all about that now. People usually did forget Ishmael's humble origin in his exalted presence. I use the word "exalted" with truth, as it applied to his air and manner. The judge certainly forgot that Ishmael was not Society's gentleman as well as "nature's nobleman," when, taking him through the crowd, he said:

"I shall introduce you to some young ladies. The first one I present you to will be Miss Tourneysee, the daughter of General Tourneysee. You must immediately ask her to dance; etiquette will require you to do so."

"But," smiled Ishmael, "I am already engaged to dance the next set with Bee."

"You verdant youth. So, probably, is she—Miss Tourneysee, I mean—engaged ten sets deep. Ask her for the honor of her hand as soon as she is disengaged," replied the judge, who straightway led Ishmael up to a very pretty young girl, in blue crêpe, to whom he presented the young man in due form.

Ishmael bowed and proffered his petition.

The case was not so hopeless as the judge had represented it to be. Miss Tourneysee was engaged for the next three sets, but would be happy to dance the fourth with Mr. Worth.

At that moment the partner to whom she was engaged for the quadrille, then forming, came up to claim her hand, and she arose and slightly courtesied to Judge Merlin and Ishmael Worth, and walked away with her companion.

Ishmael looked around for his own lovely partner, and Bee, smiling at a little distance, caught his eye. He bowed to Judge Merlin and went up to her and led her to the head of one of the sets about to be formed.

In the meantime, "Who is he?" whispered many voices, while many eyes followed the stranger who had come among them.

Among those who observed the entrance of Ishmael was the Viscount Vincent. Half bending, in an elegant attitude, with his white-gloved hand upon the arm of the sofa where Miss Merlin reclined, he watched the stranger. Presently he said to her:

"Excuse me, but—who is that very distinguished-looking individual?"

"Who?" inquired Claudia. She had not noticed the entrance of Ishmael.

"He who just now came in the room—with Judge Merlin, I think. There, he is now standing up, with that pretty little creature in white with the golden ringlets."

"Oh," said Claudia, following his glance. "That 'pretty little creature' is my cousin, Miss Middleton."

"I beg ten thousand pardons," said Vincent.

"And her partner," continued Claudia, "is Mr. Worth, a very promising young—" She could not say gentleman; she would not say man; so she hesitated a little while, and then said: "He is a very talented young law student with my papa."

"Ah! do you know that at first I really took him for an old friend of mine, an American gentleman from—Maryland, I believe."

"Mr. Worth is from Maryland," said Claudia.

"Then he is probably a relative of the gentleman in question. The likeness is so very striking; indeed, if it were not that Mr.—Worth, did you say his name was?—is a rather larger man, I should take him to be Mr. Brudenell. I wonder whether they are related?"

"I do not know," said Claudia. And of course she did not know; but notwithstanding that, the hot blood rushed up to her face, flushing it with a deep blush, for she remembered the fatal words that had forever affected Ishmael in her estimation.

"His mother was never married, and no one on earth knows who his father was."

The viscount looked at her; he was a man accustomed to read much in little; but not always aright; he read a great deal in Claudia's deep blush and short reply; but not the whole; he read that Claudia Merlin, the rich heiress, loved her father's poor young law student; but no more; and he resolved to make the acquaintance of the young fellow, who must be related to the Brudenells, he thought, so as to see for himself what there was in him, beside his handsome person, to attract the admiration of Chief Justice Merlin's beautiful daughter.

"He dances well; he carries himself like my friend Herman, also. I fancy they must be nearly related," he continued, as he watched Ishmael going through the quadrille.

"I am unable to inform you whether he is or not," answered Claudia.

While they talked, the dance went on. Presently it was ended.

"You must come up, now, and speak to Claudia. She is the queen of the evening, you know!" said Ishmael's gentle partner.

"I know it, dear Bee; and I am going to pay my respects; but let me find you a seat first," replied the young man.

"No, I will go with you; I have not yet spoken to Claudia this evening," said Bee.

Ishmael offered his arm and escorted her across the room to the sofa that was doing duty as throne for "the queen of the evening."

"I am glad to see you looking so well, Bee! Mr. Worth, I hope you are enjoying yourself," was the greeting of Miss Merlin, as they came up.

Then turning towards the viscount, she said:

"Beatrice, my dear, permit me—Lord Vincent, my cousin, Miss Middleton."

A low bow from the gentleman, a slight courtesy from the lady, and that was over.

"Lord Vincent—Mr. Worth," said Claudia.

Two distant bows acknowledged this introduction—so distant that Claudia felt herself called upon to mediate, which she did by saying:

"Mr. Worth, Lord Vincent has been particularly interested in you, ever since you entered the room. He finds a striking resemblance between yourself and a very old friend of his own, who is also from your native county."

Ishmael looked interested, and his smiling eyes turned from Claudia to Lord Vincent in good-humored inquiry.

"I allude to Mr. Herman Brudenell of Brudenell Hall, Maryland, who has been living in England lately. There is a very striking likeness between him and yourself; so striking that I might have mistaken one for the other; but that you are larger, and, now that I see you closely, darker, than he is. Perhaps you are relatives," said Lord Vincent.

"Oh, no; not at all; not the most distant. I am not even acquainted with the gentleman; never set eyes on him in my life!" said Ishmael, smiling ingenuously; for of course he thought he was speaking the exact truth.

But oh, Herman! oh, Nora! if he from the nethermost parts of the earth—if she from the highest heaven could have heard that honest denial of his parentage from the truthful lips of their gifted son!

"There is something incomprehensible in the caprices of nature, in making people who are in no way related so strongly resemble each other," said Lord Vincent.

"There is," admitted Ishmael.

At this moment the music ceased, the dancers left the floor, and there was a considerable movement of the company toward the back of the room.

"I think they are going to supper. Will you permit me to take you in, Miss Merlin?" said Lord Vincent, offering his arm.

"If you please," said Claudia, rising to take it.

"Shall I have the honor, dear Bee?" inquired Ishmael.

Beatrice answered by putting her hand within Ishmael's arm. And they followed the company to the supper room—scene of splendor, magnificence, and luxury that baffles all description, except that of the reporter of the "Republican Court Journal," who, in speaking of the supper, said:

"In all his former efforts, it was granted by everyone, that Devizac surpassed all others; but in this supper at Judge Merlin's, Devizac surpassed himself!"

After supper Ishmael danced the last quadrille with Miss Tourneysee; and when that was over, the time-honored old contra-dance of Sir Roger de Coverly was called, in which nearly all the company took part—Ishmael dancing with a daughter of a distinguished senator, and a certain Captain Todd dancing with Bee.

When the last dance was over, the hour being two o'clock in the morning, the party separated, well pleased with their evening's entertainment. Ishmael went up to his den, and retired to bed: but ah! not to repose. The unusual excitement of the evening, the light, the splendor, the luxury, the guests, and among them all the figures of Claudia and the viscount, haunting memory and stimulating imagination, forbade repose. Ever, in the midst of all his busy, useful, aspiring life he was conscious, deep in his heart, of a gnawing anguish, whose name was Claudia Merlin. To-night this deep-seated anguish tortured him like the vulture of Prometheus. One vivid picture was always before his mind's eye—the sofa, with the beautiful figure of Claudia reclining upon it, and the stately form of the viscount, leaning with deferential admiration over her. The viscount's admiration of the beauty was patent; he did not attempt to conceal it. Claudia's pride and pleasure in her conquest were also undeniable; she took no pains to veil them.

And for this cause Ishmael could not sleep, but lay battling all night with his agony. He arose the next morning pale and ill, from the restless bed and wretched night, but fully resolved to struggle with and conquer his hopeless love.

"I must not, I will not, let this passion enervate me! I have work to do in this world, and I must do it with all my strength!" he said to himself, as he went into the library.

Ishmael had gradually passed upward from his humble position of amanuensis to be the legal assistant and almost partner of the judge in his office business. In fact, Ishmael was his partner in everything except a share in the profits; he received none of them; he still worked for his small salary as amanuensis; not that the judge willfully availed himself of the young man's valuable assistance without giving him due remuneration, but the change in Ishmael's relations to his employer had come on so naturally and gradually, that at no one time had thought of raising the young man's salary to the same elevation of his position and services occurred to Judge Merlin.

It was ever by measuring himself with others that Ishmael proved his own relative proportion of intellect, knowledge, and power. He had been diligently studying law for more than two years. He had been attending the sessions of the courts of law both in the country and in the city. And he had been the confidential assistant of Judge Merlin for many months.

In his attendance upon the sessions of the circuit courts in Washington, and in listening to the pleadings of the lawyers and the charges of the judges, and watching the results of the trials—he had made this discovery—namely, that he had attained as fair a knowledge of law as was possessed by many of the practicing lawyers of these courts, and he resolved to consult his employer, Judge Merlin, upon the expediency of his making application for admission to practice at the Washington bar.

CHAPTER LV.

A STEP HIGHER.

He will not wait for chances,
For luck he does not look;
In faith his spirit glances
At Providence, God's book;
And there discerning truly
That right is might at length,
He dares go forward duly
In quietness and strength,
Unflinching and unfearing,

The flatterer of none,
And in good courage wearing,
The honors he has won.
—*M.F. Tupper*.

Ishmael took an early opportunity of speaking to the judge of his projects. It was one day when they had got through the morning's work and were seated in the library together, enjoying a desultory chat before it was time to go to court, that Ishmael said:

"Judge Merlin, I am about to make application to be admitted to practice at the Washington bar."

The judge looked up in surprise.

"Why, Ishmael, you have not graduated at any law school! You have not even had one term of instruction at any such school."

"I know that I have not enjoyed such advantages, sir; but I have read law very diligently for the last three years, and with what memory and understanding I possess, I have profited by my reading."

"But that is not like a regular course of study at a law school."

"Perhaps not, sir; but in addition to my reading, I have had a considerable experience while acting as your clerk."

"So you have; and you have profited by all the experience you have gained while with me. I have seen that; you have acquitted yourself unusually well, and been of very great service to me; but still I insist that law-office business and law-book knowledge is not everything; there is more required to make a good lawyer."

"I know there is, sir; very much more, and I have taken steps to acquire it. For nearly two years I have regularly attended the sessions of the courts, both in St. Mary's county and here in the city, and in that time have learned something of the practice of law," persisted Ishmael.

"All very well, so far as it goes, young man; but it would have been better if you had graduated at some first-class law school," insisted the old-fashioned, conservative judge.

"Excuse me, sir, if I venture to differ with you, so far as to say, that I do not think a degree absolutely necessary to success; or indeed of much consequence one way or the other," modestly replied Ishmael.

The judge opened his eyes to their widest extent.

"What reason have you for such an opinion as that, Ishmael?" he inquired.

"Observation, sir. In my attendance upon the sessions of the courts I have observed some gentlemen of the legal profession who were graduates of distinguished law schools, but yet made very poor barristers. I have noticed others who never saw the inside of a law school, but yet made very able barristers."

"But with all this, you must admit that the great majority of distinguished lawyers have been graduates of first-class law schools."

"Oh, yes, sir; I admit that. I admit also—for who, in his senses, could deny them?—the very great advantages of these schools as facilities; I only contend that they cannot insure success to any law student who has not talent, industry, perseverance, and a taste for the profession; and that, to one who has all these elements of success, a diploma from the schools is not necessary. I think it is the same in every branch of human usefulness. Look at the science of war. Remember the Revolutionary times. Were the great generals of that epoch graduates of any military academy? No, they came from the plow, the workshop, and the counting house. No doubt it would have been highly advantageous to them had they been graduates of some first-class military academy; I only say it was found not to be absolutely necessary to their success as great generals; and in our later wars, we have not found the graduates of West Point, who had a great theoretic knowledge of the science of war, more successful in action than the volunteers, whose only school was actual practice in the field. And look at our Senate and House of Representatives, sir; are the most distinguished statesmen there graduates of colleges? Quite the reverse. I do not wish to be so irreverent as to disparage schools and colleges, sir, I only wish to be so just as to exalt talent, industry, and perseverance to their proper level," said Ishmael warmly.

"Special pleading, my boy," said the judge.

Ishmael blushed, laughed, and replied:

"Yes, sir, I acknowledge that it is very special pleading. I have made up my mind to be a candidate for admission to the Washington bar; and having done so, I would like to get your approbation."

"What do you want with my approbation, boy? With or without it, you will get on."

"But more pleasantly with it, sir," smiled Ishmael.

"Very well, very well; take it then. Go ahead. I wish you success. But what is the use of telling you to go ahead, when you will go ahead anyhow, in spite of fate? Or why should I wish you success, when I know you will command success? Ah, Ishmael, you can do without me; but how shall I ever be able to do without you?" inquired the judge, with an odd expression between a smile and a sigh.

"My friend and patron, I must be admitted to practice at the Washington bar; but I will not upon that account leave your service while I can be of use to you," said Ishmael, with earnestness; for next to adoring Claudia, he loved best for her sake to honor her father.

"That's a good lad. Be sure you keep your promise," said the judge, smiling, and laying his hand caressingly on Ishmael's head.

And then as it was time for the judge to go to the Supreme Court, he arose and departed, leaving Ishmael to write out a number of legal documents.

Ishmael lost no time in carrying his resolution into effect. He passed a very successful examination and was duly admitted to practice in the Washington courts of law.

A few evenings after this, as Ishmael was still busy in the little library, trying to finish a certain task before the last beams of the sun had faded away, the judge entered, smiling, holding in his hand a formidable-looking document and a handful of gold coin.

"There, Ishmael," he said, laying the document and the gold on the table before the young man; "there is your first brief and your first fee! Let me tell you it is a very unusual windfall for an unfledged lawyer like you."

"I suppose I owe this to yourself, sir," said Ishmael.

"You owe it to your own merits, my lad! I will tell you all about it. To-day I met in the court an old acquaintance of mine—Mr. Ralph Walsh. He has been separated from his wife for some time past, living in the South; but he has recently returned to the city, and has sought a reconciliation with her, which, for some reason or other, she has refused. He next tried to get possession of their children, in order to coerce her through her affection for them; but she suspected his design and frustrated it by removing the children to a place of secrecy. All this Walsh told me this morning in the court, where he had come to get the habeas corpus served upon the woman ordering her to produce the children in court. It will be granted, of course, and he will sue for the possession of the children, and his wife will contest the suit; she will contest it in vain, of course, for the law always gives the father possession of the children, unless he is morally, mentally, or physically incapable of taking care of them—which is not the case with Walsh; he is sound in mind, body, and reputation; there is nothing to be said against him in either respect."

"What, then, divided him from his family?" inquired Ishmael doubtfully.

"Oh, I don't know; he had a wandering turn of mind, and loved to travel a great deal; he has been all over the civilized and uncivilized world, too, I believe."

"And what did she do, in the meantime?" inquired Ishmael, still more doubtfully.

"She? Oh, she kept a little day-school."

"What, was that necessary?"

"I suppose so, else she would not have kept it."

"But did not he contribute to the support of the family?"

"I—don't know; I fear not."

"There was nothing against the wife's character?"

"Not a breath! How should there be, when she keeps a respectable school? And when he himself wishes, in getting possession of the children, only to compel her through her love for them to come to him."

"Seething the kid in its mother's milk, or something quite as cruel," murmured Ishmael to himself.

The judge, who did not know what he was muttering to himself, continued:

"Well, there is the case, as Walsh delivered it to me. If there is anything else of importance connected with the case, you will doubtless find it in the brief. He actually offered the brief to me at first. He has been so long away that he did not know my present position, and that I had long since ceased to practice. So when he met me in the courtroom to-day he greeted me as an old friend, told me his business at the court, said that he considered the meeting providential, and offered me his brief. I explained to him the impossibility of my taking it, and then he begged me to recommend some lawyer. I named you to him without hesitation, giving you what I considered only your just meed of praise. He immediately asked me to take charge of the brief and the retaining fee, and offer both to you in his name, and say to you that he should call early to-morrow morning to consult with you."

"I am very grateful to you, Judge Merlin, for your kind interest in my welfare," said Ishmael warmly.

"Not at all, my lad; for I owe you much, Ishmael. You have been an invaluable assistant to me. Doing a great deal more for me than the letter of your duty required."

"I do not think so, sir; but I am very glad to have your approbation."

"Thank you, boy; but now, Ishmael, to business. You cannot do better than to take this brief. It is the very neatest little case that ever a lawyer had; all the plain law on your side; a dash of the sentimental, too, in the injured father's affection for the children that have been torn from him, the injured husband for the wife that repudiates him. Now you are good at law, but you are great at sentiment, Ishmael, and between having law on your side and sentiment at your tongue's end, you will be sure to succeed and come off with flying colors. And such success in his first case is of the utmost importance to a young lawyer. It is in fact the making of his fortune. You will have a shower of briefs follow this success."

"I do not know that I shall take the brief, sir," said Ishmael thoughtfully.

"Not take the brief? Are you mad? Who ever heard of a young lawyer refusing to take such a brief as that?—accompanied by such a retaining fee as that?—the brief the neatest and safest little case that ever came before a court! the retaining fee a hundred dollars! and no doubt he will hand you double that sum when you get your decision—for whatever his fortune has been in times past, he is rich now, this Walsh!" said the judge vehemently.

"Who is the counsel for the other side?" asked Ishmael.

"Ha, ha, ha! there's where the shoe hurts, is it? there's where the pony halts? that's what's the matter? You are afraid of encountering some of the great guns of the law, are you? Don't be alarmed. The schoolmistress is too poor to pay for distinguished legal talent. She may get some briefless pettifogger to appear for her; a man set up for you to knock down. Your case is just what the first case of a young lawyer should be—plain sailing, law distinctly on your side, dash of sentiment, domestic affections, and all that, and certain success at the end. Your victory will be as easy as it will be complete."

"Poor thing!" murmured Ishmael; "too poor to employ talent for the defense of her possession of her own children!"

"Come, my lad; pocket your fee and take up your brief," said the judge.

"I would rather not, sir; I do not like to appear against a woman—a mother defending her right in her own children. It appears to me to be cruel to wish to deprive her of them," said the gentle-spirited young lawyer.

"Cruel; it is merciful rather. No one wishes really to deprive her of them, but to give them to their father, that she may be drawn through her love for them to live with him."

"No woman should be so coerced, sir; no man should wish her to be."

"But I tell you it is for her good to be reunited to her husband."

"Her own heart, taught by her own instincts and experiences, is the best judge of that."

"Ishmael don't be Quixotic: if you do, you will never succeed in the legal profession. In this case the law is on the father's side, and you should be on the law's."

"The law is the minister of justice, and shall never in my hands become the accomplice of injustice. The law may be on the father's side; but that remains to be proved when both sides shall be heard; but it appears to me that justice and mercy are on the mother's side."

"That remains to be proved. Come, boy, don't be so mad as to refuse this golden opening to fame and fortune! Pocket your fee and take up your brief."

"Judge Merlin, I thank you from the depths of my heart for your great goodness in procuring this chance for me; and I beg that you will pardon me for what I am about to say—but I cannot touch either fee or brief. The case is a case of cruelty, sir, and I cannot have anything to do with it. I cannot make my debut in a court of law against a poor woman,—a poor mother,—to tear from her the babes she is clasping to her bosom."

"Ishmael, if those are the sentiments and principles under which you mean to act, you will never attain the fame to which your talents might otherwise lead you—never!"

"No, never," said Ishmael fervently; "never, if to reach it I have to step upon a woman's heart! No! by the sacred grave of my own dear mother, I never will!" And the face of Nora's son glowed with an earnest, fervent, holy love.

"Be a poet, Ishmael, you will never be a lawyer."

"Never—if to be a lawyer I have to cease to be a man! But it is as God wills."

The ringing of the tea-bell broke up the conference, and they went down into the parlor, where, beside the family, they found Viscount Vincent.

And Ishmael Worth, the weaver's son, had the honor of sitting down to tea with a live lord.

The viscount spent the evening, and retired late.

As Ishmael bade the family good-night, the judge said:

"My young friend, consult your pillow. I always do, when I can, before making any important decision. Think over the matter well, my lad, and defer your final decision about the brief until you see Walsh to-morrow."

"You are very kind to me, sir. I will follow your advice, as far as I may do so," replied Ishmael.

That night, lying upon his bed, Ishmael's soul was assailed with temptation. He knew that in accepting the brief offered to him, in such flattering terms, he should in the first place very much please his friend, Judge Merlin—who, though he did not give his young assistant anything like a fair salary for his services, yet took almost a fatherly interest in his welfare; he knew also, in the second place, that he might—nay, would—open his way to a speedy success and a brilliant professional career, which would, in a reasonable space of time, place him in a position even to aspire to the hand of Claudia Merlin. Oh, most beautiful of temptations that! To refuse the brief, he knew, would be to displease Judge Merlin, and to defer his own professional success for an indefinite length of time.

All night long Ishmael struggled with the tempter. In the morning he arose from his sleepless pillow unrefreshed and fevered. He bathed his burning head, made his morning toilet, and sat down to read a portion of the Scripture, as was his morning custom, before beginning the business of the day. The portion selected this morning was the fourth chapter of Matthew, describing the fast and the temptation of our Saviour. Ishmael had read this portion of Scripture many times before, but never with such deep interest as now, when it seemed to answer so well his own spirit's need. With the deepest reverence he read the words:

"When he had fasted forty days and forty nights, he was afterwards an hungered.

"The devil taketh him up into an exceeding high mountain, and showeth him all the kingdoms of the world and the glory of them;

"And saith unto him, All these things will I give thee if thou wilt fall down and worship me.

"Then saith Jesus unto him, Get thee hence, Satan: for it is written, Thou shalt worship the Lord thy God, and him only shalt thou serve.

"Then the devil leaveth him, and behold, angels came and ministered unto him."

Ishmael closed the book and bowed his head in serious thought.

"Yes," he said to himself; "I suppose it must be so. The servant is not greater than the Master. He was tempted in the very opening of his ministry; and I suppose every follower of him must be tempted in like manner in the beginning of his life. I, also, here in the commencement of my professional career, am subjected to a great temptation, that must decide, once for all, whether I will serve God or Satan! I, too, have had a long, long fast— a fast from all the pleasant things of this world, and I am an hungered—ah, very much hungered for some joys! I, too, am offered success and honor and glory if I will but fall down and worship Satan in the form of the golden fee and the cruel brief held out to me. But I will not. Oh, Heaven helping me, I will be true to my highest convictions of duty! Yes—come weal or come woe, I will be true to God. I will be a faithful steward of the talents he has intrusted to me."

And with this resolution in his heart Ishmael went down into the library and commenced his usual morning's work of answering letters and writing out law documents. He found an unusual number of letters to write, and they occupied him until the breakfast bell rang.

After breakfast Ishmael returned to the library and resumed his work, and was busily engaged in engrossing a deed of conveyance when the door opened and Judge Merlin entered accompanied by a tall, dark-haired, handsome, and rather prepossessing-looking man, of about fifty years of age, whom he introduced as Mr. Walsh.

Ishmael arose to receive the visitor, and offer him a chair, which he took.

The judge declined the seat Ishmael placed for him, and said:

"No, I will leave you with your client, Ishmael, that he may explain his business at full length. I have an engagement at the State Department, and I will go to keep it."

And the judge bowed and left the room.

As soon as they were left alone Mr. Walsh began to explain his business, first saying that he presumed Judge Merlin had handed him the retaining fee and the brief.

"Yes; you will find both there on the table beside you, untouched," answered Ishmael gravely.

"Ah, you have not had time yet to look at the brief. No matter; we can go over it together," said Mr. Walsh, taking up the document in question, and beginning to unfold it.

"I beg you will excuse me, sir; I would rather not look at the brief, as I cannot take the case," said Ishmael.

"You cannot take the case? Why, I understood from Judge Merlin that your time was not quite filled up; that you were not overwhelmed with cases, and that you could very well find time to conduct mine. Can you not do so?"

"It is not a question of time or the pressure of business. I have an abundance of the first and very little of the last. In fact, sir, I have been but very recently admitted to the bar, and have not yet been favored with a single case; I am as yet a briefless lawyer."

"Not briefless if you take my brief; for the judge speaks in the highest terms of your talents; and I know that a young barrister always bestows great care upon his first case," said Mr. Walsh pleasantly.

"Pray excuse me, sir; but I decline the case."

"But upon what ground?"

"Upon the ground of principle, sir. I cannot array myself against a mother who is defending her right to the possession of her own babes," said Ishmael gravely.

"Oh, I see! chivalric! Well, that is very becoming in a young man. But, bless you, my dear sir, you are mistaken in your premises. I do not really wish to part the mother and children. If you will give me your attention, I will explain—" began the would-be client.

"I beg that you will not, sir; excuse me, I pray you; but as I really cannot take the case, I ought not to hear your statement."

"Oh, nonsense, my young friend! I know what is the matter with you; but when you have heard my statement, you will accept my brief," said Walsh pleasantly, for, according to a well-known principle in human nature, he grew anxious to secure the services of the young barrister just in proportion to the difficulty of getting them.

And so, notwithstanding the courteous remonstrances of Ishmael, he commenced and told his story.

It was the story of an egotist so intensely egotistical as to be quite unconscious of his egotism; forever thinking of himself—forever oblivious of others except as they ministered to his self-interest; filled up to the lips with the feeling of his rights and privileges; but entirely empty of any notion of his duties and responsibilities. With him it was always "I," "mine," "me"; never "we," "ours," "us."

Ishmael listened under protest to this story that was forced upon his unwilling ears. At its end, when the narrator was waiting to see what impression he had made upon his young hearer, and what comment the latter would make, Ishmael calmly arose, took the brief from the table and put it into the hands of Mr. Walsh, saying, with a dignity—aye, even a majesty of mien rarely found in so young a man:

"Take your brief, sir; nothing on earth could induce me to touch it!"

"What! not after the full explanation I have given you?" exclaimed the man in naïve surprise.

"If I had entertained a single doubt about the propriety of refusing your brief before hearing your explanation, that doubt would have been set at rest after hearing it," said the young barrister sternly.

"What do you mean, sir?" questioned the other, bristling up.

"I mean that the case, even by your own plausible showing, is one of the greatest cruelty and injustice," replied Ishmael firmly.

"Cruelty and injustice!" exclaimed Mr. Walsh, in even more astonishment than anger. "Why, what the deuce do you mean by that? The woman is my wife! the children are my own children! And I have a lawful right to the possession of them. I wonder what the deuce you mean by cruelty and injustice!"

"By your own account, you left your wife nine years ago without provocation, and without making the slightest provision for herself and her children; you totally neglected them from that time to this; leaving her to struggle alone and unaided through all the privations and perils of such an unnatural position; during all these years she has worked for the support and education of her children; and now, at last, when it suits you to live with her again, you come back, and finding that you have irrecoverably lost her confidence and estranged her affections, you would call in the aid of the law to tear her children from her arms, and coerce her, through her love for them, to become your slave and victim again. Sir, sir, I am amazed that any man of—I will not say honor or honesty, but common sense and prudence—should dare to think of throwing such a case as that into court," said Ishmael earnestly.

"What do you mean by that, sir? Your language is inadmissible, sir! The law is on my side, however!"

"If the law were on your side, the law ought to be remodeled without delay; but if you venture to go to trial with such a case as this, you will find the law is not on your side. You have forfeited all right to interfere with Mrs. Walsh, or her children; and I would earnestly advise you to avoid meeting her in court."

"Your language is insulting, sir! Judge Merlin held a different opinion from yours of this case!" exclaimed Mr. Walsh, with excitement.

"Judge Merlin could not have understood the merits of the case. But it is quite useless to prolong this interview, sir; I have an engagement at ten o'clock and must wish you good-morning," said Ishmael, rising and ringing the bell, and then drawing on his gloves.

Jim answered the summons and entered the room.

"Attend this gentleman to the front door," said Ishmael, taking up his own hat as if to follow the visitor from the room.

"Mr. Worth, you have insulted me, sir!" exclaimed Walsh excitedly, as he arose and snatched up his money and his brief.

"I hope I am incapable of insulting any man, sir. You forced upon me a statement that I was unwilling to receive; you asked my opinion upon it and I gave it to you," replied Ishmael.

"I will have satisfaction, sir!" exclaimed Walsh, clapping his hat upon his head and marching to the door.

"Any satisfaction that I can conscientiously afford you shall be heartily at your service, Mr. Walsh," said Ishmael, raising his hat and bowing courteously at the retreating figure of the angry visitor.

When he was quite gone Ishmael took up his parcels of letters and documents and went out. He went first to the post office to mail his letters, and then went to the City Hall, where the Circuit Court was sitting.

As Ishmael walked on towards the City Hall he thought over the dark story he had just heard. He knew very well that, according to the custom of human nature, the man, however truthful in intention, had put the story in its fairest light; and yet how dark, with sin on one side and sorrow on the other, it looked! And if it looked so dark from his fair showing, how much darker it must look from the other point of view! A deep pity for the woman took possession of his heart; an earnest wish to help her inspired his mind. He thought of his own young mother, whom he had never seen, yet always loved.

And he resolved to assist this poor mother, who had no money to pay counsel to help her defend her children, because it took every cent she could earn to feed and clothe them.

"Yes, the cause of the oppressed is the cause of God! And I will offer the fruits of my professional labors to him," said Nora's son, as he reached the City Hall.

Ishmael was not one to wait for a "favorable opportunity." Few opportunities ever came to him except in the shape of temptations, which he resisted. He made his opportunities. So when the business that brought him to the courtroom was completed, he turned his steps towards Capitol Hill. For he had learned from the statements of Judge Merlin and Mr. Walsh that it was there the poor mother kept her little day-school. After some inquiries, he succeeded in finding the schoolhouse—a little white frame building, with a front and back door and four windows, two on each side, in a little yard at the corner of the street. Ishmael opened the gate and rapped at the door. It was opened by a little girl, who civilly invited him to enter.

A little school of about a dozen small girls, of the middle class in society, seated on forms ranged in exact order on each side the narrow aisle that led up to the teacher's desk. Seated behind that desk was a little, thin, dark-haired woman, dressed in a black alpaca and white collar and cuffs. At the entrance of Ishmael she glanced up with large, scared-looking black eyes that seemed to fear in every stranger to see an enemy or peril. As Ishmael advanced towards her those wild eyes grew wilder with terror, her cheeks blanched to a deadly whiteness, and she clasped her hands and she trembled.

"Poor hunted hare! she fears even in me a foe!" thought Ishmael, as he walked up to the desk. She arose and leaned over the desk, looking at him eagerly and inquiringly with those frightened eyes.

And now for the first time Ishmael felt a sense of embarrassment. A generous, youthful impulse to help the oppressed had hurried him to her presence; but what should he say to her? how apologize for his unsolicited visit? how venture, unauthorized, to intermeddle with her business?

He bowed and laid his card before her.

She snatched it up and read it eagerly.

Ishmael Worth,
Attorney-at-Law.

"Ah! you—I have been expecting this. You come from my—I mean Mr. Walsh?" she inquired, palpitating with panic.

"No, madam," said Ishmael, in a sweet, reassured, and reassuring tone, for compassion for her had restored confidence to him. "No, madam, I am not the counsel of Mr. Walsh."

"You—you come from court, then? Perhaps you are going to have the writ of habeas corpus, with which I have been threatened, served upon me? You need not! I won't give up my children—they are my own! I won't for twenty writs of habeas corpus," she exclaimed excitedly.

"But, madam—" began Ishmael soothingly.

"Hush! I know what you are going to say; you needn't say it! You are going to tell me that a writ of habeas corpus is the most powerful engine the law can bring to bear upon me! that to resist it would be flagrant contempt of court, subjecting me to fine and imprisonment! I do not care! I do not care! I have contempt, a very profound contempt, for any court, or any law, that would try to wrest from a Christian mother the children that she has borne, fed, clothed, and educated all herself, and give them to a man who has totally neglected them all their lives. Nature is hard enough upon woman, the Lord knows! giving her a weaker frame and a heavier burden than is allotted to man! but the law is harder still—taking from her the sacred rights with which nature in compensation has invested her! But I will not yield mine! There! Do your worst! Serve your writ of habeas corpus! I will resist it! I will not give up my own children! I will not bring them into court! I will not tell you where they are! They are in a place of safety, thank God! and as for me—fine, imprison, torture me as much as you like, you will find me rock!" she exclaimed, with her eyes flashing and all her little dark figure bristling with terror and resistance, for all the world like a poor little frightened kitten spluttering defiance at a big dog!

Ishmael did not interrupt her; he let her go on with her wild talk; he had been too long used to poor Hannah's excitable nerves not to have learned patience with women.

"Yes, you will find me rock—rock!" she repeated; and to prove how much of a rock she was, the poor little creature dropped her head upon the desk, burst into tears, and sobbed hysterically.

Ishmael's experience taught him to let her sob on until her fit of passion had exhausted itself.

Meanwhile one or two of the most sensitive little girls, seeing their teacher weep, fell to crying for company; others whispered among themselves; and others, again, looked belligerent.

"Go tell him to go away, Mary," said the little one.

"I don't like to; you go, Ellen," said another.

"I'm afraid."

"Oh! you scary things! I'll go myself," said a third; and, rising, this little one came to the rescue, and standing up firmly before the intruder said:

"What do you come here for, making our teacher cry? Go home this minute; if you don't I'll run right across the street and fetch my father from the shop to you! he's as big as you are!"

Ishmael turned his beautiful eyes upon this little champion of six summers, and smiling upon her, said gently:

"I did not come here to make anybody cry, my dear; I came to do your teacher a service."

The child met his glance with a searching look, such as only babes can give, and turned and went back and reported to her companions.

"He's good; he won't hurt anybody."

Mrs. Walsh having sobbed herself into quietness, wiped her eyes, looked up and said:

"Well, sir, why don't you proceed with your business? Why don't you serve your writ?"

"My dear madam, it is not my business to serve writs. And if it was I have none to serve," said Ishmael very gently.

She looked at him in doubt.

"You have mistaken my errand here, madam. I am not retained on the other side; I have nothing whatever to do with the other side. I have heard your story; my sympathies are with you; and I have come here to offer you my professional services," said Ishmael gravely.

She looked at him earnestly, as if she would read his soul. The woman of thirty was not so quick at reading character as the little child of six had been.

"Have you counsel?" inquired Ishmael.

"Counsel? No! Where should I get it?"

"Will you accept me as counsel? I came here to offer you my services."

"I tell you I have no means, sir."

"I do not want any remuneration in your case; I wish to serve you, for your own sake and for God's; something we must do for God's sake and for our fellow creatures'. I wish to be your counsel in the approaching trial. I think, with the favor of Divine Providence, I can bring your case to a successful issue and secure you in the peaceful possession of your children."

"Do you think so? Oh! do you think so?" she inquired eagerly, warmly.

"I really do. I think so, even from the showing of the other side, who, of course, put the fairest face upon their own cause."

"And will you? Oh! will you?"

"With the help of Heaven, I will."

"Oh, surely Heaven has sent you to my aid."

At this moment the little school clock struck out sharply the hour of noon.

"It is the children's recess," said the teacher. "Lay aside your books, dears, and leave the room quietly and in good order."

The children took their hoods and cloaks from the pegs on which they hung and went out one by one—each child turning to make her little courtesy before passing the door. Thus all went out but two little sisters, who living at a distance had brought their luncheon, which they now took to the open front door, where they sat on the steps in the pleasant winter sunshine to eat.

The teacher turned to her young visitor.

"Will you sit down? And ah! will you pardon me for the rude reception I gave you?"

"Pray do not think of it. It was so natural that I have not given it a thought," said Ishmael gently.

"It is not my disposition to do so; but I have suffered so much; I have been goaded nearly to desperation."

"I see that, madam; you are exceedingly nervous."

"Nervous! why, women have been driven to madness and death with less cause than I have had!"

"Do not think of your troubles in that manner, madam; do not excite yourself, compose yourself, rather. Believe me, it is of the utmost importance to your success that you should exhibit coolness and self-possession."

"Oh, but I have had so much sorrow for so many years!"

"Then in the very nature of things your sorrows must soon be over. Nothing lasts long in this world. But you have had a recent bereavement," said Ishmael gently, and glancing at her black dress; for he thought it was better that she should think of her chastening from the hands of God rather than her wrongs from those of men. But to his surprise, the woman smiled faintly as she also glanced at her dress, and replied:

"Oh, no! I have lost no friend by death since the decease of my parents years ago, far back in my childhood. No, I am not wearing mourning for anyone. I wear this black alpaca because it is cheap and decent and protective."

"Protective?"

"Ah, yes! no one knows how protective the black dress is to a woman, better than I do! There are few who would venture to treat with levity or disrespect a quiet woman in a black dress. And so I, who have no father, brother, or husband to protect me, take a shelter under a black alpaca. It repels dirt, too, as well as disrespect. It is clean as well as safe, and that is a great desideratum to a poor schoolmistress," she said, smiling with an almost childlike candor.

"I am glad to see you smile again; and now, shall we go to business?" said Ishmael.

"Oh, yes, thank you."

"I must ask you to be perfectly candid with me; it is necessary."

"Oh, yes, I know it is, and I will be so; for I can trust you, now."

"Tell me, then, as clearly, as fully, and as calmly as you can, the circumstances of your case."

"I will try to do so," said the woman.

It is useless to repeat her story here. It was only the same old story—of the young girl of fortune marrying a spendthrift, who dissipated her property, estranged her friends, alienated her affections, and then left her penniless, to struggle alone with all the ills of poverty to bring up her three little girls. By her own unaided efforts she had fed, clothed, and educated her three children for the last nine years. And now he had come back and wanted her to live with him again. But she had not only ceased to love him, but began to dread him, lest he should get into debt and make way with the little personal property she had gathered by years of labor, frugality, self-denial.

"He says that he is wealthy, how is that?" questioned Ishmael.

A spasm of pain passed over her sensitive face.

"I did not like to tell you, although I promised to be candid with you; but ah! I cannot benefit by his wealth; I could not conscientiously appropriate one dollar; and even if I could do so, I could not trust in its continuance; the money is ill-gotten and evanescent; it is the money of a gambler, who is a prince one hour and a pauper the next."

Then seeing Ishmael shrink back in painful surprise, she added:

"To do him justice, Mr. Worth, that is his only vice; it has ruined my little family; it has brought us to the very verge of beggary; it must not be permitted to do so again; I must defend my little home and little girls, against the spoiler."

"Certainly," said Ishmael, whose time was growing short; "give me pen and ink; I will take down minutes of the statement, and then read it to you, to see if it is correct."

She placed stationery before him on one of the school-desks, and he sat down and went to work.

"You have witnesses to support your statement?" he inquired.

"Oh, yes! scores of them, if wanted."

"Give me the names of the most important and the facts they can swear to."

Mrs. Walsh complied, and he took them down. When he had finished and read over the brief to her, and received her assurance that it was correct, he arose to take his leave.

"But—will not all those witnesses cost a great deal of money? And will not there be other heavy expenses apart from the services of counsel that you are so good as to give me?" inquired the teacher anxiously.

"Not for you," replied Ishmael, in a soothing voice, as he shook hands with her, and, with the promise to see her again at the same hour the next day, took his leave.

He smiled upon the little sisters as he passed them in the doorway, and then left the schoolhouse and hurried on towards home.

"Well!" said Judge Merlin, who was waiting for him in the library, "have you decided? Are you counsel for the plaintiff in the great suit of Walsh versus Walsh?"

"No," answered Ishmael, "I am retained for the defendant. I have just had a consultation with my client."

"Great Jove!" exclaimed the judge, in unbounded astonishment. "It was raving madness in you to refuse the plaintiff's brief; but to accept the defendant's——"

· "I did not only accept it—I went and asked for it," said Ishmael, smiling.

"Mad! mad! You will lose your first case; and that will throw back your success for years!"

"I hope not, sir. 'Thrice is he armed who hath his quarrel just,'" smiled Ishmael.

At the luncheon table that day the judge told the story of Ishmael's quixotism, as he called it, in refusing the brief and the thumping fee of the plaintiff, who had the law all on his side; and whom his counsel would be sure to bring through victoriously; and taking in hand the course of the defendant, who had no money to pay her counsel, no law on her side, and who was bound to be defeated.

"But she has justice and mercy on her side; and it shall go hard but I prove the law on her side, too."

"A forlorn hope, Ishmael, a forlorn hope!" said Mr. Middleton.

"Forlorn hopes are always led by heroes, papa," said Bee.

"And fools!" blurted out Judge Merlin.

Ishmael did not take offense, he knew all that was said was well meant; the judge talked to him with the plainness of a parent; and Ishmael rather enjoyed being affectionately blown up by Claudia's father.

Miss Merlin now looked up, and condescended to say:

"I am very sorry, Ishmael, that you refused the rich client; he might have been the making of you."

"The making of Ishmael. With the blessing of Heaven, he will make himself! I am very glad he refused the oppressor's gold!" exclaimed Bee, before Ishmael could reply.

When Bee ceased to speak, he said:

"I am very sorry, Miss Merlin, to oppose your sentiments in any instance, but in this I could not do otherwise."

"It is simply a question of right or wrong. If the man's cause was bad, Ishmael was right to refuse his brief; if the woman's cause was good, he was right to take her brief," said Mrs. Middleton, as they all arose from the table.

That evening Ishmael found himself by chance alone in the drawing room with Bee.

He was standing before the front window, gazing sadly into vacancy. The carriage, containing Miss Merlin, Lord Vincent, and Mrs. Middleton as chaperone, had just rolled away from the door. They were going to a dinner party at the President's. And Ishmael was gazing sadly after them, when Bee came up to his side and spoke:

"I am very glad, Ishmael, that you have taken sides with the poor mother; it was well done."

"Thank you, dear Bee! I hope it was well done; I do not regret doing it; but they say that I have ruined my prospects."

"Do not believe it, Ishmael. Have more faith in the triumph of right against overwhelming odds. I like the lines you quoted—' Thrice is he armed who feels his quarrel just!' The poets teach us a great deal, Ishmael. Only to-day I happened to be reading in Scott—in one of his novels, by the way, this was, however—of the deadly encounter in the lists between the Champion of the Wrong, the terrible knight Brian de Bois Guilbert, and the Champion of Right, the gentle knight Ivanhoe. Do you remember, Ishmael, how Ivanhoe arose from his bed of illness, pale, feeble, reeling, scarcely able to bear the weight of his armor, or to sit his horse, much less encounter such a thunderbolt of war as Bois Guilbert? There seemed not a hope in the world for Ivanhoe. Yet, in the first encounter of the knights, it was the terrible Bois Guilbert that rolled in the dust. Might is not right; but right is might, Ishmael!"

"I know it, dear Bee; thank you, thank you, for making me feel it also!" said Ishmael fervently.

"The alternative presented to you last night and this morning was sent as a trial, Ishmael; such a trial as I think every man must encounter once in his life, as a decisive test of his spirit. Even our Saviour was tempted, offered all the kingdoms of this world, and the glory of them, if he would fall down and worship Satan. But he rebuked the tempter and the Devil fled from him."

"And angels came and ministered to him," said Ishmael, in a voice of ineffable tenderness, as the tears filled his eyes and he approached his arm toward Bee. His impulse was to draw her to his bosom and press a kiss on her brow—as a brother's embrace of a loved sister; but Ishmael's nature was as refined and delicate as it was fervent and earnest; and he abstained from this caress; he said instead:

"You are my guardian angel, Bee. I have felt it long, little sister; you never fail in a crisis!"

"And while I live I never will, Ishmael. You will not need man's help, for you will help yourself, but what woman may do to aid and comfort, that will I do for you, my brother,"

"What a heavenly spirit is yours, Bee," said Ishmael fervently.

"And now let us talk of business, please," said practical little Bee, who never indulged in sentiment long. "That poor mother! You give her your services—gratuitously of course?"

"Certainly," said Ishmael.

"But, apart from her counsel's fee, will she not have other expenses to meet in conducting this suit?"

"Yes."

"How will she meet them?"

"Bee, dear, I have saved a little money; I mean to use it in her service."

"What!" exclaimed the young girl; "do you mean to give her your professional aid and pay all her expenses besides?"

"Yes," said Ishmael, "as far as the money will go. I do this, dear Bee, as a 'thank offering' to the Lord for all the success he has given me, up to this time. When I think of the days of my childhood in that poor Hill hut, and compare them to these days, I am deeply impressed by the mercy he has shown me; and I think that I can never do enough to show my gratitude. I consider it the right and proper thing to offer the first fruits of my professional life to him, through his suffering children."

"You are right, Ishmael, for God has blessed your earnest efforts, as, indeed, he would bless those of anyone so conscientious and persevering as yourself. But, Ishmael, will you have money enough to carry on the suit?"

"I hope so, Bee; I do not know."

"Here, then, Ishmael, take this little roll of notes; it is a hundred dollars; use it for the woman," she said, putting in his hand a small parcel.

Ishmael hesitated a moment; but Bee hastened to reassure him by saying:

"You had as well take it as not, Ishmael. I can very well spare it, or twice as much. Papa makes me a much larger allowance than one of my simple tastes can spend. And I should like," she added, smiling, "to go partners with you in this enterprise."

"I thank you, dear Bee; and I will take your generous donation and use it, if necessary. It may not be necessary," said Ishmael.

"And now I must leave you, Ishmael, and go to little Lu; she is not well this evening." And the little Madonna-like maiden glided like a spirit from the room.

The next morning Ishmael went to see his client. He showed her the absolute necessity of submission to the writ of habeas corpus; he promised to use his utmost skill in her case; urged her to trust the result with her Heavenly Father; and encouraged her to hope for success.

She followed Ishmael's advice; she promised to obey the order, adding:

"It will be on Wednesday in Easter week. That will be fortunate, as the school will have a holiday, and I shall be able to attend without neglecting the work that brings us bread."

"Are the children far away? Can you get them without inconvenience in so short a time?" inquired Ishmael.

"Oh, yes; they are in the country, with a good honest couple named Gray, who were here on the Christmas holidays, and boarded with my aunt, who keeps the Farmer's Rest, near the Center Market. My aunt recommended them to me, and when I saw the man I felt as if I could have trusted uncounted gold with him—

233

he looked so true! He and his wife took my three little girls home with them, and would not take a cent of pay; and they have kept my secret religiously."

"They have indeed!" said Ishmael, in astonishment; "for they are my near relatives and never even told me."

CHAPTER LVI.

TRIAL AND TRIUMPH.

Let circumstance oppose him,
He bends it to his will;
And if the flood o'erflows him,
He dives and steins it still;
No hindering dull material
Shall conquer or control
His energies ethereal,
His gladiator soul!
Let lower spirits linger,
For hint and beck and nod,
He always sees the finger
Of an onward urging God!
—*M.F. Tupper.*

Like most zealous, young professional men, Ishmael did a great deal more work for his first client than either custom or duty exacted of him.

Authorized by her, he wrote to Reuben Gray to bring the children to the city.

And accordingly, in three days after, Reuben arrived at the Farmer's Rest, with his wagon full of family. For he not only brought the three little girls he was required to bring, but also Hannah, her children, and her nurse-maid Sally.

As soon as he had seen his party in comfortable quarters he walked up to the Washington House to report himself to Ishmael; for, somehow or other, Reuben had grown to look upon Ishmael as his superior officer in the battle of life, and did him honor, very much as the veteran sergeant does to the young captain of his company.

Arrived in Ishmael's room, he took off his hat and said:

"Here I am, sir; and I've brung 'em all along."

"All Mrs. Walsh's little girls, of course, for they are required," said Ishmael, shaking hands with Gray.

"Yes, and all the rest on 'em, Hannah and the little uns, and Sally and Sam," said Reuben, rubbing his hands gleefully.

"But that was a great task!" said Ishmael, in surprise.

"Well, no, it wasn't, sir; not half so hard a task as it would have been to a left them all behind, poor things. You see, sir, the reason why I brung 'em all along was because I sort o' think they love me a deal; 'pon my soul I do, sir, old and gray and rugged as I am; and I don't like to be parted from 'em, 'specially from Hannah, no, not for a day; 'cause the dear knows, sir, as we was parted long enough, poor Hannah and me; and now as we is married, and the Lord has donated us a son and daughter at the eleventh hour, unexpected, praise be unto him for all his mercies, I never mean to part with any on 'em no more, not even for a day, till death do us part, amen; but take 'em all 'long with me, wherever I'm called to go, 'specially as me and poor Hannah was married so late in life that we aint got many more years before us to be together."

"Nonsense, Uncle Reuben! You and Aunt Hannah will live forty or fifty years longer yet, and see your grandchildren, and maybe your great-grandchildren. You two are the stuff that centenarians are made of," exclaimed the young man cheeringly.

"Centenarians? what's them, sir?"

"People who live a hundred years."

"Law! Well, I have hearn of such things happening to other folks, and why not to me and poor Hannah? Why, sir, I would be the happiest man in the world, if I thought as how I had all them there years to live long o' Hannah and the little uns in this pleasant world. But his will be done!" said Gray, reverently raising his hat.

"The little girls are all right, I hope?" inquired Ishmael.

"Yes, sir; all on 'em, and a deal fatter and rosier and healthier nor they was when I fust took 'em down. Perty little darlings! Didn't they enjoy being in the country, neither, though it was the depth of winter time? Law, Ish—sir, I mean—it's a mortal sin ag'in natur' to keep chil'en in town if it can be helped! But their ma, poor thing, couldn't help it, I know. Law, Ish—sir, I mean—if you had seen her that same Christmas Day, as she ran in with her chil'en to her aunt as is hostess at the Farmer's. If ever you see a poor little white bantam trying to cover her chicks when the hawk was hovering nigh by, you may have some idea of the way she looked when she was trying to hide her chil'un and didn't know where; 'cause she daren't keep 'em at home and daren't hide 'em at her aunt's, for her home would be the first place inwaded and her aunt's the second. They was all so flustered, they took no more notice o' me standin' in the parlor 'n if I had been a pillar-post,'till feeling of pityful towards the poor things, I made so bold to go forward and offer to take 'em home 'long o' me, and which was accepted with thanks and tears as soon as the landlady recommended me as an old acquaintance and well-beknown to herself. So it was settled. That night when you come to spend the evening with us, Ish—sir, I mean—I really did feel guilty in having of a secret as I wouldn't tell you; but you see, sir, I was bound up to secrecy, and besides I thought as you was stopping in Washington City, if you knowed anythink about it you might be speened afore the court and be obliged to tell all, you know."

"You did quite right, Uncle Reuben," said Ishmael affectionately.

"You call me Uncle Reuben, sir?"

"Why not, Uncle Reuben? and why do you call me sir?"

"Well—sir, because you are a gentleman now—not but what you allers was a gentleman by natur'; but now you are one by profession. They say you have come to be a lawyer in the court, sir, and can stand up and plead before the judges theirselves."

"I have been admitted to the bar, Uncle Reuben."

"Yes, that's what they call it; see there now, you know, I'm only a poor ignorant man, and you have no call to own the like o' me for uncle, 'cause, come to the rights of it, I aint your uncle at all, sir, though your friend and well-wisher allers; and to claim the likes o' me as an uncle might do you a mischief with them as thinks riches and family and outside show and book-larning is everythink. So Ish—sir, I mean, I won't take no offense, nor likewise feel hurted, if you leaves oft calling of me uncle and calls me plain 'Gray,' like Judge Merlin does."

"Uncle Reuben," said Ishmael, with feeling, "I am very anxious to advance myself in the world, very ambitious of distinction; but if I thought worldly success would or could estrange me from the friends of my boyhood, I would cease to wish for it. If I must cease to be true, in order to be great, I prefer to remain in obscurity. Give me your hand, Uncle Reuben, and call me Ishmael, and know me for your boy."

"There, then, Ishmael! I'm glad to find you again! God bless my boy! But law! what's the use o' my axing of him to do that? He'll do it anyways, without my axing!" said Reuben, pressing the hand of Ishmael. "And now," he added, "will you be round to the Farmer's this evening to see Hannah and the young uns?"

"Yes, Uncle Reuben; but first I must go and let Mrs. Walsh know that you have brought her little girls back. I suppose she will think it best to leave them with her aunt until the day of trial."

"It will be the safest place for 'em! for besides the old lady being spunky, I shall be there to protect 'em; for I mean to stay till that same said trial and hear you make your fust speech afore the judge, and see that woman righted afore ever I goes back home again, ef it costs me fifty dollars."

"I'm afraid you will find it very expensive, Uncle Reuben."

"No, I won't, sir—Ishmael, I mean; because, you see, I fotch up a lot o' spring chickens and eggs and early vegetables, and the profits I shall get offen them will pay my expenses here at the very least," said Reuben, as he arose and stood waiting with hat in hand for Ishmael's motions.

Ishmael got up and took his own hat and gloves.

"Be you going round to see the schoolmist'ess now, sir—Ishmael, I mean?"

"Yes, Uncle Reuben."

"Well, I think I'd like to walk round with you, if you don't mind. I kind o' want to see the little woman, and I kind o' don't want to part with you just yet, sir—Ishmael, I mean."

"Come along, then, Uncle Reuben; she will be delighted to see her children's kind protector, and I shall enjoy your company on the way."

"And then, sir—Ishmael, I mean—when we have seen her, you will go back with me to the Farmer's and see Hannah and the little uns and spend the evening long of us?"

"Yes, Uncle Reuben; and I fancy Mrs. Walsh will go with us."

"Sartain, sure, so she will, sir—Ishmael, I mean."

It was too late to find her at the schoolhouse, as it would be sure to be closed at this hour. So they walked directly to the little suburban cottage where she lived with one faithful old negro servant, who had been her nurse, and with her cow and pig and poultry and her pet dog and cat. They made her heart glad with the news of the children's arrival, and they waited until, with fingers that trembled almost too much to do the work, she put on her bonnet and mantle to accompany them to the Farmer's.

The meeting between the mother and children was very affecting. She informed them that, this being Holy Thursday evening, she had dismissed the school for the Easter holidays, and so could be with them all the time until she should take them into court on Wednesday of the ensuing week.

Then in family council it was arranged that both herself and the children should remain at the Farmer's until the day of the trial.

As soon as all this matter was satisfactorily settled Ishmael arose and bid them all good-night, promising to repeat his visit often while his relatives remained at the hotel.

It was late when Ishmael reached home, but the drawing-room was ablaze with light, and as he passed its open door he saw that its only occupants were the Viscount Vincent and Claudia Merlin. They were together on the sofa, talking in low, confidential tones. How beautiful she looked! smiling up to the handsome face that was bent in deferential admiration over hers. A pang of love and jealousy wrung Ishmael's heart as he hurried past and ran up the stairs to his den. There he sat down at his desk, and, bidding vain dreams begone, concentrated his thoughts upon the work before him—the first speech he was to make at the bar.

Ishmael worked very hard the day preceding the trial; he took great pains getting up his case, not only for his own sake, but for the sake of that poor mother and her children in whom he felt so deeply interested.

No farther allusion was made to the affair by any member of Judge Merlin's family until Wednesday morning, when, as they all sat around the breakfast table, the judge said:

"Well, Ishmael, the case of Walsh versus Walsh comes on to-day, I hear. How do you feel? a little nervous over your first case, eh?"

"Not yet; I feel only great confidence in the justice of my cause, as an earnest of success."

"The justice of his cause! Poor fellow, how much he has to learn yet! Why, Ishmael, how many times have you seen justice overthrown by law?"

"Too many times, sir; but there is no earthly reason why that should happen in this case."

"Have you got your maiden speech all cut and dried and ready to deliver?"

"I have made some notes; but for the rest I shall trust to the inspiration of the instant."

"Bad plan that. 'Spose the inspiration don't come? or 'spose you lose your presence of mind? Better have your speech carefully written off, and then, inspiration or no inspiration, you will be able to read, at least."

"My notes are very carefully arranged; they contain the whole argument."

"And for the rest 'it shall be given ye in that hour, what ye shall speak,'" said Beatrice earnestly.

They all arose and left the table.

"Thank you, dearest Bee," said Ishmael, as he passed her.

"God aid you, Ishmael!" she replied fervently.

He hurried upstairs to collect his documents, and then hastened to the City Hall, where Mrs. Walsh and her children were to meet him.

He found them all in the ante-chamber of the courtroom, attended by a bodyguard composed of Reuben, Hannah, and the landlady.

He spoke a few encouraging words to his client, shook hands with the members of her party, and then took them all into the courtroom and showed them their places. The plaintiff was not present. The judges had not yet taken their seats. And the courtroom was occupied only by a few lawyers, clerks, bailiffs, constables, and other officials.

In a few minutes, however, the judges entered and took their seats; the crier opened the court, the crowd poured in, the plaintiff with his counsel made his appearance, and the business of the day commenced.

I shall not give all the details of this trial; I shall only glance at a few of them.

The courtroom was full, but not crowded; nothing short of a murder or a divorce case ever draws a crowd to such a place.

The counsel for the plaintiff was composed of three of the oldest, ablest, and most experienced members of the Washington bar. The first of these, Mr. Wiseman, was distinguished for his profound knowledge of the law, his skill in logic, and his closeness in reasoning; the second, Mr. Berners, was celebrated for his fire and eloquence; and the third, Mr. Vivian, was famous for his wit and sarcasm. Engaged on one side, they were considered invincible. To these three giants, with the law on their side, was opposed young Ishmael, with nothing but justice on his side. Bad look-out for justice! Well, so it was in that great encounter already alluded to between Brian and Ivanhoe.

Mr. Wiseman, for the plaintiff, opened the case. He was a great, big, bald-headed man, who laid down the law as a blacksmith hammers an anvil, in a clear, forcible, resounding manner, leaving the defense—as everybody declared—not a leg to stand upon.

"Oh, Mr. Worth! it is all over with me, and I shall die!" whispered Mrs. Walsh, in deadly terror.

"Have patience! his speech does not impress the court as it does you—they are used to him."

Witnesses were called, to prove as well as they could from a bad set of facts, what an excellent husband and father the plaintiff had been; how affectionate, how anxious, how zealous he was for the happiness of his wife and children—leaving it to be inferred that nothing on earth but her own evil tendencies instigated the wife to withdraw herself and children from his protection!

"Heaven and earth, Mr. Worth, did you ever hear anything like that? They manage to tell the literal truth, but so pervert it that it is worse than the worse falsehood!" exclaimed Mrs. Walsh, in a low but indignant tone.

"Aye," answered Ishmael, who sat, pencil and tablets in hand, taking notes; "aye! 'a lie that is half a truth is ever the blackest of lies.' But the court is accustomed to such witnesses; they do not receive so much credit as you or they think."

Ishmael did not cross-examine these witnesses; the great mass of rebutting testimony that he could bring forward, he knew, must overwhelm them. So when the last witness for the plaintiff had been examined, he whispered a few cheering words to the trembling woman by his side, and rose for the defendant. Now, whenever a new barrister takes the floor for the first time, there is always more or less curiosity and commotion among the old fogies of the forum.

What will he turn out to be? that is the question. All eyes were turned towards him.

They saw a tall, broad-shouldered, full-chested young man, who stood, with a certain dignity, looking upon the notes that he held in his hand; and when he lifted his stately head to address the court they saw that his face was not only beautiful in the noble mold of the features, but almost divine from the inspiring soul within.

Among the eyes that gazed upon him were those of the three giants of the law whom he had now to oppose. They stared at him mercilessly—no doubt with the intention of staring him down. But they did not even confuse him; for the simple reason that he did not look towards them. They might stare themselves stone blind, but they would have no magnetic influence upon that strong, concentrated, earnest soul!

Ishmael was not in the least embarrassed in standing up to address the court for the first time, simply because he was not thinking of himself or his audience, but of his client, and her case as he wished to set it forth; and he was not looking at the spectators, but alternately at the court and at the notes in his hand.

He did not make a long opening like the Giant Wiseman had done; for he wished to reserve himself for the closing speech in final reply to the others. He just made a plain statement of his client's case as it is in part known to the reader.

He told the court how, at the age of fifteen, she had been decoyed from her mother's house and married by the plaintiff, a man more than twice her age; how when she had come into her property he had squandered it all by a method that he, the plaintiff, called speculation, but that others called gambling; how he had then left her in poverty and embarrassment and with one child to support; how he remained away two years, during which time her friends had set his wife up in business in a little fancy store. She was prospering when he came back, took up his abode with her, got into debt which he could not pay, and when all her stock and furniture was seized to satisfy his creditors, he took himself off once more, leaving her with two children. She was worse off than before; her friends grumbled, but once more came to her assistance, set her up a little book and news agency, the stock of which was nearly all purchased on credit, and told her plainly that if she permitted her husband to come and break up her business again they would abandon and leave her to her fate. Notwithstanding this warning, when at the end of seven or eight months he came back again she received him again. He stayed with her thirteen months; and suddenly disappeared without bidding her good-by, leaving her within a few weeks of becoming the mother of a third child. A few days after his disappearance another execution was put into the house to satisfy a debt contracted by him, and everything was sold under the hammer. She was reduced to the last degree of poverty; her friends held themselves aloof, disgusted at what they termed her culpable weakness; she and her children suffered from cold and hunger; and during her subsequent illness she and they must have starved and frozen but for the public charities, that would not let anyone in our midst perish from want of necessary food and fuel. When she recovered from her illness, one relative, a widow now present in court, had from her own narrow means supplied the money to rent and furnish a small schoolroom, and this most hapless of women was once more put in a way to earn daily bread for herself and children. Nine years passed, during which she enjoyed a respite from the persecutions of the plaintiff. In these nine years, by strict attention to business, untiring industry, she not only paid off the debt owed to her aged relative, but she bought a little cottage and garden in a cheap suburb, and furnished the house and stocked the garden. She was now living a laborious but contented life and rearing her children in comfort. But now at the end of nine years comes back the plaintiff. Her husband? No, her enemy! for he comes, not as he pretends, to cherish and protect; but as he ever came before, to lay waste and destroy! How long could it be supposed that the mother would be able to keep the roof over the heads of her children if the plaintiff were permitted to enter beneath it? if the court did not protect her home against his invasion, he would again bring ruin and desolation within its walls. They would prove by competent witnesses every point in this statement of the defendant's case; and then he would demand for his client, not only that she should be secured in the undisturbed possession of her children, her property, and her earnings, but that the plaintiff should be required to contribute an annual sum of money to the support of the defendant and her children, and to give security for its payment.

"That's 'carrying the war into Africa' with a vengeance," whispered Walsh to his counsel, as Ishmael concluded his address.

He then called the witnesses for the defendant. They were numerous and of the highest respectability. Among them was the pastor of her parish, her family physician, and many of the patrons of her school.

They testified to the facts stated by her attorney.

The three giants did their duty in the cross-examining line of business. Wiseman cross-examined in a stern manner; Berners in an insinuating way; and Vivian in a sarcastic style; but the only effect of their forensic skill was to bring out the truth from the witnesses—more clearly, strongly, and impressively.

When the last witness for the defendant had been permitted to leave the stand Wiseman arose to address the court on behalf of the plaintiff. He spoke in his own peculiar sledge-hammer style, sonorously striking the anvil and ringing all the changes upon law, custom, precedent, and so forth that always gave the children into the custody of the father. And he ended by demanding that the children be at once delivered over to his client.

He was followed by Berners, who had charge of the eloquence "business" of that stage, and dealt in pathos, tears, white pocket handkerchiefs, and poetical quotations. He drew a most heart-rending picture of the broken-spirited husband and father, rejected by an unforgiving wife and ill-conditioned children, becoming a friendless and houseless wanderer over the wide world; in danger of being driven, by despair, to madness and suicide! He compared the plaintiff to Byron, whose poetry he liberally quoted. And he concluded by imploring the court, with tears in his eyes, to intervene and save his unhappy client from the gulf of perdition to which his implacable wife would drive him. And he sank down in his seat utterly overwhelmed by his feelings and holding a drift of white cambric to his face.

"Am I such an out-and-out monster, Mr. Worth?" whispered Mrs. Walsh, in dismay.

Ishmael smiled.

"Everybody knows Berners—his 'madness' and 'suicide,' his 'gulf of perdition' and his white cambric pocket-handkerchief are recognized institutions. See! the judge is actually smiling over it."

Mr. Vivian arose to follow—he did up the genteel comedy; he kept on hand a supply of "little jokes" gleaned from Joe Miller, current comic literature, dinner tables, clubs, etc.—"little jokes" of which every point in his discourse continually reminded him, though his hearers could not always perceive the association of ideas. This gentleman was very facetious over family jars, which reminded him of a "little joke," which he told; he was also very witty upon the subject of matrimonial disputes in particular, which reminded him of another "little joke," which he also told; but most of all, he was amused at the caprice of womankind, who very often rather liked to be compelled to do as they pleased, which reminded him of a third "little joke." And if the court should allow the defendant the exclusive possession of her children and a separate maintenance, it was highly probable that she would not thank them for their trouble, but would take the first opportunity of voluntarily reconciling herself to her husband and giving him back herself, her home, and her children, which would be equal to any "little joke" he had ever heard in his life, etc., etc., etc.

The audience were all in a broad grin. Even Mrs. Walsh, with her lips of "life-long sadness," smiled.

"You may smile at him," said Ishmael, "and so will I, since I do not at all doubt the issue of this trial; but for all that, joker as he is, he is the most serious opponent that we have. I would rather encounter half a dozen each of Wisemans and Berners than one Vivian. Take human nature in general, it can be more easily laughed than reasoned or persuaded in or out of any measure. People would rather laugh than weep or reflect. Wiseman tries to make them reflect, which they won't do; Berners tries to make them weep, which they can't do; but Vivian with his jokes makes them laugh, which they like to do. And so, he has joked himself into a very large practice at the Washington bar."

But the facetious barrister was bringing his speech to a close, with a brilliant little joke that eclipsed all the preceding ones and set the audience in a roar. And when the laughter had subsided, he finally ended by expressing a hope that the court would not so seriously disappoint and so cruelly wrong the defendant as by giving a decision in her favor.

CHAPTER LVII.

THE YOUNG CHAMPION.

Then uprose Gismond; and she knew
That she was saved. *Some* never met
His face before; but at first view
They felt quite sure that God had set
Himself to Satan; who could spend
A minute's mistrust on the end?

This pleased her most, that she enjoyed
The heart of her joy, with her content
In watching Gismond, unalloyed
By any doubt of the event;
God took that on him—she was bid
Watch Gismond for her part! She did.
—Browning.

Ishmael waited a few minutes for the excitement produced by the last address to subside—the last address that in its qualities and effects had resembled champagne—sparkling but transient, effervescent but evanescent. And when order had been restored Ishmael arose amid a profound silence to make his maiden speech, for the few opening remarks he had made in initiating the defense could scarcely be called a speech. Once more then all eyes were fixed upon him in expectancy. And, as before, he was undisturbed by these regards because he was unconscious of them; and he was calm because he was not thinking of himself or of the figure he was making, but of his client and her cause. He did not care to impress the crowd, he only wished to affect the court. So little did he think of the spectators in the room, that he did not observe that Judge Merlin, Claudia, and Beatrice were among them, seated in a distant corner—Judge Merlin and Claudia were watching him with curiosity, and Bee with the most affectionate anxiety. His attention was confined to the judges, the counsel, his client, and the memoranda in his hand. He had a strong confidence in the justice of his cause; perfect faith in the providence of God; and sanguine hopes of success.

True, he had arrayed against him an almost overpowering force: the husband of his client, and the three great guns of the bar—Wiseman, Berners, and Vivian, with law, custom, and precedent. But with him stood the angels of Justice and Mercy, invisible, but mighty; and, over all, the Omnipotent God, unseen, but all-seeing!

Ishmael possessed the minor advantages of youth, manly beauty, a commanding presence, a gracious smile, and a sweet, deep, sonorous voice. He was besides a new orator among them, with a fresh original style.

He was no paid attorney; it was not his pocket that was interested, but his sympathies; his whole heart and soul were in the cause that he had embraced, and he brought to bear upon it all the genius of his powerful mind.

I would like to give you the whole of this great speech that woke up the Washington court from its state of semi-somnolency and roused it to the sense of the unjust and cruel things it sometimes did when talking in its sleep. But I have only time and space to glance at some of its points; and if anyone wishes to see more of it, it may be found in the published works of the great jurist and orator.

He began to speak with modest confidence and in clear, concise, and earnest terms. He said that the court had heard from the learned counsel that had preceded him a great deal of law, sentiment, and wit. From him they should now hear of justice, mercy, and truth!

He reverted to the story of the woman's wrongs, sufferings, and struggles, continued through many years; he spoke of her love, patience, and forbearance under the severest trials; he dwelt upon the prolonged absence of her husband, prolonged through so many weary years, and the false position of the forsaken wife, a position so much worse than widowhood, inasmuch as it exposed her not only to all the evils of poverty, but to suspicion, calumny, and insult. But he bade them note how the woman had passed through the fire unharmed; how she had fought the battle of life bravely and come out victoriously; how she had labored on in honorable industry for years, until she had secured a home for herself and little girls. He spoke plainly of the arrival of the fugitive husband as the coming of the destroyer who had three times before laid waste her home; he described the terror and distress his very presence in the city had brought to that little home; the flight of the mother with her children, and her agony of anxiety to conceal them; he dwelt upon the cruel position of the woman whose natural protector has become her natural enemy; he reminded the court that it had required the mother to take her trembling little ones from their places of safety and concealment and to bring them forward; and now that they were here he felt a perfect confidence that the court would extend the ægis of its authority over these helpless ones, since that would be the only shield they could have under heaven. He spoke noble words in behalf not only of his client, but of woman—woman, loving, feeble, and oppressed from the beginning of time—woman, hardly dealt with by nature in the first place, and by the laws, made by her natural lover and protector, man, in the second place. Perhaps it was because he knew himself to be the son of a woman only, · even as his Master had been before him, that he poured so much of awakening, convicting, and condemning fire, force, and weight into this part of his discourse. He uttered thoughts and feelings upon this subject, original and startling at that time, but which have since been quoted, both in the Old and New World, and have had power to modify those cruel laws which at that period made woman, despite her understanding intellect, an idiot, and despite her loving heart a chattel—in the law.

It had been the time-honored prerogative and the invariable custom of the learned judges of this court to go to sleep during the pleadings of the lawyers; but upon this occasion they did not indulge in an afternoon nap, I assure you!

He next reviewed the testimony of the witnesses of the plaintiff; complimented them on the ingenuity they had displayed in making "the worst appear the better cause," by telling half the truth and ignoring the other half; but warned the court at the same time

"That a lie which is half a truth, is ever the blackest of lies,
That a lie which is all a lie may be met and fought with outright;
But a lie which is part a truth, is a harder matter to fight."

Then he reviewed in turn the speeches of the counsel for the plaintiff—first that of Wiseman, the ponderous law-expounder, which he answered with quite as much law and a great deal more equity; secondly, that of Berners, the tear-pumper, the false sentiment of which he exposed and criticised; and thirdly that of Vivian, the laugh-provoker, with which he dealt the most severely of all, saying that one who could turn into jest the most sacred affections and most serious troubles of domestic life, the heart's tragedy, the household wreck before them, could be capable of telling funny stories at his father's funeral, uttering good jokes over his mother's coffin.

He spoke for two hours, warming, glowing, rising with his subject, until his very form seemed to dilate in grandeur, and his face grew radiant as the face of an archangel; and those who heard seemed to think that his lips like those of the prophet of old had been touched with fire from heaven. Under the inspiration of the hour, he spoke truths new and startling then, but which have since resounded through the senate chambers of the world, changing the laws of the nations in regard to woman.

Nora, do you see your son? Oh, was it not well worth while to have loved, suffered, and died, only to have given him to the world!

It was a complete success. All his long, patient, painful years of struggle were rewarded now. It was one splendid leap from obscurity to fame.

The giants attempted to answer him, but it was of no use. After the freshness, the fire, the force, the heart, soul, and life in Ishmael's utterances, their old, familiar, well-worn styles, in which the same arguments, pathos, wit that had done duty in so many other cases was paraded again, only bored their hearers. In vain Wiseman appealed to reason; Berners to feeling; and Vivian to humor; they would not do: the court had often heard all that before, and grown heartily tired of it. Wiseman's wisdom was found to be foolishness; Berner's pathos laughable; and Vivian's humor grievous.

The triumvirate of the Washington bar were dethroned, and Prince Ishmael reigned in their stead.

A few hours later the decision of the court was made known. It had granted all that the young advocate had asked for his client—the exclusive possession of her children, her property, and her earnings, and also alimony from her husband.

As Ishmael passed out of the court amid the tearful thanks of the mother and her children, and the proud congratulations of honest Reuben and Hannah, he neared the group composed of Judge Merlin, Claudia, and Beatrice.

Judge Merlin looked smiling and congratulatory; he shook hands with young barrister, saying:

"Well, Ishmael, you have rather waked up the world to-day, haven't you?"

Bee looked perfectly radiant with joy. Her fingers closed spasmodically on the hand that Ishmael offered her, and she exclaimed a little incoherently:

"Oh, Ishmael, I always knew you could! I am so happy!"

"Thank you, dearest Bee! Under Divine Providence I owe a great deal of my success to-day to your sympathy."

Claudia did not speak; she was deadly pale and cold; her face was like marble and her hand like ice, as she gave it to Ishmael. She had always appreciated and loved him against her will; but now, in this hour of his triumph, when he had discovered to the world his real power and worth, her love rose to an anguish of longing that she knew her pride must forever deny; and so when Ishmael took her hand and looked in her face for the words of sympathy that his heart was hungering to receive from her of all the world, she could not speak.

Ishmael passed out with his friends. When he had gone, a stranger who had been watching him with the deepest interest during the whole course of the trial, now came forward, and, with an agitation impossible to conceal, hastily inquired:

"Judge Merlin, for Heaven's sake! who is that young man?"

"Eh! what! Brudenell, you here! When did you arrive?"

"This morning! But for the love of Heaven who is that young man?"

"Who? why the most talented young barrister of the day—a future chief justice, attorney-general, President of the United States, for aught I know! It looks like it, for whatever may be the aspirations of the boy, his intellect and will are sure to realize them!"

"Yes, but who is he? what is his name? who were his parents? where was he born?" demanded Herman Brudenell excitedly.

"Why, the Lord bless my soul alive, man! He is a self-made barrister; his name is Ishmael Worth; his mother was a poor weaver girl named Nora Worth; his father was an unknown scoundrel; he was born at a little hut near—Why, Brudenell, you ought to know all about it—near Brudenell Hall!"

"Heaven and earth!"

"What is the matter?"

"The close room—the crowd—and this oppression of the chest that I have had so many years!" gasped Herman Brudenell.

"Get into my carriage and come home with us. Come—I will take no denial! The hotels are overcrowded. We can send for your luggage. Come!"

"Thank you; I think I will."

"Claudia! Beatrice! come forward, my dears. Here is Mr. Brudenell."

Courtesies were exchanged, and they all went out and entered the carriage.

"I will introduce you to this young man, who has so much interested you, and all the world, in fact, I suppose. He is living with us; and he will be a lion from to-day, I assure you," said the judge, as soon as they were all seated.

"Thank you! I was interested in—in those two poor sisters. One died—what has become of the other?"

"She married my overseer, Gray; they are doing well. They are in the city on a visit at present, stopping at the Farmer's, opposite Center Market."

"Who educated this young man?"

"Himself."

"Did this unknown father make no provision for him?"

"None—the rascal! The boy was as poor as poverty could make him; but he worked for his own living from the time he was seven years old."

Herman had feared as much, for he doubted the check he had written and left for Hannah had ever been presented and cashed, for in the balancing of his bankbook he never saw it among the others.

Meanwhile Ishmael had parted with his friends and gone home to the Washington House. He knew that he had had a glorious success; but he took no vain credit to himself; he was only happy that his service had been a free offering to a good cause; and very thankful that it had been crowned with victory. And when he reached home he went up to his little chamber, knelt down in humble gratitude, and rendered all the glory to God!

CHAPTER LVIII.

HERMAN BRUDENELL

My son! I seem to breathe that word,
In utterance more clear
Than other words, more slowly round
I move my lips, to keep the sound
Still lingering in my ear.

For were my lonely life allowed
To claim that gifted son,
I should be met by straining eyes,
Welcoming tears and grateful sighs
To hallow my return.

But between me and that dear son
There lies a bar, I feel,
More hard to pass, more girt with awe,
Than any power of injured law,
Or front of bristling steel.
—*Milnes*.

When the carriage containing Judge Merlin, Claudia, Beatrice, and Mr. Brudenell reached the Washington House the party separated in the hall; the ladies went each to her own chamber to dress for dinner, and Judge Merlin called a servant to show Mr. Brudenell to a spare room, and then went to his own apartment.

When Herman Brudenell had dismissed his attendant and found himself alone he sat down in deep thought.

Since the death of Nora he had been a wanderer over the face of the earth. The revenues of his estate had been mostly paid over to his mother for the benefit of herself and her daughters, yet had scarcely been sufficient for the pride, vanity, and extravagance of those foolish women, who, living in Paris and introduced into court circles by the American minister, aped the style of the wealthiest among the French aristocracy, and indulged in the most expensive establishment, equipage, retinue, dress, jewelry, balls, etc., in the hope of securing alliances among the old nobility of France.

They might as well have gambled for thrones. The princes, dukes, marquises, and counts drank their wines, ate their dinners, danced at their balls, kissed their hands, and—laughed at them!

The reason was this: the Misses Brudenell, though well-born, pretty, and accomplished, were not wealthy, and were even suspected of being heavily in debt, because of all this show.

And I would here inform my ambitious American readers who go abroad in search of titled husbands whom they cannot find at home, that what is going on in Paris then is going on in all the Old World capitals now; and that now, when foreign noblemen marry American girls, it is because the former want money and the latter have it. If there is any exception to this rule, I, for one, never heard of it.

And so the Misses Brudenell, failing to marry into the nobility, were not married at all.

The expenditures of the mother and daughters in this speculation were enormous, so much so that at length Herman Brudenell, reckless as he was, became alarmed at finding himself on the very verge of insolvency!

He had signed so many blank checks, which his mother and sisters had filled up with figures so much higher than he had reckoned upon, that at last his Paris bankers had written to him informing him that his account had been so long and so much overdrawn that they had been obliged to decline cashing his last checks.

It was this that had startled Herman Brudenell out of his lethargy and goaded him to look into his affairs. After examining his account with his Paris banker with very unsatisfactory results, he determined to retrench his own personal expenses, to arrange his estates upon the most productive plan, and to let out Brudenell Hall.

He wrote to the Countess of Hurstmonceux, requesting her to vacate the premises, and to his land-agent instructing him to let the estate.

In due course of time he received answers to both his letters. That of the countess we have already seen; that of the land-agent informing him of the vast improvement of the estate during the residence of the Countess of Hurstmonceux upon it, and of the accumulation of its revenues, and finally of the large sum placed to his credit in the local bank by her ladyship.

This sum, of course, every sentiment of honor forbade Herman Brudenell from appropriating. He therefore caused it to be withdrawn and deposited with Lady Hurstmonceux's London bankers.

Soon after this he received notice that Brudenell Hall, stocked and furnished as it was, had been let to Mr. Middleton.

The accumulated revenues of the estate he devoted to paying his mother's debts, and the current revenues to her support, warning her at the same time of impending embarrassments unless her expenses were retrenched.

But the warning was unheeded, and the folly and extravagance of his mother and sisters were unabated. Like all other desperate gamblers, the heavier their losses the greater became their stakes; they went on living in the best hotels, keeping the most expensive servants, driving the purest blooded horses, wearing the richest dresses and the rarest jewels, giving the grandest balls, and—to use a common but strong phrase—"going it with a rush!" All in the desperate hope of securing for the young ladies wealthy husbands from among the titled aristocracy.

At length came another crisis; and once more Herman Brudenell was compelled to intervene between them and ruin. This he did at a vast sacrifice of property.

He wrote and gave Mr. Middleton warning to leave Brudenell Hall at the end of the year, because, he said, that he himself wished to return thither.

He did return thither; but it was only to sell off, gradually and privately, all the stock on the home-farm, all the plate, rich furniture, rare pictures, statues, vases, and articles of virtu in the house, and all the old plantation negroes—ancient servants who had lived for generations on the premises.

While he was at this work he instituted cautious inquiries about "one of the tenants, Hannah Worth, the weaver, who lived at Hill hut, with her nephew"; and he learned that Hannah was prosperously married to Reuben Gray and had left the neighborhood with her nephew, who had received a good education from Mr. Middleton's family school. Brudenell subsequently received a letter from Mr. Middleton himself, recommending to his favorable notice "a young man named Ishmael Worth, living on the Brudenell estates."

But as the youth had left the neighborhood with his relatives, and as Mr. Brudenell really hoped that he was well provided for by the large sum of money for which he had given Hannah a check on the day of his departure, and as he was overwhelmed with business cares, and lastly, as he dreaded rather than desired a meeting with his unknown son, he deferred seeking him out.

When Brudenell Hall was entirely dismantled, and all the furniture of the house, the stock of the farm, and the negroes of the plantation, and all the land except a few acres immediately around the house had been sold, and the purchase money realized, he returned to Paris, settled his mother's debts, and warning her that they had now barely sufficient to support them in moderate comfort, entreated her to return and live quietly at Brudenell Hall.

But no! "If they were poor, so much the more reason why the girls should marry rich," argued Mrs. Brudenell; and instead of retrenching her expenses, she merely changed the scene of her operations from Paris to London, forgetting the fact everyone else remembered, that her "girls," though still handsome, because well preserved, were now mature women of thirty-two and thirty-five. Herman promised to give them the whole proceeds of his property, reserving to himself barely enough to live on in the most economical manner. And he let Brudenell Hall once more, and took up his abode at a cheap watering-place on the continent, where he remained for years, passing his time in reading, fishing, boating, and other idle seaside pastimes, until he was startled from his repose by a letter from his mother—a letter full of anguish, telling him that her younger daughter, Eleanor, had fled from home in company with a certain Captain Dugald, and that she had traced them to Liverpool, whence they had sailed for New Tork, and entreated him to follow and if possible save his sister.

Upon this miserable errand he had revisited his native country. He had found no such name as Dugald in any of the lists of passengers arrived within the specified time by any of the ocean steamers from Liverpool to New

York, and no such name on any of the hotel books; so he left the matter in the hands of a skillful detective, and came down to Washington, in the hope of finding the fugitives here.

On his first walk out he had been attracted by the crowd around the City Hall; had learned that an interesting trial was going on; and that some strange, new lawyer was making a great speech. He had gone in, and on turning his eyes towards the young barrister had been thunderstruck on being confronted by what seemed to him the living face of Nora Worth, elevated to masculine grandeur. Those were Nora's lips, so beautiful in form, color, and expression; Nora's splendid eyes, that blazed with indignation, or melted with pity, or smiled with humor; Nora's magnificent breadth of brow, spanning from temple to temple. He saw in these remarkable features so much of the likeness of Nora, that he failed to see, in the height of the forehead, the outline of the profile, and the occasional expression of the countenance, the striking likeness of himself.

He had been spellbound by this, and by the eloquence of the young barrister until the end of the speech, when he had hastened to Judge Merlin and demanded the name and the history of the débutante.

And the answer had confirmed the prophetic instincts of his heart—this rising star of the forum was Nora's son!

Nora's son, born in the depths of poverty and shame; panting from the hour of his birth for the very breath of life; working from the days of his infancy for daily bread; striving from the years of his boyhood for knowledge; struggling by the most marvelous series of persevering effort out of the slough of infamy into which he had been cast, to his present height of honor! Scarcely twenty-one years old and already recognized not only as the most gifted and promising young member of the bar, but as a rising power among the people.

How proud he, the childless man, would be to own his share in Nora's gifted son, if in doing so he could avoid digging up the old, cruel reproach, the old, forgotten scandal! How proud to hail Ishmael Worth as Ishmael Brudenell!

But this he knew could never, never be. Every principle of honor, delicacy, and prudence forbade him now to interfere in the destiny of Nora's long-ignorant and neglected, but gifted and rising son. With what face could he, the decayed, impoverished, almost forgotten master of Brudenell Hall go to this brilliant young barrister, who had just made a splendid debut and achieved a dazzling success, and say to him:

"I am your father!"

And how should he explain such a relationship to the astonished young man? At making the dreadful confession, he felt that he should be likely to drop at the feet of his own son.

No! Ishmael Worth must remain Ishmael Worth. If he fulfilled the promise of his youth, it would not be his father's name, but his young mother's maiden name which would become illustrious in his person.

And yet, from the first moment of his seeing Ishmael and identifying him as Nora's son, he felt an irresistible desire to meet him face to face, to shake hands with him, to talk with him, to become acquainted with him, to be friends with him.

It was this longing that urged Mr. Brudenell to accept Judge Merlin's invitation and accompany the latter home. And now in a few moments this longing would be gratified.

In the midst of all other troubled thoughts one question perplexed him. It was this: What had become of the check he had given Hannah in the hour of his departure years ago?

That it had never been presented and cashed two circumstances led him to fear. The first was that he had never seen it among those returned to him when his bankbook had been made up; and the second was that Hannah had shared the bitter poverty of her nephew, and therefore could not have received and appropriated the money to her own uses.

As he had learned from the judge that Hannah was in Washington, he resolved to seek a private interview with her, and ascertain what had become of the check, and why, with the large sum of money it represented, she had neglected to use it, and permitted herself and her nephew to suffer all the evils of the most abject poverty.

CHAPTER LIX.

FIRST MEETING OF FATHER AND SON.

Oh, Christ! that thus a son should stand
Before a father's face.
—*Byron.*

While Mr. Brudenell still ruminated over these affairs the second dinner-bell rang, and almost at the same moment Judge Merlin rapped and entered the chamber, with old-fashioned hospitality, to show his guest the way to the drawing room.

"You feel better, I hope, Brudenell?" he inquired.

"Yes, thank you, judge."

"Come then. We will go down. We are a little behind time at best this evening, upon account of our young friend's long-winded address. It was a splendid affair, though. Worth waiting to hear, was it not?" proudly inquired the judge as they descended the stairs.

They entered the drawing room.

It was a family party that was assembled there, with the sole exception of the Viscount Vincent, who indeed had become a daily visitor, a recognized suitor of Miss Merlin, and almost one of their set.

As soon as Mr. Brudenell had paid his respects to each member of the family, Lord Vincent advanced frankly and cordially to greet him as an old acquaintance, saying:

"I had just learned from Miss Merlin of your arrival. You must have left London very soon after I did."

Before Mr. Brudenell could reply, Judge Merlin came up with Ishmael and said:

"Lord Vincent, excuse me. Mr. Brudenell, permit me—Mr. Worth, of the Washington bar."

Herman Brudenell turned and confronted Ishmael Worth. And father and son stood face to face.

Herman's face was quivering with irrepressible yet unspeakable emotion; Ishmael's countenance was serene and smiling.

No faintest instinct warned Nora's son that he stood in the presence of his father. He saw before him a tall, thin, fair-complexioned, gentlemanly person, whose light hair was slightly silvered, and whose dark brown eyes, in such strange contrast to the blond hair, were bent with interest upon him.

"I am happy to make your acquaintance, young gentleman. Permit me to offer you my congratulations upon your very decided success," said Mr. Brudenell, giving his hand.

Ishmael bowed.

"Brudenell, will you take my daughter in to dinner?" said Judge Merlin, seeing that Lord Vincent had already given his arm to Mrs. Middleton.

Herman, glad to be relieved from a position that was beginning to overcome his self-possession, bowed to Miss Merlin, who smilingly accepted his escort.

Judge Merlin drew Bee's arm within his own and followed. And Mr. Middleton, with a comic smile, crooked his elbow to Ishmael, who laughed instead of accepting it, and those two walking side by side brought up the rear.

That dinner passed very much as other dinners of the same class. Judge Merlin was cordial, Mr. Middleton facetious, Lord Vincent gracious, Mr. Brudenell silent and apparently abstracted, and Ishmael was attentive—a listener rather than a speaker. The ladies as usual at dinner-parties, where the conversation turns upon politics, were rather in the background, and took an early opportunity of withdrawing from the table, leaving the gentlemen to finish their political discussion over their wine.

The latter, however, did not linger long; but soon followed the ladies to the drawing room, where coffee was served. And soon after the party separated for the evening. Herman Brudenell withdrew to his chamber with one idea occupying him—his son. Since the death of Nora had paralyzed his affections, Herman Brudenell had loved no creature on earth until he met her son upon this evening. Now the frozen love of years melted and flowed into one strong, impetuous stream towards him—her son—his son! Oh, that he might dare to claim him!

It was late when Mr. Brudenell fell asleep—so late that he overslept himself in the morning. And when at last he awoke he was surprised to find that it was ten o'clock.

But Judge Merlin's house was "liberty hall." His guests breakfasted when they got up, and got up when they awoke. It was one of his crochets never to have anyone awakened. He said that when people had had sleep enough, they would awaken of themselves, and to awaken them before that was an injurious interference with nature. And his standing order in regard to himself was, that no one should ever arouse him from sleep unless the house was on fire, or someone at the point of death. And woe betide anyone who should disregard this order!

So Mr. Brudenell had been allowed to sleep until he woke up at ten o'clock, and when he went downstairs at eleven he found a warm breakfast awaiting him, and the little housewife, Bee, presiding over the coffee.

As Bee poured out his coffee she informed him, in answer to his remarks, that all the members of the family had breakfasted and gone about their several affairs. The judge and Ishmael had gone to court, and Mrs.

Middleton and Claudia on a shopping expedition; but they would all be back at the luncheon hour, which was two o'clock.

CHAPTER LX.

HERMAN AND HANNAH.

She had the passions of her herd.
She spake some bitter truths that day,
Indeed he caught one ugly word,
Was scarcely fit for her to say!
—*Anon.*

When breakfast was over Mr. Brudenell took his hat and walked down the Avenue to Seventh Street, and to the Farmer's in search of Hannah.

In answer to his inquiries he was told that she was in, and he was desired to walk up to her room. A servant preceding him, opened a door, and said:

"Here is a ge'man to see you, mum."

And Mr. Brudenell entered.

Hannah looked, dropped the needlework she held in her hand, started up, overturning the chair, and with a stare of consternation exclaimed:

"The Lord deliver us! is it you? And hasn't the devil got you yet, Herman Brudenell?"

"It is I, Hannah," he answered, dropping without invitation into the nearest seat.

"And what on earth have you come for, after all these years?" she asked, continuing to stare at him.

"To see you, Hannah."

"And what in the name of common sense do you want to see me for? I don't want to see you; that I tell you plainly; for I'd just as lief see Old Nick!"

"Hannah," said Herman Brudenell, with an unusual assumption of dignity, "I have come to speak to you about——Are you quite alone?" he suddenly broke off and inquired, cautiously glancing around the room.

"What's that to you? What can you have to say to me that you could not shout from the housetop? Yes, I'm alone, if you must know!"

"Then I wish to speak to you about my son."

"Your—what?" demanded Hannah, with a frown as black as midnight.

"My son," repeated Herman Brudenell, with emphasis.

"Your son? What son? I didn't know you had a son! What should I know about your son?"

"Woman, stop this! I speak of my son, Ishmael Worth—whom I met for the first time in the courtroom yesterday! And I ask you how it has fared with him these many years?" demanded Mr. Brudenell sternly, for he was beginning to lose patience with Hannah.

"Oh—h! So you met Ishmael Worth in the courtroom yesterday, just when he had proved himself to be the most talented man there, did you? That accounts for it all. I understand it now! You could leave him in his helpless, impoverished, orphaned infancy to perish! You could utterly neglect him, letting him suffer with cold and hunger and sickness for years and years and years! And now that, by the blessing of Almighty God, he has worked himself up out of that horrible pit into the open air of the world; and now that from being a poor, despised outcast babe he has risen to be a man of note among men; now, forsooth, you want to claim him as your son! Herman Brudenell, I always hated you, but now I scorn you! Twenty odd years ago I would have killed you, only I didn't want to kill your soul as well as your body, nor likewise to be hanged for you! And now I would shy this stick of wood at your head only that I don't want Reuben Gray to have the mortification of seeing his wife took up for assault! But I hate you, Herman Brudenell! And I despise you! There! take yourself out of my sight!"

Mr. Brudenell stamped impatiently and said:

"Hannah, you speak angrily, and therefore, foolishly. What good could accrue to me, or to him, by my claiming Ishmael as my son, unless I could prove a marriage with his mother? It would only unearth the old,

246

cruel, unmerited scandal now forgotten! No, Hannah; to you only, who are the sole living depository of the secret, will I solace myself by speaking of him as my son! You reproach me with having left him to perish. I did not so. I left in your hands a check for several—I forget how many—thousand dollars to be used for his benefit. And I always hoped that he was well provided for until yesterday, when Judge Merlin, little thinking the interest I had in the story, gave me a sketch of Ishmael's early sufferings and struggles. And now I ask you what became of that check?"

"That check? What check? What in the world do you mean?"

"The check for several thousand dollars which I gave you on the day of my departure, to be used for Ishmael's benefit."

"Well, Herman Brudenell! I always thought, with all your faults, you were still a man of truth; but after this——"

And Hannah finished by lifting her hands and eyes in horror.

"Hannah, you do severely try my temper, but in memory of all your kindness to my son——"

"Oh! I wasn't kind to him! I was as bad to him as you, and all the rest! I wished him dead, and neglected him!"

"You did!"

"Of course! Could anybody expect me to care more for him than his own father did? Yes, I wished him dead, and neglected him, because I thought he had no right to be in the world, and would be better out of it! So did everyone else. But he sucked his little, skinny thumb, and looked alive at us with his big, bright eyes, and lived in defiance of everybody. And only see what he has lived to be! But it is the good Lord's doings and not mine, and not yours, Herman Brudenell, so don't thank me anymore for kindness that I never showed to Ishmael, and don't tell any more bragging lies about the checks for thousands of dollars that you never left him!"

Again Herman Brudenell stamped impatiently, frowned, bit his lips, and said:

"You shall not goad me to anger with the two-edged sword of your tongue, Hannah! You are unjust, because you are utterly mistaken in your premises! I did leave that check of which I speak! And I wish to know what became of it, that it was not used for the support and education of Ishmael. Listen, now, and I will bring the whole circumstance to your recollection."

And Herman Brudenell related in detail all the little incidents connected with his drawing of the check, ending with: "Now don't you remember, Hannah?"

Hannah looked surprised, and said:

"Yes, but was that little bit of dirty white paper, tore out of an old book, worth all that money?"

"Yes! after I had drawn a check upon it!"

"I didn't know! I didn't understand! I was sort o' dazed with grief, I suppose."

"But what became of the paper, Hannah?"

"Mrs. Jones lit the candle with it!"

"Oh! Hannah!"

"Was the money all lost? entirely lost because that little bit of paper was burnt?"

"To you and to Ishmael it was, of course, since you never received it; but to me it was not, since it was never drawn from the bank."

"Well, then, Mr. Brudenell, since the money was not lost, I do not so much care if the check was burnt! I should not have used it for myself, or Ishmael, anyhow! Though I am glad to know that you did not neglect him, and leave him to perish in destitution, as I supposed you had! I am very glad you took measures for his benefit, although he never profited by them, and I never would have let him do so. Still, it is pleasant to think that you did your duty; and I am sorry I was so unjust to you, Mr. Brudenell."

"Say no more of that, Hannah. Let us talk of my son. Remember that it is only to you that I can talk of him. Tell me all about his infancy and childhood. Tell me little anecdotes of him. I want to know more about him than the judge could tell me. I know old women love to gossip at great length of old times, so gossip away, Hannah—tell me everything. You shall have a most interested listener."

"'Old women,' indeed! Not so very much older than yourself, Mr. Herman Brudenell—if it comes to that! But anyways, if Reuben don't see as I am old, you needn't hit me in the teeth with it!" snapped Mrs. Gray.

"Hannah, Hannah, what a temper you have got, to be sure! It is well Reuben is as patient as Job."

"It is enough to rouse any woman's temper to be called old to her very face!"

247

"So it is, Hannah; I admit it, and beg your pardon. But nothing was farther from my thoughts than to offend you. I feel old myself—very old, and so I naturally think of the companions of my youth as old also. And now, will you talk to me about my son?"

"Well, yes, I will," answered Hannah, and her tongue being loosened upon the subject, she gave Mr. Brudenell all the incidents and anecdotes with which the reader is already acquainted, and a great many more with which I could not cumber this story.

While she was still "gossiping," and Herman all attention, steps were heard without, and the door opened, and Reuben Gray entered, smiling and radiant, and leading two robust children—a boy and a girl—each with a little basket of early fruit in hand.

On seeing a stranger Reuben Gray took off his hat, and the children stopped short, put their fingers in their mouths and stared.

"Reuben, have you forgotten our old landlord, Mr. Herman Brudenell?" inquired Hannah.

"Why, law, so it is! I'm main glad to see you, sir! I hope I find you well!" exclaimed Reuben, beaming all over with welcome, as Mr. Brudenell arose and shook hands with him, replying:

"Quite well, and very happy to see you, Gray."

"John and Mary, where are your manners? Take your fingers out of your mouths this minute,—I'm quite ashamed of you!—and bow to the gentleman," said Hannah, admonishing her offspring.

"Whose fine children are these?" inquired Mr. Brudenell, drawing the shy little ones to him.

Reuben's honest face glowed all over with pride and joy as he answered:

"They are ours, sir! they are indeed! though you mightn't think it, to look at them and us! And Ishmael—that is our nephew, sir—and though he is now Mr. Worth, and a splendid lawyer, he won't turn agin his plain kin, nor hear to our calling of him anythink else but Ishmael; and after making his great speech yesterday, actilly walked right out'n the courtroom, afore all the people, arm in arm long o' Hannah!—Ishmael, as I was a-saying, tells me as how this boy, John, have got a good head, and would make a fine scollard, and how, by-and-by, he means to take him for a stoodient, and make a lawyer on him. And as for the girl, sir—why, law! look at her! you can see for yourself, sir, as she will have all her mother's beauty."

And Reuben, with a broad, brown hand laid benignantly upon each little head, smiled down upon the children of his age with all the glowing effulgence of an autumnal noonday sun shining down upon the late flowers.

But—poor Hannah's "beauty"!

Mr. Brudenell repressed the smile that rose to his lips, for he felt that the innocent illusions of honest affection were far too sacred to be laughed at.

And with some well-deserved compliments to the health and intelligence of the boy and girl, he kissed them both, shook hands with Hannah and Reuben, and went away.

He turned his steps towards the City Hall, with the intention of going into the courtroom and comforting his soul by watching the son whom he durst not acknowledge.

And as he walked thither, how he envied humble Reuben Gray his parental happiness!

CHAPTER LXI.

ENVY.

Well! blot him black with slander's ink,
He stands as white as snow!
You serve him better than you think
And kinder than you know;
What? is it not some credit then,
That he provokes your blame?
This merely, with all better men,
Is quite a kind of fame!
—*M.F. Tupper.*

Mr. Brudenell found Ishmael in the anteroom of the court in close conversation with a client, an elderly, care-worn woman in widow's weeds. He caught a few words of her discourse, to which Ishmael appeared to be listening with sympathy.

"Yes, sir, Maine; we belong to Bangor. He went to California some years ago and made money. And he was on his way home and got as far as this city, where he was taken ill with the cholera, at his brother's house, where he died before I could get to him; leaving three hundred thousand dollars, all in California gold, which his brother refuses to give up, denying all knowledge of it. It is robbery of the widow and orphan, sir, and nothing short of that!"—she was saying.

"If this is as you state it, it would seem to be a case for a detective policeman and a criminal prosecution, rather than for an attorney and a civil suit," said Ishmael.

"So it ought to be, sir, for he deserves punishment; but I have been advised to sue him, and I mean to do it, if you will take my case. But if you do take it, sir, it must be on conditions."

"Yes. What are they?"

"Why, if you do not recover the money, you will not receive any pay; but if you do recover the money, you will receive a very large share of it yourself, as a compensation for your services and your risk."

"I cannot take your case on these terms, madam; I cannot accept a conditional fee," said Ishmael gently.

"Then what shall I do?" exclaimed the widow, bursting into tears. "I have no money, and shall not have any until I get that! And how can I get that unless I sue for it? Or how sue for it, unless you are willing to take the risk? Do, sir, try it! It will be no risk, after all; you will be sure to gain it!"

"It is not the risk that I object to, madam," said Ishmael very gently, "but it is this—to make my fee out of my case would appear to me a sort of professional gambling, from which I should shrink."

"Then, Heaven help me, what shall I do?" exclaimed the widow, weeping afresh.

"Do not distress yourself. I will call and see you this afternoon. And if your case is what you represent it to be, I will undertake to conduct it," said Ishmael. And in that moment he made up his mind that if he should find the widow's cause a just one, he would once more make a free offering of his services.

The new client thanked him, gave her address, and departed.

Ishmael turned to go into the courtroom, and found himself confronted with Mr. Brudenell.

"Good-morning, Mr. Worth! I see you have another client already."

"A possible one, sir," replied Ishmael, smiling with satisfaction as he shook hands with Mr. Brudenell.

"A poor one, you mean! Poor widows with claims always make a prey of young lawyers, who are supposed to be willing to plead for nothing, rather than not plead at all! And it is all very well, as it gives the latter an opening. But you are not one of those briefless lawyers; you have already made your mark in the world, and so you must not permit these female forlornities that haunt the courts to consume all your time and attention."

"Sir," said Ishmael gravely and fervently, "I owe so much to God—so much more than I can ever hope to pay, that at least I must show my gratitude to him by working for his poor! Do you not think that is only right, sir?"

And Ishmael looked into the face of this stranger, whom he had seen but once before, with a singular longing for his approval.

"Yes! I do! my—I do, Mr. Worth!" replied Brudenell with emotion, as they entered the courtroom together.

Late that afternoon Ishmael kept his appointment with the widow Cobham, and their consultation ended in Ishmael's acceptance of her brief. Other clients also came to him, and soon his hands were full of business.

As the Supreme Court had risen, and Judge Merlin had little or no official business on hand, Ishmael's position in his office was almost a sinecure, and therefore the young man delicately hinted to his employer the propriety of a separation between them.

"No, Ishmael! I cannot make up my mind to part with you yet. It is true, as you say, that there is little to do now; but recollect that for months past there has been a great deal to do, and you have done about four times as much work for me as I was entitled to expect of you. So that now you have earned the right to stay on with me to the end of the year, without doing any work at all."

"But, sir—"

"But I won't hear a word about your leaving us just yet, Ishmael. I will hold you to your engagement, at least until the first of June, when we all return to Tanglewood; then, if you wish it, of course I will release you, as your professional duties will require your presence in the city. But while we remain in town, I will not consent to your leaving us, nor release you from your engagement," said the judge.

And Ishmael was made happy by this decision. It had been a point of honor with him, as there was so little to do, to offer to leave the judge's employment; but now that the offer had been refused, and he was held to his engagement, he was very much pleased to find himself obliged to remain under the same roof with Claudia.

Ah! sweet and fatal intoxication of her presence! he would not willingly tear himself away from it.

Meanwhile this pleasure was but occasional and fleeting. He seldom saw Claudia except at the dinner hour.

Miss Merlin never now got up to breakfast with the family. Her life of fashionable dissipation was beginning to tell even on her youthful and vigorous constitution. Every evening she was out until a late hour, at some public ball, private party, concert, theater, lecture room, or some other place of amusement. The consequence was that she was always too tired to rise and breakfast with the family, whom she seldom joined until the two o'clock lunch. And at that hour Ishmael was sure to be at court, where the case of Cobham versus Hanley, in which Mr. Worth was counsel for the plaintiff, was going on. At the six o'clock dinner he daily met her, as I said, but that was always in public. And immediately after coffee she would go out, attended by Mrs. Middleton as chaperone and the Viscount Vincent as escort. And she would return long after Ishmael had retired to his room, so that he would not see her again until the next day at dinner. And so the days wore on.

Mr. Brudenell remained the guest of Judge Merlin. A strange affection was growing up between him and Ishmael Worth. Brudenell understood the secret of this affection; Ishmael did not. The father, otherwise childless, naturally loved the one gifted son of his youth, and loved him the more that he durst not acknowledge him. And Ishmael, in his genial nature, loved in return the stranger who showed so much affectionate interest in him. No one perceived the likeness that was said by the viscount to exist between the two except the viscount himself; and since he had seen them together he had ceased to comment upon the subject.

Reuben Gray and his family had returned home, so that Mr. Brudenell got no farther opportunity of talking with Hannah.

The Washington season, prolonged by an extra session of Congress, was at length drawing to a close; and it was finished off with a succession of very brilliant parties. Ishmael Worth was now included in every invitation sent to the family of Judge Merlin, and in compliance with the urgent advice of the judge he accepted many of these invitations, and appeared in some of the most exclusive drawing rooms in Washington, where his handsome person, polished manners, and distinguished talents made him welcome.

But none among these brilliant parties equaled in splendor the ball given early in the season by the Merlins.

"And since no one has been able to eclipse my ball, I will eclipse it myself by a still more splendid one—a final grand display at the end of the season, like a final grand tableau at the close of the pantomime," said Claudia.

"My dear, you will ruin yourself," expostulated Mrs. Middleton.

"My aunt, I shall be a viscountess," replied Miss Merlin.

And preparations for the great party were immediately commenced. More than two hundred invitations were sent out. And the aid of the three great ministers of fashion—Vourienne, Devizac, and Dureezie—were called in, and each was furnished with a carte-blanche as to expenses. And as to squander the money of the prodigal heiress was to illustrate their own arts, they availed themselves of the privilege in the freest manner.

For a few days the house was closed to visitors, and given up to suffer the will of the decorator Vourienne and his attendant magicians, who soon contrived to transform the sober mansion of the American judge into something very like the gorgeous palace of an Oriental prince. And as if they would not be prodigal enough if left to themselves, Claudia continually interfered to instigate them to new extravagances.

Meanwhile nothing was talked of in fashionable circles but the approaching ball, and the novelties it was expected to develop.

On the morning of the day, Vourienne and his imps having completed their fancy papering, painting, and gilding, and put the finishing touches by festooning all the walls and ceilings, and wreathing all the gilded pillars with a profusion of artificial flowers, at last evacuated the premises, just it time to allow Devizac and his army to march in for the purpose of laying the feast. These forces held possession of the supper room, kitchen, and pantry for the rest of the evening, and prepared a supper which it would be vain to attempt to describe, since even the eloquent reporter of the "Republican Court Journal" failed to do it justice. A little later in the evening Dureezie and his celebrated troupe arrived, armed with all the celebrated dances—waltzes, polkas, etc.—then known, and one or two others composed expressly for this occasion.

And, when they had taken their places, Claudia and her party came down into the front drawing room to be ready to receive the company.

On this occasion it was Miss Merlin's whim to dress with exceeding richness. She wore a robe of dazzling splendor—a fabric of the looms of India, a sort of gauze of gold, that seemed to be composed of woven sunbeams, and floated gracefully around her elegant figure and accorded well with her dark beauty. The bodice of this gorgeous dress was literally starred with diamonds. A coronet of diamonds flashed above her black ringlets, a necklace of diamonds rested upon her full bosom, and bracelets of the same encircled her rounded arms. Such a glowing, splendid, refulgent figure as she presented suggested the idea of a Mohammedan sultana rather than that of a Christian maiden. But it was Miss Merlin's caprice upon this occasion to dazzle, bewilder, and astonish.

Bee, who stood near her like a maid of honor to a queen, was dressed with her usual simplicity and taste, in a fine white crêpe, with a single white lily on her bosom.

Mrs. Middleton, standing also with Claudia, wore a robe of silver gray.

And this pure white on one side and pale gray on the other did but heighten the effect of Claudia's magnificent costume.

The fashionable hour for assembling at evening parties was then ten o'clock. By a quarter past ten the company began to arrive, and by eleven the rooms were quite full.

The Viscount Vincent arrived early, and devoted himself to Miss Merlin, standing behind her chair like a lord in waiting.

Ishmael was also present with this group ostensibly in attendance upon Beatrice, but really and truly waiting every turn of Claudia's countenance or conversation.

While they were all standing, grouped in this way, to receive all comers, Judge Merlin approached, smiling, and accompanied by an officer in the uniform of the United States army, whom he presented in these words:

"Claudia, my love, I bring you an old acquaintance—a very old acquaintance—Captain Burghe."

Claudia bowed as haughtily and distantly as it was possible to do; and then, without speaking, glanced inquiringly at her father as if to ask—"How came this person here?"

Judge Merlin replied to that mute question by saying:

"I was so lucky as to meet our young friend on the Avenue to-day; he is but just arrived. I told him what was going on here this evening and begged him to waive ceremony and come to us. And he was so good as to take me at my word! Bee, my dear, don't you remember your old playmate, Alfred Burghe?" said the judge, appealing for relief to his amiable niece.

Now, Bee was too kind-hearted to hurt anyone's feelings, and yet too truthful to make professions she did not feel. She could not positively say that she was glad to see Alfred Burghe; but she could give him her hand and say:

"I hope you are well, Mr. Burghe."

"Captain! Captain, my dear! he commands a company now! Lord Vincent permit me—Captain Burghe."

A haughty bow from the viscount and a reverential one from the captain acknowledged this presentation.

Then Mrs. Middleton kindly shook hands with the unwelcome visitor.

And finally Claudia unbent a little from her hauteur and condescended to address a few commonplace remarks to him. But at length her eyes flashed upon Ishmael standing behind Bee.

"You are acquainted with Mr. Worth, I presume, Captain Burghe?" she inquired.

"I have not that honor," said Alfred Burghe arrogantly.

"Then I will confer it upon you!" said Claudia very gravely. "Mr. Worth, I hope you will permit me to present to you Captain Burghe. Captain Burghe, Mr. Worth, of the Washington bar."

Ishmael bowed with courtesy; but Alfred Burghe grew violently red in the face, and with a short nod turned away.

"Captain Burghe has a bad memory, my lord!" said Claudia, turning to the viscount. "The gentleman to whom I have just presented him once saved his life at the imminent risk of his own. It is true the affair happened long ago, when they were both boys; but it seems to me that if anyone had exposed himself to a death by fire to rescue me from a burning building, I should remember it to the latest day of my life."

"Pardon me, Miss Merlin. The circumstance to which you allude was beyond my control, and Mr.—a— Word's share in it without my consent; his service was, I believe, well repaid by my father; and the trouble with me is not that my memory is defective, but rather that it is too retentive. I remember the origin of——"

"Our acquaintance with Mr. Worth!" interrupted Claudia, turning deadly pale and speaking in the low tones of suppressed passion. "Yes, I know! there was a stopped carriage, rifled hampers, and detected thieves. There was a young gentleman who dishonored his rank, and a noble working boy who distinguished himself in that affair. I remember perfectly well the circumstances to which you refer."

"You mistake, Miss Merlin," retorted Burghe, with a hot flush upon his brow, "I do not refer to that boyish frolic, for it was no more! I refer to——"

"Mr. Burghe, excuse me. Mr. Worth, will you do me the favor to tell the band to strike up a quadrille? Lord Vincent, I presume they expect us to open the ball. Bee, my dear, you are engaged to Mr. Worth for this set. Be sure when he returns to come to the same set with us and be our vis-à-vis," said Claudia, speaking rapidly.

Before she had finished Ishmael had gone upon her errand, and the band struck up a lively quadrille. Claudia gave her hand to Lord Vincent, who led her to the head of the first set. When Ishmael returned, Bee gave him her hand and told him Claudia's wish, which, of course, had all the force of a command for him, and he immediately led Bee to the place opposite Lord Vincent and Hiss Merlin.

And Captain Burghe was left to bite his nails in foiled malignity.

But later in the evening he took his revenge and received his punishment.

It happened in this manner: New quadrilles were being formed. Claudia was again dancing with Lord Vincent, and they had taken their places at the head of one of the sets. Ishmael was dancing with one of the poor neglected "wallflowers" to whom Bee had kindly introduced him, and he led his partner to a vacant place at the foot of one of the sets; he was so much engaged in trying to entertain the shy and awkward girl that he did not observe who was their vis-à-vis, or overhear the remarks that were made.

But Claudia, who, with the viscount, was standing very near, heard and saw all. She saw Ishmael lead his shy young partner up to a place in the set, exactly opposite to where Alfred Burghe with his partner, Miss Tourneysee, stood. And she heard Mr. Burghe whisper to Miss Tourneysee:

"Excuse me; and permit me to lead you to a seat. The person who has just taken the place opposite to us is not a proper associate even for me, still less for you."

And she saw Miss Tourneysee's look of surprise and heard her low-toned exclamation:

"Why, it is Mr. Worth! I have danced with him often!"

"I am sorry to hear it. I hope you will take the word of an officer and a gentleman that he is not a respectable person, and by no means a proper acquaintance for any lady."

"But why not?"

"Pardon me. I cannot tell you why not. It is not a story fit for your ears. But I will tell your father. For I think the real position of the fellow ought to be known. In the meantime, will you take my word for the truth of what I have said, and permit me to lead you to a seat?"

"Certainly," said the young lady, trembling with distress.

"I regret exceedingly to deprive you of your dance; but you perceive that there is no other vacant place."

"Oh, don't mention it! Find me a seat."

This low-toned conversation, every word of which had been overheard by Claudia who, though in another set, stood nearly back to back with the speaker, was entirely lost to Ishmael, who stood at the foot of the same set with him, but was at a greater distance, and was besides quite absorbed in the task of reassuring his timid schoolgirl companion.

Just as Burghe turned to lead his partner away, and Ishmael, attracted by the movement, lifted his eyes to see the cause, Claudia gently drew Lord Vincent after her, and going up to the retiring couple said:

"Miss Tourneysee, I beg your pardon; but will you and your partner do myself and Lord Vincent the favor to exchange places with us? We particularly desire to form a part of this set."

"Oh, certainly!" said the young lady, wondering, but rejoiced to find that she should not be obliged to miss the dance.

They exchanged places accordingly; but as they still stood very near together, Claudia heard him whisper to his partner:

"This evening I think I will speak to your father and some other gentlemen and enlighten them as to who this fellow really is!"

Claudia heard all this; but commanded herself. Her face was pale as marble; her lips were bloodless; but her dark eyes had the terrible gleam of suppressed but determined hatred! In such moods as hers, people have sometimes planned murder.

However, she went through all the four dances very composedly. And when they were over and Lord Vincent had led her to a seat, she sent him to fetch her a glass of water, while she kept her eye on the movements of Captain Burghe, until she saw him deposit his partner on a sofa and leave her to fetch a cream, or some such refreshment.

And then Claudia arose, drank the ice-water brought her by the viscount, set the empty glass on a stand and requested Lord Vincent to give her his arm down the room, as she wished to speak to Captain Burghe.

The viscount glanced at her in surprise, saw that her face was bloodless; but ascribed her pallor to fatigue.

Leaning on Lord Vincent's arm, she went down the whole length of the room until she paused before the sofa on which sat Miss Tourneysee and several other ladies, attended by General Tourneysee, Captain Burghe and other gentlemen.

Burghe stood in front of the sofa, facing the ladies and with his back towards Claudia, of whose approach he was entirely ignorant, as he discoursed as follows:

"Quite unfit to be received in respectable society, I assure you, General! Came of a wretchedly degraded set, the lowest of the low, upon my honor. This fellow——"

Claudia touched his shoulder with the end of her fan.

Alfred Burghe turned sharply around and confronted Miss Merlin, and on meeting her eyes grew as pale as she was herself.

"Captain Burghe," she said, modulating her voice to low and courteous tones, "you have had the misfortune to malign one of our most esteemed friends, at present a member of our household. I regret this accident exceedingly, as it puts me under the painful necessity of requesting you to leave the house with as little delay as possible!"

"Miss Merlin—ma'am!" began the captain, crimsoning with shame and rage.

"You have heard my request, sir! I have no more to say but to wish you a very good evening," said Claudia, as with a low and sweeping courtesy she turned away.

Passing near the hall where the footmen waited, she spoke to one of them, saying:

"Powers, attend that gentleman to the front door."

All this was done so quietly that Alfred Burghe was able to slink from the room, unobserved by anyone except the little group around the sofa, whom he had been entertaining with his calumnies. To them he had muttered that he would have satisfaction; that he would call Miss Merlin's father to a severe account for the impertinence of his daughter, etc.

But the consternation produced by these threats was soon dissipated. The band struck up an alluring waltz, and Lord Vincent claimed the hand of Beatrice, and Ishmael, smiling, radiant and unsuspicious, came in search of Miss Tourneysee, who accepted his hand for the dance without an instant's hesitation.

"Do you know"—inquired Miss Tourneysee, with a little curiosity to ascertain whether there was any mutual enmity between Burghe and Ishmael—"do you know who that Captain Burghe is that danced the last quadrille with me?"

"Yes; he is the son of the late Commodore Burghe, who was a gallant officer, a veteran of 1812, and did good service during the last War of Independence," said Ishmael generously, uttering not one word against his implacable foe.

Miss Tourneysee looked at him wistfully and inquired: "Is the son as good a man as the father?"

"I have not known Captain Burghe since we were at school together."

"I do not like him. I do not think he is a gentleman," said Miss Tourneysee.

Ishmael did not reply. It was not his way to speak even deserved evil of the absent.

But Miss Tourneysee drew a mental comparison between the meanness of Alfred's conduct and the nobility of Ishmael's. And the dance succeeded the conversation.

Claudia remained sitting on the sofa beside Mrs. Middleton, until at the close of the dance, when she was rejoined by the viscount, who did not leave her again during the evening.

The early summer nights were short, and so it was near the dawn when the company separated.

The party as a whole had been the most splendid success of the season.

***

CHAPTER LXII.

FOILED MALICE.

Through good report and ill report,
The true man goes his way,
Nor condescends to pay his court
To what the vile may say:

Aye, be the scandal what they will,
And whisper what they please,
They do but fan his glory still
By whistling up a breeze.
—*M.F. Tupper.*

The family slept late next day, and the breakfast was put back to the luncheon hour, when at length they all, with one exception, assembled around the table.

"Where is Mr. Worth?" inquired the judge.

"He took a cup of coffee and went to the courthouse at the usual hour, sir," returned Powers, who was setting the coffee on the table.

"Humph! that hotly contested case of Cobham versus Hanley still in progress, I suppose," said the judge.

At this moment Sam entered the breakfast room and laid a card on the table before his master.

"Eh? 'Lieutenant Springald, U.S.A.' Who the mischief is he?" said the judge, reading the name on the card.

"The gentleman, sir, says he has called to see you on particular business," replied Sam.

"This is a pretty time to come on business! Show him up into my office, Sam."

The servant withdrew to obey.

The judge addressed himself to his breakfast, and the conversation turned upon the party of the preceding evening.

"I wonder what became of Burghe? He disappeared very early in the evening," said Judge Merlin.

"I turned him out of doors," answered Claudia coolly.

The judge set down his coffee cup and stared at his daughter.

"He deserved it, papa! And nothing on earth but my sex prevented me from giving him a thrashing as well as a discharge," said Claudia.

"What has he done?" inquired her father.

Claudia told him the whole.

"Well, my dear, you did right, though I am sorry that there should have been any necessity for dismissing him. Degenerate son of a noble father, will nothing reform him!" was the comment of the judge.

Mr. Brudenell, who was present, and had heard Claudia's account, was reflecting bitterly upon the consequences of his own youthful fault of haste, visited so heavily in unjust reproach upon the head of his faultless son.

"Well!" said the judge, rising from the table, "now I will go and see what the deuce is wanted of me by Lieutenant—Spring—Spring—Spring chicken! or whatever his name is!"

He went upstairs and found seated in his office a beardless youth in uniform, who arose and saluted him, saying, as he handed a folded note:

"I have the honor to be the bearer of a challenge, sir, from my friend and superior officer, Captain Burghe."

"A—what?" demanded the judge, with a frown as black as a thunder-cloud and a voice sharp as its clap, which made the little officer jump from his feet.

"A challenge, sir!" repeated the latter, as soon as he had composed himself.

"Why what the deuce do you mean by bringing a challenge to *me*—breaking the law under the very nose of an officer of the law?" said the judge, snatching the note and tearing it open. When he had read it, he looked sternly at the messenger and said:

"Why don't you know it is my solemn duty to have you arrested and sent to prison, for bringing me this, eh?"

"Sir," began the little fellow, drawing his figure up, "men of honor never resort to such subterfuges to evade the consequences of their own acts."

"Hold your tongue, child! You know nothing about what you are talking of. Men of honor are not duelists, but peaceable, law-abiding citizens. Don't be frightened, my brave little bantam! I won't have you arrested this time; but I will answer your heroic principal instead. Let us see again—what it is he says?"

And the judge sat down at his writing table and once more read over the challenge.

It ran thus:

Mansion House, Friday.

Judge Merlin—Sir: I have been treated with the grossest contumely by your daughter, Miss Claudia Merlin. I demand an ample apology from the young lady, or in default of that, the satisfaction of a gentleman from yourself. In the event of the first alternative offered being chosen, my friend, Lieutenant Springald, the bearer of this, is authorized to accept in my behalf all proper apologies that may be tendered. Or in the event of the second alternative offered being chosen, I must request that you will refer my friend to any friend of yours, that they may arrange together the terms of our hostile meeting.

I have the honor to be, etc.,

Alfred Burghe.

Judge Merlin smiled grimly as he laid this precious communication aside and took up his pen to reply to it.

His answer ran as follows:

Washington House, Friday.

Captain Alfred Burghe: My daughter, Miss Merlin, did perfectly right, and I fully endorse her act. Therefore, the first alternative offered—of making you the apology you demand—is totally inadmissible; but I accept the second one of giving you the satisfaction you require. The friend to whom I refer your friend is Deputy Marshal Browning, who will be prepared to take you both in custody. And the weapons with which I will meet you will be the challenge that you have sent me and a warrant for your arrest. Hoping that this course may give perfect satisfaction,

I have the honor to be, etc.,

Randolph Merlin.

Judge Merlin carefully folded and directed this note, and put it into the hands of the little lieutenant, saying pleasantly:

"There, my child! There you are! Take that to your principal."

The little fellow hesitated.

"I hope, sir, that this contains a perfectly satisfactory apology?" he said, turning it around in his fingers.

"Oh, perfectly! amply! We shall hear no more of the challenge."

"I am very glad, sir," said the little lieutenant, rising.

"Won't you have something before you go?"

The lieutenant hesitated.

"Shall I ring for the maid to bring you a slice of bread and butter and a cup of milk?"

"No, thank you, sir!" said Springald, with a look of offended dignity.

"Very well, then; you must give my respects to your papa and mamma, and ask them to let you come and play with little Bobby and Tommy Middleton! They are nice little boys!" said the judge, so very kindly that the little lieutenant, though hugely affronted, scarcely knew in what manner to resent the affront.

"Good-day, sir!" he said, with a vast assumption of dignity, as he strutted towards the door.

"Good-day, my little friend. You seem an innocent little fellow enough. Therefore I hope that you will never again be led into the sinful folly of carrying a challenge to fight a duel, especially to a gray-headed chief justice."

And so saying, Judge Merlin bowed his visitor out.

And it is scarcely necessary to say that Judge Merlin heard no more of "the satisfaction of a gentleman."

The story, however, got out, and Captain Burghe and his second were so mercilessly laughed at, that they voluntarily shortened their own furlough and speedily left Washington.

The remainder of that week the house was again closed to company, during the process of dismantling the reception rooms of their festive decorations and restoring them to their ordinarily sober aspect.

By Saturday afternoon this transformation was effected, and the household felt themselves at home again.

Early that evening Ishmael joined the family circle perfectly radiant with good news.

"What is it, Ishmael?" inquired the judge.

"Well, sir, the hard-fought battle is over at length, and we have the victory. The case of Cobham versus Hanley is decided. The jury came into court this afternoon with a verdict for the plaintiff."

"Good!" said the judge.

"And the widow and children get their money. I am so glad!" said Bee, who had kept herself posted up in the progress of the great suit by reading the reports in the daily papers.

"Yes, but how much money will you get, Ishmael?" inquired the judge.

"None, sir, on this case. A conditional fee that I was to make out of my case was offered me by the plaintiff in the first instance, but of course I could not speculate in justice."

"Humph! well, it is of no use to argue with you, Ishmael. Now, there are two great cases which you have gained, and which ought to have brought you at least a thousand dollars, and which have brought you nothing."

"Not exactly nothing, uncle; they have brought him fame," said Bee.

"Fame is all very well, but money is better," said the judge.

"The money will come also in good time, uncle; never you fear. Ishmael has placed his capital out at good interest, and with the best security."

"What do you mean, Bee?"

"'Whoso giveth to the poor, lendeth to the Lord.' Ishmael's services, given to the poor, are lent to the Lord," said Bee reverently.

"Humph! humph! humph!" muttered the judge, who never ventured to carry on an argument when the Scripture was quoted against him. "Well! I suppose it is all right. And now I hear that you are counsel for that poor devil Toomey, who fell through the grating of Sarsfield's cellar, and crippled himself for life."

"Yes," said Ishmael. "I think he is entitled to heavy damages. It was criminal carelessness in Sarsfield & Company to leave their cellar grating in that unsafe condition for weeks, to the great peril of the passers-by. It was a regular trap for lives and limbs. And this poor laborer, passing over it, has fallen and lamed himself for life! And he has a large family depending upon him for support. I have laid the damages at five thousand dollars."

"Yes; but how much do you get?"

"Nothing. As in the other two cases, my client is not able to pay me a retaining fee, and it is against my principles to accept a contingent one."

"Humph! that makes three 'free, gratis, for nothing' labors! I wonder how long it will be before the money cases begin to come on?" inquired the judge, a little sarcastically.

"Oh, not very long," smiled Ishmael. "I have already received several retaining fees from clients who are able to pay, but whose cases may not come on until the next term."

"But when does poor Toomey's case come on?"

"Monday."

At that moment the door opened, and Powers announced:

"Lord Vincent!"

The viscount entered the drawing room; and Ishmael's pleasure was over for that evening.

On Monday Ishmael's third case, Toomey versus Sarsfield, came on. It lasted several days, and then was decided in favor of the plaintiff—Toomey receiving every dollar of the damages claimed for him by his attorney. In his gratitude the poor man would have pressed a large sum of money, even to one-fifth of his gains, upon his young counsel; but Ishmael, true to his principle of never gambling in justice, refused to take a dollar.

That week the court adjourned; and the young barrister had leisure to study and get up his cases for the next term. The extra session of Congress was also over. The Washington season was in fact at an end. And everybody was preparing to leave town.

Judge Merlin issued a proclamation that his servants should pack up all his effects, preparatory to a migration to Tanglewood; for that chains should not bind him to Washington any longer, nor wild horses draw him to Saratoga, or any other place of public resort; because his very soul was sick of crowds and longed for the wilderness.

But the son of Powhatan was destined to find that circumstances are often stronger than those forces that he defied.

And so his departure from Washington was delayed for weeks by this event.

One morning the Viscount Vincent called as usual, and, after a prolonged private interview with Miss Merlin, he sent a message to Judge Merlin requesting to see him alone for a few minutes.

Ishmael was seated with Judge Merlin in the study at the moment Powers brought this message.

"Ah! Lord Vincent requests the honor of a private interview with me, does he? Well, it is what I have been expecting for some days! Wonder if he doesn't think he is conferring an honor instead of receiving one? Ask him to be so good as to walk up, Powers. Ishmael, my dear boy, excuse me for dismissing you for a few minutes; but pray return to me as soon as this Lord—'Foppington'—leaves me. May Satan fly away with him, for I know he is coming to ask me for my girl!"

It was well that Ishmael happened to be sitting with his back to the window. It was well also that Judge Merlin did not look up as his young partner passed out, else would the judge have seen the haggard countenance

256

which would have told him more eloquently than words could of the force of the blow that had fallen on Ishmael's heart.

He went up into his own little room, and sat down at his desk, and leaning his brow upon his hand struggled with the anguish that wrung his heart.

It had fallen, then! It had fallen—the crushing blow! Claudia was betrothed to the viscount. He might have been, as everyone else was, prepared for this. But he was not. For he knew that Claudia was perfectly conscious of his own passionate love for her, and he knew that she loved him with almost equal fervor. It is true his heart had been often wrung with jealousy when seeing her with Lord Vincent; yet even then he had thought that her vanity only was interested in receiving the attentions of the viscount; and he had trusted in her honor that he believed would never permit her, while loving himself, to marry another, or even give that other serious encouragement. It is true also that he had never breathed his love to Claudia, for he knew that to do so would be an unpardonable abuse of his position in Judge Merlin's family, a flagrant breach of confidence, and a fatal piece of presumption that would insure his final banishment from Claudia's society. So he had struggled to control his passion, seeing also that Claudia strove to conquer hers. And though no words passed between them, each knew by secret sympathy the state of the other's mind.

But lately, since his brilliant success at the bar and the glorious prospect that opened before him, he had begun to hope that Claudia, conscious of their mutual love, would wait for him only a few short years, at the end of which he would be able to offer her a position not unworthy even of Judge Merlin's daughter.

Such had been his splendid "castle in the air." But now the thunderbolt had fallen and his castle was in ruins.

Claudia, whom he had believed to be, if not perfectly faultless, yet the purest, noblest, and proudest among women; Claudia, his queen, had been capable of selling herself to be the wife of an unloved man, for the price of a title and a coronet—a breath and a bauble!

Claudia had struck a fatal blow, not only to his love for her, but to his honor of her; and both love and honor were in their death-throes!

Anguish is no computer of time. He might have sat there half an hour or half a day, he could not have told which, when he heard the voice of his kind friend calling him.

"Ishmael, Ishmael, my lad, where are you, boy? Come to me!"

"Yes, yes, sir, I am coming," he answered mechanically.

And like one who has fainted from torture, and recovered in bewilderment, he arose and walked down to the study.

Some blind instinct led him straight to the chair that was sitting with its back to the window; into this he sank, with his face in the deep shadow.

Judge Merlin was walking up and down the floor, with signs of disturbance in his looks and manners.

A waiter with decanters of brandy and wine, and some glasses, stood upon the table. This was a very unusual thing.

"Well, Ishmael, it is done! my girl is to be a viscountess; but I do not like it; no, I do not like it!"

Ishmael was incapable of reply; but the judge continued:

"It is not only that I shall lose her; utterly lose her, for her home will be in another hemisphere, and the ocean will roll between me and my sole child,—it is not altogether that,—but, Ishmael, I don't like the fellow; and I never did, and never can!"

Here the judge paused, poured out a glass if wine, drank it, and resumed:

"And I do not know why I don't like him! that is the worst of it! His rank is, of course, unexceptionable, and indeed much higher than a plain republican like myself has a right to expect in a son-in-law! And his character appears to be unquestionable! He is good-looking, well-behaved, intelligent and well educated young fellow enough, and so I do not know why it is that I don't like him! But I don't like him, and that is all about it!"

The judge sighed, ran his hands through his gray hair, and continued:

"If I had any reason for this dislike; if I could find any just cause of offense in him; if I could put my hand down on any fault of his character, I could then say to my daughter: 'I object to this man for your husband upon this account,' and then I know she would not marry him in direct opposition to my wishes. But, you see, I cannot do anything like this, and my objection to the marriage, if I should express it, would appear to be caprice, prejudice, injustice—"

He sighed again, walked several times up and down the floor in silence, and then once more resumed his monologue:

257

"People will soon be congratulating me on my daughter's very splendid marriage. Congratulating me! Good Heaven, what a mockery! Congratulating me on the loss of my only child, to a foreigner, whom I half dislike and more than half suspect—though without being able to justify either feeling. What do you think, Ishmael? Is that a subject for congratulation. But, good Heaven, boy! what is the matter with you? Are you ill?" he suddenly exclaimed, pausing before the young man and noticing for the first time the awful pallor of his face and the deadly collapse of his form.

"Are you ill, my dear boy? Speak!"

"Yes, yes, I am ill!" groaned Ishmael.

"Where? where?"

"Everywhere!"

The judge rushed to the table and poured out a glass of brandy and brought it to him.

But the young man, who was habitually and totally abstinent, shook his head.

"Drink it! drink it!" said the judge, offering the glass.

But Ishmael silently waved it off.

"As a medicine, you foolish fellow—as a medicine! You are sinking, don't you know!" persisted the judge, forcing the glass into Ishmael's hand.

Ishmael then placed it to his lips and swallowed its contents.

The effect of this draught upon him, unaccustomed as he was to alcoholic stimulants, was instantaneous. The brandy diffused itself through his chilled, sinking, and dying frame, warming, elevating, and restoring its powers.

"This is the fabled 'elixir of life.' I did not believe there was such a restorative in the world!" said Ishmael, sitting up and breathing freely under the transient exhilaration.

"To be sure it is, my boy!" said the judge heartily, as he took the empty glass from Ishmael's hand and replaced it on the waiter. "But what have you been doing to reduce yourself to this state? Sitting up all night over some perplexing case, as likely as not."

"No."

"But I am sure you overwork yourself. You should not do it, Ishmael! It is absurd to kill yourself for a living, you know."

"I think, Judge Merlin, that, as you are so soon about to leave Washington, and as there is so little to do in your office, I should be grateful if you would at once release me from our engagement and permit me to leave your employment," said Ishmael, who felt that it would be to him the most dreadful trial to remain in the house and meet Claudia and Vincent as betrothed lovers every day, and at last witness their marriage.

The judge looked annoyed and then asked:

"Now, Ishmael, why do you wish to leave me before the expiration of the term for which you were engaged?"

And before Ishmael could answer that question, he continued:

"You are in error as to the reasons you assign. In the first place, I am not to leave Washington so soon as I expected; as it is arranged that we shall remain here for the solemnization of the marriage, which will not take place until the first of July. And in the second place, instead of there being but little to do in the office, there will be a great deal to do—all Claudia's estate to be arranged, the viscount's affairs to be examined, marriage settlements to be executed,—I wish it was the bridegroom that was to be executed instead,—letters to be written, and what not. So that you see I shall need your services very much. And besides, Ishmael, my boy, I do not wish to part with you just now, in this great trial of my life; for it is a great trial to me, Ishmael, to part with my only child, to a foreigner whom I dislike and who will take her across the sea to another world. I have loved you as a son, Ishmael. And now I ask you to stand by me in this crisis—for I do not know how I shall bear it. It will be to me like giving her up to death."

Ishmael arose and placed his hand in that of his old friend. His stately young form was shaken by agitation, as an oak tree is by a storm, as he said:

"I will remain with you, Judge Merlin. I will remain with you through this trial. But oh, you do not know—you cannot know how terrible the ordeal will be to me!"

A sudden light of revelation burst upon Judge Merlin's mind! He looked into that agonized young face, clasped that true hand and said:

"Is it so, my boy? Oh, my poor boy, is it indeed so?"

"Make some excuse for me to the family below; say that I am not well, for that indeed is true; I cannot come into the drawing room this evening!" said Ishmael.

And he hastily wrung his friend's hand and hurried from the room, for after that one touch of sympathy from Claudia's father he felt that if he had stayed another moment he should have shamed his manhood and wept.

He hurried up into his little room to strive, in solitude and prayer, with his great sorrow.

Meanwhile the judge took up his hat for a walk in the open air. He had not seen his daughter since he had given his consent to her betrothal. And he felt that as yet he would not see her. He wished to subdue his own feelings of pain and regret before meeting her with the congratulations which he wished to offer.

"After all," he said to himself, as he descended the stairs "after all, I suppose, I should dislike any man in the world who should come to marry Claudia, so it is not the viscount who is in fault; but I who am unreasonable. But Ishmael! Ah, poor boy! poor boy! Heaven forgive Claudia if she has had anything to do with this! And may Heaven comfort him, for be deserves to be happy!"

CHAPTER LXIII.

THE BRIDE-ELECT.

She stands up her full height,
With her rich dress flowing round her,
And her eyes as fixed and bright
As the diamond stars that crown her,—
An awful, beautiful sight.

Beautiful? Yes, with her hair
So wild and her cheeks so flushed!
Awful? Yes, for there
In her beauty she stands hushed
By the pomp of her own despair.
—*Meredith.*

Judge Merlin walked about, reasoning with himself all day; but he could not walk off his depression of spirits, or reason away his misgivings.

He returned home in time to dress for dinner. He crept up to his chamber with a wearied and stealthy air, for he was still dispirited and desirous of avoiding a meeting with his daughter.

He made his toilet and then sat down, resolved not to leave his chamber until the dinner-bell rang, so that he should run no risk of seeing her until he met her at dinner, where of course no allusion would be made to the event of the morning.

He took up the evening paper, that lay upon the dressing-table by some chance, and tried to read. But the words conveyed no meaning to his mind.

"She is all I have in this world!" he sighed as he laid the paper down.

"Papa!"

He looked up.

There she stood within his chamber door! It was an unprecedented intrusion. There she stood in her rich evening dress of purple moire-antique, with the bandeau of diamonds encircling her night-black hair. Two crimson spots like the flush of hectic fever burned in her cheeks, and her eyes were unnaturally bright and wild, almost like those of insanity.

"Papa, may I come to you? Oh, papa, I have been waiting to speak to you all day; and it seems to me as if you had purposely kept out of my way. Are you displeased, papa? May I come to you now?"

He opened his arms, and she came and threw herself upon his bosom, sobbing as if her heart would break.

"What is the matter, my darling?"

"Are you displeased, papa?"

"No, no, my darling! Why should I be? How could I be so unreasonable? But—do you love him, Claudia?"

"He will be an earl, papa."

"Are you happy, Claudia?"

"I shall be a countess, papa!"

"But—are you happy, my dear, I ask you."

"Happy? Who is? Who ever was?"

"Your mother and myself were happy, very happy during the ten blessed years of our union. But then we loved each other, Claudia. Do you love this man whom you are about to make your husband?"

"Papa, I have consented to be his wife. Should not that satisfy you?"

"Certainly, certainly, my child! Besides, it is not for my rough, masculine hand to probe your heart. Your mother might do it if she were living, but not myself."

"Papa, bless me! it was for that I came to you. Oh, give me your blessing before I go downstairs to—him, whom I must henceforth meet as my promised husband."

"May the Lord bless and save you, my poor, motherless girl!" he said, laying his hand on her bowed head.

And she arose, and without another word went below stairs.

When she entered the drawing room she found the viscount there alone. He hastened to meet her with gallant alacrity and pressed his lips to hers, but at their touch the color fled from her face and did not return. With attentive courtesy Lord Vincent handed her to a seat and remained standing near, seeking to interest and amuse her with his conversation. But just as the tête-à-tête was growing unsupportable to Claudia, the door opened and Beatrice entered. Too many times had Bee come in upon just such a tête-à-tête to suspect that there was anything more in this one than there had been in any other for the last six months. So, unconscious of the recent betrothal of this pair, she, smiling, accepted the chair the viscount placed for her, and readily followed Claudia's lead, by allowing herself to be drawn into conversation. Several times she looked up at Claudia's face, noticing its marble whiteness; but at length concluded that it must be only the effect of late hours, and so dropped the subject from her mind.

Presently the other members of the family dropped in and the dinner was served.

One vacant chair at the table attracted general attention. But, ah! to one there that seat was not vacant; it was filled with the specter of her murdered truth.

"Where is Mr. Worth?" inquired Mrs. Middleton, from the head of the table.

"Oh! worked himself into a nervous headache over Allenby's complicated brief! I told him how it would be if he applied himself so unintermittingly to business; but he would take no warning. Well, these young enthusiasts must learn by painful experience to modify their zeal," said the judge, in explanation.

Everyone expressed regret except Claudia, who understood and felt how much worse than any headache was the heart-sickness that had for the time mastered even Ishmael's great strength; but she durst utter no word of sympathy. And the dinner proceeded to its conclusion. And directly after the coffee was served the viscount departed.

Meanwhile Ishmael lay extended upon his bed, clasping his temples and waging a silent war with his emotions.

A rap disturbed him.

"Come in."

Powers entered with a tea tray in his hands, upon which was neatly arranged a little silver tea-service, with a transparent white cup, saucer, and plate. The wax candle in its little silver candlestick that sat upon the tray was the only light, and scarcely served to show the room.

Ishmael raised himself up just as Powers sat the tray upon the stand beside the bed.

"Who has had leisure to think of me this evening?" thought Ishmael, as he contemplated this unexpected attention. Then, speaking aloud, he inquired:

"Who sent me these, Powers?"

"Miss Middleton, sir; and she bade me to say to you that you must try to eat; and that it is a great mistake to fast when one has a nervous headache, brought on by fatigue and excitement; and that the next best thing to rest is food, and both together are a cure," replied the man, carefully arranging the service on the stand.

"I might have known it," thought Ishmael, with an undefined feeling of self-reproach. "I might have known that she would not forget me, even though I forgot myself. What would my life be at home without this dear little sister? Sweet sister! dear sister! Yes, I will follow her advice; I will eat and drink for her sake, because I know she will question Powers and be disappointed if she finds that I have not done justice to this repast."

"Will you have more light, sir?" asked the footman.

"No, no, thank you," replied Ishmael, rising and seating himself in a chair beside the stand.

The tea was strong and fragrant, the cream rich, the sugar crystalline, and a single cup of the beverage refreshed him. The toast was crisp and yellow, the butter fresh, and the shavings of chipped beef crimson and tender. And so, despite his heartache and headache, Ishmael found his healthy and youthful appetite stimulated by all this. And the meal that was begun for Bee's sake was finished for his own.

"Tour head is better now, I hope, sir?" respectfully inquired Powers, as he prepared to remove the service.

"Much, thank you. Tell Miss Middleton so, with my respects, and say how grateful I feel to her for this kind attention."

"Yes, sir."

"And, Powers, you may bring me lights now."

And a few minutes later, when Powers had returned with two lighted candles and placed them on the table, Ishmael, who knew that not an over tasked brain, but an undisciplined heart, was the secret of his malady, set himself to work as to a severe discipline, and worked away for three or four hours with great advantage; for, when at twelve o'clock he retired to bed, he fell asleep and slept soundly until morning.

That is what work did for Ishmael. And work will do as much for anyone who will try it.

It is true in the morning he awoke to a new sense of woe; but the day had also its work to discipline him. He breakfasted with Bee and her father and the judge, who were the only members of the family present at the table; and then he went to the City Hall, where he had an appointment with the District Attorney.

That morning the engagement between Lord Vincent and Claudia was formally announced to the family circle. And Bee understood the secret of Ishmael's sudden illness. The marriage was appointed to take place on the first of the ensuing month, and so the preparations for the event were at once commenced.

Mrs. Middleton and Claudia went to New York to order the wedding outfit. They were gone a week, and when they returned Claudia, though much thinner in flesh, seemed to have recovered the gloom that had been frightened away by the viscount's first kiss.

The great responsibility of the home preparations fell upon Bee. The house had to be prepared for visitors; not only for the wedding guests; but also for friends and relatives of the family, who were coming from a distance and would remain for several days. For the last mentioned, new rooms had to be made ready. And all this was to be done under the immediate supervision of Beatrice.

As on two former occasions, Miss Merlin called in the aid of her three favorite ministers—Vourienne, Devizae, and Dureezie.

On the morning of the last day of June Vourienne and his assistants decorated the dining room. On the evening of the same day Devizae and his waiters laid the table for the wedding breakfast. And then the room was closed up until the next day. While the family took their meals in their small breakfast room.

During the evening relatives from a distance arrived and were received by Bee, who conducted them to their rooms.

By this inroad of visitors Bee herself, with the little sister who shared her bed, were driven up into the attic to the plain spare room next to Ishmael's own. Here, early in the evening, as he sat at his work, he could hear Bee, who would not neglect little Lu for anything else in the world, rocking and singing her to sleep. And Ishmael, too, who had just laid down his pen because the waning light no longer enabled him to write, felt his great trouble soothed by Bee's song.

CHAPTER LXIV.

CLAUDIA'S WOE

Ay, lady, here alone
You may think till your heart is broken,
Of the love that is dead and done,
Of the days that with no token,
For evermore are gone.

Weep, if you can, beseech you!
There's no one by to curb you:

His heart cry cannot reach you:
His love will not disturb you:
Weep?—what can weeping teach you?
—*Meredith.*

Sitting within the recess of the dormer window, soothed by the gathering darkness of the quiet, starlight night, and by the gentle cadences of Bee's low, melodious voice, as she sung her baby sister to sleep, Ishmael remained some little time longer, when suddenly Bee's song ceased, and he heard her exclamation of surprise:

"Claudia, you up here! and already dressed for dinner! How well you look! How rich that maize-colored brocade is! And how elegant that spray of diamonds in your hair! I never saw you wear it before! Is it a new purchase?"

"It is the viscount's present. I wear it this evening in his honor."

"How handsome you are, Lady Vincent! You know I do not often flatter, but really, Claudia, all the artist in me delights to contemplate you. I never saw you with such brilliant eyes, or such a beautiful color."

"Brilliant eyes! beautiful color! Ha! ha! ha! the first frenzy, I think! The last—well, it ought to be beautiful. I paid ten dollars a scruple for it at a wicked French shop in Broadway! And I have used the scruple unscrupulously!" she cried, with a bitter laugh as of self-scorn.

"Oh, Claudia—rouged!" said Bee, in a tone of surprise and pain.

"Yes, rouged and powdered! why not? Why should the face be true when the life is false! Oh, Bee," she suddenly broke forth in a wail of anguish; "lay that child down and listen to me! I must tell someone, or my heart will break!"

There was a movement, a low, muffling, hushing sound, that told the unwilling listener that Bee was putting her baby sister in the bed. Ishmael arose with the intention of leaving his room, and slipping out of hearing of the conversation that was not intended for his ears; but utterly overcome by the crowding emotions of his heart, he sank back in his chair.

He heard Bee return to her place. He heard Claudia throw herself down on the floor by Bee's side, and say:

"Oh, let me lay my head down upon your lap, Bee!"

"Claudia, dear Claudia, what is the matter with you? What can I do for you?"

"Receive my confidence, that is all. Hear my confession. I must tell somebody or die. I wish I was a Catholic, and had a father confessor who would hear me and comfort me, and absolve my sins, and keep my secrets!"

"Can any man stand in that relation to a woman except her father, if she is single, or her husband, if she is married?" asked Bee.

"I don't know—and I don't care! Only when I passed by St. Patrick's Church, with this load of trouble on my soul, I felt as if it would have done me good to steal into one of those veiled recesses and tell the good old father there!"

"You could have told your heavenly Father anywhere."

"He knows it already; but I durst not pray to him! I am not so impious as that either. I have not presumed to pray for a month—not since my betrothal."

"You have not presumed to pray. Oh, Claudia!"

"How should I dare to pray, after I had deliberately sold myself to the demon—after I had deliberately determined to sin and take the wages of sin?"

"Claudia! Oh, Heaven! You are certainly mad!"

"I know it; but the knowledge does not help me to the cure. I have been mad a month!" Then breaking forth into a wail of woe, she cried: "Oh, Bee! I do not love that man! I do not love him! and the idea of marrying him appalls my very soul!"

"Good Heaven, Claudia, then why—" begun Bee, but Claudia fiercely continued:

"I loathe him! I sicken at him! His first kiss! Oh, Bee! the cold, clammy touch of those lips struck all the color from my face forever, I think! I loathe him!"

"Oh, Claudia, Claudia, why, in the name of all that is wise and good, do you do yourself, and him, too, such a terrible wrong as to marry him?" inquired the deeply-shocked maiden.

"Because I must! Because I will! I have deliberately determined to be a peeress of England, and I will be one, whatever the cost."

"But oh! have you thought of the deadly sin—the treachery, the perjury, the sacrilege; oh! and the dreadful degradation of such a loveless marriage?"

"Have I thought of these things—these horrors? Yes; witness this tortured heart and racked brain of mine!"

"Then why, oh, why, Claudia, do you persevere?"

"I am in the vortex of the whirlpool, and cannot stop myself!"

"Then let me stop you. My weak hand is strong enough for that. Remain here, dear Claudia. Let me go downstairs and report that you are ill, as indeed and in truth you are. The marriage can be delayed, and then you can have an explanation with the viscount, and break it off altogether."

"And break my plighted faith! Is that your advice, young moralist?"

"There was no faith in your plighted word, Claudia. It was very wrong to promise to marry a man you could not love; but it would be criminal to keep such a promise. Speak candidly to his lordship, Claudia, and ask him to release you from your engagement. My word on it he will do it."

"Of course, and make me the town talk for the delight of all who envy me."

"Better be that than an unloving wife."

"No, Bee! I must fulfill my destiny. And, besides, I never thought of turning from it. I am in the power of the whirlpool or the demon."

"It is the demon—the demon that is carrying you down into this whirlpool. And the name of the demon is Ambition, Claudia; and the name of the whirlpool is Ruin."

"Yes! it is ambition that possesses my soul. None other but the sins by which angels fell would have power to draw my soul down from heaven—for heaven was possible to me, once!" And with these last words she melted into tears and wept as if the fountains of her heart were broken up and gushing through her eyes.

"Yes," she repeated in the pauses of her weeping. "Heaven was possible for me once! Never more, oh, never, never more! Filled with the ambition of Lucifer I have cast myself out of that heaven. But alas! alas! I have Lucifer's ambition without his strength to suffer."

"Claudia, dear Claudia!"

"Do not speak to me. Let me speak, for I must speak, or die! It is not only that I do not love this viscount, but, oh, Bee!" she wailed in the prolonged tones of unutterable woe, "I love another! I love Ishmael!"

There was a sudden movement and a fall.

"You push me from you! Oh, cruel friend! Let me lay my head upon your lap again, Bee, and sob out all this anguish here. I must, or my heart will burst. I love Ishmael! His love is the heaven of heavens from which Ambition has cast me down. I love Ishmael! Oh, how much, my reason, utterly overthrown, may some time betray to the world! This love fills my soul. Oh, more than that, it is greater than my soul; it goes beyond it, into infinitude! There is light, warmth, and life where Ishmael is; darkness, coldness, and death where he is not! To meet his eyes,—those beautiful, dark, luminous eyes, that seem like inlets to some perfect inner world of wisdom, love, and pure joy; or to lay my hand in his, and feel that soft, strong, elastic hand close upon mine,— gives me a moment of such measureless content, such perfect assurance of peace, that for the time I forget all the sin and horror that envelopes and curses my life. But to be his beloved wife—oh, Bee! I cannot imagine in the life of heaven a diviner happiness!"

A low, half-suppressed cry from Bee. And Claudia continued:

"It is a love that all which is best in my nature approves. For oh, who is like Ishmael? Who so wise, so good, so useful? Morally, intellectually, and physically beautiful! an Apollo! more than that, a Christian gentleman! He is human, and yet he appears to me to be perfectly faultless."

There was a pause and a low sound of weeping, broken at last by Claudia, who rustled up to her feet, saying:

"There, it is past!"

"Claudia," said Bee solemnly, "you must not let this marriage go on; to do so would be to commit the deadliest sin!"

"I have determined to commit it, then, Bee."

"Claudia, if I saw you on the brink of endless woe, would I not be justified in trying to pluck you back? Oh, Claudia, dear cousin, pause, reflect—"

"Bee, hush! I have reflected until my brain has nearly burst. I must fulfill my destiny. I must be a peeress of England, cost what it may in sin against others, or in suffering to myself."

"Oh, what an awful resolution! and what an awful defiance! Ah, what have you invoked upon your head!"

"I know not—the curse of Heaven, perhaps!"

"Claudia!"

"Be silent, Bee!"

"I must not, cannot, will not, be silent! My hand is weak, but it shall grasp your arm to hold you back; my voice is low, but it shall be raised in remonstrance with you. You may break from my hold; you may deafen yourself to my words; you may escape me so; but it will be to cast yourself into—"

"Lawyer Vivian's 'gulf of perdition'! Is that what you mean? Nonsense, Bee. My hysterics are over now; my hour of weakness is past; I am myself again. And I feel that I shall be Lady Vincent—the envy of Washington, the admiration of London, the only titled lady of the republican court, and the only beauty at St. James!" said Claudia, rustling a deep courtesy.

"Claudia—"

"And in time I shall be Countess of Hurstmonceux, and perhaps after a while Marchioness of Banff; for Vincent thinks if the Conservatives come in his father will be raised a step in the peerage."

"And is it for that you sell yourself? Oh, Claudia, how Satan fools you! Be rational; consider: what is it to be a countess, or even a marchioness? It is 'distance lends enchantment to the view.' Here in this country, where, thank the Lord, there is no hereditary rank,—no titles and no coronets,—these things, from their remoteness, impress your imagination, and disturb your judgment. You will not feel so in England; there, where there are hundreds and thousands of titled personages, your coveted title will sink to its proper level, and you will find yourself of much less importance in London as Lady Vincent, than you are in Washington as Miss Merlin. There you will find how little you have really gained by the sacrifice of truth, honor, and purity; all that is best in your woman's nature—all that is best in your earthly, yes, and your eternal life."

"Bee, have you done?"

"No. You have given me two reasons why I think you ought not to marry the viscount: first, because you do not love him, and secondly, because you do love—someone else. And now I will give you two more reasons why you should not marry him—viz., first, because he is not a good man, and, secondly, because he does not love you. There!" said Beatrice firmly.

"Bee, how dare you say that! What should you know of his character? And why should you think he does not love me?"

"I feel that he is not a good man; so do you, I will venture to say, Claudia. And I know that he marries you for some selfish or mercenary motive—your money, possibly. And so also do you know it, Claudia, I dare to affirm."

"Have you anything more to say?"

"Only this: to beg, to pray, to urge you not to sin—not to debase yourself! Oh, Claudia, if loving Ishmael as you profess to do, and loathing the viscount as you confess you do, and knowing that he cares nothing for you, you still marry him for his title and his rank, as you admit you will—Claudia! Claudia! in the pure sight of angels you will be more guilty, and less pardonable than the poor lost creatures of the pavement, whose shadow you would scarcely allow to fall across your path!"

"Bee, you insult, you offend, you madden me! If this be so—if you speak the truth—I cannot help it, and I do not care. I am ambitious. If I immolate all my womanly feelings to become a peeress, it is as I would certainly and ruthlessly destroy everything that stood in my way to become a queen, if that were possible."

"Good heavens, Claudia! are you then really a fiend in female form?" exclaimed the dismayed girl.

"I do not know. I may be so. I think Satan has taken possession of me since my betrothal. At least I feel that I could be capable of great crimes to secure great ends," said Claudia recklessly.

"And, oh, Heaven! the opportunity will be surely afforded you, if you do not repent. Satan takes good care to give his servants the fullest freedom to develop their evil. Oh, Claudia, for the love of Heaven, stop where you are! go no further. Your next step on this sinful road may make retreat impossible. Break off this marriage at once. Better the broken troth—better the nine days' wonder—than the perjured bride, and the loveless, sinful nuptials! You said you were ambitious. Claudia!" here Bee's voice grew almost inaudible from intense passion—"Claudia! you do not know—you cannot know what it costs me to say what I am about to say to you now; but—I will say it: You love Ishmael. Well, he loves you—ah! far better than you love him, or than you are capable of loving anyone. For you all his toils have been endured, all his laurels won. Claudia! be proud of this great love; it is a hero's love—a poet's love. Claudia! you have received much adulation in your life, and you will receive much more; but you never have received, and you never will, so high an honor as you have in Ishmael's love. It is a crown of glory to your life. You are ambitious! Well, wait for him; give him a few short years and he will attain honors, not hereditary, but all his own. He will reach a position that the proudest woman may be proud to share; and his wife shall take a higher rank among American matrons than the wife of a mere nobleman can reach in England. And his untitled name, like that of Cæsar, shall be a title in itself."

264

"Bee! Bee! you wring my heart in two. You drive me mad. It cannot be, I tell you! It can never be. He may rise—there is no doubt but that he will! But let him rise ever so high, I cannot be his wife—his wife! Horrible! I came of a race of which all the men were brave, and all the women pure! And he—"

"Is braver than the bravest man of your race! purer than the purest woman!" interrupted Bee fervently.

"He is the child of shame, and his heritage is dishonor! He bears his mother's maiden name, and she was—the scorn of his sex and the reproach of ours! And this is the man you advise me, Claudia Merlin, whose hand is sought in marriage by the heir of one of the oldest earldoms in England, to marry! Bee, the insult is unpardonable! You might as well advise me to marry my father's footman! and better, for Powers came at least of honest parents!" said Claudia, speaking in the mad, reckless, defiant way in which those conscious of a bad argument passionately defend their point.

For a few moments Bee seemed speechless with indignation. Then she burst forth vehemently:

"It is false! as false as the Father of Falsehood himself! When thorns produce figs, or the deadly nightshade nectarines; when eaglets are hatched in owls' nests and young lions spring from rat holes, then I may believe these foul slanders of Ishmael and his parents. Shame on you, Claudia Merlin, for repeating them! You have shown me much evil in your heart to-night; but nothing so bad as that! Ishmael is nature's gentleman! His mother must have been pure and lovely and loving! his father good and wise and brave! else how could they have given this son to the world! And did you forget, Claudia, when you spoke those cruel words of him, did you forget that only a little while ago you admitted that you loved him, and that all which was best in your nature approved that love?"

"No, I did not and do not forget it! It was and it is true! But what of that? I may not be able to help adoring him for his personal excellence! But to be his wife—the wife of a—Horrible!"

"Have you forgotten, Claudia, that only a few minutes ago you said that you could not conceive of a diviner happiness than to be the beloved wife of Ishmael?"

"No, I have not forgotten it! And I spoke the truth! but that joy which I could so keenly appreciate can never, never be mine! And that is the secret of my madness—for I am mad, Bee! And, oh, I came here to-night with my torn and bleeding heart—torn and bleeding from the dreadful battle between love and pride—came here with my suffering heart; my sinful heart if you will; and laid it on your bosom to be soothed; and you have taken it and flung it back in my face! You have broken the bruised reed; quenched the smoking flax; humbled the humble; smitten the fallen! Oh, Bee, you have been more cruel than you know! Good-by! Good-by!" And she turned and flung herself out of the room.

"Claudia, dear Claudia, oh, forgive me! I did not mean to wound you; if I spoke harshly it was because I felt for both! Claudia, come back, love!" cried Bee, hurrying after her; but Claudia was gone. Bee would have followed her; but little Lu's voice was heard in plaintive notes. Bee returned to the room to find her little sister lying awake with wide-open, frightened eyes.

"Oh, Bee! don't do! and don't let she tome bat. She stares Lu!"

"Shall Bee take Lu up and rock her to sleep?"

"'Es."

Bee gently lifted the little one and sat down in the rocking-chair and began to rock slowly and sing softly. But presently she stopped and whispered:

"Baby!"

"'Es, Bee."

"Do you love cousin Claudia?"

"'Es, but she wates me up and stares me; don't let she tome adain, Bee."

"No, I will not; but poor Claudia is not happy; won't you ask the Lord to bless poor Claudia? He hears little children like you!"

"'Es; tell me what to say, Bee." And without another word the little one slid down upon her knees and folded her hands, while Bee taught the sinless child to pray for the sinful woman.

And then she took the babe again upon her lap, and rocked slowly and sung softly until she soothed her to sleep.

Then Bee arose and rustled softly about the room, making her simple toilet before going to the saloon to join the guests.

CHAPTER LXV.

ISHMAEL'S WOE.

And with another's crime, my birth
She taunted me as little worth,
Because, forsooth, I could not claim
The lawful heirship of my name;
Yet were a few short summers mine,
My name should more than ever shine,
With honors all my own!
—*Byron.*

Ishmael sat in the shadows of his room overwhelmed with shame and sorrow and despair. He had heard every cruel word; they had entered his ears and pierced his heart. And not only for himself he bowed his head and sorrowed and despaired, but for her; for her, proud, selfish, sinful, but loving, and oh, how fatally beloved!

It was not only that he worshiped her with a blind idolatry, and knew that she returned his passion with equal strength and fervor, and that she would have waited for him long years, and married him at last but for the cloud upon his birth. It was not this—not his own misery that crushed him, nor even her present wretchedness that prostrated him—no! but it was the awful, shapeless shadow of some infinite unutterable woe is Claudia's future, and into which she was blindly rushing, that overwhelmed him. Oh, to have saved her from this woe, he would gladly have laid down his life!

The door opened and Jim, his especial waiter, entered with two lighted candles on a tray. He sat them on the table and was leaving the room, when Ishmael recalled him. What I am about to relate is a trifle perhaps, but it will serve to show the perfect beauty of that nature which, in the midst of its own great sorrow, could think of the small wants of another.

"Jim, you asked me this morning to write a letter for you, to your mother, I think."

"Yes, Master Ishmael, I thank you, sir; whenever you is at leisure, sir, with nothing to do; which I wouldn't presume to be in a hurry, sir, nor likewise inconvenience you the least in the world."

"It will not inconvenience me, Jim; it will give me pleasure, whenever you can spare me half an hour," replied Ishmael, speaking with as much courtesy to the poor dependent as he would have used in addressing his wealthiest patron.

"Well, Master Ishmael, which I ought to say Mr. Worth, and I beg your pardon, sir, only it is the old love as makes me forget myself, and call you what I used to in the old days, because Mr. Worth do seem to leave me so far away—"

"Call me what you please, Jim, we are old friends, and I love my old friends better than any new distinctions that could come between us, but which I will never allow to separate us. What were you about to say, Jim?"

"Well, Master Ishmael, and I thank you sincere, sir, for letting of me call you so, I was going for to say, as I could be at your orders any time, even now, if it would suit you, sir; because I have lighted up all my rooms and set my table for dinner, which it is put back an hour because of Master Walter, who is expected by the six o'clock train this evening; and Sam is waiting in the hall, and I aint got anything very partic'lar to do for the next hour or so."

"Very well, Jim; sit down in that chair and tell me what you want me to write," said Ishmael, seating himself before his desk and dipping his pen in ink.

Yes, it was a small matter in itself; but it was characteristic of the man, thus to put aside his own poignant anguish to interest himself in the welfare of the humblest creature who invoked his aid.

"Now then, Jim."

"Well, Master Ishmael," said the poor fellow. "You know what to say a heap better'n I do. Write it beautiful, please."

"Tell me what is in your heart, Jim, and then I will do the best I can," said Ishmael, who possessed the rare gift of drawing out from others the best that was in their thoughts.

"Well, sir, I think a heap o' my ole mother, I does; 'membering how she did foh me when I was a boy and wondering if anybody does for her now, and if she is comfortable down there at Tanglewood. And I wants her to know it; and not to be a-thinking as I forgets her."

Ishmael wrote rapidly for a few moments and then looked up.

"What else, Jim?"

"Well, sir, tell her as I have saved a heap of money for her out'n the presents the gemmen made me o' Christmas, and I'll bring it to her when I come down—which the ole 'oman do love money, sir, better than she do anything in this world, 'cept it is me and old marster and Miss Claudia. And likewise what she wants me to bring her from town, and whether she would like a red gownd or a yallow one."

Ishmael set down this and looked up.

"Well, Jim?"

"Well, sir, tell her how she aint got no call to be anxious nor likewise stressed in her mind, nor lay 'wake o' nights thinking 'bout me, fear I should heave myself 'way, marrying of these yer trifling city gals as don't know a spinning wheel from a harrow. And how I aint seen nobody yet as I like better'n my ole mother and the young lady of color as she knows 'bout and 'proves of; which, sir, it aint nobody else but your own respected aunt, Miss Hannah's Miss Sally, as lives at Woodside."

"I have put all that down, Jim."

"Well, sir, and about the grand wedding as is to be to-morrow, sir; and how the Bishop of Maryland is going to 'form the ceremony; and how the happy pair be going to go on a grand tower, and then going to visit Tanglewood afore they parts for the old country; and how she will see a rale, livin' lord as she'll be 'stonished to see look so like any other man; and last ways how Miss Claudia do talk about taking me and Miss Sally along of her to foreign parts, because she prefers to be waited on by colored ladies and gentlemen 'fore white ones; and likewise how I would wish to go and see the world, only I won't go, nor likewise would Miss Claudia wish to take me, if the ole 'oman wishes otherwise."

Ishmael wrote and then looked up. Poor Jim, absorbed in his own affairs, did not notice how pale the writer's face had grown, or suspect how often during the last few minutes he had stabbed him to the heart.

"Well, sir, that is about all I think, Master Ishmael. Only, please, sir, put it all down in your beautiful language as makes the ladies cry when you gets up and speaks afore the great judges theirselves."

"I will do my best, Jim."

"Thank you, sir. And please sign my name to it, not yourn—my name—James Madison Monroe Mortimer."

"Yes, Jim."

"And please direct it to Mistress Catherine Maria Mortimer, most in general called by friends, Aunt Katie, as is housekeeper at Tanglewood."

Ishmael complied with his requests as far as discretion permitted.

"And now, sir, please read it all out aloud to me, so I can hear how it sound."

Ishmael complied with this request also, and read the letter aloud, to the immense delight of Jim, who earnestly expressed his approbation in the emphatic words:

"Now—that—is—beautiful! Thank y', sir! That is ekal to anything as ever I heard out'n the pulpit—and sides which, sir, it is all true, true as gospel, sir. It is just exactly what I thinks and how I feels and what I wants to say, only I aint got the words. Won't mother be proud o' that letter nyther? Why, laws, sir, the ole 'oman 'll get the minister to read that letter. And then she'll make everybody as comes to the house as can read, read it over and over again for the pride she takes in it, till she'll fairly know it all by heart," etc., etc., etc.

For Jim went on talking and smiling and covering the writer all over with gratitude and affection, until he was interrupted by the stopping of a carriage, the ringing of a door bell, and the sound of a sudden arrival.

"There's Master Walter Middleton now, as sure as the world! I must run! Dinner'll be put on the table soon's ever he's changed his dress. I'm a thousand times obleeged to you, sir. I am, indeed, everlasting obleeged! I wish I could prove it some way. Mother'll be so pleased." And talking all the way downstairs, Jim took himself and his delight away.

Ishmael sighed, and arose to dress for dinner. His kindness had not been without its reward. The little divertisement of Jim's letter had done him good. Blessed little offices of loving-kindness—what ministering angels are they to the donor as well as the receiver! With some degree of self-possession Ishmael completed his toilet and turned to leave the room, when the sound of someone rushing up the stairs like a storm arrested his steps.

Then a voice sounded outside:

"Which is Ishmael's room? Bother! Oh, here it is!" and Bee's door was opened. "No! calico! Ah! now I'm right."

And the next instant Walter Middleton burst open the door and rushed in, exclaiming joyfully, as he seized and shook the hands of his friend:

"Ah, here you are, old fellow! God bless you! How glad I am to see you! You are still the first love of my heart, Ishmael. Damon, your Pythias has not even a sweetheart to dispute your empire over him. How are you? I have heard of your success. Wasn't is glorious! You're a splendid fellow, Ishmael, and I'm proud of you. You may have Bee, if you want her. I always thought there was a bashful kindness between you two. And there isn't a reason in the world why you shouldn't have her. And so her Royal Highness, the Princess Claudia, has caught a Lord, has she? Well, you know she always said she would, and she has kept her word. But, I say, how are you? How do you wear your honors? How do the toga and the bays become you? Turn around and let us have a look at you." And so the affectionate fellow rattled on, shaking both Ishmael's hands every other second, until he had talked himself fairly out of breath.

"And how are you, dear Walter? But I need not ask; you look so well and happy," said Ishmael, as soon as he could get in a word.

"Me? Oh, I'm well enough. Nought's never in danger. I've just graduated, you know; with the highest honors, they say. My thesis won the great prize; that was because you were not in the same class, you know. I have my diploma in my pocket; I'm an M.D.; I can write myself doctor, and poison people, without danger of being tried for murder! isn't that a privilege? Now let my enemies take care of themselves! Why don't you congratulate me, you——"

"I do, with all my heart and soul, Walter!"

"That's right! only I had to drag it from you. Well, so I'm to be 'best man' to this noble bridegroom. Too much honor. I am not prepared for it. One cannot get ready for graduating and marrying at the same time. I don't think I have got a thing fit to wear. I wrote to Bee to buy me some fine shirts, and some studs, and gloves, and handkerchiefs, and hair oil, and things proper for the occasion. I wonder if she did?"

"I don't know. I know that she has been overwhelmed with care for the last month, too much care for a girl, so it is just possible that she has had no opportunity. Indeed, she has a great deal to think of and to do."

"Oh, it won't hurt her; especially if it consists of preparations for the wedding."

A bell rang.

"There now, Ishmael, there is that diabolical dinner-bell! You may look, but it is true: a dinner-bell that peals out at seven o'clock in the evening is a diabolical dinner-bell. At college we dine at twelve meridian, sharp, and sup at six. It is dreadful to sit at table a whole hour, and be bored by seeing other people eat, and pretending to eat yourself, when you are not hungry. Well, there's no help for it. Come down and be bored, Ishmael."

They went down into the drawing room, where quite a large circle of near family connections were assembled.

Walter Middleton was presented to the Viscount Vincent, who was the only stranger, to him, present.

Claudia was there, looking as calm, as self-possessed and queenly, as if she had not passed through a storm of passion two hours before.

Ishmael glanced at her and saw the change with amazement, but he dared not trust himself to look again.

The dinner party, with all this trouble under the surface, passed off in superficial gayety. The guests separated early, because the following morning would usher in the wedding day.

CHAPTER LXVI.

THE MARRIAGE MORNING.

I trust that never more in this world's shade
Thine eyes will be upon me: never more
Thy face come back to me. For thou hast made
My whole life sore.
Fare hence, and be forgotten.... Sing thy song,
And braid thy brow,
And be beloved and beautiful—and be
In beauty baleful still ... a Serpent Queen
To others not yet curst in loving thee

268

As I have been!

—Meredith.

Ishmael awoke. After a restless night, followed by an hour't complete forgetfulness, that more nearly resembled the swoon of exhaustion than the sleep of health, Ishmael awoke to a new sense of wretchedness.

You who have suffered know what such awakenings are. You have seen someone dearer than life die; but hours, days, or weeks of expectation have gradually prepared you for the last scene; and though you have seen the dear one die, and though you have wept yourself half blind and half dead, you have slept the sleep of utter oblivion, which is like death; but you have at last awakened and returned to consciousness to meet the shock of memory and the sense of sorrow a thousand times more overwhelming than the first blow of bereavement had been.

Or you have been for weeks looking forward to the parting of one whose presence is the very light of your days. And in making preparations for that event the thought of coming separation has been somewhat dulled; but at last all is ready; the last night has come; you all separate and go to bed, with the mutual injunction to be up early in the morning for the sake of seeing "him"—it may be some brave volunteer going to war—off; after laying awake nearly all night you suddenly drop into utter forgetfulness of impending grief, and into some sweet dream of pleasantness and peace. You awake with a start; the hour has come; the hour of parting; the hour of doom.

Yes, whatever the grief may be, it is in the hour of such awakenings we feel it most poignantly.

Thus it was with Ishmael. The instant he awoke the spear of memory transfixed his soul. He could have cried out in his agony. It took all his manhood to control his pain. He arose and dressed himself and offered up his morning worship and went to the breakfast room, resolved to pass through the day's fiery ordeal, cost what it might.

Claudia was not at breakfast. In fact, she seldom or never appeared at the breakfast table; and this morning of all mornings it was quite natural she should be absent. But Mrs. Middleton and Bee, Judge Merlin, Mr. Middleton, Mr. Brudenell, Walter, and Ishmael were present. It was in order that people should be merry on a marriage morning; but somehow or other that order was not followed. Judge Merlin, Mrs. Middleton, and Bee were unusually grave and silent; Mr. Brudenell was always sad; Ishmael was no conventional talker, and therefore could not seem other than he was—very serious. It was quite in vain that Mr. Middleton and Walter tried to get up a little jesting and badinage. And when the constraint of the breakfast table was over everyone felt relieved.

"Remember," said Mrs. Middleton, with her hand upon the back of her chair, "that the carriages will be at the door at half-past ten; it is now half-past nine."

"And that means that we have but an hour to get on our wedding garments," said Walter. "Bee, have you got my finery ready?"

"You will find everything you require laid out on your bed, Walter."

"You are the best little sister that ever was born. I doubt whether I shall let Ishmael, or anyone else, hate you until I get a wife of my own; and even then I don't know but what I shall want you home to look after her and the children!" rattled Walter, careless or unobservant of the deep blush that mantled the maiden's face.

"Ishmael," said the judge, "I wish you to take the fourth seat in the carriage with myself and daughter and Beatrice. Will you do so?"

Ishmael's emotions nearly choked him, but he answered:

"Certainly, if you wish."

"The four bridesmaids will fill the second carriage, and Mr. and Mrs. Middleton, Mr. Brudenell and Walter the third, I do not know the arrangements made for our other friends; but I dare say it is all right. Oh, Ishmael, I feel as though we were arranging a procession to the grave instead of the altar," he added, with a heavy sigh. Then correcting himself, he said: "But this is all very morbid. So no more of it."

And the judge wrung Ishmael's hand; and each went his separate way to dress for the wedding.

Meanwhile the bride-elect sat alone in her luxurious dressing room.

Around her, scattered over tables, chairs, and stands, lay the splendid paraphernalia of her bridal array—rich dresses, mantles, bonnets, veils, magnificent shawls, sparkling jewels, blooming flowers, intoxicating perfumes.

On the superb malachite stand beside her stood a silver tray, on which was arranged an elegant breakfast service of Bohemian china. But the breakfast was untasted and forgotten.

There was no one to watch her; she had sent her maid away with orders not to return until summoned by her bell.

269

And now, while her coffee unheeded grew cold, she sat, leaning forward in her easy-chair, with her hands tightly clasped together over her knees, her tumbled black ringlets fallen down upon her dressing gown, and her eyes flared open and fixed in a dreadful stare upon the far distance as if spellbound by some there.

To have seen her thus, knowing that she was a bride-elect, you might have judged that she was about to be forced into some loathed marriage, from which her whole tortured nature revolted.

And you would have judged truly. She was being thus forced into such a marriage, not by any tyrannical parent or guardian, for flesh and blood could not have forced Claudia Merlin into any measure she had set her will against. She was forced by the demon Pride, who had taken possession of her soul.

And now she sat alone with her sin, dispossessed of all her better self, face to face with her lost soul.

She was aroused by the entrance of Mrs. Middleton—Mrs. Middleton in full carriage-dress—robe and mantle of mauve-colored moire-antique, a white lace bonnet with mauve-colored flowers, and white kid gloves finished at the wrists with mauve ribbon quillings.

"Why, Claudia, is it possible? Not commenced dressing yet, and everybody else ready, and the clock on the stroke of ten! What have you been thinking of, child?"

Claudia started like one suddenly aroused from sleep, threw her hands to her face as if to clear away a mist, and looked around.

But Mrs. Middleton had hurried to the door and was calling:

"Here, Alice! Laura! 'Gena! Lotty! Where are you?"

Receiving no answer, she flew to the bell and rang it and brought Claudia's maid to the room.

"Ruth, hurry to the young ladies' room and give my compliments, and ask them to come here as soon as possible! Miss Merlin is not yet dressed."

The girl went on her errand and Mrs. Middleton turned again to Claudia:

"Not even eaten your breakfast yet. Oh, Claudia!" and she poured out a cup of coffee and handed it to her niece.

And Claudia drank it, because it was easier to do so than to expostulate.

At the moment that Claudia returned the cup the door opened and the four bridesmaids entered—all dressed in floating, cloud-like, misty white tulle, and crowned with wreaths of white roses and holding bouquets of the same.

They laid down their bouquets, drew on their white gloves and fluttered around the bride and with their busy fingers quickly dressed her luxuriant black hair, and arrayed her stately form in her superb bridal dress.

This dress was composed of an under-skirt of the richest white satin and an upper robe of the finest Valenciennes lace looped up with bunches of orange flowers. A bertha of lace fell over the satin bodice. And a long veil of lace flowed from the queenly head down to the tiny foot. A wreath of orange flowers, sprinkled over with the icy dew of small diamonds, crowned her black ringlets. And diamonds adorned her neck, bosom, arms, and stomacher. Her bouquet holder was studded with diamonds, and her initials on the white velvet cover of her prayer-book were formed of tiny seed-like diamonds.

No sovereign queen on her bridal morn was ever more richly arrayed. But, oh, how deadly pale and cold she was!

"There!" they said triumphantly, when they had finished dressing her, even to the arranging of the bouquet of orange flowers in its costly holder and putting it in her hand. "There!" And they wheeled the tall Psyche mirror up before her, that she might view and admire herself.

She looked thoughtfully at the image reflected there. She looked so long that Mrs. Middleton, growing impatient, said:

"My love, it is time to go."

"Leave me alone for a few minutes, all of you! I will not keep you waiting long," said Claudia.

"She wishes to be alone to offer up a short prayer before going to be married," was the thought in the heart of each one of the party, as they filed out of the room.

Did Claudia wish to pray? Did she intend to ask God's protection against evil? Did she dare to ask his blessing on the act she contemplated?

We shall see.

She went after the last retreating figure and closed and bolted the door. Then she returned to her dressing bureau, opened a little secret drawer and took from it a tiny jar of rouge, and with a piece of cotton-wool applied it to her deathly-white cheeks until she had produced there an artificial bloom, more brilliant than that of her happiest days, only because it was more brilliant than that of nature. Then to soften its fire she powdered her face with pearl white, and finally with a fine handkerchief carefully dusted off the superfluous particles.

Having done this, she put away her cosmetics and took from the same receptacle a vial of the spirits of lavender and mixed a spoonful of it with water and drank it off.

Then she returned the vial to its place and locked up the secret drawer where she kept her deceptions.

She gave one last look at the mirror, saw that between the artificial bloom and the artificial stimulant her face presented a passable counterfeit of its long-lost radiance; she drew her bridal veil around so as to shade it a little, lowered her head and raised her bouquet, that her friends might not see the suspicious suddenness of the transformation from deadly pallor to living bloom—for though Claudia, in an hour of hysterical passion, had discovered this secret of her toilet to Beatrice, yet she was really ashamed of it, and wished to conceal it from all others.

She opened the door, went out, and joined her friends in the hall, saying with a cheerfulness that she had found in the lavender vial:

"I am quite ready for the show now!"

But she kept her head lowered and averted, for a little while, though in fact her party were too much excited to scrutinize her appearance, especially as they had had a good view of her while making her toilet.

They went down into the drawing room, where the family and their nearest relations were assembled and waiting for them.

Bee was there, looking lovely as usual. Bee, who almost always wore white when in full dress, now varied from her custom by wearing a glacé silk of delicate pale blue, with a white lace mantle and a white lace bonnet and veil. Bee did this because she did not mean to be mustered into the bride's service, or even mistaken by any person for one of the bridesmaids. Beyond her obligatory presence in the church as one of the bride's family, Bee was resolved to have nothing to do with the sacrilegious marriage.

"Come, my dear! Are you ready? How beautiful you are, my Claudia! I never paid you a compliment before, my child; but surely I may be excused for doing so now that you are about to leave me! 'How blessings brighten as they take their flight,'" whispered the judge, as he met and kissed his daughter.

And certainly Claudia's beauty seemed perfectly dazzling this morning. She smiled a greeting to all her friends assembled there, and then gave her hand to her father, who drew it within his arm and led her to the carriage.

Ishmael, like one in a splendid, terrible dream, from which he could not wake, in which he was obliged to act, went up to Bee and drew her little white-gloved hand under his arm, and led her after the father and daughter.

The other members of the marriage party followed in order.

Besides Judge Merlin's brougham and Mr. Middleton's barouche, there were several other carriages drawn up before the house.

Bee surveyed this retinue and murmured:

"Indeed, except that we all wear light colors instead of black, and the coachmen have no hat-scarfs, this looks quite as much like a funeral as a wedding."

Ishmael did not reply; he could not wake from the dazzling, horrible dream.

When they were seated in the carriage, Claudia and Beatrice occupied the back seat; the judge and Ishmael the front one; the judge sat opposite Bee, and Ishmael opposite Claudia.

The rich drifts of shining white satin and misty white lace that formed her bridal dress floated around him; her foot inadvertently touched his, and her warm, balmy breath passed him. Never had he been so close to Claudia before; that carriage was so confined and crowded—dread proximity! The dream deepened; it became a trance—that strange trance that sometimes falls upon the victim in the midst of his sufferings held Ishmael's faculties in abeyance and deadened his sense of pain.

And indeed the same spell, though with less force, acted upon all the party in that carriage. Its mood was expectant, excited, yet dream-like. There was scarcely any conversation. There seldom is under such circumstances. Once the judge inquired:

"Bee, my dear, how is it that you are not one of Claudia's bridesmaids?"

"I did not wish to be, and Claudia was so kind as to excuse me," Beatrice replied.

"But why not, my love? I thought young ladies always liked to fill such positions."

Bee blushed and lowered her head, but did not reply.

Claudia answered for her:

"Beatrice does not like Lord Vincent; and does not approve of the marriage," she said defiantly.

"Humph!" exclaimed the judge, and not another word was spoken during the drive.

It was a rather long one. The church selected for the performance of the marriage rites being St. John's, at the west end of the town, where the bridegroom and his friends were to meet the bride and her attendants.

They reached the church at last; the other carriages arrived a few seconds after them, and the whole party alighted and went in.

The bridegroom and his friends were already there. And the bridal procession formed and went up the middle aisle to the altar, where the bishop in his sacerdotal robes stood ready to perform the ceremony.

The bridal party formed before the altar, the bishop opened the book, and the ceremony commenced. It proceeded according to the ritual, and without the slightest deviation from commonplace routine.

When the bishop came to that part of the rites in which he utters the awful adjuration—"I require and charge you both, as ye shall answer at the dreadful day of judgment, when the secrets of all hearts shall be disclosed, that if either of you know any impediment why ye may not be lawfully joined together in matrimony, ye do now confess it. For be ye well assured, that if any persons are joined together, otherwise than God's word doth allow, their marriage is not lawful,"—Bee, who was standing with her mother and father near the bridal circle, looked up at the bride.

Oh, could Claudia, loving another, loathing the bridegroom, kneel in that sacred church, before that holy altar, in the presence of God's minister, in the presence of God himself, hear that solemn adjuration, and persevere in her awful sin?

Yes, Claudia could! as tens of thousands, from ignorance, from insensibility, or from recklessness, have done before her; and as tens of thousands more, from the same causes, will do after her.

The ceremony proceeded until it reached the part where the ring is placed upon the bride's finger, and all went well enough until, as they were rising from the prayer of "Our Father," the bride happened to lower her hand, and the ring, which was too large for her finger, dropped off, and rolled away and passed out of sight.

The ceremony ended, and the ring was sought for; but could not be found then: and, I may as well tell you now, it has not been found yet.

Seeing at length that their search was quite fruitless, the gentlemen of the bridal train reluctantly gave up the ring for lost, and the whole party filed into the chancel to enter their names in the register, that lay for this purpose on the communion table.

The bridegroom first approached and wrote his. It was a prolonged and sonorous roll of names, such as frequently compose the tail of a nobleman's title:

Malcolm—Victor—Stuart—Douglass—Gordon—Dugald, Viscount Vincent.

Then the bride signed hers, and the witnesses theirs.

When Mr. Brudenell came to sign his own name as one of the witnesses, he happened to glance at the bridegroom's long train of names. He read them over with a smile at their length, but his eye fastened upon the last one—"Dugald," "Dugald"? Herman Brudenell, like the immortal Burton, thought he had "heard that name before," in fact, was sure he had "heard that name before!" Yes, verily; he had heard it in connection with his sister's fatal flight, in which a certain Captain Dugald had been her companion! And he resolved to make cautious inquiries of the viscount. He had known Lord Vincent on the Continent, but he had either never happened to hear what his family name was, or if he had chanced to do so, he had forgotten the circumstances. At all events, it was not until the instant in which he read the viscount's signature in the register that he discovered the family name of Lord Vincent and the disreputable name of Eleanor Brudenell's unprincipled lover to be the same.

But this was no time for brooding over the subject. He affixed his own signature, which was the last one on the list, and then joined the bridal party, who were now leaving the church.

At the door a signal change took place in the order of the procession.

Lord Vincent, with a courtesy as earnest and a smile as beaming as gallantry and the occasion required, handed his bride into his own carriage.

Judge Merlin, Ishmael, and Beatrice rode together.

And others returned in the order in which they had come.

Ishmael was coming out of that strange, benumbed state that had deadened for a while all his sense of suffering—coming back to a consciousness of utter bereavement and insupportable anguish—anguish written in such awful characters upon his pallid and writhen brow that Beatrice and her uncle exchanged glances of wonder and alarm.

But Ishmael, in his fixed agony, did not perceive the looks of anxiety they turned towards him—did not even perceive the passage of time or space, until they arrived at home again, and the wedding guests once more began to alight from the carriages.

The party temporarily separated in the hall, the ladies dispersing each to her own chamber to make some trifling change in her toilet before appearing in the drawing room.

"Ishmael, come here, my lad," said the judge, as soon as they were left alone.

Ishmael mechanically followed him to the little breakfast parlor of the family, where on the sideboard sat decanters of brandy and wine, and pitchers of water, and glasses of all shapes and sizes.

He poured out two glasses of brandy—one for himself and one for Ishmael.

"Let us drink the health of the newly-married couple," he said, pushing one glass towards Ishmael, and raising the other to his own lips.

But Ishmael hesitated, and poured out a tumbler of pure water, saying, in a faint voice:

"I will drink her health in this."

"Nonsense! put it down. You are chilled enough without drinking that to throw you into an ague. Drink something, warm and strong, boy! drink something warm and strong. I tell you, I, for one, cannot get through this day without some such support as this," said the judge authoritatively, as he took from the young man's nerveless hand the harmless glass of water, and put into it the perilous glass of brandy.

For ah! good men do wicked things sometimes, and wise men foolish ones.

Still Ishmael hesitated; for even in the midst of his great trouble he heard the "still, small voice" of some good angel—it might have been his mother's spirit—whispering him to dash from his lips the Circean draught, that would indeed allay his sense of suffering for a few minutes, but might endanger his character through all his life and his soul through all eternity. The voice that whispered this, as I said, was a "still, small voice" speaking softly within him. But the voice of the judge was bluff and hearty, and he stood there, a visible presence, enforcing his advice with strength of action.

And Ishmael, scarcely well assured of what he did, put the glass to his lips and quaffed the contents, and felt at once falsely exhilarated.

"Come, now, we will go into the drawing room. I dare say they are all down by this time," said the judge. And in they went.

He was right in his conjecture; the wedding guests were all assembled there.

And soon after his entrance the sliding doors between the drawing room and the dining room were pushed back, and Devizac, who was the presiding genius of the wedding feast, appeared and announced that breakfast was served.

The company filed in—the bride and bridegroom walking together, and followed by the bridesmaids and the gentlemen of the party.

Ishmael gave his arm to Beatrice. Mr. Brudenell conducted Mrs. Middleton, and the judge led one of the lady guests.

The scene they entered upon was one of splendor, beauty, and luxury, never surpassed even by the great Vourienne and Devizac themselves! Painting, gilding, and flowers had not been spared. The walls were covered with frescoes of Venus, Psyche, Cupid, the Graces, and the Muses, seen among the rosy bowers and shady groves of Arcadia. The ceiling was covered with celestial scenery, in the midst of which was seen the cloudy court of Jupiter and Juno and their attendant gods and goddesses; the pillars were covered with gilding and twined with flowers, and long wreaths of flowers connected one pillar with another and festooned the doorways and windows and the corners of the room.

The breakfast table was a marvel of art—blazing with gold plate, blooming with beautiful and fragrant exotics, and intoxicating with the aroma of the richest and rarest viands.

At the upper end of the room a temporary raised and gilded balcony wreathed with roses was occupied by Dureezie's celebrated band, who, as the company came in, struck up an inspiring bridal march composed expressly for this occasion.

The wedding party took their seats at the table and the feasting began. The viands were carved and served and praised. The bride's cake was cut and the slices distributed. The ring fell to one of the bridesmaids and provoked the usual badinage. The wine circulated freely.

Mr. Middleton arose and in a neat little speech proposed the fair bride's health, which proposal was hailed with enthusiasm.

Judge Merlin, in another little speech, returned thanks to the company, and begged leave to propose the bridegroom's health, which was duly honored.

Then it was Lord Vincent's turn to rise and express his gratitude and propose Judge Merlin's health.

This necessitated a second rising of the judge, who after making due acknowledgments of the compliments paid him, proposed—the fair bridesmaids.

And so the breakfast proceeded.

They sat at table an hour, and then, at a signal from Mrs. Middleton, all arose.

The gentlemen adjourned to the little breakfast parlor to drink a parting glass with their host in something stronger than the light French breakfast wines they had been quaffing so freely.

And the bride, followed by all her attendants, went up to her room to change her bridal robe and veil for her traveling dress and bonnet; as the pair were to take the one o'clock train to Baltimore en route for New York, Niagara, and the Lakes.

She found her dressing room all restored to the dreary good order that spoke of abandonment. Her rich dresses and jewels and bridal presents were all packed up. And every trunk was locked and corded and ready for transportation to the railway station, except one large trunk that stood open, with its upper tray waiting for the bridal dress she was about to put off.

Ruth, who had been very busy with all this packing, while the wedding party were at church and at breakfast, now stood with the brown silk dress and mantle that was to be Claudia's traveling costume, laid over her arm.

Claudia, assisted by Mrs. Middleton, changed her dress with the feverish haste of one who longed to get a painful ordeal over; and while Ruth hastily packed away the wedding finery and closed the last trunk, Claudia tied on her brown silk bonnet and drew on her gloves and expressed herself ready to depart.

They went downstairs to the drawing room, where all the wedding guests were once more gathered to see the young pair off.

There was no time to lose, and so all her friends gathered around the bride to receive her adieus and to express their good wishes.

One by one she bade them farewell.

When she came to her cousin, Bee burst into tears and whispered:

"God forgive you, poor Claudia! God avert from you all evil consequences of your own act!"

She caught her breath, wrung Bee's hand and turned away, and looked around. She had taken leave of all except her father and Ishmael.

Her father she knew would accompany her as far as the railway station, for he had said as much.

But there was Ishmael.

As she went up to him slowly and fearfully, every vein and artery in her body seemed to throb with the agony of her heart. She tried to speak; but could utter no articulate sound. She held out her hand; but he did not take it; then she lifted her beautiful eyes to his, with a glance so helpless, so anguished, so imploring, as if silently praying from him some kind word before she should go, that Ishmael's generous heart was melted and he took her hand and pressing it while he spoke, said in low and fervent tones:

"God bless you, Lady Vincent. God shield you from all evil. God save you in every crisis of your life."

And she bowed her head, lowly and humbly, to receive this benediction as though it had been uttered by an authorized minister of God.

CHAPTER LXVII.

BEE'S HANDKERCHIEF.

"I would bend my spirit o'er yon."
"I am humbled, who was humble!
Friend! I bow my head before you!"
—*E.B. Browning.*

But a mist fell before Ishmael's eyes, and when it cleared away Claudia was gone.

The young bridesmaids were chattering gayly in a low, melodious tone with each other, and with the gentlemen of the party filling the room with a musical hum of many happy voices.

But all this seemed unreal and dreadful, like the illusions of troubled sleep. And so Ishmael left the drawing room and went up to the office, to see if perhaps he could find real life there.

There lay the parcels of papers tied up with red tape, the open books that he had consulted the day before, and the letters that had come by the morning's mail.

He sat down wearily to the table and began to open his letters. One by one he read and laid them aside. One important letter, bearing upon a case he had on hand, he laid by itself.

Then rising, he gathered up his documents, put them into his pocket, took his hat and gloves and went to the City Hall.

This day of suffering, like all other days, was a day of duties also.

It was now one o'clock, the hour at which the train started which carried Claudia away.

It was also the hour at which a case was appointed to be heard before the Judge of the Orphan's Court—a case in which the guardianship of certain fatherless and motherless children was disputed between a grandmother and an uncle, and in which Ishmael was counsel for the plaintiff. He appeared in court, punctually to the minute, found his client waiting for him there, and as soon as the judge had taken his seat the young counsel opened the case. By a strong effort of will he wrested his thoughts from his own great sorrow, and engaged them in the interests of the anxious old lady, who was striving for the possession of her grandchildren only from the love she bore them and their mother, her own dead daughter; while her opponent wished only to have the management of their large fortune.

It was nature that pleaded through the lips of the eloquent young counsel, and he gained this case also.

But he was ill in mind and body. He could scarcely bear the thanks and congratulations of his client and her friends.

The old lady had retained him by one large fee, and now she placed another and a larger one in his hands; but he could not have told whether the single banknote was for five dollars or five hundred, as he mechanically received it and placed it in his pocketbook.

And then, with the courteous bow and smile, never omitted, because they were natural and habitual, he turned and left the courtroom.

"What is the matter with Worth?" inquired one lawyer.

"Can't imagine; he looks very ill; shouldn't wonder if he was going to have a congestion of the brain. It looks like it. He works too hard," replied another.

Old Wiseman, the law-thunderer, who had been the counsel opposed to Ishmael in this last case, and who, in fact, was always professionally opposed to him, but, nevertheless, personally friendly towards him, had also noticed his pale, haggard, and distracted looks, and now hurried after him in the fear that he should fall before reaching home.

He overtook Ishmael in the lobby. The young man was standing leaning on the balustrade at the head of the stairs, as if unable to take another step.

Wiseman bent over him.

"Worth, my dear fellow, what is the matter with you? Does it half kill you to overthrow me at law?"

"I—fear that I am not well," replied Ishmael, in a hollow voice, and with a haggard smile.

"What is it? Only exhaustion, I hope? You have been working too hard, and you never even left the courtroom to take any refreshments to-day. You are too much in earnest, my young friend. You take too much pains. You apply yourself too closely. Why, bless my life, you could floor us all any day with half the trouble! But you must always use a trip-hammer to drive tin tacks. Take my arm, and let us go and get something."

And the stout lawyer drew the young man's arm within his own and led him to a restaurant that was kept on the same floor for the convenience of the courts and their officers and other habitues of the City Hall.

Wiseman called for the best old Otard brandy, and poured out half a tumblerful, and offered it to Ishmael. It was a dose that might have been swallowed with impunity by a seasoned old toper like Wiseman; but certainly not by an abstinent young man like Ishmael, who, yielding to the fatal impulse to get rid of present suffering by any means, at any cost, or any risk, took the tumbler and swallowed the brandy.

Ah, Heaven have mercy on the sorely-tried and tempted!

This was only the third glass of alcoholic stimulants that Ishmael had ever taken in the whole course of his life.

On the first occasion, the day of Claudia's betrothal, the glass had been placed in his hand and urged upon his acceptance by his honored old friend, Judge Merlin.

On the second occasion, the morning of this day, of Claudia's marriage, the glass had also been offered him by Judge Merlin.

And on the third occasion, this afternoon of the terrible day of trial and suffering, it was placed to his lips by the respectable old lawyer, Wiseman.

Alas! alas!

On the first occasion Ishmael had protested long before he yielded; on the second he had hesitated a little while; but on the third he took the offered glass and drank the brandy without an instant's doubt or pause.

Lord, be pitiful!

And oh, Nora, fly down from heaven on wings of love and watch over your son and save him—from his friends!—lest he fall into deeper depths than any from which he has so nobly struggled forth. For he is suffering, tempted, and human! And there never lived but one perfect man, and he was the Son of God.

"Well?" said old Wiseman as he received the glass from Ishmael's hand and sat it down.

"I thank you; it has done me good; I feel much better; you are very kind," said Ishmael.

"I wish you would really think so, and go into partnership with me. My business is very heavy—much more than I can manage alone, now that I am growing old and stout; and I must have somebody, and I would rather have you than anyone else. You would succeed to the whole business after my death, you know."

"Thank you; your offer is very flattering. I will think it over, and talk with you on some future occasion. Now I feel that I must return home, while I have strength to do so," replied Ishmael.

"Very well, then, my dear fellow, I will let you off."

And they shook hands and parted.

Ishmael, feeling soothed, strengthened, and exhilarated, set off to walk home. But this feeling gradually passed off, giving place to a weakness, heaviness, and feverishness, that warned him he was in no state to appear at judge Merlin's dinner table.

So when he approached the house he opened a little side gate leading into the back grounds, and strayed into the shrubbery, feeling every minute more feverish, heavy, and drowsy.

At last he strayed into an arbor, quite at the bottom of the shrubberies, where he sank down upon the circular bench and fell into a deep sleep.

Meanwhile up at the house changes had taken place. The wedding guests had all departed. The festive garments had had been laid away. The decorated dining room had been shut up. The household had returned to its usual sober aspect, and the plain family dinner was laid in the little breakfast parlor. But the house was very sad and silent and lonely because its queen was gone. At the usual dinner-hour, six o'clock, the family assembled at the table.

"Where is Ishmael, uncle?" inquired Beatrice.

"I do not know, my dear," replied the judge, whose heart was sore with the wrench that had torn his daughter from him.

"Do you, papa?"

"No, dear."

"Mamma, have you seen Ishmael since the morning?"

"No, child."

"Nor you, Walter?"

"Nor I, Bee."

Mr. Brudenell looked up at the fair young creature, who took such thought of his absent son, and volunteered to say:

"He had a case before the Orphans' Court to-day, I believe. But the court is adjourned, I know, because I met the judge an hour ago at the Capitol; so I suppose he will be here soon."

Bee bowed in acknowledgment of this information, but she did not feel at all reassured. She had noticed Ishmael's dreadful pallor that morning; she felt how much he suffered, and she feared some evil consequences; though her worst suspicions never touched the truth.

"Uncle," she said, blushing deeply to be obliged still to betray her interest in one whom she was forced to remember, because everyone else forgot him, "uncle, had we not better send Powers up to Ishmael's room to see if he has come in, and let him know that dinner is on the table?"

"Certainly, my dear; go, Powers, and if Mr. Worth is in his room, let him know that dinner is ready."

Powers went, but soon returned with the information that Mr. Worth was neither in his room nor in the office, nor anywhere else in the house.

"Some professional business has detained him; he will be home after a while," said the judge.

But Bee was anxious, and when dinner was over she went upstairs to a window that overlooked the Avenue, and watched; but, of course, in vain. Then with the restlessness common to intense anxiety she came down and went into the shrubbery to walk. She paced about very uneasily until she had tired herself, and then turned towards a secluded arbor at the bottom of the grounds to rest herself. She put aside the vines that overhung the doorway and entered.

What did she see?

Ishmael extended upon the bench, with the late afternoon sun streaming through a crevice in the arbor, shining full upon his face, which was also plagued with flies!

She had found him then, but how?

At first she thought he was only sleeping; and she was about to withdraw from the arbor when the sound of his breathing caught her ear and alarmed her, and she crept back and cautiously approached and looked over him.

His face was deeply flushed; the veins of his temples were swollen; and his breathing was heavy and labored. In her fright Bee caught up his hand and felt his pulse. It was full, hard, and slowly throbbing. She thought that he was very ill—dangerously ill, and she was about to spring up and rush to the house for help, when, in raising her head, she happened to catch his breath.

And all the dreadful truth burst upon Bee's mind, and overwhelmed her with mortification and despair!

With a sudden gasp and a low wail she sank on her knees at his side and dropped her head in her open hands and sobbed aloud.

"Oh, Ishmael, Ishmael, is it so? Have I lived to see you thus? Can a woman reduce a man to this? A proud and selfish woman have such power so to mar God's noblest work? Oh, Ishmael, my love, my love! I love you better than I love all the world besides! And I love you better than anyone else ever did or ever can; yet, yet, I would rather see you stark dead before me than to see you thus! Oh, Heaven! Oh, Saviour! Oh, Father of Mercies, have pity on him and save him!" she cried.

And she wrung her hands and bent her head to look at him more closely, and her large tears dropped upon his face.

He stirred, opened his eyes, rolled them heavily, became half conscious of someone weeping over him, turned clumsily and relapsed into insensibility.

At his first motion Bee had sprung up and fled from the arbor, at the door of which she stood, with throbbing heart, watching him, through the vines. She saw that he had again fallen into that deep and comatose sleep. And she saw that his flushed and fevered face was more than ever exposed to the rays of the sun and the plague of the flies. And she crept cautiously back again, and drew her handkerchief from her pocket and laid it over his face, and turned and hurried, broken-spirited from the spot.

She gained her own room and threw herself into her chair in a passion of tears and sobs.

Nothing that had ever happened in all her young life had ever grieved her anything like this. She had loved Ishmael with all her heart, and she knew that Ishmael loved Claudia with all of his; but the knowledge of this fact had never brought to her the bitter sorrow that the sight of Ishmael's condition had smitten her with this afternoon. For there was scarcely purer love among the angels in heaven than was that of Beatrice for Ishmael. First of all she desired his good; next his affection; next his presence; but there was scarcely selfishness enough in Bee's nature to wish to possess him all for her own.

First his good! And here, weeping, sobbing, and praying by turns, she resolved to devote herself to that object; to do all that she possibly could to shield him from the suspicion of this night's event; and to save him from falling into a similar misfortune.

She remained in her own room until tea-time, and then bathed her eyes, and smoothed her hair, and went down to join the family at the table.

"Well, Bee," said the judge, "have you found Ishmael yet?"

Bee hesitated, blushed, reflected a moment, and then answered:

"Yes, uncle; he is sleeping; he is not well; and I would not have him disturbed if I were you; for sleep will do him more good than anything else."

"Certainly. Why, Bee, did you ever know me to have anybody waked up in the whole course of my life? Powers, and the rest of you, hark ye: Let no one call Mr. Worth. Let him sleep until the last trump sounds, or until he wakes up of his own accord!"

Powers bowed, and said he would see the order observed.

Soon after tea was over, the family, fatigued with the day's excitement, retired to bed.

Bee went up to her room in the back attic; but she did not go to bed, or even undress, for she knew that Ishmael was locked out; and so she threw a light shawl around her, and seated herself at the open back window, which from its high point of view commanded every nook and cranny of the back grounds, to watch until Ishmael should wake up and approach the house, so that she might go down and admit him quietly, without disturbing the servants and exciting their curiosity and conjectures. No one should know of Ishmael's misfortune, for she would not call it fault, if any vigilance of hers could shield him. All through the still evening, all through the deep midnight, Bee sat and watched.

When Ishmael had fallen asleep, the sun was still high above the Western horizon; but when he awoke the stars were shining.

He raised himself to a sitting posture, and looked around him, utterly bewildered and unable to collect his scattered faculties, or to remember where he was, or how he came there, or what had occurred, or who he himself really was—so deathlike had been his sleep.

He had no headache; his previous habits had been too regular, his blood was too pure, and the brandy was too good for that. He was simply bewildered, but utterly bewildered, as though he had waked up in another world.

He was conscious of a weight upon his heart, but could not remember the cause of it; and whether it was grief or remorse, or both, he could not tell. He feared that it was both.

Gradually memory and misery returned to him; the dreadful day; the marriage; the feast; the parting; the lawsuit; the two glasses of brandy, and their mortifying consequences. All the events of that day lay clearly before him now—that horrible day begun in unutterable sorrow, and ended in humiliating sin!

Was it himself, Ishmael Worth, who had suffered this sorrow, yielded to this temptation, and fallen into this sin? To what had his inordinate earthly affections brought him? He was no longer "the chevalier without fear and without reproach." He had fallen, fallen, fallen!

He remembered that when he had sunk to sleep the sun was shining and smiling all over the beautiful garden, and that even in his half-drowsy state he had noticed its glory. The sun was gone now. It had set upon his humiliating weakness. The day had given up the record of his sin and passed away forever. The day would return no more to reproach him, but its record would meet him in the judgment.

He remembered that once in his deep sleep he had half awakened and found what seemed a weeping angel bending over him, and that he had tried to rouse himself to speak; but in the effort he had only turned over and tumbled into a deeper oblivion than ever.

Who was that pitying angel visitant?

The answer came like a shock of electricity. It was Bee! Who else should it have been? It was Bee! She had sought him out when he was lost; she had found him in his weakness; she had dropped tears of love and sorrow over him.

At that thought new shame, new grief, new remorse swept in upon his soul.

He sprang upon his feet, and in doing so dropped a little white drift upon the ground. He stooped and picked it up.

It was the fine white handkerchief that on first waking up he had plucked from his face. And he knew by its soft thin feeling and its delicate scent of violets, Bee's favorite perfume, that it was her handkerchief, and she had spread it as a veil over his exposed and feverish, face. That little wisp of cambric was redolent of Bee! of her presence, her purity, her tenderness.

It seemed a mere trifle; but it touched the deepest springs of his heart, and, holding it in both his hands, he bowed his humbled head upon it and wept.

When a man like Ishmael weeps it is no gentle summer shower, I assure you; but as the breaking up of great fountains, the rushing of mighty torrents, the coming of a flood.

He wept long and convulsively. And his deluge of tears relieved his surcharged heart and brain and did him good. He breathed more freely; he wiped his face with this dear handkerchief, and then, all dripping wet with tears as it was, he pressed it to his lips and placed it in his bosom, over his heart, and registered a solemn vow in Heaven that this first fault of his life should also, with God's help, be his last.

Then he walked forth into the starlit garden, murmuring to himself:

278

"By a woman came sin and death into the world, and by a woman came redemption and salvation. Oh, Claudia, my Eve, farewell! farewell! And Bee, my Mary, hail!"

The holy stars no longer looked down reproachfully upon him; the harmless little insect-choristers no longer mocked him; love and forgiveness beamed down from the pure light of the first, and cheering hope sounded in the gleeful songs of the last.

Ishmael walked up the gravel-walk between the shrubbery and the house. Once, when his face was towards the house, he looked up at Bee's back window. It was open, and he saw a white, shadowy figure just within it.

Was it Bee?

His heart assured him that it was; and that anxiety for him had kept her there awake and watching.

As he drew near the house, quite uncertain as to how he should get in, he saw that the shadowy, white figure disappeared from the window; and when he went up to the back door, with the intention of rapping loudly until he should wake up the servants and gain admission, his purpose was forestalled by the door being softly opened by Bee, who stood with a shaded taper behind it.

"Oh, Bee!"

"Oh, Ishmael!"

Both spoke at once, and in a tone of irrepressible emotion.

"Come in, Ishmael," she next said kindly.

"You know, Bee?" he asked sadly, as he entered.

"Yes, Ishmael! Forgive me for knowing, for it prevented others finding out. And your secret could not rest safer, or with a truer heart than mine."

"I know it, dear Bee! dear sister, I know it. And Bee, listen! That glass of brandy was only the third of any sort of spirituous liquor that I ever tasted in my life. And I solemnly swear in the presence of Heaven and before you that it shall be the very last! Never, no, never, even as a medicine, will I place the fatal poison to my lips again."

"I believe you, Ishmael. And I am very happy. Thank God!" she said, giving him her hand.

"Dear Bee! Holy angel! I am scarcely worthy to touch it," he said, bowing reverently over that little white hand.

"'There shall be more joy in heaven over one sinner that repenteth, than over ninety and nine just persons who need no repentance.' Good-night, Ishmael!" said Bee sweetly, as she put the taper in his hand and glided like a spirit from his presence.

She was soon sleeping beside her baby sister.

And Ishmael went upstairs to bed. And the troubled night closed in peace.

The further career of Ishmael, together with the after fate of all the characters mentioned in this work, will be found in the sequel to and final conclusion of this volume, entitled, "Self-Raised; or, From the Depths."

Made in the USA
Columbia, SC
10 December 2024

48928405R00154